ALSO BY NOIRE

URBAN EROTIC TALES
G-Spot
Candy Licker
Thug-A-Licious
Baby Brother (with 50 Cent)
Hood
Hittin' the Bricks
Unzipped
B4 the G-Spot: The Legend of Granite McKay

FLIRTY DIRTIES
Thong on Fire
Maneater (with Mary B. Morrison)
Lifestyles of the Rich and Shameless (with Kiki Swinson)
Natural Born Liar
Sexy Little Liar
Dirty Rotten Liar
Red Hot Liar

URBAN EROTIC QUICKIES
From the Streets to the Sheets

COMING SOON
A New York State of MINEZ! (with Reem RAW)
Stone Cold Liar

NOIRE

G-Spot 2:
The Seven Deadly Sins
An Urban Erotic Serial Tale Told in 7 Parts

THE ALL-IN-ONE VERSION

A Big-Ass Book

by
Noire

www.AskNoire.com
www.GSpot2.com
www.TheGSpotSaga.com

Urban Erotic Noire Publications

G-Spot 2: The Seven Deadly Sins is a work of fiction. Names, characters, places, and incidents are the product of the author's imagination or are used fictitiously. Any resemblance to actual events, locales, or persons, living or dead, is entirely coincidental.

<u>G-Spot 2: The Seven Deadly Sins (The All-In-One Version)</u>
Pride: The 1st Deadly Sin
Betrayal: The 2nd Deadly Sin
Greed: The 3rd Deadly Sin
Envy: The 4th Deadly Sin
Lust: The 5th Deadly Sin
Trickery: The 6th Deadly Sin
Revenge: The 7th Deadly Sin
Revenge: The 7th Deadly Sin Alternate Ending

First Printing January 2015

ISBN- 13: 978-0-9830936-8-8
ISBN- 10: 0-9830936-8-7

Printed in the United States of America

10 9 8 7 6 5 4 3 2 1

Visit our websites at:
www.GSpot2.com
www.NoireStore.com
www.AskNoire.com
www.TheGSpotSaga.com

A Note from Noire

Hey fam!

Once again, the urban erotic train is rolling into the station! Thank you for loving the G-Spot Saga. It's the first and longest running saga in the urban fiction genre and brings back the favorite cast of characters that you have grown to know and love. So many of you wrote and asked if G-Spot 2: The Seven Deadly Sins would one day be available as one unified collection, and here it is!

Between the pages of this Big-Ass Book you will find all 7 parts of the Deadly Sins: Pride, Betrayal, Greed, Envy, Lust, Trickery, Revenge AND Revenge the Alternate Ending (an orginal Noire twist).

In addition, you'll also be treated to an excerpt from **"B4 the G-Spot: The Legend of Granite McKay"**, which gives you an up close and personal look at Harlem's most feared and notorious drug kingpin. I've also included an excerpt from **"A New York State of MINEZ!"**, the brand new banga written by me and artist and actor Reem RAW.

Big ups for showing your love and giving me your support every time the urban erotic train blows its whistle. Y'all are some true riders and loyal friends, and I lub ya beyond words! Now dig into these pages and read more about Juicy Monique Stanfield, the hottest chick in urban fiction. Remember, this here ain't no romance, it's an urban erotic tale!

Demand Quality and Stay Black,

NOIRE

Sign up for my email contact list at **bit.ly/noiresignup**
Like my Facebook page at **bit.ly/noirefanpage**
Follow me on Twitter at **twitter.com/AskNoire**

G-Spot: An Urban Erotic Tale by Noire

In the beginning...

Have you ever rolled over in the middle of the night and realized you were doing shit you swore you'd never do? Sexing brother you vowed you'd never touch? Bending backward and stooping lower than you ever thought you'd stoop? Well, if you can feel me even a little bit, then let me hit you with a story that might just blow your mind. And I swear, as crazy as it sounds, every word of it is true. Let me take you to the G-Spot. A gentlemen's club in the heart of Harlem. A place where playa-hating and disrespect can cost you your life, and betrayal guarantees you a fate worse than death. My name is Juicy Monique Stanfield. I lost my soul in the G-Spot and this is my story...

G-Spot 2: The Seven Deadly Sins by Noire

In the beginning...

Have you ever rolled over in the middle of the night and been so damn thankful you just broke down and cried? Did you praise God for delivering you from a grimy Dungeon and blessing you with a tiny taste of heaven? Did you wake up every morning chillin' in the arms of the one you loved? Snuggled deep in the sheets like nothing could ever hurt you? That shit felt perfect, didn't it? So perfect, that you let your guard down and stopped looking over your shoulder, right? But then... did you get caught slippin? Did you start waking up in the darkness gripxped by fear? Your body trembling in terror? Did you lay there paralyzed, with prophecy lurking over your head and holding you prisoner? Did you feel doomed to a punishment that you knew you didn't deserve? Did you search desper- ately for a way out, but no matter how far you ran, you just couldn't outrun your fate? Come hang out with me for a minute, y'all. Sit down and get com- fortable as I tell you what happened when I hauled ass outta Harlem and ran smack into my destiny. My name is Juicy Monique Stanfield. I escaped from the G-Spot, and this is the *rest* of my story...

PART ONE
OF NOIRE'S BLOCKBUSTER
URBAN EROTIC SERIAL TALE!

Juicy is back and she's hotter than ever!

Harlem hasn't been the same since the notorious Granite "G" McKay was brutally murdered in a back room of the G-Spot Social Club. In the aftermath, not only has G's massive cache of doe gone missing, but Juicy has skipped town with Gino...G's very own son!

And now Ace and Pluto, two of G's most gutter henchmen, are hell-bent on finding the enormous pile of greenbacks that G stashed away while building his grimy empire. To make things worse, Money-Making Monique, the G-Spot's top stripper and Juicy's sexy, conniving rival, is hell-bent on getting some payback of her own. Can Juicy and Gino find happiness as they try to build a new life together? Or will mayhem, murder, and the bitter wrath of the streets track them down to get what's due?

WARNING!

This here ain't no romance
It's an urban erotic tale
When things got hot in Harlem
Gino and Juicy had to bail
They headed west to Cali
Where the sun shines everyday
But back at home a plot was brewing
To send their plans astray
They dipped real quick, but they weren't slick
They could run, but they couldn't hide
Check your ego at the door
'Cause the 1st Deadly Sin is **PRIDE**

Find out more in...

G-SPOT 2: THE SEVEN DEADLY SINS
Pride: The 1st Deadly Sin

The Urban Erotic Serial Saga Begins!

NOIRE

G-Spot 2:
The Seven Deadly Sins
An Urban Erotic Serial Tale Told in 7 Parts

PRIDE: THE 1ST DEADLY SIN

by

Noire

www.AskNoire.com
www.GSpot2.com
www.TheGSpotSaga.com

CHAPTER 1

California Dreamin'

The young girl ran like the devil was after her.

And he was, too. He chased her down 136th Street all the way to Lenox Avenue. He ran her past pizza parlors, hair salons, and Italian icee stands. Past corner boys and street yummies working hard on the grind. The thick crowds parted as the good people of Harlem fell back in terror. They knew this devil. They knew him well. And they feared him just as much as the innocent young girl did.

Up ahead someone yelled out the young girl's name. She glanced down Lenox Avenue and saw her whole family standing behind the window of the Dominican beauty parlor where she used to wash hair.

Grandmother, Jimmy, Cara, Dicey, and even Aunt Ree. They were all there in her terrifying dream. Huddled together at the window looking worried in the face. Peeping the devil on her tail, they started jumping up and down and beckoning with their arms. They screamed for her and reached for her. They begged her to run like hell.

The young girl's feet were heavy as she fled toward the beauty shop. There was safety on the other side of those swinging doors, and if she made it inside she might just live.

But if she got caught...a bitter chill crept down her spine. If she didn't get inside that shop then the devil was going to ride her until she wished she was dead.

The sun beamed down on her as she fled. A Johnny pump was open near the corner and a bunch of little kids played in its gushing spray. The girl darted past them and her feet splashed in the cold water. She had just stepped up on the curb when the devil's hot breath scorched the back of her neck.

Flinching, she slipped and fell in the wet gutter. The skin of her knees ripped on the gritty pavement. She sat up soaked and terrified. She wiped her hands on her shorts, and to her horror the icy water was now steaming-hot and had turned red and slick like blood.

She yelped in disgust, and that evil-ass devil laughed dead in her ear. He scared her so badly that she almost surrendered right then and there. But she couldn't. Because her people were waiting for her in that beauty shop. They were screaming for her. Crying. Begging her to move.

"You betta *run*, goddammit!" Dicey stood in the doorway and hollered. Her eyes bulged in her pie-face and when she opened her mouth the girl saw a mangled stump of flesh where her friend's tongue should have been.

"Run, Juicy-Mo! *Run!* You seent how that evil mothafucka did me, right? Don't you let him get a hold of you too!"

Jumping to her feet, the young girl scurried onto the sidewalk. With the devil hot on her tail, she sprinted toward the open arms of her old friend and the safety of the beauty parlor. Seconds later she lunged through the doorway. Her friend grabbed her hands and pulled her inside, and then pushed something soft and warm into her palm.

"I made it!" The young girl cried, sinking to the floor in exhausted relief. "I made it!"

She crawled past Dicey and further into the safety of the beauty shop. She looked toward the window for the rest of her family, but suddenly the front door banged shut, and just like in a dream... everything changed.

The girl blinked and glanced around. She was in a familiar place, but it wasn't a salon full of Dominican hair stylists. No, she was someplace else. In a fancy, expensive joint. Then suddenly she knew.

And that's when the terror hit her.

She was at the G-Spot. The hottest gentlemen's club in Harlem. She glanced around the posh room. Everything about it screamed sex, money, danger, and drugs. Kingpins and high-stake rollers stood around wearing diamond Rolexes and high-priced clothing, and half-naked dancers aimed to please.

The girl glanced down. The floor she was kneeling on was spotless and made of real marble. Stripper music played in the background and the smell of Hennessy and crisp dollar bills floated in the air.

Oh hell no, the young girl thought, trembling in fear. She wasn't in a beauty parlor. And it wasn't Dicey who had snatched her inside either.

Her throat closed up when she saw the hellacious pair of alligator shoes that were suddenly right in front of her. She was scared to imagine who they belonged to, and she forced herself look up from her knees.

She shivered as her eyes climbed a pair of long legs clad in the finest of fabric. The devil might have been a liar, but he sure looked good and he smelled good too.

His teeth were bone-white and his hands were rough and black. Evil rolled off him, and she could tell he was pissed by the way he twirled the huge onyx ring on his middle finger.

Her eyes traveled further up his thick, muscled-up chest and paused near his throat. A raging pulse beat visibly under his smooth dark skin, just below his jaw line.

"Get moving, you nasty bitch!" said the devil. His voice scraped her ears like hot gravel and the girl knew she was going straight to hell.

"*Move*, hoe!" The devil swung his foot and planted it deep in her stomach. She collapsed, and he grabbed her by the hair and hauled her down a hallway and into a crowded room full of people.

The blue lights were dim, and the odor of smoldering hash and sweet Philly blunts filled the air. The crowd had been waiting patiently for the devil. They fell silent as he approached, and she could tell the devil had their love and their respect too.

He barked a series of orders, and suddenly the music stopped and all the lights came on. The devil dragged her out to the middle of a large stripper stage. The girl's mouth went dry as she peered at the waiting crowd.

Her family had front row seats. A bloody sheet was draped over her mother's slender, creamy shoulders. Grandmother had mortician's makeup caked all over her face, and Jimmy-Jo and Aunt Ree both wore hats to hide the bullet-trimmed portions of their skulls that were no longer there.

Something warm pulsed and throbbed in the girl's clenched fist. She uncurled her fingers and stared at the soft, wet thing she'd been holding.

It was Dicey's tongue.

She yelped and flung it to the floor. The devil laughed, then stomped it like a fat cockroach under his shoe.

He held his hand high in the air and signaled to the multitudes. The room grew cold and still. He spoke in a rumbling voice that sparked terror, even in the hearts of the dead.

"Listen up!"

The devil growled from his fine, evil mouth. "This is Juicy-Mo from 136th Street. I'm gonna ask y'all once and I expect the mothafuckin' truth. Who in here done had them some of this? I wanna know if anybody up in here ever sucked her or fucked her. If any of you bitches ever rubbed your clit on her. I wanna know if anybody ever had they fingers in her. Their *tongue*! Let me know right dammit *now*, if any mothafucka up in here done so much as *smelled* this pussy!"

The young girl cringed as nearly everyone in the room jumped up hollering, "Me! Me! *Me*! I did! I did! Yeah, I fucked her! I sucked her! I licked her too! Hell fuckin' *yeah* I got me some of that! Me too! Me too! That's a *community* pussy! I got me a lil bit too!"

Her baby brother stood up in the front row and the girl cried out at the sight of him. The bright lights shone down on his injuries and she moaned with grief. Jimmy raised his hand and wiggled his broken fingers in the air.

Her brother had nothing but love for the devil as he laughed and yelled, "Man, every niggah in *Harlem* done tapped that ass! That bitch gives some real *dead* head!"

The crowd cracked up laughing, and the girl could only weep as the devil gazed down at her with a dark, evil stare.

He was going to kill her.

She could see it in his eyes.

Fast as lightning, he snatched her by the throat and cut off her breath. She didn't even struggle as his monster blows rained down on her head and he called her every kind of stank bitch and nasty hoe he could muster. He pummeled her face, her chest, and sought out her tender gut.

And when the devil finally flung her over on her stomach and began unbuckling his belt, the young girl just lay there helplessly. In total submission. She was ready to die. The will to live flew right out of her as he yanked her naked hips high in the air. His penis was black and erect, and poised to ram her straight into nightmare hell.

But the girl didn't fight back, and she certainly didn't refuse the devil.

There was no need to.

Because if the pretty young girl hadn't been taught a damn thing during the two years she'd been Granite "G" McKay's woman, she had definitely learned one thing was true: come hell or high water, the devil always got his due.

$$$$$

I woke up in bed with my nightgown tangled around my neck. Somehow I'd ripped it off in my sleep and gotten caught up in it. I struggled to catch my breath. A scream pushed against my throat and my heart banged so hard I thought my chest was about to explode. My nightmare had felt real as hell. I was so convinced it was actually happening that my fists were balled up and my booty-cheeks were clenched tight.

For a moment I was right back where it had all started. Back in Harlem. Back inside the G-Spot, the high-rolling nightclub where I had lost my soul and almost lost my life.

I glanced over and saw Gino snuggled under the sheets beside me, and suddenly everything began shifting back into focus.

They had come to me in my dreams again. My family. Grandmother, Cara, Aunt Ree, Dicey, and worst of all, Jimmy. Not the way they were when they were alive and loving me, but the way they were in death. The way G wanted me to see them, and most of all to remember them. Twisted, sliced, bloodied, broke down, shot up. Brutalized.

It had been six months since the night I'd run out of the G-Spot with nothing but a filthy sheet wrapped around me and a nasty tube sock pressed between my legs. Six months since the life I was living had cost me almost everything and everybody I had ever loved.

Something inside me broke wide open and the fear and pain came flying out. My tears were hard and silent. The kind of cries an innocent girl makes when she's been crushed in her soul.

I had been a naïve and sheltered seventeen-year-old schoolgirl when Granite McKay rescued me from my grandmother's raggedy apartment on 136th Street, and took me and my brother Jimmy to his luxurious penthouse on Central Park West.

G might have been an old hustler, but he was top shelf all the way. Between his shiny new whips and imported tailor-made clothes, G was legendary and had absolute power on the streets of Harlem.

At the age of forty-six he had conquered a New York City Kingdom and he ruled it with a perfect balance of fear and respect. People on the streets had love for G. He knew exactly how to take care of the community and he was real generous when he wanted to be. G was real rich and he surrounded himself with nice things. He had turned me on to the finest stuff money could buy. When we moved to Central Park West, G hired two maids and a driver. He paid a stylist to do my hair, and a Swedish woman to massage my body and keep my skin soft just in case he felt like touching me.

But just because a man had money it didn't mean he could put his thing down the right way. G was rich, but he was set in his ways too. I was just a delicious piece of eye candy to him, and the only thing he allowed me to do was sit up on a barstool and look good every night.

So while I liked what G was giving me, I wasn't satisfied with the *way* he was giving it to me. G was like a big bucket of ice-cold water, and my young body was sizzling hot, burning straight on fire. A buster like him couldn't help but want to splash on me and put out my flames.

So, yeah. I had been really stupid while I was busy thinking I was so smart, but if I'd had even a little bit of sense on the cap, I would have never let Granite McKay take me up on the G-Spot stage and announce to the world that I was his. I had felt so lucky for getting chosen by the King of Harlem! But let's face it. If Lady Luck had really been on my side, she would've told me to break up out of the G-Spot and run for my life.

CHAPTER 2

Yₒᵤ a'ight?"

I shivered as Gino reached for me in the darkness. I felt his strong hands rubbing my back, and then trailing down my arms.

"Was it another nightmare?" His voice was deep with sleep but tight with worry.

"Yes." I wiped my tears on my pillow and took a deep breath and then blew it out real slow. "But I'm okay, baby. I'm straight."

I had started having nightmares about G right after we escaped from Harlem and moved to L.A. It made Gino uncomfortable to know that his father was still taking up space in my head.

"That niggah was chasin' you again, huh?"

I shrugged. My nightmares were always about me running down the streets of Harlem with G hot on my tail. The details sometimes changed a little bit from dream to dream, but in the end it was always the same: I had betrayed the great Granite McKay and he wanted me dead.

Gino pulled me toward him until I was snuggled in his strong arms. I melted against his warm, chocolate skin and he held me close as our hearts beat to one solid rhythm.

Gino was G's son in a whole lot of ways. He was hardbody and street certified, but he wasn't grimy like G, and he didn't hate women like his father did. Gino loved me, and I was crazy in love with him. He was one-hundred-percent down for me, and I was grateful for that.

But way down deep in my heart I still didn't feel safe, no matter how far away we had run. It wasn't that I didn't think my man could handle his. Gino was from Brooklyn and he could scrap with the best of them. He would die for me. I knew he would. But I just couldn't shake the feeling that somehow G was going to find a way to come back from the dead and kill us both.

Gino felt me trembling and got upset. "Yo, I can't have you walking around here scared every day, Juicy. G is long gone. What went down in Harlem is over. You're safe now, sugar. I'm here, and I got you. We left the past in the past, and we're building us a whole new life. Your nightmare is over, so cut all that dreaming shit out, baby girl. I don't wanna hear nothing else about G, a'ight?"

I nodded, but it was easier for Gino to say all that than it was for my mind and my heart to believe it. Gino hadn't been through what I had been through. He hadn't seen what I had seen. *I* was the one who had been fucked and beaten and chained to a bed with strange men shooting cum in my hair down in that dark, scary Dungeon. *I* was the one who had watched my baby brother murder G, and then stand next to me and blow his own brains out. True, Gino had gotten some too, but I had gotten the worst of it. I guess that was only right since I was the violator and the cheater. The dick-crazy young chicken who had been scandalous enough to love both a father and his only son.

"Look, Juicy. Maybe you should go talk to somebody," Gino said quietly, his voice a little gentler. "You know, somebody who can get up in your head and help you figure some of this shit out."

I shrugged quickly. He was talking about taking me to see a shrink, but I wasn't interested in that at all. My grandmother had been born and raised in the Deep South. She'd taught me all about evil hags and restless spirits. G was just mad and haunting me from the grave, and there wasn't a damn thing a doctor could do about it.

Gino sat up and leaned against the headboard, then pulled me up next to him. His chest was ripped with muscles and he held me tightly in his arms. "Listen, we've got a topnotch health plan through The Organization, Juicy. Ain't no shame in getting help when you need it, baby."

I shook my head. Gino just didn't get it. He might know a lot about architecture and all that college stuff, but he didn't know shit about prophecy. Couldn't no doctor with a bunch of fancy degrees save me from what was coming after me. My dreams were pure-dee prophecy and I knew it. They were a divine forecast of what was yet to come. Grandmother had sworn by the saying *warning before destruction* and lately warning bells had been ringing loud enough to make me go deaf in both my ears.

Gino got frustrated. "So, you just gonna lay up here shook and scared every goddamn night?"

I grabbed my pillow and folded it in half, then slid it behind my head. I knew Gino loved me, but he just couldn't deal with all the places my mind took me when I closed my eyes to go to sleep. He was right though. Coming out to the West Coast was supposed to be about building us a better future. A better life.

And aside from my nightmares, things had been going really good for me and Gino. For the first time in my life I was running free, like a regular young girl. Me and Gino did all the fun things that couples our age were supposed to do. We went to the movies, roller-skating, bike riding, and Gino even took me out on the golf course with him so I could learn how to swing a club. Our love was chill and easy because we really liked being together, and even after all the drama we had gone through in New York, our relationship was still strong.

In fact, we were so tight that Gino had just put a ring on my finger, and before you knew it I would be Mrs. McKay for real.

Mrs. Gino McKay.

And if that wasn't enough to rock the universe, in about five months we were gonna have us a cute little…Fear came rushing down on me again. I turned my back on Gino because I didn't want him to see how bad I was shaking.

"Yo, for real, Juice-baby…you gotta get some help," he said, peeping my tears. And then I heard a warning in his voice. "Cause I ain't tryna go through no more of that other shit we just went through, a'ight?"

I closed my eyes in embarrassment. He was talking about me getting high in the Compton beauty shop where I sold my JuicyOriginal dresses.

"It's not even like that," I mumbled as my hand moved under the covers and rested

14

on my tight stomach. "I haven't smoked weed in a long time, Gino. And I'm never gonna smoke it again."

"How do I know that, Juicy? That niggah G is in your head again, and you still running back and forth selling stuff in Compton every day. You can't be sure about what you will or won't go back to doing again."

I didn't like the way Gino was doubting me, but I couldn't even get mad at him. Getting high was new for me. I had tried to be slick with my little puff-puff game, but Gino was too hood for that. He had caught on real quick when I started coming home with red eyes and a dumb look on my face.

But it had been the nightmares that had me doing all sorts of crazy things. All that constant running from G in my sleep, and those murderous memories of Dicey and Jimmy that wouldn't leave me alone.

I thought about the baby that had been growing in my stomach for the past four months. I'd only recently found out I was pregnant, and I planned to surprise Gino with the good news on our wedding day.

"For real," I said firmly. I reached out and slipped my fingers between his. "I'm done with all that, baby. I swear I am." I wanted to say more, but I didn't wanna ruin his surprise. "You're just gonna have to trust me, baby. Just trust me."

I could tell he still had his doubts, although I couldn't believe he hadn't already figured it out. The thing was, I didn't look pregnant. Even though my hips had spread and my butt was banging like a hammer, my stomach was barely bulging.

But I couldn't wait to see the look on Gino's face when I told him. I knew my man would be beaming with pride when he found out his seed had been deeply planted. I knew Gino would be the right kind of father to our tyke. The kind of father that neither one of us had ever had.

But what about me? With a junkie mama like Cara, and a mental-case like James Joseph for a daddy, what kind of mother was I gonna be? I thought about how Grandmother had tried to bring me and Jimmy up with morals and common sense. It didn't work. Her body wasn't even cold yet when I ran off with G and shit all over the life lessons she had worked so hard to instill in me.

As Gino stroked my hair and rubbed my back, I closed my eyes and wished Grandmother was here to help me shake off the doom I felt rising inside.

I really needed her right now. I needed a hot cup of her milk-and-honey tea, and a warm slice of her sweet potato pie. I needed that old lady to pull out her crooked-tooth comb and scratch my scalp until I fell asleep sitting between her wise old legs.

I hated that I'd been so damned hard-headed, and that our lives had turned out so wrong despite all that praying and ass-whipping she used to do. Grandmother had been sanctified and saved by grace. She had put herself in Jesus' hands.

But my destiny was still chasing me. It was moving toward me like a raging storm. *Warning before destruction.* Yeah, no matter what Gino said my nightmare wasn't over. Somebody was still gonna catch a bad one. And since Jimmy was dead and gone, that somebody had to be me.

CHAPTER 3

The morning sun flooded our bedroom with its warm golden rays, and I felt Gino's tongue probing my lips before I could open my eyes. At first all I could think about was how nasty he was to be playing around in my morning breath, but then a spark of heat flushed through me that had nothing to do with the rising sun.

"Stop..." I whined, twisting away from him. The sheets were nice and warm from our night-time body heat, and I stretched my legs for a quick second, and then pushed my head under my pillow.

"C'mere, girl," he said, cupping my hip and pulling me closer so I could feel his wood poking me in the ass. All traces of my nightmare were gone as I squeezed my eyes tighter and giggled, then rolled over and brought my knees up between us.

"C'mon now," Gino said as he humped on me and tried to pull my panties down. "I gave you a little sumpthin' yesterday, so now it's your turn to give me a lil sumpthin' today."

I smirked like I didn't know what time it was.

"Oh, it's like that? You gave me some dick last night so now I gotta give you some coochie this morning, huh?"

"That's right," Gino whispered as he moved on me. "Lemme get a lil snacky snack..." he said as his fingers crept between my legs.

"Cut it out..." I tried to pretend that I wasn't itching to bounce up and down on that thick chocolate pole that was sticking out from his boxers. "Why are you always feeling on me anyway?"

I moaned as his strong hands cupped my ass and squeezed my cheeks before sliding between my crack and massaging my pussy. "Stop, *Gino*...."

I was acting stuck-up, but I loved every minute of it and Gino knew it. I was one of those extra-sexual chicks. I had been focused on my clitoris and craving sex from the time I was thirteen-years-old. Now that I had a real man in my bed, if I didn't get my hips rocked at least every other day then I just didn't feel right.

Back when I was with G sex had always been an act of desperation. He was a thirty-second man, and I used to be so ashamed of myself for humping him like a dog as I tried to get me a quick nut.

But with Gino, sex was everything I had ever dreamed it could be. Instead of masturbating all the time and writing my deepest fantasies in my Juicy Journal, my man kept me busy trying to think up fun and freaky sexcapades so we could act them out together. G might have busted my cherry, but until Gino made love to me, I was truly still a virgin.

And there were absolutely no sexual no-no's in Gino's book either. He was bold and creative with his mash game, and anything I wanted to try, any position, any flava, he was all for it. Fuck a Naughty Girls party! Me and Gino loved to shop together for all kinds of interesting sex toys, and at night we read real nasty books to each other while we played in bed. And right now he was about to tear our bed up as he played in my wet pussy like a horny teenager with a foot-long hard-on.

"Ga'head and touch it," he pushed my hand down on his dick as I moaned and sighed and licked my lips. "You know you like it."

Gino was in his prime. He could go morning, noon, and night. He cupped my big titties as we slid around in the silk sheets that smelled like sweet after-sex and rose-scented powder. My nipples tingled and grew hard under his caress. "You like this shit, don't you, Juicy?" He rubbed the head of his throbbing dick on my hot thigh, and it was so hard it felt amazing. "Ga'head, baby girl. Tell me how much you like it..."

I told him all right. In fact, I got to moaning in a foreign language as he licked my aching nipples and then dove under the covers and stuck his warm tongue in my navel.

"Oh, shit..." I threw my arms above my head and spread my legs as wide as they would go. My hips started thrusting in eager circles as I anticipated that first hot flick of his tongue on my wet lower lips. "I like it, baby..." I confessed as I gripped his soft, wavy hair and urged him to get down lower. "I like it, Gino...I like it..." He cupped my ass-cheeks in his big palms, but he was moving too slow and I damn near climbed up his face trying to get my pussy sucked.

Gino zeroed in on my clit, taking it between his lips and flicking it until it swelled and pulsated inside his mouth. Sweet fire shot through me and I arched my back and pressed myself deeper into his face as my first orgasm tore through me so hard it curled my toes. "Ahhh!" I moaned. "I like it, I like it, goddamn, baby! I *like* it!"

"I like it too," he moaned, sliding two fingers inside me as deeply as they would go. He withdrew them to rub my wet clit, then slid them back inside me. The next time he pulled them out he added another finger, and those three fingers went to work on my g-spot until I screamed and arched my back and a gush of hot cum shot all over his fingers.

"Oh, *baby*!" I wailed. I gripped his wrist and my hips humped feverishly as he slowed his rhythm. He slid his fingers out of me and brought them to his lips. He licked the last two, but held his pointer finger out to me so I could get a taste.

"You so damn sweet, baby," he told me as he leaned forward and covered my lips with his. "So damn sweet..."

I wanted to taste his cum too, but he wasn't having it. Gripping his meat with both hands, Gino pressed the tip of his dick to my wet hole, then spread my juices over my clit in a circular motion.

I felt myself stiffening down there. My clit became swollen and that delicious fire sparked up in me again.

"Put it in," I told him as the head of his dick sloshed around in my stuff. He slid his fat cap inside me, but then stopped. I felt his wood vibrating at the entryway to my tunnel, and I clamped down with my muscles and squeezed and contracted until he groaned and tiny beads of sweat popped out on his forehead.

"*Umphh!*" he grunted as he penetrated me with a deep, hard thrust. His hips moved back and forth as he pounded my pussy with the short, rough strokes he knew got me off. I spread my legs even wider, then lifted them straight up in the air before wrapping them tightly around his waist.

"Give it to me, baby," I urged, my hands clamping down on his bulging triceps as my hips rose from the bed to match his strokes. "Gimme that cum, Gino," I begged. "Fill my pussy up!"

And that's exactly what he did too. Gino seemed to forget all about me as he gripped my ass then pummeled my pelvis with his. I knew his nut was rising when he started digging and grinding, thrusting as deep as he could go, then holding himself in place and swirling his dick around inside me.

That combination of moves ignited a wave of pleasure in my clit, and my nails raked down his back as sweet release flooded both of us.

"I'm cumming, baby," Gino yelled. He banged my wet pussy two more times, real hard. "I'm cumming, Juicy," he panted as his sweat and love mixed with mine and clung to our flesh. "Yeah, baby. All this good cum is for you!"

$$$$$

I was a native New Yorker down to my bones, but as I zipped down the streets of L.A. I looked just like any other yummy from the Sunshine State. I was heading to Compton, to my girlfriend DarQuese's hair salon. I had on a pair of designer jeans and a white tank top. The California sun was hot on my shoulders as I dropped the top and floored the gas pedal in my sweet, two-door BMW sports convertible.

Gino had surprised me with the car as my Valentine's Day gift, and the money-green whip with the buttery cream interior was really something hot. Gino had named it the Green Gotcha because he said it caught mad looks and got everybody's attention.

My body was still tingling from Gino's lovemaking as I drove down the suburban streets and entered the highway. My loose hair blew in the breeze as the little Green Gotcha responded to my commands. Six months ago nobody could have told me I would have a driver's license and be pushing my very own whip, and I smiled as I thought about the day Gino had presented me with the car as a gift of his love.

"Happy Valentine's Day, baby," Gino had said as he opened our front door. His sexy brown eyes had been full of pride as he gazed at the spanking new special edition Beemer parked in our driveway.

"Damn, Gino!" I'd screamed as I ran outside. "This little mami is sweet!"

He held out his hand and a key clicker dangled from his finger. "Damn right she's sweet," he said, following me outside. "I paid cold cash for this little Green Gotcha and she's all yours."

"But I thought you said we were gonna keep it low?" I had asked as I circled the two-door whip slowly, checking it out from all angles. "This ain't hardly low."

Thanks to the countless bricks of cash that G had stashed in Grandmother's grave, Gino could afford to buy me practically any car he wanted to buy. For the first time in my life I had more money than I knew what to do with. In fact, we had rolled into Cali with so much cash that finding someplace safe to stash it had become one of our biggest issues.

Gino had landed a plush job just two days after we arrived in L.A. Some big-shot land development organization had sent him an email saying they were looking for an architect to design some new structures. Gino had jumped all over it, and The Organization had hired him right away.

The head boss was a tall, chunky Italian guy named Frankie Sanvenero. He was from Brooklyn, like Gino, which we thought was a cool coincidence. Big Frank had six brothers and too many nephews to count, and all of them had relocated out west to work for him.

Gino's first interview with them took place on a members-only golf course, and he had come home open like a book. He said The Organization's business plan was tighter than anything he had ever seen on Wall Street and that they didn't even consider going after a contract unless the starting bid was at least three mil.

It wasn't long before me and Gino started hanging out with the Sanveneros, especially Frank, who was about fifty, and his cute wife Renata, who was a lot younger than him. Frank was real tall with jet-black hair, beautiful blue eyes, and a big jolly belly, and Renata was about my height, but very neat and petite with blond-streaked curls.

One of Frank's nephews was a tall, buff dude about our age. His name was Salvatore McCain, but everybody called him Slick Sallie. Him and Gino had connected on the Brooklyn tip, and since Sallie didn't have a car and they were both die-hard Knicks fans, they rode to work together every day and played one-on-one basketball almost every weekend.

The Organization had become our family on the West Coast, and they looked out for us. They had even helped us get a sweet, two-bedroom condo in a gated subdivision. It wasn't Central Park West, but it was a long way from 136th Street and I was feeling it.

One of the first things Gino had insisted on when we got to Cali was that we keep the Feds off us. That meant we had to make sure we didn't do like Hansel and Gretel and leave a trail of breadcrumbs leading to our front door. If we were going to hide our shitload of cream and stay off the Fed's radar, we would have to stash G's cash out of sight and live mostly off the money we earned legally.

We knew better than to go near a bank with all that drug loot, so as soon as we moved into our condo Gino went and installed a fireproof metal safe in the crawl space in the attic. He stacked about a hundred and fifty grand inside that baby, but he took the rest out of the house for safekeeping.

"We'll use the money in the attic as our emergency stash," he had explained. "But we gotta bury the rest for when we retire, Juicy. And I mean we gotta bury it real deep."

"Oh, God," I had muttered feeling sick to my stomach. "We're not gonna hide it in no dead person's grave, are we?" Just thinking about how G had stashed all his dirty greenbacks in Grandmother's casket made me want to throw up.

Gino had shaken his head. "Nah. I'm not putting it in no grave, but I *am* putting it underground. Sallie's moms got a wine cellar in her house. I'm gonna stash it in the dirt down there."

I had to think about that one real hard.

"I don't know, Gino…they might call him Slick Sallie for a reason. You trust that white dude like that? Every time I see him he's got a gun sticking outta his clothes somewhere. He looks like a dabbler to me."

"Nah, Sal don't be getting high. He drives too fast so he lost his license and he's always bumming a ride, but other than that he's straight. Dude looks out for me at work all the time."

He saw the doubtful way I was eyeing him.

"What? You think I should stash it with Frankie and Renata instead?"

I shook my head real quick. "Nah. Frank's your boss. He's real nice, but I don't want him and Renata all up in our business like that."

"A'ight, then I got this," Gino said. "Sallie might be slick but he ain't no fool. He's gonna know where the safe is stashed, but he won't have the combination. You'll be the only one who can get up in it."

"But what if something happens and I need to get my hands on the money for some reason?"

"Then you just call Sallie and he'll bring the safe to you. It'll be just like this one, but bigger. And don't worry, it'll have the exact same combination that this one has."

And now, looking at the pricey green sports car made it pretty obvious that Gino had recently dipped his fingers into that retirement safe. We had already agreed that there weren't gonna be any wild shopping sprees, or big cash purchases for expensive items, so I was kinda surprised that he had spent so much money to get me a Beemer.

"But are you feelin' it?" Gino had wanted to know as I climbed inside the fresh whip and checked out all the little bells and whistles and special features.

"Hell yeah I'm feeling it," I admitted as I pushed down on the brake and the gas with both feet at the same time. "But I don't even know how to drive, baby!"

Gino had shrugged. "That's only because you're a New Yorker and nobody ever taught you. You're real smart, Juicy. You'll be spinning this baby in no time."

Something inside of me had still resisted.

"But won't a BMW and your brand new SUV sitting side-by-side in the driveway look like too much? You musta dropped a hunk for this baby."

Gino had nodded. "A gwap," he bragged proudly, "but that's what you got a dude like me for, baby. To give you the best."

"*I know*," I insisted. "But what about the Feds?"

"Don't worry about none of that," Gino had told me. "If the Feds come knocking then The Organization will cover for us."

I had accepted Gino's logic, and now as I gripped the creamy leather steering wheel, I snuck a glance at my diamond engagement ring and wondered if the Feds or anybody else was watching our spending habits and clocking our doe.

The ring was a sick hunk of diamond-shaped ice that stretched from the base of my finger damn near all the way up to my knuckle. It had belonged to Gino's mother back in the day. In fact, it was the engagement ring that G had given her before their wedding. Gino's aunt had sent it to us when he called to tell her we were getting married. She said it was part of a custom-designed set that G had gotten made somewhere in Asia.

I would have been just as happy with a smaller, less lavish ring, and sometimes I wondered if Gino was trying to compete with his father by showering me with expensive gifts all the time when we were supposed to be hiding our money and keeping it low.

I mean, really. The condo, the sports car, the ring. All that flossing. I didn't require none of that stuff because Grandmother had raised me and Jimmy humble and brought us up Vienna-sausage poor. But like his father, Gino always insisted on giving me the best. Finery might have been in his blood, but there was something about a man's ego that I just didn't understand. Being proud wasn't something that came naturally to me because I'd been taught that pride was the mother of all sins. It always went before a deadly fall.

I exited the freeway, turned the corner, and zoomed toward my girlfriend's beauty parlor. A young corner boy who was leaning against a light pole stood up straight as I drove past. He whistled at the Green Gotcha in envy and admiration.

I smiled at him. I guess me and Gino did have a lot to be proud of. My ride was sweet and there was no denying it. Green on the outside and cream on the inside. It was hard to knock that.

CHAPTER 4

The first time I laid eyes on DarQuese Middleton I almost freaked straight out. I had walked through the doors of the Hella Hot House of Hair and asked to speak to the owner. The girl at the front counter had smiled and pointed me toward a giant stylist who was wet-wrapping a customer's hair in the last chair.

"Hi," I'd said, faking confidence as I strode over to her station. She was tall as hell. Probably six-four. Her back was to me, and she was working magic with her sweet-smelling wrap lotion.

"My name is Juicy Stanfield. I just moved here from New York. I was wondering if I could speak to you about some business for a minute."

She stood up straight and turned toward me, and I got so shook I almost ran back out the door.

The entire right side of her face looked like some burnt cheese that had slid off a pizza. Her eye was almost melted shut, and her cheek drooped low with folds of excess skin that cascaded down to her jaw.

I had to force myself to stand there without cringing, but when she turned and faced me with a smile, to my surprise the left side of her face was totally beautiful. The skin was smooth and tight. The features were soft and feminine. She was gorgeous. But she was horrible-looking too. I didn't know this chick, or know a damn thing about her story, but the conflict between the two sides of her face just about blew my mind.

"Hell yeah, you can push your dresses outta here," DarQuese quickly agreed when I told her about my JuicyOriginal line of trend-setting urban wear. Just looking at her I could tell she was into fashion and was probably one of those high-maintenance chicks who spent at least three hours getting dressed every morning. She had long legs, pert titties, and a high, muscular ass. Her shoulder-length permed hair was some of the silkiest I had ever seen. Her shit was tight all the way around.

I had followed her into a back room that she used as an office, and I tried to focus on the good side of her face as I quickly ran down my profit-sharing business proposition.

She waved her hand to shut me up before I was halfway through. "Alright, alright. I'll give you a shot. But quit with all that bullshit about splitting your profits and shit. How you gonna stay in business talkin' silly nonsense like that? You designed all them clothes, didn't you? You bought the fly material. You sewed everything together. Give me one good reason why I should be trying to eat off your back?"

I had shrugged, surprised. "Ummm…because it's your shop? And they're your customers?"

DarQuese smirked. "My customers come in here because I have low prices and my stylists are the shit. I might do my business in the hood, but I'm a professional, baby.

I don't double and triple book appointments, and I damn sure don't start working on somebody's head first thing in the morning and make them sit around all day waiting for me to finish it. My customers are loyal, but they're also smart. So, if your gear is as hot as you say it is, and if this is the only shop in Compton where ladies can buy it, then that just gives them one more good reason to keep coming through my door."

I liked this girl already! All the other beauty shops I'd gone in had been full of hostile sistahs who had looked at me like I was begging for the stray hairs they swept up off the floor. I knew my fashion sense was hot. I knew I could sew, and I knew I made the kind of gear that sexy young chicks with big breasts and banging booties looked good in. But the owners and their stylists had stared me down the minute I started talking about us doing business together, and I knew they were checking out my big booty and talking shit about me before I could get back out the door. But not DarQuese. She seemed friendly and real generous.

I nodded at her. "Oh, my collection is hot," I said with assurance. "You can believe that. It's flamin' hot."

DarQuese nodded back. "Okay, cool. We'll see. If you're a real hustler then you're probably used to selling shit all up outta your trunk. Why don't you bring a few pieces inside? Let's see if these Compton sistahs got a taste for some of your East Coast flava."

$$$$$

You woulda thought I was giving away free creamy crack the way them Compton girls crowded around trying to get at my JuicyOriginals.

I had 'em lined up.

I sold out of everything in my car in less than fifteen minutes. Chicks were snatching my hot little dresses and sizing them up, and some even asked DarQuese if they could go in her backroom and try on a few pieces. I knew I had them open when they started whipping out cell phones and calling their homegirls. They were asking what size they wore, and taking pictures with their phones and text messaging them all across town.

DarQuese had laughed and brushed me off when I offered to split my profits with her again. She was real cool, and she put me in the mind of my old friend, Dicey.

Like Dicey, she was street smart and had a lot on the cap. And just like Dicey, she became somebody I could really talk to. But unlike Dicey, DarQuese wasn't gonna get her throat slit and her tongue cut out just for schooling me and being my friend.

Hanging out in DarQuese's shop became one of my favorite things to do, but it also made me kinda homesick for Harlem too. She had five stylists working her chairs, and like the Dominican shop where I used to wash hair back in Harlem, there was always plenty of good food, good gossip, crazy chicks, and banging music up in there too.

Meeting DarQuese ended up being one of the best things to happen to me in Cali. She had lived in Philly and Brooklyn too, so she could be really loud and ghetto and sometimes she used her height to back females down, but as Quese had proven on the first day I met her, she was also one of the realest people I could ever know.

CHAPTER 5

It was after ten a.m. when I turned onto DarQuese's street. It was a busy block with a whole lot of small stores and specialty shops, and the upbeat energy and flava in the air put me in the mind of 125th Street in Harlem. I pulled into a parking spot a few doors down from the shop, put my top up, and made sure to lock my car door when I got out.

I was heading toward the beauty shop when a guy standing across the street shouted my name. I didn't even have to look to know who it was. His voice was so deep and hard you couldn't mistake him for nobody else.

Dude's name was Pit, and he was a real buff, real mean little midget. Pit stood about four-and-a-half feet tall, and every inch of him was muscled-up gangsta. He owned an urban clothing store across the street from DarQuese's shop, and he was forever trying to get me to buy a pair of the stylish, custom-designed sneakers that he sold.

"What it do, Juicy?" he hollered, lifting his chin at me. I lifted mine back and kept it moving. Sneakers and hoodies weren't the only things Pit traded for cash. He was deep in the local drug game, and the two or three urban clothing stores he owned in Compton were just money-washing fronts for the real product of value that he moved on the streets.

I frowned when I saw him running over to cut me off. He stood in front of me rocking on his heels and grinning like a little boy who was about to beg for a piece of candy.

He lifted his chin again. "Yo, when you gonna let me holla at you, shawty? You and me can do some real nasty thangs together, ma."

I rolled my eyes at his tired ass. Pit had been trying to get at me since the first day I met him.

"You fresh around here, right?" he had asked me one day as I was going into Quese's shop. "What's ya name, baby?"

"Juicy," I had answered.

Pit had chuckled and peered around me so he could see my ass. "Juicy, huh?" He chuckled again. "I bet the fuck you is."

I had gone inside the shop and asked DarQuese who in the hell the nasty little short dude was.

"Oh, that's Pit," Quese had told me. "My homeboy. That's his urban clothing joint across the street."

I'd laughed. "Pit, like in armpit?"

DarQuese had rolled her eyes. "You stupid, Juicy."

"No, for real. I'm just trying to figure him out. Pit, like in pit-i-ful?"

She smirked. "That shit ain't funny, Juicy. It's Pit, as in Pit-bull. And don't be forming no ignorant-ass opinions about him because he's little, neither. He's a boss on the streets and he's a real man. He keeps order around here. If it wasn't for Pit them crazy thugs out there slanging rock on the corner would be shaking me down for my cash bag every night. Pit makes sure them niggahs fall back when they see me coming."

It didn't take me long to figure out that Pit and DarQuese had some shit going. And it was a whole lot more than just business like she tried to pretend.

"He don't judge me!" she had screamed on me one day when I pushed her into admitting they were fuck buddies. "He's a fuckin' man and I'm a woman! He don't look at my flaws, and I don't look at his neither!"

I had swallowed real hard because I had basically forgotten that she was disfigured. She had confided in me that her ex-boyfriend had thrown gasoline on her when she was sleeping and lit a match, but I hardly ever focused on the scarred side of DarQuese's face anymore. I just didn't notice it. She had become beautiful all the way around to me. Yeah, I knew most people would be real pressed about being all burnt up like that, but DarQuese always seemed so confident about herself, like her scars weren't even there.

But for real, I couldn't even imagine her tree-tall ass getting banged up by some funny-looking troll Pit's size, but she assured me that the only thing short on Pit was his legs. Quese said she'd been with countless men who were way shorter than her, and she swore everybody was exactly the same height when they were mashing it up in the sheets.

Looking down at Pit now, I still couldn't see it.

"So, me and you gonna holla a lil bit or what?" Pit repeated, still blocking my path.

Ignoring that noise, I stepped around him and he reached out and grabbed my left hand.

"What's this little shit, five carats?" He crushed my fingers together as he eyed my engagement ring.

"No," I said coldly and snatched my hand away. "It's ten."

"Only *ten* fuckin' carats?" Quick as hell, he grabbed my hand again. "Yo," he laughed, "that niggah you got is straight slippin' Juicy. You worth at least twice that, ma. Tell him to come work for me so he can upgrade this lil knuckleduster shit. Your back action alone is worth ten carats. We ain't even factoring in them big titties, that hair, and your gorgeous face, baby doll."

I snatched away from him again and walked toward the shop. Pit was just mad because I wouldn't give him no play.

"Oh, so it's like that?" he yelled as I strutted down the block with my nose in the air. "You just gonna play me like that?"

I couldn't help thinking about how G would have slumped him just for letting his eyeballs roll over me. Let alone talking to me like that. I knew better than to tell Gino that Pit had dissed my ring, though. He would've taken it as a diss to me, a diss to his moms, and in a crazy way, a diss to G too.

Because as good a man as Gino was, he was still a McKay, and in some ways it was like father, like son. Gino had a lot of G's protective instincts when it came down to me. L.A. might not be his hood, but Gino was the type of gorilla who traveled with his own zoo. It just wasn't worth it, risking Gino's job and his status at The

Organization by bringing him all the way to Compton to beat some ignorant midget's ass.

Besides, I knew I had a nice chunk of ice hanging off my finger. Granite McKay had top-shelf tastes, and the only kind of diamond he would have slid on Gino's moms was the best of the best.

Ignoring Pit as he kept up his little beef, I stepped calmly into DarQuese's shop and closed the door behind me.

$$$$$

Walking into DarQuese's beauty salon was like walking into Grandmother's kitchen. It was so comfortable that I wanted grab a big black frying pan and make me a fried baloney sandwich on Wonder bread.

There was some old-school R&B music playing over the speakers, and the whole joint was decorated in a real fly combination of red, white, silver, and black.

"Hey, Teenie," I greeted the cute young girl who worked at the front counter.

"What's up, Juicy!" she smiled. "Today is Thursday. That means your big day is almost here, girl! You excited?"

I grinned and nodded. I was crazy excited! I really, really was! Where I came from chicks didn't hardly think about getting married. Usually a girl just had a couple of baby daddies and then called it a day.

"Where's the honeymoon going down at?" Teenie asked.

"Acapulco, Mexico," I told her grinning. "And I can't wait to hit the beach!"

A few minutes later I was leaning back in DarQuese's sink getting my hair washed. I loved the way she scrubbed my scalp and pulled her strong fingers through my tangled curls.

"I tried on my Maid-of-Honor dress last night," Quese said, giggling. "It's fitting me like a mutha, girl. Especially in the back. You carrying that baby all in your ass, Juicy, but you ain't gonna be the only big-booty star at the show, my sistah! I might find me a husband too."

With my eyes closed, I smirked. "I sure hope you do," I said, then muttered under my breath, "then maybe you can drop Pit's stray ass off at the dog pound where you got him from."

"Ow!" I yelped when she yanked my hair.

"I heard that shit, Juicy. I can't help it if you don't understand about me and Pit. We got us a nice thing going on."

"Does Pit know that?"

She jerked my head again.

"What? You must want me to get with one of them little-dick white dudes your man be chilling with. Them shiesty-ass Italians."

"They're not shiesty, Quese. They're businessmen. Just like you're a businesswoman. That's all."

Her fingers almost scratched the skin off my scalp as she snorted, "Yeah, okay. That's how much you know."

"I do know," I said, jerking my head to the side.

"No, Juicy," DarQuese said dryly. She yanked my head back over the sink, and then mushed down on my forehead to keep it where she wanted it. "You don't know shit. I peeped all their games when y'all had that cookout that time. Especially that white boy, Sallie. He was tryna eat my pussy that day, you know."

I bust out laughing. "Quese, please. Sal is real regular. I don't even think he likes sistahs that way."

"He ain't gotta like us to wanna fuck us, Juicy. For real, you better watch his ass 'cause he's got a reputation on the track. Shit, ain't none of them Italians clean! They be frontin' like they some big-shot corporate executives when they're really just a crew of con-artists living the high life off somebody else's dime."

I shrugged. DarQuese was just jealous because me and Renata Sanvenero had been hanging out a lot. I'd made a mistake and brought her to the shop with me one day when I was dropping off some dresses, and that shit had pissed Quese off. She had stunted real hard with Renata, towering over her and grilling her with the hood-face real mean-like, and I didn't understand where all that heat was coming from. Renata might have been white, but she was definitely cool. She always went out of her way to look out for me since I was new to Cali and all. Quese really went nuts when she found out I had asked Renata to be one of my bridesmaids.

"Damn, Juicy! You ain't gotta be asking no white girl to be in your wedding! I know you ain't got no family out here or nothing, but if you need to fill up the church I can call some of my cousins and their friends to come eat up all your food."

"But most of your cousins are already coming to the wedding, Quese. Plus, I didn't ask Renata because I needed to fill up my bridal line," I told her. "I asked her because she's good people and I like her."

That had pissed Quese right off.

"We gone see about all that shit," she had muttered under her breath.

And now, I sat back with my head in the sink as she slathered a deep-conditioner in my hair. I was dying to bust Pit out and tell her how he had just now tried to push up on me again, but Quese was in a good mood today and I didn't wanna ruin it. She was buttering up my hair for free, like she always did, and she had promised to shape my eyebrows with hot wax since I was too chicken to go for all that thread-cutting stuff.

Fuck Pit, I told myself as DarQuese wrapped a towel around my head and led me from the sink over to the hair dryer. I wasn't about to let no dude come between me and my new friend. After all, if Quese was digging him so hard then he couldn't be all that bad.

Nah. He couldn't be.

CHAPTER 6

Meanwhile, Back in Harlem

It was late Saturday night and Money-Making Monique sat on a stool at the G-Spot Social Club sipping from a cold bottle of beer. The shitty tips she'd earned had put her in a funky mood and blown her high. She had smoked some chronic and slurped back two Incredible Hulks right before going onstage, but after snatching up just a few wrinkled twenty dollar bills from the filthy floor she was ready to curse all them stingy, meat-beating niggahs out.

She glanced around the club with her bottom lip poked out. Even after six months of bad luck and hard knocks, it was still hard for her mind to grasp what her eyes clearly saw: The G-Spot was a dump. It had fallen off. Way off.

At the height of its magnificence, back when Granite McKay was still alive and running things with a concrete fist, the G-Spot had been one of the premiere gentlemen's clubs on the East Coast. Pimps, ballers, kingpins, Hollywood stars, and professional athletes had eagerly dropped a grand just for the privilege of stepping through the door.

G had run his shit so tight the club operated like a well-oiled cash machine, and everybody on his payroll ate until they were full. He'd had a loyal crew of hardbody soldiers who had been down with him from his roots, and every last one of his strippers worked like hell to get customers to buy out the bar and keep the sheets stank and hot too.

Pairing up with a luscious stripper named Honey Dew, Monique had been G's top money-maker. Honey Dew had mad control over her pussy muscles and could grip a soda bottle with her twat, but Monique was the headliner who had the kind of phatty package that kept the heat-meter spiked on high every single night. With a thick blooming onion, and her trademark fishnet stockings, shot-callers used to drop prime dollars just to watch her bend over and step outta her panties.

And along with her make-a-niggah-cum moves and multiple ill na-na striptease routines, Monique had been blessed with something that none of the other dancers in the G-Spot could even come close to competing with.

Three titties.

Her two normal breasts were plump and round like cantaloupes, and sat in the regular position on her chest. But that third titty, the one that was the size of a twelve-year-olds and drove all the freaky niggahs wild, was right in the middle. Some called it a birth defect, but Monique called it a blessing. It was ultra-sensitive and sat up much higher than the other two, and when the clients were respecting her game and tossing their tips right, she would fuck their heads up by gripping her two big titties with both hands, as she stretched her tongue downward and slurped the hell outta that little one.

But the days of cash-bomb dropping ballers in the G-Spot were over. Without G

28

around to drive the train, what remained of his crew had lost their focus and fallen off the tracks. Monique looked at the stage in disgust. The marble floors that used to be clean enough to eat off were now straight filthy. The Spot had gone from being Harlem's only celebrity-exclusive establishment with a cover charge of a grand at the door and another grand to purchase chips, to being a grimy hole in the wall where any old regular niggah could slide in for a C-note as long as he bought at least two drinks before the end of the night.

Monique flicked some nasty, booger-looking thing off the edge of the bar and frowned. One of the first things to go had been Greco's cleaning crew, and unless a miracle happened and they struck some kinda gold, the security team was about to be out the door too.

It was like the entire ecosystem in Harlem had collapsed the moment G died. And even though Ace and Pluto, G's two main henchmen, were all fucked up behind the G-Spot's downfall, Monique was devastated way beyond repair. She had been straight hysterical over G's death because her life had been thoroughly ruined. Every last one of her big, brilliant dreams had been deaded, and all because of one stupid little bitch who didn't know the rules of the game or the value of her pussy.

Juicy Stanfield.

Just thinking about that little Harlem rat got Monique so depressed she felt like going back to the tiny roach-trap she shared with Pluto and sticking her head in the fuckin' oven.

But instead, she snapped her fingers above the bar and signaled to Bizzie to bring her another round. She'd already been onstage six times since the doors opened earlier that afternoon, and she needed to get her head buzzed if she was gonna make it through her last few sets of the night.

"Bitch I see you!" Bizzie based as Monique snapped for him twice, then twice again. He took his time coming down to her end of the bar. "A'ight. This is five so far tonight," Bizzie warned, sliding her another beer. "You know Pluto's new rule. Strippers and hoes got a two-drink limit."

"Fuck Pluto!" Monique snarled. She couldn't believe this shit. Back when Cooter's stuttering ass was bartending she had gotten free drinks all night long, no questions asked. Shit, a hoe got thirsty when she was out there mashing hard. Besides, the bar used to rake in so much doe from the customers that they didn't sweat the little bit extra the bitches drank up.

She looked at Bizzie and rolled her eyes. He was short and skinny, and had a damn curly kit in his ashy hair. Even Cooter, with his slow-talking self, had been a better bartender than this sweet-ass was. Out of all the jobless niggahs in Harlem, she didn't know why Pluto had put Bizzie on. Pluto wasn't no G, that was for sure. And neither was his sidekick, Ace. Both of them small-time niggahs balled up together coulda fit inside the toe of one of G's alligator shoes.

Because no matter how coldblooded he had been, no matter how cruel or how merciless his heart was, G had always been about his bizzness. He was the perfect combination of guns and gloss. Of danger and dapper. He was a ruthless OG, but he was a suave, charismatic gentleman too. G had lived by a code that gutter niggs like Ace and Pluto couldn't even conceive of. That's why his clientele had felt like it was a privilege to walk into his joint and empty their wallets at the door. Some of the richest and most powerful boss-men in the country had wilted like hot bitches at G's feet. He'd had 'em all sprung. G had been more than just a kingpin or a boss. He had been a living legend, and he'd elevated the hustler's game to a level that had never before been seen in Harlem and would probably never be seen again. But all that was over now.

Thanks to that dumb bitch Juicy and her slow-ass brother Jimmy, G was toast and so was everything Monique had ever worked for. Over the past few months she had watched the Spot's main crew break for the doors like roaches scattering under a light. And she couldn't blame them neither. All the shine and the status of the place was gone. They'd plummeted down from a multi-million dollar operation to some real low-level ma-and-pa shit, and no matter how loyal and dedicated a soldier was, couldn't nobody afford to work for free.

And not one area of the Spot had survived untouched either. The hoes suffered, the bar suffered, and the kitchen was ready to close completely down.

But what was worse, the cut room upstairs had damn near halted production too. What had once been a major drug cutting and distribution operation on the top floor of the G-Spot was now just a big old half-empty room filled with triple-beam scales and other drug-manufacturing paraphernalia. The fiends on the streets had to find alternate trap boys to cop their product from, because G's old corner boys were almost always dry.

G had always played all his cards close to his chest and nobody, not even Ace or Pluto, knew how to make contact with his main supplier. Nobody that is, except his right-hand man Moonie. But Moonie, just like G's mysterious connect, had gone deep underground, and not a soul knew how to find him.

And with the drug game up for grabs, every small-time hustler in Harlem had gone into desperation mode. Cooter had hooked up with that crazy come-up named Flex and tried to muscle in on G's old drug turf in the projects, and both of them niggahs had gotten beat down and buck-shot full of holes. Flex's shit was critical for a minute, but Cooter had taken a fatal ass-kicking and died laying in the street. Face down, brains bashed in, dead with his shoes on.

Monique took a long swig of brew and dug around in her shoe and retrieved the clipped roach she had stashed under the arch of her foot. Yeah, times were hard, and her blood went to boiling every time she thought about how laced her shit woulda been if it wasn't for that bitch Juicy. She lit her joint and pulled on it so hard the tip steamed red and a stray seed popped out and landed on her thigh.

Shit! Monique cursed and quickly brushed the hot ember from her lap. These days she couldn't even get her head right without getting burnt. She glanced around the club. There was no way in fuck she woulda been sitting up at the bar smoking no chronic if G was still alive. But he wasn't alive.

That niggah was dead. Dead as shit.

CHAPTER 7

There was no disputing the fact that G was dead, but what Monique didn't know was that someone real close to G was still alive.

One night a few weeks later, after the doors to the G-Spot had closed, the bar was counted down, and all the dried cum had been washed out of the sheets, Monique walked into G's office. Her feet were throbbing and her coochie was scuffed as she plopped down into a soft leather chair and sparked up a Newport.

Pluto, the three hundred pound bitch-beater she called her man, was hunched over G's desk going through the mail. Monique could feel the meanness radiating off him. He was like this every night after counting up the day's take. Short on money and ready to fight.

She sat quietly while he shuffled through the stacks of bills that still came to G's post office box. She was tired and ready to go home, but she knew better than to interrupt him. The last time she opened her mouth while he was trying to read something he had thrown a stapler at her and damn near knocked out her front tooth.

He tore open a letter and his lips started moving as he slowly read. Monique shook her head as she heard his dumb ass struggling to sound out some of the words. She eyed him on the sly. No matter which way she looked at him there was nothing cute about Pluto. They had been together for a good minute now, and even though Pluto was mean and violent, Monique stayed with him because he was also powerful and dangerous.

Pluto had been one of the strongest lieutenants in the G-Spot's army. Next to Moonie he was the closest thing G had to a friend, and G had trusted him as far as he could trust anyone. Ace had been a big part of all that too. Both of them had taken oaths of complete loyalty to G, and each had lived up to that vow until the day G died.

Monique shifted in her chair as Ace entered the office. She could see why him and Pluto were so tight. They were an even match. One was just as ugly as the other one.

"Close ya fuckin' legs," Ace snapped at her. "Your damn pussy stanks." He turned to his boy. "You ready to roll, man?"

"Yo, hold da fuck up," Pluto said. His lips were still moving as he continued to read from the piece of stationary he held in his hand. "Check this shit out," he said standing up from G's chair. "Yo, man," he tried to pass the piece of paper off to his partner. "You ain't even gonna believe this shit..."

Ace waved him off. "Ga'head. I'm good, man. Just read it to me."

Illiterate ass! Monique smirked. With dumb and dumber running the Spot no wonder it had turned out worse than a girl's home run by a crew of broke-dick pimps.

"Nah, slime. You gotta read it. You ain't gonna believe this shit!" Pluto insisted.

"Niggah just read it! Who's it from?"

"It's from some place called Sunny Hills Sanatorium. It's way up in Canada."

Hearing this, Monique jumped up to take a peek as Pluto moved his finger under the sentences and began sounding his words out like a first grader:

"Dear Mr. McKay. Greetings from the Sunny Hills Sana-to-rium for Restor...a...restora...tive Care. We are hon-red that you have been a valued pa-tron of our services for more than ten years. Your on-going de...deci...de-ciseeon to settle your account's..."

Monique couldn't take it no more. She ignored Pluto and read on silently over his shoulder.

Your ongoing decision to settle your account's annual balance in advance has made it possible for us to provide your wife with topnotch professional care. Unfortunately, it has come to our attention that your balance has been depleted and your account is now seriously past due.

Here at Sunny Hills Sanatorium we rely solely on the financial support of clients like you to ensure we can provide for the unique needs of your loved one. In order to continue offering our quality services to Mrs. Salida McKay, you will have ten days from the date of this letter to remit your past due balance in full. If you wish to maintain a suite at our facility you will be required to remit full payment for the next twelve months at this time as well.

If you are unable to do so, it will be with great sadness and profound regret that we will be forced to discharge Mrs. Salida McKay from our facility. We have truly enjoyed our long-term relationship with you. We hope to continue providing you with the security and peace of mind of knowing your loved one is receiving the absolute best mental and physical health care possible.

Sincerely,
Joseph Gordon
Director, Sunny Hills Sanatorium for Restorative Care

About a dozen of the words written on the paper flew off and embedded themselves in Monique's brain. They were the twelve most important words she had heard in the last six months.

We will be forced to discharge Mrs. Salida McKay from our facility.

Monique just couldn't believe it. A ghost straight outta G's past was alive and kickin'.

And as she would soon find out, that ghost was alive, kickin', slickin', trickin', and best of all, *crazy* as hell!

CHAPTER 8

Unlike his father, there was always something sexually freaky going on up in Gino's head. After all those years I'd spent fantasizing about how wonderful dick could be and the hundreds of ways I'd dreamed of getting my stuff beat up, I felt lucky to fall in love with a dude who had just as much erotic creativity as I did.

"Ease down on it," Gino whispered. His strong hands gripped my waist as he lowered me onto his thick, straining dick.

Our wedding was right around the corner and we were sitting in a bathtub full of warm, bubbly water. At least Gino was. I was crouched over him, backing my ass down on him so he could hit it from behind the way I liked it.

The hot soapy water added a whole different aspect to getting nasty in the tub. I peeked between my thighs and licked my lips as Gino's dark manhood thrust up outta the big white bubbles and slid deeply inside me.

Sparks shot through my pussy like the water was electrified. Titties jiggling, I raised and lowered myself slowly, riding him like he was a giant black thoroughbred. Behind me, Gino moaned against my neck, then nibbled my ear. I gasped as he gently pinched my nipples with his wet fingertips, the soapy water making his slippery friction that much more exciting.

Suddenly, Gino lifted me completely off of him and pushed me forward. I pressed my palms to the bottom of the tub and balanced my weight until I was almost on my knees. Gino got up on his knees too, and he entered me again with one long, deep stroke. A stroke so hard and delicious that my pussy hiccupped twice and then I came just like that.

"Yeah, baby girl," he moaned in my ear. "Get yours..." But that little nut hadn't done a damn thing for me, and he knew it. I was ready for round two as Gino reached in front of me and cupped a handful of suds then massaged it all over my aching, swollen clit.

"That's it," he said as his lips trailed hot, wet kisses down my back. "Get some more, Juicy." He sucked hickeys from my neck down to the crack of my ass while his dick worked like an underwater jack-pump, drilling a nice hot hole in my pussy.

I got me another small nut before Gino lifted me from the water and wrapped me in a thick beach towel. He carried me into our bedroom and lay me on the bed, then lifted one of my legs over his shoulder and gave my pussy two deep licks.

"Is this what you want?" he teased, parting my curly hairs with his tongue.

Hell yeah, I wanted that, but I wanted something else first.

"C'mere," I told him, swinging my legs around and pushing him back on the bed until he was laying flat on his back. All that beautiful black dick coming off of him looked like a long marble mountain of perfection to me. It was thick and perfectly shaped, and the veins running along the side throbbed like his dick had a migraine headache.

I gobbled that shit up.

Gone were the days when I had to practice sucking dick on a cucumber. I had the real thing now, and Gino's dick was the only one that I had ever willingly sucked.

My man really deserved this neck pussy, and I slurped that thang half to death. I planted hot kisses up and down his shaft, then covered the smooth, mushroom-shaped head with my lips and swirled my wet tongue around the rigid rim as I gripped the base in my hand and jacked him slow and tight.

Gino sighed and cupped my cheeks. His fingers trailed down my neck. He pumped in and out slowly; making sure the tip of his dick deeply penetrated that trap door in my throat on each stroke. I hummed all over that baby, slurping and sucking it like there was gold in the center and I was desperate to strike it rich. I felt his nut rising, and Gino felt it too.

He tapped my chin and then extracted himself slowly from my mouth. He stood up, and I lay down on my stomach and brought my right knee up to my chest. I bit into the pillow as Gino inched into me just a little at a time. My pussy was thumping to a nasty beat, and Gino got down to my favorite song.

My juices sloshed each time he pushed his meat into me, and the wet, splashing sounds my coochie hole made when his nuts smacked against me drove both of us crazy.

"Ahhh..." I growled deep in my throat. Gino placed his hand on the flat of my back and pressed down gently as he worked his dick between my thick ass-cheeks. Trying his best not to come, he pulled out and smacked my ass.

I shivered as my flesh jiggled.

He smacked me again, this time on the other cheek. The sound of his hand slapping my booty combined with the heat flaring up on my sensitive skin was so erotic I started humping and rubbing my pussy on the sheets and I almost came again.

Gino spanked me with one hand and guided his pole between my buns. I bucked up and opened wide, pointing my asshole up in the air as my pussy bubbled and begged him to get back inside!

He climbed on top of me, and the sensation of his pubic hairs scraping against my ass cheeks is what sent me over the edge. My clit started throbbing in triple time, and when Gino reached under me and pinched my nipples while pounding me into the mattress, we both started bucking like horses.

"Ooohh..." Gino moaned behind me as I slobbered all over the bed. "I luh this tight pussy, Juicy. I luh the hell outta this pussy."

All I could do was lay there and nod. I felt just like I was riding a warm wave on a magical river of love. Because between the slobber trickling out of my mouth and the hot cum gushing from between my legs, I had wet the whole damn bed up.

$$$$$

I had already decided not to tell Gino about how Pit had been pushing up on me, or about all the shit he had talked about my engagement ring, but I didn't have to because as it turned out Pit told Gino himself.

My wedding was only two days away and DarQuese had promised to do something cold with my hair.

"You know I don't usually get pressed out by what's sitting on a chick's head, but you got some real pretty hair, Juicy," she said as she rubbed a thick, creamy shampoo through my curls and smoothed it down to my ends with a rat-tail comb.

"Your shit is obedient, you know? It does exactly what a stylist tells it to do. I'm about to tell this baby to be butter for you on Saturday, okay?"

I laughed and enjoyed the sensation her hands were creating all over my head.

"Oh," she said. "I forgot to tell you. Cynthia swung by earlier. She left an envelope for you. She said you was holding something for her."

Damn! I sat up and sucked my teeth. I had forgotten all about Cynthia. She was a beautiful big girl that I'd been sewing for lately. Her sister hosted a lot of hood fashion shows, and I'd designed three figure-flattering dresses for Cynt that I was supposed to bring with me and leave at the shop for her today.

"I forgot," I told Quese, covering my mouth. "I totally forgot."

"How did you forget to sew her stuff, Juicy? The show is tonight. You know that girl is depending on you!"

"No," I shook my head quickly. "I already finished the dresses. I just left them at home and forgot to bring them with me."

"Oh," DarQuese said, pulling me back in the chair. She plunged her hands into my hair again. "Well, shit. That ain't no problem. Just call your man and tell him to do you a solid. Ask him to run Cynt's stuff over here and tell him you'll pay him with free pussy for the rest of his life."

Gino was right on it. My call had caught him and Sallie coming out of a business meeting, and he agreed to swing by our condo to pick up the dresses and bring them down to the shop for me.

"A'ight," he chuckled when I told him what Quese had said about him getting free pussy for life. "I'm counting on that, baby. For real."

"Wait!" I said, trying to catch him before he hung up. "Be careful about how you carry those dresses, okay? Cynt's modeling them tonight so make sure you don't let them get wrinkled. Just leave them on the hanger and hook it in the backseat of your ride."

Gino didn't know it, but I had been pushing my JuicyOriginals non-stop so I could buy him a dope wedding gift. At least three nights a week I would fuck him real good, then go in my sewing room and stay on my machine until daybreak.

I had full access to our bank account so I could have easily whipped out my debit card, but I was determined to buy my man something with money that I had earned on my own.

The black onyx ring that G used to twirl on his finger had been a wedding gift from Gino's mom. Gino had seemed real proud when he talked about his mother buying that ring, and I had found a jeweler to design him an onyx and diamond ring that was twice as grand as the one G had worn.

I was planning on surprising Gino with it on our wedding day, right before I told him about our baby. Our future was looking damn good and I couldn't wait to reveal all the surprises I had for my man!

I was sitting under the dryer with a hot oil treatment in my hair when I saw Teenie jump up from the front desk and jet toward the door. A second later, two chicks who had been waiting to get their eyebrows waxed were right behind her. They waved for DarQuese to hurry up and come see what was going on, and that's when I jumped up and ran over to the door too.

I almost blacked out when I saw what was happening. Gino and Slick Sallie were standing outside in business suits and white shirts, and Gino was about to give Pit a beat down. My man had Cynthia's dresses slung carelessly over his shoulder, and him and Pit were going in hard.

"What the hell is going on?" I yelled as I pushed past DarQuese and went to stand beside my man.

"Everything is chill, Juicy," Gino said calmly. He gave me a quick kiss. "I got this, baby."

Pit started laughing. He was standing there with one of his friends, showing his ass and trying to flex for his audience.

"Sup, Juice," Pit said. "I was just telling ya man here how I could help him get an upgrade on that tiny speck of glass he got a dime like you flossin'. Looks like some shit he pulled outta a Happy Meal."

Pit's lil posse started laughing, and then Slick Sallie bust out with a stupid joke of his own.

"Are you crazy, dude? That's at least a hundred grand hanging off Juicy's finger!" He laughed. "As broke as I am, I'd jack her for that ring myself if I thought I could get away with it."

Gino didn't laugh at all. Instead, he swelled up on Pit. The two of them went back to beefing, but I got distracted from what they were saying because the guy standing next to Pit looked real familiar.

Oh, hell yeah. I'd definitely seen him before. He was an ex-NBA player who used to ball hard in Philly back when I first got with G.

I tried to ignore him and focus on the drama going down between Gino and Pit, but dude kept staring at me with this wicked look in his eyes. He was tatted up Philly-style and still sporting his trademark cornrows. He was still fine as shit too. I could tell he recognized me, but I turned my head and tried to play him off.

"Hey ma," he said softly. I knew damn well he was talking to me. But I didn't want no trouble. I swear to God I didn't. Me and Gino were fresh in town and this wasn't our hood. I igged that fool as hard as I could.

"Hey, ma," he said again, and this time he was loud-talking over Pit and Gino and pointing dead at me. "Don't I know you from somewhere?"

I gave him the dumb look and shook my head, no. Quese, Teenie, and a bunch of Hella Hot's customers were standing there catching every word that sailed by, and all I wanted him to do was shut up.

Instead, he looked over at Pit and bust out laughing. "Yo, man. I *know* this chick. Shawty is a firecracker. Hot as hell. Sweet too. I got me some of that in a club back in New York, ak. Mami got a cute little monkey on her, word."

Everybody out there shut the hell up and stared at me. I couldn't even look at Gino. I was so ashamed I wanted to shrivel up and disappear. I'd only willingly fucked two men in my whole life: G and Gino. None of them other perverts who had raped and abused me counted. Me and Gino had both agreed on that. But what about this dude? He was the first man to ever eat my pussy! Did he count?

"I don't know what you talking about," I lied hotly. "I'm not even from around here."

He cracked up laughing. "Oh, I know where you from baby girl! The same place you was from when I slurped your shit out."

"Yo, muh'fucka–" Gino stepped up on dude and amped right the fuck out. "You said you slurped somebody's shit?" He was way thicker and taller than the Philly baller and he got in that ass about ten feet deep, drilling Mister Cornrows with a blow so fast and hard it sent his skinny ass rolling over the hood of a parked car.

"Oh, shit!" Pit squealed as Gino went after the dude, stalking him out into the street. The baller swung a few hood blows, and a lucky one caught Gino on the chin. Cynthia's dresses got slung straight to the ground as Gino snatched the dude up, flung him back onto the parked car, and then smashed his grill into the front bumper about ten times straight.

The Philly dude wasn't no punk, but he had absolutely no wins. He might have been a fleet-footed baller, but the fast-fisted Brooklyn brawler was way too much for him to handle.

With his muscles straining under his suit jacket, Gino pulled his arm back and pounded his fist into the guy's face until it was completely covered in blood. He didn't stop until the guy was stretched out across the hood of the parked car spitting blood out of his busted-up mouth.

Dude was defeated. "I thought I knew her," he kept saying over and over again like he was dazed and confused. "I made a mistake...I thought I knew her..."

"Stop lying!" I hollered, although I was the one lying my ass off. "I've never even seen you before! You was just trying to take the heat off Pit because his little ass was about to bite off more than he could shit out!"

"Fuck you, *bitch*!" Pit hollered.

Gino bent down to Pit's level and slammed his big fist into the midget's grill.

Cursing, Pit rushed at Gino. His buff little muscles bulged and flexed as he bear-hugged Gino's knees and tried to force him off his feet and swing him to the ground.

But Gino was way too solid for that, and he scooped Pit up in a quick headlock that lifted him right off his feet. "Lemme school you for a minute, lil niggah," Gino barked. His forearm dug into Pit's throat as the midget's feet dangled in the air. Pit struggled to breathe, kicking his legs wildly and swinging short, desperate punches.

"I don't usually fight lil kids," Gino told him, "but I don't give a fuck how stunted yo' ass is. Disrespect my woman again and I'ma treat you like a full-grown man and lay ya tiny ass down, ya heard?"

Gino turned him loose and Pit hit the ground hard. He rolled over on his stomach, but before he could get up Gino bent down and punched him in the back of his head with so much force it sounded like he'd swung a bat.

Pit yelped and tried to crawl away, but Gino capped him with a sweet roundhouse that almost sent his eyeball flying to the back of his skull.

Cupping his eye, Pit rolled over on his back again and howled, and then he reached down in the front of his pants like he was fumbling for his burner.

"Yo, yo, *yo!*" said a cold voice. "That better be your dick you fixing to pull out, my man."

All eyes swung over to Slick Sallie, who was posted up in a wide-legged stance.

He'd been standing there quietly the entire time, but now a shiny silver Glock was suddenly in his hand and he had it trained dead on Pit.

"Calm down, Cowboy," Sallie said, checking Pit cold. "I'm the chief gunslinger on the block right now. So fight with your hands, my dude. Fight with your *hands*."

The sight of the smooth white boy brandishing a gat made the danger all too real for me.

"Y'all stop! Y'all stop!" me and DarQuese both yelled. A small crowd had started to gather, and a couple of young dudes were laughing at the sight of Pit sweating and clutching his bulging eye.

Pit jumped to his feet and glared at the young boys. Something dark entered his eyes, and his sinister expression told me that this cat had been laughed at before. He had been laughed at a lot.

And he didn't like it.

"Yo, you fuckin' snuck me, son!" Pit bitched at Gino as he paced back and forth. "You *snuck* me! You got that one, but I'ma sneak you back. Yeah, I'ma put something on you that'll sit you down, muh'fucka. Just watch. Me and you gone both be the same fuckin' size!"

Me and DarQuese gave each other a look. Enough was definitely enough. She stepped up to Pit, and I got in front of Gino and put my hand on his hard shoulder.

"C'mon, baby," I said in a whisper. "Look at all these people out here watching us. This guy isn't worth it. We're supposed to be keeping it low, remember?"

A cop car rolled by, and Slick Sallie stuck his gun hand behind his back and waved pleasantly at the white police officers with his other hand.

Pit shook DarQuese off then stormed across the street bitching and fussing the whole time. "Your ass is minez, niggah!" he screamed at Gino. "You and ya fuckin' white boy is both gonna get served!"

Sallie just laughed. "That little guy has a whole lot of mouth," he said.

Gino nodded, and then he walked over to where he had slung Cynthia's dresses in the street. Keeping his eye on Pit, Gino picked up the dresses and brushed them off before handing them to me.

And then out of nowhere, Gino turned back to the baller with the cornrows. Dude was still sprawled all over the parked car trying to pull himself together.

"Yo, my niggah," Gino spit smoothly although fire still raged in his eyes. "Check this out. C'mere, Juicy." He grabbed my hand and posted me up right in front of the Philly baller. "You sure my baby ain't sweet, ak?"

I grilled dude hard, fronting like crazy. I knew he wasn't the type to run away from a fight. He was a risk-taker, and danger was in his blood. I'd known that the night he violated G's territory up in the G-Spot, but that didn't stop me from letting him munch me out.

I was shocked when he frowned with his blood-crusted lips and shook his head.

"Nah, Chief," he said to Gino. "I don't know if ya girl is sweet or not, ak. Cause I ain't never tasted her."

I went limp with relief. I wanted to thank him for biting his tongue. Instead, I took Gino's arm. The killer look he was still giving the baller told me it was time for us to dip.

Sallie and Gino stayed outside while me, Quese, Teenie, and all their nosy customers went back in the beauty shop. I was too embarrassed to meet anyone's eyes as I took off my plastic smock and got my purse from the cabinet under Quese's station.

"Oh, so you're leaving now?" she asked dryly. I could tell she was real salty over the drama that had just gone down between our men.

"Yeah. I have to go with Renata to take a last-minute look at the menu for my wedding dinner tomorrow night."

Her lips got all twisted. "I don't even wanna know how much you're paying that trick to cook, Juicy! I told you I coulda got my aunts to fry some chicken, and make some collard greens and macaroni and cheese for you real cheap."

"Oh, I'm not paying her," I said. "The Organization is hosting the wedding for us remember? Renata's catering all the food for me."

DarQuese frowned for a quick second, but then the unscarred half of her face smiled.

"I wanna be mad at your ass, Juicy, but I just can't. You know I don't like that white girl, but you're my friend and regardless, I'm happy for you."

"Thanks, Quese," I said. "That means a lot to me." And it really did, because the situation between Pit and Gino was bad enough. I didn't want there to be any static between me and her too.

She eyed my hair. "You sure you gotta go? Sit back at the sink and let me rinse you real quick."

I shook my head. "Thanks, but I'm good. I need to get outside and make sure Gino is calm. I can rinse my hair in the shower when I get home."

DarQuese opened her top drawer and took out an envelope. "This is from Cynt."

"Cool," I said without opening it because I knew Cynthia's money was always good. "So, I'll see you tomorrow night?" I asked. "You're gonna close up early so you can make it to the dinner on time, right?"

She smirked. "You mean you want me to cut my paper short just because a white chick is gonna feed us some dried-out chicken that we probably ain't gonna be able to chew anyway?"

All I could do was shake my head.

"You are truly crazy," I said as I headed for the door. "But I have a feeling that once you get a chance to chill with Renata you're really going to like her."

"*Shiiiit*," I heard DarQuese drawl. "No I won't."

I glanced over my shoulder, and her arms were crossed over her little titties. I was almost out the door as she said it again.

"No the hell I won't."

CHAPTER 9

Renata and her husband Frankie lived in a gated community about ten minutes away from our condo. Unlike me and Gino, they didn't even try to hide their money, and if G hadn't already exposed me to the finer things in life my mouth would've been hanging open each time I walked through their doors. But as it was, the gorgeous travertine floors and shiny granite countertops didn't impress me. Neither did the chic furniture or expensive paintings that hung from every wall.

What did impress me though was Renata. I had never been tight with a white girl before and at first I didn't know how to take her. I judged Renata to be about thirty-five, but she looked damn good for her age. She jogged and lifted weights and all that, and she was forever sipping on bottled water and protein shakes.

Renata didn't have a job, but Frankie was the boss man of The Organization so she stayed laced from head to toe. She was always inviting me to go with her to get a facial or get our nails done, or to just lounge in the sauna and get massaged at the clubhouse while our corporate men worked out big deals on the golf course.

I knew Renata could probably tell I had been born poor and raised in the hood, but she didn't even blink when I told her I was from the heart of Harlem. She was like yeah, Harlem is real cool and then she told me Frankie and his brothers, and even the Asian attorney named Jason who worked with them, had all been down with some kind of high-powered family business back in Brooklyn. She said Frankie had recently sold off some assets and decided to relocate to someplace warm and expand his business on both coasts.

Of course, I wasn't about to tell her why me and Gino had left the Empire State. I didn't want her all up in my business, and she didn't ask me about anything either. Renata wasn't the prying type, and I appreciated her not trying to get up under my left titty. After having to sneak and do everything my whole life, first under Grandmother's roof and then under G's, I wasn't in the mood to keep telling a bunch of lies. I was about to turn twenty years old soon, and after all the drama I had been through I didn't owe anybody any bullshit stories.

I'd gone home to shower and change clothes, and now Renata and I were heading to the caterers to give them final approval for my menu items. Afterward, she was taking me to an exclusive health spa for a mud wrap and a water massage.

I got to her house a few minutes early, and she was dressed in pink sweats and talking on her cell phone when she answered the door. The house had a breezy, open design, and it was always crisp and clean and smelled like the maid had just left. She smiled and waved me toward the living room. "Make yourself comfortable, Juicy. The remote is on the table. I'll be right back."

I kicked off my shoes and sank down into a yellow leather sofa that felt like a cream puff on my ass. I turned on the television and channel surfed until I landed on the Braxton Family Values show. I really loved it! Toni and her sisters were a trip, and they made me wish I had some sisters to love and argue with. I was deep into the show when Renata's house phone rang. A number popped up on the big screen. It said "Blocked" but it had an 804 area code with the rest of the numbers showing in a line of seven x's. I wasn't gonna answer it until Renata yelled, "Hey Juicy, can you get that? It's probably Nunna, my grandmother in Brooklyn!"

I hopped up and snatched the phone off the base. "Hello," I said, pressing the receiver to my ear. "You've reached the Sanvenero residence. Can I help you?"

There was a long, long pause on the other end, and I was just about to say hello again when a man's deep voice growled, "Yo, who dis?"

Before I could answer the line went dead. Dude had hung up. Renata flounced back into the living room carrying a small gym bag. She had changed into a black tube top and a pair of tight white jeans. Her hair was pulled back in a ponytail with a thick white scrunchie around it.

"Who was it?" she asked.

I shrugged, the dead phone still in my hand. "I don't know, but I don't think it was your grandma."

"Oh, hell," Renata said, chuckling. "You would've known if it was my Nunna. You would've known for sure."

"The area code was 804, but the rest of the number came up blocked on the caller ID," I told her. "It was a man, though. He sounded Black. He asked me who I was, and then he hung up."

Renata's bag hit the floor. She narrowed her eyes and gave me a real funny look. "Did you tell him anything?"

I shook my head. "No, I didn't get a chance to say anything because he hung up on me."

The phone rang again and Renata snatched it from my hand. She clicked the talk button real fast, but not fast enough where I didn't peep the caller ID as it flashed on the television screen. It was a blocked number again, just like the last time, and it had the same 804 area code too.

"Hold on," she said into phone. "It's my Nunna," she told me, pressing the phone to her chest as she dug into her purse. "From Brooklyn." She passed me the keys to her whip. "I'll meet you in the car. Cut the air on," she added, turning away, "because the seats are probably hot."

I caught the hint and headed toward the door. But as I was on my way out, I heard her say something crazy about FedEx arriving soon to pick up a crate of blood oranges.

I knew damn well there was no 804 area code in Brooklyn, and the way Renata was acting was real suspicious. I couldn't believe she was messing around on her husband, but on the real, if she was getting drilled by some dark meat from the Big 804, that was between her and Frankie. I didn't even wanna know about it. Hell, this wasn't Harlem, and I was no longer that fast young girl who always had to be in the know. Determined to mind my own bizz and give Renata the same respect she had always given me, I tipped out of her crib and closed the door behind me.

CHAPTER 10

Huddled in a back room of the G-Spot, they approached their plan like three blind mice. Late into the night Pluto, Ace, and Monique fussed like a bunch of bitches over how they could best use Salida to their advantage. A hundred different scenarios had been argued back and forth, and shortly before dawn they'd finally settled on a strategy. Although they had different approaches they wanted to take, all three schemers had agreed that Salida getting kicked out of that mental hospital was like getting a gift straight from G's grave.

They figured with G's ex-wife back on the scene it was only natural that she would be anxious to see her only son right away. And it was also only natural that Gino would raise his head to answer his mother's loving call. And wherever Gino was hiding Juicy – and G's money – were sure to be somewhere close by.

Ace and Pluto saw eye-to-eye when it came to picking up Salida and bringing her back to New York so they could position her to their advantage. But after that is where they split.

Ace wanted to use Salida as bait to lure Gino out of hiding just as bad as Monique and Pluto did. But he also wanted to set her up in a chill little crib and treat her in a manner that was befitting of Granite McKay's wife.

"Yeah, our paper might be a lil short," Ace insisted, "but whatever ends we got coming through the door is because G stacked shit up that way. Salida is his rightful heir, yo, and we gotta set her up lovely 'cause that's what G woulda expected us to do. Anything short of that is gonna be like shitting on our manz."

Pluto, on the other hand was like, fuck no.

"He put her in a *nut-house*, my nig! That chick is prolly crazy as shit. Yo, we gotta trust G. That niggah knew exactly what the fuck he was doing when he banished her ass from the Empire! He stashed her out there in no-man's-land for a *reason*, slime."

Pluto shook his head. "I'm down to go spring her ass outta that hospital joint and all, but I'm cool on the rest of that shit. She's got mad family out in Brooklyn, right? Well then she should stay out there and leave Harlem the fuck alone. Let them Puerto Rican muh'fuckas take her in and set her up. She's they blood, not ours."

Manipulation was Monique's middle name so she had been sure to keep quiet during this part of the discussion and let the two big men duke it out. She waited until each of them had feverishly argued their case, and then she calmly suggested a compromise that she believed would satisfy them both.

"Y'all know Salida's been stuck out there in that crazy-house by herself for a minute now," she said quietly. "She might not wanna be on her own just yet. Maybe we can take her to her sister's crib in Brooklyn so she can be around her family and they can look out for her, but then send somebody to bring her to the Spot every night if she wants to come out here."

Both men had chewed on her suggestion for a few moments, and then nodded their approval. Yeah, Monique gave herself a little pat on the back. It was a decent compromise, but in all honesty Monique didn't give a damn what Ace or Pluto wanted.

Ace talked that all bullshit about putting Salida up out of loyalty to his manz, but Monique scoffed at that shit. Why be loyal to somebody who wasn't here to do you a solid or to be loyal back to you? Monique didn't feel she owed G shit. If anything that niggah owed *her*. Getting her all souped up and then dying! G had promised to send her and Pluto down to Baltimore to spark up the G-Spot 2, where she was gonna be the head boss-bitch sitting on a throne and running things. And then that niggah goes and gets himself shot!

Of course Monique wanted them to find G's money, but she wanted something else too. She wanted to get a bitch back. She wanted a piece of that bitch Juicy.

So while Ace and Pluto thought she was sitting around with an empty little head, she was busy scheming and planning. Just a' planning and scheming. Damn straight. No more sitting up in that grimy-ass Spot feeling sorry for herself. It was time to take the bull by the horns and ride him until he fell the hell out.

Matter fact, it was past time.

$$$$$

Monique opened the door to G's office and blew a big fat bubble. "Y'all ready?" she asked, smacking her pink Bazooka and working it around in her mouth. Her hair was spiraled-curled tight and bouncy, and her perfume floated above her in an invisible sugar cloud.

Pluto looked up from the money he was counting and grilled her, but Monique didn't give a damn. His stank ass wasn't gonna ruin her mood today. They were about to go for a real long car ride and she was hyped like hell. She'd only been out of New York City twice in her entire life, and she'd never been out of the country at all.

She had on some stylish but comfortable traveling gear, and had packed a bag full of snacks for the road. Pluto could buck his eyeballs all he wanted to. Monique was ready to roll.

"Are y'all ready?" she grinned at him and asked again.

"We ready when I say we ready!" he barked from his fat face. And then he switched it up and whined, "I'm hungry, Mo-Mo. Didn't I tell you to make me something to eat?"

Monique grinned again and reached into her travel bag. Six o'clock on a Monday morning was not the right time to be cramming your face with tacos, but it was what her man had a taste for, so it was what Monique had fixed.

She pulled out six stuffed beef and chicken soft tacos wrapped in aluminum foil. They were still nice and hot, and she passed them to Pluto as she popped her bubblegum and sang a little tune under her breath.

"What you so happy for?" he barked, snatching the food. "You wanna be singing all early in the fuckin' morning? How about we drop you off at a studio so you can sing all fuckin' day!"

Monique ignored him and kept right on carrying her tune. She even snapped her fingers a couple of times and gyrated her juicy ass. Pluto's noise-talking was bouncing all off of her today. He could say whatever the fuck he wanted to say. She was in no danger of being left behind, and they both knew it.

"I got my photo ID and my driver's license in my purse, Daddy," she said just to remind him of how important she was to the success of their plans. Both Pluto and Ace had multiple felonies on their records, and neither could cross the border into Canada without getting detained.

"Don't worry, Daddy," Monique sighed and cooed. "I remember everything you told me, and I'm gonna hop over there and pick up our package, then hop right back out, okay?"

Pluto was steady getting busy on his tacos. He nodded a few times and said happily, "This shit good, Mo-Mo. "Real good."

Monique smiled. She knew she could burn. Her man loved damn near everything she cooked, and when it came to food he wasn't shy about giving up the compliments.

Thirty minutes later Ace was pushing G's custom-designed Mercedes north toward Canada. He was in a bad mood and he hadn't been sleeping right since getting that letter from the sanitarium. He'd been up the last few nights steaming over all the shit that had happened over the past six months. He'd gone back and forth between feeling like a weak bitch for losing all the doe his niggah G had stashed away, and being pissed off at the thought of Gino and Juicy laid up on some tropical fuckin' island living large and spending that shit.

Ace had been one of the closest people in the world to G. Not as close as Moonie, nah he couldn't front and say that, but he had definitely come in second place on G's trusted capo list.

Him, Moonie, Pluto, and G had been a four-man crew when all that cash got stashed in a mausoleum out in Woodlawn Cemetery after Juicy's grandmother died. In fact, he had helped G haul the old lady's dead body outta the coffin and stuff her into the trunk of his whip. Later that night, he'd ridden with G and Pacho out to the landfill and tossed the dead bitch off on top of a mound of rotting trash.

But Harlem had exploded in a fireball after G got shot, and Ace and Pluto had both gotten knocked in a flash. The cops had raided Pluto's crib and caught him with his pants down, but Ace had gotten done even worse. He'd gotten busted going to check on his sick Grandma. And when the bullets started flying, it had been Grandma who ended up slumped over in her rocker with a metal slug through her forehead.

Hot rage ran through Ace as he thought about how he'd had to cool it on Rikers for a month before his lawyer finally got him out. But by that time it was too late. He had rushed over to his boss's crib straight outta lock up and busted opened the wall safe. He had known there wasn't gonna be a whole lotta doe in G's home stash, but he *had* expected to find some decent pocket change. Most of all, he had expected to find a very special key, and when that shit wasn't there, he had rushed out to Woodlawn Cemetery and used a sledgehammer to break into a crypt. Ace had known he was fucked by the weight of the metal drawer when he pulled it out. It was too light to hold a body, and it was damn sure too light to hold over half a million dollars in cold hard cash.

He shook with rage as he remembered staring up at the ceiling in the mausoleum.

He'd flung a vase of dead flowers against the wall, then snatched up a folding chair and started swinging it like a bat. He'd cursed and screamed and beat the shit outta the walls and the floor until there was no more strength left in him.

There was no question in Ace's mind about who had pulled a grand larceny on G's hard earned stash. If he coulda gotten hold of Gino's dirty ass he would have snapped his fuckin' neck. But Gino had dipped. That marked niggah had grabbed Juicy and fled the city just like a little bitch.

I shoulda popped him when I had a chance, Ace thought bitterly. Right before his murder, G had given Ace an order to take Gino to the airport and put him on a plane. And when Ace had asked his boss what he should do if Gino bucked and didn't wanna go, G's eyes had been colder than ice when he'd said, "Then kill him."

"And that's what I shoulda did," Ace said out loud. If he had sunk a hot one in Gino when he had him in his sights, the money woulda still been sitting in the crypt when he got outta jail, and him and Pluto would be rolling in it right now. "Yeah," Ace muttered under his breath, his voice thick with rage and regret. "That's exactly what the fuck I shoulda did."

CHAPTER 11

Pulling up to the Canadian checkpoint, Monique eyeballed her reflection in the rearview mirror. Not only did she look cooler than ice, she looked young, sexy, and absolutely stunning. The line of cars waiting to cross the border had been mad long, but she wasn't nervous and she wasn't stressed. She had no reason to be. Her ID was in order, the paperwork on the whip was in order, and most important, the vehicle was totally clean. No drugs had ever come close to it because that had been one of G's strictest rules.

Monique flashed the skinny white border agent a 'fuck-me' smile and he sent her one right back. She had dropped Ace and Pluto off at a mall in a small town nearby, and then followed the directions on her GPS until she came to the border crossing.

She handed over her paperwork, and when the agent directed her to get out so the car could be inspected, she climbed out cooperatively and stood there crunching on a Chick-o-Stick she had stashed in her bag.

Less than ten minutes later she had cleared customs and was on her way. According to the GPS the sanitarium was twenty-five miles north, so Monique sat back in the plush leather seats and purred. Handling the luxury whip was like riding a nice fat dick, and she enjoyed the feel of the powerful car as it moved at her command.

Sunny Hills was on a large, fenced-in compound. Monique had to show the letter they'd sent G, along with her photo ID, before they would let her pass through its heavy, well-guarded gates.

When she pulled onto the grounds she was shocked by what she saw. A huge, modern estate situated on what looked like miles of rolling green grass. Employees dressed in fancy uniforms walked around looking like butlers and maids. There was a slick swimming pool with bright blue water, several cabanas, and shaded tables where patients were laid out getting back rubs and hip massages.

This ain't no regular nut-house! Monique thought, taking it all in. Hospital, hell. G musta been dropping a gwap every year to keep his wife stashed away at a slamming resort like this. Escorted by an attendant, Monique breezed into the administrative office and filled out a stack of discharge paperwork for Salida McKay.

When she was done, they assigned her another attendant who escorted her down to the area where Salida was being housed. This attendant was a Black woman who looked to be about sixty.

"I'm so glad you came to get Mrs. McKay out of here," the hefty woman said, her short legs moving fast. "Are you her daughter?"

"Oh no," Monique said quickly and then lied, "I'm her niece, Monique. She was married to my uncle."

"Mr. McKay? Oh, what a fine man! He used to come around here all the time, just loaded down with shopping bags and boxes full of expensive clothes jewelry. He made sure he kept his wife looking good and living in style, too. It's been a while since I've seen him though. A lot of family members seem to just up and stop coming to visit sometimes."

"Well, he upped and died," Monique said flatly. "That's why he stopped coming."

The attendant frowned.

"Did he get sick? It happens. Our patients outlive their family members all the time. Most of them have healthy bodies. It's their mental state that keeps them here." They crossed the street and headed up a grass-lined walkway. Monique waited as the attendant used a key-card to unlock the side door of a small, ancient-looking building.

"We're here," the older woman said brightly, and led her into a stifling hot lobby. "This part ain't as nice as what you saw out front. This is where they keep the ones who can't pay their bill no more."

Monique looked around and nodded. Now this was more like it. She'd seen a couple of nut-houses in city hospitals and most of them were just like this: run down, dark, and low-budget.

"For years Mrs. McKay stayed in one of the finest suites on the property," the attendant went on. "But about a month ago they waited until it got real late at night, then they packed her things up and stuck her way back here where the real broke patients stay. I wasn't here, but I heard they had to drag the poor thing out of her room kicking and hollering. She'd been living there so long her suite was the only home she really knew."

The attendant stopped outside of room 126 and knocked three times on the door. When there was no answer she swiped her key-card through the slot and Monique heard the lock click open.

"Don't worry," the attendant whispered behind her hand. "She's been getting her medication every single day. It's against the law for us to withhold anti-psychotic drugs just because the family can't pay."

Monique nodded. She had no fuckin' idea what kinda fool she was gonna see when the door swung open, but she wasn't prepared for what was waiting on the other side.

Salida McKay sat in a metal folding chair by the window. Her hair was piled on her head in a mass of soft, natural curls and she was dressed to slay in a slinky maroon designer dress. Her legs were crossed elegantly at the knee and a pair of bammin' chic silver stilettos with a six-inch heel were on her slender feet.

"Mrs. McKay!" the attendant called out brightly. "You have a visitor. It's your niece, Monique! She's come to take you home!"

Salida took her time turning to face them, and when she did Monique saw exactly why she had been the only bitch that G had ever wifed.

She was beautiful. She was more than beautiful. She had some shit about her that screamed, "*Royalty*!" Like she deserved to be bathed and oiled and fanned by servants.

But gorgeous or not, Salida had some crazy shit going on with her too. Monique had seen that buggy look in the eyes of sickos around Harlem her whole life. She wasn't sure if Salida was gonna bust her out and get stupid because she'd never seen her before, or if she was sane enough to use this opportunity to get the fuck outta jail while she had the chance. She found out real quick.

"Monique, huh?" Salida smirked, looking Monique slowly up and down.

Watching her cunning eyes, Monique could tell there were still a few slick cylinders clicking in the old bird's brain.

"Yes," she answered sweetly. "I came to get you, Aunty. Uncle Granite sent me."

"Where is he?"

Monique didn't know what the hell to say. "Um, he couldn't make it so I came instead."

Salida stared at her real hard for a second and then uncrossed her legs and stood up, displaying her full, magnificent splendor.

Goddamn, Monique thought, begrudgingly giving up mad appreciation for what she saw. Salida was an older version of Juicy. Her body was succulent and luscious. Her slick maroon gown fit her curves like a tailored glove. Simply put, she was a prime stunna. She looked delicious. In fact, she looked damned delicious, and even as jealous of other chicks as Monique was, she had to give the bitch that.

She watched as Salida swung her sweet round hips across the room like she was a bikini model on somebody's fashion runway.

"It's about time you got your ass here," Salida said crisply, like she had been expecting Monique for months. "Grab my things from the closet, and don't forget my minks."

She sat back down and crossed her legs daintily as Monique and the attendant scurried to throw her personal items into two large designer suitcases that were stored under the bed.

"She don't mean no harm bossing you around like that," the old Black attendant whispered as her and Monique packed Salida's gear. There was expensive jewelry, silk dresses, lingerie, and top-label designer shoes out the ass. "Mrs. McKay just has terrible mood swings. Up one day, and down the next. You never know what you're gonna get out of her. It's part of her mental condition, so be sure she stays on her medication at all times."

As they were on the way out the door Salida spoke to Monique over her shoulder.

"I don't know where you're going, Monique, but I'm from New York. New York City, in the United States. Do you know where that is?"

"Oh yes, ma'am," Monique said sweetly. I know New York City like the back of my hand."

Salida nodded. "Good. Take me there." And then she added, "You got a cigarette?"

Monique, with her arm full of Salida's shoes, clothes, and all the other random shit the older lady had accumulated over the years, nodded yes.

Salida looked satisfied.

"Good," she said dryly. "Light me one."

CHAPTER 12

It wasn't Harlem they were heading for as Monique re-crossed the border with Salida riding shotgun in G's luxury whip. Instead, they were Brooklyn bound. But first, they had to make a quick stop.

"Why are you stopping here?" Salida asked as Monique pulled into the mall parking lot where she had left the two main men in her life. "You taking me shopping or something?"

"No, we're not going shopping but I'm picking up some people who really wanna see you, Mizz Salida," Monique said. "They gonna roll with us the rest of the way to the city."

She texted Pluto and let him know they were waiting outside, and when him and Ace walked out the mall and headed toward the car it was all Monique could do not to bust out laughing.

"What...the...*fuck?*" Salida said slowly, narrowing her insane eyes and blowing smoke from her nose as she watched the two fat men waddle their way over to the car. Salida was smoking up all her damn cigarettes, but Monique didn't care. This trick was funny!

"Who are those two clowns coming to see?"

Monique giggled as she climbed out the driver's seat so Ace could get in. "You. They coming to see you."

Salida sat right where she was as the two men approached. Ace came straight over to her window wearing a big smile on his face. He had been with G the longest and had known Salida very well back in the day.

"Sup, Mizz Salida," the big man said. Seeing her brought back memories of the good old days with G and he took her hand in his and kissed it respectfully. "It's Ace. Remember me?"

"Hello, Arnold," Salida replied calmly. "Yes, it has certainly been a long time."

Ace walked around the car and climbed into the driver's seat, and Pluto stepped up to her window next.

"How you doing, Mizz Salida? I'm Pluto. G was my dawg. Me and you met a long time ago but you prolly don't remember me." He opened her door and held out his hand like he was gonna help her get out.

"Oh, I remember you," Salida said, and there was no mistaking the coldness in her voice. "I remember you very well."

Perched in her seat like a goddess, Salida reached out and pulled her door shut, leaving Pluto standing out there with his hand still held out.

Monique giggled her ass off in the back seat, happy to see Pluto get dissed.

"Take me home." Salida glanced at Ace, then turned and looked out the window at the dumbfounded Pluto. She blew some more smoke out her nose. "What you standing there looking stupid for? Climb your big ass in the backseat and let's go."

$$$$$

The ride back to the city was interesting. Monique was fascinated by Salida. Mama was a boss! She was still sexy at damn near forty-five, and even though she had been doped up and locked away for years, the stress of it didn't hardly show on her at all.

"Where's Granite?" Salida asked about ten minutes into their journey. Pluto had climbed angrily into the backseat next to Monique. He kept looking over at her all crazy-like. Monique knew he was daring her to grin so he could bust her one. It was all she could do to hold her giggles in too. It wasn't everyday that big bad Pluto got bitch-checked by a female.

"Is he at that club?"

"Umm, which club, Mizz Salida?" Ace played dumb. "You talking about the G-Spot?"

"Yeah," she said. "The G-Spot. I know all about that place. Who you think told him to buy it and how to set it up? Is he still running it?"

Ace swallowed hard. "Yeah, the Spot is still pretty hot. It's not all it could be, but it's still generating."

"I didn't ask you all that," Salida replied, irritated. "I said is Granite still running his club?"

Monique almost felt bad for Ace when she heard how hard he sighed.

"I don't know how to tell you this, Mizz Salida, but G is dead. We buried him six months ago. I can take you to see his grave if you want me to, and I'm sorry you gotta find out like this, but that's what it is. G is dead."

Salida kept right on puffing on her cigarette. "How'd he die?"

"Somebody killed him. He got shot."

Salida got real quiet for a while. And then she scared the shit outta all of them when she threw her head back and bust out laughing.

"I knew it! I knew it! I *knew* that black bastard was dead! That's why they let me outta that hell-hole! He always said the only way I would ever see the streets again would be over his dead body!"

Smiling, she blew a long trail of smoke out of her nose. "So who did it? *Good* for that mothafucka!" She laughed. "Who did it? Huh? Who did it?"

Ace was too shocked. "Mizz Salida! That ain't right! Laughing at ya man like that! I just told you he's dead!"

Salida bucked and came hard out of Brooklyn. "Oh, *fuck you, Arnold!* What ain't right is what that niggah did to *me!* Telling my little boy I was crazy! Separating a mother from her damn child! *That's* what ain't right! And where's my damn son? Where's my Gino?"

Ace raised his hand in the air and shook his head. "Look, I'm sorry but I'on't know where the fuck Gino's at, and I'on't know shit about nothin' personal between you and G! Word. I'm just saying...it ain't right to be laughing because the man got killed."

Salida laughed again and her voice sounded like a whole bucket of ice cubes clinking together.

"That niggah *better* be dead," she said, coldly. "Taking my baby away from me. I wish whoever shot him would have shot him twice. Once for whatever he did to them, and once for all the shitty little things he did to me."

They rode in silence after that. When they finally arrived in Brooklyn Ace passed Salida a fat envelope stuffed with money.

"This is just a lil sumpthin' to hold you for a minute," he told her. "It ain't a whole lot considering how long you been gone, but you should be able to get you an apartment or a lil car or whatever you want."

Monique could tell by the look on Ace's face that he was mad as fuck, but he told her to go ahead and take Salida upstairs while him and Pluto waited in the car.

Salida's sister lived on the fifth floor of a big apartment building. They were a large family of Puerto Ricans, and some of them looked like they were mixed with Black. After dragging Salida's suitcases up the steps, Monique niggah-knocked on the door. When it opened she saw a room filled with people who were sitting around eating, playing dominos, and talking shit in both Spanish and English real loud.

They rushed the door when they saw Salida standing there, and everyone started wailing and crying like crazy. Monique elbowed her way inside and stood in the middle of the living room looking and feeling out of place. She had never been all that fond of Brooklyn. It was so big and crazy compared to Harlem, and in her opinion Brooklyn tricks were grimier and more cut-throat than those in any other borough.

She only planned to stay for a hot minute, because even though Salida's people were jumping up and down and crying and singing with joy at seeing her alive, a few of her female relatives were sitting around looking at Monique like she was a dark stain on a piece of used toilet tissue.

"Call me," Monique told Salida as she broke for the door. She had already written her phone number on a slip of paper and given it to the older woman. "I'll have somebody swing by and bring you to the G-Spot whenever you feel like hanging out, okay?"

"The *G-Spot?*"

A lady who was hugging on Salida spit loudly and with mad attitude. Monique glared at the woman and her eyes almost popped out her head when she thought she was seeing double. This chick and Salida looked *just alike*. From head to toe, they could have been beautifully stunning, identical twins.

"Isn't that G's old place?" the woman demanded.

"It's okay, Lourdes," Salida said.

"Uh-*uh!* Hell no, it's *not* okay!" Lourdes glared at Monique with Salida's exact same eyes. "That's G's place, right? The place where they tried to kill Gino? Why would my sister wanna go there?"

"*Gino!*" Salida entire face lit up at the mention of his name. "Where is my son?" she demanded loudly. "Is he here? Where's my Gino?"

Salida's crazy eyes darted around the room and Monique's did too. The joint was packed out but there was no Gino in sight.

"Gino, Gino, Gino, Gino..." Salida sang in a high-pitched voice. "*Gino, Gino, Gino, Gino, Gino...*"

"Your son's away at college," Lourdes said, gently placing her arms around Salida as she tried to hush her and steer her toward a back room.

Monique paused with her hand on the doorknob. She cocked her ears like a hunting dog as she listened closely, hoping to learn Gino's whereabouts.

"Gino's doing fine," Lourdes continued when Salida kept calling her son's name and refused to budge from where she stood. "Your son is happy, and he's doing really good in school. Getting all A's."

"But he should *be* here!" Salida wailed. "I'm his *mama*. He's my *baby!* I wanna *see* him!" she pleaded with tears in her eyes.

"Soon," her sister said gently, soothing Salida like she was a sleepy child. "Please don't cry. You'll see Gino soon. I promise." Suddenly Lourdes turned and glared at Monique. There was no mistaking the 'get the fuck out already!' look on her face.

Monique knew the deal. She opened the door and stepped outside. She was closing the door slowly behind her when she heard Lourdes say to Salida, "Gino is doing fine, *chica*. Come. Sit with me and I'll tell you all about him."

CHAPTER 13

Two nights later, at the stroke of midnight on Wednesday night to be exact, Monique closed the door on fuck room number 3 and pushed a wrinkled fifty-dollar bill down into her bra. She had just finished flat-backing in one of the G-Spot's hottest rooms, and she was still damn near broke. She was heading to the bathroom to wash up when she heard a big commotion going on at the front door.

A tall, regal woman had pushed past Greco and swept through the doors lugging two expensive suitcases behind her.

"What's wrong, Mizz Salida?" Monique cried out as she hurried over to the distraught woman. "Hey, what happened? Why didn't you call me so I could send a car down to pick you up?"

"Gimme a drink," Salida demanded, abandoning her suitcases and marching over to the bar. She snapped her finger at Bizzie, who opened his sissy-ass mouth to curse her out. He thought better of it when Ace walked up and checked him with a quick nod.

Monique and Ace waited while Bizzie poured Salida a double shot of hen dog. She tossed it back like it was sweet tea, and then slammed her glass on the bar and signaled for another one.

"You okay, Mizz Salida?" Ace asked, his big hand patting her shoulder. "What happened? Somebody been fuckin' with you?"

Monique passed Salida a cigarette and Ace pulled out his lighter and sparked it.

"I need somewhere to stay," Salida said after exhaling a thick funnel of smoke from her nose.

"Sure," Monique cooed sweetly. She looked Salida over and thought about that envelope full of money that Ace had given her. *Bitch, get a hotel!* "That ain't no problem. You can stay with me and Pluto. We got plenty of room. Things ain't working out for you in Brooklyn?"

Salida sniffled, and to Monique's surprise tears began streaming from the older woman's eyes as she sobbed into her hands.

Mrs. McKay suffers from terrible mood swings...up one minute, down the next...you never know what you're gonna get out of her...be sure to keep her on her medication at all times....

"Mizz Salida," Monique cooed, putting her arm around the crying woman, "you sure you should be drinking liquor while you taking all that medication?"

Salida stopped crying and looked up sharply. "What goddamn medication? I threw all that shit in the trash! They pushed them damn pills into me for over ten years. I ain't taking so much as a *vitamin* for the rest of my life!"

"Okay, then what's wrong, Mizz Salida? Why you so sad?"

"Who the hell said I was sad?" Salida snapped, glancing around in confusion. "Who said it?"

53

A bent, bitter look crossed her face as her tears dried up. "Those bitches don't know me. They think they can hide my baby from me like I'm crazy. Do I look dead to you?" she demanded.

Monique shook her head quickly. Mama was straight up coo-coo, but her interest had suddenly shot up to the highest peak. "Nah, you look real live from where I'm sitting at, Mizz Salida. But what bitches you talking about? Who's been hiding your baby? Gino's a big man now. You not talking about your sisters, are you?"

Salida ignored the slick young girl in her ear. She had already peeped her game and would give Monique her full attention later. When she could be useful. Right now she was just a mouthpiece. Talking all out of her ass.

She puffed on her cigarette and tried to concentrate as random thoughts and phrases floated around in her head. It had only been two days since she'd left the hospital and she was still drugged up and confused. But soon she would be better. Very soon. She laughed inside. Damn right there was a reason G had locked her up all those years ago and tried to throw away the goddamn key. And it wasn't because she was crazy like he told everybody, neither.

No, it was because she was smart. Way smarter than his ass was. If it hadn't been for her slick advice and cunning counsel G would still be wandering around Harlem scratching out a hustle under Big Sonny.

Salida motioned for Bizzie to bring her another drink. When it came she flung it back and then held the empty glass up to her lips until the very last residue of liquor dripped onto her outstretched tongue. She'd been living in a dark tunnel for more than ten long years, but now that she was off all those psycho-buster mental pills she was counting on her slick mind and her devious wit to come back in full force.

Yes. Salida shook her head again and willed herself to focus and control her thoughts. Yes, *yes.* She was coming back! She knew her knack for scheming and calculating might return very slowly, but she also believed her skills would come back stronger and more potent than ever!

$$$$$

After slipping away from Salida and going to wash up, Monique reappeared at the bar smelling clean and fresh, and ready to get her buzz on. She usually popped a tab of X or something to help her get through the long nights of grinding on her back, but she decided to stick to Grey Goose and juice so she could keep a focused eye on Salida.

With her hair laid nicely and styling a short red freak 'em dress, Monique had just sat down at the bar when one of the G- Spot's former strippers came over to chat.

"Hey Mo," Nae-Nae greeted her and climbed up on the stool beside her. "What's good homegirl?"

"Long time no see," Monique said eyeing the ex-church-girl-turned-stripper with a big grin. "Girl, what you doing up this way? I heard you moved down to Brooklyn. Where's that cute little fella of yours?"

Nae-Nae smiled at the mention of her son. "You should see Maleek. He's almost two now and talking like I don't know what. He's still staying down the street with my mother. You know my father opened a jewelry store in Brooklyn after he got kicked outta the church. I work down there with him during the week and I come up here to be with my baby on the weekends."

"Yeah, I heard about your old devilish dick-slanging pops," Monique said with a wicked glint in her eye. "Papa was a rolling stone, wasn't he? While you was up in here stripping on the stage, his old nasty ass was tearing up some poon-poon in the pulpit!"

Nae-Nae's face fell and she looked embarrassed. "Yeah, well ain't none of us perfect. We all have our troubles in this life. My daddy was a pastor, but he's still a man. Hey," she said, perking up a little bit and pointing down the bar to change the subject. "What's she doing up in here? She's from Brooklyn."

"Who?" Monique asked as she scanned the row of patrons who were sitting where Nae-Nae pointed.

"That real pretty Puerto Rican lady in the blue," Nae-Nae said, and started waving at Salida. "She's so nice! I cleaned a *stupid*-sick engagement ring for her about a week ago."

"Nah," Monique shook her head. "You didn't clean no ring for that trick because she just got out the nut-house two days ago."

"Oh yes I did," Nae-Nae insisted. "That's her. She waited while I cleaned the ring, and me and her talked for the longest. She's so damn pretty there's no way I could forget that face."

Monique's eyebrows furrowed as her mind shifted into high gear. "You said you cleaned an *engagement* ring for her?"

"Yep. It was a block of straight-up ice. She said her nephew was getting married out in Los Angeles and she wanted it nice and shiny so she could send it to him." Nae-Nae shook her head. "But on the real, that thang was *sick*, Mo-Mo. It made all the tiny shit my father sells look like little ice chips."

"Hmm…" Monique was deep in thought. "Are you sure it was her?"

Nae-Nae glanced down the bar again. "Hell yeah. I can go over there and get with her right now. I know she remembers me because we ran our mouths together forever."

"No-no-no-*no!*" Monique said, hand-checking Nae-Nae before she could slide off her stool. "I believe you. Did she mention her nephew's name?"

Nae-Nae shook her head. "Nah, I ain't ask her all that. She just said he was getting married in L.A. and that she was sending him his mother's ring. It was her, though. I swear to God it was her."

Monique squeezed her thighs together as she tingled with glee inside. It was a long shot, but she was damn near willing to make a bet on it. If the woman Nae-Nae had spoken to was who Monique thought she was, then she could see why Nae-Nae had mistaken her for Salida. Monique had met her too, and them two pretty Puerto Rican divas looked *just alike!*

$$$$

Monique had fixed up her couch like it was a queen's throne for Salida. She topped it with freshly ironed sheets, four fluffy goose-down pillows, and a thick purple velour blanket that had never been used.

An insomniac would have gotten a good night's sleep on that bad boy, but Salida never closed her eyes the whole damn night. And this Monique knew because she'd snuck out into the living room several times to check.

No wonder G kept her bugged-out ass on lock, Monique thought as she peeked around the fish tank and spied on Salida. That nut was sitting straight up on the couch still dressed in her cute blue dress. She was rocking back and forth and crying one minute, then cursing somebody out real good under her breath the next.

Yawning and pretending like she couldn't sleep, Monique walked through the living room in a pair of yellow bikini panties and a matching t-shirt and went into the kitchen. She took a box of instant hot cocoa out the cabinet and turned around and held it up so Salida could see it.

"Want some?"

Salida nodded, and Monique spent the next five minutes microwaving two big cups full of hot chocolate until they were steaming.

After adding milk and sugar to the mix, she carried both mugs over to the couch where Salida sat and put them on the table. Then she plopped down on the purple blanket where her houseguest was still rocking back and forth and went to work.

"It must be real hard being back in New York after being gone for so long. Everything probably looks real strange to you. I bet you missed a lot of people too. Especially your son."

Monique picked up her mug from the table and held it carefully. Salida was rocking so damn hard she was scared she might make her spill the hot liquid all over herself.

"He was around here not too long ago, you know," Monique said slyly. "Me and him used to hang out a lot."

"Gino?" Salida stopped rocking. "You talking about my boy?"

Monique nodded and sipped. "Yeah. He's a grown-ass man now, though. He's even taller than G was, and swole up too. Real smart dude. G woulda had him running things in Harlem by now if it wasn't for that bitch Juicy."

"Juicy?" Salida sniffed. She snatched a cigarette from the open pack on the table and lit it.

Monique shrugged. "Hell yeah. Juicy. She's just some low-down young bird from 136th Street. Your sisters didn't tell you about her? She's the chick who got between G and Gino. She had 'em tearing at each other's throats all out in the streets and shit. Them two was real tight before Juicy came along and ruined everything. You shoulda seen how close they used to be. Gino loved his father, and G was *always* bragging on his son."

Salida kept smoking, but now tears were in her eyes. "But how could G turn his back on our baby like that?" she moaned, her face crumpling with pain. "What happened to the two of them?"

"Like I said...." Monique got ready to spin a long tale, "That young bitch Juicy came along and ripped them apart. Some kinda way she caught G slippin'. She got in real deep with him and got him open. Man, Juicy had G tricking up all his money on her and her brother, and leaving Gino out of everything! I guess Gino musta started feeling real lost and left out behind that shit. He told G he was gonna have to choose between his son and his bitch. Juicy probably saw her dollars turning into cents, because the next thing everybody knew she started banging Gino! After that, the father-son relationship was definitely over. From what I heard, Juicy's brother is the one who murdered G. I think the cops was looking for Juicy to see if she had anything to do with it, but her and Gino ran off somewhere together."

Monique spent the next twenty minutes dropping funky loads of bullshit into Salida's ear. She told her all kinds of dirty, scandalous lies about Juicy, making up shocking incidents of greed and manipulation as she went along. She really sold that shit, too. She invented devastating tales of betrayal between Gino and G. She painted a picture of Juicy that was so ugly and evil that by the time she finished yapping Salida's eyes were red from crying and her lips were tight with rage.

"So," Monique finally concluded. She had the mother in Salida on boil, and she could actually feel the steam coming off the older woman. "Nobody knows where Gino and Juicy ran off to. Ain't nobody been able to find them. But from what people say, Juicy ain't never gonna let Gino come back to Harlem. You probably ain't *never* gonna get your son back, Mizz Salida. That's word. *Never.*"

Hearing that, Salida cried out like she had been punched. She snatched Monique's cigarettes from the table and took the last one out of the pack.

"Oh, my poor Gino," she said pounding the tip of the cigarette on the table before sparking it up and puffing on it real hard. "My baby boy is lost to me!" she wailed, her eyes running like a faucet. "G was supposed to take care of him! How could he let a piece of tail tear them apart?"

I got her crazy ass going! Monique cheered inside. Now all she had to do was find a way to get some of that cash outta Salida's pocketbook and her work would be done.

Her chance came at about ten o'clock that morning. Her and Salida had stayed up talking for hours, and Monique had just gone back to her room and dozed off good when she heard the bathroom door slam shut. She jumped out of bed and peered down the hall before tiptoeing past the fish tank.

The living room was empty, and the sound of water running in the bathroom sink met her ears. Quicker than shit, she dashed across the room and over to Salida's big-ass pocketbook and rifled through the bag.

There was all kinds of shit in there! An open bag of onion and garlic potato chips, some red nail polish, a wad of balled up tissue, a pack of purple Violet candy, and…a fat-ass envelope stuffed with doe.

The sound of the flushing toilet made Monique jump. She slid a chunk of hundred-dollar bills outta the cash-fat envelope and pushed them down inside the crotch of her panties. Her naked titties jiggled under her t-shirt as she darted back toward her bedroom. She was right by the fish tank when the bathroom door opened and Salida stepped out.

"Good morning, Mizz Salida," Monique whirled around and said brightly, but the look on the older woman's face stopped her in her tracks. Salida's eyebrows were furrowed, her nostrils flared, and her lips were pressed into a hard, vicious line. *This chick is bent*, Monique thought. *Straight bent.* "What's the matter?" she asked, and for once she was seriously concerned.

Them damn tears were long gone. Salida looked like somebody in that bathroom had picked her pocket, fucked her man, and slapped the shit outta one of her kids.

"Get the hell outta my way," Salida hissed, and elbowed past Monique. She stormed into the living room, grabbed her suitcases and her purse, and fifteen seconds later she was banging into shit as she tried to get out the front door.

No this crazy heffah didn't just throw me a 'bow in my own damn house, Monique thought as she caught the heavy door before it slammed. She watched as Salida took off down the hallway and toward the elevators.

"Where you going, Mizz Salida?" Monique called out. "You going back to Brooklyn?"

"No, dummy," Salida said sarcastically. "I'm going to Queens."

"Well, do you need a ride? Queens is kinda far."

Salida acted like she didn't hear her. She sat her suitcases upright and pounded the elevator call button about fifty times straight.

Monique tried again. "Mizz Salida, I can wake Pluto up so he can ride with you downstairs. You want me to call you a cab?"

"I ain't taking no damn cab."

"Then Pluto can drive you. Or Ace."

No answer.

Monique stood and watched from her doorway until the elevator arrived. She started to tell her it cost a lot of money to catch a taxi back to Brooklyn, but then she said fuck it. That trick had an envelope stuffed full of duckets in her bag. She coulda caught herself a hundred cabs.

Monique waited until Salida had gotten on the elevator, and as soon as it closed she slammed her door and locked it. Taking the money out of her panties, she dashed into the kitchen to get on her computer. And while Pluto snored in the next room, Monique spent the next hour and a half on the Internet searching for florists in the Los Angeles area and writing down their phone numbers.

Businesses were just beginning to open on the West Coast when Monique started making her calls. She was damn near at the bottom of her long list before she struck gold, but when she did finally hit it, she hit it right outta the mothafuckin' park!

"Thank you so much!" she gushed to the clerk at Inez Florist. "Wedding planning can be so *nerve-wrecking*! My assistant usually handles these matters but she had a death in the family and had to leave town. The bride is severely allergic to daffodils, and I just wanted to make sure that none were ordered for her. So what time did you say the delivery for Juicy Stanfield was scheduled for? Nine o'clock this Saturday morning? So, if today is Thursday then that's the day after tomorrow, right? *Perfect!* And what location would that be? Oh, Crown Baptist Church? *Right again!* Would you happen to know that street address offhand? 1914 Cynthia Avenue? *Got it.* Thanks so much, darling. Have a great day!" Tossing the phone across the room, Monique darted into her bedroom to shake Pluto awake.

"Get the fuck up!" she yelled, tugging him by a hunk of fat that hung from his upper arm. "Wake up, Pluto! C'mon, baby, sit up. I got something to tell you!" She punched him real hard, and then smacked both of his plump cheeks until they jiggled. A glob of spit flew from his lip and landed on her arm. She wiped it in his hair before smacking him again.

"Wake the fuck up, Pluto! Wake up now! I know where Juicy is, goddammit! Gino too! I know where them mothafuckas is hiding at, Pluto, so wake your big ass up and get Ace on the phone so I can tell y'all!"

$$$$$

Ace was absolutely sure that the way he wanted to proceed was the best way to go, but Pluto swore all out that he was the one who had the better plan. They knew they had to get their hands on Gino in order to find out where G's money was, but the issue of where to snatch him, and how to go about it, was still up in the air.

"Yo, we can handle this shit on our own," Pluto said with mad confidence.

"Nah, man," Ace insisted, waving his boy off. "Me and you can't do it. Yeah, we can fly out there and be waiting to go hard once they asses get got, but if they spot us they gonna buck us. Gino ain't stupid, yo. His eyes are rotating man. He's looking over his shoulder, between his legs, and under both his fuckin' nuts. I'm telling you. It's gotta be somebody they don't know, yo."

"Nah, I really think me and you can handle this, slime! The wedding is on Saturday and we can fly out tonight. One of us can go in the church and get at 'em, and the other one can wait outside. If they see us then they just fuckin' see us! Our tools just gotta be aimed on blast." Pluto growled and remembered the sight of G with half his chest blown away. "Matter fact, my hammer's gonna be the last goddamn thing either one of them muh'fuckas ever see!"

"Niggah is you *crazy?*" Ace barked. "Why the fuck we gone kill 'em for? You think Gino and Juicy are just walking around with all G's paper stuffed in they pockets? They got that shit stashed outta sight somewhere! It's *hid,* niggah! We gotta make Gino tell us where the money is, fam! We need that muh'fucka to stay alive for a minute 'cause dead men tell no tales!"

"Well, if me and you ain't gone do it then we gotta fly some Harlem soldiers out there to handle it real quick," Pluto insisted. "Some warriors we know and trust."

"Hell no!" Ace refused. "I know some cats out that way that can handle it better. My cousin has a good crew. They'll be putting in work on their own turf. In their own hood. That's how it should go."

Monique stayed out of it. She chilled in the corner and pretended to file her fingernails and let the goonies try to figure it out. She had done her part by giving them the date of Juicy and Gino's wedding and the address to the church. As long as they moved fast she didn't really care how they handled their bizz. Who went in, who stayed out, who got popped, and who got dropped...She was cool with whatever, just as long as they found out what they needed to know and then brought the cheddar - and Juicy - on home to mama.

CHAPTER 14

Although Grandmother had kept me and Jimmy on our knees when we were growing up, I still wasn't all that religious. And Gino wasn't religious neither. I would've been cool with going down to the Justice of the Peace to get married, but Gino wasn't having it. It wasn't like we knew enough people out in Cali to draw a big crowd or nothing, but the guys from The Organization liked to celebrate and socialize, and they looked for any old excuse to throw a party.

Renata had acted a pure fool for my wedding dinner. The Crown Baptist Church had a very large and beautiful banquet room that they rented out to the community, and Renata had catered food from almost every gourmet restaurant in the city.

The hall was decorated in our wedding theme, which was a gathering of different cultures. There were colorful little flags from a lot of different countries hanging everywhere, and the centerpieces were done up in flags that represented all the members of our wedding party.

Tomorrow, Gino would be wearing a white tux with a Kente-print bow-tie to represent the continent of Africa, and his best man and two groomsmen were wearing black tuxes with bow-ties that repped the countries they came from. Frank's bow-tie had red, green, and white stripes like the Italian flag, Jason's tie was red with little golden-yellow stars because his family was from China, and Slick Sallie's bow-tie was bright green and had a bunch of smiling leprechauns all over it as a tribute to his Irish father. It was odd for a wedding, but it was what Gino wanted and I really didn't object.

After all that shit DarQuese had talked about the food, you should have seen her aunts, uncles, and cousins getting their grit on. They were killing the buffet stations that Renata had arranged by tasty themes.

There was a table for fruits and desserts, one for soul food, and one stacked with lobster, shrimp, and Alaskan King crab legs. There were also tables loaded with Mexican food, an assortment of Italian dishes, Chinese food, pasta, and a real big table overflowing with barbeque ribs.

I was glad to see a server posted up at each station because folks were trying to fix stupid to-go plates. All the guests seemed to be real impressed. Everybody kept saying that if the food was this good at the wedding dinner, then they couldn't wait until tomorrow to see what the reception menu was going to be like.

Everything was going perfectly until a little situation jumped off outside in the parking lot that pissed me off. I couldn't believe folks were clowning and trying to turn my classy catered dinner party into a straight-up hood classic.

It turned out that somebody had been smoking weed in the bathroom. The church lady who had rented us the building came over and told me she had smelled marijuana as she was walking down the hall. When she went into a bathroom to investigate, she busted a bunch of young girls puffing dutches and sniffing blow, and she chased them all outside.

Cynthia and Renata both insisted on coming with me to check it out, and when I opened the front door and peeked outside I saw a bunch of people having their own little party in the parking lot.

It was about five or six of Quese's little guttersnipe teenage cousins. They had some music pumping, and their grown asses were out there smoking, drinking, and letting some young thugs feel all over their behinds. I got real mad when I saw who was with them.

"What the hell are *you* doing here?" I hollered at a dude who was busy getting down on a barbequed rib.

It was Pit. He was sitting on the hood of a car and chewing on our catered food. I couldn't believe he had rolled up with his crew to crash my wedding dinner, and I automatically got mad with DarQuese because she had to be the one who had told him where we would be.

Pit peeped me staring at him from the doorway and licked his lips, then stuck up his middle finger.

"Yo, tell ya fuckin' man he's gonna get sat down!" he yelled, trying to impress the young girls who were now laughing and sitting all over my dinner guests' cars. "Y'all muh'fuckas about to take a honeymoon to *hell!*" he said. "For real, darling. You better enjoy ya little party tonight, Juice, because trust me, the honeymoon is about to be a nightmare!" Then that fool opened his mouth and laughed long and hard. Real hysterical like.

"Um...sorry, but none of them were invited so they're not our guests," I told the church lady calmly as I ignored Pit's childish ass and closed the door. Cynthia was from the hood, but I was embarrassed that Renata had witnessed all that. I didn't want her to think me and Gino were all about hanging out with trifling drug dealers and under-age cokeheads.

The incident almost put a cloud over my night, but I fought it off. *Forget about it*, I told myself, because overall the night was going really smooth. What Pit and his friends did outside was outside. Inside, a whole banquet room full of people were laughing and grubbing, and having a real good time together. Black, Italian, Puerto Rican, it didn't matter. Tonight the world belonged to me and Gino, and that meant tonight the world was good and right.

$$$$$

That is, until Gino got all suspicious and messed everything up. I still hadn't told him I was pregnant but I don't know how he didn't guess it. My stomach was still real flat, but I was sleeping a whole lot, I had to run and pee every thirty minutes, and even though I'd heard about women who lost their appetite when they were pregnant, the exact opposite seemed to be going down with me.

I had never been crazy over food, but for the past few weeks I had been munching like a mutha. I mean I was putting it down at all hours of the day and night. Food didn't make me sick. Not eating is what got my stomach all tossed up.

One of Quese's cousins had just fixed me a big fat-man plate that was overflowing with a little bit of something from every food station. I was sitting at the bridal table with Cynt and Teenie and stuffing my face hard when Cynt put her hand on my arm.

"Juicy, you and Gino be real careful when y'all leave here tonight, okay?" Cynt said quietly. "I caught Quese crying at the shop earlier today. Pit's been going at her ass."

I stopped eating. "Pit went at Quese because of me and Gino?"

"You're her girl, Juicy," Cynt said with a shrug. "Pit is territorial, just like a dog. Quese is the one who brought y'all around on his turf."

"He's a fuckin' bully," I said, remembering the aggressive way he had approached me from the gate. Pit didn't care that I was his girl's friend. He would have eaten my pussy right in Quese's shop if I had let him.

"Look, Pit is the one who started all that drama with Gino when he talked shit about my engagement ring," I told Cynt. "How did he think he could step to me like that and my man wasn't gonna raise up on him?"

Cynthia shrugged again. "I went to school with Pit when we was little, Juicy, and even as a second grader he was an evil-ass bastard. You know how cruel kids can be. They mean and they don't give a fuck about nobody's feelings. Well, if somebody even looked like they was teasing Pit back then, or even made like they was laughing at him because he was short, that dude got swole and got them back. A brick upside the head when you wasn't looking. A poke in the leg with a real sharp pencil. The book bag hanging off your back suddenly set on fire...somebody always had to pay whenever Pit got clowned."

"That's not my fault," I said, picking up my fork. "Quese needs to smash him like a bug, then walk away and leave him alone."

I had just dug into my plate again when the doors swung open and I saw Gino walk in with Slick Sallie.

"Excuse me, ladies," Gino said to Cynt and Teenie as Sallie walked off into the crowd. "I need to holla at Juicy in private real quick." Cynt and Teenie got up, and Gino sat down beside me and nodded at my packed plate.

"The whole hallway smells like sticky out there," he said quietly. "You straight?"

His voice was calm and his words had love in them, but Gino couldn't fool me. I knew exactly what he was thinking and what he was trying to say, and it was way more than I could handle at that point.

"What?" I paused with a sweet-and-sour shrimp halfway to my mouth and got defensive. "I don't see you clocking nobody else's fuckin' plate."

He backed off. "Never mind, Juicy. I didn't mean nothing. Just forget it."

I wasn't buying that. He *did* mean something. He had smelled that Cush and come running to see if the scent was coming off of me. And since I was sitting around surrounded by food and stuffing my face, he had jumped right to the conclusion that I must have smoked some sticky and gotten the munchies.

I got pissed off because I had already given him my word that I wasn't smoking anymore, and I felt that should've been good enough. But then again, I had also told him I'd never fucked with nobody else but him and his father, yet some stray niggah had claimed to know what I tasted like right up in his face.

Gino hadn't gotten over that, and neither had I. Even though the baller from Philly had walked it back and denied it, I knew it still bothered Gino and he still wondered. It bothered me too. That was the only lie I had ever told my man and I felt real bad about it.

But I was still mad. "Just so you know, some of DarQuese's cousins got caught smoking blunts in the bathroom," I told him. "It wasn't *me!*"

I didn't tell Gino that Pit was outside in the parking lot eating our food and getting lifted with them young chicks. Pit was probably the one who had brought them the weed and the blow too. But I wasn't mad enough to tell Gino that.

"I didn't accuse you of nothing, Juicy," he said.

"But you don't really trust me, do you?" I asked, my voice getting small and tight. "I know you trust me some, but not all the way, right?"

"Hey, baby," Gino put his hand over mine and assured me. "That's not true. I do trust you."

I sighed. No he didn't. Not the way I trusted him. "You wanna know why I've been eating so much and acting this way lately?" I asked him. Forget the surprise announcement. This wasn't the way I had planned it, but if I was going to be Gino's wife then I really needed him to trust me all the way without any barriers.

Truthfully, sometimes I didn't believe I was good enough for Gino. He had traveled a lot and lived other places. He was educated and sophisticated, and had class and swagger. I was just his father's ex-chicken from 136th Street. But if we were going to spend the rest of our lives together, then I needed him to know without a doubt that he could trust my word on *everything*. That he could count on me not to take any more drugs, or see any other men, or put our child in any kind of danger whatsoever.

"The reason I've been acting all crazy is because—"

"*Sshhh...*" Gino said, leaning forward to kiss me quiet. "I *trust* you, Juicy-Mo," he said. He pressed his lips to mine again. "I swear to God, I do. You ain't gotta explain *nothing* to me, girl. I *trust* you. It's you and me against the world, baby. Just us two."

I took a deep breath and made myself chill as he pulled me close and kissed the sweet-and-sour sauce from my lips. The only thing I wanted in this world was to be Gino's wife and to have his baby. In less than twenty-four hours me and my man would take that ultimate walk down the aisle, and everything would be all good. Yes, I told myself as Gino embraced me in his arms. In less than twenty-four hours the rest of our lives would be set, and every last one of our dreams would come true.

CHAPTER 15

The sun was shining brightly above the church parking lot where two stylish white limousines idled in wait. The young drivers were clean-shaven and professionally dressed, and they appeared to be busily wiping specks of road dust from their glistening chrome rims.

Around them, wedding guests streamed steadily into the church, smiling happily and chattering non-stop. The women were dressed in vibrant colors and large fashionable hats, and the men wore tailored suits and rented tuxedos.

"I gotta take a piss," said the taller of the two drivers. He was known as Zero on the streets of Los Angeles because of the number of witnesses he was known to leave behind at the scene of a crime. He glanced around slyly, then pulled out his gat and chambered a round in the head.

"Yo!" The slim, lighter-skinned dude frowned at the sight of the gun. "Stick with the plan," he warned. "Remember what the fuck Ace told you." He knew how hot-headed Zero could be. Niggah would get sent on a mission to deliver a verbal message and his trigger-happy ass would end up laying a whole house down.

"Yo, you can leave the tool in the whip, man. The time for that'll come later on when we rolling out to the airport, remember?"

"Man, shut the fuck up Izz," Zero barked at his partner, and moved toward the entrance of the church. "You ain't no fuckin' boss."

Zero liked the way his burner felt on his waist. He knew what the fuck he was doing. He'd been standing right there in the old fabric warehouse when Ace and Pluto had laid out the plan the night before.

"Zero, we gonna need you to pick up Gino in the morning," Ace had instructed, "and Izz, you'll be driving Juicy. Stay real cool until after the wedding reception, ya dig? We gonna snatch 'em up when they leave for their honeymoon. Izz, you gonna be the one driving them to the airport. Take the detour I showed you on the map, and then pull over in the alley. That's when Zero's gonna hop in and take control in the backseat. Don't fuck 'em up too bad, just handle shit until you get 'em here. Bring 'em inside, and then me and Pluto will take over from there."

Zero had his instructions cold memorized. He glanced at Izz over his shoulder and laughed. "Off brand muh'fucka," he said, and then with a slick grin playing on his lips, he disappeared through the double doors and into the cool interior of the church.

Left outside alone, Izzy shook his head. "That niggah is *unstable*," he muttered under his breath. "Straight unstable."

$$$$$

Izzy damn sure had one thing right. There was some serious instability in the air, because while the two contracted killers had been busy going at each other, neither of them had noticed the stocky midget who hopped out of the Range Rover and slipped through a side door that had been left unlocked just for him.

CHAPTER 16

The groom knew it was bad luck to mess around with the bride before the wedding, but he had an itch going for her that he really needed to scratch. In just a few hours they would be headed to Acapulco for their honeymoon, but his baby was so sweet and fine that just the thought of her waiting down the hall had his dick standing straight up on rock.

Dressed to bang in his three thousand dollar custom-sewn white tux and a Kente-print bow-tie, he waited until his best man and one of his groomsmen went upstairs, then booked out of his dressing room and crept quickly down the corridor of the church's basement.

All he wanted to do was slide up in the bride's dressing room and get his lick on for a hot minute, and then he'd be out.

He grinned broadly as he walked past his second groomsman. Standing in a wide-legged stance, his man was loitering in the corridor and talking on his cell phone. His tux was tapered and his bright green bow-tie had lucky little leprechauns all over it. He raised his arm to wave and his jacket hiked open, giving the groom a peek at the ever-present gat on his waist.

Nodding, the groom moved on, and moments later he stood outside the bridal suite with his ear pressed to the door. He frowned. He had expected shit to be popping with about a thousand chicks running off at the mouth at once, but the soft chords of chapel music were the only sounds to be heard.

He raised his fist to knock, but then he changed his mind. Slowly, he twisted the knob and pushed the door open. He broke out in a smile the moment he saw her. Wearing an exquisite gown made of white lace, she was all alone and sitting at a dressing table with her back to him. Their eyes met in the mirror and all hell broke loose.

"*Boy!*" She jumped up from her chair and almost tripped over the long hem of her gown. She stumbled, caught up in the layers of snow-white fabric. "What are you doing in here?"

"Sshhh--!" The groom reached out and steadied her on her feet and then pulled her into his arms. "Nothing," he said guiltily, nibbling at the corners of her lips. "What was you doing?"

"I was *praying*!"

The groom grinned. He kissed her again as his hands roamed her body. "Okay, let's pray together real fast. And then I'm gonna get me a little bit, cool?"

"Are you crazy?" she pushed him away, laughing. "You ain't even supposed to *see* me before the wedding! It's bad luck!"

"Sshhh...relax, baby...chill..." He pressed his nose to her neck and inhaled deeply, enjoying the sensations she ignited in him. His baby had been real sensitive lately and even the smallest thing seemed to hurt her heart. He hated to see her upset, or in any kind of pain. He loved the hell outta this girl. They'd been through a lot together and he would never do anything to hurt her.

He licked her neck and pulled her closer. She had his nose open so wide that he could smell her soul, and it smelled like a lifetime of happiness.

"Stop boo..." she moaned as his fingers brushed lightly against her nipples. "Quese just ran upstairs to get something. She's gonna be back in a second..."

The groom ignored her. Her mouth was talking noise but the hands gripping his thighs and pulling him closer were saying something totally different.

He abandoned her full breasts and ran his fingers down her bare back and over the mound of her ass. She smelled like strawberries and the fabric of her dress was like nothing he had ever felt before. He parted her lips with his tongue, and delved into her mouth, exploring the warm wetness he had come to know so well.

She murmured a soft protest. "Boy, you're gonna jack up my makeup..."

"Sshhh...just let me get some real quick..." he whispered, giving less than a damn about her makeup. His baby was so gorgeous she didn't have to wear none of that shit anyway. She had a natural beauty that nothing a man made and put in a bottle could compete with.

He squeezed her tighter, crushing her against his chest. She moaned again as his lips trailed down her silky skin. Pushing his nose down the front of her dress, he nipped the swollen mounds of her breasts.

"Uh-uh," she whispered, swaying against him as he lifted the miles of material that pooled around her ankles. "It's almost time to go upstairs...we got people up there waiting..."

Their hands were tangled in lace as the bride fought to keep her wedding dress down and the groom fought for what he wanted: to feel that softness she was hiding underneath.

She sighed deeply, and when he felt her body relax he grinned because he knew he had her. The groom chuckled. His baby liked to fuck just as much as he did. He was about to marry one of those "come-get-it-anytime-anywhere" type of chicks and he loved it.

"Yeah, that's it," he said with approval as she gave in to him. He gripped her hips, and then slid his hands together and cupped her thick, fluffy ass.

"Sshhh..." he muffled the last of her protests with slight pressure from his lips. "Just let me taste a little bit..." He lowered his aim, planting kisses down her body as he headed south of her navel. "Just let me lick it baby..."

Bracing herself against her chair, the bride spread her legs and leaned back as her man squatted down and lifted her wedding dress. He gathered its bulk above her waist and stared at the stark white garter belt and G-string she wore beneath her clothing. Her tummy was flat and her waist was cinched. Her hips were perfect, and her lower lips were neatly shaved.

He glanced up at her and saw the sexual heat in her eyes and sucked in his breath. He knew what she liked and he was just about to give it to her.

But suddenly she paused. Listening.

"Somebody's coming!" she whispered, pulling him to his feet and yanking down her dress. "DarQuese is back!"

The groom listened too, but what he heard was the ominous click-clack of a cocking gat. He was on the move even before the door burst open. A gun blast shattered the silence as he leaped on top of his woman, completely covering her with his large frame.

Pop! Pop! Pop!

A hot slug penetrated his lower back and the groom flinched and wrapped himself around his bride, enveloping her in his protective embrace. The bullet sped through his body and continued on its path, piercing the bride-to-be's precious tummy.

The groom toppled forward and both of them went down, knocking over the chair and sending makeup vials and water bottles flying off the counter.

Helpless under his weight, the bride absorbed the force of the impact. Her slender back splintered painfully against the chair, and the base of her head slammed into the dressing table as they plummeted to the floor. She lay beneath him stunned, bleeding, and writhing in agony.

"Stay down, baby," the groom gasped. His full weight crushed her and his lips were warm against her ear. He groaned loudly and reached for her hand, lacing his fingers through hers. "I got you, baby girl," he panted. "Just stay down."

The room spun in looping circles as the bride battled her throbbing pain and the approaching darkness that was slowly snuffing out her light. Warm blood seeped from her body as she fought to stay conscious. She tried to hold tight to her man's hand, but both of them were slowly losing their grip.

A voice raked over the young lovers as they lay bleeding together on the dressing room floor, and even through her fiery haze of pain the bride felt an icy finger of fear run down her spine.

"Gino..." she whimpered, breathing hard beneath him.

"Stay down..." the groom whispered one final time. "I got you, baby. Just stay..."

Footsteps sounded as the shooter stormed over to the downed couple. Their hands were lifted roughly, and the bride's ring-finger was bent and twisted until the ten-carat hunk of ice she wore slid free. Pinned beneath her man, the last voice the beautiful, young, almost-bride-to-be heard before her world pitched to black belonged to a killer.

"That's right," the shooter rasped in a cold, greedy voice. "Stay down and give me that goddamn ring."

CHAPTER 17

Izzy was sweatin'.

Fifteen minutes had passed since his man Zero had disappeared through the church doors, and every few seconds he glanced toward the building hoping to see that long-legged niggah coming back out. A huge batch of colorful flowers had arrived from Inez Florist, and a preacher and a bunch of little kids had just been dropped off at the front door.

Izzy was reaching into his jacket pocket to get his cell phone, when the shit hit the fan. He heard the screams even before the front door of the church burst open. His stomach tightened into a hard ball as a skinny old woman in a lime green hat and matching shoes ran outside screaming, "They got shot! They got shot! Lord, *Jesus*! Call an ambulance! They got shot!"

At least twenty-five people erupted out the door right behind her, and a young mother screamed as her little girl tripped and fell and got trampled by the fleeing crowd.

"Ohhhh *damn*!" Izz muttered under his breath. That crazy *muh'fucka*! This shit had Zero written all over it. He'd told him not to go in there fuckin' nothing up!

The faint sound of sirens could be heard in the distance. Izz didn't know if it was an ambulance or the police, and he was way too smart to wait around and find out.

He ran over to his limo and snatched open the door. Shouts and wails were coming from inside the church, and Izzy knew that anybody on the scene when the cops got there was gonna get grilled. And just how the fuck was he supposed to explain the two dead muh'fuckas in the trunk that him and Zero had popped for their chauffeur uniforms and their extra-long whips?

"Stupid-ass niggah!" Izz spit. He had just slammed the door and put the limo in drive when he saw Zero running out the church holding up his pants. Izz shifted the gear to park again, and then jumped back out and ran toward his partner-in-crime.

"Yo, muh'fucka! What the fuck did you just do?"

There was no mistaking the look of confusion on Zero's face as he shrugged and tried to zip up his pants. "I took a *shit*, niggah!" he barked. "All I did was take a fuckin' *shit*!"

Izz shook his head. "Then what the fuck just happened in there, man?" he demanded. "You ain't pop 'em, did you? Yo, niggah! Don't tell me you went in there and blasted them muh'fuckas!"

The truth shone bright in Zero's killer eyes as he shook his head and jetted toward his ride.

"Nah, slime," he spit over his shoulder. "I ain't shoot 'em! Word is bond, I didn't!"

He nodded toward the panicked crowd that was pouring out the church's doors.

"But *some* fuckin' body did!"

TO BE CONTINUED...

Order

BETRAYAL: THE 2ND DEADLY SIN
at
www.Amazon.com or www.BN.com

**PART TWO
OF NOIRE'S BLOCKBUSTER
URBAN EROTIC SERIAL TALE!**

Juicy-Mo's dreams have all been shattered!

Drama and danger continue to follow Juicy and Gino!
On what should have been the happiest day of their lives the beautiful young lovers, who fled the streets of New York City, are once again marked for murder!

With Ace, Pluto, and Money-Makin' Monique determined to get their hands on G's stash of doe, will Gino and Juicy realize their dreams of marriage and a lifetime of happiness? Or will the wrath of the streets sneak up on them to collect the debt they owe?

WARNING!

This here ain't no romance
It's an urban erotic tale
A hater's on the loose
And the situation's frail
From out of town
They gunned them down
The lovers took a fall
A gwap is on the line and G's homeboyz want it all!
So if the script gets flipped, down-side-up
And you can't tell foe from friend
Watch your back and trust no man
'Cause **BETRAYAL** is this Sin!

Find out more in…
G-SPOT 2: THE SEVEN DEADLY SINS
Betrayal: The 2nd Deadly Sin

The Urban Erotic Serial Saga Continues!

NOIRE

G-Spot 2:
The Seven Deadly Sins
An Urban Erotic Serial Tale Told in 7 Parts

BETRAYAL: THE 2ND DEADLY SIN

by
Noire

www.AskNoire.com
www.GSpot2.com
www.TheGSpotSaga.com

CHAPTER 1

My wedding guests never did get to see me in my white designer bridal dress. Instead, two days after I was supposed to get married I woke up in a hospital bed wearing a plain old cotton nightgown.

I opened my eyes in a state of total confusion. Machines beeped all around me. I had tubes coming out of everywhere. I tried to sit up but my body felt weighted down, and a white-hot bolt of pain drilled into the deepest part of my stomach.

I held my breath, sweating through the agony. The beeping machines scared me, and I closed my eyes again. My thoughts were hazy and all over the place. Nothing was making sense, and I figured I must've had one of those crazy dreams again.

But this dream had taken place in my bridal suite. Gino had snuck up on me while I was praying. He was trying to get him some, and he had just pulled up my dress and pushed his face between my legs when I heard somebody coming. Gino had stood up to listen too, and then out of nowhere the door busted wide open.

In a flash, Gino spun around and damn near jumped on top of me. A popping noise exploded in the air, and then something hot thumped deep in my belly.

The next thing I knew we were on the floor. Gino's body was covering mine and he was holding my hand. I felt myself fading off. Gino was whispering softly in my ear, but I couldn't stay focused. Everything started going black.

The beeping machine cut into my thoughts and I opened my eyes and saw a nurse walking out of my room. And that's when I knew my dream was actually my reality, and suddenly I was wide-awake. Now I remembered! I remembered it *all*, and immediately my heart reached for Gino.

Gino!

I actually heard myself gasp as he fell on top of me. I felt his body jerk when the bullet sank, first into him, and then into me, piercing my stomach like a spear. I felt us falling together. And then the ground jumped up to catch us like it was a brick mattress. Gino's body was all dead weight as he covered my heart with his.

Please God, I prayed as I lay in that hospital bed more scared than I had ever been in my entire life. The searing pain in my belly was now throbbing all the way down in my booty.

Lord, I know I ain't been right. I'm trifling and I'm a sinner. I admit that. But if you gotta punish me, if you gotta take something away from me, let it be the baby! Take it. Just take it. Me and Gino can have us another one. Just please, I squeezed my eyes closed and prayed so hard my whole body trembled. *Please don't take Gino. Please don't take my man!*

I must have fallen back to sleep because the next time I opened my eyes there were two doctors looking down at me. I struggled to sit up, and one of them took my hand and told me to hold still.

"Try not to move," he said, gently. "You're in the hospital and you're safe. We have a security guard outside your door, and everything is going to be fine."

My back hurt like hell and my gut was just crazy sore. I slid my hand over my belly and I was shocked to feel the thick bandages that were taped to my skin. But as bad as I was aching, I didn't give a damn about myself. I could still feel Gino pulling me into his arms as the gun boomed behind him. I could feel his lips, wet on my ear, as he used his body like it was a shield just for *me*.

"Gino..." I whispered as the other doctor came closer and stood beside my bed. She had red hair and big blue eyes. She reached for my hand and her skin felt soft and cool.

I licked my lips and my eyes searched hers.

"Where's Gino?"

She squeezed my hand.

"He's here," she said softly. "I'm sorry, but the bullet passed straight through you and it caused quite a bit of damage. You're having a boy, Juicy. We operated on both of you, and we hope your son will cooperate by staying in your womb for a while longer so he can develop more fully."

"Where's Gino?" I cried out as loud as I could, but my voice was barely a whisper in the room. I'd heard what the hell she said about a baby boy and an operation, but couldn't she see I didn't care about none of that?

"Gino?" I pleaded weakly. My eyes darted all over her face. "*Gino!*"

"He's in intensive care," she finally told me. Her blue eyes looked so, so, so sad, and that scared the hell out of me because doctors weren't supposed to get emotional, even when shit was real bad.

She said, "Gino was shot in the back. The bullet passed through his body and into your stomach. He suffered severe damaged to some of his internal organs."

She shook her head and sighed as she continued. "We have a fine team of surgeons here and they repaired things as best they could. But I won't lie. It looks pretty bad. Right now it's touch-and-go. We'll know more about his condition over the next forty-eight hours. For the time being, all we can do is wait. And pray."

Wait and pray. Pray and wait. I closed my eyes and that's exactly what I did. All those long nights that Grandmother had kept me and Jimmy on our knees were about to pay off. I knew how to pray.

And I knew how to beg too.

I begged God for Gino's life.

There wasn't a drop of shame in me as I kissed up to the man upstairs. My lips moved frantically as I gave Him a list of all the reasons why Gino's life had beauty and promise. Why his soul was special and worthy.

I didn't give a damn about myself. And at that moment I didn't care about my baby boy, neither. I just wanted my man to be okay. I wanted him to *live*. There was no way I could make it without Gino. I didn't even wanna think about being in a world without him there to love me and keep me warm. For the first time in my life I knew what it was to really, really *need* somebody. And not just to set me up in a fancy crib, or to splurge on me at expensive restaurants, or to keep me laced up lovely with designer shit on my back neither.

Nah, I needed Gino the way the sun needs the moon. The way a flower needs rain. The way a woman needs her man.

Please God...

I begged and begged, over and over again.
Please God...
Don't take him. Please, touch him. *Heal* him!
Please God...
I'll do anything. Anything! Just don't take him.
Please God...
With Gino's name on my lips, I drifted off into a fitful sleep.
Please God...

$$$$$

The next time I opened my eyes Renata was standing there.

"Where's Gino?" I asked hoarsely. She had been right by my side, holding my hand as I slept.

Slowly she shook her head. "He's still fighting, Juicy. The police think it was a robbery attempt. Somebody must have snuck into your dressing room. Most of your guests were already upstairs in the chapel, and it was your friend DarQuese who found you. She walked in and saw you and Gino lying on the floor covered in blood. She ran upstairs screaming and Frankie heard her and called an ambulance."

DarQuese. The sound of that bitch's name filled my whole body with rage and I started trembling under the sheets.

"Did they catch Pit?" I whispered. It took every bit of strength I had just to speak, but right then nothing could have kept me quiet.

Renata frowned. "Pit?

"DarQuese's man. The midget. He was outside the church getting high with all those young girls last night, remember?"

She shook her head. "It was dark out there, and I didn't get a good look at him. But the police questioned everybody." Renata shrugged. "But you know how it is. Nobody saw anything."

"*Uh-huh!*" I shrieked. I tried to raise myself up on one elbow, but my stomach muscles screamed, burning like they were on fire.

"*DarQuese* saw something!" I insisted as I remembered how anxious she had been to get out of my dressing room. She had claimed she needed to go upstairs and get something real quick, and now I knew that something had been *her man!*

I inhaled deeply, trying to breathe through my pain. "Quese saw who shot us, didn't she?"

Renata shook her head again. "I don't know, Juicy. I didn't get a chance to talk to her. All I know is that she came running upstairs to Frankie. She was crying and screaming that you and Gino were both dead. And just like everybody else, she claimed she didn't see anything."

That was some bullshit and I knew it! As bad as I was hurting my blood was on boil. DarQuese was a low-life schemer! No wonder that bitch had two sides to her face! She was the one who had brought Pit up to the church to shit on my rehearsal dinner, and I knew damn well she'd brought him to spray me and Gino at our wedding too! I closed my eyes as my body was racked with waves of pain. Wasn't nobody fuckin' stupid. Quese could stunt all she wanted to, but that bitch knew exactly who had shot me and Gino.

"So where is she?" I asked, opening my eyes again. I had been laying in this bed for a minute now, and the only familiar face I'd seen so far had been Renata's. "Has Quese been up here to see about me?"

Renata shook her head. "I really don't know where she is, Juicy. I haven't seen her at all. But you need to relax, *cara*. You've lost a lot of blood, and the doctors aren't sure what's really what with you just yet. And besides, you have your baby to think about too. Congratulations! We were all surprised to hear that you were expecting. I'm told you're having a boy."

I nodded. "Gino doesn't even know yet," I said sadly as my heart filled with regret. "I was gonna surprise him with the news right after we got married."

"Well, there will still be plenty of opportunities to tell him later," Renata said. "I don't want you to worry about anything, okay? There'll be enough time to figure everything out when you and Gino are both a little stronger."

I was still mad and scared and gripped in sorrow all at the same time, but I was doped up and in crazy pain too. I opened my mouth to rage some more, but that groggy sense of heaviness settled over me and once again I fell off into a deep sleep.

CHAPTER 2

I had a couple of new visitors when I woke up. Two white cops. DTs from the violent crimes division, they said.

"How are you feeling?" the younger one asked, and I could tell he really wanted to know. They were both dressed in street clothes, and they looked like pure white boys.

"Shitty," I answered. My mouth was dry and my lips felt crusty, and when I frowned after licking them, the younger cop took a cup of water from the night table and held it gently to my mouth so I could take a sip.

"You know why we're here," the older cop said. He stared at me intently, like the shooter's name was about to appear on my forehead.

"Tell us everything you remember about what happened before you and your boyfriend were shot."

My fiancé! I wanted to scream. Gino wasn't just my boyfriend! He had been about to wife me. He was gonna be my husband.

"It was real hectic," I whispered, remembering how excited everybody had been for us. "I was downstairs in my dressing room, and Gino—" my voice caught in my throat, "Gino was supposed to be in his dressing room too."

"So you two were alone?" the younger dude asked, as he scribbled on a small white pad. "It was just a few minutes before your wedding, and there was no one else in the dressing room with you guys?"

"Yeah," I nodded. "My bridesmaids had already gone upstairs to get lined up. My maid of honor had just stepped out to check on something, and I was in there by myself. Praying. Until Gino knocked on the door."

"And then what happened?"

I tried to shrug my shoulders but even that slight movement hurt like hell.

"Nothing happened," I lied, remembering how Gino's lips had felt on my thighs, and how his hands had been all up my dress and between my legs as he tried to lick me out.

"We were just standing around talking, and the next thing I knew the door banged open and then Gino jumped all over me. He covered me up. He was holding me close to him when I felt his body jerk, and then my stomach got real hot and we both went down to the floor." A tear slipped from my eye. "I guess that's when we got shot."

"Did you see anyone?" The older cop was still staring at me hard. "Can you identify the person who shot you?"

I shook my head.

"No," I told him as my mind whirled fast on rewind and I recalled all the drama that had gone down over the past couple of weeks. "I didn't see anybody. But I know who it was."

"So who was it?"

I didn't even hesitate.

"It was this dude named Pit. He's a midget gangsta from Compton. Either he shot us, or he got one of his boys to do it. But it was my homegirl who set us up."

Just thinking about DarQuese cut my heart like glass. In just six short months I had really trusted Quese. Loved her and trusted her just like a sister, and in return she had betrayed me.

"Friend who?" the cop asked.

"DarQuese Middleton." I spit that two-faced, long-legged scheming bitch's name off my tongue. "My so-called maid of honor."

$$$$$

I was exhausted again by the time they finished grilling me. They wanted to know everything, and I wanted them to know everything too. I didn't hold anything back. They told me a cop had been posted outside my door ever since they brought me in, and that I was safe and could speak to them freely because L.A.'s finest was there to protect me.

I almost laughed behind that one. I'd seen the way G used to buy and pay for cops in New York all the time, so I knew all that protection talk was a joke. But I didn't care. I told them all about how Pit had been riding me. How him and Gino had scrapped when Pit tried to shit all over my engagement ring.

"Where's the ring now? In patient property?" the older cop asked, lifting my hand. "You were probably unconscious when they brought you in, so you might not remember. I can check your inventory sheet."

I shook my head.

"Whoever shot us took my ring," I told them. "Me and Gino were on the floor when somebody said 'give up your ring' and then snatched it off my finger. I think I passed out right after that."

"You said you didn't see anyone, but did you recognize the voice? Would you be able to identify it if you heard it again?"

I shook my head once more. It hurt like hell to move but I fought the pain.

"I doubt it. Gino was heavy on top of me and everything was happening so fast. It seemed like the voice was coming from miles away."

Before the detectives left I gave them the address to DarQuese's beauty shop, and told them Pit owned an urban clothing store right across the street. In fact, I told them everything I thought might help them. Forget all that 'stop snitchin' nonsense. That was for honor between thieves. Me and Gino were innocents. It was nothing except greed and envy that had made Pit come at our throats. And for him to just gun us down like two stray dogs, and almost kill our baby too?

All that bitter grief was too much for my heart to hold. I lay there twitching. Crying and twitching. Tears just ran from my eyes like water. I tried to say a few more prayers for Gino but my words seemed empty. Like I was only begging and praying because I was in trouble and needed help. I wondered if God was even paying me any attention, or if this was the wrath of the Lord that Grandmother used to speak of when she was whipping my ass for being sneaky and grown.

My whole body felt like it was on fire. I trailed my fingers lightly across my stomach, and moaned at the swelling and throbbing soreness. I thought about Gino, laying somewhere in this same hospital, yet out of my reach and so far away.

The white female doctor, the one who had been standing over me the first time I woke up, came to see me a lot. Her name was Doctor Atgrove, and she seemed to have a lot of sympathy for me. "I can't tell you a whole lot right now," she'd said just a day or so earlier, "but there is some concern about Gino's spinal cord. The bullet shattered two vertebrae in his lower lumbar, and even if he survives his soft tissue injuries there's a possibility that he could be paralyzed from the waist down. But we won't know much of anything unless he comes out of his coma."

I refused to even hear that. I didn't even care about the possibility that he might be paralyzed. I just wanted Gino to *live*. I wanted my man to hold me in his arms again. To be with me. To flow through life with me. If he ended up paralyzed it wouldn't mean a damned thing to me. I just needed Gino to fight and fight hard.

I needed my man to stay alive.

CHAPTER 3

Monique was getting her gushy on. While the dog was away the alley cat was damn sure out to play. She leaned over the buff, high-yellow young dude whose dick she was riding, and licked his pink nipple until it stiffened under her tongue.

Monique grinned. She was a maneater. She craved meat. Young, hard, muscled-up meat. She glanced down at the big-boned tyke as they fucked. He was Pluto's nephew. A young'un. A light-bright redbone too. He was no more than eighteen, and that's just how she liked 'em. She kept a crew of come-up niggahs just like him on a string, using them to pull all kinds of devious capers that she concocted when she was being sneaky and slick.

Technically, the young crew worked for Ace and Pluto, slanging rock and banging heads out on the streets. But Monique had found a way to stimulate their fragile egos and manipulate their juvenile, impressionable minds. She simply gave their young asses for free what hundreds of grown men were required to pay top dollar for.

"Oooh, goddamn!" the boy muttered below her as she bucked around on his juiced-up dick. It had been a minute since she'd had anything so long and stiff up in her, and all them dildos and other stage props she used in her freak 'em routines didn't hardly count.

She pressed her titties to the young boy's chest and smashed them up. He slid his hands up from her bodacious ass and hugged her tight in his arms as he pumped his dick up inside her and expanded her inner walls. He crossed his arms behind her and hugged her shoulders.

They rocked it like that for a few seconds, but then Monique broke free and reared back again. This wasn't nothing but a fuck, and she needed his young ass to know it. All that hugging shit was too damned tender. It was nice, but it was still tender.

"Fuck me from the back," Monique demanded as she dislodged herself from the young hood and got on her hands and knees. Who the fuck did he think he was hugging on? Didn't this fool know she was his Uncle Pluto's bitch?

And speaking of Pluto, Monique wondered why the fuck he hadn't called her yet. By now him and Ace shoulda snatched all the feathers outta those two stupid-ass lovebirds in California! Getting married! Tryna be all extra. They was already fucking. Why the hell did they need to get married just to do more of that?

She couldn't wait until Ace and Pluto got back to New York with G's money. She got off just thinking about the stacks of crisp cash that they were gonna steal back from Gino.

And Juicy.

Monique giggled as she gyrated. Juicy's stupid ass was gonna get sliced up. Monique had instructed Ace and Pluto to bring that run-through trick back to Harlem right along with the doe. There was an extra-sharp razor blade and a real pissy mattress waiting downstairs in the Dungeon, and Juicy's name was written on both of them.

Monique gasped as dude slid his wet dick deeply up in her. This was just how a young dude was supposed to fuck, she thought with approval. He'd been banging her for the past thirty minutes, and aside from the sweat running in rivers from their bodies, he didn't seem tired and he was still holding on to his nut.

The bed rocked beneath them and Monique moaned as her nipples scraped against the sheets. She pressed her chin to her chest, then stuck out her tongue and licked her third, most sensitive nipple.

Taking her hint, the corner boy reached beneath her and rubbed her stomach, then brought his hands up to weigh her full breasts. He twisted her nipples and Monique went wild. He moved his hands back down until they cupped her round hips, then he slapped her bouncy ass and sent a thrill shooting all the way up to her little titty.

"Do that again!" she bossed him, tooting that na-na up to meet his frantic thrusts. She reached between her legs and squeezed her dripping clit, then arched her back and sighed with pleasure.

"Yeah," she muttered as he inserted his thumb deep into her ass and fucked both her holes. He ain't half-bad for a young'un, Monique mused as his other hand cracked like a whip on her ass cheek and he spanked-fucked her toward another nut. "Do that shit again!" she demanded. "And again and again and again..."

$$$$$

While Monique was busy getting fucked, her man Pluto was ready to fuck somebody up. Instead of buying a truck and driving back to the East Coast loaded down with cash like they'd planned, Pluto and Ace had been forced to catch a red-eye flight and sky up outta L.A. with a quickness.

The temperature had gotten real hot on the streets after Gino and Juicy got popped. Some crazy shit jumped off with the Mob that had even the most seasoned hardbodies looking for a safe hole to crawl into.

"I told you," Pluto said for the hundredth time since they'd jetted to the airport and hopped on the first plane smoking back east. They had just touched down at LaGuardia Airport, and the thought of going back to Harlem and telling Monique they had failed to complete their mission was giving Pluto some serious heartburn.

"We shoulda used our own squad," he fussed. "We coulda flown Swish or Domni or one of them other level-headed soldiers out to Cali, and no shit like this woulda went down."

Ace looked at his longtime boy like he was a two-year-old idiot.

"How many times I gotta tell you it wasn't us? That wasn't our shit, man! Zero didn't get nowhere near Juicy and Gino in that church! He told you that. Even Izz believed him. That niggah Zero is a patient, but he ain't stupid.

"Besides," Ace shrugged as they walked from the airport terminal to the parking lot. "You saw how shaky shit got out there on them L.A. corners. Even the Crips and the Bloods went into hiding."

"That's because them Cali niggahs fucked shit up!"

"Yo," Ace exploded with frustration. "It wasn't us! Rabb already explained that shit, niggah! How many times you gotta be told the same damn thing?"

Ace's cousin Rabbit had been real nervous when they swung by his crib to tell him his manz had fucked up their job.

"Word, my niggahs didn't fuck it up," Rabb had insisted. The thick-necked, brawny killer had snatched Ace and Pluto off his porch before they could ring the doorbell, and they had sat dumbfounded in his darkened living room as he peered out through his closed venetian blinds like a scared little bitch.

"Somebody beat my dudes to it, that's what happened," Rabbit told them. "Word on the block is that ya boy Gino made some enemies around here. He caught the attention of a click outta Compton. They prolly the ones who put him down."

Ace had bucked. "So what? Y'all niggahs suckin' Compton dick now? Them niggahs got you peeping out ya window and holding ya nuts now?"

Rabb had frowned and shook his head. "Nah, fuck them sherm-ass Compton niggahs," he said quietly. "Don't nobody give a fuck about that set. It's them white boys everybody is checking for right now. Them *mafia* niggahs. I heard they out there *stalking* dudes. Them fools is on the prowl."

"Over what?"

"Not over what. Over who. They looking for ya boy's shooter, man. And when they find him they gonna lay him and his whole posse down. Ya boy Gino was they niggah. He was protected. Wasn't nobody supposed to touch him."

Ace and Pluto had given each other a smirked-out New York look. Neither one of them believed that bullshit. G had always been in deep and smoove with several Mob families, and Gino wasn't big enough to spark their interest or their protection. It just didn't make no sense.

Nah, this wasn't that type of crime, Pluto concluded as they walked around the airport parking lot searching for their whip. If the boyz they hired didn't do it, then the local click that was gunning for Gino prolly did. Yeah. The bullet that hit Gino had some Cali niggah's fingerprints all over it. He was almost sure of it.

CHAPTER 4

Mad as hell didn't even describe what Monique was when Ace and Pluto came back to New York by airplane. The plan had been for them to leave their whip at the airport and fly out to the West Coast. Once they got their hands on the cash, they were supposed to buy a truck and transport G's money back home.

But a quick call to Pluto verified that once again, all Monique's dreams had been slain. Them niggahs had just flown in on a plane to LaGuardia, and Monique knew there was no way in fuck they had rolled outta L.A. carrying more than half a million dollars in their check-on luggage.

And that meant they had failed.

Monique was past mad. She was furious. She shoulda known better than to send two stupid men to do a smart woman's job! Them bumbling-ass niggahs had gone all the way to California just to come home empty-handed. And not only didn't they get the money, they didn't get that bitch Juicy neither.

The death-look on Pluto's face should have been enough to check her tongue when he walked in the front door, but Monique was too far gone to value her life.

"What do you mean somebody shot him?" she demanded when Pluto told her Gino had taken a hot one.

"Just what I said. That niggah got popped. He's in the hospital. They got po-po posted on him and ere'thang."

Monique's eyes narrowed. "And what about Juicy?"

Pluto shrugged as he took off his shoes and wiggled his cheesy toes around in the air.

"She's in the same hospital. She got hit too."

Monique couldn't bear to believe this shit. What had she done to deserve this? Why couldn't she get the things she wanted out of life? What kinda fucked up luck did she have?

"So, you mean to tell me that all that money..." she breathed heavily in anger. "All that fuckin' money they stole from us...*they still got it?*"

Pluto didn't answer. He picked up his shoes and started walking toward their bedroom.

But Monique wasn't finished. Hell no, she wasn't.

"Hold up," she said, walking behind him. "So, you telling me that after all that work I put in, fuckin' with that crazy-ass Salida, pumping Nae-Nae's dumb ass for information and then calling every fuckin' florist in L.A., ...after all that fuckin' *work*, you and Ace lose ya heads and shoot Gino's ass, but neither one of y'all is smart enough to make him give up the cash first? Damn, Pluto! What the fuck is wrong with you? You was supposed to have this shit all planned out!"

She didn't even see the first blow coming. Pluto had already walked past her when he swung. That big-belly niggah pirouetted on his toes like a fleet-footed ballerina.

His four fat knuckles drilled into her temple, dropping her to her knees. Monique could only clutch her head and gasp for air. The scream she wanted to let out was pushed back down her throat by Pluto's knee as he brought it up and thrust it into her mouth. Her front teeth sank into his flesh drawing blood, and Monique shrieked and fell over backward. She lay there helplessly, knees bent, arms outstretched, and her blood-filled mouth open wide.

"Bitch, don't you *ever*," Pluto panted in rage above her. "Ever! As long as your black ass is alive and licking my balls, tell me nothing about planning shit out! I'm the master fuckin' planner up in here. And you better not never forget it!"

There was no mistaking the killer intentions in his eyes, and Monique had enough sense to roll over real quick and cover her face.

Pluto's next blow came down hard in the center of her back. It almost stopped her heart. But there was no sense in screaming. Wasn't nobody gonna come save her no way.

Monique balled up and protected herself the best way she could. She understood why Pluto had to check her for getting outta pocket. And in a perverse way, she knew she deserved it too. But she had meant every damn thing she said! Them niggahs shoulda stuck to the plan!

Scurrying all over the floor, Monique took her ass-whipping like a natural woman. And the whole time Pluto was beating her, she didn't even cry. She couldn't. She was too busy scheming and conniving and formulating some grand, brand new plans of her own.

CHAPTER 5

I was dreaming again, but this time it wasn't no nightmare. I was back in New York with Gino.

He was sitting on a bench in Central Park, and I was across the street on the corner, waiting for the light to change.

It was wintertime, and a deep layer of snow was on the ground.

"Hurry up, Juicy," Gino hollered, grinning with his fine self. My heart started beating real fast. Gino wasn't shot! There was nothing wrong with him! He had on a bad-ass gray wool coat and some jeans and a pair of Timbs. He got up from the bench and walked toward me. Still grinning, he picked up a handful of loose snow and packed it between his palms. He laughed at the scared look on my face and waited till a car sped past, and then he threw the snowball softly in my direction.

I hollered like his little flimsy snowball was a giant asteroid about to take me out, and Gino cracked up laughing. Then he gave me a sexy wink and ran into the park.

"I'ma get you!" I yelled, trying to act like I was mad. The traffic light changed and I ran across the street and chased after him. Gino was still laughing but he kept getting further and further ahead, pulling me deeper into the park.

The snow sucked at my feet. Gino was straight dusting me, even though he was walking normally and I was booking.

"Wait up!" I called out to him. "Hey Gino! Wait up!"

"Catch up!" he turned around and yelled with a big grin. "You gotta run faster, Juicy. *Faster!*"

The distance between us grew much greater. Gino was turning into a shadowy blur against the winter whiteness of the park. He was getting so far away I could barely see him.

"Wait for me..." I whined as my legs pumped harder. I lifted my knees and my feet came down hard in the slurping snow. "Gino...wait..."

I was whimpering now. It had gotten darker outside. Much darker. Like somebody had pulled a blanket over the sky. My chest felt tight. Like my heart had swelled up. The air had turned so damned cold I could barely breathe.

Then suddenly the world went completely dark.

Ahead of me, where Gino should have been, was just an endless black road. I was running blind. I could feel his presence just up the way, but no matter how fast I moved I just couldn't catch up with him.

And then I heard his voice. He spoke to me as clear as day in my head and in my heart.

Juicy, he said sadly. *Ahh...Juicy. My baby. I love you, girl. I'll always love you.*

"Gino!" I screamed and ran deeper into the heavy darkness.

That's right. Come closer to me, baby. I wanna hold you so bad. I wanna feel you just one more time. I'm right here, Juicy. Can't you see me?

It was pitch black and he was so far away! My legs wanted to move faster, but I was freezing like never before, and I was tired. Oh, damn, was I tired.

Juicy! My man's voice bounced all around me in the darkness.

I'm waiting for you, baby. I'm holding on… I'm trying, Juicy… I'm trying…

"Juicy."

I need you, Juicy, Gino said. I could feel his heart reaching for me across what seemed like an ocean of ice-cold miles. *Juicy, I need you…*

"Juicy!"

I opened my eyes. Renata was standing by my bed and she looked worried.

"Juicy?" she said my name again. "You were crying out in your sleep, honey. Are you in pain? Do you need more medication?"

"Gino," I muttered. My body trembled from head to toe. The coldness in my dream had been real. I realized I'd brought it with me to wakefulness as I lay there crying and shivering, my teeth chattering uncontrollably.

"Oh my God! You're shaking," Renata soothed me with her strong, even voice. She pulled an extra blanket from the end of the bed and spread it out over me. She smoothed my hair back from my forehead and took my hands in hers. "So cold, Juicy," she said gently. "Your hands are so cold."

"Gino," I muttered again. "I gotta see Gino."

Renata shook her head and patted my hand.

"Not yet, Juicy. It isn't safe for you to move around yet. But don't worry. Frank has been sitting with Gino every day. In fact, he's with him right now. Gino's condition hasn't really changed, but at least he's still alive."

"I gotta see him, Renata!" Fear had me whining like a baby. "He needs me."

The icy terror from my dream was pounding deep in my bones, and all I knew was that I had to be by Gino's side.

"Please help me," I begged her. "Take me to him, Renata. Take me to my man."

Renata gave me a look and opened her mouth like she was gonna tell me no, then she closed it again and nodded.

"Okay," she said, and I was lifted by the glare of determination that had entered her eyes. "I understand how bad you want to see him, Juicy, and I think you should. It might do you both some good. I'll go down to the nurse's station and talk somebody into taking you upstairs to the ICU."

$$$$$

Renata had done her part in talking to the doctors, but all those fools could bark about was the liability they would face if I got out of bed and something went wrong for me or the baby.

Why couldn't they understand that I didn't care about any of that? Two doctors and a nurse rushed up in my room when Renata came back. I guess they figured if they rolled up on me like a gang it would be easier to get me to accept them telling me no.

"I'm sorry," one of the doctors said, crossing his arms. He was the ob-gyn doctor whose job it was to make sure that me and Gino's baby stayed alive. His tight-ass wouldn't even let me get out of the bed to go sit on the toilet and pee. Instead, I had to lay flat on my back and use a nasty bedpan.

"It's just too risky, Juicy. Your body is still traumatized. Your cervix is very dilated. Even if we were able to transport you upstairs, the trauma of seeing Gino in his condition is likely to cause both you and the baby a lot of distress. I just can't recommend it."

The other doctor backed him up with a nod. She was the surgeon who had operated on me.

"He's right, Juicy. I understand how concerned you are about Gino, but right now your baby's health is our priority. You simply cannot leave your bed."

I cut up like a true project chick up in there.

"This baby is *your* fuckin' priority!" I screeched. I was spitting mad. Sweating bullets and slinging hot tears all over the room. "My priority is *Gino*! Y'all can't keep me away from him! You don't have the *right* to keep me away from him! Gino needs me. I need him. I don't care what I have to do. I'm seeing him!"

The cop who was posted outside my door stuck his head inside, and ignoring the doctors, asked me if everything was okay.

"Oh, it's about to *be* okay!" I snapped, wiping my nose with the end of the sheet. I struggled to sit up in the bed and winced in pain as I tried to slide my legs around. "'Cause I'm getting the fuck outta here!"

"You can't be serious," the male doctor said.

"Oh, she's serious," Renata answered.

I grilled both those damned doctors down.

"Bring me my papers! Bring me my *mothafuckin'* papers! I'm signing myself *out!*"

That got their attention.

By the time I scooted my naked butt to the edge of the bed and my feet were dangling down about to touch the floor, everybody in the room understood that I was not bullshitting! The nurse rushed over to my side, and both doctors started backpedaling, eating all the words they had just spoken.

"Okay, okay," the surgeon said. She put her arm around my shoulder and lifted my legs back onto the bed. "Don't do this," she said softly. "Please don't hurt yourself like this. We'll take you to see Gino. Let me get the staff to bring us a wheelchair and I'll have an attendant get you seated in it safely."

But the ugly man-doctor still wasn't having it. "I don't advise that," he said sharply. "The fetus—"

The female doctor shut him down with just one look. "It doesn't matter what you advise. Her fiancé and the father of her child is upstairs fighting for his life. He's fighting for *their* lives. Do you have any idea what this must be like for Juicy? To have to lie in bed helplessly while Gino fights his battle alone? We're taking her upstairs. In my personal and professional opinion, by his side is exactly where she needs to be."

CHAPTER 6

My whole body hurt as they placed me in the wheelchair, but I took the pain without even flinching.

While Renata had been downstairs with me, Frank had been visiting Gino, so she jetted upstairs to tell him to leave so that I could go in. She told me there was a cop posted up to guard Gino too, but since Gino was up there with the critically ill patients he could only have one visitor every other hour.

"Are you cold?" the hospital attendant asked me kindly. He was a heavy-set, freckle-faced white guy, and I was thankful that his hands had been so gentle and compassionate when he lifted me off the bed.

I waved away the blanket he was offering me. I was shivering and goose bumps had popped up all over my skin, but there wasn't but one thing on my mind, and that was getting close to my man.

Gino needed me. This I knew for sure.

I could feel him calling out to me with his heart, and every ounce of me was focused strictly on getting up there and answering that call.

The attendant turned the wheelchair around cautiously, and pointed me toward the door.

"Can you move a little faster?" I asked him. Both doctors gave him a look, and I got even more pissed off when they both shook their heads, no.

I waited while they signed the papers giving me permission to leave the floor, and then we bounced.

My police guard walked behind us as the attendant pushed me down an endless hall and through several sets of double doors. When we got to the elevators I saw we were on the third floor. Renata had told me the intensive care unit was on five, and if I could have jumped up outta that chair and ran up those two flights of stairs I would have.

Finally, the elevator came and we got on. We only had to go up two floors, but in my mind it was taking us forever. I closed my eyes and started praying again. I didn't open them until I felt the elevator stop on the fifth floor.

The intensive care unit was all lit up. Family members of the sick and dying were standing around in the hallway pushing coins into vending machines, and talking on cell phones while they waited to see their loved ones.

Down the hall, I could see Renata and Frank standing outside of a room across from the nurse's station, and my heart started pounding real hard as we got closer. Even with the seriousness of our situation I was hyped with the anticipation of seeing Gino again.

But just as they were wheeling me toward his room, Renata peeped us coming down the hall and she rushed over to stand in my path.

"What's going on?" I asked, frowning. There was a commotion going on in the room behind her and I peered past her and tried to get a look inside.

"Is Gino in there?"

Renata nodded. I didn't see the cop that was supposed to be standing guard over Gino, but now a bunch of medical people were leaving the room with blank expressions on their faces.

"What's going on?" I asked her again. "All them doctors wasn't in there for Gino, was they?"

Renata didn't answer. She just stared at me with a real funny look in her eyes.

I glanced over my shoulder and barked at the dude who was pushing my wheelchair. "Push me in there, please! Take me in that goddamn room!"

But Renata stood in front of me like a mountain. She was blocking hard, and I wasn't having it. I leaned forward to push her out the way, and that's when the first pain hit me. It was real low in the bottom of my stomach, and it shot out of my tailbone like a ball of fire.

"Ouch!" I yelped and doubled over, my chest almost touching my knees.

"What's wrong?" Renata said. Her eyes went from looking sad to looking worried quick fast.

"Nothing," I gasped. Suddenly there was pressure building inside me like I needed to use the bathroom. I pressed my hands to the seat of the wheelchair and lifted my butt up a little bit, trying to relieve the pain.

Gino.

"Get outta my way," I muttered to Renata. I had come to see Gino. Why the fuck was she standing in my way?

My stomach cramped again. Harder this time. Hard as shit! I needed to use the bathroom, and my whole body broke out in a sweat from trying to hold my bowels in.

"Renata, *move!*" I tried to raise my voice, but I was hurting so bad that all I could do was whisper. "I gotta see Gino. Get out my way."

"Please don't go in that room, Juicy," Renata said softly. "Gino is not there anymore."

"What?" I glanced around, confused. We'd gotten off the elevator on the right floor. The pain rocking my stomach was messing with my head.

"He's not in there? Then where the fuck is he?" I demanded loudly. The hallway got real quiet. A few people who were standing around stopped talking and stared at me, but I didn't give a damn.

"He..." she started. "He...he..."

Tears slipped from Renata's eyes and ran down her cheeks.

Fear pounded in my heart and I straight wailed.

"Renata!!! Tell me where my man is!!!"

"He's dead, Juicy!" she blurted. The words slipped from her mouth and felt colder than the blood that was now rushing through my veins.

"His blood pressure fell and his heart just couldn't go on. He didn't make it, *cara*. Gino is dead."

Grief washed over me in a giant, suffocating wave. It snatched all the air from my lungs. I felt like I was being smothered under an enormous pillow. But then, a searing pain and a numbing dizziness overtook me. I gripped the arms of the wheelchair and trembling, I pushed myself to my feet.

I staggered over to the doorway, and almost fell inside the room. Wasn't nobody rushing around anymore. I took one look at the patient, and then that blistering pain shot through me again. I almost collapsed, but Renata was right by my side, catching me before I could fall.

I stepped deeper into the room and stared down at the man who was stretched out in the hospital bed, but I didn't recognize him. He wasn't Gino. He wasn't *my* Gino.

His features looked stressed and puffy. Tubes was all in his mouth and nose. The last time I'd seen my man he was smiling and dressed in a fly tuxedo. His haircut was fresh and shiny, his slight goatee had been trimmed real tight, and his eyes had been full of promise for the life we were gonna build together.

The guy laying there on the bed looked way different. His moustache was growing in, and his beard was thicker. His curly hair looked dry, but his eyelashes were still long and beautiful.

"Gino," I whimpered. I leaned over him, and then collapsed with my upper body across his legs. In my mind I knew it was Gino. The dude I loved with everything in me. But my heart...my heart just couldn't, just wouldn't believe it.

"Please, ma'am," the attendant said. He had rolled my wheelchair over to the bed, and now he urged me to sit down.

"Gino...wake up..." I whispered quietly. I pressed my cheek tight against the fading warmth of his arm.

"I'm pregnant," I finally told him. "You're gonna be a father. We're having a baby, Gino. A little boy."

I reached over and pushed my trembling hand under his still one. I was praying he would take it and acknowledge me and what I'd just said. Praying he would squeeze my fingers just one more time. But his hand never moved.

"Wake up, baby," I urged him in a whimper. My soul was one big ball of pain, and I couldn't tell if I was hurting more in my stomach or in my heart. "You can wake up now, Gino. I'm here. I'm right here."

"He fought hard," Renata whispered softly. She settled both her hands on my back and began rubbing my shoulders gently. "He fought very hard, Juicy. But he just couldn't make it."

"Nooo..." I moaned loudly. I shook Renata off then stretched out across Gino again as I prayed to God and kissed his cheeks and squeezed his lifeless hand. "He ain't gone...he can't be gone..."

Suddenly, my stomach felt boxer-punched. I gasped, then everything inside of me caved in as hot, bitter liquid rushed up from my throat.

I gagged and wretched, unable to breathe. I didn't even wanna breathe. Renata and the attendant were all over me as they tried to get me to sit back down in the wheelchair. They called my name, held my shoulders, and patted my tear-streaked cheeks. Everything around me was spinning, but I held on tight to Gino. I couldn't breathe and I couldn't think. I was caught in the middle of another nightmare. Just another stupid crazy nightmare that would end if I could just wake the hell up.

I squeezed my eyes shut tight, but when I opened them again Renata was still there. She was trying to pull me off the bed. Her face was wet with tears too.

"No, please," I whimpered softly, clutching Gino's muscular thigh through the sheets as I fought to hold on to the only guy I had ever loved.

"Don't let this be true, Renata. Please, God. Don't let this be true! I NEED HIM..." I wailed. "I need him...I need him...I need him..."

My voice grew soft and tiny. My eyes silently begged her to make this not be true.

"I need him."

"He's gone, Juicy," was all Renata whispered, and as her words crashed down and shattered my heart, a puddle of warm liquid burst out of my coochie. I lay back against Gino's body and gapped my legs open wide.

My bowels heaved, and I didn't have any other choice except to bear down and push.

I need him.

There was a crazy knot bulging between my legs, then a ball of something hot and mushy slid right out of me. I was terrified. I glanced at Renata. I glanced at Gino.

And then I closed my eyes and screamed.

CHAPTER 7

Pluto couldn't stand smart bitches, which was why he had hooked up with Monique in the first place. The only lips he wanted to see flapping on a chick were her pussy lips, and the sight of Salida all of a sudden strutting around the G-Spot tryna run the joint like a capo was starting to really fuck with him.

"We can be broke as hell, but we ain't gotta be nasty," she had chastised him one day as he came out of G's private bathroom. It had been two weeks since him and Ace had come back from Cali empty-handed, and outta nowhere this broad had been underfoot 24/7. "You just take your grown-man ass right back in there and flush that toilet and wash your hands," Salida bossed him.

Pluto had wanted to put his foot up in her ass, but instead he went back inside the bathroom and did exactly what she said.

He just didn't fuckin' get it. Somebody musta told Salida that since she was G's wife she was entitled to run shit, because suddenly that bitch thought she was in control. That whipped niggah Ace had called some bullshit-ass emergency meeting and let Salida stand up there and talk shit like she was a true Queenpin. Ace had sat there staring at her like Salida was his kinny-garden teacher or something, and Pluto was stunned when his manz let it be known that he would check the first muh'fucka to get outta pocket with her too.

"I don't know how Granite was running things when he was alive," Salida said with her nose turned up, "but his ass is dead now and this situation is critical."

She had spent the past week going through every single file cabinet in G's office, and examining his computer files with a magnifying glass too.

"It's a whole lot worse than I thought it was around here," she said, giving Ace and Pluto both the snake eye. "You two done fucked the cut room up so bad it's almost dry. Y'all also missed the last two payments to the chief of police, and now it's going to cost us double just to keep the cops in our pocket.

"On top of that," she pressed on, rubbing shit in, "since neither one of y'all were smart enough to find out who G was getting all his dope from, your lil boys on the street are running out of product and sending our loyal customers jetting over to the competition."

She glared at Pluto. "Did you know the liquor license had expired?"

He shook his head dumbly.

"Well it did, genius. And from what I've learned, it takes big-time money to get it renewed under the table."

She got on Greco next.

"I guess pussy ain't selling at a premium no more, huh? Tell me why our girls are never fully booked? Every time I look up them hoes are watching movies, eating cookies, and running off at the mouth. This ain't no damn sorority house! Hell, the IRS is hounding us for back taxes, and if we don't make a payment soon we're gonna have to walk away from some of G's other businesses too."

Salida paused to let that sink in, and then said, "So, we're about to make some big time adjustments around here. We're going to start with the cut room. It's mine now. I'm gonna run it." She held out a sheet of paper. "But I also made of list of some other things that are gonna have to change…"

Pluto sat there on boil as Salida spouted off at the mouth. Disbelief spread over him as she read from her shitty little list. Not only was this throwed-off bitch tryna completely get rid of the cover price at the door, she wanted to overhaul the G-Spot so that it catered to a set of young musicians, rising ballers, and come up playas and pimps.

"So yeah, we're gonna have to kill the cover charge altogether," Salida declared, taking a seat behind G's great big desk and propping her slender legs up and crossing them at the knee. "That's the only way to get customers to come back. Then once they get to liking all the new set-up we've got, then we'll raise the door charge back up again. Hell," she chuckled evilly, "we'll double it."

Pluto almost jumped on that bitch over the next thing outta her mouth.

"So tomorrow morning, Pluto, I want you to go get me some of those dumb-ass boys you got working half-days selling crack. Send their asses upstairs to the cut room. We're about to turn this mutha out."

Later that night Ace shrugged shit off when Pluto bitched about Salida's long list and her grand plans for the cut room. Ace thought she was right on point.

"Salida's got some real live ideas, ak," he told Pluto as they shot a game of pool. "Times are changing, man. Me and Greco was just talking about that shit the other day. The old heads are falling off. It's all about the tykes and the young'uns now."

"Hell, nah," Pluto protested ready to put Salida's 7:30 mental ass on a bus straight back to the nuthouse. He was about to line her up in his crosshairs, and he was truly itching to pull the trigger. "She's fuckin' everything up," he insisted. "That broad is tryna do too much."

"I don't think so," Ace disagreed. "Look around, niggah. You see any fuckin' body large chillin' up in here? Bizz is bad, man. If anything we gotta do *more*. We done walked away from the bakery and the rib shack. The cleaners, the fish joint, and the check cashing place are gonna be dead in a month. Yo, Salida got a nose for sniffing out business, and I think we should let her use it."

Pluto jumped off his stool and shook his head. "We don't need that bitch! All we need is a big buy, ak! If we can just flood the streets with product like we used to do, there'll be so much doe rollin' in it'll bust down the fuckin' door!"

"Yeah, flooding the streets would work," Ace admitted calmly as he lined his cue stick up and tapped his ball into a corner pocket, "but me and you ain't got the connections to be making that kind of quality buy. If Salida wants to restock the cut room with club drugs, then I say we should go for it. We can't dominate in every sector no more like G used to do, man. Them come-ups is getting their hands on big-time product at cut-rate prices while we over here just scraping up the crumbs. Fucking with these lil low-level suppliers is gonna cost us in the long run, ak. Our territory done already been reduced by more than half. Remember, we gotta pay them taxes and pay our crew too, my niggah. So, if Salida can run the cut room half as good as G did, then I see it as more doe in our pockets and more power to her."

The next morning Pluto had reluctantly sent a few members of his street crew upstairs with brooms, mops, and bottles full of Lysol. The cut room was in shambles, but not a single one of those corner boys had bitched or complained as Salida worked the shit outta them. She had them scrubbing floors and washing walls like they were a crew of janitors, and she watched over them like a jailer the whole time.

Later on that night, Pluto snuck upstairs to see what he could see. Standing in the middle of a complex room that had once been a bustling, vibrant hub of drug activity brought it all to a head for him. The G-Spot was his home, and a sad realization washed over him as burning tears of rage came to his eyes.

Things were never gonna be the same again. They had gone from the mountaintops down to the grimy gutters, and if they didn't do something drastic they risked losing everything.

The fucked up part was, as bad as he hated to admit it, Salida's vision was probably dead on. They were gonna have to make some desperate moves just to survive, but that didn't mean he was gonna lay down and roll over for G's old piece of pussy, though.

Pluto figured he would play Salida's game for as long as it took to get their cash right. But once their business was back on the map and the cream was once again stacked mile high, Salida was gonna be lined up in his crosshairs for real, and all grimy bets would be off.

CHAPTER 8

Cara. Aunt Ree. Grandmother. Dicey. Jimmy. And now Gino and our precious, unborn baby boy, too.

You would think I'd get used to losing the people I loved, but Gino's death and my miscarriage cut me so deep that I didn't think I was ever gonna be right again.

Back in downstairs in my own room I stretched out flat in that hospital bed and just soul-cried. I grieved so hard that I was literally trying to die. I was just begging God to take me. Begging him. I couldn't see anything except a big black hole of emptiness where my life had once been. All that madness I'd survived in Harlem...losing Grandmother, the rapes and beatings, Jimmy blowing his brains out all over me...None of it even came close to touching what I was feeling now. Seeing Gino stretched out in that hospital bed like that...all swole up and with no life left in him. It just hurt so bad. I prayed to God to please just make my heart stop beating so I could escape my pain too.

Renata came to visit me a lot.

Most of the time I didn't even talk to her. She still came. She would sit beside me and stare out the window, while I laid in the bed staring at the wall.

Sometimes she held my hand. Sometimes she just let me be. Sometimes I cried. And sometimes she cried too.

At some point she asked me what I wanted to do about planning a funeral for Gino. I didn't know what to do. I couldn't even think about putting my man in the cold ground.

So Big Frank handled it. He called around and made all the arrangements and said The Organization would pick up the expenses.

None of this is real, I told myself a week later as I sat in the chapel of the same church that me and Gino had planned to get married in. I had been out of the hospital for two days, and Renata had taken me straight to her plush crib and set me up in one of her caked-up guest rooms.

This is just another one of them crazy-ass nightmares, that's all, I told myself. And as they rolled Gino's casket down the aisle, I closed my eyes and pictured me and him holding hands and walking down that same aisle. Together, the way we had planned. With a wedding song playing, and all our guests smiling happily at the promise of our union of love.

This is just another bad dream that'll go away as soon as the sun comes up.

Organ music played softly in the chapel as our friends walked past Gino's royal blue grand deluxe coffin to pay their last respects. It was a real small crowd. Just a few people that me and Gino had met over the past few months. There was security out the ass though, and of course all the staff at The Organization had showed up to say goodbye with their families.

I understood why most of the people who had shown up for our wedding were missing-in-action for Gino's funeral. Wasn't no lobster and barbeque ribs being served afterward, and most of them were scared to come in case the church got shot up again. But still, for somebody as large and full of life as Gino had been, I felt like the whole place should have been packed out.

But what really hurt me to my heart was that none of Gino's family was here to see him laid to rest. Instead, with his mother and father both dead, my man was going to be buried way out in some lonely cemetery in Cali. Where almost nobody really knew him except me.

"That's the way it has to be," Renata had told me when I started crying because she wouldn't let me call Gino's aunts and tell them he'd been killed.

"His aunts love him! They deserve to know what happened to him!"

"Tell me," Renata had asked bluntly, "where is Gino's mother?"

I shrugged. "I guess dead. She disappeared when Gino was just a kid. A lot of people say G killed her."

"Okay, there's your answer. You don't think the people who are loyal to G might find out that Gino's gone and come after you too? That's the main thing Gino was worried about, wasn't it? Protecting you?"

"But they're his aunties. They love him," I insisted weakly. "The least I can do is call them."

Renata shook her head with a quickness. "You're gonna have to trust me, okay Juicy? I know it's hard for you to think straight right now, but please trust me. Whoever you and Gino were running from six months ago is probably still after you today. In fact, they're probably more of a threat to you now than ever before because Gino isn't around to protect you."

I got defensive. Renata was real cool, but she didn't know me like that.

"What makes you think we were running from somebody?" I asked her with my New York attitude showing. Right from the jump me and Gino had agreed not to confide in anybody about our troubles back home in Harlem. "I told you we came out west so Gino could find a job."

"Yeah? Well, Gino told Frankie a different story, Juicy. In fact, Gino told Frank the truth about everything. But don't worry. We're not here to judge you. Nothing about our lives is squeaky clean either, so your secrets are safe with us. But we can't keep *you* safe if you don't listen to us."

"But his family..."

Renata's voice was firm. "I know it hurts, but you've gotta leave the past in the past, Juicy. You can't tell *anybody* that Gino is dead. Absolutely nobody. In fact, you should forget about New York City and everybody in it. I did, and I'm surviving. Gino was smart enough to get you out of there. I'm sure he loved his family, but he knew better than to tell them where you guys were hiding. There was a reason for that."

I was so hurt and weak that I just gave up. She was probably right anyway. After all that ducking and dipping me and Gino had done trying to make sure we didn't leave any tracks leading back to Harlem, we had run smack into the same kind of trouble we had been running away from in the first place.

And now, as I watched the last few mourners file past Gino's coffin, a big fat tide of tears flowed from my eyes.

"Juicy," Frank said softly. He was standing over me, holding out his arm. "Come on, dear. It's time to say goodbye to Gino."

Somehow I reached out and clutched Frank's warm, steady hand. My feet felt like rubber noodles as I took small, shaky steps toward the front of the room.

Dear God. You know how much I need him.

I pressed my hand to my empty stomach. My baby was gone, and my man was too. My whole body started shivering, and the closer we got to the open casket the colder the air around me got. It was like I could feel the chill coming off of Gino's dead body. All the heat in his big heart, all the comfort and warmth in his strong arms and in his big smile, was gone.

It's just another crazy nightmare, Juicy. Everything will be cool when the sun comes up.

But as I listened to the funeral music being played on the organ and gazed at Gino's body stretched out stiffly in his casket, I knew that was a lie. The sun was *never* gonna come up over my head again. No matter where I went, or what I did, the sun would never, ever shine on me again.

Tears bubbled up outta me from a place I didn't even know I had.

I need him.

They dripped from my eyes and slid down my face.

I need him.

They splattered on my breasts and wet up my hands.

I stared down at my man with anguish radiating from my eyes. Gino looked just like he was sleeping. He was dressed in a navy blue French-cut suit that he had planned to wear to a formal dinner during our honeymoon. His skin was chocolate-smooth. His wavy hair was jet-black and shiny. A sparkly diamond glittered from his ear, and the onyx wedding band I had bought for him was on his ring finger.

I moaned and gasped.

"Let it out, Juicy," Renata whispered softly. She stood on the other side of me and used her handkerchief to wipe my snotty nose. "It's okay to let your pain out."

But I couldn't let it out, and I couldn't keep it in neither. I couldn't breathe and I couldn't think. All I could do was feel. And what I felt was a pain so deep and so fuckin' unbearable that it nearly split me down the middle. I felt my chest tearing in two. My throat clogged. My skull throbbed and my knees gave away.

I need him!

I reached for Gino. I mean I really, really, really *reached* for my man. And the moment I touched him all my pain disappeared. The room got quiet and my whole body went numb. The coldness swallowed me up, and the last thing I felt was my knees bumping hard against his casket.

And then God was finally merciful to me.

I didn't feel anything else. I passed out.

CHAPTER 9

You like this shit, don't you baby? You want it like this? Or you want me to stroke it right there?"

Marguerita Gonzales was in poon-poon heaven. Her man Dutchy Gaines was hittin' her sweet brown pussy from every angle imaginable.

"Right there, *papi*...ooowie...oh yes!" She crawled onto her hands and knees and backed her shapely hips up to meet his powerful thrusts, "Fuck me right there..."

"I got you!" Dutchy panted, spreading her brown ass-cheeks and widening her sopping pink slit. Her small titties jiggled under his onslaught as he pounded her so good her head bounced off the wall.

"Ouch! Ouch! Ouch!" Rita squealed. Her forehead was getting dented, but she was steady pumping her hips, loving her joy ride and refusing to let a little pain slow her down.

"You want me to quit?" Dutchy teased, slowing his grind. He revved his hips behind her, stirring her juices with his love stick. Her snatch was warm and soft like a fresh-baked bun. "You still with me or you need a break?"

Rita shook her head furiously.

"Don't stop!" she moaned, pushing against him forcefully with her soft, fluffy ass. "No breaks, baby. Just fuck this pussy. Bang this pussy up!"

Rita loved the feel of Dutchy's heavy balls slapping against her wetness, and there was no way in hell she wanted him to stop. "Keep going," she ordered him as he gripped the base of his dick and slowly pulled it from her sucking cave. Tendrils of sweet juice dripped onto the sheets as he rubbed the erect, helmet-shaped head of his dick between her ass-cheeks and probed her sensitive hole.

Rita sucked in her breath at the tingling sensation his slippery dick created as he slid it from her wet pussy and up to her puckered starfish. Aiming low, Dutchy stuck the head in her pussy, then quickly extracted it and probed her asshole. Groaning, he swiped his dick downward again and shoved the head right back into her gaping pussy, and then he quickly withdrew and pushed gently against her back door again.

Rita began humming with glee as her asshole got creamy and wet from her sticky pussy juices. Over and over again Dutchy probed her asshole just enough to stimulate her without actually entering her, and just the thought that he might stretch her out back there excited Rita to no end.

Sensing her orgasm building, Dutchy licked his thumb, and then rubbed it around her booty hole. Without warning, he slipped it deep inside her ass while plunging his dick into her pussy at the same time.

Rita yelped as the odd sensation turned her out. Reaching between her legs, she massaged her swollen clit with two fingers as she clenched his thick thumb with her anal muscles, and milked his dick with her pussy muscles too.

"Ooooow, *papi*! Yes, ouch! Oh *papi*...go deeper."

Sparks flew through Rita's body as her clitoris pulsated and her asshole got ruffed out by Dutchy's finger. She swirled her hips frantically, then bucked backward to take Dutchy in deeper as his hard dick slammed against her cervix.

Withdrawing slightly, Dutchy bucked his hips and pounded his rod deeply inside her again. His pelvis smacked into her ass hard enough to break her tailbone and she loved every stroke.

Rita felt sparks shoot up her spine and out of her pointed nipples. "Ooowie, ooowie, ooowie!" she screeched. She reached up and pinched one of her breasts real hard. Electricity surged through her. She stuck her fingers between her legs and caught some of the syrup that was spilling from their bodies. She sniffed her fingers and moaned, then stuck them in her mouth and sucked greedily. The sweetness blew her mind. Her eyes rolled back in her head, and her nut was just about to pop off when her cell phone jangled and vibrated on her night table.

Licking her lips, Rita slowed her rhythm for a moment.

"Fuck that phone!" Dutchy barked as he gripped her hips and banged up in her with deep, wet strokes. He rocked his pelvis from side-to-side, allowing his dick to sweep every corner of her inner cave.

The phone rang again, and when Rita strained to see it, Dutchy cupped her breasts and pulled her toward him until she was upright and on her knees. With her back pressed to his muscular chest, he inhaled the glorious scent of her sweaty hair, then bit down gently on her shoulder and sucked her soft flesh in passion.

The phone rang a third time, and as good as she was getting fucked Rita just couldn't help it. School had just started back up and her baby sister Chub had been coughing a lot, and her other sister, Nooni, had been cutting classes and getting high. The call could have been coming from the school nurse, or maybe from a pissed-off teacher.

Rita scooted close to the edge of the bed as Dutchy ignored the interruption and continued to beat her pussy up deliciously from the back. She squeezed her thighs together and rotated on that dick. He was almost there and so was she. Wrapped up in her own pleasure, Rita was just about to say fuck the phone, when it rang again. She took one more peek and finally caught a glimpse of the name flashing on the caller ID.

It said, *Naughty Girl*, and just those two little words were enough to dry Rita's pussy up and cold-stop her on her knees.

Dislodging herself from her man's pumping dick, she yelped and lunged for the phone. And when she clicked the talk button and breathlessly yelled hello, she found out that it wasn't the school nurse on the line, like she'd feared, and it wasn't no damn teacher calling about her hard-headed, hot-in-the-ass little sister Nooni, neither.

It was Juicy.

$$$$

Fifteen minutes later Rita was rushing down the streets of Harlem with her heart aching in her chest. In the eight months since Juicy had dropped a gwap of cash on her kitchen table and then dipped out of New York, she had only heard from her girl one time.

Once.

And even then, she hadn't really been sure it was her. Rita remembered it like it was yesterday. Juicy and Gino had been gone for almost a month when she got a call from a number that had a California area code. When she answered the phone there was nobody on the line. At least nobody was talking.

Something in her gut had told her it was Juicy on the other end. Calling to let her know she was okay. And as hot as the streets had been after G got ganked, Rita had understood why her girl was playing it so safe.

Rita knew firsthand the kind of danger Juicy had faced in Harlem. She'd jumped between Juicy and G up in their crib on Central Park West one day, and that homicidal niggah had cracked their foreheads together and tried to make an omelet out of their brains. When Rita finally came to her senses G said if he ever saw her face again her family would be reading about her murder in the newspaper.

It didn't even sound like a threat, it sounded like a promise, and Rita had believed that shit too. Yeah, Juicy was smart to lay low and stay outta range. No matter how much bank she was holding, if G's niggahs ever caught up with her, her life would have been worth less than two cents.

Acting on her hunch, Rita had saved the strange number in her contact list under the name, "Naughty Girl." She'd chosen that name because she had taken Juicy to her very first sex toy party, and it had been funny as hell to watch her girl getting wide open on a bunch of fake dicks.

But now, after talking to Juicy and hearing the raw agony in her voice, and finding out that Gino had been murdered and her girl was ass-out and all alone, couldn't nothing stop Rita from getting out to the West Coast.

The minute she hung up the phone she had jumped into her clothes and hit the door. Dutchy had been dazed like, 'what up with that?' but he was a good dude, and the look on her face must have told him that shit was critical.

"Where you going, baby?" he'd asked, stroking his still-hard dick.

Rita splashed some water on her crotch and pulled on a pair of jeans she found on the floor as she thought about how to answer. Dutchy was big-time in law enforcement. His whole family was. His father, four uncles, and two aunts had all worn uniforms. And every last one of his six brothers were either cops, or detectives, or corrections officers, and Dutchy himself worked as a New York City probation officer. Rita decided against putting him down on anything just yet. Giving him too much info about Juicy's situation could be a bad thing. For both of them.

"I gotta run up to the high school."

"Something up with your sister?" he asked.

Rita had nodded, and it wasn't a total lie. Her teenaged sister Nooni was a habitual hell-raiser who was forever getting in trouble. Rita was going up to the school to get her, but not because the girl had done anything wrong, though. She was heading out to pick up Nooni, and then swinging by the elementary school to get her youngest sister, Chub, so she could drop them both off with the Cuban babysitter who lived down the block.

Rita promised herself she would explain more to Dutchy later, but right now she had to roll and roll fast. Because Juicy really needed her, and no matter what kind of drama was going on in her own world, she had to catch a flight to California so she could be there for her girl.

$$$$$

"But I don't want you to leave," Chub whined. Her bottom lip was poked out and she followed Rita from room to room singing her sad little song.

Rita stuck a tube of toothpaste in her Fendi travel kit, then zipped it up and put the bag inside her matching suitcase. She turned and ran her fingers through her baby sister's hair. Chub's smooth skin looked like dusty cinnamon, and her hair was jet black and crazy curly, just like Rita's.

"I won't be gone for long," she promised. "Probably two weeks. Maybe three."

Rita eyed the gear she'd neatly placed in her suitcase and checked off a mental list to make sure she had everything. She wasn't taking a whole lot. Wasn't no need to. This wasn't a socializing or sightseeing trip, so she wasn't going to be partying or hanging out, or doing anything except taking care of Juicy.

Juicy.

Rita's heart ached when she remembered how gutter-scorched her friend had sounded over the phone. All the life had been gone from Juicy's voice. She sounded like somebody who was already dead, but had lost her way crawling toward a dark, muddy grave.

Rita checked her wallet and made sure her two credit cards and her driver's license was good to go. She had already stopped by the bank and taken out enough cash to pay the babysitter for a good minute, and now all she had to do was throw a few more items in her suitcase and grab a jacket to wear on the airplane.

"Are you going back to Puerto Rico?" little Chub asked suspiciously. "Cause if you are, that's not fair because you promised I could go with you again."

The little girl had poked her finger through the belt loop on the back of Rita's jeans and was leaning backward, her weight almost dragging Rita down.

Rita laughed, then turned around to face her.

"Nah," she said gently, cupping her hands around her baby sister's fat cheeks. Chub was a little eat-o-holic. She had been placed in a foster home after Rita had knifed their father to death and gotten sent to jail. By the time Rita had been cleared of the justifiable homicide charges and had come back home to take care of her sisters, the damage had already been done. Chub was hoarding food and sneaking candy and snacks like crazy. In just one sitting the nine-year-old could suck down enough grub to make a grown man fat.

Rita kissed the child's smooth forehead.

"I'm not going to Puerto Rico. I would never go without you," she reassured her sister. "I promise."

Chub frowned, then chewed on the collar of her yellow and green shirt.

"Then where are you going?"

Rita shrugged.

"Somewhere else," she said. "To check out a friend. But don't worry. Mrs. Moreno is going to take good care of you. You'll get to stay with Lucie and Charlize every night and have lots of fun, okay?"

Chub was clingy and nervous. The doctors said she overate and hoarded food because she suffered from a fear of abandonment.

Rita was concerned about the little girl, but nowhere near like she was worried about her other sister, Nooni. That chick was like a shooting star. Aiming fast and reckless, and at all the wrong targets.

"I'm almost eighteen and I don't need no babysitter," Nooni had bitched, poking her lip out when Rita told her she was going away for a few weeks and her and Chub would be staying with Mrs. Moreno.

"Besides, Mrs. Moreno is stinky. Her house smells like old lady pussy, and her bathroom is nasty."

"If you don't like the way her bathroom looks then clean it up," Rita told her.

"But why can't I just stay home?" the teen protested. Her jet-black curly hair was pulled back in a ponytail and she had on a t-shirt that had pink bulls-eye targets over both of her bulging young breasts.

"I'm not no little kid, Rita! You don't have to pay nobody to watch me. I'm old enough to watch my damn self."

Bullshit, Rita had thought. To be so cute and prissy Nooni was real loose with herself. She had some wide hips and a tiny waist like Rita's, except she had an even plumper bubble-ass to go along with them. The girl was all attitude and no street sense. All it took was one whiff of her fresh pussy and a street niggah could actually smell how naïve she was. The scent of young, dumb, stupidity just floated straight up out of her crotch.

Rita wrapped a bottle of shampoo in a plastic bag and placed it in her suitcase. She knew Mrs. Moreno was no match for Nooni, but Dutchy had promised to check on the girls every couple of days and make sure Nooni stayed in pocket.

Rita knew she was lucky to have a dude like him to support her, but Dutchy didn't know everything about her past and she liked it like that. He was the type of dude who wanted his woman to be hot and seasoned, but not ghetto and funky. Rita was afraid that if he knew about all the shit she had gone through with her father he would look at her differently, and probably not in a good way either.

But she couldn't worry about any of that right now. She had to make sure Nooni was straight. She planned to take all the house keys with her when she left, and double-lock all the windows too. That way Nooni wouldn't be able to get back inside the apartment while she was gone. She could just see the girl trying to scheme and con Mrs. Moreno into letting her come back to the house to pick up a schoolbook or something else she supposedly "forgot." That would be all she wrote. Mad dudes would be crawling all over the crib, and Nooni and her hood rat little girlfriends would be up in there partying like guttersnipes and having naked-twister orgies out the ass.

Rita was real nervous about the whole situation. Ever since her sister had started fucking with a cut-throat young drug dealer named Maleek, the girl had been dabbling in all kinds of trouble. Stealing, getting high, skipping classes, even sneaking out the window and climbing down the fire escape at night. Anything to get in the streets and roll around with the sleazy little dogs on the corner.

It had all come to a head when Rita came home early one afternoon and busted Nooni and her thugged-out boyfriend getting bizzy in her living room. That long-legged street niggah Nooni was so in love with had her naked and on her knees sucking the skin off his dick, while he reclined on Rita's brand new leather sofa with his hands propped behind his head like he was up in his own damn crib.

At first Rita couldn't believe what she was seeing. Maleek was moaning his ass off as Nooni's head jutted like a pigeon and she gave up that wet neck pussy like a natural hoe.

Rita had blacked out. She knocked the shit outta Nooni and told her to get up off her knees and put on some clothes, while Nooni screamed that Rita wasn't her damn mother and couldn't tell her whose dick she could suck.

Throughout it all, Maleek had stayed calm and moved real easy, like his ass wasn't pressed out and he wasn't in no kind of rush. It was hard to believe that he was even younger than Nooni was with his baby face and ice-cold killer glare. He had the nerve to let his eyes roll all over Rita's hips before he gripped his hard, wet dick and wiped it dry on her favorite sofa pillow. His soulless eyes never left hers as he slowly maneuvered his wood around and tucked it back inside his drawers.

"Look at that piece of shit!" Rita had screamed on her sister as Maleek sauntered his tall, skinny ass out the door without saying a word to either one of them. "You over here putting his raw dick in your mouth after he just pulled it outta some stank bitch's ass! He's too young for you anyway! That piece of trash don't give a fuck about you, Nooni! He don't love you!"

"He do so love me!" Nooni had screamed. "And he ain't got no other bitches! Maleek is *my* man and I'm his fuckin' boo!"

Rita had been too done. They'd actually come to blows behind that shit, and for the first time ever Nooni had swung on her and punched her in the face.

Rita got hot just thinking about that punch. She had fallen back against the wall and then got up and kicked Nooni's ass straight in. She'd beaten her sister so bad that their next-door neighbor had to come over and pull her off the youngster. Rita didn't know what was going to happen in a few weeks when Nooni turned eighteen and she could no longer legally control her wild ass. It was probably gonna be on and poppin' up in their crib 24/7.

Yeah, it was a real bad time to be jetting off and leaving Nooni with nothing but opportunities to fuck and connive on her hands, but what else could Rita do? Juicy needed her, and she had to be there for her girl. She just had to. She sighed as she zipped her suitcase closed and lifted it off the bed. She was only one person, and she had to give of herself where she was needed the most.

And right now, that was definitely out in California. Her sisters would be cool until she got back. Everything would work out fine. Nooni was just gonna have to go along with the program. No matter how grown the girl thought she was, she was just gonna have to stay her hot little ass at Mrs. Moreno's crib and chill until Rita got back.

CHAPTER 10

Her big sister hadn't even made it outta Harlem good before Nooni started trippin'. She jetted out of Mrs. Moreno's apartment with the sounds of the old lady fussing in Spanish ringing in her ears. Feeling free as a bird, she walked down the streets of Harlem swinging her hips and enjoying the attention her tight jeans and sexy, curvaceous body attracted from the young boys on the block and the grown men in their shiny new whips.

Fifteen minutes later she ran up the stairs to her friend Cheyvon's project apartment and knocked on the door. The two girls caught the train uptown to 149th Street and spent the whole day boosting cheap outfits and eating pizza slices and Italian-style heroes.

It was getting dark outside by the time they returned to Harlem with their stolen goods. Nooni had picked up a couple of pairs of jeans, two skirts, and an ultra-sheer white mini dress that had an open slit from the neckline to right below her navel. Cheyvon had boosted three skirts, a cute dress, and a cheap bottle of perfume for her grandmother.

The thrill of stealing was physically exciting, and it had Nooni's coochie nice and slippery. Maleek was heavy on her mind, and the last thing she felt like doing was ending her night by knocking on Mrs. Moreno's front door.

"You staying in the house tonight?" she asked Cheyvon.

"Hell no," was the answer she got.

"Good, 'cause there's gonna be a real hot party over at T.C.'s Place. Maleek and his set are gonna be up in there. He thinks I'm on lock down with a fuckin' babysitter tonight so I wanna roll up and surprise him."

Cheyvon frowned. "T.C.'s Place? You mean that pool hall over on St. Nick where Thug and the 'Licious Lovers used to spit? Where all them people got killed?"

Nooni nodded. "Yeah. That was Trust Chambers and his wife, Miss Lady. Thug-A-Licious was their godson. My hair dresser, Miss Vyreen, used to work for T.C., and she got shot up in there too."

Cheyvon frowned some more. "And they opened that place back up again?"

"Oh hell yeah," Nooni shrugged, trying to sound much growner and wiser than she really was. "Why not? They got all the dead bodies up outta there and besides, it's the only place in town where the cops won't come fuckin' with us about underage drinking and stuff."

"Then that's what's up," Cheyvon agreed. "Yeah, okay, I'll come. Maybe I can do like you did and hook me one of them thug dudes with the knotty pockets."

"Cool," Nooni said, "but I ain't tryna go all the way home and then come all the way back over here, though. Can I take a shower and get dressed at your crib?"

"Uh-huh," Cheyvon answered. "Hell yeah. But hold up. What you wearing? One of them hoochie-ass outfits you just stole? You know I can't let you roll up in no club pulling all the good looks away from me!" Cheyvon laughed, but she was serious about that shit. Hanging out with Nooni was fun, but most dudes couldn't even see her when her girl was on the scene.

Nooni giggled. "Chey, please. You can have all them little club pups for yourself. Maleek is my man, and the only eyes I want checking for my booty are his."

"Oh, I didn't know you and Maleek was still kickin' it like that," Cheyvon said innocently. "I thought he was messing around with that real bowlegged girl named Ashanti from 145th Street."

Nooni's eyes narrowed as her heart fell. It was Ass-Almighty Ashanti this week, it had been Big Titty Tameeka last week, and it would probably be Dick-Sucking Dominique next damn week. Maleek was down with a strong street crew, and even though he was young, he balled so hard that females just pulled off their thongs and dropped them at his feet.

Nooni rolled her eyes as Cheyvon's words sank in. Maleek was a pussy hound, but he was real jealous and controlling too. He messed around behind her back like mad, but just let him catch her even thinking about another dude. His ass would go gorilla. He'd stretch her *and* the niggah she was scoping straight out on the ground.

"I said," Cheyvon repeated, cutting into Nooni's anguished thoughts, "ain't Maleek with Ashanti now?"

Checking herself, Nooni smirked and chuckled. "Hell no he ain't with her," she said, playing her role. "His ass is with *me*. Ashanti ain't nobody special. Maleek don't mess with that nasty, camel-toe hoe." Nooni laughed. "You didn't hear what they said about her? That trick gave Dirty Legs the crabs! She had his ass on itch mode. I know Maleek is a hoe, but he ain't stupid enough to be digging around in no ass-dumpster like her. I don't care how fat her booty is. My pockets is puffed up too!"

Cheyvon looked doubtful, but she nodded and agreed anyway. "C'mon," she said as they walked around the corner and toward her project building. "Forget Ashanti. Her booty is big, but her teeth are shot out. You got me ready to party now! Let's go cop us a little piff so we can slip into our new gear and hit da club."

$$$$$

It was warm for September and T.C.'s Place was busting at the seams. Young Harlemites who wanted to feel and act grown, but couldn't get past security at other clubs pushed into the newly re-opened pool hall in droves.

On paper, T.C.'s Place had been re-classified as a youth development center, but in reality it was run by a powerful Harlem drug sect, and it was a hot spot for everything an under-aged teen could hope to get into.

The pool hall had lost its liquor license when its owners Trust and Lady Chambers were gunned down in a brutal robbery, but that didn't stop its young patrons from sneaking in alcohol and other forms of get-high by the bagful.

Nooni and Cheyvon got cleared through security and the metal detectors and paid their five-dollar cover charge, and then stepped inside. Styling their boosted gear and letting their long hair swing down their backs, they knew they looked good and the appreciative comments and stares from the young trap boys on the scene just confirmed it.

T.C.'s Place had been partially remodeled. One whole side of the hall had been cleared of pool tables and replaced with tables, booths and bucket chairs. The other side of the room was still set up the way T.C. had left it, with ornate pool tables positioned in a long row, and endless pool cues racked against the wall. A small dance floor sat in the middle of the room, and couples were out there moving hard to all the latest cuts.

Nooni and Cheyvon shook their hips to the loud rap music that blared from the speakers as they looked around for some familiar faces to click up with.

"It's time to get buzzed," Cheyvon declared, passing Nooni one of the small bottles of rum she'd stashed in her purse. Security frisked for guns and knives and shit at the front door, but they didn't give a damn about liquor. The entire club was getting lifted. Yay was in the air big time, and a few chicks were popping X and sipping on colorful liquid they had poured into empty water bottles.

Nooni took the small bottle of alcohol from her girl and cracked the top. Taking a deep breath, she turned it up to her lips and throated the liquid fire straight down from the first drop to the last.

"So is ya man up in here?" Cheyvon sipped from her bottle and hollered over the music. Her head was on a swivel as she tried to spot Nooni's infamous young baller, Maleek, a cat so brutal he had dudes twice his age giving him mad respect. "Do you see him?"

Nooni froze in place as her eyes scanned the crowd. "Yeah," she muttered, swallowing hard. "I see his ass."

She narrowed her eyes and angled her chin toward the VIP booths. "He's over there with the willies, see him? He's got on a red fitted."

Cheyvon stared in that direction. "Oh, I see him now. Yo, who's that bitch sitting all up in his lap? She looks just like that crab-ass chick, Ashanti!"

Nooni felt flushed as the alcohol burned in her stomach and slowly buzzed her head. She stared at the scene in the booth. There were some major drug dealers and hustlers surrounding Maleek, and that bitch Ashanti was right in the thick of it, laughing and grinning and bouncing all around in Maleek's lap.

Nooni sighed. Once again her man had broken her heart and betrayed her trust. He was so disrespectful! He'd told her the only reason he was coming out tonight was to take care of a little business, yet here he was ballin' in a booth with a 'rilla bitch riding his dick. Well, disrespect was a two-way street, and Nooni was about to show him that.

"Let's walk around," Nooni told Cheyvon as she strutted through the crowd and rolled her ass in her see-through white mini dress. Underneath it she had on a bright red thong, and no bra. She plastered a big smile on her face and made sure she bumped her hip against almost every horny dude she passed.

All eyes were glued to her smooth brown skin, wavy hair, and vicious young curves as she switched over to the VIP area. Ignoring Maleek, she flashed a sexy grin at a few of his boys who were secretly clocking for her, and then moved down to the next booth where a crew of hoods from the other side of Harlem sat puffing sticky and getting toasted.

"What's up, y'all?" she cooed. Giggling, she draped her arms over the back of the booth and the ballers sitting there turned around in surprise.

"How y'all doing tonight?"

Before they could answer, Nooni sashayed around to the front of the booth and struck a sexy pose. Her silhouette of plump breasts, a tiny waist, and wide, curvy hips made all five dicks in the booth jump on instant rock.

"We good, beautiful," replied the guy sitting closest to her. He took a pull from his blunt, then extended his hand and passed it to Nooni. "What's your name, baby?" he asked, rising to his feet.

"I'm Nooni. I saw a bunch of fine ballers sitting over here without no chicks, and I started wondering if I was in the right place tonight."

They laughed with her as their hungry young eyes roamed the curves of her body.

"We was talkin' a little bizz and just waiting for a dream like you to float by," joked the guy who had slid her the yay. Looking down at her, he grinned and sized her up with lust leaking from his eyes.

Nooni gave him a once over and dismissed him right away. He was tall and kinda cute in the face, but he was also light in the ass and had a goofy air about him. Not only wouldn't Maleek get jealous over a sherm like him, he would sense the lack of competition and smash dude with absolutely no remorse.

She scanned the other four dudes in the booth and zeroed in on one. He was light-skinned and had real pretty eyes. He was built solid and had a rugged look about him, and while his gaze let her know he liked what he saw, he sipped his beer coolly, like he wasn't really all that interested.

"You wanna dance?" Nooni hit on him with her softly stated question.

He paused with his beer bottle halfway to his mouth, then shrugged. "Yeah, aiight. I'll dance witcha, baby."

His manz on the left got up to let him out the booth, and when dude stood up Nooni was damn pleased by what she saw. He was real tall and real buff too. He looked a little bit older than her and niggah was packing muscles all up under his gear. His hair was curly and under the glow of the club lights his eyes looked like they were light gray. He grinned down at her and she was almost blinded by his ultra-bright smile. His hand snaked around her waist and slid up to her hip. Without a word, he turned Nooni toward the dance floor, and then grabbed her hand and confidently led the way.

Chillin' in the next booth with his posse, Maleek had Ashanti's nice warm ass in his lap and a clear view of Nooni as she gyrated her hips on the edge of the dance floor with some niggah from across town.

His boy Grip nudged him and then nodded toward the floor.

"Sup wit' Nooni?"

Not a trace of emotion or even a flicker of expression crossed Maleek's face. No, the danger surging inside him was visible only in his eyes, and if Nooni hadn't been so busy cheesing up in that yellow niggah's face she woulda seen that.

"Ain't nothing," he told Grip calmly. "She just out there playin' that's all."

Ashanti squirmed around and dug her ass deeper into his groin. The erection she'd been enjoying had almost completely subsided.

"Playin' my ass," she giggled as she peeped Nooni's game. The sun-baked Puerto Rican chick was out there getting vicious on the dance floor. Her hips were crucial, and she was swiveling them shits and booty-rocking her partner like they were about to get bizzy. "Them two look ready to start fuckin' out there!" Ashanti joked loudly.

Maleek scowled and stood up abruptly.

"Hey!" Ashanti hollered as she tumbled out of his lap. "You ain't gotta chase behind that bitch!" she yelled at Maleek's back as he strode toward the dance floor. "She just tryna make you jealous!"

Maleek stormed right past Nooni and her dance partner as they bumped their bodies to the sexy beat. Nooni had backed up against the dude, prompting him to reach down and grip her hips as he bounced with the bass and grinded his dick on the sweet mound of ass she was offering him.

From the corner of her eye, Nooni caught a quick glimpse of Maleek as he strode past. His gaze was aimed straight ahead, but she peeped mad rage in the set of his jaw and knew somebody's ass was about to get treated!

"Hey," she turned around to face her dance partner and gave him a nervous smile, "I gotta go to the bathroom real quick, okay?"

Sweat ran down his sand-colored face and buff neck, and he flashed his pretty grin down at her before pulling her into his strong arms.

"You ain't gone just leave me out here dancing all by myself, are you?" he asked, grinning sexily. His hands slid down Nooni's back and cupped her thick ass. His hard wood pressed through the slit in her dress and into her toned stomach. "The track is almost over. Let's finish what we started, girl."

Nooni had just opened her mouth to protest when she glanced past him and saw Maleek running up on dude from behind.

There was no time to warn him, no time to even scream.

She watched helplessly as Maleek seemed to move in slow motion. He leaned back on his right leg, then threw his weight forward and swung his arm around in a large arc.

The first pool ball he hurled struck dude square on the back of the head. He lurched forward, stumbling into Nooni, who ducked instinctively and pressed her face into his broad chest for cover. Dude shook his head in confusion, and when he turned to look over his shoulder the second pool ball caught him on his temple, bursting his skin, and sending bright red blood splattering from a spot above his eye.

All hell broke loose as thugs and hoods rushed over from tables and booths to stand with those in their set. Nooni got knocked on her ass as one of Maleek's goonies bum-rushed the guy she'd been dancing with, and then there was nothing but screams, grunts, swinging pool cues, and deadly pool balls whizzing through the air.

"Bitch! Get your fuckin' ass up!"

Fire was burning in her tailbone, and with her cute lil dress riding up over her hips, Nooni looked up and saw Maleek coming after her with a killer glare in his eyes. She flipped over on her stomach and grabbed some niggah's pants leg and pulled herself up as she tried to get away.

Chaos had broken out on the dance floor, and every table and booth in the joint had been abandoned as hood nigs got theirs in.

Ignoring her pain, Nooni tried to yank her mini dress down below her ass and run at the same time, but Maleek was on her. He swung his foot and planted it square in the crack of her ass, sending pain shrieking through her lower back and causing her to land face-down on the ground again. She was bracing herself for the death-blow she knew was coming, when the thick end of a pool cue cracked across Maleek's head and spun him around, drawing him back into the fight.

"C'mon!" Cheyvon was suddenly crouching down beside Nooni as she tried to help her friend get up. "These fools is wildin'! We gotta get the fuck outta here!"

Led by Cheyvon, Nooni stumbled toward the door with a wave of other young chicks. They pushed their way outside, and as Cheyvon supported her, Nooni clutched her aching booty-bone and staggered around the corner toward the housing projects.

"What you go over there and stunt with that yellow dude like that for?" Cheyvon yelled. "Look at what y'all started! That niggah Maleek was about to be on your ass!"

"Maleek is the one who started it," Nooni muttered under her breath. Her heart felt broken as she rubbed the sore spot on her back. "He don't love me like he says he do," she wailed in grief. "It's all good for him to fuck with other bitches, but he gets real stupid whenever a dude acts like he wants to fuck with me!"

"*Uhhhh*-huh," Cheyvon pursed her lips and agreed. "I know exactly what you mean. But that's the way these Harlem niggahs roll, girl. That's just the way they roll."

$$$$$

Even though she was heartbroken, Noni actually went to school the next day, although she didn't stick around for long.

"Uh-uh," her good friend Bubbles told her as they strutted out of their third period science class and headed toward the school's lunchroom. "We outta here girl. I heard about the big fight that went down at T.C.'s Place last night," Bubbles said as she grabbed Nooni's arm and swung her around in the opposite direction.

Nooni winced as she thought about how Maleek had kicked her up the ass in the club, and then probably spent the rest of the night getting his bone waxed by that cootie-coochie bitch Ashanti.

"Where we going?" she asked gloomily as she followed her friend. They were both juniors when they should have been seniors, but after cutting so many classes they'd come up short on credits.

"Don't worry about it," Bubbles said mysteriously as she strutted in her hoe heels and switched her ass down the school's corridor. A sick and sexy stunna, Bubbles stayed pressed out in the latest fashions, and like Nooni, she was prissy as hell and meticulous about her hair and nails.

But unlike Nooni, Bubbles was an only child, and her single mother worked two nursing jobs tryna keep her daughter looking fresh and feeling good. That left Bubbles with a whole lot of time to do whatever she wanted, and usually that included getting high and hanging out in the streets with grown men.

"I texted my friend," Bubbles said with a sneaky smile. "Friend who?" Nooni asked.

"One of the guys who was fighting up in T.C.'s Place last night. I hate I missed that shit! My moms took the night off from work and I couldn't sneak out. My friend is fine as hell girl, and he's waiting for us outside."

"He got a car?"

Bubbles smirked. "Hell yeah he got a car! What I look like? I don't be fuckin' with no busted niggahs, Nooni! Bitch you know me better than that."

"Yeah, what-the-fuck-ever!" Nooni couldn't help but giggle as they waited until the security guard's back was turned, then cut across a hallway and dipped out of a side door. Laughing, the pair hauled-ass down a stone-lined concrete path, swinging their back packs and hoping security wouldn't spot them before they could make it off school grounds.

A beat-up two-door black Honda was waiting for them at the corner. It had Jersey license plates and a chrome bumper, and the right front fender was dented and painted gray.

"Damn girl, don't tell me this is your friend," Nooni said, eyeballing the busted ride with her lips turned down and her nose turned up. "Uh-uh, Bubbles. Hell no. I ain't getting my gear all grimy riding around in that lil piece of shit."

"Shut up! I don't see your boojie ass coming up with no plans or no rides!"

Nooni was still frowning when she followed her friend over to the car. It was some kinda throwback hatchback. A young, light-skinned dude with gray eyes and cute dimples was sitting behind the wheel with his seat pushed all the way back, low-riding. A Band-Aid halfway covered a bruise over his temple, and another large, egg-shaped bruise stood out like a hill on the back of his head, courtesy of Maleek.

Bubbles opened the door, and the guy reached over and popped a lever letting the passenger seat flip forward. Nooni was embarrassed over the scene she'd caused in the club the night before, but she wasn't gonna let him see it. She smirked and stepped carefully into the back row. The pleather seats were ripped and belching foam. She was straight disgusted as her feet sank into a thick pile of empty soda bottles, fast food wrappers, and all kinds of random trash that had been dumped on the floor and on top of the badly stained seat cushions too.

Nooni rolled her eyes. Her stolen designer gear was about to be straight filthy and she shivered when she went to put on her seatbelt and saw how stained and nasty it was.

Releasing the lever, she said fuck buckling up. She was so skeeved out she couldn't even bring herself to sit all the way back, forget about letting the seatbelt touch her. She was about to climb her ass right back out the car, but then Bubbles pulled the front passenger seat upright and plopped down in it, grinning up in the driver's face like he was pushing a Porsche.

"Sup, baby?" the dude said to Bubbles as he pulled out into traffic. His seat was leaning back so far that Nooni felt like he was riding in the back with her.

He glanced at Bubbles, then nodded at Nooni and flashed her a handsome, thuggish grin. "Hey, gorgeous. How you doin' today?"

Bubbles giggled. "Nooni, this is Truth. Truth, Nooni."

Nooni smirked again. "Yeah, we already met."

Truth glanced over his shoulder at her again. She'd looked damn good when he was buzzed in the club last night, but he was really seeing her now. His gray eyes roamed over her smooth brown skin, high, firm breasts, and the spread of her curvy thighs.

"We sure did, and you still lookin' fine, baby," he grinned and nodded. "Real fine."

Truth turned the music up mad loud. He drove with one hand as he sparked up a blunt. He puffed on it a few times and then passed it to Bubbles. She took a couple of long tokes, then sent it to Nooni in the backseat.

The trio rode around getting nice and lifted. Before long, Nooni felt herself relaxing. She took a deep breath and allowed herself to unwind. She even sat back in the grimy seat. And even though her feet had sunk ankle-deep in the pile of stanking trash, she was steady patting them to the music's banging beat.

It wasn't long before Truth and Bubbles started getting it on in the front seat. Nooni puffed a fresh blunt as she watched Truth steer with one hand and unbuckle his belt with the other. Moments later, Bubbles had dipped her head in his lap. As Nooni watched, they rode down the busy streets of Harlem with Bubbles bobbing and slobbing on Truth's long, yellow joint.

After a while, the cush had Nooni high and horny too. Forgetting about her heartache over Maleek, she thought about how Truth's big hands had felt rubbing all over her in the club while they were dancing, and she couldn't help but stare jealously as her girl throated his thang like it was a sugary bomb pop. It was rock-hard and glistening wet with spit, and Truth moaned as he drove, palming Bubbles' head with his free hand as he rotated his hips and fucked up into her mouth.

It didn't take him long to bust his nut. By the time Bubbles swallowed his load and was coating her swollen lips from a tube of cherry-red gloss, Truth was sliding her a yard that he'd peeled off a knot he'd taken outta his sock, and they were pulling up outside of a nightclub.

"What's this?" Nooni asked, peering out the dirt-caked window as Truth turned off the ignition and opened his door. "Where we going?"

"This is my chill joint," he replied smoothly. "They call it the G-Spot. Whattup? You was feeling that lil kiddie action over at T.C.'s Place last night, but you too young to handle a grown man's club?"

Nooni smirked as he moved his seat forward and she followed him out on the driver's side. She stood up and made a show of wiggling her succulent ass around as she hiked up the waistband of her tight designer jeans. "I ain't too young for a damn thing," she said, eyeing Truth's crotch. She was drooling for the cash in his sock, and for that snake she'd seen him tuck back inside his pants too. Truth grinned and slung his arm over her shoulder. "So you ain't got no problem chillin' wit' a niggah like me for a minute?" he said as they walked toward the nightclub's front door.

"Nah," Nooni shrugged, feeling herself. "I ain't got no problems with nothing," she said, her gaze lowered, her eyes still glued to his dick. "Except for one thing," she giggled, ignoring the hater look on Bubbles' face. "The next time you feel like driving me and my homegirl around I'm riding up in the front."

CHAPTER 11

Even though it was early afternoon the G-Spot was alive and kicking and everything about it looked spectacular to Nooni's untrained eyes. She didn't see the filthy windows, the grime on the floor, or the greasy fingerprints and smears that were all over the once-glistening fuck poles.

There were people walking around drinking, smoking, and doing all kinds of other illicit shit. Led by Truth, Nooni and Bubbles pranced into the club strutting in their tight jeans and high heels like they were grown women who hung out in titty joints every other day.

Truth took them over to a booth near the bar. Bubbles sat on one side of the crusty table while Nooni and Truth slid in next to each other on the opposite side.

"What you ladies drinking?" Truth asked smoothly.

They looked at each other and bust out giggling. Sneaking a little Pink Champale into school was one thing, but drinking real liquor at a bar on a school morning was even better.

"Y'all got some Ciroc Coconut?" Bubbles asked, sticking a piece of gum in her mouth.

"We got whatever you want."

Bubbles grinned. "Well that's what I want!"

"I want me a Ciroc Dragonberry," Nooni said.

"Yo, Bizz!" Truth hollered at a skinny dude behind the bar. "Let's get the liquid luvin' flowing over here, my slime! Nah'mean? For the ladies!"

$$$$$

"Bitch, are you sure that's her sister? Don't be playing with me! You know I can't stand that fuckin' chick."

"That's her! I'm telling you. That's *her.*"

Monique stood in the doorway of the G-Spot's closed-down kitchen and eyed the two teeny-boppin' chickenheads who were getting tipsy with her young stud, Truth.

The little hoes couldn'ta been more than seventeen, if that. Monique couldn't help but chuckle inside. If G could see these two sweet pieces of jailbait sitting up in his spot that niggah would be bitching about his liquor license and kicking a hole in his coffin!

Monique peered closely at the beautiful young girl they were scoping out.

"She do look like her, though. Same skin color. Same hair."

"That's because they're sisters!" Honey Dew insisted. "Rita is the oldest, this chick here is in the middle, and then they have a real little sister too."

Monique's lip twisted. "So where the hell is Rita while her sister is playing hookey up in a damn club?"

112

"I ain't seen her in a minute," Honey Dew said, grilling the two young girls over Monique's shoulder. She tipped her beer up and slurped from the neck, then shrugged. "The last I heard, somebody said Rita moved outta her old apartment. She got a new place now. I think she moved in after Juicy and Gino dipped."

Honey Dew took another sip from her bottle. "She's still right here in Harlem though, so she didn't go too far."

"Oh, hell yeah!" Monique whispered gleefully as the young chick stood up and walked out on the dance floor with Truth. "That's her! That's Rita's sister 'cause they shaped just alike. That bitch got a real cute ass. What's her name again?"

Honey Dew frowned and shook her head. "Fuck if I remember. Nah-Nah. Nu-Nu. Nee-Nee." She shrugged. "Some stupid shit like that."

Monique couldn't take her eyes off the stunning young brown thing. She was a cocoa-colored Puerto Rican. Obviously mixed with black. The young girl who had come in with her was pretty too. She had real light skin and silky hair down to her ass.

Look at these lil hot mamas, Monique laughed inside. They were gorgeous all right. And grown as hell, too. They had their hot asses up in a men's club when they shoulda been sitting up in school tryna learn something. Monique loved it.

"You sure that's her, right?" she asked Honey Dew again. She just couldn't believe something this good could be falling right into her lap.

Honey Dew sighed and passed Monique her beer. "Bitch, look at her! She looks just like a little Rita. Plus, I already fuckin' told you. It's her. I know 'cause she used to hang out with a girl who stays next door to me. Some young chick named Bashira. Rita used to pick her sister up from there all the time."

Monique nodded, a cunning look glowing in her eyes.

"I sure hope you right 'cause I owe that bitch Rita one. She tried to get my brother Maurice locked up over some bullshit back in the day."

Honey Dew nodded right back. "My next door neighbor can't stand Rita neither. She came home and caught this here chick—Nooni! Yeah, I remember now—her name is Nooni—giving little Bashira dick-sucking lessons with a banana. Trust me. That's her."

Monique took a swig from the beer bottle and watched the girls dance and suck down free liquor from the bar.

"Oh, I know that lil bitch can suck some dick," she nodded. "That's how she got my brother knocked. Rita caught her giving Maurice some head and called the fuckin' cops. Like he was raping her or some shit. I oughtta beat that lil bitch's ass right now."

"You oughtta start *thinking*, is what you oughtta do," a silky, but strong feminine voice said behind them.

Monique and Honey Dew both whipped around. Salida had snuck up on them and dipped on their conversation without either one of them realizing it.

"Hey Mizz Salida," Monique said sweetly. "What's going on?"

Salida smirked, turning up her pretty lips.

"The cash register, baby. That's what's going on." Salida nodded toward the teenagers who were out on the dance floor getting loose with Truth.

"I heard what y'all was saying just now. Why you wanna kick that baby's ass?"

Monique ran the situation down real quick. "The one in the white shirt is Nooni. Her sister, Rita, used to run real tight with Juicy before G got killed."

"Is that right?" Salida asked, perking up at the mention of Juicy's name.

"Yeah. That lil bitch got my brother knocked when Rita caught them fuckin' and called the cops on him."

"And this girl, Rita, you say she's Juicy's friend?"

"Yeah. They partners. Homegirls. Juicy used to bring Rita around here every now and then when G was alive. Her and her little college friends would sit up in G's VIP booth looking stupid and acting like they was the shit."

"So, Juicy and Rita are tight, but are they *friends?*"

"Yeah, they friends," Monique shrugged. "As much as two bitches can be friends anyway."

"Uh-huh."

"Matter of fact, Rita was the one Juicy went running to the night her brother shot G."

Salida stared. "How do you know that?"

"'Cause I followed her ass! I came down here even though Ace had kicked my ass and told me to stay home. At first I was sitting in my car in the alley out back, and I watched them take off with G's body in the trunk of his Benz. When I drove around front I got the shit shocked outta me when I saw Juicy come busting out the door. She was asshole-naked with just a sheet wrapped around her."

Honey Dew shook her head sadly. "It was a shame the way they did Juicy. They had that girl tied to a pole down in that Dungeon for days. I can still hear her screaming. How the hell did she get out?"

Monique shrugged. "I don't know, but I saw her jet. She jumped in a bootleg taxi, and when they pulled off, I followed they asses."

Salida asked, "And where'd they go?"

"I just told you! They went to Rita's house! I saw that bitch open her front door and let Juicy in!"

Salida nodded. "So Rita and Juicy look out for each other like that, huh? That's good. That's even better than good."

"Yeah. That's why I was just telling Honey Dew I should go over there and bust Nooni's lil ass. Give her something to take back to her sister."

Salida waved her hand and shook her head real fast.

"Nah, nah, nah, darling. Forget about busting her ass. That's not how you win at this kind of game. Like I said, you need to start *thinking!*"

"A bitch like me," Monique snapped, "is always fuckin' thinking!"

"Then think on this," Salida said slickly. "We've got us a cute young goose who can lay us a fat golden egg, and all you can think about is kicking her ass."

Monique shrugged. "Then maybe I'll put her out on the track, or throw her young tail in one of the fuck rooms and make her flatback for some dollars instead. That's what G woulda done. Headlined her ass. We gotta take the Spot back to what it used to be. That's the only way we gonna get our pockets back right again."

Salida disagreed.

"Listen, can't no one chick sell enough ass to get this place back up on its feet. I don't care how hot her pussy is. But what we *can* do is use her. We can use what we got, to get what we want!"

"And how we gonna do that?"

"Oh," Salida said mysteriously. "There's more than one way to kill a cat. But first we're gonna go fishing. And that little hottie sitting over there is gonna be our prime piece of bait."

"Hmm..." Monique mused as Salida took her aside and broke it all the way down so she could understand it. The more Monique listened, the more impressed she was with Salida and her plan. No wonder G had locked this scheming bitch up way outta the country and tried to throw away the damn key!

Salida strategized like a man. She was way slicker than G was. Far more ruthless. If G hadn't drugged her up and stashed her in that nut-house Salida woulda had his black ass out on the track turning tricks and bringing her the money!

"So," Monique said, trying to wrap her head around the crazy-ass scenario Salida had just dropped on her. "You saying there's a way we can use Nooni, and get her to use her sister Rita, so we can get our hands on some big-time money?"

"That's correct. About two hundred grand to start."

Monique shook her head at the thought of all those zeros. "I just don't see it, Mizz Salida. That bitch Rita ain't paid. She ain't got that kind of cash."

"No, she doesn't," Salida coldly agreed.

"But her good friend Juicy does."

CHAPTER 12

Nooni mighta thought she was street slick, but she didn't have nothing on Money-Making Monique. At seventeen-years-old, she was miles behind the seasoned stripper, but she admired her swagger on sight.

Monique wiggled her delicious body over to the table where Nooni and Bubbles now sat chatting with Truth.

"Hey, cutie."

"Sup, Mo," Truth joked, raising his chin and wincing as he tossed down a shot-glass full of straight gin.

"Shut up," Monique said playfully, popping her chewing gum between her back teeth. "You cute, Truth, but ain't nobody talking to you." She flashed Nooni and Bubbles a bright smile.

"I was talking to *her*," she said, nodding at Nooni. "Welcome to the G-Spot, cutie. Look at your pretty eyes and all that curly hair! You're gorgeous, honey. What's your name?"

Nooni swallowed hard. She couldn't believe the beautiful lady with the butter weave and bombastical body was giving her props. She was awestruck and flattered, and Bubbles had to kick her under the table to get her to answer.

"N-Nubia," she stuttered, smiling back. "My name is Nubia, but they call me Nooni."

Monique slid into the booth next to Bubbles and sparked up some chocolate sticky.

"So why y'all not in school?" she asked, puffing first and then passing the blunt across the table to Nooni. "All that reading and writing shit is boring as hell, ain't it?" she added quickly, just so they knew she wasn't tryna preach to them or chastise them for playing hookey and cutting classes.

Nooni could barely speak. She was overly impressed by Monique's flawless brown skin, perfect false eyelashes, and three-inch diamond-studded fake nails.

Monique was sucking up the adoration with glee. She liked being admired by young girls. She liked tickling their ears and dumping dog shit in their empty heads. Salida had been right. There was more than one way to skin a cat. It was much smarter to use Rita's little sister as their tool than it was to get mad and beat her ass. She spent the next two hours happily wooing Nooni and Bubbles, soaking their throats with liquor and filling their heads up with whimsical nonsense. The kind of dumb shit that young girls loved to hear.

"Check it out," Monique said, feeling a little bit tipsy herself after matching Truth drink for drink. "I know y'all got school and homework and studying and all that type of bullshit going on. But are either one of y'all interested in making some extra money?"

Monique laughed inside as all four bright eyes in the two guttersnipe faces lit up.

"Yeah," both girls said together. "Hell, yeah!"

"See," Monique explained, lying her black ass off, "I'm a party planner. I put together erotic events for paid niggahs who got swole pockets. Can y'all young heffahs dance?"

Heads got to bobbing up and down.

"Well, we don't do no whole lotta freaky shit or nothing like that. You know, no fucking or dick sucking is required. But you *will* have to strip. And you'll have to shake that ass a lil bit too. You know, it ain't nothing serious. You just wiggle outta your panties and smack the crotch under them niggah's noses. Humph. After that, their old asses are usually straight for the rest of the night."

"Both of these honeys got plenty of ass," Truth laughed. "I believe they can handle that."

Monique nodded. "True, true. Problem is, I only got one opening left. Most of our parties are way out in Philly, or sometimes down in Atlantic City. I can only fit one more girl in my whip."

She looked from Nooni to Bubbles, then back to Nooni again.

"So who's it gonna be?"

Monique snickered to herself as the girls damn near brawled trying to get chosen, "Me! Me! Me!"

She gazed thoughtfully up at the ceiling for a moment, and then batted her false eyelashes as she looked from girl to girl.

"Y'all both real cute. But stand up and lemme see who got the best shape."

The young girls almost broke their necks as they scurried to get out of the booth. Standing in front of Monique, they struck pose after pose, tooting up their asses and arching their slender backs trying to make their high, young titties look even bigger.

Monique laughed.

"All right, all right. It's gonna be hard to decide. But since I have to choose, I pick.... Hold up. Hey, Truth. You a street playa, so what you think? If you had to fuck either one of these two honeys, which one would it be?"

Truth grinned, his sexy eyes red from weed and alcohol as he peeped Monique's shiesty game.

He licked his lips. "I'd pick her," he said, pointing not at the girl who had slobbed his dick down in the car on the way over, but at her girlfriend, whose pretty eyes and sexy grin had promised she would do much, much more.

"Nooni," he said with a big grin. "Yeah. I'd pick Nooni."

CHAPTER 13

It was a windy, overcast day when Rita touched down in Los Angeles. She had never been on an airplane before, and she spent the entire flight worrying. Not about the pilot, or whether the plane was gonna stay up in the air like it was supposed to. Nah. She was worried mostly about Juicy, but also about the two younger sisters that she had left back in Harlem.

She caught a taxi from the airport to an address in a plush neighborhood where Juicy was staying. She was surprised when a white chick answered the door.

"You must be Rita," the white lady said.

Rita nodded.

"I'm Renata. Juicy's upstairs. Come on in."

The crib was just as plush as the neighborhood, and Rita couldn't help but admire what she saw. She was a Harlem girl, born and raised. She'd never been inside a house this grand before. Because of Juicy's generosity, Rita had been able to move her sisters from the shabby tenement their father had raised them in, to a nice, spacious apartment building not too far away. Her new place was laid out, but it was nothing like this.

She followed Renata up a winding staircase. The steps were made of marble and the handrails were carved from deep, dark cherry wood. She was led to the doorway of an airy bedroom with high ceilings and two skylights, and her breath caught in her throat when she looked inside.

Rita knew life had been real hard for Juicy lately, but nothing could have prepared her for the actual sight of her girl.

Juicy was a wreck.

She had lost so much weight her collarbone stuck out like a rail from one shoulder to the other. Her cheeks were flat, and her eyes looked lost and sunken deep in her head.

But it wasn't her physical appearance that startled Rita the most. It was the pain coming out of her friend's soul. It overflowed from Juicy's eyes, and Rita had never seen anything like it before.

She rushed over to the bed where Juicy sat, and they hugged and cried. Rita made soft, comforting noises as Juicy clung to her like she was drowning.

"I'm so glad you came," Juicy said through her tears. "I couldn't call nobody else. I couldn't even tell nobody that Gino was dead. There was nobody else I could really trust."

Rita rocked her friend in her arms. "I'm glad you called me, Juicy. You should have called me sooner, though. I can't believe you waited almost two months! I would've jetted out here right away if I had known. You didn't have to suffer by yourself all this time, girl. I could have been here for you."

Juicy wiped her eyes. "I wasn't alone. Renata made me come home with her straight from the hospital."

Rita glanced toward the door. "Who the hell are these white people?" she asked in a dropped voice. "Why they doing all this for you?"

Juicy sighed. "They're a group of businessmen from New York, and they're some of the best people I've ever known. Gino worked for them. He got real tight with his boss's nephew, and since we were out here by ourselves with no friends they just kinda adopted us and started treating us like family."

"That's real unusual for Italians," Rita said, doubtfully. "Especially the ones I know in New York."

"I know," Juicy said, nodding. "But they're good people, Rita. Like you said, it's been almost two months and they've been taking care of me the whole time. The Sanveneros might be Italian, but they're legit. They loved Gino, and he loved them back."

"Well, I'm glad somebody out here had your back," Rita shrugged, then nodded. "Going through all that stress by yourself would have been ten times worse."

Juicy hadn't been back to her crib since Gino was murdered, but she told Rita she was ready to go home so she could try to pick up the pieces she'd left behind.

"Cool, I came out here strictly for you," Rita said. "So whatever you wanna do, wherever you wanna go, it's all good with me. Just say the word."

Juicy said the word, but Renata wasn't trying to hear it.

"I have another bedroom that you can use, Rita," she said. "You're welcome to visit as long as you like, but Frank and I both think it's best if Juicy continues to stay with us. We can keep her safe here. We can protect her."

But Juicy wasn't down with that.

She wanted to go home. Home to the bed that she and Gino had slept in every night, and home to the unfulfilled promise of what their lives would have been like together if he had lived.

Slick Sallie hugged Juicy real tight before she left, and Big Frankie gave her what looked like a pink cell phone.

"It's a stun gun," he told her. "Believe me, your problem has already been taken care of, but I want you to keep this near you at all times."

Juicy nodded. "I appreciate everything you and Renata and Sal have done for me," she told Frank as she picked up her small bag. "Y'all looked out for me and treated me better than people I've known my whole life. But I can't hide out here forever. I have to figure out my next move. I've gotta make some decisions."

Renata jumped in and protested a little bit more, but in the end she respected her friend's wishes. There were tears in her eyes as she drove them to Juicy's house. She held Juicy in her arms for a real long time before saying goodbye, and Rita could tell the white chick really had mad love for Juicy in her heart.

Settled down in Juicy's crib, Rita had a sense of déjà vu. She remembered the night that Juicy had escaped from the G-Spot like it was yesterday. She remembered how torn-down her friend had looked when she jumped out of that taxi, raped and beaten and wearing nothing but a sheet.

Juicy looked almost as bad as that now.

Not only was she grieving for Gino and the baby boy she'd lost, she was still recovering from her surgery and barely eating enough to keep any meat on her bones.

"It's gonna be alright," Rita whispered over and over as Juicy walked around the crib whimpering and touching Gino's things. It was all just the way he had left it. From his toothbrush on the sink, to his shoes under the bed. Gino's spirit was definitely in that house. The essence of him was in all the stuff he had left behind, and it made Juicy break all the way down to know he wasn't coming back.

Rita followed closely as Juicy roamed the house just crying and touching. Rita let her be, simply reaching out to catch her friend when her legs got too weak and she couldn't stay on her feet. She had never seen anybody cry so hard or so long, and there was no way to stop the tears of sympathy from falling from her own eyes.

Juicy's grief seemed to know no end. She told Rita that the two months since Gino's death felt like two short hours to her heart. Hiding away at Renata's crib hadn't given her a proper outlet to mourn, and seeing and touching and smelling Gino's earthly possessions made something inside her die all over again.

Rita did her best to be strong and supportive. She turned the hot water on in the shower, and helped her girl get undressed. Juicy stood there in front of her naked, and Rita winced at the sight of the stitched-up bullet wound right below her girl's navel. It was twisted and purplish, and she could tell how bad it had hurt just by the way it looked.

"I lost my baby," Juicy wept pitifully. She pressed her hands to her empty womb as Rita stared at her surgical scar. "I wanted that baby, Rita. I wanted him so, so, *bad.*"

Silently, Rita poured shower gel on a cloth and smoothed it over Juicy's back, breasts, and arms. She squeezed suds all over her, then she propped Juicy up in the shower and washed her hair, angling the showerhead so she could get a good rinse. She had just gotten Juicy out of the water and was gently drying her off with a big fluffy towel when her girl began talking again.

With trembling lips, Juicy opened her mouth and told her friend everything that had happened. From the moment her and Gino left New York, until the day she watched her man get put in the ground.

Through it all, Rita just couldn't believe what she was hearing. The lost hopes and dreams...the senselessness of it all was just heartbreaking.

"So all of this went down just because some guy was jealous and wanted to push up on you?"

Juicy shrugged her shoulders miserably.

"I don't know. I've been thinking maybe it wasn't just about Pit, though. Maybe it was my fault. There's something fucked up about me, Rita. I make niggahs act crazy."

"That's not true, Juicy. You can't blame yourself for what that psycho fool did."

Juicy sniffed, her eyes and nose were both red. "But I *do* blame myself. There's something about me that attracts bad energy. The way I look. How I dress. How I walk... Maybe some kind of vibe I be giving off. I can't explain it, Rita, but it's there. It's like I have bad luck or something."

Rita shushed her with a hug. "Juicy, you don't have no control over what some fool-ass niggah decides to do! All you want is the same thing every other chick like us wants. A good education, a nice dude to chill with, some friends to hang out with, and to have a little fun. It's not your damn fault that men like G and Pit want to control a bitch's next breath! And it ain't bad luck when you catch a lot of fucked up breaks in life, neither. It's just life, Juicy. *Life.* Pit musta been fried in the head to do what he did. That's probably why somebody took him out."

Juicy wiped her eyes on her towel and sighed. "I don't know who got to him, but I'm glad he's gone. Renata said the cops found him hanging in his own shower. His throat was slit and somebody had chopped off his right hand."

"Damn..."

"I know...Renata thinks somebody left Pit's body like that to send a message. Two of his homeboys got took down too. Execution style."

Rita shuddered. "So, what happened to his girl? Your so-called friend? The chick who was doing your hair?"

"I don't even know," Juicy shrugged and shook her head. "I guess she skied up. I sent Renata looking for her a few weeks ago, but she came back and said Quese's shop was boarded up and she was nowhere to be found."

Rita sighed. No matter which way she looked at Juicy's situation it looked real bad for her girl. She was out on the West Coast all alone, with no real friends or family, but she couldn't go back to New York either. Not while niggahs were still gunning for her head.

They spent the next two weeks just chilling and lounging around at Juicy's crib. Rita cooked a bunch of different dishes, but Juicy barely ate anything. She was sad and she cried a lot. She went back and forth between feeling guilty about everything, to wanting to die so she wouldn't have to feel anything at all.

"I begged God to take me," Juicy confessed one night as they walked on a beach. "I asked Him to either strike me dead, or give me the courage to take myself out. And you know what, Rita?" she asked, her voice full of misery. "I'm so fucked up that God doesn't even want me."

There was no self-pity in Juicy's words. Only sorrow. But instead of trying to find ways to comfort her all the time, Rita held back and let her girl just get it all out. Shit, if anybody had a right to feel sad, it was Juicy. She had suffered a whole lot to be so damn young.

"It's gonna get better," was all Rita could think of to say. And in her heart, she believed it. On the real, with all the crazy shit that had happened to her girl lately, it for damn sure couldn't get no worse.

CHAPTER 14

So what now?" Salvatore McCain asked his uncle. He'd been pacing back and forth in front of the window ever since Renata left the house with Juicy and her beautiful Hispanic girlfriend who was visiting from New York.

Frank shrugged. "Nothing changes, Sallie. We keep an eye on Juicy, and we help her out the best we can. Oh yeah," he added. "We tell Fat Paul to set up some security around her condo. If she needs us, we're there."

Sallie frowned. He was still mad about being run out of New York City. The weather was a lot better in California, but his friends—and his hustle—was on the East Coast, and that was where he wanted to be.

"We're there for how long? C'mon, Uncle Frank. It's over! Gino's dead, and the trash that killed him got put down for a nice long nap. We paid our debt, and now it's over."

Narrowing his eyes, Frank stared at his nephew. The kid was a half-Irish bum. If Sallie wasn't his sister's son Frank would have knocked some principles into the boy's head.

As the leader of his family Frank wasn't gonna tolerate having his decisions questioned by some snot-nosed little asshole. He had moved twenty-seven members of his immediate family from one coast to the other in the blink of an eye. He'd arranged new identities for everybody, and set them up with legitimate jobs and front businesses so they could re-establish their normal criminal activities. Keeping the family running smoothly was a full-time occupation, and Frank didn't need a spoiled little shit like Sallie adding to his troubles.

"It ain't over until I say it is," Frank said with firm authority. "We made a deal and we're sticking to it. That's how The Organization does business, Salvatore. No matter how long it takes."

"But you made a deal with a fuckin' moolie!" Sallie shot off. He despised Blacks and his entire family knew it.

Frank's patience was growing thin. Like most of the family's younger soldiers Sallie was near-sighted and hotheaded. His generation, if left to their own impulsive devices, would buck the time-honored traditions and run La Cosa Nostra right back into the barren grounds of Italy where it had originated.

Of course, Sallie wasn't a member of the ruling council, but Frank sure was. He had vivid memories of the night The Organization was tipped off to an impending federal sting. It was a full-scale, complex operation that involved several federal agencies, and within a matter of days it would have crippled and taken down his entire clan.

Most ignorants believed the mob had all but disappeared from New York City, and that's exactly what Frank and the other members of their ruling council wanted them to think. Over the past twenty years La Cosa Nostra had adjusted and adapted to the new criminal landscape. They'd gone deep undercover while maintaining dominance in the drug trade, and the idiots who thought they were irrelevant were the same idiots whose money they gladly raked in.

So, when Frank got word that the Feds were sniffing at his door, he and the senior members of The Organization had been grateful for the advance warning. They'd gone to work hiding assets and destroying damning evidence. And as a result of their quick actions they'd not only eluded the Feds with their finances intact, they'd escaped with their lives and their freedom too.

"I'm serious," Sallie pressed the issue. "I say fuck the moolie."

"Look, you fuckin' retard!" Frank exploded, snatching his nephew in the collar. "Did you forget that 'moolie' saved your miserable little life? Do I have to remind you about the caches of guns and the warehouse full of dope we moved? And what about all the money we hid away? If it wasn't for that moolie we'd be spending the rest of our lives in a federal fucking pen! He looked out for us like a man. And we're going to respect him. Like men."

Even with the meaty fist at his throat Sallie still disagreed. "I understand all that, Uncle Frankie, but we already did our part! Our deal ended at Gino's funeral. I say we send this guy a couple of blood oranges and then we call it even. It's done! Juicy can look out for herself."

Frank trembled, he was very close to the edge.

"Our deal *included* Juicy," he spit. "She's under our protection. And she's going to stay that way! End of discussion."

"But what are we getting out of it?"

Frank barely controlled his temper. "That man could have been killed for what he did for us. Looking out for the girl is the least we can do. Besides," he said, releasing Sallie and running his beefy hand through his mop of jet-black hair, "Juicy's a nice kid and Renata likes her. She likes her a lot."

CHAPTER 15

Nooni felt like the winning contestant on a television game show. She was finally getting over her love for Maleek, and for the past two weeks her and Bubbles had cut out of school every day to jet over to the G-Spot to hang out with Truth.

Drinking, smoking, and fucking was all they had on their minds, and it didn't even faze Nooni when Mrs. Moreno fussed her out in Spanish for coming home way after midnight and waking up late for school every day.

Nooni knew her shit was veering off the chart, but she didn't care. There was too much fun shit going on to worry about school or anything else. There was always a shopping trip with Monique to go on, or nice restaurants to floss at, and ballers out the ass to rub shoulders with when she went to live parties with some of the dancers at the G-Spot.

Her sister Rita had been blowing her spot up like mad, though. She left worried messages on her cell phone day and night, but as soon as Nooni saw her number on the caller ID she'd hit ignore, and then text Rita and give her some bullshit story like her phone was dying and she couldn't find her charger.

Nooni was playing a dangerous game and she knew it, but what she didn't know was that somebody else was playing their own little dangerous game too.

A game of cat and mouse.

She was sitting on a barstool between Monique and Bubbles when Truth walked over from the DJ booth where he'd been jamming.

"Whaddup," he said, eyeing her with a sexy grin.

Nooni blushed. The swagger on this dude was amazing. He stepped up on her and kissed her, snaking his tongue deep into her mouth.

Monique puffed on a blunt and watched as her young lover slobbed Nooni down. She crossed her legs and grinned at the sight of his tongue slithering all over the stupid chick's eager lips.

Nooni's knees damn near buckled just from his kiss. Truth had been laying that yellow dick down on her deep and hard, and Monique completely understood why the young girl was bent and strung out on that good shit.

"Yo," Truth said breaking the kiss. A hot look was in his eyes as he bit his lower lip. "We gonna holla, Mo." He took Nooni's hand and they headed toward the fuck rooms. "I gotta take care of some bidnizz with my girl real quick."

Monique was shivering with excitement as Truth led Nooni away, and she couldn't stop herself from giggling when he winked over his shoulder and gave her a swagged-out grin.

"That low-down Puerto Rican bitch!" Bubbles muttered, crushing her cigarette out on the bar. "I was sucking Truth's dick first!"

Monique turned to the pretty young girl and let out an evil laugh. "Shut up, chicken. You ain't special. Every hoe up in here done sucked Truth's dick. And that's

124

the truth!"

$$$$$

While Truth was busy soldiering hard for Nooni, Salida had made a true soldier out of Monique. Although Ace and Pluto had come up short during their trip to California, Salida had looked at the situation from a completely different angle and devised herself an alternate plan. She'd been off her medication for a minute now, and while she still had a few fucked up periods of hazy thinking, she was becoming more and more like her old self every day.

"The only way to get our hands on some quick money is to think and plan, you hear me?" she schooled Monique. "Think and plan!"

Monique agreed, but she kept quiet. Hell, she had already done her thinking and planning when she sent Ace and Pluto after Gino and Juicy. But she knew better than to tell Salida that. Shit, if Salida ever found out that Monique had sent the goonies to California to pop her only son, she would probably pull out a tool and shoot Monique right between the eyes. Salida was just that throwed off.

"If we play our cards the right way," Salida continued intensely, "then Rita, Juicy, *and* the money will jump straight into our hands without us moving a muscle."

"How the hell is all that gonna happen?" Monique wanted to know.

"Trust me," Salida told her. "You'll know my plan is working because you won't have to approach Rita at all. That bitch will walk straight up to you and start talking."

Monique had rubbed her hands together in anticipation of that big day.

And while Monique was anticipating, Salida was busy thinking about their future operations. She had already decided to use part of the money they were gonna pull in to get the G-Spot's cut room back up to full operations. But not the way it used to be. After just a few weeks of watching television, surfing the internet, reading blogs, and hanging out in chat rooms, Salida had decided that the era of selling drugs G's way had passed.

The color of Harlem was slowly changing, and so were its tastes. Crack would always be king to a certain group of addicts, but Salida planned to upgrade the G-Spot's drug operations to include the kind of club drugs that were cheaper and easier to get than cocaine. She was interested in the kind of drugs that more and more young people were beginning to like.

Quaaludes, ecstasy, roofies, special k, and especially meth, were all the rage with the kids who were starting to hang around Harlem today. Salida wanted to include all that shit on the menu at the G-Spot, and she had even figured out how to cook up the meth herself.

Monique knew what she wanted to do with her share of the take too. She also knew what she was gonna do to Juicy once she got her razor blade against that bitch's throat. And it wasn't gonna be pretty, neither. Nah, it wouldn't be pretty at all.

But they had to do all of the first things, first. Divide and conquer, is what Salida had instructed Monique to do with their two new protégés, and she set about getting Bubbles outta the picture in a hurry.

The tough little chicken didn't appreciate getting cut from the squad, though. She nutted up and made Truth get physical when he tried to shake her off, and he ended up having to mush her face into a light pole so she could get the message.

With Bubbles mad as hell, but gone, Monique instructed Truth to concentrate all his efforts on making Nooni feel comfortable so she could let her guard down.

She told him to keep the girl as high as possible, and to fuck her little lights out so that when it came time to put the moves on her she would bend in whatever direction they wanted.

That same night, after he busted Bubbles in the grill and left her staggering near the corner of her block, Truth took Nooni back to the small apartment where his Uncle Pluto lived with Monique.

"Don't you put that young heffah in my bed," Monique had warned Truth earlier. "Y'all can eat anything you find in the house, and you can fuck her in whichever room you wanna fuck her in—except mine."

Truth and Nooni made themselves at home in Monique's living room on her sleeper sofa. They partied at the G-Spot most of the time, and stayed out of Pluto's way whenever he came home to eat or sleep.

Nooni had never known a dude like Truth before. She had only fucked with a handful of guys in the past, but other than Maleek, none of them had been about the streets the way Truth was. For one thing, he was only two years older than she was, but he wasn't no regular come up. He was certified. Already he had made a name for himself that was ringing bells on the streets, and he was down with one of the leading sets in Harlem.

Two days later, Nooni walked out of Mrs. Moreno's apartment, never to return. She waited while Truth stuffed her small suitcase into his junky-ass trunk, then she climbed into the car beside him and sipped on his pineapple soda as he drove her back to Monique's apartment where they had been chilling off and on for days.

"Yo, shawty, you said you wanna be wit' a niggah, right?" Truth asked, squeezing her thigh as he drove.

Nooni nodded quickly. Damn right she did. Truth was nothing like that jealous, cheating-ass, Maleek. Her sister had been right. Maleek was too young and immature for her anyway! But this cat Truth was the bizz. He was so cold she wanted to be with him every single fuckin' day and sleep with him all night too.

"Then lemme hear you say it," he demanded. "Don't be nodding your head like no baby, Nooni. I'm a man and you a woman. Tell me what the fuck you want."

"I wanna be with you," Nooni declared. "Yeah, I do. I wanna be with you."

"Good," Truth said. "Then you better act like it. If anybody asks you any questions, you tell 'em you got put outta that old lady's crib and I helped you find someplace to stay, aiight? Act like you wanna be with ya niggah! Ya heard?"

Nooni was all for it.

Monique was in the kitchen frying chicken livers and stirring grits when they walked in. She fixed a plate for Pluto real quick, then turned off the pots and teetered into the living room on her six-inch stilettos and posted up in front of the young lovers who were sharing a set of headphones as they listened to some N.J.S. cuts by Reem Raw on Truth's iPod.

"What's good?" Monique asked, posing magnificently before them with her hands on her sexy hips.

Nooni's eyes went back and forth between Monique and Truth, like what the fuck. Monique was damn near naked. She looked like a piece of Pepto-Bismol coated chocolate. All she had on was a hot pink push-up bra and a matching fishnet-and-lace thong, but she wasn't the least bit pressed out about Truth's eyeballs rolling all her delicious cocoa-puffed ass.

"Oh," Monique laughed, busting Nooni's look. "I'm a stripper, honey," she waved her hand and grinned at the young girl. "I take my shit off for a living. I grind my pussy on a pole every night, so Truth done already seen everything I got." She didn't tell Nooni that Truth had also tasted and fucked everything she had too.

"Yo, Mo," Truth said, nodding at the suitcase he had dropped near the door. "Nooni ain't got nowhere to go. Her sister went outta town and left her with some old lady. The old bat started trippin' when I went to drop Nooni off, and then she told her to get all her shit and get the fuck out."

Monique faked a look of concern.

"For real? She put you out? That's messed up! So, where did your sister go? When is she coming back?"

Nooni bit the bait.

"She went to California or something. She said she had to go see about one of her sick friends."

"And she left you back here with some old lady who put you out in the street knowing you ain't got nowhere else to stay?"

Nooni looked up at Truth. He took a hit from the blunt he had just lit and then passed it to her.

"Yeah," the young girl said. She toked the chronic and nodded her head, remembering what Truth had told her to say. "Yeah," she squinted as she slowly exhaled the heavy, acrid smoke. "That's exactly what that old bitch did."

$$$$$

Nooni had been born to hang out in the G-Spot. She loved the excitement and the vibe. The strippers and hoes were all real cool, and lounging around drinking and smoking everyday made her feel loose and free.

The only thing that made her nervous was being around the beautiful older woman Salida. Nooni straight stuttered and lost all her lil cool if Salida so much as looked at her. It was obvious that Salida was a boss bitch, and Nooni felt like the femme fatale was peering through her eyes and seeing straight into her brain, and it was intimidating and very confusing.

"Don't pay her no attention," Monique had whispered when Salida rolled up on them while they were watching skin flicks in the XXX cinema room. Salida had barked on all the hoes to get their asses back to work, and warned them that she would be collecting their liquor tabs out of their nightly pay.

"She's a mean-ass bird, but she's smart and she definitely got a mind for business," Monique had confided as she sat cross-legged on a sofa and smoked yay from a bong.

Monique was playing a role for Nooni, but she really meant what she had said about Salida being smart. That bitch was psycho-smart. They had become partners of a sort, and it delighted Monique to see how crafty and conniving Salida was, and how little respect she had for Ace and Pluto.

"Both of them buffalo butts are dumb as hell," Salida had declared a couple of days earlier. "You better decide whose team you're on right here and now, Monique, because when the drama goes down it's gonna go all the way down!"

Monique had wasted no time assuring Salida that she was on her team. Shit, loyalty to Pluto wasn't even on her mind. If the right opportunity floated by that niggah would drop her on her head and step on her neck.

"Mizz Salida is pretty," Nooni told Monique as they watched the elegantly dressed woman with the upswept hair saunter regally around the club. As low-down as the G-Spot had sunk, Salida carried herself like she was a high-society hostess catering to bankrolling clientele in a luxurious Las Vegas nightclub or something. "But she's scary, though. Real scary."

"No," Monique said, playing from the script that Salida had made her rehearse earlier, "what's scary is what's gonna happen if we don't get some big-time cash up in here real soon."

"Oh yeah?"

"For real. The G-Spot is in serious trouble. We owe a lotta back taxes, and if we don't pay them shits the government is gonna come put padlocks on the doors. Mizz Salida just don't wanna see us get shut down, that's all."

"Damn," Nooni exclaimed, looking around at what had practically become her new home. "I sure hope y'all don't have to close up. It's mad cool up in here. I like it."

"Yeah, but do you like it enough to help us keep the doors open?" Monique asked, passing the young chick her bong.

Nooni shrugged, then smoked. "Yeah. But what can I do? I ain't got no ends."

Monique picked up her glass of gin and juice and swirled it around until the ice cubes clinked together.

"Oh, I know you don't have no money, baby girl. You just a real sweet kid. But I bet you know somebody who has exactly the kind of heavy bank we need."

"Oh yeah?" Nooni asked, looking puzzled. "Who's that?"

"Don't worry about who it is," Monique said slyly. "Just worry about how you can help us get our hands on it. You think you can be down for that?"

Nooni nodded, and then she remembered what Truth had told her about speaking up like a grown woman.

"Yeah," she said boldly. "I'm down."

"That's what I'm talking about!" Monique grinned with excitement. "You's a real soldier, Nooni-baby. You the kind of hood chick who can make an old bitch real proud. Thanks to you, the G-Spot is gonna get saved and every last one of us is about to be paid. Now listen up, cutie-booty. This is what we need you to do..."

CHAPTER 16

Rita had been on the West Coast with Juicy for over two weeks and she had been worried about her sisters the entire time. She called Mrs. Moreno every couple of days to check on the girls, but she could only seem to reach Nooni by text message, and even that was sometimey.

Every single night after Juicy fell asleep Rita would get on the phone and talk to Dutchy for hours. She didn't tell him none of Juicy's personal business or nothing, but she did talk to him about how bad she felt for her friend, and about how worried she was about Nooni.

"She's been texting you from her own phone, right?" Dutchy asked.

"Yeah," Rita said. "But that's not the same as speaking to her. Every time I call her it goes straight to her voicemail. Then she'll text me hours later and say her battery died, or she wasn't near her phone, or some bullshit like that."

Dutchy said, "I've been by there a few times myself, but I can never catch up with her either. But you know how teenagers can be, Rita. They don't like to talk on the phone, but they'll text them little fingers down to nubs."

Rita knew Dutchy was joking so she could stop worrying so much. But it wasn't working. Rita had been a parent to her sisters for so long that she'd developed a mother's instinct. And it was only two days later that she got the phone call that she had been dreading.

It was six o'clock in the morning L.A. time when Rita rolled over in Juicy's guest bedroom and reached for her cell phone. Mrs. Moreno was babbling on the line, and she was crying so hard that Rita almost didn't understand what the old lady was trying to say.

"What do you mean Nooni went away?" she asked sleepily.

"She gone! She been gone for days!" the old Hispanic woman fretted. "Nubia, she no listen to nobody, Marguerita! That girl, she just no *listen!* I tell her to stay inside, and poof! she disappear! And just now on the tellyvision it say the police find a dead girl in the trunk of a car! I afraid, Marguerita. I afraid for you sister! I have young children here. I cannot look for her. I don't know what else to do."

"Okay, okay, calm down," Rita said. Her heart banged in her chest and she was scared as hell too. "Don't worry, Mrs. Moreno." Rita found herself breathing fast and her mouth was bone dry. "I'm on my way home. I'll be back in New York before the end of the day."

Rita felt bad for leaving Juicy so suddenly, but she had to go. Juicy offered to fly back to New York with her and help her look for Nooni, but Rita told her that would be like going on a suicide mission.

"I feel really bad about leaving you here all by yourself, Juicy. I swear I do. Promise me you'll try to think positive and relax, okay?" Rita pleaded. "I'll be in touch. And as soon as I find Nooni and put my foot up her little ass, I'll come back and see you again."

"Don't hurt her," Juicy said with a small smile. "You know I love me some Nooni. She ain't a bad kid, Rita. She's just like I was when I was her age. Dumb in the head and hot in the tail."

"That girl is wild," Rita said, exasperated. "Crazy wild."

Juicy offered to drive her to the airport, but Rita had already put her bags near the front door and called a cab. "Nooni is trying to grow up way too fast. I'm sure she's just hanging out at one of her friend's houses, but I gotta go home and see what's really going on. As soon as I get Nooni straight and I'll come back and stay with you for a few more weeks, okay?"

Juicy was trying real hard not to cry when the taxi pulled up outside, but Rita saw her tears anyway.

"Thanks for always being there for me," Juicy whispered, hugging her tightly. "You're my best friend in the world, Rita. The only person I know that I can truly trust. I love you, girl."

Rita tried to sniff back her own tears, but it didn't work. "I love you too, Juicy. And I swear I'll be back. I promise. As soon as I get everything straight with my sister, I'm coming back to California to see you."

Rita rushed out to the cab, wiping her eyes. She'd meant every word she'd said to Juicy, but little did she know the promise she had just made was straight empty. It would never come true. Rita would never return to California to see Juicy again.

$$$$$

Back in Harlem, Rita went on a manhunt. She'd wigged out up at the precinct when she went to report Nooni missing, and Dutchy had to smooth shit down so his boys wouldn't put the cuffs on her. The problem was, Nooni had been in trouble so many times that the cops were treating her disappearance like a typical runaway case, and they refused to list her as a missing or endangered minor. There was so much criminal shit going on in Harlem they weren't about to put no whole lotta energy into looking for some fast-ass teenager who probably didn't wanna be found anyway.

But Rita knew different. Nooni had her troubles, but she wouldn't just run off to parts unknown while Rita was all the way across the country. No, something was wrong. Something was very wrong. Rita could feel it deep down in her bones.

With Dutchy's help, she searched high and low for Nooni. They hit all the local strip clubs, the drug houses, the back alleys, and the late-night bars. Under the cloak of darkness Rita walked up and down the track, praying that some old predatory pimp hadn't snatched Nooni up and turned her out on the streets.

During the day she went up to Nooni's high school and talked to some of her friends, but they were no help. Dutchy had even flashed his badge a few times and threatened to haul some asses down to the precinct, but nobody cracked. Either they knew where Nooni was and they weren't gonna snitch on her, or they were telling the truth and Nooni had just disappeared.

Either way, Rita was devastated and way past desperate when she ran into an old ghost from her past.

"Hey!" she yelled, sliding to her feet. After searching Harlem for hours, she had bought a slice of pizza and was sitting on the hood of a parked car eating it when she noticed the chick.

It wasn't hard to spot her because with her fly hair, stylish gear, and the 'for sale' sign in her strut, she stood out in the afternoon crowd.

Rita abandoned the dusty old Toyota she'd been sitting on and hurried to catch up to the girl. The chick was dressed in shimmery shades of gold from her sunglasses all the way down to her designer sandals, and she walked like she was laying down in the bed fucking.

Rita couldn't stand the bitch, but she had to give it to her. She was ice-cold from the tips of her glittery fingernails to the smooth satin of her designer mini-skirt, which flapped like a flag under the mound of her stacked hips and gyrating ass.

"Hey *Monique!*" Rita yelled, catching up to her until they were walking side by side.

Monique gave Rita a shitty look out the corner of her eye and kept on working it down the block.

Rita swallowed her pride and walked faster. Here was a bitch who had her nose to the ground. If anybody knew the seedy underbelly world of Harlem, it was Monique. But Rita had to be careful. Monique was a well-trained dog. Just one sniff of desperation would make her snap and bite. Ordinarily Rita wouldn't give this twisted chick no energy, but wasn't nothing ordinary about her seventeen-year-old sister getting swallowed up in the sewers of Harlem and vanishing without a trace.

"I don't mean to bother you," Rita said calmly, "but I'm looking for my sister. Her name is Nooni. She used to mess with your brother, Maurice, remember? Have you seen her around?"

Monique strutted sexily and pretended not to hear Rita, but inside she was squealing with glee. Salida had been right! All she had to do was show up in the vicinity and this bitch had come running straight to her! Monique didn't show it, but she was so happy she wanted to jump in the air and click her heels together.

Instead, she kept her eyes aimed on forward as she maintained her evil aura and her funky strut.

"Monique, please," Rita begged. "I know you don't like me and that's cool. But Nooni is a child. She's a child and she's *missing!* Can you just tell me whether you've seen her or not?"

Despite the plea ringing in Rita's voice, the coldness of Monique's chill flowed off her in waves. She only had two sentences for Rita, and they offered no help at all.

"I'm an old hoe, Rita," Monique sniffed, aiming her nose way up in the air. "And it ain't my job to be keeping track of none of these young ones."

$$$$$

It was Friday night and Rita had just put Chub to bed when she got a call that came up blocked on her cell phone. She clicked the talk button quickly, praying it was Nooni, but the caller shocked her by laying down a line from an old Wu Tang Clan rap.

"Hello?"

"It's ten o'clock, hoe! Where the fuck is ya sister at?"

"What? Who's this?"

"I said where the fuck is ya sister at?"

"My sister? Who is this?"

Rita heard the sound of flesh being slapped, and then a girl screeched and cried out in pain.

"Don't worry about who the fuck I am. Just know I got somebody here that you really wanna get back."

A commotion sounded in the background, like somebody's ass was getting kicked. A girl shrieked loudly again. But this time she called out a name.

"Margueritaaaaa! Help!"

Rita went cold inside.

It was Nooni. There was no mistaking her voice.

"Oh my God," she whispered as she envisioned her sister tied up in somebody's basement being beaten and tortured and abused.

"Please," she begged, tears springing to her eyes. "Don't hurt her. Please don't hurt my sister!"

"That's up to you," the male voice said coolly. "I can slump this bitch right now, or you can have her back for two hundred grand. You got 24 hours to get it."

Rita screamed, "Two hundred grand? Are you fuckin' crazy? How am I supposed to come up with that kind of money?"

"I don't give a damn how you get it. But if it was my sister I'd be looking for some help from my friends. Whatever you do, don't call the cops, because if you do I'll pop this bitch and leave her dead ass burning in a garbage can. The next time you see her she'll be so fuckin' crispy you'll wanna pour barbeque sauce on her. Now, listen close and pay attention 'cause here's what I want you to do..."

$$$$$

By the time dude finished running shit down Rita was in a panic. Before he hung up there was another slapping sound and Nooni screamed again, and then the line went dead.

Rita's first thought was to dial 911, but then she checked herself.

Call the cops and I'll pop this bitch.

Rita stood there trembling and staring at the cell phone she gripped in her hand. Suddenly the reality of what was going down hit her, and it hit her real hard.

Two hundred grand...

In her head, she quickly calculated the worth of everything in her apartment, all her jewelry, and every dime in her savings account. The amount she came up with was laughable. It came out to way less than what she needed to get her sister back.

With the memory of Nooni's terrified voice echoing in her ear, Rita jumped into action. Her hands were sweaty as she punched some numbers into her phone. The first person she called was Dutchy.

You got 24 hours to get it.

And when her man's phone rang and rang until his voicemail finally picked up, Rita knew she had no other choice but to make another call.

She took a deep breath and dialed her girl.

She called Juicy.

$$$$$

Nooni was stretched out on Monique's sofa holding a sock full of ice cubes high on her right cheek. Truth had knocked the piss outta her. For real. The first time he swung she'd screamed out in fear and surprise. The second time he'd dug his fist deep into her eye. His third blow had made her pee on herself as she cried out in pain for her sister, and she lost count of all the blows after that.

"You're okay," he told her as she lay there shivering and hiccupping. Her nose was red from crying and he bent down and kissed it on the tip. "I wasn't tryna hurt you, baby, but we had to make it seem real, nah'mean?"

Her screams had sure as hell been real. Nooni closed her eyes behind the ice pack and forced herself to be chill. She was grateful for Truth's affection and his small kiss, and she told herself that was more than Maleek would have given her after he kicked her ass.

Truth had practiced what he was gonna say to Rita about five times before he actually called her, and not one of those times had he told Nooni that he was gonna really smash her, or that the beat-down Monique had filmed with her cell phone so she could sent it to Rita was gonna be the real thing.

Nooni's eyeball throbbed in her skull where he'd capped her, and she wondered if getting Juicy's money was worth all this. She knew shit was crucial and they had to pay the back taxes on the G-Spot, and that was all good. But the only reason she had really agreed to go along with the plan is because Truth said he had a lot of expensive warrants that he needed to clear up. If he didn't pay his fines he was gonna get locked up, and Nooni couldn't bear to think about him going to jail and leaving her by herself.

"Lemme see it," Monique said, taking a seat on the sofa beside Nooni. She pulled the sock gently away from the young girl's face, then sucked her breath in real quick like the sight of Nooni's bruised eye really hurt her.

"Oh, he straight fucked you up," Monique moaned, hyping the situation up. "It's already bloodshot and you gonna have a black eye too. Word."

Nooni felt another wave of tears rising in her. She talked shit to the chicks she went to school with, and she rose up a lil bit on her sister every now and then, but she wasn't no street fighter. She was delicate, built for loving, and she damn sure didn't like getting boxed around by no man.

"Don't worry," Monique told her. "You can stay with us until the bruises go away. I'll send a note to your teachers and shit. That way they won't send no truant officers out looking for you."

Monique made a sympathetic noise and pulled Nooni's head to her breast as if to comfort her. "Don't worry, baby girl. When your sister makes the drop on that money we're gonna tear you off enough to make you forget all about them little love taps Truth gave you. For real," she said, stroking Nooni's soft cheek and loving how the girl felt snuggled all up in her arms. Lying and scheming made Monique horny, and right now her pussy was popping off like a whole packet of firecrackers.

"Yeah, don't worry," she told Nooni, steadily stroking the girl's tender flesh. "Mo-Mo gonna make you forget all about Truth's mean yellow ass."

CHAPTER 17

I got up early in the morning to get ready for my overnight trip to New York. I won't lie. I was scared shitless, and I knew I was taking a really big risk with what I was about to do. But Rita had called me in a panic. There was nobody else she could turn to for the kind of help she needed, so I had to go to her.

She had been totally hysterical last night when she told me Nooni had been kidnapped and some fools were holding her for two hundred grand.

"I feel like shit even calling you when you've already been through so much, Juicy, but I just don't know what else to do!"

"Do you think somebody really has her," I asked, "or is she just hanging out and scared she might get in trouble? Did it sound real?"

"Yes," Rita had whimpered. "It sounded real as hell and they texted me a video of her too. Check your phone when we get off, I just sent it to you. Nooni was all busted up. She was screaming for me, Juicy! Somebody was beating the shit outta her! Oh, my God...two hundred grand? What the hell makes them think I have that kind of money? I just don't know what to do!"

"Calm down," I told her, and for once it was me doing the soothing instead of her. "Don't worry about the money, I got that. We're gonna get her back, Rita. Nooni's gonna be okay because we're gonna get her back."

Rita told me the guy who called had warned her not to go to the cops, but that was a no-brainer because neither one of us trusted the police to look out for Nooni anyway. They would have labeled the situation a stupid teenage prank instead of a crisis, and that would have been the end of that.

But Rita had been convinced that Nooni was in real danger. We'd stayed on the phone for over three hours putting our heads together as we tried to figure out the best way to handle the situation. Giving Rita the money she needed wasn't an issue for me, but how to get it to her was going to be tricky.

Sending it through Western Union was out because not only wouldn't they accept or pay out such a large amount for a wire transfer, if we even tried to move anything over ten grand we'd be throwing up a red flag and leaving a paper trail that could get us busted for wire fraud and failure to report income to the IRS.

Mailing two hundred grand worth of cash in a box was a dumb idea for obvious reasons, and we nixed out sending it by carrier pigeon too. We were both getting exhausted, and Rita was at the end of her rope with fear. It took some trying, but I finally convinced her to do things my way.

"Uh-uh, Juicy," Rita told me over and over again. "You can't come back here!" she insisted. "It's too much for you. You haven't even healed up from your surgery yet. Besides, New York is way too dangerous. Niggahs got long memories on these streets. You know they're still gunning for you, right? Please, let's do this *my* way, okay? I'll catch a quick flight out there and pick up the money, and then I'll come right back and make the drop."

What she was suggesting just didn't make any sense to me. Rita had it backwards. I was the one who was all alone in the world with nothing and nobody to lose. If I got caught the Feds would automatically assume I was transporting drug money, and since every dime of the loot had come from G, most if it probably was. But still, if I got caught it would only be *my* ass on the line. Rita had two younger sisters to think about. If she got caught taking two-hundred-thousand dollars worth of dirty money across state lines then all three of them would be ass out.

"And what if the crew that snatched Nooni tries to call you back while you're on the airplane? You still don't know the drop spot," I reminded her. "How are you gonna answer the phone to find out where it is if you're up in the air? Besides, they said Nooni would be dead in 24 hours, didn't they? That doesn't even give you enough time to fly out here, pick up the money, and then catch a flight back. Nah," I told her, shaking my head. "We have to do this my way, girl."

When we finally hung up I watched the video clip that Rita had forwarded me, and my heart broke wide open for Nooni. She was getting pounded for real. It reminded me of all the beatings I had suffered through when G chained me to that pole down in his Dungeon. I was even more determined to help Rita save her sister after seeing all that.

I used my cell phone to make a quick airline reservation, then I climbed up on my dresser and removed the ceiling tiles to get to the safe that Gino had stashed up there. Using the combination that he had told me to memorize, I removed several bricks of hundred dollar bills and left the rest in there. It wasn't a whole lot left, but it was enough.

I had fallen asleep thinking about the stacks of cash that Gino had locked away in another safe and left with Sallie. Shit, between that money and what I was holding there was more than enough to get Nooni back. Two hundred grand was just a drop in the bucket.

I'd gotten up so early that my stomach was too nervous to even think about eating breakfast, so I took a shower and dressed in loose clothing. In the safety of my bedroom, I re-counted the money out twice, and then I wrapped two thick towels around a hundred and fifty thousand of it and stuck it in my Gucci travel bag. I spent over an hour breaking the rest down into small stacks and taping them to my stomach, down the front and back of my legs, under my titties, and as far up my back as I could reach.

At eight o'clock I walked out the house and past Gino's SUV, which was still parked in our driveway. I climbed into my BMW and drove to a nearby Walgreens where I did a little shopping. Twenty minutes later I was on my way to the airport. I parked in the long-term lot and then sat in the Green Gotcha and began putting on my disguise.

I was shitting bricks by the time I limped into the terminal to check-in for my flight. With a brace around my neck, another one on my leg, and my left arm in a sling, I looked like a straight-up car wreck victim. I got sympathetic glances from quite a few people, but I was still paranoid as hell. It seemed like random strangers were taking extra-long looks at me. I kept peeking around, swearing all out that somebody was following me. I finally hobbled into the bathroom to put some water on my face, and when I glanced in the mirror little Juicy-Mo from 136th Street looked scared as shit and guilty as hell.

But as bad as I was shaking, I walked through the metal detector and made it through the security screening with only one small problem. The body scanner beeped twice. It scared the shit out of me until I remembered that I had forgotten to remove my necklace before putting on the brace.

The TSA dude waved me over to the side, and since I could only use one arm he was nice enough to help me unsnap my neck brace and take off my gold chain. That was the only item he required me to remove, and when I walked back through the scanner again, I was good to go.

I had only checked in one small suitcase, and I kept my cash-heavy travel bag between my feet during the entire flight. The last time I had been on a plane was when G took me and Gino on a trip to Hawaii. I couldn't help but remember how me and my man had made sweet love in paradise, and how he had given me my very first dick-induced orgasm. I also couldn't help but remember how bad G had kicked my ass the next night, or how ashamed I had been when he made me dance butt naked on a coffee table right in front of Gino. I had been so humiliated!

I boarded the plane and sat next to a young black chick and her cute baby girl. I told her I had been in a car accident, and she told me her husband was serving in Iraq and she was flying to New York to meet him for his R&R.

Listening to the love in her voice as she talked about her man, and watching her take care of her daughter was so damn hard on me. It took everything I had not to sit there and cry my heart out. I thought about Gino and our unborn son, and I knew I would never have what this girl had. Never.

But as bad as I was hurting, I knew I was doing the right thing by helping Rita and Nooni. For the past few months my life had been all about grief and rage, and totally without purpose. By forcing myself to go out into the world, even though I was scared out of my mind, I was really helping myself too.

The flight was all good and we landed in New York right on time. I texted Rita and told her I was on my way to baggage claim, and after saying goodbye to the young mother and her baby girl, I played my role and rode one of those transport carts all the way to the luggage area.

Holding my carry-on bag tightly, I stood right at the front of the crowd and waited for my suitcase to come out. I was ready to get moving, but of course I wouldn't be going anywhere near Harlem. The plan was for Rita to pick me up at baggage claim and help me out to the car with all my braces and bandages, and then she was gonna drive me to a hotel that was right next to the airport. Once we were securely behind a locked door I would hand over the money, and she would take it to Harlem so she could make the drop and try to get Nooni back.

I had made a return reservation for a flight back to Cali for six the next morning, and that meant I would be on New York soil for less than twenty-four hours, which was cool with me.

It was taking forever for the luggage to come off the plane and down the chute. My back was itching from the hundred-dollar bills that were taped to my skin, and all I could think about was getting in that hotel room so everything could be over with.

There were a whole lot of tired, anxious-looking people gathered around waiting for their luggage. I kept scanning the crowd searching for Rita, but she was nowhere in sight. New York City traffic was unpredictable, and I figured she was probably running a little late. I checked my phone to see if she had texted me back, but there was nothing.

No calls, no messages. Nothing.

A few minutes later I almost jumped outta my neck brace when I saw my designer suitcase coming toward me on the conveyor belt. Since Rita was nowhere around, I decided to grab my bag and go outside to wait for her. But just as I reached over and gripped the shiny gold handle on my suitcase, my whole world got straight fucked up.

"*There* she is!" A high-pitched voice rang out behind me and a heavy hand of authority landed on my shoulder.

"That's her! Arrest her, officer! That chick is *transporting!* She ain't nothing but a money mule, and every dime she's holding is *dirty!*"

I stood up looking shocked as shit. When I turned around I coulda sworn I was in the Twilight Zone.

Because standing between two NYPD cops and pointing her accusing finger in my facc as she tried to bury my ass deep in a New York City trick bag, was the last person in the world that I ever thought would betray me.

It was my number one homegirl. The sister I'd never had. It was my very best friend in world.

It was Rita.

TO BE CONTINUED...

Order

GREED: THE 3RD DEADLY SIN

at

www.Amazon.com or www.BN.com

PART THREE
OF NOIRE'S BLOCKBUSTER
URBAN EROTIC SERIAL TALE!

Juicy-Mo is caught in a web of lies and greed!

Real friends are hard to come by in the heart of the hood, and when two hundred grand in cash is on the line, even your closest friend might do you dirty!

Lured back into the heart of New York City, Juicy faces some harsh realities when the cuffs get slapped on her and she gets thrown in the bing.

Will Juicy come out of this with her heart and soul intact? Or will these gut-wrenching acts of greed set her up for even more drama?

WARNING!

This here ain't no romance
It's an urban erotic tale,
Paper chasers gettin' doe
While Juicy's stuck in jail!
Don't let 'em catch you sleepin'
Cause they're schemin' for ya stash
Sticky fingers reachin'
In ya pockets for your cash!
Even when they're fat and full
They want more than they need
They're plottin' on your paper too
This Deadly Sin is **GREED!**

Find out more in...
G-SPOT 2: THE SEVEN DEADLY SINS
Greed: The 3rd Deadly Sin

The Urban Erotic Serial Saga Continues!

NOIRE

G-Spot 2:
The Seven Deadly Sins
An Urban Erotic Serial Tale Told in 7 Parts

GREED: THE 3RD DEADLY SIN

by

Noire

www.AskNoire.com
www.GSpot2.com
www.TheGSpotSaga.com

CHAPTER 1

My mouth was hanging wide open as the police made their move on me.

"Wait a goddamn minute!" I hollered as a fat white cop ripped my suitcase from my hand. A black DT in plainclothes was there too, and without a word he snatched the phony sling off my arm and slapped a pair of cuffs on me.

"What the hell are y'all *doing*?" I shrieked as the brothah bent me over and hiked my arms up behind my back. "*Rita*!" I screamed as she took off walking ahead of me. "Rita! What the fuck is going on?"

I stumbled through the terminal way too shocked to care about the nosy people who were pointing and staring at me. As the cops shoved me along I didn't give a damn about the gwap of cash that was hidden in my Gucci bag, or the stacks of hundred dollar bills that were taped to my body neither.

Nah, my heart was on petro, and my mind was lost in a tunnel of confusion. The only thing that was coming through loud and clear was the fact that I had been played. Set up. Stabbed in the back. Straight up *betrayed*.

I couldn't believe it. It just didn't seem real.

But as those cops muscled me through the crowd behind Rita and the tall DT, the truth was colder than ice.

"Rita!" I screamed again as I struggled in my handcuffs. "*Rita*! What's going on?"

She had taken my suitcase from the white cop and now the DT was wheeling it behind him with my carry-on bag sitting on top.

"Stop fuckin' *playing*, Rita!" I shrieked. "Why the hell am I getting arrested?"

My girl didn't even look back. She just kept right on booking up ahead of us like she'd never seen me before. Her high heels stabbed the floor fast and furious as she hauled ass through the crowded baggage claim area and toward the exit doors. Just before she stepped outside, she glanced back at me one quick time. She didn't say a word, but the guilty look in her eyes was enough to say it all.

As soon as we hit the sidewalk Rita and the black dude hopped into a bright red Mustang. I heard a ripping sound as one of the white cops loosened the Velcro on my neck brace and yanked it off. Flinging it in the gutter, he mushed my head down and tossed me in the back seat of the squad car that was parked right behind them.

"You ain't gotta fuckin' manhandle me!" I snapped.

"Be quiet, bitch," was all he said.

I changed my tune real quick as the cops climbed in the front seat and we pulled off behind the Mustang. "Listen officers," I attempted to explain through the bulletproof partition. "There must be some kinda mistake. This has to be a big mistake! The girl up there in that red car is my best friend," I said. "I swear to God I'm not a money mule. I'm supposed to be helping her, that's all. *Helping* her."

They cold igged me as we followed the Mustang off the airport grounds.

What the hell is happening? I tried to find a way to rationalize this shit so it would make some sense. But as I rode handcuffed in the backseat of that squad car I realized that *nothing* made any sense, and that's when I got so scared my whole body started shaking.

What the *fuck* was Rita *doing?*

Something about this just wasn't right...I could feel it all in my bones. I had never been to jail in my life, and I could hear Grandmother in my ear promising that if I ever got arrested she would disown my little ass.

I knew two-hundred-grand wasn't a whole lot of paper in the drug game, but it was definitely way more than you could legally transport across state lines. The fact that the money had come from G's criminal operations made it dirty enough to put my ass straight *under* a jail, and that freaked me out. It wasn't like I could lie and say I had hit the lottery back in Cali, or that I'd gotten a phat income tax refund or nothing legitimate like that.

Nah, there was only one logical reason that a nineteen-year-old black chick like me would be carrying bank the way I was carrying it.

Drugs.

And if I knew it then the cops damn sure knew it too.

I was boxed in and fuming mad, but my heart had been cut real deep too. Tears filled my eyes and rolled down my cheeks. How could Rita *do* some shit like this to me? She knew how bad I had been hurting! She knew what kind of heart-wrecking shit that I had gone through. She knew I had just lost my baby *and* my man!

That *greedy* fuckin' bitch! Her phony ass had been a red-carpet actress playing a role when she came out west to see me. I thought about the way she had fed me and bathed me and comforted me... All that fake-ass sympathy! It wasn't nothing but a ploy to get up in my pockets and get next to my doe.

Yeah, my girl had tricked me out for real. Here I was trying to help her sister out of a fucked up situation, and in return she had shit on me.

I was so, so scared. I didn't wanna go to jail!

As we rode through the borough of Queens, I stared out the window with tears steady falling from my eyes. I hadn't seen or smelled New York City in about eight months, but even from the back of a police car I could tell all the flavors were still the same.

We had been zipping down the streets for only a few minutes when we made a right turn and started heading out over a body of water.

"W-w-where are y'all taking me?" I yelled to the officers on the other side of the partition.

Neither one of them answered, but I knew they had heard me. All I could do was sit in that nasty backseat with my hands cuffed behind me, just like all the other criminals who had ridden back there before me.

"For real," I yelled again as we drove onto a long ass bridge. I frowned as we started rolling over the East River with LaGuardia airport just off to our right. "Where am I going? What damn bridge is this?"

"It's the Francis Buono," the cop who was driving replied. As shook as my ass was he sounded bored as hell. "You're going the same place all the rest of the criminals go. To the Rock."

CHAPTER 2

"Calm down, baby," Dutchy Gaines said as he drove with one hand and tried to soothe Rita's nerves with the other one. His baby was wildin' out. Kicking, screaming, banging her fists on the dashboard and rocking furiously back and forth in her seat, straight going crazy.

"I *knew* something wasn't right!" Rita shrieked and stomped her feet on the floorboards. "I just *knew* it! It was Monique and her crew! Them bitches tried to set us up! They're the ones who snatched Nooni! They was scheming to get that money and to get *Juicy* too!"

"Don't worry shawty, we got this," Dutchy said calmly as he sped down the street making sure the squad car stayed in his rearview mirror. "We can handle this shit, baby." He reached for the phone clip on his waist. "Just lemme make a few calls, sugar, and everythang is gonna be straight. We gonna take good care of Juicy. Your friend is gonna be okay, baby. Word."

"But did you see the way she *looked* at me?" Rita wailed with her face contorted in pain. "She thinks I fuckin' *set her up*! My girl is gonna *hate* me!"

"She'll understand later," Dutchy muttered. "And then she'll be thanking you."

Rita could only sob as her dude made contact with his peeps. He barked all kinds of instructions into his cell phone and made the risky, complex arrangements for Juicy that Rita prayed would save her friend's life.

She was beside herself with guilt and anger. The cop car Juicy was riding in was right behind them, but Rita couldn't bring herself to glance back. Not even through the side mirror. The expression of terror and disbelief on her friend's face had punched her right in the heart. To have Juicy thinking she was a snake and had betrayed her was almost as bad as if she had actually done that shit for real.

This was so fucked up! Life had already handed Juicy more than one chick should have to bear. If there had been any other way to keep her girl safe Rita would have taken that path. But as it was, Monique and the dudes she was rolling with had caught her out there and blindsided her.

Rita had spotted them as she walked through the airport terminal looking for the flight arrival board so she could see where the baggage from Juicy's flight would be unloading. At first she had walked past it, and when she realized she missed it she quickly turned around and doubled back the way she had come.

And that's when she saw the crew from Harlem lurking on the low. Standing out in the crowd of frenzied travelers, they looked like a stalking pack of wolves on the prowl. It was Monique and three gutta-looking youngstas, and every nerve in Rita's body told her they had been scoping her out, watching her the way a hungry snake eyeballs a big fat rat.

Rita and Monique had locked eyes for a quick second, and then Monique had ducked behind an obese white lady and tried to dip into a bookstore and hide behind a magazine rack.

Rita had frozen in her tracks. She had come up in the bowels of Harlem, and suddenly her nose was straight burning from the foul odor of street grime in the air.

Instead of continuing in the direction of the arrival board, she had jetted toward the nearest exit and ran back to Dutchy's whip with a quickness.

"Monique is in there!" she'd shrieked, jumping in the ride and gripping her man's arm in terror. "That skank from the G-Spot! She's got a crew of predator-looking niggahs with her too. I coulda sworn they were following me! Why the hell would she be tracking me way out here in Queens?"

Dutchy had frowned. "I don't know but dig, the whole time I been sitting here waiting for you there's been more Harlem cats sliding through here than a little bit. Them niggahs is piled up in mad whips. Check out that black beemer SUV parked about three cars back. I peeped it when we were coming in off the highway." He peered in the rearview mirror and shook his head. "Yo, that's the same fuckin' car I seen parked outside your crib the other night when I was leaving, babe. That's word."

Rita was a college math major and had no problem adding shit up. She had a calculating brain and she studied probabilities and logic just for fun. And right now her math-mind told her that the probability of Monique, or any young gangsta, showing up at the airport looking shifty as fuck under random circumstances was almost zero. Yeah, those G-Spot bastards had been laying in the cut outside her crib, and they had followed her all the way to Queens too. Running into Monique on the street that day wasn't just a coincidence either. That chick had been out there for a reason. She didn't just "happen" to walk by. But the question was, why? Why would Monique be scoping her out, and then trail her to the airport to pick up the money from Juicy?

There was only one logical conclusion and Rita had already come to it. Them niggahs had snatched her sister Nooni, and what they wanted in return was plain as day. And as bad as Rita wanted to get her hands on that money and make the drop so she could get her little sister back, there was no way in hell she was gonna trade Juicy's life for a *goddamn* thing!

Not even for her sister.

"They're gunning for her," Rita had moaned as she sat in Dutchy's car trembling in fear. The memory of Juicy jumping out of a taxicab after breaking up outta the G-Spot popped into her mind crystal clear, and Rita shuddered with sympathy for her girl. "This shit just can't be happening! I should've never let her come back to New York!"

She had turned to her man, crying and pleading in desperation. "We gotta get her outta here, Dutchy! We've gotta do something quick. 'Cause if they catch her they're going to kill her."

So, with only fifteen minutes until Juicy's plane was scheduled to touch down on the ground, Rita and Dutchy came up with a desperate plan to save Juicy from the greedy bloodsuckers that ruled Harlem's underworld.

"It's gotta be this way," Dutchy insisted. "Don't worry, baby. I got people on the inside. Plenty of peeps. She'll be real safe. She's gonna have good eyes on her the whole time."

Dutchy had big-time law enforcement connections and the plan would probably work, but it was grimy and Rita just didn't like it. Her girl was going to freak out. She was going to be traumatized. She was going to think real bad of her.

Yeah, Dutchy reasoned with his woman as he put in call after call to members of his family who worked for various enforcement agencies all throughout the city of New York. Juicy was damn sure gonna be traumatized and all that other shit Rita was talking too. *But,* as Dutchy was quick to hip his girl, if they could get Juicy someplace where Monique and her crew couldn't follow her or get their hands on her, she was also gonna stay *alive.*

With a heavy and reluctant heart, Rita had given in. Dutchy was right. Juicy had to go to jail.

CHAPTER 3

Juicy didn't know it, but there were at least ten vehicles rolling behind her in straight-up criminal caravan.

"Y'all niggahs done *fucked* up!" Monique screamed from the passenger seat of the first car, a black SUV. "Y'all straight fucked the whole shit up!"

Truth drove furiously, darting down the city streets and cutting off traffic as he struggled to keep up with the cop car that was transporting Juicy.

Monique was in a panic as she watched her two hundred grand speeding up ahead of her and getting the hell away. This had been a major fuckin' operation and she couldn't believe how bad Rita had just fucked it up. They'd set up a dragnet and put a nice-ass bounty on Juicy's head, and there were shit-loads of youngstas riding behind her right now who were just itchin' to collect it.

Monique didn't understand it. Where the fuck did those cops come from? There had been ten carloads of slangers circling the airport terminals on the hunt for Juicy. They had been so close! So fuckin' *close*! And now her big opportunity was about to slip through her fingers.

"I *told* y'all how to do this shit!" she fumed. Her breath hitched in her throat and her whole body felt hot. "But *nooooo*. Y'all just had to fuck it up! Y'all just *had* to!"

Bilal, a dreadlocked corner boy with a killer's heart, kept quiet in the backseat, and Twan, a come-up with a reputation for being hotheaded wore a mean-mug as he stared out the window, but Truth was sick of Monique's shit and he popped right off.

"How the *fuck* did *we* fuck it up, Mo? Huh? Tell me how? Rita turned around and busted *your* greedy-ass game! So how the fuck is that all on *us*?"

"Because y'all stupid asses was walkin' all *on* her ass, that's how! Y'all idiot niggahs got too fuckin' close! Just like you getting too close to that cop car right now! Learn how to back the fuck off, stupid ass!"

Monique knew she had to do something to make this shit right, and she had to do it quick.

"Stay with they asses!" she ordered as a minivan turned the corner and cut in front of Truth.

"I thought you just said to back off?"

Monique reached over and slapped the dog shit outta him.

"Don't play with me muthafucka!" she spit in a rage. She didn't know if the rest of their caravan was still following her, but she knew she couldn't lose sight of Juicy. "Stay close enough where we can follow them, but not so close that they can peep us. I gotta know where them cops are taking her. Get closer! Go around that raggedy-ass minivan! Don't let them muthafuckas shake you!"

Truth was burning with fury but Monique didn't give a rat's ass. Her mind was everywhere at once as she tried to figure out exactly what the hell had just gone down.

Deep inside she knew Truth was right, and that Rita had peeped her at the most fucked-up moment possible. But what the hell was that crazy chick thinking, getting Juicy knocked like that? If Juicy went down then the money went down as evidence right along with her. That meant everybody was fucked. Juicy was fucked with the law, Monique and Salida were fucked outta their big plans, and Rita was fucked outta getting her sister back!

"We gotta get to her..." Monique whispered through clenched teeth. "We gotta get that goddamn *money*!"

They followed the cop car for just a couple of miles through Queens. It was a borough that Monique wasn't all that familiar with. But when the cruiser turned to go over a bridge that stretched out over a murky river, she was damn sure familiar with the sign that repped for New York's Boldest! It read, *City of New York Correction Department.*

Rikers Island.

Monique knew the joint well. She had done a couple of bids on The Rock back in the day. She had been busted on charges that ranged from prostitution to larceny, and Monique had sworn a long time ago that Rikers had seen the last of her ass.

"Go straight!" she screamed on Truth, just in time for him to avoid following the cop car as it turned onto the bridge.

"Oh hell, no, don't get on that bridge," Monique muttered as Truth swung the steering wheel and continued going straight across the intersection. "We don't *even* wanna get on that goddamn bridge!"

Two minutes later, Truth had found the highway and the BMW X5 was heading in the opposite direction.

"Where now?" he asked. His voice was filled with rage and bitterness.

Monique was about to answer him when the cell phone she'd been gripping vibrated and shook her so bad she almost dropped it down the side crevice of her seat.

Catching it, she stared at the caller ID and cursed. The last person in the world she wanted to talk to right now was Salida. Monique had no desire to be stuttering and stumbling all over her words tryna justify shit to that over-baked piece of chicken! Because on the real, no matter how she looked at it, and no matter how she attempted to snazz that shit up, there was just no good way to explain that their prized little fishy had just jumped off the fuckin' hook and was about to swim across a channel in New York's East River.

CHAPTER 4

We pulled up in the back of a wide, red-brick building. Taking my Gucci bag full of money with them, both cops got out of the car without saying a word, and when their doors slammed shut the only thing I was left with was cold silence to keep me company.

The red sports car that Rita had ridden in was parked up ahead. I sat in the backseat of the cruiser trying my best to catch a glimpse of her, but it was hard to see through that grimy Plexiglas partition.

But what I did see was the Black detective who had flashed me his badge standing outside with the two cops that had busted me. Two correction officers in uniform had joined them. A white guy, and a real tall sistah. The five of them seemed to be having a heated-ass conversation about something very important.

Me.

There was a bunch of back and forth hand moving and head shaking. The DT was hyped. He patted my Gucci bag, then pointed at each one of the officers in turn and counted off on his fingers. He leaned in close to the COs, and nodded rapidly, like he was trying to get everybody to feel what he was saying.

I guess they finally did because suddenly the detective wiped his forehead and nodded slowly. He shook hands with the cops, hugged the female correction officer, and dapped the male correction officer out. Then they all walked through a doorway and disappeared inside the building.

All I could do was sit there and wait. I'd had to pee real bad when I got off the airplane but I'd forgotten all about it when they slapped the cuffs on me. But the urge was back now. Real strong. I was so damn uncomfortable. If I leaned back in my seat the handcuffs cut into my wrists. If I leaned forward my bladder screamed from holding my pee. So, I leaned to the right against the car door and tried to find a neutral position in my misery.

They left me sitting in that car for so long that I nodded off. Yeah, I was shook, and yeah I knew I was going to jail, but I was in shock too, and my body just shut down on me. I couldn't keep my eyes open, even in the face of getting locked up.

I don't know how much time passed, but the next thing I knew the door I was leaning against was snatched open and I almost fell straight out of the car.

"Let's go." The white male correction officer who had been standing outside earlier grabbed my arm and helped me out of the car. As soon as I stood up I looked around for Rita, but the little red car that my best friend had been riding in was now gone. I looked up at the cold stone building they were about to take me in. I was so hurt and mad that I didn't care if I never saw Rita's treacherous ass again, yet still...a part of me had never felt so alone.

$$$$$

"Yo, you fuckin' with me, right?" Rabbit barked into his cell phone. He paused holding the blunt he was rolling in his hands. It was first thing Saturday morning and he hadn't had his wake up smoke yet, and these niggahs was already making noise in his ear.

"Y'all niggahs had ya eyes on her and neither one of y'all didn't see the bitch when she dipped?"

"I'm telling you man," Izzy reported through the line. "We sat outside her crib the whole fuckin' night just like we was supposed to. Nobody went inside, and she didn't come out neither. At least not until around eight o'clock this morning."

Rabb gripped the cell phone between his shoulder and his ear while he packed the seedless weed inside a cigar leaf. "That's impossible, niggah. Ace said she was taking two hundred g's to New York. That shit wasn't stashed up in her pussy, yo. Either somebody dropped it off or she went and picked it up from somewhere."

"We was on watch all night long, man. Nobody went in, and nobody came out. When she left this morning we followed her. She stopped at a Walgreen's for a minute, and then she went straight to the airport and parked her ride. She took the beemer. The green convertible."

"Did y'all go inside and check her crib?"

"Yeah, we went back and tossed it the best we could. Security musta seen us going in, though. Some old white dude came banging on the door so we had to dip out the window real quick. But from what we could see wasn't nothing in there."

Rabb cursed. After all these months this bitch was still a problem. The streets had cooled off after the mob smoked that midget from Compton, so when Ace called and gave them another crack at getting at that doe, Rabb had jumped on it.

"Yo," he told Izzy. "Go back to that fuckin' airport, man. Get up in her whip and let me know what you find. Go over that shit with a magnifying glass, you hear? Search every inch of it. I got a feeling that chick got something hiding up in that bitch."

Rabb clicked off his cell and went back to rolling his spliff. His cousin had promised him a nice piece of change if he could figure out where the girl was holding that money, and with the economy tanking and good licks getting hard to come by on the streets, Rabb wanted that paper.

$$$$$

Salvatore McCain stared out the window at the green BMW convertible that was parked in his mother's backyard. The phone call he had gotten from Juicy the night before still lingered on his mind. It had been pretty late when her home number flashed across his cell phone. He had just finished jacking his dick, and he was kicked back enjoying a Philly blunt packed with prime Columbian Gold and her call had caught him by surprise.

"Hey Sallie," Juicy had said. "I need a favor."

"Then you got one," he'd answered. Sallie had hung out with Gino and Juicy a lot before they took that hit on their wedding day, but now with Gino dead, the Juicy he had known seemed gone too.

"You know you're good for anything," he told her, playing the big-brother role. "Just tell me what you need me to do and it's done."

"I gotta make a quick run," she'd said. "I'm only gonna be gone for about a day, but I want you to look out for me just in case I need something."

Sallie had immediately grown suspicious.

"Something like what?"

"Something like that safe Gino left with you when we first came out here."

His heart had pounded. "Right. I'd forgotten about that safe," he lied. "But hell yeah. Absolutely. It's right where Gino left it. If you need it just give me a call and I'll bring it to you. But is everything cool, Juicy? You wanna tell me where you're going?"

Juicy had hesitated, and when she spoke again her words sounded real shady.

"I need to go check on a friend. It's all good. I won't be gone long."

"Does Renata know you're going?" Sallie pressed.

"Nah. You know how she can be. I didn't tell her because I don't want her to worry. Besides, I'm coming right back. She'll never even know I left."

Sallie had nodded as his mind worked to put all the pieces together. "Cool. No problem. Your secret is safe with me. Do you want me to check on your crib and bring in the mail, or maybe you need a ride to the airport or something?"

"Nah, I have an early flight so I'm gonna drive myself. But just in case something comes up, I'll text you my parking area and leave my keys under the floor mat."

"No problem. Be careful out there. You know you can count on me, so if there's anything you need, just give me a call."

Slick Sallie had taken a taxi to the airport at eight-thirty that morning, and walked over to the area that Juicy had texted to him. The key to her convertible had been right under the floor mat where she said she would leave it, and he had paid the parking fee and driven it right off the airport grounds.

Sallie had come straight home and parked the car behind his mother's orchard house, and for the last hour he had been sitting there staring at it. He appeared to be calm and deep in thought, but in reality his heart was pounding and his blood was surging with excitement.

It was as if something spiritual had come over him as he thought about the possibilities that had opened up for him. It was almost divine. Like a lucky lottery ticket had fallen into his lap complete with all the winning numbers.

Sallie lit a blunt and took three long puffs. Then he clipped it in an ashtray and forced himself to breathe deeply. Nobody knew Juicy had left town except him. This was his prime opportunity, and he needed to be clear-minded and level headed so he could take full advantage of it. His destiny had just manifested, and there was no way he was gonna let it slide through his fingers. Slick Sallie knew exactly what he had to do. And for the next thirty minutes he sat staring at the sexy green convertible he had stolen from the airport, as he came up with his grand, life-changing plan.

$$$$

"Yo, man, her car is gone."

"Niggah what you mean her fuckin' car is gone?"

"It ain't there. Me and Zero looked all over the parking lot. Somebody musta took that shit. It's gone."

Rabbit shook his head.

"Man, ain't nobody take that car. Y'all was just lookin' in the wrong place. You must be at the wrong terminal, stupid ass. Ace said that chick got locked down as soon as she got to New York so I know she ain't come back here and moved no car. That shit is right where she left it. Go back and look again."

"I'm telling you," Izz protested. "That shit ain't there! We crisscrossed and circled that lot so many fuckin' times that security musta got suspicious. Cop cars started swinging through left and right and we had to break out 'cause Zero had some powder and two dirty gats on him. But for real, slime, I saw where that bitch parked at. Her shit ain't there no more. I swear it's gone."

"Muthafucka!" Rabbit kicked over a garbage can in his small kitchen. "It's gotta be there, fool! Y'all niggahs just didn't look good enough. A'ight. Don't go back today 'cause security is prolly on the lookout now. Wait 'til tomorrow night when it gets dark outside, then go back and look again. I swear to God, Izz, if I gotta go through there and find that ride myself I'ma slump both of y'all niggahs! Word!"

"A'ight," Izzy sighed even though he knew what he knew. "We'll go back out there tomorrow, right after it gets dark."

CHAPTER 5

Growing up in Harlem I had heard a whole bunch of horrors stories about Rikers but I had never stepped foot on the island before, not even on a visit.

A lot of girls around my way got sent to The Rock for various petty crimes, mostly dealing with selling ass or buying drugs, or occasionally for cutting some niggah with the sharp edge of a beer bottle.

But no matter how scary the jailhouse stories had sounded, they were nothing compared to the Kool-Aid my heart was pumping as the cops led me into the Rose M. Singer Center for women.

"Keep your mouth shut in there," the male C.O. warned me as he opened the door and pushed me inside. He was a skinny white dude with a patchy red birthmark on his nose. "Don't offer no extra information, and don't tell nobody your real name."

"What?" I was straight confused.

"You carrying?" he asked, stopping me right outside another doorway.

"Huh?" I said dumbly.

"You got anything on you? Knives, needles, anything sharp that's gonna stick me or hurt me?"

I shook my head. "No. But I got some money on me."

His eyebrows shot up. "There's more? Where?"

I swallowed hard. "All over me."

He took me into a small room and patted me down in a quick, but thorough manner before taking the cuffs off me. He had been all about the bizz when he told me to spread 'em, but then out of nowhere he told me to strip too.

I didn't know what was up, but I knew something was shady. I thought he was gonna try to bust a look at my titties or something, but all he did was order me to take off my clothes and remove all the bills that were taped to my body and put them on the table. He even turned his back and gave me the privacy to do it.

"I'm done," I said when I had finally gotten all the money off me. Most of it was damp from my sweat but he didn't seem to give a fuck as he took a trash bag out of a small garbage can near the door. He emptied the trash into the naked can, then dumped the money into the trash bag and tied the end in a knot.

"If anybody asks, you're being detained for transporting," he told me as he handcuffed me again and led me out of the room. "Not money, but drugs." He chuckled. "Every fuckin' body is in here for drugs."

"But don't I get a chance to make bail?"

"Nope. You're not even going before a judge."

"But hold up, don't I get to make a phone call?"

"Negative again. No calls and no visitors."

I opened my mouth to say something else, but he shut me right up.

151

"Listen. You can do this my way or you can do it the hard way, all right? My way? You got no priors. You get a nice private cell complete with the finest protection our hardworking corrections department can provide. In a couple of weeks you'll be arraigned for carrying a small amount of crack cocaine, and the judge will offer you a ninety-day treatment program and eventually expunge the charge from your record. Simple.

"The hard way? You go down for theft, transporting drug money, money laundering, and every other RICO charge we can strum up against you. Plus, we'll take our special protection off you. You're a fine ass chick. Every dyke in the joint will be looking to wife you. And at some point, during the middle of the night, somebody might wanna have a little conversation with you. You know, some of that pillow talking y'all ladies like to do. Ain't no telling who might slip in your bed and get comfy under your covers. Now, did you catch all that, or do you need to write it down?"

My situation was real clear and I submitted to it real quick. His way sounded a whole lot better than the hard way, and when he finally turned me over to the Black female correction officer I kept my mouth shut and walked inside the facility, not as Juicy Monique Stanfield, but under the bogus name of Yvette Williams.

$$$$$

"This shit is just unbelievable," Salida snapped as she paced the floor in the cut room. Her strides were long and measured, like a panther that was just about to fuck up its prey. She lit another cigarette and blew the smoke out her nose.

To say she was pissed off wouldn't have been saying shit. Salida hated stupid bitches. She could work with ignorance and she could even overlook incompetence, but stupidity just fucked her up all the way around.

It had been a real smooth plan, using Rita to get to Juicy. They'd had cars full of hoods at the airports, and almost a hundred young come-ups from the G-Spot roster had been spread out all over town just a' waiting for Juicy to hit the streets. They had sent crews to every business that G had either owned or shook down. Pizza shops, cleaners, bodegas, restaurants and check cashing places, they'd put the word out on Juicy everywhere. The order was to snatch up any chick that so much as looked like Juicy and bring her ass in and collect a cash reward.

But even with all that street power they'd failed. Juicy had slipped through their fingers and was now locked up in jail, where not even they could get to her.

Salida smirked as she paced. They had already gone over the scenario three or four times, but she kept on grilling Monique because she knew the stripper was lying out of her ass.

"So," she went in again on the greased-up bitch sitting next to her desk. "You're trying to tell me that Rita spotted Truth right before Juicy's plane landed?"

Monique nodded as Salida sat down at her desk and unlocked her top drawer and slid it open.

"I swear that's what happened," Monique said. "I warned him to fall back so she wouldn't see him but that niggah is young and hardheaded! He was driving all up in their trunk on the way there, and when we got inside the airport terminal he was damn near stepping on the back of Rita's shoes."

Salida stared at her. She didn't know what the hell G had been thinking when he hired Monique, but everything about her idiot-ass was completely wrong for the new direction Salida planned to take the G-Spot in.

There was no denying that Monique's lush chocolate body was fuckable and built for comfort, but Salida was trying to create a whole new image for the G-Spot. She was about to brand that baby. Make it a real franchise. Get some white pussy up in the house. Some Puerto Ricans and some Asians too.

Monique started flapping her gums some more. "And you know what else, Mizz Salida? That dumb-ass boy got the nerve to holla about how he wanna be equal partners with us. You just can't tell these lil pissy-tail niggahs nothing these days, ain't that right Mizz Salida? These lil niggahs think they got the plans all figured out."

Partners? The older woman glared at Monique with a look of pure disgust on her face. With us?

Salida lost it. She reached over and mushed the shit outta Monique. She rammed her dome so hard Mo's neck snapped back and her head cracked against the wall.

"It was your stupid-ass who fucked up the plan!"

For a second Monique looked stunned, and then her hood instincts kicked in. She jumped outta her seat and reached down in her back pocket at the same time. She was about to flick her pocketknife open, but she pulled up short when she saw Salida's hand resting on something cold and black in her top drawer.

"Oh, so you strapped, huh, Mizz Salida?" Monique breathed heavily. She wasn't nobody's punk, and bitches didn't mush her everyday and get away with it. Not even old bitches. But Monique was a lot smarter than Salida thought she was. She knew if she bucked she was gonna be in a gunfight, and the only thing she had on her right now was a pocketknife.

Danger danced in Monique's cold eyes, but there was a shred of fear there too. And it was that tiny slice of weakness that Salida honed in on.

"You don't want none of this," Salida said calmly. Even if she hadn't checked Monique with her piece, Salida would have taken the young hoe's pocketknife and stuck it down her throat. "I swear to God you don't want none."

Monique nodded as she stared at the .38 Special that was now in Salida's hand. The door to the cut room slam-locked from the inside, and the only key that could open it was on a bright pink coil around Salida's wrist.

But the old broad had it right. Monique didn't want none. Salida had a crazy bug crawling around in her head. Monique could see it shining bright in her eyes, and regardless of her personal pride or anything else, Monique wanted to live to see another day.

Salida smirked as she waited for Monique to make a move. She nodded when she saw the survival senses creep into Monique's eyes as the girl sat her ass back down in the chair.

Things had just changed drastically between the two women and both of them knew it. Salida knew she still needed Monique to do some things, and Monique damn sure needed her. But a mush wasn't something most Harlem girls could brush off and forget about. Salida had disrespected Monique in a major way, and she was gonna have to play her extra close from now on. But she was good with that. There was more than one way to cook a bitch's coochie, and later, when the time was exactly right, Salida was gonna burn Monique's ass like a cat on a hot tin roof.

CHAPTER 6

This shit is all fucked up," Ace muttered under his breath as he sat tossin' 'em back at the bar Saturday afternoon. It was a good thing he hadn't put Pluto down on the little side deal he had cut with his cousin Rabbit. Not only had his plan gone bad, but Juicy had gotten knocked before Salida's plan could work too, and now they were ass-out all the way around.

Ace shook his head and tossed back another shot of Hen-dawg straight-up. He had hesitated in going behind Pluto's back and cutting the outside deal, but his son was on some other shit these days and they just didn't see eye-to-eye the way they used to. Salida had convinced him their situation was too critical to wait around for a buster to see the light, and Ace had agreed. He'd kept his manz in the dark, and that had ended up being a good thing because his Cali niggahs had messed shit up again.

"This shit is all fucked up," Ace muttered again. And he meant that shit.

$$$$$

"Oh, so you mean between the two of y'all smart mouth bitches y'all couldn't come up with one solid plan?"

If Monique thought she had been hot when Ace and Pluto came up short when they went out to Cali, that was nothing compared to the way Pluto clowned now that the shoe was on the other foot.

They were driving through Harlem and all Monique could do was stare out the window as her man beefed so hard spit flew outta his mouth with each word. She hadn't even told him that she had gotten her forehead mushed, or about the gat Salida had pulled on her either. She was saving that bomb so she could drop it during another battle.

"It was your nephew's fault," Monique lied. "He got too damn hyped and he didn't follow the plan."

"Truth is a tyke!" Pluto came at her. "You gonna send a young'un like him to put in a man's work?"

Monique shrugged. "Salida told me to send him."

"I don't know why you listened to Salida's psycho ass anyway!" Pluto fumed. "You thought getting that money was gonna be easy didn't you? What? You thought you and Salida was gonna do something me and Ace couldn't do?"

Monique watched the urban scenery flash by as the big fella pushed the whip down the avenue at top speed.

"I bet that greedy bitch sent your dumb ass inside to make the pick-up too, didn't she? That way, if somebody got caught holding all that dirty loot it wouldn't be her!"

The same thought had crossed Monique's mind too, but it was a risk she had been

155

willing to take. She'd reasoned that it was better to make the run herself and get the money in her hands, than it was to trust Salida to bring the money back and dish her off a fair share.

"That bitch got you and Ace both eating out ya own asses! I keep telling y'all G stuck her ass up on a high shelf for a reason! The bitch is throwed-off! 7:30! Straight-up crazy!"

Pluto jerked the steering wheel and took a corner so hasty it felt like the car was careening on two tires. Monique reached up and held on to the overhead handle and prayed he didn't clip no old-ass lady tryna cross the street and bounce her off his bumper.

"I'm telling you, Miss Dumbness," he warned, spinning the steering wheel with one hand so he could shake his fat finger in her face with the other one. "You better stop following behind Salida's ass, ya heard? She's gon' fuck you up, Mo! Word. That bitch don't even like you. I see the way she be grilling you when you ain't looking. It's ill, man. You keep running your mouth to her and doing whatever she says. She's gonna walk your clueless ass right off a cliff!"

Monique knew better than to challenge Pluto's theory. He would open the car door and toss her ass out so fast she'd be eating concrete for dinner. Instead, she tried to soothe him the best way she knew how. She catered to his ego and most of all to his stomach.

"Yep, you been telling me," she said in an agreeable tone. "And I been listening, Daddy. I know you're way smarter than Mizz Salida is. And I'ma be real careful around that bitch from now on," she said. And she was dead serious about that shit too.

Monique had seen the future when Salida got her up in the cut room and bitched her out for messing everything up. Monique wasn't the type who could take a whole lotta down-talking from no female, and she hadn't liked the way Salida had flashed that tool on her not one bit either.

That bitch was deranged, and she was getting stranger every day. Monique had figured since their plan was shot she could send Nooni back home, but that nut had damn near cracked open at the suggestion of cutting the young girl loose.

"Hell no! Nooni ass ain't going nowhere! She still has work to do. Home, hell. If she goes anywhere it'll be right downstairs on that mattress in the Dungeon!"

Monique couldn't tell if Salida was serious about doing Nooni like that or not, but she didn't put it past her.

Pluto sped up through an intersection and ran a red light. Tires squealed loudly as a transit bus hit its brakes as it tried not to crash into them.

"How about this," Monique suggested, giving Pluto a big smile. He was still furious and breathing hard. "I'ma run you a nice hot bath later on tonight when we get home, and while you in there having fun with your bubbles I'ma make you some fried potatoes with onions, and some of them real spicy shicken wings you like so much."

Pluto poked his bottom lip out and frowned. "You gone put some honey on them shicken wings?"

"Uh-huh," Monique giggled and nodded. "I'ma put some honey on them, some Lawry's, a little garlic salt, and some Texas Pete's too. You gonna love 'em."

Pluto cracked a small grin.

"Yummy," he said in a little boy's voice. "I love your shicken wings, but I don't think I can wait until tonight, though. I'm hungry right now. You hungry, Mo-Mo? You feel like eating you some shicken sausage?"

Monique knew the drill.

"I'm starving, Daddy," she said sweetly. She reached over and felt around under his massive stomach until she found his belt buckle. Expertly, she got it loose and Pluto jumped in quickly to help unbutton his pants.

Monique reached into his drawers and extracted his sticky dick. It was already wet at the top, and it felt like a hot pickle in her hand.

"Eat it," Pluto urged as he stepped on the gas and the whip lurched forward even faster.

Monique knew she had a dilemma. The last thing she wanted was for this fool to lose his top and go crashing into a damn building. But she was worried about something else, too. There was only about two inches between Pluto's bulging stomach and the steering wheel. Where the fuck was she supposed to put her head while she sucked his stank dick?

Make do, Monique, she told herself. She was a real creative bitch at heart. *Just make do.*

Taking a deep breath she jacked Pluto's dick to the side, then stuck her head down into funky land and got to grindin' his nasty sausage.

CHAPTER 7

Jail was a grimy, cold place to be.

I didn't care how they tried to dress the joint up with a mildewed mop or a fresh coat of paint. It was nasty. The food was shitty, the showers were dirty...the whole scene was a lesson on how to live like a dog.

I had grown up in Harlem so I was used to junkies, hoes, and thieves, but nothing in my life had prepared me for the hopelessness that hung thick in the air at Rikers.

Being G's woman had made me soft. He had gotten me used to sleeping on plush mattresses and bathing in deep tubs filled with hot, bubbly water. Coming up in here was like being dropped onto another planet. I felt like an alien who didn't understand the language, the reasoning, or the rules.

Right away I noticed that the guards did a whole lot of barking. Most of them were just regular dudes and chicks who had probably grown up in the projects too, but right now they were roaming around and flossing large and in charge, and they looked down on the inmates like we were some gutter scum that had come up out of a clogged toilet.

My face burned with embarrassment as they fingerprinted me and made me strip naked and squat down to the floor. The humiliation alone was enough to make me break down and cry, but I knew I had to be strong. Predatory bitches were probably already scouting me for signs of weakness, and I forced myself not to show them none.

One thing I knew for sure I wasn't gonna do was be nobody's damn jailhouse wifey. I wasn't a fighter, and I had never started trouble in my life, but when this grimy-looking trick with buck teeth and bumpy skin rubbed up against me as we waited on line I told her I would beat the brakes off her ass if she touched me again, and I meant that shit too.

Almost everybody around me seemed real comfortable and familiar with the procedures. Like they had been here before and none of it was that big of a deal. Some of them went through the line doing what they needed to do without even being told. I didn't wanna ask any stupid questions and let everybody know it was my first time being locked up so I just followed directions and kept my mouth closed.

I did my best to stay to myself but you know how it is. People don't never wanna just let you be. I had so many hood chicks coming at me asking who I was, what I was in for, did I have a man, did I have a bitch, did I have any money, was I looking for a good lawyer, did I know a good lawyer...that shit was exhausting.

They put me in a cell that was so little I could almost stretch my arms out and touch both walls. It had a thin, plastic-covered mattress on an iron rack, a small closet, a desk, a tiny sink, and a dirty white toilet with half a roll of tissue sitting on the floor next to it.

I sat down on the hard mattress and looked around. The floors were nasty, the walls were grimy, and all I wanted to do was go home. I closed my eyes and started praying for help. Why, I don't know, because it seemed like God had forsaken me a long time ago.

"I need to talk to somebody," I told a Puerto Rican CO later that night when it was time for us to take a shower. "I didn't get my mandatory phone call when I came in here."

He grinned like I was a real comedian.

"Yeah, okay," he said, ushering me along with a bitch-be-for-real smirk on his face. "I'll make sure I tell somebody about that."

The showers were the free-for-all type, where everybody and their mama could peep your naked ass. I ran through that water like hot lightening. I barely stopped to rub the rough bar of soap under my arms and between my legs, and I know for damn sure I didn't get a good rinse off.

That first night of being locked up in a small, musty cell damn near killed me. I was too freaked out to lay down and sleep, and I couldn't keep still neither. That locked door was fucking with me. What if there was a fire and nobody let me out?

I was so scared. I dropped down to the floor by the door and started crying. My tears just fell. I balled up in a knot and thought about Gino. I was so ashamed of myself, and I was glad he couldn't see me like this. Me and him should have been buying baby clothes and cribs and all that type of stuff together, instead he was in the ground and I was sitting up in jail.

I rocked back and forth on my hands and knees on that dirty-ass floor, and I cried and I prayed, and then I cried and I prayed some more. In the deepest part of my grief I coulda sworn I heard Gino's voice. My man was whispering to me, trying to comfort me. Stay strong, Juicy. *Hold on, baby. Just stay strong...*I cried so hard that I fell asleep with my mouth open and my face wet.

I must have stretched out on the floor at some point because in the middle of the night my mind started playing tricks on me. I was dreaming again, and this time instead of running, I had already been caught. I was locked downstairs in the Dungeon at the G-Spot, beaten and tricked out with my arm chained to a pole.

I woke up in a panic. The floor was cold and hard. Terror jumped up in my throat and my swollen eyes darted all around the tiny cell. Sweat covered my body as I stared up at the door. A thin rectangle of light came in from the tier outside, and I shivered in fear as I waited to hear G coming after me with a bunch of horny gangstas who were all just dying to fuck me. I jumped up and started banging on the door as hard as I could.

"Help!" I screamed at the top of my lungs, my voice high and shattering as it bounced off the cold walls.

"Help! Help! *Help!*" I shrieked and banged over and over again, even louder. My voice was so pitiful and it held so much terror that I barely recognized it myself. "Let me out! Please! Somebody...help!" I cried and whimpered like a baby as I beat the hell outta that door. "Please, please! Open the door and let me out! Oh God help me! Please let me *out!*"

"Shut up and go to sleep," a gruff voice came from the cell on my left. It was more sleepy than mean. "You all right, girl," she said. "Everything is cool. Ain't nobody fuckin' with you. Just take your ass to sleep."

It took me a few minutes, but I eventually started to calm down. I was finally able to stop crying when I realized that whoever had spoken was right. Wasn't no crew of gangsta niggahs coming to rape me, I realized in the darkness. I wasn't beat down and locked away in the basement of the G-Spot. My ass was under arrest and locked away in jail.

I staggered over to the hard bed and collapsed down on it, and with my fists clenching the thin wool blanket I'd been given, I did what the chick in the cell next to me had told me to do. I closed my eyes and drifted off to sleep.

CHAPTER 8

I'll keep you my dirty little secret..." Slick Sallie sang along with his favorite band, The All American Rejects. It was almost dark but he was completely comfortable cruising the mean streets of Compton with the top down on the flashy, green BMW convertible.

The neighborhood was crime-ridden and dilapidated, but Sallie felt absolutely no fear as he leaned back in the plush leather seats and nodded his head to the sounds of the nerdy white-boy band that blared from the speakers.

He drove slowly but deliberately, and both his expensive whip and his pale skin attracted curious stares from the young dope dealers and stick-up kids who were clustered on almost every corner.

Sallie grilled the thugs the same way they grilled him. There was raw aggression in their eyes, but there was mutual respect there too because Sallie wasn't the type of white boy who punked out in the presence of dangerous Black men..

Sallie turned his white-boy music up louder and sang off-key at the top of his lungs. He was totally aware that one well-placed bullet fired from the gat of any one of the corner thugs would smash his dome like a tomato. But life on the streets was tough. If it went down it just went down.

But even from a distance he could tell how much they admired him. Slick Sallie with his white skin, flashy car, and cocky demeanor symbolized the best of American greed, power, and materialism. And what urban hoodfella didn't respect that?

Greed was Sallie's middle name. Hardbody power oozed from his pores. He flowed with the kind of swagger that let you know you were in the presence of a man with muscle and clout. Which was why when he pulled up near a dark corner where working girls peddled their goodies, a whole slew of half-naked chicks swarmed around his ride like flies on a honey bun.

"That's right," Sallie laughed as the excited whores beat each other back trying to be the first to get up in his ride. He knew what they were thinking: Here was a young, clean-cut white boy who was paid in the pockets and would get his shit off in five minutes flat!

Boy, were they *wrong*!

"That's right, ladies," he repeated. "Come to Papa!"

A thick, brown-skinned young thing who was jostling in the middle of the pack caught Sallie's attention.

"Hey, fall back!" he told a scrawny geriatric hoe who had thrown her long skinny leg over the side of the passenger door and was trying to climb in beside him.

"I want that one," he pointed. "Yeah," he confirmed when the hot-cocoa young beauty aimed her thumb at her own chest and smiled.

"Yeah," Slick Sallie said. His eyes raked down her small waist and curvy hips and his voice was already growing thick with anticipation. "That's right. I want *you*."

$$$$$

Sallie hated the thought of spending his good money on a grimy motel room when Juicy's spacious two-bedroom condo was just sitting there empty, but he couldn't risk getting caught slumming around in her territory. His uncle Frankie had a security guard keeping an eye on the place, and Sallie had no doubt that if he pulled up in the hot green beemer the old guy would have been on the horn ratting to his uncle in two seconds flat.

Of course, he could have fucked the whore in the car, or up against a brick wall, or right out there in the open on the streets if he really wanted to, but what he had planned for tonight required the utmost privacy.

He drove to one of the hot-sheet motels he frequented whenever he cruised in these parts. After parking in a shadowy corner of the lot, he paid for the room by the hour and took the young girl inside.

"You want some water?" Sallie nodded toward a rusted-out sink as she stood in the middle of the stuffy room and stripped off her short skirt and skimpy top. He sucked in his breath at the sight of her bodacious curves and flawless, milk chocolate skin.

Staring at him from green contact lenses, she shook her head no, and her cheap hairweave moved stiffly back and forth around her shoulders.

Sallie walked up on her and cupped the soft hunks of her bare ass.

"I need the money first," she said in a shy, tender voice.

Sallie nodded. He'd chosen the right one tonight. She sounded so young and sweet. Not rough and worn-out like most of the hookers on the track.

He dug into his back pocket and pulled out a twenty, which he set on the nightstand. He would give her a little bit more later on if she didn't put up a fuss or object to what he wanted to do to her.

Sallie pulled back the worn, dingy sheets on the bed and told her to get in and lay flat on her back with her legs spread open and her arms stretched out over her head.

"I'm gonna tie you up," he said calmly, "but I swear I'm not gonna hurt you."

The girl bucked and propped herself up on her elbows.

"I can't let you tie me up," she said, panic rising in her voice.

"Relax." Sallie pushed her back down gently. He pulled a jumble of flexi-cuffs from his pocket and quickly fastened her right wrist to the bedpost. "I'll pay you double," he said, digging into his back pocket again. He pulled out two more twenties and tossed them on the night table next to the first one. "No, make that triple. And I swear to God I'm not gonna hurt you."

Moments later Sallie had the girl tied up spread-eagle. He stared down at her luscious black body and could hardly keep himself from attacking her.

"I'm not gonna hurt you..." he whispered over and over as he pulled off his clothing and stretched out naked on top of her. "I'm not gonna hurt you."

She was so warm and soft that it was unreal, and the contrast between their skin tones freaked him out. He could feel her trembling beneath him, and he pecked small, tender kisses on her forehead, cheeks, and chin.

And then he moved lower.

He licked the girl's neck, and trailed his tongue all the way from her collarbone to her erect left nipple.

Sallie sighed as he cupped her firm breast and took the small raisin in his mouth. He sucked and licked like crazy, swallowing every so often, swearing all out that her dark skin truly tasted like sweet milk chocolate.

He squeezed her plump titties close together and lapped back and forth at her nipples. His dick was harder than a diamond and it pulsated with the hot blood that had engorged its pink, mushroom-shaped head.

Sallie hadn't been lying when he told the girl that he wasn't going to hurt her. He wasn't. Fucking a black chick was his number one fantasy, and there was no white girl who tasted anywhere near as good, or who could even come close to satisfying his insatiable craving for chocolate pussy.

He dropped his head lower and licked a wet trail down her tight stomach and stuck his tongue in her navel. The smell of her cheap perfume rose from her crotch, but that wasn't what Sallie's nose craved at all.

Moaning, he inserted his pale finger into her slick snatch and marveled at how thick and creamy her juices were. He slid his finger in and out of her as her hips gyrated on the bed and her pelvis rose to meet his thrusts.

Sallie nodded with approval as small noises of delight came from the young girl's throat. He wasn't the average trick, this he knew. Most men picked up girls off the street seeking their own pleasure. But Sallie, in his own perverted way, was a pleasure-giver. His sexual fantasies involved being with this type of girl in a way that would never be acceptable in his real life.

The girl's slit was now hot and dripping as he fingered her deeply and stroked her clit. He could smell her now, too. That special scent that he'd been craving was now rising from her body and Sallie knew it was time for him to do exactly what he'd come to do.

He parted his lips and dove face first into her black pussy. He rubbed his lips, nose, forehead and chin all over her creamy genitals. Her pubic hair was nothing like the long, plastic-like weave strands on her head. It was thick and puffy. Coarse and kinky. Just the way he loved it.

His tongue found her swollen clit and swirled it like it was a chocolate tootsie pop. Using both hands, Sallie spread her pussy lips wider and furiously licked at the luscious hunk of chocolate with the sweet pink center. He fucked her with his tongue until she arched her back and screamed out and shuddered, and only then did he let himself go, spurting his load onto the shabby sheets and whipping his tongue back and forth against her pulsating clit.

Even before the last drop of sperm had ejaculated from his dick, Sallie's mood had completely changed. The girl lay there smiling, covered in sweat and panting. Her perfect breasts heaved and jiggled as she struggled to catch her breath in the wake of her intense orgasm.

A feeling of deep shame washed over Sallie like an icy ocean. He staggered to his feet and glared down at the girl with a fearsome sneer. He pulled on his clothes without saying a word, and slipped into his shoes.

He was heading out the door when the girl spoke.

"Hey!" she said, her after-sex voice husky and sweet as she wiggled her hands and feet around in the restraints. "Don't you have to do something for me?"

That's right. Sallie turned around.

He walked back to the bed and stood over her. The sight of her filthy black skin filled him with hot disgrace, and the sour leftovers from her pussy juice lingered in his mouth and made his tongue itch.

Without warning he pulled his fist back and buried it in the pit of her stomach as hard as he could.

The girl *umphed* and farted as her eyeballs rolled up in her head. Sallie gut-drilled her again, and the air left her lungs as her stomach caved in and she went limp in her restraints.

Wordlessly, Sallie turned around once more. He swept all three of his wrinkled twenty-dollar bills off the nightstand, then left the disgusting Black whore choking on her own vomit as he walked out the door. His first stop was gonna be the chop shop, and right after that he was heading directly back to the airport.

$$$$$

"No shit?" Mick Sanvenero asked, his liquored-up voice full of respect as he stared at the large metal safe. "Gino left this with you?"

Slick Sallie nodded as he stood in his mother's basement. It was three o'clock in the morning and he had just dropped Juicy's car back off at the airport and parked it very close to where he had gotten it from earlier that day.

Mick swigged from his shot glass. "How much loot you figure is in there?"

"Half a mil." Sallie shrugged. "Probably more."

Mick whistled. "Damn! Does the broad know you're busting it? What if she comes back looking for it?"

"She's not coming back," Sallie muttered under his breath as he thought about the pipe bomb that had been wired to the ignition switch in Juicy's sexy green BMW just a couple of hours ago.

After abandoning the dirty moolie prostitute at the motel, Sallie had driven to a chop shop run by a member of the Gambino crime family and watched as an explosive device was placed under the hood of the green beemer and rigged to the ignition of the idling car.

"Whatever you do," the shop's owner, Big Earl, had warned him, "don't cut off the car until you're ready to get out of it. Because if for some reason you do turn it off and then you try to turn it back on..." The beefy-necked Italian threw his head back and laughed, "Boom! Smithereens! All gone! Both you and the car."

Sallie had driven straight back to the airport. He'd placed the keys under the floor mat where Juicy had left them, then called his cousin Mick for a ride home.

"You're really gonna crack that shit?" Mick asked as Sallie studied the physical mechanisms of the safe. "I thought Uncle Frankie told everybody to stay cool with the chick?"

Sallie shrugged. Fuck Frankie and all his talk about La Cosa Nostra, respect, honor, and the old ways. It pissed Sallie off that they had run outta New York City like mutts with their tails tucked between their legs. Instead of running scared, they should have swissed somebody's fuckin' cheese and left a bunch of bullet-dotted bodies on the ground behind them.

"Yo, Sallie," Mick whined again. "You're pretty sure Juicy isn't gonna come back blabbing to nobody that we did this, right buddy?"

Sallie gave his cousin a long, hard stare. Mick was slow, and he was a scary little shit too. But he was faithful and loyal, and Sallie knew his cousin would die before he snitched on him.

"I already told you she's not coming back, Mikhail," Sallie assured him. And then he whispered under his breath, *"Because if she comes back...BOOM! She's dead."*

$$$$$

Three hours later the sun was just about to come up and Mick was leaning against a wine barrel fast asleep. Sallie was covered in sweat, and Gino's safe sat battered and hacked at, but still firmly intact in the middle of the floor.

No matter which way Sallie had tried to breach the damn thing, through the locking mechanism or by cutting into its iron core, he couldn't get to the money inside to save his life.

Wiping his face, Sallie remembered a strange telephone call he had received about eight months earlier. An old business partner from New York had been on the line asking him to help stash something Gino needed to hide.

Sallie had owed his moolie friend a solid in a major way, so he had agreed. But now, sitting in a pile of metal shavings with his hands so damn ripped up that they were starting to bleed, Sallie couldn't help but laugh.

He was almost positive that his old friend had predicted his greed, and had helped Gino find a fuckin' safe that was stronger than Fort Knox.

Sallie shook his head. There was more than one way to crack a nut. Nothing was impossible, and there was a whole lotta money in that goddamn safe. He could practically smell it. And as soon as he came up with a way to bust that baby open, every dime of it was gonna be his.

CHAPTER 9

I had been in jail for less than twenty-four hours and I was already desperate to get the hell out. It felt like I had just drifted off to sleep good when I was awakened by the sound of the COs stomping up and down the hall and hollering for everybody to get up. I dragged myself to my feet and we went through the same type of headcount that we'd gone through several times the day before, and as I would learn, we would go through every single day that our asses belonged to the Department of Correction in the City of New York.

Day two was no better than day one. Most of the women who were in with me looked desperate and beaten down by life. There were no ax-murderers, terrorists, or corporate white-collar criminals that I could see. Just a bunch of tired-looking minority females who had fallen down on their luck and landed flat on their asses.

After breakfast, they made me line up with a bunch of other women. We watched as a chain-gang of busted-looking hoes, junkies, winos, and thieves were led staggering off a bus and into the building. They were handcuffed one to the next, and the bored-to-death guards were screaming at them to shut the hell up and stay in one straight line.

We took some mug shots, and then we were all taken to an infirmary area where they made us sit in some kind of body-scanning chair that x-rayed our insides to make sure we weren't bringing in contraband in our coochies or up our butts.

"Williams!" one of the COs barked as she looked down at a clipboard. She was a real cute chocolate-skinned sister and her navy-blue uniform fit her curves like a cat suit. "You were supposed to come through here yesterday," she bitched at me. "How come you're just getting in here today?"

I shrugged with my eyes popped open wide. Shit, I wasn't no career criminal! I didn't know none of the jailhouse rules! Besides, I wasn't in charge of myself. Cause if I was, I woulda given myself a mandatory phone call and let myself out the side fuckin' door!

The tall Black female CO that I'd seen the day before was all over it.

"I got her," she said, quickly. She reached for my arm and led me toward another line. "There was a mix up with her paperwork but we're fixing it right now."

The nametag on her uniform said Gaines, and she had been outside with the white guy, CO Allen, who had made me give him my money when I came in the door.

"Don't say shit," she whispered me a warning. "Just roll with everybody else."

The next thing they did was give me a physical exam where I peed in a cup and let them take my blood. They said they were testing me for pregnancy, HIV, and a bunch of other diseases.

I got to see a mental health counselor after that.

"Are you having thoughts of suicide?"

166

"No."

"Do you feel like hurting yourself or anyone else?"

I stared at her. Damn straight I wanted to hurt some fuckin' body. *Rita*! But if I told this chick how I really felt she would send the people in the white coats to get me. Instead, I told her about the shady way my arrest had gone down.

"I don't think they did me right," I said.

"Who?"

"The cops who arrested me."

"Did they abuse you, physically, emotionally, sexually, or otherwise?"

"No, but I never even went to a precinct. They brought me straight here from the airport. They didn't even read me my rights."

She sighed, and I saw a little smirk on her lips.

She thought I was mental.

"Our officers are professional. Every inmate they arrest is read their Miranda rights. That's the law."

"Well, they didn't read me mine. I never got to make a phone call neither."

The smirk grew bigger as she scribbled something in my chart.

"And, nobody asked me if I wanted a lawyer."

She put her pen down and folded her hands on her desk. She shook her head and her Black Diamond hairweave moved like feathers below her jaw line.

"So, your complaint is that you were arrested without being read your rights, you were refused a telephone call and denied access to legal counsel?"

"Yeah," I said, nodding. "And I came in here with two-hundred grand in cash on me too."

Now she really smirked. This chick was used to dealing with drug addicted, mentally ill inmates who worked the system and lied and boosted for a living. She gave me the bitch-you-are-deranged look, and let out a big sigh.

"I'll be sure to annotate all that in your chart," she said, waving me off and beckoning to the chick behind me. "Next!"

As the day went on I noticed there was a big difference between how the male COs treated us and how the females did. Mostly all of us were either Black or Puerto Rican, including the guards. The male officers in here were just like men everywhere. The only difference was they wore a uniform and a badge, and were paid to keep us in check.

But they were still doggish. They stared at our asses and our breasts, and the look in their eyes was the same universal look you could find in any man's eyes if he wanted to fuck you.

The female guards were special though. These chicks were steady flossing and flouncing. Letting the inmates know without a doubt that they had it all over us, and that free pussy trumped jailhouse pussy seven days a week.

I didn't give it no energy. I just kept my mouth closed and did whatever they told me to do because I wasn't trying to get yelled at by none of these power-tripping tricks and get thrown in the hole.

But what I *was* trying to do was figure out a way to get the hell out of here. Even with my tiny bit of jailhouse knowledge I knew something wasn't right about the way things had gone down. And it wasn't just about Rita and the way she got me knocked, neither.

The CO who brought me in had told me it would be a couple of weeks until I went before the judge. I was so torn down that I'd lose my mind if I had to stay locked up in here for that long. Weeks were definitely out of the question. I couldn't see myself handling this shit for too much longer. Not even for another day.

CHAPTER 10

Chiney Jackson was getting her lower-lips glossed. The cum-slick face of her jailhouse lover was buried deeply between her thighs, and Chiney shuddered with pleasure as her engorged clit was tongued with hot passion.

"Just like that," Chiney whispered as she threw her head back and rotated her pussy all over the girl's wet mug. They were in a corner of their cell and she was standing with her back pressed against one wall, and her leg propped up on the wall opposite her. They had skipped their shower so Chiney could get her a little quickie, but this bitch ate pussy so good Chiney didn't ever want it to end.

Her lover slipped her middle finger deep into Chiney's twat. Chiney reached down and pushed her hand away. She was the type of stud who didn't require penetration in order to cum. She preferred to have her top done, her knob slobbed, her mannish lil dick sucked.

Chiney pushed down on the girl's head and humped. Her juices were leaking everywhere. The girl gulped and slurped, trying to catch every drop of nookie nectar Chiney released, shivering as it spilled from her mouth and ran down her chin.

"Ahhh, *shittttt….*" Chiney hissed between her clenched teeth as she rotated on the girl's twirling tongue and gently pulled on her own nipples. "You lick that shit so damn good…"

She felt a nut sparking off deep inside her pussy and her face grew flushed. Beads of sweat formed on her breasts, and soft mewing sounds fell from her slack lips. Chiney was in pussy paradise. She was an extreme squirter, and if her bitch kept it up she was gonna get a load of hot cum shot down her throat.

"Don't stop," she whispered, urging the girl to lick her out faster. "Oh, yeah….baby please don't stop!" And to Chiney's delight, the girl didn't.

$$$$$

Like I said, I couldn't see myself riding out another day in jail, but I did. I already felt like I had lost about five pounds. Most of the food was too damn nasty to eat, and I was scared all the stress was gonna make my period come down.

I had only been behind bars for a hot minute when the wolves decided to make a move on me. I still hadn't accepted the hard bed, the scratchy blanket, or the white porcelain toilet bowl that sat all out in the middle of the floor, and those open showers were too damn much for me too.

Most of the women were just trying to wash up and get clean and they kept their focus on doing that, but there were some man-looking predators who stood around licking their lips as they schemed on our soaped-up goodies.

I didn't have any money on my commissary account so I had to work with the hygiene items that the jailers gave me. Shampoo was out of the question, and one night while I was standing under the shower spray rubbing a rough bar of soap through my hair I noticed it had gotten real quiet all of a sudden.

I wiped at my eyes, then opened them up real quick. Almost all the other girls had gotten the hell up out the door.

I froze as this tall, dude-looking chick walked up on me butt naked. She was cinnamon brown with chiseled thighs, high titties, and a six-pack stomach. I knew from the swagger in her approach that there could be no mistaking her purpose. She was a straight-up stalker, and my heart started pounding. I had heard plenty of Big Bertha jailhouse stories about screaming chicks getting held down in the bathroom while some dyke got up in that coochie.

The girl coming toward me was real butch too. She stood over six feet, had muscles out the ass, and she wore her hair cut real low like a lot of stud females were doing these days.

I got ready to fight as she stepped up close. I didn't know what her first move was gonna be but she wasn't getting none of my pussy, I knew that much for sure.

I tried to cover my titties and my coochie as the mannish looking chick looked me up and down.

"What's your name, pretty girl?" she asked smiling at me with her wolf-ass teeth. I remembered my friend Dicey telling me that the only way she had survived in prison was by demanding her respect. So I grilled that butch right back and hoped my bark was bigger than her bite.

"Don't worry about my fuckin' name," I spit, swelling up and bracing my hands on my naked hips.

She had me stretched out on my back in two seconds flat. She pinned me to the wet shower floor and started feeling me up. Her hands slid all over my soapy skin. Her strong legs had me on lock.

"Get the fuck offa me!" I screamed as loud as I could. I fought like she was trying to kill me.

But she was laughing her ass off. Cracking the hell up. With her rock-hard forearm braced across my throat, she squeezed my left titty then giggled and dug her fingers up under my arm trying to tickle me.

"Bitch!" I screamed, twisting and bucking my body from side to side. "Let me go!"

We were like two soapy sumo wrestlers, arms and legs everywhere. Just like a dude, she forced my legs apart with one knee. Then she clamped my arm up above my head, and slid her hand down my stomach and thrust her middle finger deep into my pussy.

"Get off!" I snapped my knees together and bucked so hard everything except my head left the floor. "Get the fuck *off*!"

I started swinging wild killer blows at her. I punched her in her head about ten times, and all that bitch did was giggle. She was humping the hell out of my thigh, too. In fact, the harder I fought, the funnier that shit got to her. Grinding her wet pussy all over my leg, she grabbed at every part of me she could get hold of. I kicked at her and pulled my knees up to my chest and she reached down and dug in my stuff. I yelped and straightened my legs and she gripped my ass cheek and licked my nipple.

I started crying then. It was obvious that she wasn't really trying to fuck me, but both of us knew she could have if she really wanted to.

In a desperate move I lunged up and bit into her shoulder. That heffah leaned down and bit me right back. I screamed and we got to tussling again. She was straight tearing me up. Every time I thought I had some wins she used her muscled up arms and pinned me back down, then tickled my sides and tried to get her fingers up inside my pussy again.

"Help!" I cried out over and over again. "Help!" I was worn out and getting weaker, but she was still cock-strong and laughing. The skin on my back was all scraped up from the rough shower grout, and I was just about to collapse in defeat when a voice boomed loud in the room.

"Psycho! Man, get the fuck up offa her!"

The dude-chick froze on top of me and I used that moment to swing my knee up between our slippery bodies and kick her dead in her chest.

She fell off me but she was in no way hurt.

"Man, why you always fuckin' around like that?" my rescuer barked.

"I was just playing," Psycho said in a crazy girlie high-pitched voice. "I wasn't tryna get none. I was just tickling her that's all."

Playing my ass! I scooted far away from her as I could get. "You better not put your fuckin' hands on me no more!" I screeched. "Touch me again bitch, you hear? I will *kill* your nasty ass!"

"Psycho didn't mean no harm," the chick who had come to my defense claimed. She was a dude too. Light-skinned and chunky, but real pretty in the face. "She just be playing like that sometimes."

"Well I don't play that shit!" I snapped climbing shakily to my feet.

All I wanted was to get the hell out of that shower. For all I knew both of these dyke bitches could be planning to jump me and take turns fucking me.

My hands were trembling as I reached for my towel and headed fast for the door. I was pumped with fear and breathing like I had just run up to the top floor in a project building.

"Yo, hold up," the light-skinned girl said behind me.

I looked back, but I was still moving forward.

"I know you," she said, narrowing her eyes as she peered at me. "Yo, you from Harlem, right? We went to the same high school. Your name is Juicy, ain't it?"

I turned around and took a real good look at her. She was young. Just a little younger than me. Maybe Jimmy's age. She was a boy. Straight duded out. But pretty. Her piercing eyes held no ill will.

"Yeah," I said, forgetting all about the fake name I had come in the door with. "Yeah. I'm Juicy."

She grinned real wide. "Damn, it's been a minute girl! You probably don't remember me 'cause I was just a sophomore when you were a senior, but I'm Chiney. Chiney Jackson. I think I'm in the cell right next door to you. Do you remember my brother Trey? They used to call him Messiah back in the day. All the girls around our way used to sweat him. Brown-skinned, mad tall, real fine. He used to ball real hard with a skinny dude from Manhattanville named Mayhem?"

She watched me run the names through my memory and come up blank.

171

"Well, whatever," she said. "You might not remember me and Trey, but I know damn well you remember my other brother. His name was Cooter. Cooter Jackson. He used to work the bar over at the G-Spot."

CHAPTER 11

I ain't feeling this shit no more, Nooni thought miserably as she touched that sweet spot between her legs. Truth had just gotten his nut and rolled over, but once again she had been left hanging and she needed to cum so bad it wasn't funny.

With all the fucking, shopping, and getting high she was doing Nooni was definitely living the kind of life that she had been looking for.

Partying with ballas in the club every night was all good, but she missed the high school scene and her best friend Bubbles, and all the silly little teenage drama they used to get into.

Nooni missed her sisters too.

Yeah, Chub was fat and greedy, and Rita was all the time yapping on her to stop cutting class and to carry herself with respect, but that's how sisters did it and Nooni was starting to realize that. Besides, she was sick of sleeping on the sofa bed in Monique's living room. She couldn't hardly catch a good Z the way Pluto's fat ass snored, and the air was starting to get tight between all of them in the small apartment anyhow.

Everybody had been extra-hyped and excited when they had been plotting on how to use Nooni to get some ransom money, but now that the plan was dead there wasn't nothing but bad attitudes and sour faces in the crib.

Mizz Salida had been real cool about it though, and she had complimented Nooni for playing her role as a kidnap victim real good. She had even given her a bunch of money and told her to buy herself an iPod, a new Android phone, and some fresh new clothes as a gift for her eighteenth birthday too.

"So what now?" she asked Truth as he lay facing the wall beside her. He had been acting real cold toward her ever since him and Monique had come back from the airport empty-handed. Nooni had heard them cursing each other out in the G-Spot, with Monique blaming Truth for fucking everything up, and him denying that shit and blaming her right back.

Nooni had been drinking at the bar while they argued. Truth came over and snatched her up, and brought her back to the quiet apartment. After taking a shower together and smoking a whole bunch of chronic, they engaged in some real strange sex.

Nooni had really wanted it to be good for both of them, but Truth had just gone for his like she wasn't even there. There was no way she could cum with him just pounding all on her like that, in fact she hadn't been able to cum with Truth for a minute now and that shit was real frustrating.

She had almost cried tonight as he banged her hard and furious, battering her pussy and slapping her ass cheeks so hard he left red welts on her creamy skin. She had taken the pain and rode with it, but afterward she had been dying for him to hold

173

her, or to at least throw his leg over hers so they could snuggle and be close like a real couple. Hell, any kind of affection would have let her know that Truth was still feeling her and she wasn't just some random piece of meat he was mashing.

"Truth!" she backhanded him on the shoulder. "I asked you what's gonna happen now? What's our next move?"

He mumbled something into the pillow, but he didn't move.

"I didn't hear you," she said, raising up on one elbow. She put her hand on his arm and he shook her off.

"Why you acting like that?"

"Like what?"

"Like you acting."

He raised up on his elbow and spit, "What? I gotta act some special kinda way around you?"

"That's not what I'm saying. It's just that you been igging me a lot lately and I don't know why. You don't even think about how I'm feeling when we have sex, and it's like you can't even look me in the face or something."

Truth rolled over and grilled her.

"Happy now?"

Nooni shrugged. "I guess so. But you still didn't answer my question. What's gonna happen now?"

"Happen with what?"

"With us. With you and me. With the money we don't have. With us staying here with Monique."

He shook his head, then lay back and stared up at the ceiling.

"I don't know, Noons," he sighed and said truthfully. "Monique fucked our shit up. She tried to put it all on me, but it was her. That bitch is too greedy and she got too happy. She made moves like the money was already in our pockets. Man, she fucked around and let your sister peep her game at the airport. It was a wrap after that. Now everybody is ass out."

"I know," Nooni said quietly. "I heard." Disappointment washed over her. And a little bit of fear, too. It had never been her intention to run off and get involved in no fake hostage situation, or to have her sister walking around worried sick about her forever. She had convinced herself that after Juicy gave Rita the money then everybody would get their little cut and she could quietly ease herself on back to her crib.

"So how y'all gonna get paid now? What about all your warrants? Are you gonna get locked up?"

She sounded scared and Truth shrugged. "Don't worry," he said, patting her firm, naked thigh. Her body was so stunning it had him ready to fuck again. "I already talked to Salida about all that and she's on it. That old broad is smart, Noons," Truth said as stuck his fingers between her legs and got ready to hit that wet pussy again. "Trust me, she's gonna come up with something real good for all of us."

$$$$$

Monique came through her front door pissy drunk. She had just cursed all them niggahs out in the G-Spot, and Pluto had snatched up one of his dun duns and told him to drive her ass home.

She didn't get it. Ace and Salida were tryna blame her for messing everything up when it wasn't even her fault! She staggered down the hall and stopped when she saw what was going on in her living room. Truth's naked yellow ass was pumping like a jack-rabbit as he dug Nooni's gushy out. Nooni was spread eagle on the pull-out sofa and moaning at the top of her lungs, and Monique could actually hear that wet pussy sloshing as Truth pounded up in them guts.

Monique stood in the shadows as the young couple fucked. Truth groaned real loud when he got his nut, and a few seconds later he climbed out the bed and walked into the bathroom and turned on the shower.

In a flash Monique stripped outta her club clothes. She crept over to the couch and slipped under the covers where Nooni lay breathing hard.

"Wha—" the young girl almost jumped outta her skin when she realized Monique was on her.

"Shhh!" Monique warned and pushed Nooni back down as she tried to sit up. "Just shut the fuck up and roll with this."

Ignoring the girl's protests, she thrust her hand between Nooni's sweaty legs and rubbed her wet, swollen pussy. Truth's cum spilled out of her tunnel making everything down there nice and slick.

"Monique, stop!" Nooni cried out, snapping her legs shut.

Monique finger-fucked her deeply, plunging in and out of her pussy as she sucked Nooni's stiff nipple.

Heat pulsated through Nooni's body and for a second she opened up. She was so damned confused and she needed to cum so bad. Fire was boiling between her legs and her pussy was now thumping. Monique was licking and sucking her titties exactly right, and on their own her hips started thrusting upward to meet Monique's stroking fingers, which were now smearing hot juices all over her swollen clit.

Nooni let her legs fall open wider and Monique slid two fingers deeper into her softness. Her breath caught in her throat as Monique flicked the tip of her erect nipple back and forth with her tongue. Nooni's clit blinked and throbbed as her pussy muscles clamped down on Monique's probing fingers. She fucked upward in a furious motion as Monique's hand moved up and down beneath the covers. Hot cum shot out of her and Nooni arched her back and squealed with pleasure. Monique was just about to climb on top of her when Nooni caught herself.

And Truth caught them too.

"Yo what the fuck is y'all doing?" he exploded as he flipped on the light. He stood over them with a towel wrapped around his waist and the anguished sound of betrayal in his voice was like ice water over Nooni's soul.

"*Nooni*!" he yelled looking down at them in disbelief. "*Monique*!"

"I'm sorry..." Nooni rolled over and started crying. She was ashamed beyond words and she buried her face in her hands. "I'm so sorry!"

"Yo! What the fuck was y'all *doing*?"

Monique sat up with a smirk on her face.

"Don't even try it, Truth," she slurred. "You know I been wanting to fuck Nooni for a good minute now. You was down with all this shit from the gate so don't act like you all innocent now."

Truth exploded, and beads of water rolled down his muscular chest and shoulders. "Fuck what I *used* to be down with, you drunk bitch! Nooni don't roll like that. She don't wanna get fucked by no girl!"

Monique laughed, then stood up and stretched. Even with him pissed off and raging, the sight of her gorgeous brown body was enough to make Truth's dick jump.

"Nooni might not wanna get fucked by no girl," Monique said as she weaved across the room butt-naked. She bent over to pick up her clothes and her pussy blossomed open like a beautiful new flower. "But she damn sure liked it when this girl made her cum."

$$\$\$\$\$\$$$

Salida had already laid out her plan and conducted all her research, and now she was ready to get things popping. She had hooked up with a motivated drug dealer who promised to sell her all the X, special k, roofies, xan, and other club drugs she could handle, but Salida knew the only way to generate some real money was by producing her own poison.

Since she was new to the game, she had decided to start out with methamphetamine. White people's crack. The gentrification of Harlem had become so widespread that white folks were now walking around like they owned the place. And except for the housing projects and the slums that surrounded them, they did.

Salida didn't have a problem with crackers coming in and buying up all the property that Blacks had dogged out, trashed the fuck up, and then abandoned. In fact, she respected the real-estate moguls for being all about business.

But, she was an ambitious businesswoman too, and if meth is what the white junkies liked then that's exactly what she planned to give them. All she wanted them to do was keep coming back for more.

And it wasn't just white people's pockets that Salida wanted to tap either. Asian, Mexican, Puerto Rican, Arab...she didn't give a damn where the money rolled in from as long as it rolled in heavy.

Unlike the two dumb-asses who had taken over for G, Salida had nothing but ambition and big dreams on the brain. She didn't want just a lil bit, she wanted it all, and she wanted it fast too. She would never be satisfied with nickels and dimes if quarters and dollars were out there for the taking. Some might say Salida had caught herself a bad case of the greedies, but she preferred to think of herself as being eternally hungry. The thirst was just in her. It ran through her blood. No matter how much fortune she was holding in her right hand, she was always, always looking around to see if she could get more, more, more for her left hand too.

But she wasn't about to go off half-cocked with her shit. She was too smart for that. She would be starting out very small. Baby-stepping her way through a process that had the potential to make millions of dollars in a very short period of time. Salida took pride in being thorough and in doing things in a strategic way, so she was gonna be moving very slowly.

She had discovered an interest in computers since leaving the nuthouse, and she'd quickly become an information junkie who loved the Internet too. So when it came to club drugs, Salida had already read about enough blown up home-cooked meth labs to know she was dealing with something lethal. Sure, she wanted to make a truckload of money, but she didn't plan on killing herself in the process. Her goal was to cook for herself and keep all her profits, and eventually to become a major distributor and cook for other dealers too.

She'd already purchased a small amount of ephedrine from some Mexicans on the black market, and gathered some red phosphorous, a solution of lye, and a bunch of other chemical ingredients. She had made Ace get at ten of G's most trusted cut room workers and tell them to report for duty. Under her detailed guidance and instructions, they had opened all the windows in the cut room and plugged in three industrial fans, and then for the first time in a long time, the G-Spot crew got busy producing, cutting, and packaging drugs again.

"Yo, that crystal ain't nothing to fuck with," Pluto had bitched when he came upstairs to grumble about the foul smell that had customers complaining down at the bar. He had looked around at all the plastic jugs, glass jars, flasks, and various open containers of chemicals and shook his head. "See, this is why we need to stick to fish scale and powder, goddammit! All them fumes mixing together gone kill y'all stupid muh'fuckas up in here."

"Shut the hell up," Salida said calmly as she slammed the door in his fat, ugly face. "I know what the hell I'm doing."

But as it turned out, as careful and as thorough as she had tried to be, Salida didn't know exactly what she was doing and after everything had cooked down all she ended up with was a stank, oily mess on her hands.

Staring down at all her wasted time and money, Salida laughed out loud. She was far from mad, and she wasn't discouraged neither. In fact she was energized and encouraged.

"No problem," she muttered as she eyed the bad batch of meth and tried to figure out what the hell she had done wrong.

"I'ma get this shit down pat," she reassured herself as she prepared to ride out to Three Brother's Funeral Home for a late-night meeting with her connect. "All a bitch needs is a little bit more money and a little bit more practice."

CHAPTER 12

It was still warm for fall in California, and the Sanveneros were having a pool party. Renata appeared crisp and cool on the outside, but inside she was beside herself with worry.

Three of Frank's brothers and their wives were sitting in the shade drinking martinis, and their nephews Sallie, Mick, and Joey, along with about ten of their young friends, were jumping in and out of the large, circular swimming pool.

It was a relaxing day. The beer was flowing, the grill was hot, and everyone was laughing and splashing and having a good time.

Everybody except Renata. Excusing herself from the group, she called Frank into the kitchen to help her get more ice, and she blurted out exactly what was on her mind.

"I think something's wrong, "she told her husband. "I haven't been able to get in touch with Juicy for almost two days and I have a funny feeling in my stomach." Renata sighed and ran her fingers through her lush, perfectly layered hair. "I mean, she's not answering her home phone, and her cell phone must be turned off because my calls roll straight to voicemail. I just don't understand, Frankie. Where in the world could she be?"

Frank shrugged as he held the ice bucket under the freezer's high-tech dispenser. "She's probably just relaxing. Maybe she took a little vacation. Things have been rough for her. You can't blame a young girl for wanting to get away for a little while."

Renata shook her head. She placed a fresh jar of olives on the tray, and reached into the pantry for a stack of bar napkins.

"So you think she would take a vacation without telling me? Where? And with who? Other than us she doesn't have one good friend in the whole damn state. Besides, Juicy wouldn't go anywhere without telling *somebody*," she said with certainty.

Frank sighed. He had no idea where Juicy was. If it was up to him he would have forgotten all about her, but his wife's protectiveness of the girl, and the promise Frank had made to his old east coast associate, hung like a weight around his neck.

"I just get so afraid for her sometimes," Renata confided, her voice dropping. "It's like she just disappeared or something." She thought for a moment, then asked, "What about the security guy who's watch her condo? Has he seen her?"

Frank sighed and raked his fingers through his hair. "I asked him this morning like you told me to. He said Juicy went out early yesterday." Frank left out the part the old guy had said about seeing someone near Juicy's condo later that morning because when he went to check it out nobody was there.

Frank passed his wife the ice bucket and took the heavy tray from her hands. "We did everything we could do for Juicy. She's an adult and she chose to leave our house and live on her own. She can do that you know."

"I know, I know," Renata nodded. "I just have a bad feeling about this, that's all."

She led the way to the poolside patio and set out the ice, olives, and napkins. Settled once more in her lounge chair, she lit a cigarette and inhaled on it deeply before releasing the smoke through her nose.

"You know," she turned to Frank and continued. "That girl is all alone in the world. We're the only ones who would notice if she disappeared off the face of the Earth. I think we should take a ride over to her condo and see if everything is okay."

Frank sighed again and tossed back a Martini. He had no desire to get off his ass on a warm lazy Sunday, but as the head of his family it was his job to run around and put out other people's fires.

"All right." He glanced around at his clan as they ate, drank, and splashed around in his swimming pool. "Richie's got the grill and Sallie and Paulie can handle the kids in the pool. Let me get the keys to the condo, and I'll take you over there."

$$\$\$\$\$\$$$

By the time they arrived at the condo it was getting dark outside. Gino's car was sitting in the driveway but Juicy's car was gone. A couple of envelopes stuck out of the curbside mailbox. Renata got the mail and put it in her purse, and Frank unlocked the door with the extra key he had held back after he sold Gino the condo.

He opened the door and was shocked by what he saw. The place had been tossed. Furniture had been thrown everywhere, sofa cushions were sliced and gutted, closets had been ransacked, and every cabinet in the kitchen had been flung open and had its contents spilling out.

"Oh my God!" Renata covered her mouth.

"Stay here!" Frank ordered and pulled out his piece. He swept through the apartment looking for signs of static, although his instincts told him whoever had been here was already long gone.

The master suite had been hit hard. Juicy's king-sized bed had been torn apart, and the mattress was propped against the wall with all the stuffing hanging out. The dresser had been knocked over and was lying flat on its back with all the drawers pulled out. Lamps, paintings, perfumes and toiletries were scattered on the floor, and the bedroom closet looked like it had been attacked by somebody who was searching for something important.

Frank was heading back to the living room when the cordless phone caught his eye. The message indicator was blinking. He pressed the button and listened as an automated message played.

When the message ended Frank removed the phone's handset from the base then hit the redial button to see what number had been dialed last. The phone rang three times before it was answered.

"How the hell did you get home from the airport?" a voice on the other end demanded. The clear sounds of splashing water and a real lively backyard party could be heard in the background. "You were supposed to drive your own car home, Juicy!"

Frank frowned. He recognized the voice on the other end of the line. He recognized it, and he didn't like it at all.

Without a word he placed the handset back on its base. He waited a few seconds and just as he expected the phone rang and shattered the silence in the condo.

Frank looked at the caller ID. It showed a California area code but the number was blocked. He clicked the talk button, then pressed the phone to his ear and waited.

"Juicy? Juicy! Did somebody give you a ride home?" the caller sounded shocked. "Juicy? Why didn't you just drive your own fuckin' car?"

Once again Frank disconnected the call and put the phone back on the charger without saying a word. He didn't want to alarm his wife, but the family had a problem. A very big problem. The man on the other end of the line didn't know who Frank was, but Frank sure as hell knew him.

Frank locked the door behind them as they left the ransacked condo. There was a frown on his face as he mentally pieced the puzzle together. "There was a message on Juicy's phone," he told Renata.

"From who?"

"The Los Angeles International Airport. It was a recording. It said a car registered to Juicy's address had exceeded its allotted time in a 24-hour lot and that they were gonna tow it if it wasn't moved right away."

"So she took a flight somewhere?" Renata said, surprised. "You mean she left L.A.? Why didn't she tell me? And where the hell could she have gone?"

"I don't know," Frank said. "But her car is at the airport."

"I have her key," Renata said quickly. "She gave me a set after Gino died."

"I need to use your cell phone," Frank said.

"Where's yours?" Renata said as she dug into her purse.

"I think I left it by the pool. I need to make a call."

"Make it quick. My battery is almost dead."

Frank took his wife's phone and punched in a number. His nephew answered on the first ring.

"Aunt Renata, what's up?"

"Sallie, it's Frank. We're on our way to pick up Juicy's car. Stay at the house until I get back. We need to talk."

"You're going to the airport? Why? Wait! Don't—"

Click.

"Phone died," Frank said, handing it back to his wife. "Let's go get this car before they tow the damn thing away."

$$$$$

"Yo, fuck that niggah!" Zero barked as Izzy pushed the ride down the highway. Darkness had fallen and the cold-blooded killer had other moves on his mind. "Why we going back out there when we already looked all over the place? If the whip ain't there, then that shit just ain't there!"

"Chill, my niggah," Izz said as he glanced in his rearview mirror checking for cops. Zero was riding dirty, and the last thing he wanted was for this idiot to get all hyped up and start wildin'.

"Man, all this ridin' back and forth is a waste of fuckin' time, yo! I got other moves to make, nah'mean?"

Izzy igged his partner-in-crime and turned the music up real loud. The boom of the bass vibrated the car's frame and shook the windows. He hit the gas pedal hard and the car lurched and picked up speed as they changed lanes and approached the airport exit.

"Yo, man. If we find it I'm taking that shit. Word. I'ma hotwire that bitch and push it all damn night."

Izz had no expectations of finding the green BMW convertible. Zero was on point, that shit just wasn't there, but they had a job to do so fuck all that whining. Izz was a soldier. He took his orders and followed them. All that waaa-waaa shit wasn't gonna throw him off his mission. Nah, they were gonna hit that parking lot hard, and they were gonna find that goddamn whip if it was the last damn thing they did.

CHAPTER 13

Chiney actually was in the cell right next to mine, and we stayed up half the night talking through a small hole in the sheetrock. The crack was up high, so we both had to stand up and talk with our mouths close to the wall, but just having somebody halfway familiar to talk to made being uncomfortable worthwhile.

When I thought back hard enough I kinda remembered Chiney and her group of friends from high school, but in all that time I'd had no idea that she was Cooter's little sister.

I found out that Chiney and Jimmy were the same age, and that the two of them had actually messed around a little bit back in junior high school before Chiney got all butchy and started pushing up on females.

Chiney was cool, though. I liked her right away. She knew all about the drama I had gone through with G in the G-Spot. She said every damn body in Harlem knew about it. She told me that a lot of people had felt real sorry for me when word got out about what G had done to me. She also said that no matter how hard folks had smiled all up in G's face and kissed his ass when he was alive, a whole lot of them had been real damn happy when they found out he was dead.

Chiney was locked up on a parole violation and only had a month left to serve. She was definitely a butch, but that didn't bother me because she wasn't coming at me with nothing but friendship.

So, instead of laying down on that hard ass bunk and crying myself to sleep, I stood facing the wall as me and Chiney took some crazy trips down memory lane. As bad as I missed Gino, and as much as I hated jail, I actually laughed once or twice when she reminded me of something wild that Jimmy had done or said.

"Your brother was fine, but he was crazy as shit you know," she laughed. "I fucked with dudes back then, and one time he snuck me inside your crib so I could give him some pussy. But then your grandmother came home. We heard her coming up the stairs and Jimmy made me go up on the roof and hide."

"Speaking of brothers," I began, but then I had to swallow real hard to pull myself together. Me and Chiney had something real important in common, I realized. We had both lost our brothers because of G and his coldblooded way of life.

"I was real sorry to hear about your brother Cooter. He was real good to me. I think he just felt sorry for me. He used to look out for me all the time. "Matter fact," I closed my eyes for a quick second and I could've sworn I smelled that pissy mattress in the funky Dungeon of the G-Spot.

"As a matter of fact," I continued, "It was Cooter who helped me get out of the G-Spot when the rest of them niggahs wanted to kill me."

"For real?"

I nodded as a tear slid down my face. "Yeah. It was the night that Jimmy shot G and then killed himself. They were getting ready to go get rid of the bodies. Cooter came downstairs with a key. He unlocked my chains and gave me an envelope full of cash that Moonie had left for me. Cooter said he was just doing for me what he wished somebody had done for your sister Charlene."

I could hear Chiney's sigh of sorrow through the crack in the wall. "Charlene was so young when she died. She never really got to live at all. Yeah, she was hardheaded and wild, but it seems like God woulda protected her, you know? The way he protects babies and fools."

I understood how she felt. Just last night Grandmother had come to me in my dream. I had laid my weary head in her lap and asked her what I had done that was so wrong that God had to punish me like this. Grandmother had stroked my hair and told me, "God loves you, Juicy. He chastises, but he also rewards. You just keep the faith, baby. Fight the good fight. Your reward is coming."

"You know, after Charlene died my moms was useless," Chiney said sadly. "She was in so much pain she just couldn't do shit for the rest of us. So, we took care of ourselves. I hated G. We all did. I used to dream about burning the G-Spot down. Just burning that bitch down to the ground with everybody in it." She paused for a second and then asked, "Was you really fucking G's son like everybody said you was?"

"Yep," I went on and 'fessed right up. "Gino was my man. I loved him. And he loved me." I thought about our baby, then quickly pushed him out of my mind. "We were planning to get married. But we never got a chance to take our vows though...."

"Married? How old are you?" she asked.

I paused and swallowed hard.

"I'm twenty," I told her. "As a matter fact, my birthday is today."

"Damn," she said. "This is a fucked up place to celebrate but happy birthday anyway."

"Thanks," I took a deep breath and wiped the tears from my eyes and changed the subject. "Anyway, like I said, I'm sorry your brother is dead, Chiney."

I thought about how Jimmy had shot and killed two men just to save me. "And I'm sorry my brother is dead too," I added. "In a way, I owe my life to both of them."

"Yeah. Harlem has a way of chewing good people up," Chiney said. "And then shitting them back out. Are you sure you don't remember my other brother, Trey? He played mad ball back in the day. His friend Mayhem got shot at a basketball game and Trey killed the dudes who shot him. It was on the news and everything, and people all over Harlem was talking about it for a real long time."

"Ohhh, I remember!" I nodded as a picture of a real fine dude with the same beautiful eyes as Chiney's popped into my head. I used to see him ballin' at Rucker Park back when I was in middle school, and I'd had a big crush on him too.

"Yeah, I do remember Trey. I think I was in the middle of my freshman year when all that happened. I remember him getting locked up, but didn't he get back out just a couple of years later?"

"Yeah, he did. They kept Trey down for about two years, but then his conviction got overturned when a new prosecutor dropped the charges. But even still, Trey wasn't the same no more after that. Everything about him had changed."

I nodded again in the darkness, even though I knew she couldn't see me. I could definitely understand people changing. Life had knocked me down on my ass too, and nothing about me would ever be the same again either.

CHAPTER 14

Antonio "Trey" Jackson was putting in work. It was six o'clock in the morning and a fine little honey was moaning on her hands and knees as she took his ten-inch wood from the back.

Nicole was a corporate attorney. They'd met while Trey was in jail fighting a murder charge. The two had stayed in touch while Trey was locked up, and when he came home from upstate and enrolled at Harvard Law School they hooked up as study partners and fuck buddies.

"Aye! Aye! Aye!" Nicole screeched. She peered over her shoulder as Trey pounded his dick inside her all the way down to the root. She lifted herself up on her toned arms and threw that ass back at him, bucking and grinding and taking his battle meat like a real troop.

"Fuck this pussy!" she panted, clenching his dick between her magnificent ass cheeks. "Fuck this goddamn pussy!"

Trey let her have it. Clenching every muscle in his six-pack, he banged up in her guts until she squealed in surprise and tried to run from his dick. Locked together like stuck dogs, they bounced all over his bed getting sweatier by the second.

Nicole reached between her legs and spread her fingers on either side of Trey's big dick and squeezed. Gathering their juices, she massaged her tingling clit and grit her teeth as her second orgasm tore through her and she soaked Trey's condom with her cum.

"This your pussy, baby," she panted, tossing her hips. "Take it! Fuck it any way you wanna fuck it! It's yours, Trey. I swear to God, it's yours."

Trey pulled out of her sucking hole and tapped her on the hip. Her hair had sweated out and random strands stuck to her face. Following his directions, Nicole flipped onto her back and pointed her long, beautiful legs toward the ceiling.

She stared up at Trey's chiseled, athletic physique. Every damn thing about him was perfect. His dark brown skin, his rocked-up muscles, and the neat, velvety dreadlocks that hung down past his shoulders.

"You fuck so good, Trey," she moaned. "Your black ass is fine as hell and you got a big dick! You the best baby! Yum! Your dick is the best!"

Trey grinned and his even white teeth flashed in the near-darkness. He gripped his dick at the base and checked to make sure his condom was still good, and then he splayed Nicole's legs over his broad shoulders and went in hard again.

He groaned as his balls slapped her ass and her juices sloshed out and soaked them. The heat coming off her was amazing and Trey's knees shook as his dick strained and swelled as he banged her walls from one side to the other.

Trey reached down and dipped his finger in Nicole's puddle of juices and brought it to his lips and sucked. Moments later he lowered himself down on top of her and kissed her lips, then moved further down and licked her collar bone as she grinded hard and gripped his muscular ass, drawing him in even deeper.

They mashed it up, both of them growling, moaning, and making ugly faces as they fucked the sheets off his bed. Trey grit his teeth as he felt a big one building in his nuts. Nicole felt it coming too, and she wrapped her legs around his waist and held on tight as he impaled her pussy over and over again.

"*Arghh!*" Trey struggled for control as his dick jerked and skeeted, filling the condom with a gallon of warm cum. Nicole sure had some good pussy. His dick stayed hard long after the last drop had been squeezed from his nuts, and if he didn't have someplace to be in a couple of hours he woulda changed his condom and gone in for round two.

Trey knew exactly what Nicole wanted next, and for about ten minutes he let her have it. Pulling her into his arms, he stroked her back, hair, and legs, and she snuggled close to him enjoying that beautiful after-sex glow, their wet bodies sticking together as their breathing returned to normal.

Eleven minutes later Trey glanced at the clock on his dresser. It was time for her to go. He slid his arm out from under Nicole's head and prepared himself for the twenty questions. It was always the same thing with the women in his life, and Trey always had the same truthful answers. Yes, they were beautiful. Hell yeah, he dug the shit outta them. No, he wasn't in love, but yeah, he definitely cared.

Trey got up and walked into his bathroom. He peeled off the soggy condom and flushed it down the toilet, and then turned the shower on high. He waited until the water was flowing nice and hot, then he went back into his bedroom to get Nicole so he could rub soap all over her body before he asked her to leave. Thirty minutes later they were both showered and dressed and Nicole was standing on the other side of his door.

"So you're gonna call me later, right?" she asked, standing on her tippy toes as she reached for a goodbye kiss.

"Nah," Trey told her truthfully. "I got a lot to do today. I'll holla at you tomorrow though."

Nicole was a real dime. He kissed her, then touched her hair as she turned away.

Trey called her back. "Yo, hold up for a minute, okay?" He dipped back inside his apartment and went into his bedroom. He attacked the bed slowly but thoroughly, running his hands under the sheets, between the mattress and the box-spring, and even behind the headboard.

He found what he was looking for wedged deep inside his pillowcase, and he retrieved the skimpy red panties and sniffed them as he headed back to the door.

"You forgot something." He grinned and handed Nicole her underwear. The last time she spent the night he'd found one of her earrings stashed in his silverware drawer, and few of his other girls were always good for leaving a bra or some stockings or even an unopened tampon under the cushions of his sofa.

Busted, Nicole grinned sweetly.

"You can't blame a girl for trying," she said.

Trey understood. He pressed his lips to hers again, and then stepped back inside his crib and closed the door.

Trey locked his door and shook his head. He'd been through this type of thing countless times with countless beautiful girls, but no matter how good his chicks threw him the pussy, or how much they schemed and tried to hook him or catch him out there sleepin', Trey was a solo roller.

Yeah, he loved him some gushy, and hell yeah, he treated all his honeys like they were his queens, but Trey Jackson didn't have no woman.

And he wasn't looking for one neither.

$$\$\$\$\$\$$$

Trey Jackson coulda been any damn thing he wanted to be. A doctor, a dentist, an athlete, an accountant...all of that and more coulda been in his future, and even though he had a law degree from one of the most prestigious schools in the country, in the city of New York Trey was best known as an ex-convict and a killer.

He glanced around *Second Chances*, the first Harlem barbershop he had bought and opened. He'd done all right for himself, and it hadn't taken him long to open a *Third Chances* and a *Fourth Chances* too, and all of his shops were highly profitable anchors in the community.

Two years ago Trey had been a major player on the floor of the New York Stock Exchange. He had a nose for picking winners, and he'd made a lot of money while the market was in an upswing. He'd hung all of that profit and excitement up for a chance to chase his real dream, and even though he wasn't trading commodities anymore, Trey was content with the path in life that he had chosen. It had had its share of pitfalls and hard knocks, but he had learned to take shit on the chin, and he wouldn't have wanted things any other way.

It was early Monday morning and as usual he was heading out to Queens for the day. He had stopped by all three of his shops and took care of some business so his managers would be straight while he was gone for the day. Confidence was in his stride as he walked down the streets and watched his beloved Harlem wake up to greet a new day. This was his town. The blood of his family had run in its gutters, and he claimed a stake in it.

Standing just over six-feet-three and packing a little over two hundred pounds of iron-hard muscle, Trey looked just like the beast that he was. Church ladies, winos, and corner boys alike greeted him with mad street love as he walked by, and he had a smile, a strong dap, or a casual 'what it do' for almost everybody he ran across too.

"Sup, Leek," Trey walked up on a street-hardened young trap boy who was putting in early morning work on a busy corner.

The tall, slim kid barely glanced his way as he spoke back. "What it do, Trey?"

"It do what it do," Trey responded with a grim look on his face as he paused to eye the young'un. "Yo, I heard your moms was back in the hospital, man. I'ma swing over there and check her out later on. How's she doing?"

The boy shrugged like his eighty-pound mama laying on her death bed in Harlem Hospital was a real small thing. "I guess she a'ight."

Trey watched as Maleek conducted his street bizz. Their families went way back, and the boy was deep in his heart. No matter how many kids Trey had helped save from the grimy clutches of Harlem's trenches, it fucked him up that Maleek who had fallen headfirst into the gutter, and he took the boy's fearless devotion to the street life as a personal failure.

"Yo check it out," Trey went at him. No matter how hard the boy tried to tune him out, Trey was either gonna try or die.

"I'm about to put together an all-star team at The Crossover. We could use a starting point guard with good speed and sick handles. Your skill set is ice-cold, Lil Leek. We're gonna be ballin' in front of a lot of big time coaches, yo. You could pick up right where your brother left off."

"Nah, I'm good," the teenager said, keeping his eyes glued to the action on the street. Posted up with his hands thrust into his pockets, he looked just like all the other life-hardened sons of the ghetto who sold tan goods in Harlem.

"I know you good, man. But you could be even better. You could shine out there!"

The kid shrugged again as he stepped forward to get at a customer. "I'm shining pretty bright right here where I'm at."

Trey didn't respond. He watched as the sixteen-year-old transacted some quick bizz with a bone-thin, fast-walking girl who couldn't have been much older than he was. Their transaction was a slick blur as money and drugs changed hands in just a fraction of a second.

Trey peered up the block and spotted a squad car coming down the ave.

"Yo, Jake is riding," he warned as he eyed the police cruiser approaching at a fast clip. "You prolly gon' wanna stash that work."

Maleek turned and jetted, walking briskly in the opposite direction.

Trey held his ground as the cop car slowed down. The officer who was riding shotgun aimed a menacing look at Maleek's retreating back, but the car kept on rolling.

Trey chuckled as he watched them go.

Bum muh'fuckas.

As much as the local police were gunnin' for young'uns like Maleek who populated the streets with illegal drugs, they hated Trey and his partners even more.

It was understandable when you considered that businessmen like Trey fucked with the side stash in the police force's pockets. The local grocery store, your favorite deli, even your friendly neighborhood funeral home had to pay up for protection in this town.

But the little bit of cash that was strong-armed from small businesses was just the cherry on top of the police force's sundae. It was the big willies who paid out the ass. Ice Man Reynolds, Big Sonny Dawson, Granite McKay, Hurricane Jackson…all of Harlem's major kingpins had laid out premium dollars to keep their protection up and the local police force in pocket.

And since shit rolled downhill, of course the willies had to get their money back, so they robbed small business owners to reimburse themselves for what they had dished off to the cops.

But entrepreneurs like Trey refused to cough up the kickbacks. Instead, they formed their own security coalition and handled their own bizz.

Trey walked the few short blocks to the community center and gym he had founded. He stopped out front and looked up at the illuminated basketball logo that was superimposed over a bridge and read, The Crossover Community Center.

He'd started the center so he could help local kids and athletes learn job skills so they could stay off the streets. Trey did all kinds of things to make sure that every kid who wanted something better was given the opportunity to have it. He took up collections from local business, organized fundraisers and clothing drives. He put his money where his heart was too. Almost every barber who worked a chair at one of his shops had come through his center. Trey paid their tuition through barber school, and gave each one of them a full set of barber's tools as a graduation gift.

The Crossover Community Center had cost Trey a nice hunk of change to get it up and running, but what went on inside the building was worth every dime he'd spent and more. Although the hypnotic lure of drugs, gang banging, and easy money reigned supreme all over Harlem, under Trey's guidance The Crossover Community Center had become a life preserver for Black and Hispanic youths who were drowning in the gutters of New York City.

It was more than just a gym. The Crossover was a memorial to the friend he'd lost, and a bridge between a past life of crime and hopelessness, and a future filled with promise and potential.

Trey unlocked the front door to the center and stepped inside. For a long moment he stood in the foyer and stared up at the front wall. Centered on a basketball mural was a huge, custom-framed oil print that had been painted from a photo taken years earlier.

The picture was of two happy-go-lucky athletes sporting haircuts from back in the day. They wore matching yellow jerseys and their sweat-drenched brown faces were practically exploding in smiles.

Mayhem and Messiah. M&M. Double Trouble. The Twin Towers. The Dynamic Duo. Whatever you wanted to call them, they had been two peas in a muh'fuckin' pod.

Trey had gotten the name "Messiah" because he was a savior on the court who always delivered, and him and his man Mayhem had wreaked havoc on the hardwood from junior high school all the way through college.

Trey shook his head as the memories flooded him. His boy Mayhem had fought a battle with the streets and the streets had won. But it was just another tragedy in a highly tragic town. Another waste of talent and another waste of life. It seemed like so long ago, but at the same time it seemed like just yesterday....

It was halftime and the cheerleaders had just run out on center court when Mayhem made his move toward the side door. It was a local hoop tournament and he played in it every year over the winter break. They were up 67 to 42, smashing the shit out of a team that nobody else in college hoops had been able to beat. The coach was giving a rah-rah speech, and the sound of the screaming crowd was still echoing in his ears when Mayhem faded toward the back of the locker room and disappeared into the shadows.

He was coming right back. He was still in his court shoes, and he'd be back in the gym before anybody noticed he was gone.

Except somebody did notice.

Somebody had eyes on him. And when Mayhem dipped out the door and into the cold New York City night, that somebody dipped out right behind him.

Messiah Jackson just didn't get down like that. A man could only push his luck so far before that shit ran out. For almost four years his nig Mayhem had been playin' both ends of the bridge between his future and his past. They had less than three months to go before college graduation, and there was a lotta buzz going up about both of them getting into the league as top-tier second-round draft picks.

That NBA cream was finally about to rise, and it was gonna rise for both of them. All they had to do was be patient for a little while longer. Just hold off until graduation. Leave the streets behind and put everything on the basketball court.

Messiah had watched his friend drift toward the back of the room while the coach gave his half-time speech. Even though he loved his town he didn't love everything about it, and the greed and impatience that drove Mayhem to transact drugs in college was something he had no love for at all.

"Yo, come off that hustle," he had warned his nig. "Give it up. That little change you be makin' ain't shit compared to how you gon' be rolling when you get to the league, man. Don't let this little street grind throw you off ya game. It ain't worth it."

"I got mouths to feed, niggah," his boy had shot back. "I gotta look out for my moms and Lil Leek too, ya know?"

Nah, Messiah didn't know. But when his boy dipped outta that locker room he'd dipped too. He'd hung back in the shadows and watched his friend jog across the street to an overflow parking lot where a black Hummer waited. It had chrome rims and a sports pack, and Messiah had seen it many times before.

A U-Haul truck sped past him. He used it for cover as he crossed the street too. He was standing behind a Toyota van when he heard the words he had been waiting to hear.

"Nah, I'm done," Mayhem told the two dudes who had been his links to the street life for the past four years. "You can keep that package Peedee 'cause it's a wrap. It's over, man. I'm out."

One of the dudes just laughed. "C'mon, my niggah. You been around long enough to know how we flow. You don't just walk up outta this game, baby. You get carried out."

Shit moved real fast after that.

Them niggahs pounced and violence exploded in the cold night air. Messiah didn't even remember moving his feet. But somehow he got over there. They fought in a blur of tussling bodies, with Mayhem and Messiah swinging killer blows on K-Dawg and Peedee, two of the most feared drug dealers in Harlem.

It was Double-Trouble time, and just like on the court, they attacked. Mayhem handled one and Messiah handled the other.

It wasn't until he had Peedee pinned against a parked car that Messiah saw the gat in dude's hand. He lunged for it, and a shot rang out behind him before he got close enough to touch it.

It was about survival of the fittest after that. He clenched his big hand around Peedee's gun-fist, and with both of their trigger fingers fighting for position Messiah came out the winner.

He swung around just in time to see his manz clutching his stomach and rolling around on the cold ground. Mayhem's yellow jersey was dark with blood as K-Dawg stood over him and prepared to take aim again.

"Noooo!" Messiah screamed into the darkness, but not so much as a whisper came outta his mouth. Crushing Peedee's hand, he swung the pistol toward K-Dawg and squeezed one off. Then he jerked his arm down and dug the barrel of the gun into Peedee's gut and squeezed again.

By the time the boom of the bullets stopped echoing in the bitter night air, there was only one man left standing in that cold, inner city parking lot. One man left to tell the tale of how the streets could wrap their hands around ya throat and strangle your dream before it had a chance to take its first breath.

And that man was Trey "Messiah" Jackson.

CHAPTER 15

Rita undid her seat belt the moment the car came to a stop. She had spent the past few days grinding hard for Juicy and for Nooni too.

"You sure you're gonna be okay up in there?" Dutchy asked. Instead of parking on the other side of the bridge and taking the bus over, they had just pulled up in a private parking area not far from the Rosie building on Rikers Island.

Dutchy was worried about letting his baby go inside on a visit by herself. Rita was just too precious and fragile to be stepping behind the walls of a violent jail.

"Yeah." Rita nodded, keeping her eyes down. "I'll be fine."

Jail didn't scare her. She'd had a little bit of contact with the justice system herself. Rita had vivid memories of her fifteenth birthday when her father came into her room in the middle of the night just the way he usually did.

She could still feel his blood on her naked body as she held open her sheets and, for the first time, welcomed him in. He had been coming to her for ten whole years. But this time, instead of suffering another incestuous rape, Rita had thrust a butcher knife into her father's chest and held it there.

"I just wanna get Juicy out of there…" Rita stared toward the red brick building and said in a small voice.

Dutchy agreed. "I know, baby. Just a little while longer. We gotta keep working on it until something looks good."

Rita nodded. As much as she had been relying on Dutchy over the past couple of weeks she had also been doing her own homework and trying to come up with some of her own resources too. If it was up to her she would have taken Juicy straight to her crib and guarded her friend with her Glock 24/7, but Dutchy told her that shit would be like committing a double suicide.

"The last place we wanna stash Juicy is up in your crib, baby. That's the first place they're gonna look for her. Them niggahs get a hint that you're hiding her and they'll pull a kick door and lay your whole house down before you can get off a single shot. Nah, Rita. Juicy can't come to the crib, baby. It ain't just you and her we gotta worry about. You got Chub up in there too, remember?"

As much as it hurt, Rita had to admit that Dutchy was right. She couldn't bring Juicy home with her. It was way too dangerous for everybody. But Juicy couldn't stay in jail forever neither.

"Yeah, we had to pay off a few officers to make sure Juicy stays safe on the inside, but my sister-in-law said they ain't gonna be able to keep her off the radar much longer," Dutchy had warned. "It's only a matter of time before some square peeps what's up and drops a dime on her, so we need to hurry up and figure out our next move."

Rita agreed, and unbeknownst to Dutchy, she had already made contact with

192

someone she believed was lethal enough to hold those G-Spot niggahs off and protect Juicy from all the sharks who were looking to bite her.

Taking only her ID card and a roll of quarters for the vending machine, Rita listened to Dutchy's last minute instructions.

"Remember, she ain't in there under her real name," he reminded her. "They're calling her Yvette Williams, so that's the name you gotta say when you go to sign in."

Dutchy kissed Rita's cheek, then got out and came around to her side to open her door. He held it open while she undid her seat belt and climbed out.

Smoothing down her wild curls, Rita glanced over her shoulder like she expected a stray bullet to come flying at her at any moment.

"Are you sure nobody followed us?"

Dutchy nodded. "Nah, we straight, baby," he said, pulling her close to him. "But even if they did, this is a secure parking area. Not just anybody can roll up in here."

The visitor center was packed with people who had come to visit their friends and family members. Buses pulled up regularly, and there was a long line of people waiting to get their IDs checked.

Rita knew it was a damn good thing that Dutchy had people on the inside. Otherwise, they would have had to jump on the back of the line and wait like everybody else.

"I hope we don't get caught in the count," Dutchy muttered as they waited to go through the first metal detector. There was no getting around that. Everybody had to be checked, and Rita stared as some chick started wildin' out because the guards were making her go back over the bridge and leave her contraband cell phone in her car.

"I already waited forever to ride the damn bus over here!" the girl bitched. "On top of that, I got slobbered on by your drug fuckin-sniffing dog, and now I gotta ride all the way back over the bridge again? Y'all muthafuckas is a real trip!"

It was easy to see how stressful it was for those who had loved ones in jail. Little kids were running around going crazy, and the long wait combined with the strict rules and the shitty attitudes of the guards was enough to get people mad frustrated.

Rita tried to chill and wait patiently, especially when they searched her endless times. She had left her cell phone and all that other shit back in the car. The only thing she was carrying was her ID and her quarters. She hadn't even worn any jewelry, so there was no threat of attracting any reprimands from the guards.

Since Juicy was just a detainee and not a sentenced inmate she was now allowed up to three visits a week. Rita planned on coming back as much as she could, and today she had brought a money order for a hundred dollars with her so Dutchy could take it to the cashier's office and put it on Juicy's commissary.

It was gonna be a big relief to explain everything to Juicy face to face, and Rita couldn't wait for the chance to clear everything up. She had prayed day and night that her girl was handling the situation she had put her in, and according to Dutchy's sister-in-law and his boys, Juicy was safe and sound.

Of course, Rita still worried about her, and she was still worried crazy over Nooni, too. Knowing who had snatched her sister was a long way from proving it or finding her, and Rita's fear for Nooni was real and constant. Even though her sister had just turned eighteen, Rita had gone down to the police station and told the cops that Monique was holding a minor child hostage. Two days later she went back and they claimed they sent somebody to Monique's apartment and there were no signs of Nooni living there.

The next logical place Rita thought her sister could be was the G-Spot. She remembered how G and his posse had held Juicy hostage, and just the thought of Nooni going through half of that was enough to make Rita shake in fear.

But not even Dutchy had enough pull to send the cops rushing into the Spot looking for no delinquent runaway. "Yo, them boyz is in the *pocket*," he had said, shaking his head. "And I ain't talking no low-level shit, neither. They got some real willies on the payroll at the G-Spot, baby. Ain't no cop going up in that joint unless he's tryna get his dick sucked."

That left Nooni still missing. Still out on the streets somewhere, doing who knew what. As Rita sat and waited for her visit with Juicy, she looked around the room and imagined her sister alone and hurt, being abused and terrorized by the deadliest crew in Harlem.

Rita just couldn't help it. A tear slipped from her eye and she sat there and cried.

$$\$\$\$\$\$$

It was Monday and it seemed like every other chick in the facility was hyped. It was a visitation day for everybody who had the right last name and a lot of girls were anxious to see their families.

No matter what a chick had come to jail for, no matter how busted she looked or felt inside, every hood rat wanted to show up for a visit looking like a fox. Maybe it was all just a front so the world wouldn't find out how bad this shit-hole was kicking your ass, or maybe it was just the nature of a woman. Either way, there was a whole bunch of face primping and hair styling going on in almost every cell.

I had fallen asleep feeling sorry for myself, and it was close to lunchtime when I heard somebody call my name.

"Williams! Visitor!"

I didn't even move. I knew they had made a mistake so I didn't even get excited.

"Williams!" CO Gaines stood outside of my cell barking at me like she was my mother. "I know you heard me calling your ass!"

I kept my mouth closed and stood up.

"You got a visitor," she repeated.

I tried to keep the shock off my face as I followed her to the visiting room. It was on jam when we got there and she led me to a small table that was off to one side of the room by itself.

I didn't know who or what to expect.

My eyes scanned the crowd and I took in all the New York faces, sounds, and attitudes. Almost everybody looked like they could have come right off 136th Street, just like me.

I spotted Chiney sitting at a table across the way and she lifted her chin.

"Sup, homegirl," she said. "I thought you couldn't get no visitors?"

I shrugged and shook my head to tell her I didn't know what was up.

Chiney nodded and turned away, but her visitor kept me on grill and immediately I knew exactly who he was.

Trey.

His name jumped right into my mind. It had been a long time since I'd seen him, but his eyes were still sexy and mad intense. I couldn't help but stare back. He was fine as hell with his neatly groomed locks and long-ass legs. He was a lot more muscular than I remembered, but his piercing dark eyes, chiseled lips, and thuggish chin hadn't changed a bit.

I looked away first. My eyes were steady roaming as I searched the room to see who had come to see me.

My visitor walked through the door with CO Allen. I took one look at her and rolled my fuckin' eyes. She was so shook she almost tripped over her own damn feet as she walked toward me and I thought, *good for your ass*! If she was too soft and scary to be up in a jail how they hell did she think I felt?

I felt like a real fool, is how. I had let Rita catch me out there when I was weak and grieving, and after being locked down in this shitty box I couldn't think of a damn thing Rita could say that would make me forgive her.

In fact, as long as I was locked up Rita could kiss my black ass. If she wasn't rolling in with a cache of Uzis and a helicopter to bust me out, then I didn't want to hear a damn thing she had to say.

"*Juicy*," she said softly.

I blasted her.

"You got the nerve to bring your ass up in here when you're the one who sold me out?"

Chiney turned around in her seat and looked at me like, what's up? Where's the static? Show me which bitch I need to bite!

"It wasn't like that," Rita protested. "I swear to God! I can explain everything!"

"That wasn't nothing but greed that got a' hold of you, Rita. That little bit of money was just *change*, baby! *Chicken change*! That's the price you put on our friendship when there was a whole lot more where that came from! Officer!" I stood up and started showing out as loud as I could. "Officer, I refuse this visit!"

I saw the look of shock that jumped into Rita's eyes and I turned my back on it.

"Take me back to my cell!" I barked.

"Juicy, no..." I heard her say as I turned away. "No, wait...don't leave..."

I folded my arms across my chest and kept my eyes aimed on the back wall. "Get me the fuck outta here! I wanna go back to my cell!"

It had gotten quiet in the room and I knew all the inmates and their visitors were staring at me. Fuck it. Let 'em. CO Gaines jumped on me real quick. Snatching my arm, she jacked me up on my toes and whisked me back through the doors in two seconds flat.

"You real stupid," she declared as she led me away to get strip searched before returning to my cell. "I told you to keep your mouth closed and stay easy. Besides, whatever static you got with that bitch you should have squashed it. Sitting out here for a couple of hours with your worst enemy beats sweating by yourself in your cell all damn day, dummy."

$$$$$

There was always some kinda drama popping off on The Rock, and the commotion playing out in the visiting room wasn't out of the ordinary considering you were up in a jail.

Trey had done hard time and he knew everything about the jailhouse scene was a trial of mental toughness and victory over misery.

His visit with his sister had started out all fucked up. A drug dog on the bus had sniffed him up and down as they came over the bridge, a guard had made him go to the back of the line because he was slow pulling out his ID, And for some reason he was patted down twice at every security check on his way into Rosie.

But Trey took it all in stride. He was a big dude, and no matter how tastefully he dressed or how calmly he carried himself, that element of danger that lived in him always seemed to shine right through.

He visited his sister like clockwork every Monday, and today he was planning to ask her to come live with him when her time was up on The Rock. His baby sister was real smart, but all that pill popping, smoking blunts, and the in-and-out-of-jail-on-minor-charges shit wasn't a good look for her.

He wished he woulda caught somebody selling drugs on the street to his sister, but the slangers were like roaches out there. If you saw one you knew there were at least a hundred more that were hidden in the darkness.

They camouflaged their operations in check cashing places, deli stores, dry cleaners, and one pretty major playa was rumored to be dealing his candy out of a day care center.

Hell, the streets were full of people like his sister who couldn't get their shit together, and as Trey sat in the visiting room watching the drama jump off he wasn't surprised by who was making all the noise.

He studied the fine yummy from 136th Street as she barked on the guards and demanded to be returned to her cell. His eyes roamed over her body from head to toe. She still had it. All of it. Even her baggy prison gear couldn't hide the fact that she had some phatty pockets in the back, a nice pair of titties, and a tight waistline too.

"That's Juicy," his baby sister said, following his gaze and nodding toward the chick who was now being escorted out the door. "You remember her, don't you? She went to high school with me, then she hooked up with that grimy niggah G McKay—"

"I remember her," Trey said, cutting Chiney off. His eyes hardened. "If she was stupid enough to fuck with that niggah G then I ain't surprised she ended up in here."

Just hearing G's name brought back some real hostile memories for Trey, and this Chiney knew and understood.

"Juicy ain't that bad," she said, noting the dark thunder that had entered her brother's piercing eyes. "She's just a cool chick who made some fucked up decisions about men. The same as Charlene did. The only difference is G killed Charlene, and Juicy got away with her life."

196

Trey nodded. Granite had been a wily black muthafucka. It still burned his heart that his brother Cooter had stayed loyal to G even after their sister had gone missing and was obviously dead. To sit up drinking and partying with a niggah like that night after night after night, knowing he'd put your own flesh and blood in the ground was unthinkable to Trey. And as much as he had loved his brother Cooter, G had come between them and stayed between them until the day he died.

But all that was in the past now. Cooter had made his mistakes and Trey had made his share of them too. There was nothing left to do but let the dead rest in peace and keep the living focused on living.

An image of Juicy as she was led away by the CO flashed through Trey's mind. *Backwards ass.* From what he remembered, she'd been a real flirt back in the day, but her grandmother had kept her on church-girl lock.

It was strange the way people turned out sometimes. Those who started out on top could fuck around and end up on the bottom. And sometimes, those that life shoved down into the gutters managed to rise to the top. But not Juicy Stanfield. She had gone from the G-Spot to The Rock.

What a chicken, Trey thought, shaking his head. *Such a fuckin' waste.*

Putting all thoughts of the beautiful and sexy inmate out of his mind, Trey discreetly adjusted the knot that had risen in his pants, and then shifted all of his attention back to his little sister.

CHAPTER 16

Williams! Visitor!"

I got called down for another visit the very next day, and this time I was ready to do just about anything to get out of that little ass cell. But instead of being led into the room where everybody else had their visit, the CO took me into a private booth. I wasn't surprised to see Rita waiting there, but in my heart I still felt the same way I had felt the day before.

I sat down at the table across from her. My lips were straight up twisted and I felt grimy, busted, and torn all the way down.

Rita had always been neat with her game, and today was no exception. Everything about her was perfect. Her gear was uptown and pressed. Her skin and hair looked real fresh and shiny. Like she had just showered and brushed olive oil cream through her curls.

"Juicy," she spoke first like she wanted to plead her case from the gate. "Please don't be mad at me," she begged. "I know how bad it looks but I can explain everything."

I gave her a shitty ass look. Where I came from when somebody swore all out they could explain away their dirt, it really meant they didn't have a good excuse for none of it.

"I swear on my dead mother," Rita continued.

I smirked. That dead mama shit didn't mean a damn thing to me. I had a dead mother too, and swearing on Cara's grave didn't hold no significance to me one way or the other.

"Listen to me," she said, leaning toward me. "I didn't set you up, Juicy. I was just trying to keep you alive. It was Monique. Monique from the G-Spot. Them muthafuckas put a bounty out on your head. A big one."

"What?" I broke my silence as fear and confusion banged in my chest.

"Monique is the one who snatched Nooni," Rita said miserably. "Her and the crew. All this shit was a set up. From the beginning to the end. They took my sister because they knew me and you were tight. They cooked up a scheme to use me to get next to you and your money." She gave a pained chuckle. "And it worked."

For the next ten minutes I listened as Rita ran shit down to me. She told me that Ace and Pluto had put a bull's-eye on my forehead. A target on my back. They had put my picture out all over the community and every corner boy in Harlem was gunning for me. The first person that found me was supposed to drag me into the G-Spot, and get a nice chunk of change as a reward.

By the time she finished talking I was more terrified than ever. How was I supposed to watch my back and stay alive out there when total strangers were looking to snatch me up?

"The G-Spot is all fucked up," Rita said. "Without G's muscle they practically ran that shit into the sewer. They need that money you and Gino took, Juicy. They're saying y'all stole almost a million dollars of G's stash and they're desperate to get that shit back."

Rita told me her man Dutchy had a lot of cops in his family. One of them had been talking to some snitches that were on the police payroll. They had given him some crazy-ass information and Dutchy and Rita had stayed up late nights piecing together the scenario, and now the puzzle was forming a clear and complete picture. That grimy set wanted my ass.

I sat there trembling and bewildered. Deep inside I had known this day was coming. I had never felt safe. Even way out in California. Of course G's goonies still wanted his fucking paper! They would never stop looking for that kinda cash. They knew I had it, and with Gino out of the picture it was just a matter of time before they moved in on me to get it.

"So, let's take this from the beginning so I can make sure I'm following you straight. Ace and them figured if they put a high enough price on Nooni's head that you would ask me to pay it, right?"

Rita nodded. "They made a calculated guess. Who else was I gonna turn to for that kind of bank?"

"But how did they know I was gonna come back to New York? How did they know you wasn't gonna come pick the money up yourself like you wanted to? I didn't even get the ticket in my real name."

"That's probably why they only gave me twenty-four hours to make the drop. Like you said before, they knew I wouldn't have time to get all the way to California and back and still meet their deadline. Dutchy scoped them watching my crib, and then they followed us. My dumb-ass led them straight to the airport. But the good thing is I peeped Monique when I was coming to meet you at baggage claim."

"I just couldn't let them get to you, Juicy. Not for the money, and not for Nooni neither. All I could picture was them niggahs dragging you back inside the G-Spot, and on my own life, I couldn't let that happen. So instead, we brought you out here."

"So that's where the two hundred grand went, right?" I had already figured out that CO Allen had kept the hundred grand I had taped on me I just didn't know where the other half had gone. "You and Dutchy paid off the cops to arrest me, and the guards to keep me here?"

Rita nodded. "Some of it. I still have some left. But we paid them to keep you *safe*, Juicy," she said. "We paid a whole lot of people to keep you safe." She was crying now, and all I could do was sit there and cry with her. Once again I was wrapped in a blanket of never-ending fear. Just knowing what was waiting for me on the other side of the jail walls made my tiny little cell look real good.

"So can you just get me to the airport?" I asked. "That way I can get a ticket and fly back to Cali. I left my car parked at the airport and I'll just go back home from there."

"Juicy..." a look of pure terror crept into Rita's eyes. "If your car was at the airport then I'm not sure it's safe for you to go back there."

"What do you mean? Why you say that?"

"I saw something on the news the day before yesterday. It was all over every channel, and CNN reported that the threat level was going up because of it. A green BMW blew up in the airport parking lot in L.A. It was rigged with a car bomb, and they said two people got killed."

"They blew up my damn car? And people *died*?"

The blood in my body ran ice-cold. I couldn't think straight. I didn't know who to trust. Everything was all jumbled up in my head, and now I had even more crazy doubts and suspicions about everything and everybody. Including Rita.

"So what now?" I sniffed. No matter which way I looked at my situation I was fucked from one end to the other. "I'm supposed to just stay locked up in here until Ace and Pluto forget about me and the money?"

Rita shook her head quickly.

"No, *chica*. Hell no. This was only a temporary fix. I'm getting you out of here. Believe me, I'm grinding for you, and I've got a little something in the works."

She leaned closer and confided. "I've been talking to some pretty strong playas who have a lot of manpower. They got someplace safe for you to chill, and best of all they gots no love for the G-Spot crew. They've agreed to help you lay low until we can find somewhere for you to go, cool?"

"Who are these people? More gangstas? And what about your sister? How are you gonna get her back?" As bad as I wanted to get the fuck outta jail and ditch everything about New York, I was worried for Nooni too because I knew what lay ahead for her.

A cold look came across Rita's face.

"We'll talk about that later. I don't want you to worry about none of that right now, Juicy. You just hold on while I work shit out for you, okay? We'll take care of everything else in due time. Right now my focus is on getting you outta here and finding you someplace safe to stay."

CHAPTER 17

"One of y'all niggahs is lying," Salida pointed her finger as she stood in front of the open safe in G's office. They'd just done a countdown and over ten g's was missing from the cash box. Since only the three of them could get into the safe, and only a handful of people ever came into the office, the pool of suspects was real small.

"Yo," Pluto said, swelling up on her, "don't point ya fuckin' finger over here, a'ight? I'm telling you now. I ain't been in that safe in a good minute, so whoever left the shit sitting wide open needs to figure out where the fuckin' money went."

Ace held up his hands. "Chill, y'all. That doe didn't just walk up outta here, we all know that. But on the real Salida, me and Pluto ain't got no reason to dip in the cash box. We'd be stealing from ourselves and from each other and wc ain't never got down like that."

Salida shrugged. "Who said it was y'all who stole the money? I said one of y'all forgot to lock the safe up and maybe somebody else came in here and stole it. Now somebody cop to that!"

Ace shook his head. "I been lockin' this safe up for years. Why would I all of a sudden start forgetting?"

"Well who else has been in here besides us?" Salida demanded. "I mean, Monique comes in here all the time, but she's family." She shrugged. "Nooni's been in and outta here too. Sometimes I send her back here to get a file for me or something like that, but she's definitely in here by herself a whole lot."

Pluto was silent, but Ace bit hard on that shit.

"You think that young girl been sliding her hands up in our doe? Yo, she got the heart for that kind of hustle?"

"Hell, no," Pluto shook his head. Nooni slept on his fuckin' pullout couch every night. He'd seen how shook and nervous her little ass was. "She's a mouse," Pluto said firmly. "A scared little mouse."

"I'on't know man..." Ace frowned. "You never know. Sometimes them real quiet mousy-types is the ones you gotta watch out for. Nah'mean?"

"That chick is slick," Salida nodded in agreement. "Slick and sly. I think she got us. I really do."

Pluto waved his hand like *get the fuck outta here*! "Man, that little girl ain't take that money! If she did she woulda dipped off my couch by now!"

"Well if you know for sure who *didn't* take it," Salida challenged, "then why you don't know for sure who *did*?"

"Man, I see how y'all living. Y'all tryna set that girl up!"

"That's bullshit. She did it," Salida lied, even though she knew damn well that she was the one who had dipped in the G-Spot's cash box so she could put a down payment on the club drugs she was about to start selling.

201

Her connect had promised her a shipment of ecstasy and zannies, with another shipment of 'ludes, special k, and roofies coming right after that.

Salida was covering all her bases. She'd used the cash she'd stolen from the safe as a down payment on the pills, and she'd had Truth and Bilal pull a lick on a neighborhood store so she could have enough money to buy all the ingredients she needed to manufacture her first batch of crystal meth.

And she'd gone down to the courthouse and transferred all of G's businesses that were making money into her name too. Just in case she had to flip them for some extra cash.

"Nooni ain't even grimy like that," Pluto insisted again. "This shit smells just like a set up."

"Why would we want to set that poor girl up?" Salida glared at Pluto.

She turned her back on him and spoke directly to Ace. "Nooni took that money, baby. She's been acting real sneaky lately, and every time I look up she's either modeling some new clothes, or she's walking around showing off some new phone or some other fancy electronic gadget. Where's she getting the money to buy all that expensive new shit, huh? Lil Mama is a thief, y'all. Trust me, I know one when I see one."

$$$$$

Salida slammed outta G's office as Ace and Pluto continued to argue over Nooni. They didn't know it, but she was standing right outside taking delight in every heated word they spit. She pressed her ear to the door and tried to hold back her laughter as the two fat fools went at each other's throats over the changes and upheavals she had set in place.

Salida knew exactly what she was doing. It was all about dividing and conquering. She didn't give a damn which one of them got the win, or came out on top in their little bitch-fest. If they couldn't find a way to bring in some big-time cash then there was nothing either one of them could say that would slow her stroll.

Salida was all about her paper. In fact, she was on her way out right now to hook up with her broker. Her connect was a determined hustler who operated his business from the basement of a funeral home of all places.

They'd made a few deals, and already Salida respected his ambition. He reminded her of another hungry hustler she had known pretty good back in the day.

She listened until Ace and Pluto finished talking all that shit. Then she sauntered out the side door and into a

whip parked in the alley, where Truth was waiting to take her to Three Brothers Funeral Home.

CHAPTER 18

Two days after Rita's visit, the COs came for me again. It was CO Allen with the birthmark on his nose, and of course CO Gaines.

"Let's go, Williams," Gaines said real loud, making a show of it. Rita had told me she was Dutchy's sister-in-law and that she was one of the guards who was helping me hide out, but I still didn't like her. "You just made bail, girl. Grab your shit. It's time to roll."

Rita had kept her word. I hollered goodbye to Chiney, then walked out of that cell light-footed and empty-handed because there wasn't a damn thing in there that I wanted to take with me.

I had to go through the whole process of waiting in a stinking little area while I was being processed. Next, they took me to another area where I waited with some other chicks who were getting sprung too.

"How long is this gonna take?" I asked a skinny Hispanic lady who looked like she had been inside multiple times.

She shrugged. "There might be one more bus leaving tonight but ain't no telling. If it gets too late they gonna leave our asses right here until in the morning."

"Williams!" one of the COs called out for me. "Tonight is your lucky night."

They gave me back my empty Gucci bag and the clothes I had been wearing when they brought me in. I was given my cell phone too. My battery was shot, but I didn't care. At least I had a phone.

I was nervous as I walked out the jailhouse doors. I expected Rita to be waiting outside to pick me up, but instead there was a tall, light-skinned dude with long box-braids holding open the door of a white Rolls Royce for me.

"Where is Rita?" I asked, nervous as hell. For all I knew this could be another set up. "Who are you?"

"I'm Dabu," he said evenly. "Just relax and get in the car. Rita told me to pick you up, so come on before I leave your ass here."

I was so scared my mouth went dry.

I glanced over my shoulder at the red brick building, then back at the dude who was waiting for me to hop in his ride.

"How do I know Rita sent you?"

He shrugged. "You don't. But while you standing out here bullshittin' you ain't nothing but an easy target, nah'm sayin?"

I rode in that plush whip second-guessing myself all the way back to Manhattan. What if Ace and Pluto had sent this dude? What if this fool kicked me out on a side street and Monique and her crew were waiting to kill my ass? All kinds of scenarios were running through my mind and none of them looked good.

Dabu acted like I wasn't even in his back seat as we rode. He didn't say a word to me, and I didn't say nothing else to him neither. We ended up on the streets of Spanish Harlem, and I almost freaked out when he pulled up in the parking lot of a funeral home and stopped right near the delivery door where they brought the bodies in.

"We're here," he said, turning off the ignition and opening his door.

"Umm, hold up!" I said, ready to straight panic. I stared at the sign on the building.

Three Brothers Funeral Home.

Oh, hell no. I didn't fuck with funeral homes. No way, no how!

"Umm, I'ma need to use your phone," I told him. Right then and there I decided that he was gonna have to drag me out of his whip. My ass fit real snug in those soft leather seats, and I wasn't about to budge.

"Get out," he said, coming around and holding my door open.

"No! I ain't getting out! Why the hell are we going in the damn funeral home?"

"Just come ya ass on!" he barked over his shoulder. "Or I'ma drive you around to the front and drag your ass out on the street so one of them G-Spot niggahs can get you."

I got out the car and followed him through a set of double doors that he unlocked with two keys. I grabbed the back of his shirt as we entered the dark building, and I was shaking so hard he reached back and gripped my wrist to steady me.

"Calm the fuck down, girl. You all right."

To my surprise I could hear music playing, and it wasn't funeral music neither. It was a cut by Jay-Z, and judging by the bass that was tickling my feet it sounded like it was coming from somewhere down below us.

"Who in the hell is up in here?"

"My boss."

"Look, I don't fuck with dead people," I muttered as I tiptoed behind him with my eyes squeezed half-way closed.

He laughed. "These dead people don't even know you here."

I was shitting boulders as he started leading me down a flight of stairs. The music was getting louder. The beat was bumping. I could see a light shining down there and I prayed like hell that we weren't gonna walk up on no dead bodies stretched out in open caskets.

I took a few steps and looked down again. There was somebody sitting in a chair at the bottom of the steps, just off to my left.

The first thing I noticed was the toe of his shoe. I had been stomped out with enough first-class leather to recognize imported alligator when I saw it. I knew it wasn't a dead man because his ankle was propped up on his knee and his foot was moving to the beat.

The further down I went, the more of him I saw.

My eyes traveled along the foot, past the argyle sock, and up the length of the trousers that were cut from fine Italian silk.

My knees shook as I took another step.

A cream-colored shirt was tucked into the pants, and in the lap were a pair of dark hands that were furiously twirling a familiar-looking black onyx ring.

I took another shaky step down, and what I saw in that chair hit me like a sledgehammer and I almost passed out right where I stood.

"*God, noooo!*" I screamed and clutched the railing as my bladder let go.

G was back.

TO BE CONTINUED...

Order

ENVY: THE 4TH DEADLY SIN

at

www.Amazon.com or www.BN.com

**PART FOUR
OF NOIRE'S BLOCKBUSTER
URBAN EROTIC SERIAL TALE!**

Juicy is facing a whole new set of problems!

The grimy road of life takes more crazy twists and turns when Juicy-Mo hits the bricks and lands right back in the heart of Harlem!

The chaos and danger she thought she'd escaped comes rushing back to haunt her as a blast from her past shows up in the basement of a funeral home!

What's next for the sexy Harlem stunna who just can't seem to catch a break? Will she end up stretched out cool in a box, or will she escape the clutches of her destiny and live to fight another day?

WARNING!

This here ain't no romance,
It's an urban erotic tale
Juicy's back in Harlem
And she's bout to catch some hell
She's creepin' in the basement
And that shit is smellin' foul
Drugs are flowing in the streets
And thugs are on the prowl
They're racin' for that paper,
Ain't no tellin' who's gone win
Betta check ya jealous heart
'Cause **ENVY** is a **SIN!**

**Find out more in...
G-SPOT 2: THE SEVEN DEADLY SINS
Envy: The 4th Deadly Sin**

The Urban Erotic Serial Saga Continues!

NOIRE

G-Spot 2:
The Seven Deadly Sins
An Urban Erotic Serial Tale Told in 7 Parts

ENVY: THE 4TH DEADLY SIN

by
Noire

www.AskNoire.com
www.GSpot2.com
www.TheGSpotSaga.com

CHAPTER 1

But it couldn't be G!

G's black ass was dead. I had watched Jimmy blast his whole chest open right in front of my eyes!

No, it wasn't the notorious Granite McKay sitting in that plush armchair in the basement of that funeral home, but it *was* a stone-cold killer who was dressed like G from head to toe and twirling an onyx ring on his finger.

"*Fletcher!*" I screamed real loud when I recognized who it was. A huge wave of relief washed over me at the sight of Jimmy's old friend from back in the day. "Boy! What the hell are you doing down here?"

"It's Flex, remember?" he said smoothly. He stood up and opened his arms real wide, and I was so happy that G hadn't crawled outta his wet grave to get me that I fell right into them.

"It's good to see you, Juicy-Mo," he held me close to his chest for a few seconds and then beamed at me with that same dumb, bucktoothed smile of adoration he used to give me back when he was ten.

"Boy, you almost made me pee on myself! I can't believe it's you!" I stepped back and took a good look at him while holding on tight to both of his hands.

"But what the hell are you *doing* down here?"

The last time I'd seen Fletcher Boykin I was chained to a pole in the Dungeon at the G-Spot. G had been feeling generous that day, so mad niggahs was coming through to fuck me for free, but I was bleeding and filthy, and so run-through that Flex didn't even want him none.

I glanced around in disbelief. It looked like something out of a damn horror movie down there. The walls were made of rough cinderblocks, and exposed pipes and electrical wiring crisscrossed each other and ran over our heads.

"Boy, what in the world are you doing chilling in a damn funeral home?" I was *too* creeped out. Rita must have been outta her mind for sending me to hide out in a joint full of dead bodies.

"This is where I rest," he shrugged. "C'mon." He turned toward the back wall where I saw a steel door sticking out of all that cinderblock. It had one of those real high-tech keypads on it, and it seemed like Fletcher punched in a hundred numbers before a green light flickered and he pushed the door open.

But that door only led us into a small foyer where there was another thick-ass security door waiting for us. This one looked like it was made outta concrete or some kind of rough stone, and once again, Fletcher punched a million numbers into a keypad before that door was unlocked too.

I couldn't believe there was another damn door facing us after that. Fletcher had barricaded himself down here like it was a war bunker, and I frowned at my reflection as we stood in front of a door that had a big, shiny mirror across the top half.

The door also had locks going up and down the bottom left side, and a bunch of keys jingled when Fletcher went into his pocket.

"What the hell is back there?" My voice came out real scary-like, and he laughed as he slipped key after key into the locks and turned them.

"You'll see."

He finally got all the locks opened and pushed through the door.

"I heard you were looking for someplace safe to lay your head." He opened his arms up wide and moved back so I could step inside. "Well, here it is. *Mi casa es su casa.*"

I forced my feet to move two tiny paces, and then I took a real good look around. The hallway outside had been scary as fuck, but the space that had opened up behind all those doors was straight laid. We were standing in a huge room that had been done up like an office. A long mahogany desk sat in the center of the room, and a huge crystal chandelier hung directly above it. A plush leather couch was pushed up against one wall, and a built-in marble-and-mirror bar was on the other one. There were end tables, lamps, and leather chairs on each side of the room, and the shiny floors were covered in real hardwood.

I couldn't believe my eyes.

"You mean you actually *live* down in here?" I blurted out, but what I was really thinking was, what kind of crazy fool pimps out a goddamn funeral home?

Fletcher laughed. "Hell yeah. Hot, ain't it? I been chillin' down here for a good minute now. I think it's beast."

He busted the look on my face and laughed.

"Hey, don't knock it Juicy-Mo. This joint is cool, it's comfortable, it's quiet, and it's the last fuckin' place in the world that somebody would think to come looking for me."

He had that shit right.

"Yeah," I agreed. "It sure as hell is."

"So what's been happening with you?" I asked as he led me over to sit on the couch. The last I'd heard Fletcher had gotten into some crazy static with a posse of rival drug dealers. Him and Cooter Jackson had been scheming on how to grab a share of Harlem's drug territory after G died, but their plans must have been real weak because they had both caught a bad one.

A bunch of slangers had stomped on Cooter's head until it busted open like a grape on concrete, and then some rival cats had gunned Fletcher down in the middle of the street like he was less than a dog.

He had been in the hospital on critical when me and Gino left New York, and I couldn't believe he had taken all those bullets and was still alive and standing.

"So you doing okay now?"

He looked just like a little boy when he grinned, and I remembered how he used to be in love with me when we were kids.

"A niggah like me is doing better than ever, Juicy-Mo. You know how it be. I took a few shots to the gut, but I made it through."

"Wow, Fletcher," I said. "I can't believe I'm actually sitting here talking to you!"

He pressed the back of his hand against my arm real firm. "It's Flex now," he said quietly. "Go 'head and remember that baby."

A chill zipped through me.

"*Got it,*" I said with a fake laugh. "I know you on your grown man thang these days but you're still like a little brother to me."

He grinned. "You was a real good big sister, Juicy. I used to think Jimmy was the luckiest dude in the world to be your brother, nah'mean? He got to see you every day. Eat with you, chill with you, sleep in the same house as you..." he shrugged. "Your grandmother used to look out for me all the time, Juicy, and your brother was my best friend. But I loved *all* of y'all. Y'all was my only family. The only people who ever really cared about me."

I nodded. "We're still your family. We always will be."

When me and Jimmy were growing up I could never understand why Fletcher was always up under us all the time. He used to be a big pain in my ass, and I would chase him away from our crib every chance I got.

But now that I was all by myself in the world, with no kinda roots and no real blood connections, I knew exactly how Fletcher must have felt back then. Being in the world all by yourself was hard as hell, and I was extra-happy to see him now.

I looked around at his joint again.

"Like I said, it's good to see you, but I don't know about this whole funeral home thang you got going on. Dead people scare the hell outta me."

"Don't worry, baby. They keep all the bodies upstairs in the freezer. Besides, ain't nothin' never gone fuck with you as long as I'm around, Juicy. If one of them dead niggahs comes down those stairs tryna get at you I'll kill his ass!"

I laughed with him, but my feelings were all over my face.

Fletcher chuckled. "Stop worrying, Juicy. You look just like your grandmother when you make that face. I promise, ain't nothin' in here that can hurt you. Believe me," he said seriously. "I wouldn't let it. C'mon," he grabbed my wrist and pulled me to my feet. "Come check out the rest of the place."

There was another door on the other side of the room. He punched in a code to get through that one too, then he pulled it open.

We walked down a short hall. Fletcher was just as pimped out as his crib. I peeped the hell outta him as he strolled beside me dressed up like an old-ass man. This boy wasn't but eighteen years old, and his gear was damn near retro.

I felt some kinda way as I eyeballed his expensive tailor-made suit, his polished 'gators, and the glistening diamond cuff links that sparkled at his wrists. And the onyx ring straight fucked me up. No wonder I had thought he was G when I came down those stairs. He looked like a skinny little boy playing "dress up" in his daddy's closet.

This was some brand new shit to me, because Fletcher had been one of the bummiest kids on our block. His grandmother used to put big fat yellow-ducky diaper pins up and down his shirts, and the bottom of his pants were always floating somewhere up above his bony ankles.

But when he got in the drug game he had started dressing just like all the other thugs on the street. I had gone looking for him one night in Taft projects when Jimmy first went missing. Fletcher was running a crew of trap boys from the lobby of a building, and he was suited up in baggy jeans and timbs and swaggering just like every other young hustler on the grind.

I remembered how Fletcher had called me stupid that night, and begged me to leave G and stay right there in the projects with him so he could wife me. He told me he was gonna be in charge one day and holding all the cards, and he swore he had a plan that would set me up with riches for life.

And it looked like riches was exactly what Fletcher was sitting on in his little underground palace now.

"I got me a nice little kitchen," he said, pointing toward a real slamming spread. It was done up in stone and stainless steel, and the eat-in nook had one of those fly L-shaped leather benches that hugged two walls.

"And back here is the washer and dryer and the extra bathroom. I'ma use this one, and you can go ahead and use the shower and stuff in my room, cool?"

I followed him further down the hall.

"This is my guestroom. I'ma chill in here and let you take the big room, a'ight?"

I peeked my head inside and I was real impressed by what I saw. The room was done up. It had a king-sized bed, a wall mounted television, and a real pretty bearskin rug on the floor.

We was in the basement so of course it didn't have no windows, and after coming out of jail I noticed that shit right away.

"Over here is the master bedroom," Fletcher said. He took me next door to a large room that looked like it had been furnished by a professional decorator. A small fridge was off to one side, and a bar was cattycorner on the other wall.

"You gone sleep real good in here, Juicy," he bragged. "Real good. You gonna have your own bathroom and everything."

"Thanks," I said quietly, taking it all in. Fletcher's crib put me in the mind of G's old place, just much smaller. There was marble, granite, and expensive electronics and appliances everywhere. The only difference was, G had rested in a swanky condo on Central Park West, and Fletcher was flossin' his game from the basement of a funeral home.

I walked into the bedroom and Fletcher leaned against the doorframe and eyed me down as he tapped his foot in them expensive-ass shoes. I didn't know what to think except that my dude really looked bugged. He had gone from a gutta young hood trying to come up in the game, to the ghost of G past.

And it wasn't just his clothes, neither. Everything about him screamed "Granite McKay" from head to toe. The way he walked and talked, and the scary way he twirled that onyx ring on his finger was straight G to a tee.

"You like all this?" he asked, nodding at his spread.

"Yeah. It's real nice."

"See, I told you, Juicy!"

Outta nowhere he bum rushed up in my face and got all hyped. "I *told* your ass!" he based and poked me in the chest twice with his skinny finger.

"Ow!" I shrank away from him. "Stop fuckin' poking me! You told me what?"

"I told you I was gonna be runnin' shit one day!" he said and poked me again. "I told you to have faith in me, girl! That niggah G was living on borrowed time. I could feel that shit. I seen the whole thing go down in my mind before it ever even happened! That's why I wanted you and Jimmy to jump on my team, baby. I was trying to *protect* y'all. But neither one of y'all would listen to me!"

I rubbed my chest where he had jammed his damn finger into me. What could I say? Fletcher had been dead right. And me and Jimmy had been dead wrong. Both of us had paid a price for not listening to him.

"Uh-huh. I told you I was gonna take over the G-Spot one day too, didn't I?" Fletcher gave me the crazy eye. "And I meant that shit. I still am."

Hold up. I shook my head real fast. I had been vibing with him for a minute, but I wasn't co-signing that G-Spot shit.

"Why you wanna be down with them niggahs at the Spot?" I based. "I hate that fuckin' place! Jimmy *died* up in there, Fletcher! Did you forget that shit? The only thing I wanna see the G-Spot do is burn down to the goddamn ground."

"Yo, you don't *unnerstand,* Juicy," he said moving up on me. He grabbed his nuts and hiked up the front of his pants. "I can run that joint ten times better than G did! Them niggahs up in there done let the Spot turn into a fuckin' wasteland! It's time for them to fade out and let a real boss take the throne."

I smirked. "Fletcher, please."

"Yo," he grabbed my chin and spit through clenched teeth. "It's *Flex*, Juicy. *Flex.* That old bum-ass niggah Fletcher is *dead.* Now get that in ya head, ma, 'cause I ain't gonna tell you no more."

"I don't care what your damn name is!" I jerked away and barked at him like I was the big sister and he was still a little kid. "I ain't gonna never be down with the G-Spot or nobody in it!"

He shook his head. "You better kill all that noise, Juicy. If you ain't learned nothing else I hope you done learned to put your money on me, baby girl, because I'm about to rake in a whole lot of it. Every town needs a one-stop shop for high-post entertainment. And the G-Spot is about to be mine!"

CHAPTER 2

Truth pulled out of the parking lot of Three Brother's Funeral Home just as a glistening white Rolls Royce was pulling in. Salida strained to see into the car's interior as they rolled past each other, but all she could make out was a shadowy figure sitting in the back seat.

"Hold up," she told Truth as she turned around and looked out the rear window. The bone-white whip rolled up to the side entrance that Salida had just come out of, and at this time of night whoever it was had to be going downstairs to the same place she had just left.

She watched as the car stopped and a tall young man got out. He went around to the back passenger door and opened it, and appeared to be arguing with whoever was inside.

"Go on ahead," Salida said with a shrug and waved her hand for Truth to drive on. The young drug broker she'd just picked up a bag of samples from must have been getting his pussy delivered from the hoe strip up the street. Whoever the trick was, Salida couldn't blame her for not wanting to get out of the car. Not even the most desperate hoe wanted to make her money in the basement of a goddamn funeral home.

Let the truth be told, Salida hadn't been all that anxious to go down those basement steps herself, but the love of money had overruled her apprehension and sent her tipping down those stairs where she had been promised the very best prices on all the club drugs she wanted to sell.

Salida remembered cracking up laughing the first time she laid eyes on the baby-faced dealer. She'd already known he was just as greedy and hungry as she was, but when she saw his little ass dressed to kill in a 2011 version of a zoot suit, it almost blew her mind.

She had brought G a suit just like it back in the day, and it had only taken her sharp eye a minute to sweep over the boy and see exactly what his problem was.

He had Godfathered G.

He was striving to be just like him. Salida had known G better than anybody did, and when she looked at young Flex she recognized G's style, his swagger, his tone of voice, and his insecurities. And most of all she recognized the replica of the black onyx ring he twirled on his finger. It was damn near identical to the one she had given to G on their wedding day.

But aside from the fact that G had been a seasoned gansta all down in his bones, and this lil' boy Flex was probably still pissing in his drawers, there was one real big difference between G and the adolescent kid who was trying so hard to be him.

Bitches.

There was no way in hell G would have been caught dead bringing a goddamn prostitute to his crib. G was pussy-phobic and he could only fuck a virgin. He would have never touched a woman who had already been dicked down by another man.

"Where you wanna go now, Mizz Salida?" Truth asked as he steered out of the parking lot and took a right turn on the main street.

"Take me back to the G-Spot," Salida told him as the thought of sex with G lingered on her mind. She crossed her legs at the knees and gave her unused womanhood a quick little squeeze.

Before G locked her away Salida had been a very sexual and sensual person. Defying G at every turn, she had dreamed about dick like there was no tomorrow. But all those years of being locked up, doped up, and isolated all alone had killed her urges and left her feeling drier than dust down there.

But power was one of the strongest aphrodisiacs, and lately Salida's body had started talking to her again. All those years of forced celibacy were for the birds, and her dry spell was about to end at the tip of a nice, hard dick.

Putting the right playa on pussy-lock was also part of the next phase in Salida's plan, and Ace was about to be a lucky mothafucka because tonight he'd be the very first man to fuck her behind Granite McKay.

Salida thought about G, and how pissed that niggah would be to know his right-hand man was about to knock her pretty-pretty out, and she threw her head back and laughed out loud.

"You okay, Mizz Salida?" Young Truth asked from the front seat.

Salida pumped her crossed leg a few times and sighed as pent-up sparks of passion zipped through her clit.

"I'm about to be fine," she answered, her voice low and husky as she anticipated the long-awaited sexual release she was going to receive. "You better believe Mizz Salida is about to be just fine."

CHAPTER 3

Make that money-money! Make that money-money! Make that mothafuckin' money-money, honey!

Once again Monique had the heat meter on broil in the G-Spot. Hustlers and ballers were whistling and wildin' as they enjoyed the solo act she performed on the main stage. The room was packed out, and Monique had 'em all sprung. They climbed all up on top of tables and jumped up on their chairs so they could peep her shapely onion as she twerked it in her trademark fishnet stockings.

"Yeah, baby!" a professional football player screamed as Monique did her nasty dance with her eyes squeezed closed. "That's birthday cake! Yeah gimme a slice and I'll slurp that plate!"

Monique grinned under the smoky lights. There were slumlords in the house and stockbrokers too. Politicians, pimps, and top selling performing artists out the ass were digging her game.

She loved the shit outta them.

And as long as they kept that cash raining down on the stage she would keep moving her ass to the beat.

Grown men cried into their drinks as Monique whipped her chocolate hips and made her backbone slip. Her body was simply stunning, and her silky horse-tail weave swished around her shoulders as she rolled her toned stomach and gyrated her moist pelvis at the same time.

Monique had countless moves and super-erotic choreographed routines that she performed in her stage act. She was dedicated to her grind, and she kept the G-Spot's customers digging deep into their pocket stash as she popped her hips and dipped her sweet cocoa chips.

They all wanted to fuck her, and she could understand why. There were cries of satisfaction ringing in the air as niggahs grunted and nutted right where they sat.

She got down on the floor for them and gave them a little taste of the scissor-dance that never failed to get 'em drooling.

Mo was packing a nice hump of ass, and when she turned over on her back and arched her spine, a wide patch of light was illuminated between her shoulders and her meaty booty-cheeks.

Monique could hear all the screaming coming from the crowd, but she paid the men no mind. She was up on that stage strictly for self, and as the C-notes floated down on her damp breasts and stomach, she moaned and felt her orgasm barreling through her vagina.

She sat up quickly and spread her legs wide so they could watch her pussy leak. Then she pulled back the hood on her clit, and let the little man jump right out of his boat.

Her slit oozed thick cream as she masturbated herself for the whole world to see. Her pussy became sloshing wet, and she sat in her own puddle and pushed her fingers into her softness and fucked herself as deeply as she could.

There was pure bedlam in the house.

Monique was panting on the stage as she went all out for her nut. The moans falling from her mouth were the real thing and everybody in the joint knew it. She lowered her chin to her chest and licked her third electric nipple like she was a cat going at a bowl of milk.

Monique rode the wave that was rippling inside her coochie. Her plump booty bounced around in the pool of cream that she had spilt all over the stage. She cupped her pussy and fucked into her palm as her clit became engorged just like a dick.

Then she moved her hand and bent both legs until her heels touched her ass. She let her knees fall open wide, and flicked her pearl back and forth, whimpering and cursing as she came, her clit quivering and her pussy ejaculating thin spurts of cum in the air and all over the floor.

But even before the last drop of cum shot from her snatch, Monique slumped over in sheer frustration as she realized what had happened.

She had been doing a whole lot of fantasizing lately, and as she looked out at the ten or twelve low-level squares who had shown up for a performance that used to draw hundreds, disappointment came crashing down on her. Damn right she had been fantasizing. She had been imagining the way her life used to be before the G-Spot had taken its fall.

But right now reality was staring her full in the face. The four or five twenty-dollar bills that had been tossed up on the stage weren't even worth picking up. Snatching the thong she had stripped out of, Monique got up from the dirty floor and looked out at the sorry spectacle that the G-Spot had become. Once, she'd had big dreams about giving up her stage act and rolling down to Baltimore to launch the G-Spot 2. She had been hyped about the top billing she would receive, and about her role and status as a First Lady too.

But now, all Monique wanted was what was rightfully hers. Instead of working the stage and letting these niggahs peep at her uterus, she should have been draped in finery and working the front door as the hostess of the house.

Of her own house.

Monique knew her worth, and she wasn't the type to sell herself short. She was a devastating bitch and she added value to the hustle because she was working with a real brain.

And right now her brain was telling her she was never gonna get what she wanted outta life until she dealt with the blockers that were standing in her path.

Like, that old scheming bitch, Salida. If there was ever a time that Pluto had been right about somebody, this was it. They shoulda let her grimy ass stay locked up in that nut house in Canada. G's old bitch had been trouble from the gate, and while she had Ace blinded by her shine, Pluto had seen right past Salida's pretty hair and beautiful face, and right down to the grimy streaks in her dirty-ass drawers.

And Monique hadn't forgotten about how that bitch had pulled a gat out on her. Or that disrespectful smush she had taken to the forehead neither.

Yeah, Salida had thrown everything way off balance at the G-Spot. It killed Mo to see that old trick walking around draped in designer wear and rocking white pearls, while she had to gap her legs open onstage and flick her pink pearl. The injustice of it all made hatred burn straight through Monique's heart.

Something was gonna have to be done about that bird. She needed her wings clipped off. Stepping off the side of the stage with her chest still heaving from her orgasm, Monique peered out into the tiny crowd and spotted Salida grinning up in some young playa's face with her hand all on his chest.

Biding her time, Monique headed toward the fuck rooms to take care of the customer who was waiting for her. Mizz Salida was gonna get what she had coming to her. That crafty bitch shoulda stayed disappeared. But since she didn't, she was definitely gonna have to disappear again.

Monique was gonna make sure of that.

CHAPTER 4

It had been almost a week since the green BMW convertible had exploded at Los Angeles International Airport. When the call came in from his aunt Renata's phone, Slick Sallie had snatched his cousin's car keys and raced to the scene with his heart in his throat. He had prayed that God would let him get there in time to stop his uncle Frankie from climbing behind the wheel of Juicy's car and blowing himself into raggedy little chunks.

But as fast as he had driven, he just wasn't fast enough. He saw the flashing lights and heard the sirens as he was getting off the highway, and the huge plume of smoke that had risen in the air above the parking lot was enough to let him know that he was already way too late.

"Oh no!" Sallie had screamed in a panic when he realized what he had done. "Oh God! Oh fuckin' God *no!*"

He had driven straight to an old girlfriend's house so he could drown himself in grief. And later that night, after drinking as much liquor as his stomach could possibly hold, he had cried like a baby and passed out on the bathroom floor.

By the time he woke up the next afternoon, television coverage of the airport explosion was on almost every station. Sallie had stared at the television screen in amazement as photos of the two people who'd been blown up by the detonation were shown.

To his surprise, both of the victims were killers.

They were both men. And they were both black.

Relief had washed over him like a heavy, cleansing rain. The thought that he had killed his uncle had been almost unbearable, and it was nothing but a beautiful stroke of luck when he got two phone calls later that day. One had been completely unexpected, and the other one he had long been waiting for.

Two months earlier Sallie had been in the right place at the right time, and he had weaseled his way in on a heist that could easily bring in over a million dollars in exchange for thirty minutes of simple work.

The plan had been delayed several times due to a local longshoreman's strike, and now that the port workers were back on the job, Sal's associates had been given the green light to move forward with the operation.

Parked in the shadows behind a loading dock in the Bay Area of San Francisco, Slick Sallie ran the plan down to his slow cousin Mick one last time.

"I'm gonna stay right here with you until they give me the signal and the electric fence is turned off. Then I'm going in, and I'm going in fast. You stay right here, okay? Just keep the car running, and the second my ass hits the seat cushion you step on it. Are you locked and loaded?"

Mick's hands shook as he held his Glock 17 9mm out for his cousin to see.

"Good," Sal said as his eyes swept back and forth over the dock entrance to Uniden Technology, one of largest manufacturers of computer chips in the nation.

It was late in the afternoon, right before the business was scheduled to close. Sal and Mick, along with nine other men, were dressed in all-black and wearing gloves and masks. They were waiting for their inside man, a maintenance worker who was hiding in the ceiling rafters, to cut the wires to the security alarm and hit a button to slide open the wire-meshed electric fence.

Sallie peered out the window as a thin sheen of sweat broke out on his upper lip. He was nervous, but he was excited too. A heist like this didn't go down every day, and when it did it made big news.

Sallie wasn't afraid of getting caught or arrested. Their plan had been timed perfectly and they'd be in and out of the warehouse before the employees could call for help. But what made Sallie nervous was the fact that they were about to hit some mob-protected territory.

The Milan crime family of Los Angeles was in control of this area. Uniden Technology was the biggest company on their extortion list, and Sal knew the owners paid top dollar for the level of protection their mob payouts assured them.

Ordinarily, a made man wouldn't even consider violating another mob family's territory. Respect for boundaries was one of the rules that allowed multiple Mafia families to function in small areas simultaneously.

But Sal wasn't a made fuckin' man. And since his father was just a lowly Irish son-of-a-bitch, he never would be. He secretly envied Mick and the rest of his dick-weed cousins who could trace their bloodline back to the Old World, yet walked around in this world with shit for brains.

Sallie was a million times smarter, slicker, and craftier than those clowns ever would be, yet he would never be as big-time or as respected as them simply because of the origin of his blood.

"Y-y-you sure about this, right Sallie?" Mick stuttered. "You're not gonna go in there and get yourself shot or nothing, right?"

Sal stared at his cousin. He loved Mick the way you would love a puppy. He was a simple dickhead, but he was faithful.

"Nobody's gonna hurt me, Mikail. Everything is gonna be fine. You just be ready to drive like you're at Daytona, okay?"

Minutes later the signal was given, and like the others who were waiting, Sal exited the car and crept cautiously toward the fence-line. The ten men were silent and had their weapons at the ready. The moment the metal fence slid back they rushed onto the property, and through the recently unlocked door.

Sal was near the middle of the pack as they burst into the office closest to the loading dock. Five men and one woman were busy at work, and in a flash, all ten guns were on them. Sal and his crew ordered the employees to drop their wallets and cell phones into a plastic bag, and then forced them to the floor. They were tied up and gagged, and then the team swept into the warehouse where their moving truck was backed up to the dock and waiting to be loaded.

It took less than thirty minutes for Sal and his cohorts to load massive amounts of processors and microchips onto the truck, and they moved so expertly that everything went without a hitch.

It was time to go, and Sal jumped on the back of the truck along with the other men. The rear panel of the truck remained raised so each man could hop off and make his escape at the appropriate time.

They were halfway to the fence when the shots rang out. Standing at the truck's back opening, Sal ducked instinctively. When he looked up he saw two employees running out of the warehouse. They were brandishing automatic rifles and spraying rounds in their direction.

Three members of Sal's team began returning fire, and Sal had just lifted his own weapon to blast a few rounds when he saw something that made his blood run cold.

It was his cousin Mick.

Disobeying Sal, Mikail had left the safety of the car and entered the compound, and now he was caught directly in the line of fire.

"Wait! Wait! *Wait!*" Sal shouted at the driver as the truck sped toward the fence, leaving Mick behind on the compound. "Hold up! We left somebody!" Sal screamed. "We left some fuckin' body!"

Sal reached out both his arms toward his cousin as the young man ran behind the truck with bullets flying past him in both directions.

The look on Mick's face was one of bewildered terror as he ducked and dogged in an attempt to stay alive.

"Stop the fuckin' truck!" Sal screamed and reached hysterically.

"Keep fuckin' going!" the team leader fired his weapon and barked to the driver. "They're closing the fence! Punch it! Punch the fuckin' gas! They're closing the fence!"

Sal watched in stunned silence as a round skimmed the side of Mick's lower leg. Grimacing, his cousin clutched his calf and went down to one knee.

"Run!" Sal bellowed! "Get up and run you stupid fuckin' idiot!"

The sting of hot lead got Mick moving again. He jumped to his feet and ran for the fence, favoring his shot leg with every step.

"C'mon! C'mon! C'mon!" Sal urged, but just as the moving truck lurched across the threshold of the property, the automatic fences began to slide close on their tracks.

The rest was like watching a train wreck about to happen. Mick was *almost there* when the next bullet caught him. It sank into the flesh high in his back. Screaming, he was blown forward as the impact of the blast flung him full force into the fence just as it slid to a close.

"*Nooooo!*" Sal screamed from deep in his gut. Thousands of white sparks flew in the air as Mick was bonded to the electrified fence. His body shuddered and jerked, and smoke sizzled in a cloud as 20 amps of heat flowed through him from head to toe.

Sal was helpless as the truck lurched to a stop and his partners-in-crime jumped out and raced toward their cars. His feet were stuck in place, his eyes glued to the picture of his favorite cousin doing a grotesque death dance on the voltage-heavy fence.

"Get the fuck outta here!" The team chief planted his foot in Sal's back and kicked him roughly out of the truck. Sal hit the ground hard, then got up running. He jumped behind the wheel of Mick's souped-up ride, and without another look behind him, he peeled out of the parking lot right behind the others and took off in his pre-designated direction.

CHAPTER 5

Hey, Pluto," Honey Dew came over to the bar and put her hand on his shoulder. "Something's wrong with the pipes in this joint, boo. All the damn toilets are overflowing and those plungers ain't getting it."

Pluto looked up from his rum and coke. "Go, tell Ace."

"He ain't here. He went to Burger King to get something to eat."

Pluto shrugged and tossed back his rum.

"Then go tell Truth."

"He ain't here either," Honey Dew said. "He been gone for a minute. I seen him drive off with Mizz Salida in G's car."

"C'mon, man," he shrugged her hand off his shoulder. "Y'all nasty bitches need to quit balling shit up and throwing it down the damn toilets! Y'all can't be flushing ya wigs and drawers and shit down them lil-ass holes and expect them things not to back up on you."

"It ain't us!" Honey Dew protested. "The pipes is just bad up in here! Now can you come unclog some of these nasty shitters so the hoes can pee and wipe they asses and get back to work?"

"Damn." Pluto brewed inside. The last thing he wanted to do was fuck around with some nasty toilets. He wasn't no goddamn maintenance man, and he wasn't feeling the G-Spot like that to be sticking his hands down in no shitty toilet water.

He finished his drink, and then went to the supply closet to grab a plunger and a plumber's snake. He hit every bathroom in the club and all kinds of foul shit sloshed up outta the pipes.

He went to take care of the bathroom in G's office last, and since it shared a line with the toilets in the stripper's dressing room, he knew there was gonna be a bunch of shit down in those pipes too.

But when he opened the office door all he saw was creamy cooch and glistening ass-crack. Salida was on top of G's desk butt-ass naked. She was propped up on her elbows with her legs spread wide and her head thrown back.

Ace's bag of Burger King was on G's desk but he damn sure wasn't eating it. Instead, his manz was leaning over the end of the desk puttin' in work. Salida's caramel ass was cradled in that niggah's hands, and his tongue stuck out a country mile as he licked out every inch of that bitch's snatch.

"Sssss..." Salida hissed and gyrated as Ace rotated his head and probed up in her tunnel. "Lips and tongue, you son-of-a-bitch," she bossed his ass. "Get it with your lips and tongue..."

Pluto was straight fuckin' disgusted by the wet, lapping sounds his boy's mouth made as he slurped Salida's pussy like it was a juicy piece of fruit.

Neither one of them noticed him standing there watching, and before he could

221

move Ace stood up and yanked down his pants. He grabbed his thick meat, then pushed Salida down flat on the desk and rammed it into her raw, causing the older woman to scream in pleasure as he dug over ten years worth of cobwebs outta her wet hole.

"Oooh! *Fuck* me!" Salida screamed and squeezed her plump, perfect titties. "*Fuck* me, you troll! *Fuck* me, you fat, ugly mothafucka!"

She lifted her long, beautiful legs high in the air, then brought them down and wrapped them tightly around Ace's back. "Fuck this pretty-pretty, you ape-ass, bitch! Beat it up! Fuck it right! I said fuck it *right*, goddammit!"

"Chump muh'fucka!" Pluto muttered as he stepped fully into the office and headed toward the bathroom. Ace jumped and stood up. His dick fell outta Salida with a loud sucking noise, and Pluto made sure the toilet plunger brushed against his manz ass as he passed by.

"Ay, what the fuck!" Ace barked. "Nigga you can't knock first?"

Pluto smirked as he slid his eyes over Ace's shoulder and copped a peek at Salida's fat, glistening pussy.

"Knock for what, man? I'm on the job, muh'fuckah! You digging ya head up in a shit hole and I'm about to dig my hand up in one."

Pluto walked into the bathroom and slammed the door on the loud curses that were falling outta Salida's grimy mouth. Shit was starting to make a whole lot more sense now. Yeah, now he knew why Ace was always so amped on every stupid thing that came outta 7:30's mouth.

He couldn't believe some of the shit his boy Ace was talking these days. He couldn't believe his manz was boning G's conniving old bitch neither, and Pluto wondered what other grimy secrets that niggah had been hiding from him too.

CHAPTER 6

The last 24 hours had been mad crazy and I was dog-ass tired, but that didn't stop Flex from trying to talk me to death.

"You hungry, Juicy?" he asked me. "I ain't no cook but I had my boy pick up some grub cause I know how shitty they be feeding you in the joint."

We went back in the kitchen where he pulled all kinds of good stuff out the fridge. There was Chinese food, deep fried shrimp, a whole sausage pizza, and some hot wings with blue cheese dressing. We piled our plates up and he put mine in the microwave first, and once it was hot he put his in next.

"What you wanna drink? I got come Corona, some Olde E, apple juice, quarter waters, and a Sprite."

"Sprite."

We took our plates out to the living room, and Flex started reminiscing about how good shit used to be when we were growing up.

"Our block was always on jam, man," he said all excited. His eyes lit up like he was reliving his childhood. "Your grandmother used to have some crazy rent parties! She would tell me and Jimmy to stay in the backroom, and our bad asses would sneak out in the kitchen and try to eat up all the food!"

"She used to whip the hell outta y'all too!" I laughed. "But Jimmy didn't care. That boy was hardheaded and he could take an ass whipping. It didn't matter how much she tore him up, he still did whatever he wanted to do."

"Yeah he did," Flex nodded. "I remember that day he threw your cat Fay-Fay out the window."

"Fee-Fee!" I screamed. "Her name was *Fee-Fee!*"

"Yeah, Fee-Fee. That wasn't the first time he threw her ass out there, you know. He had tossed her down a couple of times before and ain't nothing happen. He couldn't understand why she just upped and died that last time, man. It was crazy."

"*Jimmy* was crazy," I said softly, missing my brother so, *so* much.

"Did you know our mothers used to run the streets together back in the day?" he asked. "Probably before we could even remember?"

I nodded. "I think I remember hearing that. My grandmother might have told me."

"Yeah, they did. They got high together and sold pussy too. Our families was tight like that. That's why it hurt me so bad when I heard your grandmother had passed. I tried to give you some sympathy at her funeral but G had you locked up tight. I couldn't even get close to you."

I shrugged. G had been a big blocker, so I wasn't surprised.

"You know, a lot of bad shit happened to me in Harlem, but I came back strong," Flex bragged. "Even after I got shot. The game went into a tailspin after you left. The leadership was gone, and hungry niggahs was tryna come up left and right. It was

223

dog-eat-dog out there, man. Click-kill-click. But the strong survived, and now," he said proudly, "I just about *own* Harlem, girl. I got my hand on a good half of that town. I don't even go up around our old way that much no more, but I'm still runnin' things."

Good for you, I wanted to say. But instead I said, "Yeah, I heard shit got crazy. I also heard Cooter got killed. I ran into his sister on Rikers and she told me he was gone."

Flex got quiet, and his bony shoulders seemed to sag.

"Yo, that was my dude, man," he shook his head. "Next to Jimmy, he was my closest dog. And they fucked him up. All he was doing was tryna pick up a few leads so he could get put down on some action. And them niggahs pounced on him."

Flex swiped one hand down his face slowly, then said, "I got them fools, though. My dude Cooter caught a bad one, but I paid them niggahs back five times as bad. That's why don't nobody out there wanna go head up with me now, Juicy. I let it be known that if you fuck with me and my team, you and yours is getting straight smashed. And that's word."

I just looked at him. Flex was young and dumb. He was just like Jimmy had been. *Real* young, and *real* damn dumb. All that drug drama and street commotion reminded me of how much I had hated the thought of my brother grinding in the streets for G.

Except, G was way smoother with his flow than Flex could ever be. At forty-six, G had been cruel, callous, and ruthless, but he wasn't harsh, or gutter, or grimy with his game like a lot of these young hoods were. G had had a lethal, icy cool that it was gonna take Flex, no matter how fly he dressed or how many niggahs he popped, at least another thirty years of hard-knock living to perfect.

I looked down at all the food on my plate. I had piled on enough to feed two grown men, but I was full after just a few mouthfuls.

"You got some foil?" I asked, rubbing my eyes. "I'm too tired to finish."

Flex set his plate down and jumped to his feet.

"My bad, Juicy. I don't know what the fuck I was thinking. Damn, girl, I gotta remember you's a lady. You probably tired, huh? A'ight," he said, taking my plate and pulling me to my feet and back toward his bedroom. "I'ma let you get some sleep, baby, okay? The sheets are silk, girl. Fresh out the pack, a hunnid percent, word. You wanna take a hot bath? I put some nice shit for you in the bathroom, so go for it. There's warm towels, some of that bubble shit, baby powder, lotion, a couple of them fancy-type pajamas...everything is for you, Juicy. I still love the shit outta you, ma, and every single thing up *in* this bitch is for *you*."

CHAPTER 7

Ease up," Monique whispered and pushed two fingers against Bilal's sweaty forehead. She didn't know who the hell had taught his young ass how to eat pussy but they'd taught him all wrong. He was too damn rough, pressing his whole face into her stuff and making her clit sore.

"Softer," she instructed him as he dipped his face back into her warmth again. Almost every young boy who grinded for the G-Spot crew needed to be schooled on how to fuck, and Monique was just the right teacher.

She thrust her pelvis forward and pulled Bilal by his dreadlocks as she rubbed herself on his face. This time his lips were pleasing and his tongue was nice and wet as he went back to work, licking and sucking the way she liked it.

Monique let him eat her out for a while, and then she turned the tables and went to work on him. His young ass didn't know what had hit him. He couldn't do shit with all them titties and that beastly ass she was packing on her, and he was moaning and trembling as Mo put some of her specialty moves down on him until she had him weak and soft, exactly the way she wanted him.

She soaked his dick in her mouth and then gave him a slippery hand job that made his young ass start speaking in tongues. Then she climbed on top of him and rode him half to death, slamming her bomb body down on him hard enough to crack his raging nut.

But instead of letting him cum, Monique jumped off the boy and stretched out next to him. She ran her wet tongue around the lobe of his ear while her fingers twirled his erect nipples and she threw her ham-hock thigh over his groin.

"I need you to do something for me, B," she whispered hotly in his ear. "You take care of me, and I'll keep on taking real good care of you too."

As hard as the boy's dick was there was no way in hell he could resist. He was totally whipped by Monique's scent and her sexy skills, and he would have agreed to murk his own mama if it meant he could slide his throbbing dick back inside her wetness just one more time.

Monique giggled as he turned into a soft puddle of pudding in her hands. She whispered her request in his ear, and told him how happy it would make her if he would handle this one little favor for her.

Bilal groaned and quickly agreed, and when Monique climbed back on top of him and he saw those beautiful black titties, tight waist, and the shapeliest hips in the world bucking up and down on top of him, making Mo happy became the only thing in the world he wanted to do.

CHAPTER 8

Flex woke up the next morning feeling like a million dollars. Just knowing Juicy was sleeping right next door had kept him on buzz all night. He got out of bed and stood in the middle of the floor holding his dick. His eyes slid toward the wall that separated their rooms and his manhood throbbed with need.

For damn near all his life he had been fantasizing hard about Juicy. And right now, as he almost penetrated the wall with his x-rated, x-ray vision, he could just picture her laid up over there in his bed with those big, luscious titties and sexy round hips.

The good thing was, he didn't even have to use his imagination. All he had to do was rewind the tape on the cameras that he had set up all around his crib, and he could see whatever he wanted to see for himself.

He had been so happy to be around her last night that he'd shot his mouth off a mile a minute while they sat around eating dinner. He didn't shut up until she started yawning, and by then he'd almost talked her into the ground.

Juicy had gone into the master bathroom to take a bath, and Flex had stood outside the door listening to the water run and hoping she liked all the stuff he'd gotten for her. He had tried to think of everything, and he hoped she appreciated that shit because none of it was slum.

At first he had started to take one of his local guttersnipe bitches with him to shop for her, but then he realized that none of the chicks he rolled with would know how to properly adorn a queen like Juicy.

He pictured her sitting up on that stool in the G-Spot wearing the latest designer dresses and rocking icy diamonds out the ass. None of his chickens had ever flown that high, so he ended up going shopping all by himself at Neiman Marcus, trusting his own instincts and picking out finery that he thought would be good enough for her. He'd dropped a gwap in that joint without even blinking, and from the black silk panties to the classy lingerie set with the low-cut, flared-leg night pants, everything he got was high quality and befitting a jewel as precious as Juicy was.

Flex went over to a cabinet and rewound the video that had been downloaded during the night. He selected the camera from the bathroom, and gripped himself as she popped up on the screen.

Juicy was a fuckin' princess. From her head to her toes she was like royalty to him, and he didn't even look as she sat down on the toilet and peed. Watching her do that type of thang was just too disrespectful and she deserved more than that.

But he did watch Juicy wash her pussy in the bathtub, and he sighed and stroked his dick at the beautiful sight of her naked ass and titties before she put on her pajamas.

Flex remembered the day he'd gotten a call from Pluto saying G was inviting him and his boys to come by the Spot and get some of Juicy's pussy for free. He'd almost

226

blown his top when he went downstairs in that basement and saw his jewel beaten down and chained up like a mangy dog. As much as he had envied and imitated G, at that moment Flex's hatred for Harlem's number one kingpin had become eternal.

That niggah didn't deserve a thoroughbred like Juicy. It had burned Flex's heart to see her in that brutalized condition, but it had also spiked his rage to heights unknown. If Jimmy hadn't popped G then Flex knew he damn sure would have.

He had been even more devastated when he found out that Juicy had run off somewhere with G's son, but by then he was in the hospital trying to recuperate from his gut shot so he could exact his get-back on the niggahs who had popped him.

From there, it had been all uphill as Flex and his crew waged a bloody comeback that had left bodies scattered left and right, and earned him a major portion of the drug territory that had once belonged exclusively to Granite McKay.

And for the last six months Flex had been living the gangsta life. He'd been cracking heads, raking in doe, and enjoying his hard-earned street clout and chief capo status. Juicy had been the furthest thing from his mind until he started hearing shit about the fuckin' bounty that Ace and his crew had put on her head, and then Rita rolled on him saying Juicy's life was in danger and she needed someplace to hide.

There hadn't been a moment's hesitation in him when he said, hell yeah, bring her here. He knew Juicy had been run-through in the G-Spot like a regular hoe and locked up on the Rock like a regular criminal, but he didn't give a fuck about none of that. Juicy was the type of chick who could brush the grime right off her shoulders and keep on shining. As fine as she was, and the way she carried herself, you'd never know a speck of dirt had ever touched her.

Whatever Juicy had done in the past was in the past. Flex was willing to leave it there, and all he wanted in return was a rider who he could trust no matter what, and who was completely down with every aspect of his program.

Because Flex was on a mission and his cause was deeply rooted in his past. Growing up as a skinny dude with buckteeth, it had been hard for him to get his props and his share of the attention. It pissed him off that he wasn't tall with light skin and curly hair like his boy Jimmy, and he didn't have the muscles or the fearsome physical presence of a niggah like G, neither.

But what he was, was fearless. All heart. And he was smart too. He had studied the best and the brightest hustlers out there, and he was quick to learn all the lessons the street had to offer.

And there had been no better teacher than Granite McKay. Nah, Flex didn't just idolize G, he straight up *envied* that niggah. He wanted him some of everything that G had had. He wanted that respect, he wanted that control, and he damn sure wanted that money.

So he had studied G like there was gold just under the surface of his smooth dark skin. He'd memorized the purposeful way that niggah walked, the deadly confidence that rode on his words when he talked, the killer look he wore in his eyes, and the arrogant way he worked his bitches, like they had a prime commodity stuck between their legs. Flex had watched G rule over Harlem like he had been crowned a Black Caesar, and judging by the way people had bowed down at that niggah's feet, maybe he really was.

CHAPTER 9

Big Frankie was stretched out on his back getting his dick sucked just right. He had a long shlong of meat, and it was almost too much for the whore to handle. He sighed and thrust his hips at her as his stomach sloshed and jiggled from her bobbing action.

"That's it," he whispered as her wet mouth swept up and down his engorged shaft. There were all kinds of family problems that needed to be dealt with today, but right now nothing was more important to Frankie than getting his fat cock creamed.

The whore dug her nails into his thighs and gargled on the tip of his dick. Delicious sensations radiated all the way down to his balls, and Frankie was pumping his way to heaven when he got the call.

"Frank." It was his brother.

"What is it, Paulie?" he panted. He had left his younger brother back at the condo watching a ball game, and he was annoyed to see a call coming from his home phone at a time like this.

He tangled his fingers in the whore's flaming red hair as he tried to force her back into her perfect sucking rhythm. "I'm a little busy right now! W-w-what...*oh God yes keep it going*...what the fuck do you want?"

"It's Don Vito," Paulie said quietly. "He wants to meet with you."

Frank froze.

"The Don wants to see me?"

"Yeah," Paulie said. "That's what he said."

"Well, when'd he say that?" Frank barked. His erection disappeared as he tried to figure out why the top crime boss in Los Angeles was requesting a face-to-face meeting with him. "Did somebody call you? Did Don Vito call?"

"No," his brother said. He stared across the room at the three well-dressed mobsters who had walked into his brother's house without bothering to knock or ring the bell. They sat watching the ball game with their feet up on Frankie's living room table, guns in clear view. "He came by to tell you himself."

Frank had paid the whore, then rushed out of the hotel and driven back to the condo at break-neck speed. Paulie had said very little over the telephone, but the anxiety in his brother's voice and the fact that the West Coast capo had paid him a personal visit let Frank know that something very serious had gone bad.

The tree-lined street was quiet as Frankie pulled up to his house. An unfamiliar late-model sedan was parked in his designated spot, so he pulled in sideways, blocking Renata's Porsche.

The mobsters were on his porch before he could get out of his car. There were three of them, with Don Vito leading the way. Frankie stepped out the car and waited as they walked calmly down his front steps. He climbed obediently into the backseat of their sedan as one of the mobsters held open the door.

He looked back only once as they drove away from his house. His brother Paulie had come out on the porch and their eyes met briefly. And then Frank looked away, wondering if he'd ever see his family again.

$$\$\$\$\$\$$$

Flex had built himself an empire from the basement of the funeral home, and it was from G's living example that he plotted his path to success. Before making any decision he always asked himself, WWGD? *What would G do?* And he got so good at pretending to be the dead kingpin that he amassed more and more of Harlem's drug territory, and made big plans for the day that he would have it all.

But taking down drug clicks meant stacking plenty of bodies, so Flex had chosen a funeral home as his base of operations. Not only was it a great place to stash a corpse, it also allowed him to double-stack a rival's body in the fake bottom of a coffin, and bury it undetected during an actual funeral service.

Yeah, not everybody could grind like a champion knowing they were surrounded by the dead, but Flex's basement crib helped keep him on his game, because he knew the funeral home was exactly where he would end up if he fucked around and got sloppy again.

So six months earlier he had assembled himself a crew of young worthies he called his "Divine Nine." Flex had hand-selected each of them based on their deadly street rep, and then he put 'em on trial to certify their loyalty and their courage.

Every member of the Divine Nine was required to put a fresh body on a gun and sit through a round of Russian roulette.

Flex called it his gut test.

Every hoodlum he knew was willing to live by the gun, and his gut test was designed to make sure his team had the courage to die by it too. So, Flex would sit them down with a six-shooter Magnum pressed to their domes, then make them pull the trigger until he gave them permission to stop.

So far, he'd only lost two soldiers to the game of enforced suicide, and as a result Flex commanded a vicious crew of youngstas who were hardbody and street certified. They controlled the trap in his sector of Harlem and competed viciously with fell-off niggahs like Ace, Pluto, Domni, and Bop for dominance over the town's drug trade.

It was common knowledge that G McKay had cornered the largest drug market in all of Manhattan. What had made G so successful, aside from his business savvy and street rep, was the fact that he'd been in bed with the absolute biggest supplier of cocaine since anyone could remember.

But Flex didn't have the connections that G had, so he was forced to do the opposite. He'd not only found multiple sources of mid-level suppliers to keep his corners stocked, he'd also got in good with distributors of club drugs, a sweet source of side bank that most dealers overlooked.

Flex knew long-term success could only be achieved through diversification. And while crack would always be king in Harlem, the town was changing and so were the bags of some of its younger residents. Many of them had seen the devastation that crack addictions had caused in their own families. Some had even been crack babies themselves, and because of that they were looking for a new drug.

A cooler drug. A club drug. And Flex made sure he had exactly what they needed. From Xanies, to ecstasy, to roofies, and mesc, Flex was a walking pharmaceutical rep. He had his soldiers hanging around concerts and rave parties peddling pills to white kids, Black kids, Asians, Puerto Ricans...whoever. It was an excellent source of secondary income, and Flex saw the demand growing larger and larger each day.

But of course, where there was money there were also problems. Lately, Flex had been feeling some kinda way about a couple of his mid-level connects. They were some Columbian niggahs, and the last couple of times his boys rolled in to re-up them cats all of a sudden didn't speaka-no-English.

Flex knew they were testing his gangsta, which just made him even more determined to cut all those middlemen out and find one good broker. Word traveling through the street grapevine was that Ace and Pluto were sniffing around trying to find themselves a good broker too. They were looking to score the name of G's old connect, which was information that Flex, no matter how deep he dug, had never been able to come up with himself.

But he wasn't about to stop trying. He didn't give a fuck if he had to turn over every rock in the city of New York. He was gonna find that connect, and even better, he was gonna take control of the G-Spot and put Ace and Pluto down for a nice long nap.

Because see, Flex didn't just want *what* G had had. He wanted *everything* that G had had. And right now, that included total control of the drug game, total control of Harlem, and with Juicy's fine ass getting dressed right next-door in his bedroom, Flex wanted total control of G's woman too.

CHAPTER 10

The mobsters took Frankie to a deserted warehouse. It was a good thirty minutes south of L.A., and in an area that was unfamiliar to him. The warehouse was surprisingly cozy inside, and as they sat down at a table one of the younger soldiers poured drinks for everyone.

Frank tossed his liquor back quickly, and pushed his glass forward to be refilled. If he was going to be executed then he wanted to go out at least halfway buzzed.

Don Vito emptied his glass and lit a cigar, and then he spoke. "You know, Frankie, that was some pretty big trouble you were in back there in New York."

Frank nodded, but remained silent.

"They had a meeting, the New York council did. Some wanted to put you out of business, ya know, but Tommy spoke up for you. He said you were a stand-up guy. A real asset to The Organization. He called me up personally too, ya know. He asked me if I could do him a big favor and make room for you out here in Los Angeles." Don Vito toked from his cigar. "And because I always liked you, and because Tommy is my good friend, I agreed."

"The trouble in New York couldn't be avoided," Frank said coolly. "It was me or them. Nobody likes war, Don Vito. And there definitely would have been one."

"Yeah, but I stuck my neck out for you, Frankie. You came out here with your entire family, and I gave you your own territory and cut you in on some pretty sweet deals. And how did you repay me?"

"I don't know what you're talking about," Frank said honestly. "It's been a great business relationship. Our families are good together. I've opened up some good avenues for you, and contributed a lot of money to the Los Angeles operations. I don't know what the problem is. I thought we were doing fine. Can you just tell me what's going on?"

"You fucked up, Frankie! That's what's going on! What are you, retarded? You were given detailed instructions. What was so hard about following them?"

With his cigar clenched between his teeth, Don Vito counted off on his thick fingers. "You keep your toe on your own side of the fuckin' line, you don't take from nobody else's cookie jar, and you don't whack off no made men or paid politicians. Standard stuff. How could you fuck it up?"

Frank stared his boss dead in the eye.

"With all due respect, Don Vito, I have no fuckin' idea what you're talking about."

Don Vito stood up from the table and motioned for Frankie to follow him. His soldiers stood up too, and Frankie walked behind the boss with wise-guy confidence, but deep inside he was preparing himself to take a hot slug to the back of the head.

But instead of having him executed, Don Vito led him through a doorway and around a corner to a small room. They walked over to a sheet-covered form that lay on the ground, and Frankie stared down with a frown as Don Vito nudged the sheet back with the toe of his well-shined shoe.

It was Frankie's nephew.

Mick.

Or at least what was left of Mick.

The kid's face looked like an over-cooked hotdog. His tongue had exploded and his eyeballs had poached right in his skull.

"Yeah? So, what happened to him?" Frank asked casually, without a trace of emotion.

Vito puffed from his cigar and let the burnt ash fall into the corpse's face.

"He got fried on a fence at a warehouse in San Francisco. Him and some other idiots crossed over into The Milan Family's territory. It was a well-planned heist. They got away with twenty-million dollars worth of computer chips. The cameras were rolling, but your nephew here was the only piece of evidence they left behind."

Frank stared down at his brother's son. There was no way in hell Mikail could have participated in a twenty-cent heist, let alone a twenty million one. He didn't have the heart or the smarts. But Frank knew who did.

"This wasn't my job," Frank said firmly. "None of my men were involved."

Vito exploded. "Well it looks like somebody in your family is running themselves a little side operation! Do you know what kind of trouble this is gonna cause for us? Trouble that we don't need? Are you trying to start a friggin' war between us the Milans? I don't have to tell you what'll happen when the DEA gets on the trail."

Don Vito puffed from his cigar and then pointed it at Frankie's face. "You know, one of your nephews paid Big Earl Gambino a visit at his chop shop the other night."

Frank's look was blank.

"Big Earl likes to blow things up, you know. He told me he put a little boom-boom in a BMW your nephew brought by. I hear it went off at the airport and two moolies got hashed. Who the fuck were they?"

Frank just shrugged. He had no fuckin' idea.

Don Vito sighed. "Look, they ran you out of New York because of this same kind of thing. I don't know, Frankie. You're looking pretty foolish, here. Someone in your family must be a maverick. A renegade. I'd say you better get some control, Frankie. You better shut your rogue relatives down. Or we'll have to shut you down. All the way down."

Frank nodded. He was angry, but Vito was right. When you lost control over your family in this business, shit rolled straight uphill.

"I'll take care of this," Frank said firmly. He knew exactly what needed to be done. "Please give my regards to Don Milan. I'll handle this. In fact, consider it already fixed."

Don Vito nodded. "It better be. Because this is a very small world you know, Frankie, and your family is running out of places to hide."

CHAPTER 11

Juicy was still sleeping when three of Flex's top lieutenants swung by the basement crib. A text from his boy Doc's phone alerted him that the members of the Divine Nine were heading downstairs for their morning meeting, but Flex still made them go through all the security procedures before he unlocked the last door and let them in.

He greeted his street team: Doc, Stamp, Mannie, Rome, Boog, Cee-Low, Chickie, and Lil Lee. The nine of them sat around smoking blunts and discussing the financial profits from their various drug sectors.

"Yo," Doc stood up and spoke out, "we gonna need to do something about our product flow, man. Without no large-scale distributor we just gonna keep coming up short. Them fiends is buying it up faster than we can put it out there."

Lil Lee sat with her beautiful legs crossed. She was sexy to the bone and as coldhearted as they came. "Yeah, and just remember, every time we come up empty it's like giving money away, okay? Our customers have no choice but to run across town and give their bizz to them other dealers."

Flex sat there listening as his crew debated the matter back and forth. He was definitely about making his money, but just knowing Juicy was back there in his bed was a big distraction.

Doc asked, "So you wanna double up on what we usually get from Walla, or we just gonna be short this week?"

Flex had to shake his head to clear his thoughts.

"Nah, man," he said slowly. "We gotta keep up with the demand, yo. We can't be coming up short."

Flex twirled his ring. Them Columbian connects were tryna fuck him. Flex could feel it, and he could also feel the anger rising in him at the thought of it. Them south-of-the-border niggahs musta thought he was soft. They must not know what kinda beast he really was.

"Yo, Cee," he told his manz. "Run across the street to McDonald's and get some of them steak bagels, man. Get some a them potato shits too. Enough for everybody."

"Well then we gotta find another source," Doc said, steering Flex back to the matter at hand. "Or, we gotta take some off the top of all our other piles. Either way, they gonna keep wanting more than we have and business is gonna suffer."

Flex sat quietly, deep in thought.

The last thing he wanted to do was lose money. The sales from his club drugs were steadily climbing, and that was cool. In fact, he had just dished off some free samples to an old broad last night, and if she liked it she would come running back for more, thus creating an additional source of secondary income.

But he had to study the big picture and figure out how to best handle this new situation. Sure, he could do like Doc had said and shorten the supply in all of his other sectors to make up for what he was lacking in two. But that was just shuffling money around, not bringing in more of it.

Another option was to hook up with another low-level dealer, and probably get some inferior product that would turn his die-hard users off. But Flex didn't wanna risk that. His rep was solid, and he knew word of mouth was key in sending customers his way.

What Flex really wanted to do, was conduct a two-fold operation. If he could gain control of the G-Spot, he would have some of the sweetest drug territory in Harlem under his thumb. Of course, he'd inherit the same problems that Ace and Pluto had: the lack of a large enough distribution connection.

So what did he need in order to accomplish his mission? The first thing he needed was some firepower. Some clean firepower. He was gonna have to find a broker who could deliver some fresh, high-grade weaponry, because almost every piece his boys carried was dirty. Shit, most of their toolies had five and six bodies on them each. If they got caught blasting up in the G-Spot with dirty gats the cops would use their superior ballistics to connect the dots to countless other unsolved murders.

But Flex thought he might have a way around that. He knew a white dude who had tossed him off some AKs in the past. He had called this guy up to see if he had some clean burners that would fit his criteria, and dude told him he would do his best to find somebody with a fresh shipment.

After that, all Flex needed was a big, steady supply of high-quality cocaine. Finding somebody to supply it was gonna be a whole lot easier said than done, so the next thing he planned to do was twist somebody's fuckin' arm until they spit out the name of G's old connect.

$$$$$

These were the thoughts on Flex's mind when Cee-Low came back with breakfast.

Flex had just taken two meals out the bag for him and Juicy, when to his surprise the door leading to the back of his crib swung open and she was standing right there.

"Ooops!" she said with an embarrassed grin. "Sorry. I didn't know you had people out here."

Every niggah in the room was transfixed.

Wearing a black robe tied tightly over the slinky lingerie that Flex had bought for her, Juicy looked fuckably delicious with her sleep tousled hair, wide eyes, and clear, creamy skin.

"It's cool, baby," Flex said quickly. He stood up and walked over to her with the food in his hand. "I sent my manz to get you some breakfast, ma. It's nice and hot," he said, handing the steak bagel to her. "Give me a few minutes and I'll be back there to check you out."

Juicy took the food and stepped back into the living area, and Flex quickly pulled the door closed behind her. He knew his crew was swift, and by the time he turned back around, there were eyeballs on the ceiling, eyeballs on the floor, eyeballs studying chewed up fingernails, eyeballs everywhere but on the spot where Juicy had just stood.

Except for that niggah Cee-Low's eyes.

"Yo, man!" he hollered, gripping his dick and pointing toward the closed door. "I *remember* that chick! That's the bitch we banged one night in the G-Spot! She's a *baaad* piece of ass! You remember her, Flex?"

Flex's voice dropped low as he sat down on the couch. "Nah, man. That ain't her."

"Yo! I'm telling you, niggah! "That's *her!*"

Cee laughed. "I remember getting' all up in that shit..." with his face screwed up in mock sexual concentration, he gestured like he was gripping a woman's hips, then thrust his pelvis back and forth in a deep, fucking motion. "Bang! Bang! Bang! I was knockin' a hole in that soft-ass pussy!" He laughed again and reached out to Doc for some dap. "That shit was good, too. It was a little sloppy, but it was still good."

Doc refused the dap. "Man, shut the fuck up, a'ight?" He grilled the youngsta. "You heard what Flex just said, niggah. You got the wrong girl. It wasn't her."

"*Oh yes the fuck it—*"

Boom!

A hole opened up on Cee-Low's forehead and hot blood splattered the wall behind him.

Flex sat on the sofa cooler than winter, the gat he'd retrieved from between two cushions trailing smoke from its barrel.

Cee's body had flown backward, into the wall, and now his dead weight slumped to the floor as his legs collapsed and folded beneath him.

"Now," Flex looked around the room and said patiently. His voice sounded like cold death. "Any fuckin' body else up in here think they remember my queen from somewhere?"

Heads started shaking.

A chorus of, "Nah, man, I don't remember her. Yo, I ain't never seen that girl before. Me neither, I wasn't even there that night, and Nah, she don't even look familiar," rang out in the room.

"Good," Flex said, ignoring the smell of blood, shit, and hot brains that rose from Cee's body and filled the air. He set the pistol down on the end table. "I didn't think so."

Doc's eyes went to Cee-Low's body, then quickly swept the room.

The Divine Nine was back down to eight.

Flex unwrapped his steak bagel and took a big bite. "Yo, Stamp, run upstairs and tell Mr. Williams to give you a body bag 'cause we gonna need to do another double-stack. Everybody else..." he chewed with his mouth open and waved his breakfast sandwich in the air. "Let's get back to business."

CHAPTER 12

It felt like forever since the last time I had eaten me some McDonald's, and I had just bitten into the toasted bagel and was feening on the taste of salty steak and cheese when I heard the gunshot.

My heart thumped twice and I dove straight under the table.

"Don't kill us," I whispered, my eyes squeezed tight as I pulled my knees up to protect my stomach. "Please...don't..."

I was gripped in fear. Frozen in place. Tiny fingers of terror dug into the pit of my stomach as I found myself stretched out on the floor of my bridal suite once again. I lay there for hours it seemed like. Blacking out and coming to. Twisting and turning in agony. The scent of gunpowder stung my nose, and a hot pellet of lead burned like hell as it bored deep into my belly. Gripping my middle, I moaned loudly and called out for Gino.

"Juicy! Juicy! What's the matter, baby? What happened to you, girl?"

I opened my eyes.

It was Flex.

He was kneeling over me, and he looked more worried than I had ever seen him look in my life.

Oh, Gino, I thought as reality hit me. And then my tears came. They were tears of pain, but they were tears of relief too.

"Juicy! What happened?" Flex pleaded. He rolled me over onto my back and his eyes scanned my body from head to toe. "Are you hurt? Was there something wrong with the food? *What the hell happened to your stomach?"*

I raised my head slightly and saw that my pajama top had ridden up over my navel. My bullet wound, and the scar I'd gotten from my operation, looked red and angry, just an ugly reminder of all the drama that I had been through.

Flex slid his arm under my shoulders and scooted closer until my head and neck were resting on his thighs. His hand was warm and gentle as he placed it on my belly and traced my scar with his fingers.

"Oh, Juicy," he cried big tears as he held me in his arms and rocked me tenderly like a baby. I held him too. Flex mighta had his issues, but he was the closest thing I had to a family, and there was no denying that he had always loved me. We held each other close and for the first time in a long time I felt safe.

"Oh, baby," he moaned, lowering me to the floor as he stretched out beside me. "Who did this to you, ma?" he asked, patting my stomach with his lips on my ear. "Tell me, baby. Tell Flex what happened."

"Somebody shot me," I said miserably. "I got shot."

$$$$$

For the longest time I lay in Flex's arms accepting all the comfort he had to give.

"Ain't nobody never gonna hurt you again," he whispered, clutching me to his chest as we both sniffed and cried. "I swear to God, Juicy. Won't no fuckin' body ever so much as *touch* you girl. You ain't never gotta worry again. I can promise you that."

I buried my face in his chest as he stroked my hair. I was gripped in grief over my family, but I was also grateful for Flex's friendship and his love.

I'm not sure when I realized that something had changed, but at some point it did.

Flex was still stroking my hair and whispering words of comfort, but now he was pressing against me too. His dick was hard. I could feel it throbbing through his pants, and moments later he began moving his hips. Thrusting. Grinding. Poking his wood into me with a persistent, steady rhythm.

"Flex," I said softly, bringing my arms up to push him away.

"Shhhh..." he said, gripping me tighter. He covered my lips with his and began tonguing me down. His hand left my hair and slid over my shoulder, down the small of my back, over my ass, and between my cheeks. He moaned into my mouth and palmed my ass, drawing me into his body as he pushed at me with his dick.

"I'm not gonna hurt you, Juicy," he whispered, planting soft kisses on my cheek, chin, and neck. "I love you baby. I could never hurt you."

He dipped his head lower and snagged my top in his teeth, pulling it down over my titties. I gasped as his lips covered my nipple, sucking it deeply into his mouth, but my reaction was from surprise, not from pleasure.

"Flex...wait..." I leaned back and tried to break our contact. For a chick who had always been hot in the ass and who had craved sex like it was crack, I felt absolutely nothing as his tongue flicked back and forth across my hard nipple. His pushed his knee between my legs and started dry fucking me with long, slow strokes, but still, my pussy was parched and I felt nothing.

In all the months since Gino had been gone, my pussy hadn't popped not one time. It was like my womanhood, the sexual part of me, had died right along with my man.

I mean, I had been a real live professional masturbator, and I hadn't rubbed my own titties or touched myself down there not one single time. I hadn't even looked at or thought about none of the nasty stories I'd written in my Juicy Journal. My sex thing was just gone, and it didn't matter how much Flex humped on me with his big, hard dick. I just couldn't feel it.

"Flex, I can't..."

He *shhh'd* me again as his thrusts got harder and more frantic.

Flex musta been one of them premature comers. He was panting real hard now and I could tell he was about to blow a nut right in his drawers.

"C'mon, Flex," I said, trying to push him off of me. "We can't be doing this shit."

"I got protection, baby," he whispered like a real amateur. "I ain't gonna get you pregnant."

I probably would have lay there and let Flex hump me half to death just out of pure exhaustion and gratitude, but I knew I had to stop the madness when he ran me that old lame junior high school line.

"Just lemme put the head in, Juicy. Just the head, okay?"

That was it.

"*Flex!*" I practically screamed in his ear. "Get the fuck up offa me!"

It was like somebody had thrown a bucket of ice-cold water over us. Flex froze for a second, and then he pushed himself up on both arms and looked down at me and sneered.

"What? I can't touch you, Juicy? A niggah like me ain't good enough to touch you or something?"

That crazy look was back in his eyes, and I remembered the gunshot that had sent me flying under the table in the first place.

"C'mon now. You done fucked plenty of other niggahs, Juicy. So why you don't wanna give me none? Huh? What?" he said and thrust his fingers between my legs. "Your pussy too good? Or is something wrong with me?"

I pushed his hand away and shook my head real fast.

"No! I ain't saying nothing is wrong with you, boy! It's me, not you."

"*Boy?*" his eyes narrowed as he leaned back on his knees and started unbuckling his belt. The way he went at that belt did something to me. It put me right back in G's ass-dicking mode, and for the first time I felt fear. Real fear. I remembered how Flex had pushed a dude named Macaroni off the roof of our building when we were kids. They had locked his ass up behind that shit, and when he finally got out there was something real mean and crazy about little Fletcher.

"You still think I'm a fuckin' kid, don't you, Juicy? You think you fuckin' with a little boy, huh?"

"That's not what I'm not saying," I blurted out real fast as he extracted his dick from his drawers and gripped it in his hand like a snake. Flex had a monster package on him. It was almost fatter than his thigh, and just as long too, but that shit still didn't impress me.

"You think you can handle this shit, Juicy? Huh? Can you fuck with this?"

I shook my head.

"No, Flex. I can't fuck with it. I'm just not ready for all that."

Immediately his whole face changed.

"Awww, *shit!*" He bent over me with a look of deep regret in his eyes. Once again his voice was tender as he took my face in his hands.

"I'm sorry, Juicy. Damn! I'm sorry. I don't be thinking sometimes. Of course you ain't ready. You been hurt..." he scooted back, then dipped his head down and kissed my stomach. "You got all these fuckin' scars and shit...I shoulda known better. It's too soon, right? Is that what it is, Juicy? Is it just too soon?"

The look on his face was full of hope. Crazy hope, but it was still hope.

"Yeah," I nodded. "It's too soon for me, Flex. A lot of stuff went down in my life and I just need a little time to get my head right."

I lay there as he stuffed his dick back inside his pants. He fixed his clothes, and then he pulled me to my feet.

"I'm sorry," he said again. The sadness in his eyes told me that he really meant it. "I can wait for you, Juicy. I can wait."

I nodded and tried to turn away, but before I could take a step he grabbed my wrist and jerked me real close to him.

"Hey," he said softly, breathing in my face. "Whatever happened to that curly-haired niggah you ran outta New York with? G's son. What was his name again?"

My jaw felt frozen as I muttered, "Gino."

"Yeah, Gino. What ever happened to that cat?"

I shrugged and bit down on my lip before answering. "He got shot too. He died."

Flex gave me a strange look, and then he squeezed my wrist slightly and let me go. I was walking toward the bedroom when I heard him mutter something cold under his breath.

He said, "Good for that muh'fucka."

CHAPTER 13

Trey Jackson was choosey about who he banged. He had an example to set for his boys at The Crossover Community Center, so he made it his business to take everything in his life very seriously, and that included sex.

"Yummm..." he moaned deep in his throat as his date for the night sucked up a hickey on the upper region of his groin.

Raising his head slightly to watch her work, Trey ran his big hand through her curls and palmed the back of her skull like it was a basketball.

He exhaled through his mouth as Debbie's small teeth raked across his inner thigh and her nose nudged the underside of his balls. The girl had a head game on her that was almost indescribable, which was why Trey had found it hard to turn her down when she showed up at his door begging to get some pipe laid.

Debbie was a well-loved teacher at a high school on the Lower East Side of Manhattan, but she could be clingy and envious, and quick to throw down crazy accusations when she couldn't get shit exactly her way. That kind of jealousy was just part of her nature, so sometimes Trey had to be stingy with his dick and only allow her to bounce on it every now and then.

Debbie opened her mouth wide and sucked his thick meat down her throat. Trey saw her jaw trembling and straining as she did her best to take in as much of him as she could. Her hands roamed everywhere as he fucked up at her with short, hard thrusts. She stroked his thighs, massaged his six-pack, cupped his balls, and then her fingers returned to grip the base of his dick to jack and squeeze the leftover inches she just couldn't fit inside her mouth.

It had been a minute since Trey had gotten some real prime top, and what this chick was doing was almost too good for him to take. He pushed himself up on his elbows and straightened his legs, then moaned again as Debbie went to town with her tongue like she was trying to lick her way to the center of a tootsie roll pop.

Trey reached down and rubbed the juice that had dripped from her bottom lip to her chin, then he gently dislodged her from his joint and lifted her easily into his lap.

She was a petite little thing with small titties and a cute ass. Her hands were sure and quick as she rolled a magnum condom down over his erection, and when Trey positioned her dripping slit over his dick, she eased herself down on it, sighing as her pussy adjusted to his size and she attempted to handle everything he had.

Arching her back, Debbie braced her feet on either side of him, and rode him slowly at first, then deeper and harder as her honey flower blossomed and opened up to him.

Groaning softly, Trey craned his neck and captured one of her small titties in his mouth as they jiggled up and down with her bucking motions. Her skin was caramel mocha, but her nipples were dark chocolate and as sweet as hell.

He slid his rough hands down her shoulders, over her elbows, and then held tightly to her waist. Her midsection was so small that his fingertips actually touched went he brought his hands together, and her wide hips bucked feverishly back and forth.

Raising and lowering her in his lap, Trey enjoyed the wet sounds coming from her pussy, and the mutters of pleasure falling from her lips. He knew he was a big man everywhere, and he loved being able to thoroughly fuck a woman at the same time that she was pleasing him.

Right now the shaft of his dick felt like it was swollen to twice its size. Her insides were blazing hot and wet, and he felt himself losing control of his stroke.

"Damn!" he whispered. "This pussy is gooood!"

He slammed her down deeply on his rod, then stood up quickly and did a 180-degree turn around. Debbie was all warm, smooth brown skin as he lowered her to his bed. He hovered over her as she spread her legs wide, and lifted them high in the air.

Trey dove in dick first.

He felt her body shudder as he penetrated her fully, the head of his monster battering the back of her pussy walls.

"Oh! Damn!" Debbie cried. Her gorgeous body slithered beneath him like a snake as she raked long scratches down his back and ass in mindless bliss. "I love your dick, Trey! I love you, baby! This feels so damn good. I love you!"

Trey held her hips in place and bore down with all his weight, pressing into her pussy deliciously as she screamed into his chest with her release.

Second later, Trey let go too. He felt her vagina clenching and pulsating as his dick jerked inside her, spilling his seed into the tip of the condom.

Trey knew what was expected of him next. He rolled over onto his side and pulled Debbie into his arms so they could snuggle. His huge body dwarfed her tiny one as they spooned together in the aftermath of their sexual battle, and she felt sweet and warm laying in his arms. Long minutes passed before either of them said a word. Debbie broke the silence first.

"Wow," she said, pushing back deeper against his chest as she drew her knees all the way up to her chest. "I missed you, Trey. Can't no other man make me feel this good."

Trey pushed her hair up and kissed a sweet spot on the back of her neck.

"Thanks, baby," he said. "You make me feel good too."

Trey wasn't lying when he told her she made him feel good. She did. Debbie was a cool sistah. He liked her, and their sexual chemistry was off the chart.

But only the physical side of him had been satisfied tonight. The part of his heart that Trey was holding on reserve was still untouched. As much as he dug chilling with Debbie, Trey knew she wasn't the one for him. None of the ladies who were currently in his life, and who sometimes shared his bed were.

Trey Jackson was still waiting to find his queen. He was still waiting to provide sunlight for his flower, and water for his earth. He didn't know who she was, or when she would show up in his life, but he was a patient, serious man, and he'd know her when he found her.

These were the thoughts on Trey's mind when his cell phone vibrated on his nightstand. With his arms full of soft, brown flesh, he ignored it.

"You're not going to answer that?" Debbie asked.

"Nah, baby," Trey said, pulling her closer to him as his lips grazed her naked shoulder bone. "I'm chillin' with you right now. My voicemail can get it."

The phone vibrated again, and he felt Debbie go stiff in his arms.

"You can go ahead answer your phone you know, Trey." She reached over and snatched it up from the nightstand and passed it over her shoulder to him. "I already know you fucks with other women, so maybe my time is up on your clock and it's somebody else's turn now."

"C'mon, Deb," he said and stroked her arm gently as he braced for one of her insanely jealous heat rounds. "It's not even like that baby."

His phone vibrated again, and Trey glanced at the caller ID and froze.

"Hello?"

He frowned deeply as he listened to the gravelly, panicked voice on the other end of the line.

"No, I haven't seen her in a few days," he told the elderly caller, "but the last time she came by we hung out and she seemed pretty straight."

Trey listened some more.

"So was that the last time you spoke to her?"

The old man said a few words and Trey nodded.

"A'ight. I'll look around and see if I can find her. Yeah, I understand. I know, I know. I love her too."

Debbie jumped out of the bed as soon as the last few words left Trey's mouth.

"Check it out baby," he told her as he got outta the bed too and started looking for some clothes. "A situation just jumped off with one of my girls and I need to go take care of a couple of things real quick."

"You know," Debbie said completely igging what he'd said. She stuck one foot inside her panties while she balanced on her slim, pretty leg. "I'm tired of you and all your other girls, Trey. And that's real fucked up of you to lay up here next to me talking about how you love some other chick, you know."

"Debbie," Trey reached for her, and she pushed his hand away. "Hold up," he said. "It ain't even like that, baby."

"Nah, don't Debbie me. I already told you I know you fucks with other females, Trey!"

"Yeah," he answered honestly. "I do. But I've never tried to hide that from you. You told me sex was all you wanted too."

"Well I fuckin' *lied!*" she said as she pulled her jeans over her cute hips and bent over and snatched her shirt up off the floor. The pert, naked titties that he had just sucked all over bounced up and down as she moved.

Trey went in the bathroom and flushed his soggy condom down the toilet, then wiped his dick and balls off with a wet washcloth.

When he went back in his room Debbie was still standing pretty much where he had left her.

"Look, let me give you a ride home, Deb, cool?" He reached for her arm. "Or at least let me get you a cab."

She hand-checked him. "Nah, the only thing you can do for me is give up all them other chicks you got on a string! And if you can't do that then I'm out baby. Sorry. I can't help but get jealous when I'm giving you my heart and all I can get back is a piece of your body, Trey. I mean, damn! You just laid right there in the bed next to me and said you love some other girl! Don't you think I would like to hear you say you love *me* sometimes too?"

Trey nodded. He felt her. He really did. He could have broken the situation down about the pregnant thirteen-year-old dopefiend who had gone missing from her grandfather's house. And he could have told Debbie how important it was for him to go comfort the girl's scared, elderly grandfather, and maybe he coulda tried to explain why he was so damn driven to help the neighborhood kids when they found themselves caught between the streets and a hard spot. But none of that woulda changed anything between him and Debbie. When there was so much clear envy in a heart, there was no room for love or anything else.

He got dressed in silence and grabbed his wallet and his keys. Somewhere out in there wandering the dark streets of Harlem was a thirteen-year-old girl who was pregnant by her dead pimp and shooting drugs in her veins.

Debbie was a grown-ass woman and he could deal with her shit later. But right now Trey needed to call his boyz so they could get out there and try to find that lost little child of the ghetto before it was too late.

"Oh, so you're just gonna walk out on me now?" Debbie smirked and crossed her arms over her breasts when she realized that he was about to leave with or without her.

"I'm not walking out on you, baby. I have something I need to take care of. I'll call you later, Deb, okay?"

"You know what?" she exploded. "A niggah like you should *never* believe a chick when she tells you all she wants is sex! That's a bunch of bullshit, because a real woman is *never* gonna be satisfied with just some random, occasional dick from a dude like you, Trey! You best believe every bitch you're mashing it up with wants more, more, more! I don't care how much she fronts and tells you all she wants is that bone. Trust me. She wants *more*."

CHAPTER 14

I had been staying with Flex for about a week and he had been true to his word all that time. Not once had he tried to push up on me in a sexual way. Instead, he had bent over backward tryna shower me with all kinds of treats.

He'd brought an old lady named Mrs. Freeman down those rickety stairs to wash and style my hair, and after using that rough-ass bar soap on Rikers Island, I was happy as hell to feel and smell some real salon products being lathered all over my head.

The last person who had done my hair had been DarQuese, and sitting there with a towel draped over my shoulders while Mrs. Freeman combed conditioner through my hair brought back some real painful memories.

Later on, I was surprised when a bow-legged Asian chick came down the stairs with a nail kit and gave me a dope manicure and pedicure. She chatted her ass off in Chinese, and I talked right back to her in English. It felt so good to be pampered again, but then Flex messed around and told me where he'd gotten all those damn people from.

"Oh, they work upstairs for the funeral home," he said nonchalantly. "Mrs. Freeman is real cool. She hooks up the dead ladies' makeup and hair, and the Chinese chick polishes their nails."

My skin crawled at the thought that those same hands that worked on dead people had been touching all over me. But I didn't have time to get stupid about it because I was waiting for Flex to break out for a little while so I could get back on his laptop.

I had emailed Rita when he left me by myself earlier, and Miss Computer Whiz emailed me back with instructions on how to download Skype so we could talk face to face.

"Whatever you do," Rita warned me when her face popped up on the screen. "Don't pop ya head up in Harlem, Juicy. Dutchy ran into somebody working undercover on the force who's tight with Ace. Them fools don't want you dead like we first thought. They want you alive."

I got scared again. The only reason them niggahs wanted me alive was so they could torture my ass. I woulda preferred to die then let them drag me down into the Dungeon and tie me up again in the G-Spot.

"But I can't stay down here in this basement much longer," I told Rita. "Flex's black ass is crazy. He's almost as bad as G. I gotta find someplace else to go."

Rita looked real sad on the camera.

"I'll keep working on it. It's just that everybody I know and trust is right here in Harlem. Which is exactly where you don't wanna be seen."

"How's Nooni?" I asked. "I'm sorry, girl. I'm over here complaining when I shoulda been asking about your sister."

244

Rita shrugged.

"I haven't heard anything from her or anybody else. Dutchy still has a few eyes on the G-Spot, though. We're just watching and waiting, and praying too. But really, it's their move."

I heard that. I had somebody waiting on me to make a move, too. Earlier that day Flex had handed me a large box that had a dope three-thousand-dollar Fendi dress inside. It was a classy cut, in a beautiful shade of emerald green, and inside the big box was a smaller box that held a pair of cute diamond earrings and a platinum tennis bracelet. He had already bought me a couple of pairs of jeans and some cute tee shirts, but this was something way different.

"What's all this for?" I asked him. I was getting used to him sporting a different tailored suit everyday, but I hadn't worn anything this fancy in a minute. "We going somewhere?"

Flex just grinned and shook his head.

"Nah, baby. We ain't gotta go nowhere special for me to wanna put you in finery, Juicy. All this is for *us*, baby. I'm looking good for you, and I want you to look good for me too. It ain't about nobody else."

That shit creeped me right out. Flex was like a weird-ass kid trying to play big man. I wasn't about to get all dressed up just to watch movies in his basement. It had been over a week since I'd gotten out of jail, and I hadn't been above the ground not one single time.

"That's okay," I had said, turning down his gift and handing him back the box. He could keep that shit. The last thing I wanted Flex to think was that we was some kind of Bonnie and Clyde couple. "I'm good. Thanks, though."

He stared at me real hard, then started spitting like a maniac but real quiet-like.

"You know what? You's a ungrateful bitch, Juicy. You don't appreciate nothing a niggah try to do for you! Look at all the shit I got for you! You got everything you need right here. *Everything.* If you want something I ain't got, then just tell me and I'll go out and get that shit!"

I fixed his skinny black ass.

"I want a *phone charger*, Flex. I need my phone so I can make some calls. Can you go out and get me that?"

"You know," he pouted and straight igged my request, "I could be one of them sorry muh'fuckas who just gets up in your pussy and treats you like a hoe, but no. I'm treating you like a lady, Juicy. Like a real lady. And you don't even 'preciate that shit."

"I do, Flex," I insisted. "You like a little brother to me, and I appreciate everything you been doing. I just need a phone charger so I can use my phone."

His face got real twisted. "I ain't your fuckin' brother, Juicy. I ain't trying to be your brother."

I sucked my teeth. "Okay then. I just don't wanna get dressed up to sit around and watch you play no damn video games."

I walked back into my room and turned on the television, but I wasn't hardly watching it.

Instead, I was thinking. There was a time when I had been real stupid and naïve, but I wasn't any more. I saw where Flex was going with all his crazy bullshit. I saw exactly where he was trying to get me. In a corner. In a box. In a small little space where only he had access to me. A space that only *he* controlled.

But it wasn't happening. The days when I let a niggah hem me up in his fantasy were over. Flex might be throwed off, but if he pushed me hard enough I could get throwed off too. The next time he unlocked that basement door I was going out with him. There were plenty of knives in Flex's kitchen, and I didn't care what I had to do, or who I had to fuck up, the next time that door opened up I was leaving.

CHAPTER 15

Nooni's little ass needs a job," Salida told Monique. "I'm tired of her sitting around here looking pretty but not doing shit. That girl is a liar and a thief, and I want you to put her ass to work."

"Me?" Monique said, thinking about how pissed Nooni had been after she jumped in the bed and finger-fucked her until she came. "That chick is mad at me. We ain't even hardly speaking."

"Look, me and you work our asses off, right? Hell, everybody up in this joint is about a hustle except her. All that warming up barstools is out the door now, and she's gotta start bringing in some money. Besides, how the hell is she not gonna speak to you when she's living up under your roof and eating your food? You better get her ass in check real quick, honey. Don't you *ever* let a young girl play you. Remember that."

"So you want me to put her to work?" Monique asked skeptically. "Where?"

Salida grinned. "Remember when I told you how to get rid of her little friend Bubbles? By telling them you hosted private parties in Philly and Atlantic City and you only had room for one more girl?"

Monique nodded. She saw exactly where this was going and she couldn't believe Salida's predatory ass was taking it there.

"Well we're gonna follow through on all that and make it come true. I want you to rope Nooni's ass like a calf and tie her down so tight that she don't even think about going nowhere.

"I want you to put her ungrateful ass through a meat grinder so we can get her ready to work the rooms and generate some cash. If anybody can school her and get her trained up right," Salida said in a flattering tone, "I *know* you can, Monique. Blast her all over Craig's List. Hit those kinky-ass white men who like to bang hot brown bodies like hers. You're the slickest stripper in Harlem, Monique. I want you to turn Nooni's ass out and show how to make some money. *Shiiit,* she's been laying around giving up all that pussy to Truth for free, right? Well, now it's time for her to get it together and start contributing to the family business."

$$$$$

Salida had told Monique to put Nooni in a trick bag, and that's exactly what she was gonna do. She'd posted an ad on Craig's List and found just the right trick to roll with, and every detail had been planned to perfection.

"Remember," Monique told the young girl, "you gotta get the money first, then make him take off all his clothes so he can't chase you when you run out the room."

The first time Nooni hustled a trick Monique had participated in the party and they'd worn matching bob-cut wigs. Nooni's was flaming red and Monique's was light blue, and they'd had on skin-tight little cat suits in the same color. They'd drank gin and partied with the trick for a couple of hours before going in for the kill. Monique had even let him suck on her titties a little bit just to make him think he was really getting some.

But as soon as they got his clothes off and got his cash, both girls had jetted from the room taking the trick's clothes with them.

Tonight's show was gonna go down a little different. The trick had specifically asked for someone who was into role-playing. When Monique pressed him for details, she found out he was looking for somebody to whip his ass and punish him. Monique had immediately doubled the price and started prepping Nooni.

"Now I already told you this dude is a little shy," Monique said as she rubbed bright green eye shadow on the girl's upper lids. "He's one of them S&M freak who likes young bitches, and that's probably because he's got a real little dick."

Nooni looked scared, and Monique gave her an encouraging pat on the back. "Don't worry. I've partied with those types before. One dude paid me two grand just to let him stick his big toe up my ass." She shrugged. "I would come in the room with you, but he's not into the group thing, so it's gonna be a private party with just you and him tonight."

Nooni looked scared.

"Don't worry. I'll be listening out right down the hall," Monique assured her, "so if any shit jumps off I'll be standing by to squash it."

She eyed Nooni's shape as the girl stepped into a short white dress. Her lightly oiled body was deliciously firm and curved, and swollen in all the right places. "You think you can handle it?" Monique asked. She added a dab of mascara to Nooni's eyelids and studied her fake lashes with approval.

Nooni sounded stressed. "I'll try. You got a belt or something? What am I supposed to beat him with?"

"Oh, you ain't gotta worry about that," Monique told her with a wave of the hand. "These kind of guys always bring their own whips and chains and all that other crazy shit. They know what they like. You just make sure you hit him real hard wherever that fool wants you to make it hurt."

Nooni knocked on the hotel room door, and waited until her customer told her to come in. She slid the key-card through the slot, then twisted the doorknob and went inside.

The room was semi-dark, with the light from the bathroom shining into the hall.

"Um, where you at, Mister?" she called out. She was so nervous her voice trembled and her knees were knocking together too.

"I'm over here," he said, and Nooni's blood froze in her veins.

The voice was coming from the area by the desk, and he sounded like a ten-year-old white boy.

"I can't see you," Nooni said, peering into the darkness.

"You gotta come closer," he said like a child. "I've done a lot of bad things. I need you to punish me."

Nooni remembered what Monique had told her.

"I'm supposed to get the money first."

"It's on the bed," he said. "Near the wall. Take it."

Nooni walked cautiously over to the bed that was closest to her, and in the darkness she made out the neat stack of bills. She picked them up and saw that they were all hundreds. She spread them out in her hand and counted over a grand, then stuffed them inside her small white purse.

"Now, come on," the trick whined. "You promised to punish me."

Nooni stepped further into the room, and then stopped suddenly when the butt-naked white man rose to his feet.

He was tall and heavy-set, with a baldhead and a belly that covered his dick and sagged halfway down to his knees. His skin was real pale, and the wiry hairs on his chest looked like gray Brillo.

He picked up something from the bed and held it out to her.

It was an extra large pair of tweezers, and Nooni took them with a puzzled look on her face.

"Mister, what in the world do you want me to do with these?"

The trick turned his back on her, and spread his legs wide. Balancing his knees on the edge of the bed, he tooted his big asshole up in the air as his fat hairy balls dangled between his thighs.

If Nooni hadn't been so scared she would have laughed. This fool had a bunch of shiny silver stickpins embedded in his nut sack. He looked like a hairy-assed porcupine, and a shiver of disgust ran down her spine.

"The hairs on my balls," the old man gave his order in the voice of a child. "Pluck 'em."

CHAPTER 16

Chiney Jackson had gotten sprung from Rikers Island a couple of weeks ahead of schedule, and she hit the wonderful streets of Harlem rolling hard. She'd taken her little jail bid in stride, and now that she'd hit the bricks she was determined to make up for lost time.

She had promised her brother Trey she was gonna spend the morning looking for a drug treatment program to enroll in, but instead she rode her ten-speed bike up on the avenue, and looked around to see who was handling some bizz. Young Maleek was posted up on the corner grind, and he spotted her as she was peddling toward him.

"Whattup, whattup?" he greeted her, dapping her out like she was a dude for real.

Maleek was one of the few trap boys who respected Chiney for who she was. He was also one of the few who was willing to handle any transactions with her too, as most of the other hustlers were too fearful of her brother to get down with her like that.

"It's all good," Chiney said, passing him some cash in her dap. Chiney and Maleek used to be cool back in the day when Mayhem and Messiah were playing varsity ball. They'd both enjoyed the limelight of having talented, popular brothers. And they'd both suffered the loss when their brothers were suddenly gone: Mayhem to the grave, and Messiah to jail.

"Ay, what kinda music is playing in the club tonight?" she asked, speaking in code.

"Oh, the club is hot," Maleek assured her. "Got that Red Devil, baby." He tossed off a vial containing four small pills. The words Divine Nine were stamped on the outside. "See how that do you," he said, stepping off to take care of another customer. "Lemme know how you fly."

Two hours later Chiney was flying high.

She had hooked up with her booty call for the night and both of them had popped the tabs she had copped from Leek.

"Damn, baby," Chiney moaned as she gazed at the head full of weave that bobbed between her legs. Being in jail had put some constraints on her sex life, but that didn't have shit to do with how horny she was tonight.

Chiney liked to fuck when she was high, and right now, she sat on her brother's coffee table with her right leg bent and her foot resting on the edge. Her left leg was splayed out in front of her, and a fly little light-skinned honey was kneeling between her thighs giving up that wet-wet.

"Yeah," Chiney directed her lover as the girl alternated between slathering her clit with her warm tongue and sucking it between her soft lips. "Right there, baby. "Oh yeah. Jack it for Daddy. Jack it."

Chiney had a very large clit for a woman. It protruded from her vaginal lips and felt to her like what she imagined a man's dick must have felt like to him.

She leaned back on the table, letting her right leg fall open wider. The girl between her legs parted Chiney's ass cheeks and put some dressing on that salad.

Chiney felt her clit jerking. She didn't know if it was the drugs she'd ingested or the pussy she was smelling, but a spasm shot through her and her nipples began to tingle.

Pushing the girl's head away, she stood up and helped her girl get up too. They stood close together, kissing and swaying in the middle of the room.

The girl was soft and cuddly in Chiney's muscular arms. She smelled sweet, and the sensation of their nipples brushing together almost drove Chiney wild.

She lay the girl down on the floor and climbed on top of her. Yeah, she had a bedroom that she could have taken the girl to, but Chiney liked it raw and spontaneous.

She got on top of the girl and reached between them to finger her softness. Spreading the girl's lower lips, Chiney positioned herself so that her stiff, dangling clit was at the door of the girl's wet tunnel.

Moans rose in the air as the two women fucked. Their clits collided as they rubbed pussies back and forth as they got their mash on. Chiney pumped the chick just like a man would. She cupped the girl's firm breasts and squeezed her thick nipples between her fingers.

The girl moaned loud and long in Chiney's ear. Her movements became more frantic as she gripped Chiney's ass and ground her pussy around. Guiding one breast to her mouth, Chiney bit down on the girl's nipple, causing her to yelp and come hard, throwing her hands over her head as she surrendered to the pussy whipping that Chiney was putting on her.

But now, a hurricane was brewing deep in Chiney's clitoris too, and as gay as she was, she still longed to feel something thick and hard banging against her inner walls.

"Fuck me," she muttered, taking the girl's hand and placing it between her legs. Two fingers were inside her before she knew it, and as the chick stroked and sloshed her fingers around in the pool Chiney's pussy had created, Chiney locked her legs on the girl's hand, and gyrated her hips until she came too, her little man quivering as her boat got rocked and her sugar walls melted in delight.

CHAPTER 17

Monique was stretched out in the hotel bed watching television and sipping some Moet when she heard a door slam and footsteps booking outside in the hall. She glanced at her watch. Nooni had only been in the room with the trick for ten minutes, which wasn't even enough time for them to get down to any real business. She frowned moments later when there was a desperate series of knocks on her door.

"Monique!" the young girl begged from outside in the hall, "Please let me in!"

Jumping from the bed, Monique unlocked the door and flung it open.

"*Sssh!*" she whispered, snatching Nooni inside the room. The girl was crying and holding both hands near her neck. Her swirly ponytail had come undone and her makeup was smudged all over her face. "What the hell happened?" Monique demanded.

"H-h-he tried to choke me!" Nooni cried hoarsely. "At first he said he was a bottom bitch. He wanted me to punish him, but he had all kinds of needles stuck in his balls!" Then he told me to pluck out all the little hairs around his nuts," the girl squirmed, squeamish and disgusted by the memory, "but I just couldn't do that shit!"

"Why not?" Monique demanded. "Didn't he pay you first? You couldn't just snatch them hairs out and keep it moving?"

Nooni shook her head.

"I couldn't, Monique. That shit was too freaky. I'm sorry, but I just couldn't do it!"

"So you just upped and left?"

The young girl shook her head no again.

"He got mad and wanted me to give him his money back. He tried to go in my purse and we started fighting. He knocked me against the desk and started choking me. I didn't have no choice, Monique. I couldn't breathe and I couldn't get away neither. So I hit him."

Monique gave her a look. "You hit him?"

"Yeah," Nooni said nodding. "With a lamp."

"And then what happened?"

"He fell," Nooni whispered, fresh tears running from her eyes. "He fell and I think he hit his head because a whole lotta blood started gushing outta him. And that's when I ran."

Monique stared at the girl. Her scary ass coulda put them in a trick bag for sure.

"Stop crying," she told Nooni, hugging her briefly. "I'ma go see if he's okay. You stay here and change your clothes and start packing up our shit. Wash your face first," Monique told her. She slid the key-card from the dresser. "I'll be right back."

$$$$$

252

J-Ugly stood outside the trap house clenching his ass-cheeks tight. He had to take a serious shit but there were way too many customers flying at him to get off the trap anytime soon.

His boss Lil Lee had just swung by with a nice resupply, so he knew nobody else would be coming by to check for him anytime soon. His eyes darted up toward Lenox Avenue and hope surged in him at what he saw.

"Yo, Leek!" he yelled at the young cat who was about to head across the street. "Ay, slime, lemme holla at you for a minute!"

Maleek was down with the same click that J-Ugly was, but he was even lower on the food chain. J liked the boy 'cause he was cold as ice, and plus the same chick braided both of their hair, and they were cool like that.

"Yo, listen up, son," he said when Maleek got over to him. The boy was young, but he was already mad tall, and the two of them stood eye-to-eye. "I got this work on me but I need to hit the bathroom real quick. Hold this shit down for me while I run inside, and make sure my money is right when I get back out here, ya heard?"

Dope and money passed from one hand to the next, and it happened so fast the casual observer woulda missed it.

"I'll be right back," J-Ugly screwed up his handsome face as his stomach cramped with pressure. He ran up the steps and pushed through the raggedy door, then bust into the filthy crack den and hauled ass toward the bathroom.

$$$$$

"Girl you walk just like a damn duck," Taleah said as she switched her booty down Lenox Avenue. She was walking her pregnant friend to the corner store so the girl could get a bag of those hot, crunchy pork skins that she'd been craving all day.

Her thirteen-year-old girlfriend laughed. "Later for you! I'm nine-months, stupid. How the hell do you expect me to walk?"

"I'on't know but I be glad when you drop that load. It's fuckin' up my flow. Niggahs look at you and don't even wanna holla at me. Hell, I ain't the one swollen. I'm still cute."

They were just about to cross the street when Princess saw a guy she knew hustlin' from the block.

"Girl, that dude is fine as hell," she said and nodded at a tall corner boy with fresh cornrows in his hair. He was standing outside of a trap house and working hard on the grind.

"Hold up for a minute," Princess said, and waddled her way over to the dude. She said a few words, then they walked over to the building and huddled for a quick second. The next thing Taleah knew, Princess was walking up the building's front steps as fast as she could.

"Hey heffah!" Taleah hollered. "Where the hell you going?"

Princess waved her off. "Go 'head, Tee! I'ma catch up with you later, okay?"

Taleah started to say something slick, but a look from the trap boy froze her cold.

"All right then," she muttered under her breath as she turned around and headed back toward her block. "How a bitch gonna ask me to give her a walk," she said out loud, "and then just leave me hanging like that? Pregnant bitches got a lotta nerve.

They got a whole lotta nerve."

CHAPTER 18

The muffled voices of other hotel guests drifted into the hallway as Monique crept three doors down to the room where Nooni had left the trick. She inserted her keycard in the door, then waited until the small light flashed green before pushing down on the latch and going inside.

The room was cool and dim, and the first thing she did was run the back of her hand along the wall and flip on the light switch.

The trick was laying there, banged up and bloody, just like Nooni had said.

Monique stepped over to him cautiously, but even before she got up on him she knew what time it was. The naked white man was stretched out on his back with his legs cocked open and slobber coming out of his mouth. A big-ass noogie had jumped up red and swollen on the side of his head and a small pool of blood had leaked onto the floor. His torture kit was laid out neatly on one bed, and the lamp Nooni had hit him with was turn over on its side.

Eyeballing the downed white man, Monique put her hands on her hips and grinned. Salida was gonna be so happy. Opportunities like this didn't just pop up in your life everyday. She giggled. Sometimes shit was just *for* you. It just fell in your lap like a gift from your guardian sugar daddy.

Her eyes scanned the room as she devised her plan. A large pair of tweezers lay on the desk. Stepping around the white man, Monique stuck out her toe and nudged his plump nut sack. There were so many silver pins sticking outta that thing that it looked like a tomato-red pincushion.

She shook her head. Nooni was way too fuckin' soft. Monique woulda jammed those pins in his balls and had those silver hairs plucked and yanked in no time flat.

Chuckling out loud, Monique turned her back on the drunk, snoring john and strutted on out the door.

$$$$$

The knock Monique put on her room door was way more frantic and panicked than Nooni's had been.

"Open the goddamn door!" she whispered harshly, and the moment Nooni did, Monique bum-rushed inside and headed straight to the bathroom.

"Get a towel!" she barked at Nooni. "Wipe off everything you mighta touched!"

Nooni's eyes were two big scared O's.

"W-w-what happened in t-t-there?" she stammered.

"Hurry up!" Monique snapped. She moved like a tornado as she wiped down the telephone, the remote control, and the switches and knobs on all the lamps. "Put your shoes on," she told Nooni, who had wiped off the arms of the chairs, and had

255

gone into the bathroom to wipe off the hot and cold water taps. "We gotta get the fuck outta here, girl. We gotta get outta here fast."

Nooni looked so scared that Monique almost felt sorry for her dumb ass.

"Is he okay?" the frightened girl asked. Her eyes pleaded with Monique for the answer to be yes. "What happened?"

Monique stopped and grilled her. Hard.

"You know what the fuck happened in there, Nooni!" Monique lied sternly, even though she really wanted to laugh. Salida said she wanted Nooni roped up like a cow? Well her young ass wouldn't be tryna run back home or anywhere else after this!

"Bitch, you killed a *white* man! You hit him in the head and murked his ass, that's what happened! That mothafuckin' trick is *dead*."

CHAPTER 19

You're not gonna get in trouble, Taleah," Trey reassured the crying teenager who was sitting on the white leather sofa in his office. They were at the Crossover Community Center that Trey had founded to help local kids and athletes learn job skills and stay off the city streets.

The building was one of those 1930's single-story warehouses that had hundreds of very small windows along every side. The roof of the building was also constructed of thick glass, with thousands of small panes on the ceiling that let the light in and gave it an open, roomy feel.

Princess, the thirteen-year-old pregnant girl Trey mentored, had disappeared into thin air. Trey had put in some calls to his local business partners and sent a crew out on the streets to search for her.

The scared young girl sitting in front of him had been the last person to see her, but Taleah was too shook to tell him what she knew. She was afraid somebody on the streets might find out she had snitched on a dope dealer, and come looking for her to get some payback.

"Nobody is gonna find out anything about you," Trey told her. "And I can promise you that. C'mon, Taleah. Just tell us who Princess bought the dope from and where she went to get high."

"But I don't know the dude's name, Trey! I swear to God I don't. All I know is she asked me to give her a walk to the corner store up on Lenox so she could buy some skins. We was almost there when she saw a dude slanging on the corner. They walked over to the building together and she copped from him. That's it. I don't know where she went after that. She told me to go ahead and said she was gonna catch up with me later, so I left."

"Did you see which way she went?" Mr. Howell, Princess' eighty-two-year-old grandfather asked in a small, scared voice. "Baby, do you remember what street she was on when you last saw her?"

Tears ran down Taleah's face. The poor girl was so shook she was trembling.

"Please, Trey." Her nose was red as she pleaded with him. "I just don't wanna get my name in nothing, you know what I mean? Them dudes out there are crazy, and if they find out I told you something they gonna come after me and my little brother too."

"Yo, Taleah, listen." Trey kneeled down in front of the girl and held both of her slender shoulders in his large hands. "I would *never* put you in any danger. And that's word. Now, Princess is nine-months pregnant and ain't nobody seen her in almost two days. She could be in some real trouble and she might just need our help. You were damn solid to tell her grandfather y'all had been smoking weed together, but now you gotta tell it all, baby girl. Mr. Howell is an old man, and he can't handle all

257

this stress. So I need you to tell me what street Princess copped on, and which way she was heading when you left her. Tell me, Taleah. Whatever you know you gotta tell me."

Taleah took a deep breath and swallowed hard.

"I'm telling you the truth, Trey. I really don't know the dude's name. I just know he was tall and skinny, and he had cornrows going back in his hair. But I did..." she swallowed hard again. "I did see the building Princess went in. And if you come with me up on Lenox Avenue, I'll show you."

$$$$$

Trey helped Mr. Howell climb into his whip. The old man was so thin and feeble that his bones poked through the oversized shirt he wore and his belt damn near looped his thin waist twice.

"I just don't understand it," he kept shaking his gray-haired head. "She was doing so good, you know. She was off that stuff and doing good while she was hanging around up here with you. But as soon as she stopped showing up she started running the street again. You know she's my little princess, Antonio."

His thin voice was full of grief. "I was disappointed when she came home pregnant, but I accepted it as the Lord's will. Princess and that baby she's carrying are the last of my bloodline. They the only things I got left in this world."

Trey waited patiently until the elderly man got himself strapped in. His gnarled hands shook as he tried to guide the seatbelt's latch over to the lock, but somehow he got it done.

"I know, Mr. Howell." Trey said as he climbed in on the driver's side of the car. He had grown up next door to the Howell family and hung out a lot with Freda, Princess' mother. Freda had gotten shot in a drive-by years ago while she was pregnant, and although she died, Princess survived. Mr. Howell had been raising the girl by himself until a local pimp got her pregnant and tricked her out on dope.

"Don't worry," Trey told him. "I got some good eyes out there on the streets looking for your granddaughter, Mr. Howell. She's out there somewhere, and we're gonna find her."

Trey was pulling away from the curb when he felt his cell phone vibrate on his waist. He snatched it off the clip and pressed it to his ear.

"Yeah, whassup?"

It was his manz, Rain. He operated an icee stand near 116th Street, and he was calling with some real bad news.

"Yo, man. You know my oldest son's mother works at Harlem Hospital, man. I was asking around like you said, and she told me an ambulance brought a young pregnant girl in unconscious earlier today. I think this young chick might be the girl you lookin' for, man. I think this might be her."

Trey went ice-cold inside.

It felt like history was repeating itself.

He drove past the corner where Taleah said she had last saw Princess, and noted the building the girl pointed out. It was a well-known drug den, and Trey had gone up in there to pull out smoked-up kids quite a few times over the years.

Wordlessly, he dropped Taleah off at home, and then he drove down Malcolm X Blvd and took Mr. Howell inside Harlem Hospital. Two hours later, Trey held the weeping old man in his arms as they left the dank, impersonal morgue.

Thirteen-year-old Princess Howell's body had been waiting in a freezer drawer to be identified. The sight of the dead teen with her swollen belly, barely old enough to be anybody's mother, had rocked both Trey and her devastated grandfather deep down in their souls.

"I'm sorry, Mister H." Trey let the old man press his bony face against his chest as he cried like a baby. Every life lost to drugs was another painful nick in the center of Trey's heart. "I'm so fuckin' sorry!" he said.

And he was. But what Trey didn't tell the elderly man as he held him in his arms, was that he was mad as hell now, and he was on a mission too.

CHAPTER 20

Nooni was a nervous fuckin' wreck.

She knew she was a murderer, and she kept peeking at the front door like the cops were gonna bust in and arrest her at any minute. Her hands were icy cold and her heart pounded in her chest as she wandered around the G-Spot looking lost and turned out.

To make things worse, Monique had overheard Greco asking her for his cell phone back, and that chick had wilded out on her like crazy.

"You tryna *call* some fuckin' body, Nooni? Huh? Huh?" Monique slapped her upside her head and punched her in the eye. "Here I am tryna hide you and protect you, and you poppin' your lil dumb ass head up to get picked off!"

Monique had put her hands around Nooni's throat and dug her nails in deep as she squeezed the air outta her. "I ain't going to jail for you, Nooni. I shoulda just called the cops when you killed that dude, but since I didn't they can come after my ass behind that shit too, and I ain't going to jail!"

She had pressed her fingers hard against Nooni's windpipe, and when Nooni squirmed and tried to fight her off, Monique had come straight outta the projects and beat her down to the ground.

"Yo, what's up with that chick?" Ace asked Salida. He was busy tryna think of how to pinch off a few ends so his cousin Rabb could pay for Izzy's and Zero's funerals, and Salida was busy chattering in his ear about the next week's entertainment line up. They watched Nooni drag herself from the XXX cinema room and shuffle toward the staff bathrooms.

Ace shook his head. Something wasn't right. Nooni used to be a stunning and sexy young *mamacita,* and now she was dragging her ass around like a dried up little old lady.

Salida smiled inside. Unlike Ace, she knew exactly why Nooni was all shook up, and she knew exactly what to do to get the young girl to calm down and relax a little bit too. So, later that night, Salida went and found Nooni sitting alone near a pool table.

"Come with me," she said, and took Nooni by the hand. The girl's fingers were ice-cold and Salida was pleased by how much they trembled.

She led Nooni upstairs and unlocked the door to the cut-room using the key on her wristband. They walked past all the jugs and containers, and other drug-making paraphernalia, and into the small office.

"Sit down," Salida told her.

Nooni did, but she kept her eyes on the floor.

"Something is wrong with you," Salida spoke like she was a trained mental health professional, and after all those years in the nut house she had sat through enough counseling sessions to know exactly what tone to take. Her voice was calm and soothing, yet cool with authority.

"What's going on?" Salida pressed.

Nooni shook her head.

"You'd feel so much better if you let it all out and told somebody," Salida urged.

The girl looked damn near comatose. She was shivering uncontrollably, and the tips of her nails were stumped and bloody because she'd gnawed them all the way down to the meat.

Salida switched tactics.

"I see you and Truth are pretty close. I think he really cares about you."

Silence.

"Are y'all still staying in that lil ass apartment with Pluto and Monique?"

A small nod.

"You and Truth need to work harder so y'all can get your own place. Monique is cool, but two women can't live up under the same roof. Believe me, I know."

Silence.

"Are you homesick or something, Nooni? Do you miss your family?"

The girl trembled visibly.

"I bet your people are probably really worried about you."

A small tear slipped from Nooni's eye.

"You want me to ask Monique if you can go home and see your sister?"

Nooni shook her head quickly. "She already said I can't. The cops are looking for me."

More tears came then. An ocean of them.

Salida pressed the girl to her breast in a motherly embrace. She whispered soothing words as the dumb-ass who was about to become her little in-house tester wept in her arms.

"There, there, there," Salida cooed and rocked. "You don't have to cry. You're safe here with us. We'll protect you. And things will get better for you, Nooni. I promise they will. In fact, I can help you start feeling better right now. Do you trust me?" she asked, smoothing down Nooni's wild tangle of hair. "Do you trust me, Nooni?"

The girl nodded. Just once.

That was all Salida needed to see.

She reached into her top drawer and pulled out a small vial. The words Divine Nine were stamped on the outside. Shaking out two pills, she spoke gently to the crying girl.

"Open your mouth," she said softly.

Nooni obeyed. Salida placed the two pills on Nooni's tongue, and when the young girl swallowed, Salida smiled.

CHAPTER 21

Slick Sallie was thinking fast and moving even faster.

He'd driven Mick's car home after the bungled heist, but there was no time to grieve for his cousin and there was no time to wait around for the money that would come in after the microchips were sold to a company in Vietnam either.

Sallie had parked Mick's car several blocks away, and let himself into his mother's house. He'd showered and drank half a bottle of whisky, and after sleeping for a few fitful hours he'd gotten up with the sun and driven north for several hours.

After ditching Mick's car on some railroad tracks, he'd hitched a lift back to the city from a truck driver who was hauling paper goods. He hopped out about a thirty-minute walk away from his mother's house, and he was almost there when his cell phone rang.

"Uncle Frank," he said. "*Come stai?*"

"Where the fuck are you, Salvatore?"

His uncle's tone was cold and unforgiving, and Sallie sensed the danger right away.

"Uhhh," he said, stalling, "I'm actually on my way to your house," he lied. "Yeah, I should be there in a bit."

"Good," Frank said coldly. "Come quickly. I have something for you."

Sal stuck the phone down in his pants and ran the rest of the way home. There was no time to waste now. His uncle's voice had said it all. They knew about the bomb, they knew about the heist, they knew about Mick. There was gonna be fuckin' hell to pay.

Back downstairs in his mother's wine cellar, Sal once again dragged the heavy safe from its hiding space behind the dusty barrels.

"Stupid fuckin' Mick," he muttered. A tear slipped from his eye as he mourned briefly for his favorite cousin. "Retarded ass-wipe bastard."

Steeling himself for the task at hand, Sallie plugged in his brand-new hacksaw, put on a pair of goggles, and went to work.

An hour later Gino's safe sat gutted open in the middle of the floor. Without stopping to wipe the sweat from his face, Sallie plundered right in, pulling out stack after stack of money and tossing it to the floor at his feet. Quarter of a mil, his ass. There had to be hundreds of thousands crammed inside that baby, he realized. The money smelled dank, and slightly moldy, but it was definitely still spendable.

Only when the safe was finally empty did Sal use the end of his shirt to mop his dripping face and chin. He wanted to jump up and down at the sight of all the legal tender that was strewn out around him. There was more than enough there to set up an arms deal that a young drug lord in Harlem had asked him about, and to get into some other income-producing projects as well.

With one eye on the pile of dough at his feet, Sal took his cell phone off his belt and punched in a number.

"Three Brothers Funeral Home." A female voice with a strong east coast accent greeted him from the other end of the line.

Sal grinned broadly, and then asked to speak to the slick New York City drug dealer who was going to help make him a millionaire.

CHAPTER 22

Lenox Avenue was live and on fire when Trey got back from dropping Mr. Howell off at his apartment. He parked his whip in front of a Spanish bodega that was owned by one of his homeboys in the Talented Ten coalition, and then walked around the corner without a bit of urgency in his stride.

The slanga he was looking for was holding his spot down real lovely in front of the dilapidated building. Customers were walking up on him from all directions, and the deadly tan goods he sold were flowing from his hands like city water.

"Yo whatchu want, whatchu want, whatchu want," the young hustler chanted as Trey approached him. He eyed Trey's hands in search of that mean green, and he was definitely ready to conduct some bizz.

Trey never slowed his stride as he snatched the trap boy up in his collar and muscled him over to the stoop of the drug den.

"Yo, what the fuck is you doin' niggah?" the slanga struggled to get outta Trey's killer grip. He swung a wild right hook, and Trey capped him in the grill, and then head-butted him hard on the bridge of his nose.

He pounded the young'un up the stairs and flung him through the rickety front door. They tussled as Trey dragged him, kicking and fighting, all the way up to the fifth floor.

The young man looked up from his knees, then twisted and bucked on the landing when he realized he was being dragging out on the roof. He tried to leap to his feet, and Trey crushed his grill with the heel of his boot, and sent a thick stream of blood flying from his mouth.

"Yo! Who da fuck is *you?*" the young man screamed around his busted teeth. "What I do, man? What the fuck did I *do?*"

He struggled some more as Trey flung him outside on the building's roof. He got up on his hands and knees and tried to crawl away. Trey planted his foot in his ass and sent him crashing face-first into the asphalt.

Grabbing dude by the back of his shirt, Trey dragged him a couple of feet over to the edge of the roof. He lifted dude's long, skinny ass easily to his feet, and held him upright while he wobbled and panted in confusion.

"What?" The dope slanga hollered, straight bewildered. "*What?* You got some bad shit? Well just ask for another package, my niggah! You ain't gotta do all this here!"

"You like selling dope to pregnant girls and little kids, huh, muh'fucka?" Trey spit, addressing the trap boy for the very first time. "You killed a little girl, man, and her baby is prolly gonna die too. You ain't got no problem with that grimy shit huh?"

Dude shook his head. "What the fuck I look like to you, niggah? A fuckin' baby sitter? Ay! I sell my shit to whoever got money, yo! Now do I go *lookin'* for knocked up bitches and snotty-nosed kids? Nah, man, nah. But if they roll up on this block tryna conduct a transaction J-Ugly is gonna handle his!"

"Gimme what you got on you," Trey said quietly. Heat was coming outta his eyes and he was damn close to losing his grip. "All of it. Whatever you got in ya muh'fuckin' pockets, give that shit up right now."

The trap boy bucked. "Niggah is you *crazy?* Yo ass ain't *about* to stick me up without no burner, ya heard? Do you know who the fuck I rep for? Whose product you tryna gank? Man, Flex is my rowdy. I'm rolling with them Divine Nine niggahs, and you ain't *about* to get my shit!"

"A'ight," Trey said calmly. He reached behind dude's knees and scooped his long ass straight up off his feet. He cradled dude in his arms like a baby, and tipped him backwards over the ledge of the roof.

"What the fuck is you *doin'* man?" the dope slanga screeched and tried to wrap his arms around Trey's thick neck and rocked up shoulders. "Man, if you drop me off this bitch my crew is gonna *kill* your ass!"

"Oh, them niggahs can get some too," Trey said as he head-butted dude in the nose again, and flung him straight over the edge. He stepped over to the door without a backwards glance, and it slammed shut behind him right after dude's body went splat on the ground.

"Hell yeah," Trey muttered as he walked back down the stairs without an ounce of regret. "Them niggahs can get some too."

CHAPTER 23

The dark blue Ford sat idling in the darkness at the corner. Its headlights were off, and a lone figure was slouched down out of sight in the driver's seat.

In the alley behind the G-Spot, Truth sat at the wheel of a BMW as he waited for his boss lady to come out so he could give her a ride home.

It was after 4:30am and the Spot was winding down for the night. The bar had closed, and the strippers were about to leave too. Ace and Pluto were in G's office counting money and arguing over the night's pitiful earnings. Pluto was still blaming his boy for the loss of Juicy and G's cash, and Ace was tryna convince him that they still had eyes out there, and they could still find her and get paid big-time.

Truth turned on his iPod and pushed his earplugs deep in his ears as he waited. His eyes were on the door, and when it finally swung open Salida walked out carrying the bag of drug samples that she had picked up from her broker at Three Brothers Funeral Home. Truth saw her turn around and wave goodbye to Honey Dew, who had come outta the dressing room to lock the door.

As Salida strutted toward the whip in her dainty heels and sexy white dress, Truth got out so he could take her bags and open the door for her. But before he could make it around the car's front fender, a burst of blue death roared outta nowhere.

A dark sedan screeched straight down the sidewalk, clipping parked cars and knocking over garbage cans as it zoomed toward the older woman at a heart-stopping speed.

"Mizz Salida!!" Truth screamed as time seemed to go into slow-mode. Salida saw the speeding car just feet before it struck her. She froze for a second, and then turned with a look of horror on her face as she dove toward the safety of the BMW.

But she was too late.

The roaring dark slice of thunder struck her and spun her body around in a circle. It propelled her up in the air, and then sent her slamming down hard against the trunk of the BMW.

Truth screamed as his boss slid down the back bumper and hit the ground with a crunch, then rolled over like a lifeless doll in the middle of the sidewalk.

The sound of screeching tires was all he heard as he ran over to her and dropped down to his knees. He went to touch her, but her eyes were closed and blood was coming outta her nose. Scared shitless, Truth jumped up and ran over to the locked door of the G-Spot. Screaming for help, he pounded on that shit like somebody's life depended on it.

$$$$$

"*I got her!*" the driver of the dark car hollered as his front end made contact with

266

the beautiful woman crossing the sidewalk. "I hit her! I busted that bitch right on her ass!"

Peals of laughter erupted from the backseat of the car as Monique popped up from her hiding spot on the floor. She knelt on her knees and peered through the back window, giggling her ass off at the sight of Salida sliding off the back of G's old whip and rolling onto the sidewalk like a broken-up mannequin.

"Yeah!" Monique screamed at the top of her lungs as Salida's body lay outstretched on the hard concrete. "Bitch down! Bitch down! Bitch down! And that crazy bitch betta *stay* her ass down too!"

Bilal grinned. Anything that made Mo happy made him happy too. He floored the gas pedal as the Ford's front wheels jumped the curb, and moments later the car left the coarse concrete of the sidewalk, rolled onto the smooth asphalt of the city street, and disappeared into the darkness of the night.

CHAPTER 24

Flex must have felt me getting swole, because two nights after we had it out he asked me to get dressed so he could take me out to a concert. If I had known Flex drove like a damn ten-year-old I woulda never gotten in the whip with him. Instead, I found myself holding on to the door handle in his candy-apple red Hummer as Flex recklessly drove me and his boy Dabu downtown to Brooklyn.

The concert was in Prospect Park, and some of the hottest rappers on the street scene were gonna be there. The streets of Park Slope were packed when we arrived. Traffic was on jam. It was wall-to-wall niggahs. Cops were on foot and in squad cars, and NYC's mounted police rode high on horses as they stayed busy trying to direct the flow of it all.

Flex rolled into a handicap spot on Prospect Park West and told me and Dabu to hop out. He held my hand as we walked into the crowd of rap fans, and I had to admit I was excited. Following the huge herd, we strolled deep into the park, and found the band shell. We got as close as we could get, and stood in the middle of the crowd and rocked with everybody else.

I had always felt a lot older than Flex, but two years wasn't really much of a difference. I was so glad to be outta that damn basement, and out of Harlem period, that I was actually having a good time.

Brooklyn was known for being rowdy, but people were real chill in the crowd, and I was surprised that didn't no fights break out.

"Nah, man," Flex said, blocking with his hand when his dude tried to pass me the sticky they were smoking. "Juicy don't puff, niggah. She ain't no jump-off. She's a lady."

We stayed in the park until the concert was over, then we followed the huge crowd across the grass and back outside to the streets. I acted like I didn't notice when Flex grabbed my hand and threaded his fingers through mine. He swung our arms a little as we walked, and I knew he was trying to look big in front of his boy.

But when we got back to the area where he had parked the Hummer, another car was in his spot. This one had a handicapped tag hanging from the rearview mirror.

"Yo, where's your shit?" Dabu said.

"I don't know man. I thought I parked it right here."

"You did," I said. "It was right behind that beat-up Mustang. But this is a handicap zone." I pointed up at the sign. "They probably towed your shit."

Dabu started laughing and I felt Flex freeze up next to me.

"I can read that shit, Juicy," he spit, letting go of my hand. "I saw the fuckin' sign when I parked, a'ight?"

I shrugged. I had to pee and I was ready to go.

"So what are we gonna do now?" I asked him.

268

"What you mean, what we gonna do now?" he barked. "You see all these fuckin' people out here, Juicy? What you think everybody else is doing? How you they getting back to they cribs?"

I hunched my shoulders and frowned.

"I don't know. Probably the same way they got here."

That niggah cuffed me.

Standing right there on the sidewalk with fifty thousand people all around us, that little mothafucka knocked the shit outta me.

"Yo, boss," Dabu said, grabbing at Flex as I slumped against that dirty Mustang and went down to my knees. "There's a lotta heat out here, man. You might wanna chill with all that until you get back to the crib."

"I'm good," Flex said, shrugging his boy off. "Yo, D. I'ma holla at you tomorrow, man. Same time as usual. A'ight?"

Dabu shrugged and started backing away.

"You sure? You straight?"

Flex nodded. "Yeah. We both straight, ak. For real. I'll holla tomorrow."

$$$$$

My whole face was numb as Flex led me down the steps of a subway station on 7th Avenue.

It had been a long time since I'd taken an ass-kicking from any man, and I wasn't built for that type of shit no more.

There was no way in hell that I was going back to that funeral parlor with him. I knew if I did, Flex was gonna kill me down in that basement and double-stack my body in a secret compartment under somebody else's casket.

We stood waiting on the train platform with a whole bunch of other people who were coming from the concert. It was crazy crowded, and a big Rasta-looking dude with long dreads was passing out flyers and postcards for after-parties left and right. I walked up to the edge of the platform to look for the train, but the tunnel was pitch black. I couldn't wait for that iron-horse to come so I could get my ass back uptown and call Rita to come and get me.

While I looking into the tunnel and praying to see some lights, Flex came up behind me and stood real close to me. I could feel him breathing on my neck.

"You know what?" he said, in a calm, scary voice.

I didn't answer. I didn't even turn around.

"Now I know why G used to fuck you up the way he did, Juicy. I was all wrong about you, ma. But G? G prolly always knew."

I ignored his ass. Every few seconds I would lean forward and take another peek, looking desperately for the train.

"See, a bitch like you just ain't ready. You ain't ready for a niggah who can give you the whole world 'cause the only thing you can see is what's right in front of you."

Something told me to just walk away from this buggy young niggah and ask one of these big dudes standing around if I could use his phone and call Rita. I knew one of them would have let me, but I also knew Flex was strapped, and he was liable to go popping off with his pistol if I walk up on some other dude and got in his face.

Fuck it, I thought. I was gonna ask one of these females if I could use her phone. Sometimes a sistah could sense when a crazy niggah was riding you and be down to help you out.

I leaned forward and took one more peep into the tunnel, and then Flex was on my ass. He grabbed my shoulders and spun me around to face him.

"You know what that niggah Macaroni did to me that day when you left me outside in the hallway all by myself, Juicy?"

A chill ran through my bones and suddenly my feet felt like they were glued to the edge of the platform.

"You know why I pushed his ass off our roof?"

I felt a deep rumbling in my toes. The train was finally coming and a big wave of relief washed over me.

"Guess what that niggah did?" Flex demanded, leaning his body all up on me. He gripped my upper arms and squeezed hard enough to make me cringe. "Just guess what that junkie mothafucka did to me?"

"What?" I whispered. My voice came out so low I didn't think he could even hear me over the roar of the approaching train.

"Nothing," Flex laughed crazily and pressed his cheek right up against mine. "That niggah didn't do *nothing*," he repeated quietly in my ear.

And then he pushed me.

TO BE CONTINUED...

Order

LUST: THE 5TH DEADLY SIN
at
www.Amazon.com or www.BN.com

PART FIVE
OF NOIRE'S BLOCKBUSTER
URBAN EROTIC SERIAL TALE!

Juicy-Mo's on fire and she's feeling herself!

It's been a hard-knock life for Juicy-Mo Stanfield, and drama seems to find her no matter where she tries to hide. Even though she's been sprung from jail, the G-Spot Crew is still on her trail, Flex has turned into a murderous psycho, and Juicy is hurt and all alone on the treacherous streets of New York City.

Is Harlem's #1 Stunna down for the count? Now that she's weak and vulnerable, will her enemies finally catch up with her and go for their revenge? Is the magic of love and happiness a thing of the past for Juicy? Or does life hold one more trump card for the beautiful hood chick from 136th Street?

WARNING!

This here ain't no romance
It's an urban erotic tale
A scorching hot attraction
Makes you shudder and exhale!
When the wood gets good, in your 'hood
It's hard to let it go
Feenin' for some action?
Better keep it on the low!
Hookin' up and slapping skins
Is looking like a must
Juicy's thong is poppin'
In this Deadly Sin called **LUST!**

Find out more in...
G-SPOT 2: THE SEVEN DEADLY SINS
Lust: The 5th Deadly Sin

The Urban Erotic Serial Saga Continues!

NOIRE

G-Spot 2:
The Seven Deadly Sins
An Urban Erotic Serial Tale Told in 7 Parts

LUST: THE 5ᵀᴴ DEADLY SIN

by
Noire

www.AskNoire.com
www.GSpot2.com
www.TheGSpotSaga.com

CHAPTER 1

I went flying off that train platform like somebody's broken-wing bird. But I damn sure didn't hit those tracks by myself! I grabbed hold of Flex's shirt with both of my hands and his skinny, buck-toothed ass flew down there right along with me.

We landed feet first on the sooty train tracks and the moment I touched down, my ankle turned over and my knees straight-up buckled.

A bolt of white-hot pain spiked up through my right foot. I toppled over and banged my hip, and me and Flex both collapsed down there in all that grime.

Up on the platform the crowd of people went bonkers and started screaming like hell.

"*Get the fuck up!*" they shrieked and hollered. "The train is coming! Get the fuck up, y'all! The *train* is coming!"

Flex was right beside me on his knees, but when all those people started screaming he leaped up on that platform so fast it looked like his ass had ran up some invisible stairs.

I was down there all by myself now, and people were still screaming for me to get up, but I just couldn't move. I was stuck. I felt like I had floated up outta myself and I was watching some other chick crouched down on her hands and knees in that black, gritty subway dugout.

But when the crazy rumble of the train sent a hard vibration through me and I felt the damn pillars shake, everything got real as hell.

I pushed off with my hands and tried to get up on my feet, but my right leg folded under me and I toppled over again. My instincts made me twist away from the electrified third rail as mad shouts rang out and the people who were watching me from the platform screamed out in panic and fear.

"Help her!" some chick shouted. "C'mon, y'all! Somebody fuckin' *help* her!"

I tried to stand up and balance my weight on my left foot, but fear and panic had me wobbling. I was just about to tip over again when suddenly the tall dread who had been passing out all the party flyers was right down there on the tracks with me.

Dude reached out and snatched me.

He grabbed me by the back of my t-shirt and damn near yanked that shit right over my head as he took two giant leaps and scampered back on up on the platform, dragging me up with him like I was a boneless little rag doll.

Dread was flat on his back and I was laying halfway on top of him with my whole shirt hiked up around my neck and my back and bra exposed. The roar of the approaching train had gotten even louder. Dread was all the way up on the platform, but my face was just above his knees and the bottom part of my body was still hanging halfway off the ledge.

"Help," I panted as I grabbed at his belt and tried to crawl up his body with my

273

good leg. Dread grabbed my upper arms, then he squeezed me between his thighs and brought his knees up with me sandwiched tightly between them.

My face was now above his stomach. I tasted his shirt in my mouth, but my right foot was still on fire as it dangled like a hook over the platform's ledge.

"My *foot!*" I screamed.

The Rasta man lifted his head off the ground and then raised his upper body like he was doing a crunch. He shot a desperate glance toward the tunnel and then grabbed me under my arms and yanked at me one good time, and even though I screamed like holy hell, both of my feet were now safely up on the platform.

My face was directly above his and for a split second all we could do was stare at each other in horrified shock. And then a blast of hot, gritty air washed over us as the train roared into the station, speeding like a silver bullet. I squeezed my eyes closed and ducked my face into Dread's neck as tiny shards of grit and subway dirt sprayed out in all directions and bit into the skin on my bare back.

Me and Dread were both in shock. Our black asses had almost *died* together, and we laid on that platform holding on to each other like we were deeply in love.

It was straight chaos on the platform as people rushed over to us and the brakes on the train squealed loudly as it came to a stop.

It sounded like thousands of terrified New Yorkers were standing over my head screaming for somebody to call the cops and the ambulance. I was so shook that all I could do was squeeze my eyes closed and mumble my thanks in Dread's ear over and over and over again, and the next thing I knew I heard the sound of walkie-talkies and New York's Finest were on the scene trying to take control.

The cops urged me and Dread to let go of each other as they tried to roll me off of him and onto the hard concrete.

"My foot!" I screamed in agony as a fat police officer grabbed at me. He clamped one hand on my arm and the other one on my thigh, and dragged me off of Dread. "Ow! Damn, my *foot!*"

"Let her go!" a black female officer barked on him as she crouched down beside me and pulled my shirt back down over my titties. "You're okay, Miss. An ambulance is coming, and you're gonna be okay."

Me and Dread lay there side-by-side, and I was trembling like crazy as he reached out and grabbed my hand and squeezed it. The train idled at the platform with its doors still open. The stunned crowd stood around staring down at me like they couldn't believe I had made it off those tracks and was still alive. A couple of young hoodstas whipped out their cell phones and started snapping mad pictures and filming a video so they could post my near-death experience up on YouTube.

"Can you tell us what happened?" the cops grilled me and Dread, but both of us were too shook to even open our mouths. On the real, New Yorkers didn't usually tell the cops shit about shit, but a light-skinned girl with big titties and two curly ponytails went right on ahead and put it out there.

"You wanna know what happened? Some skinny mothafucka pushed her in front of the train, that's what happened! I mean that psycho-lookin' niggah just straight up *pushed* her!"

As soon as she said that shit I lifted my head up and glanced around with my heart pounding in terror. Even with mad cops strapped up with tools and standing right there beside me, I was still scared Flex's crazy ass was gonna rush up out of the crowd and get at me.

Shit, mami with the big titties had called it real correct, though. Fletcher Boykin was a psycho niggah all right. That fool had tried to kill me! An evil picture of his twisted-up buck-toothed grill flashed in my mind real quick, and after thanking God again that I was still alive, all I could do was put my head back down on that dirty-ass platform and cry.

CHAPTER 2

Flex exited the train station on 9th Street and walked down to Ninth Street against the flow of traffic. Fury bubbled all up in his throat as he thought about that bitch Juicy and how she had tried to play him low in front of his manz.

Reliving the embarrassment in his mind, he stormed down the middle of the block swinging his arms wide and praying one of these Brooklyn fools would fuck around and bump him. He would twist a niggah's noggin back and stretch him out without spittin' a single word, that's how hot his rage was.

He had blacked the fuck out so fast he didn't even remember chucking Juicy down on those damn train tracks. And her trifling ass had made him fall down there with her in all that soot and trash. He shoulda pulled out his tool and shot her ass on the spot for that one!

He had scampered up on that platform and left her grimy ass right down there where she belonged. That's what the bitch got. Fuck around lay around. Flex wasn't the one, and if Juicy had gotten smashed up when that train pulled in then she had brought it on herself. Wildin' on him like he was some kinda sherm niggah in the street. For all he knew, her dumb ass was prolly a big ball of road kill under the wheels of the F train by now.

After walking several blocks, Flex turned the corner and jogged down the steps and descended into the belly of the subway station at the next stop.

Pimp strolling and chillin' like wasn't shit up in his world, he took his time and sauntered down the crowded platform to the spot where the first train car would stop. It was almost deserted way down at this end, and Flex dug his hands in his pockets and scowled as he leaned against a pillar with his eyes focused on the blackness in the tunnel.

A range of emotions flowed through his eighteen-year-old mind, and most of them were heavy as hell. Especially all his fucked-up feelings over Juicy. She had him flipping between rage and lust so fast his young heart couldn't take it.

Flex was still fuming when the train finally came and he got on. He sat down in a two-seater next to the conductor's cab and closed his eyes and let his black thoughts roll.

All his life people had been tryna short him outta what shoulda been his. Tryna elevate over him like he was less than the next niggah or something. Even his boy Jimmy was guilty of that shit. As tight as they had been, Jimmy was one of them light-skinned pretty niggahs who got over in life just because of the way he looked.

And that's what was going on right now with Juicy. Flex knew it took bank to get a chick who looked like her to fall for a niggah who looked like him. So what was it? As fat as his pocket-knots was, did that bitch still think he was ugly or something?

He slid his lips over his buckteeth and grimaced with rage. No matter how much he loved Juicy the girl was just a regular trick. Even after G had dragged her ass through the gutter she still didn't appreciate it when a real niggah tried to elevate her status and keep her on shine.

Yeah, she had run him some ol' bullshit about her fuckin' pussy being dead inside, but Flex knew the drill. That chicken couldn't get her thang wet unless a niggah knocked her on her ass before he fucked her, and as soon as he got him another the chance that's exactly what he was gonna do.

He sat there swaying with the train as he pictured the way Juicy had looked when she was washing her sweet pussy in his bathtub. Those fat titties she had on her had looked spectacular, and he remembered how good they had tasted when he was licking and sucking them down on his kitchen floor.

Flex felt his rage subsiding and his thick dick rising. It had stiffened uncomfortably in his pants and he shifted in his seat as his balls got tight with lust for Juicy. He imagined how good it would feel to slide his meat up in her guts. He knew his package was substantial, so he'd be real gentle when he pushed the head past her tight pussy lips.

See, Juicy wasn't no regular gutter jump-off. He prolly shoulda been a little smarter in the way he had approached her. Maybe he had come at her the wrong way. Juicy didn't give a damn about niggahs who rolled in finery from the top to the bottom. She was used to all that. For a chick like her it wasn't just about possessions. It was about power. Something she could respect.

Flex coulda kicked himself right in the nuts. He shoulda known a dime like Juicy wasn't gonna be impressed by no tiny apartment in the basement of no funeral home.

He was gonna have to step his game up a little bit more. Elevate his status and his rep on the streets. Become larger and even more in charge so he could floss like G McKay with the finest bitch in Harlem on his arm.

But in order to do that Flex was gonna have to find the answer to the one question that continued to elude him. He was gonna have to find the one man who could get him mass quantities of powder at the absolute lowest cut-rate prices. He was gonna have to seal the deal with his slick white-boy partner and get his hands on that arsenal he had promised him too.

And once he was sitting on the top of the power pile and everybody else was either slumped over or bowed down, then Juicy was gonna open up them sexy legs for him and he would have her pretty slit dripping like melted butter.

Yeah, Flex thought as the overhead lights blinked and the train pitched back and forth. Just as soon as he had the guns and the distribution channels deeply on lock, then Harlem and Juicy were both gonna be his.

Just thinking about how he was gonna handle Juicy's body had his joint hot and throbbing. He closed his eyes and imagined Juicy with her creamy thighs cocked open, straddling his hips and riding his thick dick like a champ. The train rocked back and forth, making him sway gently in his seat. He thrust his hand deep in his front pocket and stroked his dick on the sly.

Lust had Flex gripped in a desperate, feverish state. He wanted to fuck Juicy more than he had ever wanted anything in his entire life. And not just to get his shit off neither. He wanted to make Juicy feel good too. He wanted to make her squirt. He would eat her pussy all night long if that's what it took. He would lick her whole ass.

All of it. He rubbed his dick and imagined sliding it straight through the deep valley snuggled between Juicy's firm, pretty breasts, and then spanking her thick nipples with the swollen head until he squirted all over her chest.

Flex could feel Juicy's soft flesh in his hands. He could taste her in his mouth. And as the train roared through the station and the lights flickered off and on, he opened his eyes briefly and whispered her name. They glazed over again as he grunted and busted a load right there in his pants, and a rush of hot, sticky cum coated his thigh.

By the time Flex's stop came and he got ready to transfer to the IRT line, thoughts of Juicy had totally consumed his body and his mind. He was sorry for pushing her down on those damn train tracks. Juicy was his girl. She always had been and she always would be. He didn't give a fuck where she went, or how far she tried to run and hide. Juicy's ass was *his,* and when he got ready to have her, he was damn sure gonna get her back.

CHAPTER 3

Yo, what the fuck was that?" Ace paused in his heated argument with his manz Pluto as the sound of a commotion came from the hallway leading to the back door. Greenbacks were stacked in short piles all over the table, and the tension between them was thicker than the cigarette smoke that rose in the air.

It was after closing time at the G-Spot, and the two men had been counting the night's take and arguing back and forth over whose fault it was that they had failed to nab Juicy.

Ace had been talking big shit, but now his hood instincts kicked in and he paused and frowned as he reached for the loaded gat he kept on his waist. Something wasn't right. Salida had just left to catch a ride home with Truth, and hearing a hint of static at the back door made the beefy-necked gangsta suspicious as he listened intently with one hand on his burner and the other hand full of doe.

He heard it again. A frantic shouting sound that shattered the quietness of the night. Ace locked eyes with Pluto for a split second, and then he dropped the cash he was counting, yanked his 9mm from his waistband, and jetted up outta G's office like that shit was on fire.

It was Truth, Ace realized as he sped down the hall. That lil niggah was hollerin' and screamin' like a lick was going down, and Ace gripped his burner tight in his meaty fist as he raced toward the back door.

His mind was on whirl with every step he took. He was ready to blast the shit outta whichever come-up click had the nuts to fuck with Truth and pull a lick on the Spot, but then cold fear washed over him as he realized that Salida was out in that back alley with Truth too.

Ace barreled outta the door with his finger heating up the trigger. His eyes darted around for signs of a stick-up crew, but instead of spotting a posse of dangerous hood niggas, he almost had a fuckin' heart attack when he spotted Salida stretched out on the sidewalk with blood coming outta her nose and her arms and legs sticking out in all different directions.

"What the fuck happened!?!" Ace roared as Truth knelt down beside her and pointed toward the corner. A pair of fading red taillights was disappearing into the dark night.

"Somebody fuckin' hit her!" Truth panted. "Them niggahs rolled up on the fuckin' sidewalk and *crashed* her ass!"

Ace pushed his burner into the back of his pants and dropped down to his knees beside his woman's motionless form. "Salida, Salida, Salida," he cried out in the emptiness of the night. She was so still he couldn't tell if she was dead or alive. Her eyes were closed and a trail of blood ran from her left nostril. Her stylish white knit dress had street grime all over it, and the front had ridden up over her hips and exposed her thigh-high stockings and her lace-trimmed ivory garter belt.

Ace reached out and tugged Salida's dress down, and then he cupped her face in his hands. Her skin was warm, and even with her hair fanned out everywhere and a huge noogie rising up on her right temple she was still beautiful.

"Yo!" he exploded on Truth. "Your dumb ass was supposed to be lookin' out for her, you stupid muh'fucka!" Ace turned to face the young blood and straight blasted on him. "How the *fuck* did you let her get hit?"

"I didn't *let* her get nothin'! I was coming around to open her fuckin' door and that fuckin' whip came outta nowhere! It was up on the sidewalk, man! That shit was movin' so fast neither one of us saw it coming!"

"But when you guarding a jewel you supposed to see *every* fuckin' thing coming, dun dun! *Every* fuckin' thing, ya heard?"

Ace's hands shook as he patted Salida's cheeks again, and a huge wave of relief flooded through him when her eyelids fluttered a few times and then slowly parted.

She coughed and tried to straighten out her legs, and then she moaned in deep pain.

"Don't move," Ace told her quickly, and his voice was real gentle. "This lil muh'fucka let you get hit by a car, baby. I'ma get you to the hospital, okay? Just don't move. Everything is gonna be all right."

"Fuck is you standin' around for?" Ace barked on Truth, furious again. "Open up the goddamn door so I can put her in the car!"

"Yo," Truth frowned as he stared at his boss lady as she grimaced and moaned on the ground. That car had knocked the shit outta her. He'd watched her fly up in the air and then slam down hard on the BMW's trunk. He wouldn't be surprised if the whip had a big dent from where she had crashed into it. And the way her head had bounced off that concrete like a handball was just fuckin' crazy.

"You sure we should move her, Ace? What if she broke something? You don't wanna just call the ambulance?" Truth shook his head and backed off a couple of steps. "I don't know about moving her, man..." he said doubtfully.

"Shut the fuck up and open the goddamn door!" Ace spit viciously. He was sweating with fear for Salida, and his head swiveled on his neck as he looked over his shoulder and hollered frantically toward the G-Spot.

"Pluto! Yo, Pluto! Come help me! Where the fuck you at, man?"

"I'm right here," his partner said quietly and stepped outta the shadows in the doorway.

"Yo, my niggah!" Ace barked suspiciously. "Fuck you doin', man? You been standing there all this time? Salida got hit by a fuckin' car! Somebody tried to ice her. Grab her legs and help me get her in the whip. And you better be gentle, muh'fucka, ya heard! Make sure you don't hurt her. Word up, my dude, you better be real fuckin' gentle!"

CHAPTER 4

They took me and Dread to the closest hospital, which was New York Methodist. The waiting room was crazy crowded. Dread wasn't hurt, so he refused to be treated, and even though I had rolled up in an ambulance I didn't have no bullet hole in my head so they parked my ass on a stretcher out in the hallway and made me wait for almost three hours.

By then my ankle had swollen up so bad my whole leg was throbbing and I was moaning and whimpering in pain. A nurse finally came and wheeled me into a little cubicle that was surrounded by a semi-circle of stained, raggedy curtains. She put me in a hospital gown and gave me a shot in my arm to help with the pain.

After a few minutes I started feeling real woozy, and I had almost fallen off to sleep when the curtains parted and a tall, shadowy dude stepped inside and walked right up to my bed.

Fletcher! was all I could think as my eyes flew open and I broke for the other side of the bed. *Fuck my ankle!* I wasn't feeling no pain as I crawled up on my knees and tried to leap my ass over the rail to get away from him.

"Pret-ty gurl," Dread grabbed me by my shoulder and pulled me back down in the bed. "You ah safe, gurl. Me no gwan hurt you. No one gwan hurt you here, gurl."

My heart pounded as I settled back on the plastic mattress. Dread pulled over a beat-up white plastic chair and held my hand as he sat down beside me. His Jamaican accent was like a song as he told me I was safe over and over until I drifted off into a doped-up sleep.

I woke up when a young hospital tech came and got me so my right leg could be x-rayed. He told Dread to wait in my cubicle, and then he wheeled me down a long hall to the radiology department. It was cold as shit in the bright room as they x-rayed my foot from all different angles, and then I got left outside on the stretcher in the hallway again.

I laid there dozing on and off for damn near forever, and the sun had come up by the time a doctor finally came to tell me that my right ankle was badly sprained and my knee was bruised, but thankfully nothing was broken.

"Pret-ty gurl," I was shocked to find Dread still waiting for me when they wheeled me back into my little cubicle. "What you gwan do now, eh? You want me should get you sum-ting?"

I shrugged. I didn't know what the fuck I was gonna do. I was just happy as hell to be alive and up outta Flex's basement. But I was still stuck between a rock and a hot spot. Hell, I was still trying to wrap my head around that fuckin' fool pushing me in front of a train! I couldn't really see too far past that.

"Hey, what's your name?" I asked Dread.

"Darren," he said in his heavy West Indian accent. "Them call me Dirty D."

281

"My name is Juicy. I'm thirsty," I told him. I felt battered. My mouth was dry as hell and my lip was swollen and painful from Flex capping me all upside my head with his fist. "I don't have any money, but can you buy me a Sprite?"

Dread nodded and pushed through the flimsy curtains like he was on a real important mission. I closed my eyes again when he walked out, but just a few seconds later the curtains slid open and a tall, brown-skinned sistah walked in.

"Good morning," she said, smiling and holding out her hand. "My name is Shay Lucas, and I'm the social worker on staff. Do you mind if I talk to you for a few minutes?

I shook her hand and I couldn't help but notice how pretty she looked in her stylish blue and gold dress. Her entire game was fresh. She smelled sweet like shower gel and perfume, and she wore her natural hair pulled back from her face and tied with a blue and gold scarf. She was playing some big gold hoop earrings and a matching gold choker, and her toned body and chocolate skin was flawless.

She sat down in the cracked plastic chair and crossed her legs, then leaned toward me with a serious look on her face.

"I understand you were brought in here by ambulance last night after a violent incident where a man pushed you onto the train tracks. Is that right?"

"Yeah," I answered. I'd been raised never to give out any info to the cops, the welfare, BCW, CPS, ACS or anybody else who came snooping around trying to be nosy, but what the hell. Lying and conniving wasn't gonna get me nowhere today. Damn-near half of Brooklyn had seen Flex knock my ass down on those train tracks. If anybody needed to be worrying about the truth getting out it was his crazy ass. "Yeah," I 'fessed right up and told her. "I got pushed in front of a train."

"I'm sorry to hear that," she said and peered at me closely. "But I'm glad you survived it. I see he bruised your face up pretty badly. Well, the city of New York has a coalition against domestic violence and it allows us to provide resources for women who need assistance leaving abusive relationships. Were you living with the man who pushed you?"

I thought for a quick second, and then nodded. "Yeah. I was staying with him in Manhattan, but I'm not going back there."

"Do you have any money? Are you employed? Do you have any assets that you can get hold of to help you out right now?"

I shook my head. I didn't have shit. Not a dime in my pockets, not a change of clothes or even a clean pair of drawers. Hell, I didn't even have a cell phone, since mine was dead and sitting on the dresser in Flex's bedroom.

Shay nodded like she understood. "Is there someplace you can go? Do you have any family or friends you think you might be safe with?"

I thought about Rita, and shook my head. With all the drama in her life and Nooni still missing, my girl had enough to worry about. Besides, I wasn't about to bring Flex and all his madness crashing down on her doorstep. Rita was the one who had hooked me up to stay in Flex's basement in the first fuckin' place, and if that fool decided to come gunning for me then Rita's crib was gonna be his very first stop.

"Nah. I don't have no family or friends around here," I said abruptly, which wasn't a lie. "I left New York a while ago and I'm just now getting back."

She nodded again. "Okay. Well, what I can offer you today is some counseling, and a temporary place to stay until you decide what you'd like to do next."

I eyed her. "A place to stay *where?*"

"New York Methodist Hospital works in partnership with several shelters around the city. I'd have to call and see exactly which site has a bed for you, but they will come pick you up and take you to a safe location."

Shay told me she was gonna head down the hall to her office and make a few phone calls while I waited for a nurse to wrap my ankle in an ace-bandage and bring me a pair of crutches. They put a big black boot on my foot and told me not to put any weight on it for forty-eight hours.

By the time Dread came back with a Sprite and a bag of barbeque Wise potato chips, I had already made up my mind. *Fuck New York*, I thought as I tore those chips up and licked the salt from my fingers. I was ready to dip as far away from this city as I could. All I needed to do was make a quick call to Cali and get a bunch of my cash wired to me, and after that I was hopping my ass on a plane and heading someplace down South, or maybe even to the Caribbean or somewhere like that.

I closed my eyes as reality came crashing down on me. I didn't have nobody. No matter where I went or how far I ran, I would still be alone.

I couldn't stop the tears as they slipped from my eyes and ran down my face. Everything that was happening to me just seemed so unfair. Sometimes when you're trying to do good, bad comes down on you hard. All I had tried to do was help Rita get Nooni back, and I couldn't believe what it was costing me. There was so much danger coming at me from so many different directions that it was a miracle I was still breathing and living above ground. I felt like a hunted animal. Between Flex and the G-Spot crew, I was liable to get shot from behind and slumped at any moment.

"Don't cry," Dread told me gently. I could tell he really felt sorry for me, and he wasn't tryna holla at me neither. "Here," he passed me a slip of paper. His phone number was written on it and he told me to call him if I ever needed him.

When Shay came back to my cubicle she asked Dread to step outside so we could talk in private. She smiled as she told me she had found a site that had a bed available for me.

"It's not a domestic violence shelter though," she said and shrugged. "It's just a regular shelter for the homeless, and you can stay there for ten days, okay?"

"Where is it?" I asked suspiciously. I wasn't taking my ass nowhere near Manhattan, and I damn sure wasn't stepping foot within ten miles of Three Brothers Funeral Home in Spanish Harlem.

"Oh, the shelter is right here in Brooklyn," she said, pushing me some papers to sign.

"Brooklyn?" I twisted my lips up at first, and then I shrugged. Why not? Shit, Manhattan was an island, and that meant if I stayed in Brooklyn there would be a body of water between me and Flex. Besides, the deck was stacked real high against me, and right now I wasn't the kind of beggar who could afford to be choosey. Better Brooklyn than the damn cemetery.

Besides, all I needed was a little bit of time. I could survive in Crooklyn for a few days while I made some calls and got me a plane ticket. And as soon as all that came through I was getting the hell outta the shiesty-ass Empire State for good.

"Cool," I told Shay as I stood up and got ready to crutch down the hall behind her.

I slid the curtain back and gave Dread a big hug and thanked him again for saving my black ass.

We broke out in our separate directions, and the only thing left for me to do was go cop a squat in the social worker's office while I waited for a ride to the shelter. "Yeah," I said under my breath. "Brooklyn'll be cool."

CHAPTER 5

I got you, baby," Ace said as he cradled Salida in his big arms and carried her up the stairs to her apartment. He unlocked the door, then flicked the light switch up with his shoulder and followed the thin stream of light past the neat kitchen and toward Salida's plush bedroom.

Him and Truth had sat up in Harlem Hospital with her for mad hours, but Ace hadn't been worried about the time on the clock. His whole body had sagged with relief when the doctors told him Salida had been real lucky. She'd bruised her hip and had suffered a mild concussion when her head hit the sidewalk, but other than that she had escaped without serious injury from the hit-and-run car accident.

"The driver just kept going, huh?" The doctor asked as he wrote Salida a prescription for painkillers and filled out some forms on his clipboard. "Did you get a good look at the car? You should probably file a police report."

Ace had shaken his head as he got behind Salida's wheelchair and held his hand out for the prescription.

"Nah, we ain't filing no reports with nobody," he'd said with his voice cold and deadly. "Trust me, I already got this, Doc," he said, as his mind replayed the actions of everybody who had been within three steps of the G-Spot that night, to include his manz Pluto. "Word up, Doc. This shit is gonna get handled."

$$$$$

And now that he had gotten Salida home and safely in her bed, handling some bizz was heavy on Ace's mind. He had grilled Truth over and over again about what had happened out there in that dark alley, and each time the young'un had come up with the same story: an unfamiliar car had roared down the sidewalk and clipped Salida, taking her legs out as it knocked her high up in the air.

Truth swore to God that he didn't get a look at the driver's face. He said the car's lights had been off, and that shit was moving too fast for him to see anything anyway.

But Ace wasn't going for that shit. Didn't no random fuckin' ride just come flying down that back-alley and smash into his lady outta the blue like that. He was Harlem born and bred, and his gut told him that Salida had been targeted. Set up. Somebody had wanted to rub her ass out, and when Ace thought about how slow his manz Pluto had been to rush to the scene, suspicion jumped straight into his heart.

Pluto. The distrust between the two of them had stretched a mile long, and it wasn't hard for Ace to picture his old friend sprinkling a few grimy words on the streets and then setting Salida up to get run over in an alley like a bitch-ass dog.

But Salida didn't have a clue when he asked her who she thought had tried to run her over and she sure didn't mention Pluto's name. So for now Ace was just gonna have to watch and wait. And the minute something looked shady in his manz camp, he was gonna pounce all over that shit.

In the bedroom, he laid Salida on her bed and started taking her clothes off like he was handling a newborn baby. He unbuttoned her soiled dress and gently pulled it over her head. Her naked breasts bounded free. They were firm and full, and looked like delicious buttermilk biscuits that had been perfectly baked.

Salida let him handle her. She was out of it, and for once her guard was down and the soft, vulnerable side of her was exposed.

"I'm not gonna hurt you," Ace whispered like a love-struck sherm as he unsnapped her sexy garter belt and rolled the white stockings down her firm, creamy thighs. His clumsy hands fumbled a few times, but they stayed gentle and loving as he slipped a nightgown over her head and adjusted it around her hips.

Ace was straight-up awestruck by Salida's beauty. He didn't know what the fuck G had been thinking. Letting a woman this fine go, and locking her up outta sight. His old boss musta been straight fuckin' bonkers. Salida was the finest bitch he had ever seen in his life.

She moaned a little bit as he propped her sore leg up on two designer pillows, and Ace sucked his breath in and flinched, gut-struck at the thought of causing her the slightest bit of pain.

"Make me a cup of tea," Salida muttered, and Ace shot outta the bedroom and obediently jetted into the kitchen. It was small, but decorated out the ass, and it was probably the cleanest kitchen he had ever been in.

He looked in the cabinet and found a box of green tea. He put two teabags in a cup of water and microwaved it until it was steaming hot. He set the cup on a saucer and stuck a spoon in it. He searched the cabinets looking for some sugar that he could dump in the cup, but then he remembered that Salida didn't like it sweet.

Back in her room he helped her sit up a little bit so she could sip the tea. He stood silently by the window and watched her, still shook by the fact that he coulda lost her preciousness under the wheels of a speeding car.

"Bring your ass over here," Salida's husky voice interrupted his loving thoughts as she demanded his attention. She was done with her tea and had set the cup on her nightstand.

She scooted down slightly in the bed, then bent her good leg and slid her foot all the way up until her heel was touching her ass. She let her leg fall open, exposing herself without a hint of shame.

Ace drooled. The swatch of her thong barely covered her fat pussy, and he got an instant hard-on as he walked over to her bed. His thick dick wanted to jump outta his drawers as a puddle of hungry saliva filled his mouth.

"Make me wet before I go to sleep," Salida demanded. Her fingers slid between her legs and she pulled her thong to one side. Ace watched through lustful eyes as she stroked her clit until it came awake and got stiff, and then she pressed it a few times before inserting her middle finger deeply inside her snatch.

He groaned as he sat down on the bed beside her. Lifting her gown above her waist, he squeezed her breast and sucked the juices off the wet finger she was offering him.

Her insides tasted sweet and bitter at the same time, and Ace's dick ached as it throbbed in his pants. He held her by the hips and lowered his face to her groin. Her end-of-the-day smell was a real turn on, and he delved into her pussy and plunged his tongue in as deeply as he could.

Salida moaned and sighed and humped under his expert head game. Her movements were limited due to her hip injury, so she held his head and pushed his face into her wetness, moving his head around in ways that excited and pleased her the most.

Ace needed that pussy. He knew he couldn't get on top of her and fuck her, but that didn't stop him from wanted to be inside of her. He wanted to feel her riding him and raping him with those beautiful, silky guts.

His tongue worked overtime as he nibbled on her clit, then dipped it into her puddle of hot juices and licked her out. They were both moaning now, and Salida screamed as her body stiffened and she climaxed, spurts of her hot cum filling his mouth.

Ace got him a nut too. His dick jerked and spasmed like crazy as he busted off hard, filling his drawers with a gigantic load of sticky semen.

He put his groin over his hand in shame, and Salida laughed at his lack of dick control.

"I can stay the night and take care of you, if you want me to," he said, ignoring her laughter as he squeezed her thigh and continued to lust for her.

"Hell naw," Salida said and pushed his hand away. "Don't *no* niggah stay all night in my house. Matter of fact, run over to Pluto's place and get Nooni's ass and bring her over here," she ordered as she thought about the latest batch of meth she needed to test. "Nooni can take care of me tonight. Just put a blanket out there on the couch and tell her lil ass I said she better sleep real light just in case I call for her in the middle of the night."

CHAPTER 6

Slick Sallie pushed Mick's souped-up car to the max as he drove down the highway heading east. He had already stopped at a gas station where he filled up his tank and bought a six-pack of bottled water and three jumbo packs of cinnamon gum.

Earlier, he'd gone to a discount cell phone dealer and filled out an application for a new account. He'd purchased a cheap throw-away phone that didn't require a contract, but still had enough bells and whistles on it to make it worthwhile.

Sallie got himself a brand new phone number, and then waited as the salesman copied all the numbers and email addresses from his old address book and transferred them to his new one.

He was gonna miss his iPhone, but it was registered under his uncle Frank's business account and Sallie was way too fuckin' smart to leave a trail behind him like that.

"We have a special program going where we'll give you a discount if you turn in your old phone," the tech said.

"Nah, I'm cool," Sallie had declined, taking both phones with him as he got back in Mick's car.

With his eyes burning from a lack of sleep, Sallie set the ride on cruise control and coasted five miles above the speed limit with the windows rolled down and the wind rushing through his hair.

Images of the past few days flashed in his mind and he thought about his cousin Mick and wondered if his aunt would ever get over the death of her son. By now, the entire family knew Sallie was responsible for Mick getting electrocuted, and if Sallie knew anything about the Sanveneros, he knew they wanted him to pay.

Rage had been broiling his Uncle Frank's voice when he called Sallie and told him to get his ass over to the house. Sallie had lied and told Big Frank that he was on his way, but instead of walking into what would have been worse than a firing squad, Sallie had hauled ass outta town with no intention of ever going back again.

In the eyes of The Organization, Sallie was now a fugitive. With dumb Mick dead and all of Sallie's dirty, underhanded deeds exposed to his family, he was officially a wanted man with a big round target on his back.

As dangerous as it was to be lined up in the mafia's crosshairs, he was also glad to be out from under Big Frank's thumb. The Sanvenero family had been ordered to stay out of New York City, but Slick Sallie was a McCain so those goddamn orders didn't apply to him.

Besides, New York was where he needed to be. There were a lot of opportunities in that town for a man who could live by his wits. There were plenty of prospects that a guy with Sallie's brains and cunning skills could explore and exploit.

One of the first things on Sallie's crooked agenda was to complete the arms deal that he was planning with a young drug dealer from Harlem. The guy was looking to get his hands on an entire fucking arsenal, and Sallie knew it was gonna be a risky exploit, but if he pulled it off the right way it would net him a shitload of cash.

Sallie had done a little business with this particular hoodlum before, but it had been mostly small-time shit. Two-bit trading. A couple of hot semi-automatics and ten or fifteen dirty revolvers.

But this time the guy wanted to do business on a whole 'nother level, and he wanted way more than a few random pieces too. He was looking to score an entire arsenal, and the most important aspect of the deal was his demand that every single gun be brand new. Unfired. Guaranteed squeaky clean.

Sallie had agreed to take the job, even though it had looked pretty impossible to get his hands on the amount of money it took to commandeer that kind of cache. But now that he was sitting on the loot that had been stuffed in Gino's safe, there was more than enough cash in his pockets for him to get down on the deal. He knew he'd have to go back-alley deep in order to broker a deal of this magnitude, but if he could get in contact with a trader he knew in Virginia and make the big buy, then he could slap a steep mark-up on the weapons and sell them at a nice profit to the drug dealer in Harlem.

Slick Sallie grinned as he envisioned the kind of cash he'd be holding. Shit, if he could pull this deal off he'd be set for life and rolling so heavy he'd never have to come down.

Fuckin' moolies, he thought as he sped down the highway. It didn't take a rocket scientist to figure out why the drug dealer up in Harlem wanted an entire arsenal of clean guns, and Sallie had no problem with the bloody battle that was sure to go down for control of Harlem's streets. In fact, he was happy to be doing his part to clean that place up. The guns he traded would go a long way towards wiping out some of the dirty moolies who were stinking up the slum-infested housing projects worse than they already stank.

Yeah, fuck Big Frank and the rest of the family, he thought with satisfaction. Sallie was making all the right moves and every one of his plans was about to fall in place.

"Suck my nuts, you lousy Sanveneros!" Slick Sallie yelled out the window as his dead cousin's car lurched forward with a zoom. "New York City, here I come!"

CHAPTER 7

I put in good work for you, didn't I, Mo?"

Young Bilal sounded real hopeful as he pounded his wood into Money-Making Monique's tight chocolate tunnel. He balanced her plump titties in his palms and they jiggled like hot water-balloons as he grunted and kept up his deep, steady strokes.

Releasing one of her titties, Bilal slid his hand over her stacked hip. His fingers crept around until they found her dripping slit. Her clit was hard and throbbing, and he pinched it a few times before digging his fingers inside her up to his third knuckle.

Pussy was real good, Bilal thought as his palm filled with Monique's dripping cream, but he liked ass so much better.

Mo's hips twerked deliciously as she glanced over her shoulder and threw her round humps at him with short, hard jerks.

Bilal's young ass almost fainted under her expert moves. He moaned as his fingers played in her gushy and he filled her backdoor with his dick at the same time.

Biting gently on the tender meat of Mo's neck, he pressed his middle finger against the thin membrane that separated her two holes, and shuddered as he felt his dick moving just on the other side, thrusting deeply in her ass.

"Oh damn..." Bilal groaned in her ear. They had snuck inside the triple X cinema room at the G-Spot and he pressed Mo up against the wall as he plundered her sweet asshole.

A necklace of drool hung from his bottom lip and rested on Monique's shoulder as she gripped his dick in the unbelievable tightness of her tunnel. "Oh, yeah...I did good," the young'un muttered like he was a school kid talking to his teacher. "I hit that bitch just like you wanted me to, Mo. I did real good."

Monique rested her forehead on the wall and smirked as she winded her hips and straight up laid her sick booty-dance on him. She was giving Bilal his promised reward for the solid he'd done for her in the G-Spot's back alley, but his lil four-inch dick probing up her ass wasn't giving her nothing but a bad attitude.

"Shut the fuck up and get yours so we can get outta here niggah," she muttered. "You did a'ight, but you ain't kill that bitch! But I bet your ass'll be dead if Ace finds out you was driving that car! Now hurry up and bust your nut, goddammit. I gotta get out there and get that old hag some lunch."

$$$$$

"You hungry, Mizz Salida?" Monique asked fifteen minutes later. She had let Bilal

290

finish getting his shit off, then washed her ass and approached Salida real sweet-like even though her hatred for the older woman was growing on a daily basis.

Salida was dripping jewels and finery and relaxing on a burgundy satin lounge chair that Ace had bought for her. He had gotten a few of his dun duns to set it up on a little platform he built next to the bar so she could oversee the happenings in the G-Spot as she rested her sprained hip.

Ace had also bought her a slim, fly-ass gold cane, and Salida sat up there waving that shit like a queen on a throne as she questioned and controlled almost everything that went down.

Sprained hip my ass, Monique thought as she smiled sweetly at the laced-up old trick, but deep inside she was steaming. Wasn't shit wrong with this throwed-off bitch. Salida hadn't broken a goddamn thing when that car hit her. She could get around just fine on her own, but Ace still had Monique and Nooni taking turns waiting on her, and both of their damn feet were worn out from running around to meet her crazy demands.

"You want me to send Nooni down the block to get you something to eat?" Monique asked, holding her hand out like she was waiting for some money. She wasn't paying for Salida's food! She'd be damned if that double-crossing bitch was gonna eat one bite off the doe she shook her naked ass for!

Monique was too steamed about Salida and her greedy, double-crossing ways. They were supposed to be partners, and by all rights Mo shoulda been pocketing a percentage of the loot that came in from the cut room operations. She had done some cut-throat shit for Salida, but so far that old wench hadn't gotten her ass up off a single dime.

"No!" Salida replied, ignoring Monique's outstretched hand. "Don't send Nooni nowhere. Tell her to bring her ass over here. I got that girl on a schedule and it's time for her to take her medicine. Send one of them corner boys over to Famous Fish Market and get me a fried whitey sandwich and a side order of jumbo shrimp. Tell 'em to make sure they put plenty of hot sauce on my fish too."

"Okay, I will," Monique said and turned away with a look of disgust in her eyes. She was hoping like hell the old bitch would choke on a fish bone, but on the real, an alley cat like Salida seemed to have nine lives. Bilal had knocked the shit outta her with his brother's car, and as Mo peeped outta the back window she coulda sworn Salida had cracked her conniving skull on the concrete and croaked.

But *noooo.* That woulda been too much like an answered fuckin' prayer! Monique had been hot as hell when Pluto came home that night talking about Salida had got hit by a car and the only thing she had was a sprained damn hip.

What the hell? Monique had wanted to scream and ask him. How was that possible? You mean that bitch's back didn't get broke? Her dome didn't shatter into a hundred pieces and her shiesty-ass brains didn't spill out all over the sidewalk? What the fuck! Wasn't old people supposed to have brittle fuckin' bones?

Monique had gone over to Salida's apartment the next morning and pretended like she was all concerned. But on the real, she just couldn't stop seeing the dark hole of the gat that Salida had pointed at her, and the whole time she was in the kitchen showing Nooni how to fix Salida some buttery grits and a bacon and cheese omelet, she was steady plotting on how to hit Salida one more time, but the next time she was gonna knock the old bird on her ass for good.

CHAPTER 8

I don't think he's going to show up," Renata whispered to her husband as they sat in the front row of the cathedral. They were having a quiet Catholic memorial service for Frank's nephew Mikail, and Renata couldn't help glancing at the door every few minutes and hoping that their other nephew, Salvatore, would walk in.

"He'd better not show up," Frank growled under his breath. "Because if he does he's a dead man."

Frank had been livid at his nephew's blatant defiance of his orders. Not just with the electronics heist and the death of his cousin Mick, but with Juicy too. He had made it clear to Sallie and everyone else that the girl was strictly off-limits. He'd given his word and put his arm of protection around the girl, and Sallie had violated that in the worse way.

If Juicy had come back to Los Angeles and tried to drive home from the airport she would have been blown to bits by the bomb that Sallie had gotten boom-rigged in her car. It had been reported all over the news, and some media outlets had even tried to tie the bombing to terrorist activity. Juicy had to have heard about it, and Renata had been trying desperately to reach her, but Frank told his wife that Juicy was probably too scared to think about coming back to California now. She probably didn't think there was anyone in the whole state that she could really trust.

Renata sighed and interrupted Frank's thoughts. "I just can't imagine where Sallie could be. Where he could have gone."

"Beats the hell outta me." Frank shrugged as he looked over his shoulder, "But if the little bastard isn't burning down in hell then he didn't go far enough."

Renata followed her husband's eyes as they watched the other mourners stream through the doors. They were mostly the mafia-type. Stern-looking Italian men in business suits who had come out to pay their respects to the idiot son of a made man.

"That worthless turd should get away with killing my son?" Frank's brother Mike had cried when he saw Mick's roasted body. "I'm a made man, Frankie! That Irish bastard should be the one laying here like a toasted marshmallow! Not my freakin' Mickie!"

And their sister, Salvatore's mother, had been no less emotional with her pleas. "Have mercy on him, Frankie!" she had cried when Frank and his brothers burst into her house looking for Sallie. The little rat didn't even have the decency to tell his own mother goodbye. Instead, he had run off and left an empty, carved-up safe in her wine cellar.

Frank had given his only sister a real long look, telling her without words exactly what he was going to do to that bum son of hers if he ever got his hands on him. Yeah. Salvatore had always been slick, but he had never been very smart. Frank would let him run for now, but the kid wouldn't get very far. And when Frank finally did catch up with him and nail him down, he was going to have the exact same mercy on Sallie that Sallie had had on Juicy and Mick. None.

CHAPTER 9

Nooni had been staying at Salida's crib and taking care of her for a good minute now and shit was getting worse and worse for her on a daily basis.

Salida had turned the girl into her own personal little drug tester, taking her from popping Divine Nine pills day and night, to smoking Salida's special home-cooked blend of crystal meth from a crack pipe all day long.

Whatever the hell was in that lethal chemical combination that Salida had her crew brewing and cooking upstairs in that cut room, it kept Nooni flying high as hell. And it kept her horny as fuck too, Nooni had to admit as she walked around the club with her young pussy leaking slippery puddles and spazzing from self-induced orgasms.

It was late night at the G-Spot, and the music was bumping from the speakers and shaking the windows in their panes. Nooni couldn't keep her fingers outta her pussy, and even though Truth had already dug her out deliciously twice during the day, she still had to slip into the bathroom and pinch her nipples and rub her stiff clit until she came over and over again.

But Salida had been watching her ass like a vulture, and after the seeing the girl dip into the ladies room and come out with her face looking red and flushed for the third time that day, Salida had decided to put her hot ass to work.

So, dressed in the plaid mini-skirt of a schoolgirl, complete with white folded-over bobby socks and chunky high-heeled shoes, Nooni moved her fine young flesh through the crowd exciting lustful men, young and old, as she followed a customer into one of the fuck rooms in the back.

While Nooni mighta looked scrumptious and luscious to the casual observer, deep inside the girl was terrified. She was coming down off an all-day high, her nerves were all fucked up, and she was getting paranoid as hell.

Every time the door opened she thought for sure she was going to jail. She was wanted by the po-po and it shook her to the bone to know they were looking for her ass so they could lock her up over that murder she had committed in Atlantic City.

The first time the two uniformed cops had shown up at the G-Spot looking for her was just two days after she left the trick dead on the hotel room floor.

Mo had taken the officers inside G's office to talk, and when they left she told Nooni that they'd grilled her half to death and flashed her two pictures of Nooni that they had gotten off the hotel's security camera.

A few days later they'd almost busted her at a stop light on 125th Street. She was riding in the whip with Truth and Mo, heading to go pick up some supplies for Salida, when Monique screamed out, "Cops!" and reached over the backseat and smushed Nooni down to the floorboards.

She had crouched down there shivering in fear as Monique flung Truth's jacket over her head and warned her to either stay her ass down, or get dragged outta the whip and hauled off to Rikers to face a murder rap.

And just a couple of hours ago, two white cops had rolled up in the G-Spot again and posted up by the back office. Nooni had walked past and saw Monique leaning up against the wall talking to them. Their eyes met and locked, and when Nooni peeped the warning look that Monique quickly shot her, she knew the drill right off the bat. A sudden surge of ice had run through her veins, completely blowing her high. Monique had jerked her head toward the fuck rooms, and Nooni had twisted the doorknob and ducked inside the closest one, and then closed the door and locked it behind her.

For the last few hours she had been shitting bricks every time the front door swung open, and when Salida called her over to her throne and told her she was gonna have to put in some work for the rest of the night, Nooni was too shook and terrified to complain.

Especially after Salida tore her off some more of that crystal yum-yum. The older woman had taken Nooni from poppin' pills, to swallowing meth, to straight up smoking that shit, and even beyond making her so horny she had to sneak in the bathroom and masturbate, the drugs made her want to forget her troubles and float away on a big fluffy cloud of don't-give-a-fuck.

And now, behind the closed doors of fuck room number four, Nooni dipped her hand in a large jar of Vaseline, then jacked her customer's crooked wood as she thought about the heavenly dick-down Truth had put on her that morning. She had worn his fuckin' ass out with her swiveling hips, and Truth had actually screamed out loud as she rode him rough-style, busting load after load until she was weak and dizzy from pleasure.

"You like this big dick, don't'chu baby?" her customer was saying as Nooni fantasized about Truth and the creamy juices of her lust began to coat her inner thighs. This was her third hand job of the night, but she wasn't as high right now as she had been earlier and this old dude's dick just didn't appeal to her.

"I know Salida said you can't do no fuckin'," he whispered and rubbed her puffy ass. "But just lemme slide my shit between them big titties you got, baby. That way you can suck it and squeeze it at the same time, you know?"

She frowned as she continued jacking his greased-up little dick.

"Sorry, I can't give you no head. This is all I'm allowed to do. Besides, you didn't pay for no titties. Only for a hand."

The tall stranger lost his head and snatched Nooni up in her collar. Moaning, he pinned her up against the wall and yanked the crotch of her panties aside and dug his long fingers inside her pussy. When he saw that shit was already sopping wet, he pushed his forearm against her throat and slammed his dick up in her. He gripped her right ass cheek and thrust himself deeply inside her, fucking the shit outta her and getting himself a nice little piece of raw trim.

Nooni had barely screamed good when Greco and his boyz busted up in the room and pulled the trick off of her. They had been posted up outside the door, and they bum-rushed the customer and went at his ass like he had stolen some bank outta the safe in G's office. They beat his narrow ass down to the ground and dragged him outta the room as Nooni stood pressed against the wall trembling in fear.

"You okay?" Greco asked, as she pulled her skirt down and straightened her thong.

Nooni nodded her head. The trick had got up in her and scared the shit outta her, but he hadn't really hurt her.

"I'm cool," she told Greco. She smoothed her curly hair back and gave him a small smile. "I'm cool."

"You sure?" Greco eyed her. "'Cause I'll fuck that niggah up permanently if you want me to."

"He just scared me, that's all. But check this out," Nooni said, thinking fast as she pulled Greco's sleeve and leaned in close to him. She had never asked him for anything before because she wasn't a hundred percent sure she could trust him. But Nooni was desperate and crashing down hard off her high. It was now or never time for her, and she knew it. "There is something you can do for me, Greco if you don't mind."

"You got it, Shawty," he said smoothly. "Whuddeva you need, you got it."

Nooni could tell Greco meant what he said. And not because he was a goddamn child molester who wanted to fuck her, neither.

"I need to make a call real quick," Nooni whispered. "I need to borrow your cell phone, Greco, but please...*please* don't tell nobody."

The older dude shrugged and popped his cell out of the case on his belt clip.

"Have at it," he said. "You can talk as long as you wanna."

Nooni was damned grateful to Greco. She had already gotten busted tryna use the phone at Salida's crib when she thought the older woman was knocked-out sleeping from all those pain pills. Nooni was supposed to be washing the dishes, but in reality she was two seconds away from sneaking on the phone when Salida appeared in the kitchen as silent as a ghost.

That old lady scared the shit outta her so bad that she dropped the cordless phone down in the sink full of soapy dishwater and let that shit stay right there until Salida got up outta the kitchen and went back to her room.

Later on she had dried the phone off as best she could and stuck it right back on the charger, praying to God that Salida wouldn't find out what she'd done. And ever since then Nooni had just been watching and waiting for the right opportunity to make herself an emergency call.

"Thank you, Greco," Nooni said nervously. She turned her back on the security dude and hurried outta the room and down the hall. But Nooni's luck was all fucked up, and just as she flipped open the phone and punched in a number, she heard somebody giggling and coming around the corner and she froze.

It was Honey Dew. Looking finer than shit and evil as all outdoors.

"You mean you bought three whole chips just to get down with little ol' me?" Honey Dew asked her trick and laughed as she pulled him by his hoody and swung her wide hips down the hall.

Nooni fumbled with the phone and tried to hide it behind her back as Honey Dew got ready to go inside fuck room number two. She was so scared she was gonna get caught that she stuck her hand under the back of her skirt and shoved the phone between her thick ass cheeks and clenched it there.

"What the hell you standing there for?" Honey Dew sneered at Nooni. She paused and stood in the doorway eyeballing Nooni's young flesh with a resentful smirk on her face. "Fuckin' spoiled-ass baby up in here giving hand jobs. All the grown and sexy bitches in the house gots'ta open up their legs for a goddamn living."

Nooni scuttled down the hall quickly, holding her hand awkwardly over the bulge sticking out from her ass. She darted past the working girls who were running the customers in and out of the back rooms as fast as they could, and walked through the main area where the bar was getting more and more crowded by the minute.

Nooni skirted around the stage, and hurried past the kitchen and toward the stairs. She glanced up at the landing near the cut room where Salida's crew brewed batches of potent chemicals and packaged club drugs for street sales and distribution.

She figured Salida's posse musta been taking a break tonight, because all the lights were off and it was dark up there. Praying she was unnoticed, Nooni crept up the steps and onto the landing. She walked over to the door and put her hand on the knob, and her heart sank as she remembered that even if the door was open and she could get inside, she wouldn't be able to get back out because that shit had been rigged to lock from the inside.

She tiptoed back toward the stairs and looked out over the railing. The club was bouncing. The ass-shaker competitions and nicest nipple contests, and all the other Las Vegas-style sex-theme parties that Salida had put in place were starting to bring in more and more clientele, which meant more money for the G-Spot, and more customers for the strippers and the hoes too.

Creeping back over to the cut room door, Nooni reached back and extracted the cell phone from her hind-cheeks. She gripped it in her trembling hand, and then she slid down to the floor with her legs gapped open and splayed out in front of her.

Tears sprang to her eyes. It had been a real long time since she had dialed the most familiar number in the world to her, and she felt worse than shit about all the heartache and drama that she had put so many people through.

Gripping the phone in her hand, Nooni punched in her sister Rita's cell phone number.

"C'mon, c'mon, c'mon!" she prayed as she waited for Greco's phone to find a signal and connect. She was relieved when she heard the hollow, static-like sound of a phone that was just about to ring.

But then suddenly, she thought she heard something else too.

Footsteps. Clumpy, uneven footsteps.

Coming up the stairs.

Nooni froze with Greco's phone pressed to her ear.

Ringggg

Ringggg

"Please, please, please," she uttered a prayer under her breath. "Hurry up and answer this shit!"

Ringggg

Ringggg

Her heart jumped into her throat as the phone was finally answered on the other end, but it was too late because whoever was coming up the stairs was now right up on the ledge.

"Hello?" came a voice over the phone line.

"Who's up here?" A stern voice rang out at the top of the landing as the awkward footsteps sounded in the darkness.

Nooni bucked and panicked.

There was no time to move and no time to lose. Snapping the phone closed, she reached under her skirt and shoved the cold metal between her legs and straight past her pussy lips. She pushed hard with one finger and clenched her pelvic muscles deeply, sucking the phone safely into her moist vaginal canal.

Guilt was all over her face as she looked up and saw Salida stepping onto the landing. The beautiful matriarch of the G-Spot tapped the steps with her elegant gold cane, and a cigarette dangled from her lips as she carried a drink in her free hand.

"What the hell are you doing up here?" Salida demanded. The cigarette bobbed between her clenched lips as she gave Nooni a long, suspicious glare.

"I...umm...I..."

Salida grilled her ass from head to toe, like she had an x-ray machine in her eyes and could see up under the young girl's clothing and detect the metal cell phone that was roughing up her pussy.

"N-n-nothing," Nooni said, thinking fast and swallowing hard. "I-I-I was feeling kinda sick so I came up here looking for you."

"Is that right?" Salida asked. The cruelty in her voice disappeared and she came off real sweet and motherly. "Well, get yourself up off that floor, honey," she said frowning as Nooni climbed to her feet. "Ladies *never* put their asses on the ground. And they sure as hell don't sit with their legs cocked wide open like that."

Salida walked past her with barely a limp as she twisted the knob, and then she held the cut room door open as she stood on her tiptoes to reach the dangling light string.

"There," she said as she clicked it on and the room was washed in bright, fluorescent light. She turned around as Nooni stepped inside behind her, and then once again she grilled the girl long and hard.

"You do look sick," Salida said gently. She passed Nooni her cocktail glass. "Here. Drink a little bit of this Cristal while I get you some special shit that I mixed up myself."

Doing as she was told, Nooni followed Salida to the small office in the back and obediently sipped the alcoholic beverage, which she recognized as expensive champagne.

Her heart started beating real fast when she realized that Salida was unlocking her desk drawer, and she swooned when the older woman pulled out a vial filled with crystal rocks and shook some into her hand. The letters on the side of the vial read STRAWBERRY SNAKE, and Nooni's palms got sweaty and her mouth dried up with anxious anticipation.

She waited while Salida reached for a pipe and put all the rocks on the screen. A cigarette lighter appeared in Salida's hand, and then suddenly the rocks were hot and swirling.

Nooni sucked that glass dick like it had sweet cum in the bottom of it. She inhaled every bit of whirling smoke, and then sucked up all the acrid residue that followed too.

"Here's your dessert," Salida teased as she handed Nooni two pills to pop.

Tossing her head back, Nooni dry-throated the drugs and then picked up Salida's glass and swallowed down the bubbly until every drop was gone.

"Good girl!" Salida praised her, grabbing her cane and heading toward the door. "I bet your sick ass is feeling just fine right now!" she laughed.

At the door, Salida stopped and looked at a row of boxes that were stacked up against the wall. They contained thousands of tiny vials that were stamped with her unique street logo and the name of her new brand, Strawberry Snake. Her plans for widespread distribution were about to become a reality, and after the extensive testing she had done on Nooni, she couldn't wait for her specially-blended product to invade Harlem's streets and capture the hearts of its residents.

Anxious to leave, Nooni made a mistake and reached for the doorknob, but Salida slapped her hand down real hard.

"When are you gonna learn that it's locked on this side, dummy?"

Nooni waited as Salida stretched out the neon-pink spiral bracelet that she always wore on her wrist. Two keys dangled from it, and Salida stuck the larger key in the lock and then pressed down on the handle and opened the door.

She spoke over her shoulder. "You's a sweet lil thing, Nooni. Anytime you start feeling bad you just come find Mizz Salida and I promise I'll make you feel better, you hear?"

"Yes, ma'am," Nooni said and grinned. Her head was good and her mood was lifted. And the cell phone jammed up in her tight pussy was starting to feel just like a dick as she bounced her gorgeous young ass back down the stairs to get ready for her next customer.

CHAPTER 10

The homeless shelter didn't look nothing like I had pictured it looking. From the outside you could have taken it to be a regular old New York brownstone, but when I got inside I was surprised at the way it was set up.

The Puerto Rican lady who came to get me from the hospital took me into an office to meet an intake counselor named Mrs. Singletary, and after she gave me an ice pack for the lumps on my face and asked me if my foot was feeling okay, she got out her little clipboard and started drilling me with a whole lot of questions about my past.

Most of what I told her was lies, and just like when I was in jail, I made up a lot of shit as I went along, but this was New York. I figured Mrs. Singletary had been around the block a few times and had probably heard all kinds of bullshit before.

She punched my bogus information into her computer, and then I half-listened as she ran down about a million New York City shelter rules.

"We have a ten-day stay limit and there are absolutely no visitors allowed. There is no smoking, drinking, and absolutely no drug use permitted during your stay. All cooking must be done in the kitchen, and all food must be consumed in the dining room."

My mind wandered as she continued talking. I wanted to listen but I was busy trying to plan my next move and figure out how much of me and Gino's cash I could get Sallie to wire me before the Feds got suspicious.

"We have a bed for you on the second floor," the intake counselor said, eyeing the boot on my foot. "You think you can make it up there?"

I nodded real quick. Hell yeah, I could make it. I could make it up them stairs, and as soon as my money got wired to Western Union, I could make it back down them bad boys too.

Matter fact, the minute I got my cash I was gonna catch a cab to the airport and buy me a one way ticket to someplace far, and then check into the airport hotel and order room service and chill until it was time for my flight to leave.

"The second floor is no problem," I assured the counselor as we walked through a little lounge area. She was one of those older ladies who still used a hot comb to straighten her salt and pepper hair. She turned around to lead the way and her pleated skirt twirled like a giant tent. Her hips were big and round, and her stockings made that soft squishing noise as her thighs rubbed together with every step she took.

I damn near fell in love with that sound and the way her ass moved. She reminded me of Grandmother and the ladies she used to hang out with in church when I was growing up. I longed to put my head down on her shoulder and confess my sins on the pulpit the way Grandmother had always urged me to do back in the day.

301

But times had changed, and all the good church ladies I knew were up in Harlem, which was the last place I was going. Instead, of putting my head on her shoulder, I glanced around the room.

"Excuse me, Mrs. Singletary. Is there a phone around here that I can use?" I asked.

She nodded and pointed at a desk up against the far wall. "You can use that one right there," she told me. "Just dial nine to get an outside line."

I sat down at the desk and dialed nine, and then I punched in the rest of the numbers as I remembered them.

The phone rang four times, then a recording came on that said, "The number you have dialed is not in service. Please check your number and dial your call again."

My ass dialed real slow and careful on the next try. I took my time and deliberately pressed every number real hard, pausing between each one to make sure I got it right. And I did. This time the phone was picked up on the second ring.

"Hello?"

The background noise was so loud that I could barely make out his voice. It sounded like he was in a wind tunnel or shouting into a fan the way me and Jimmy used to do when we was kids.

"Sallie!" I shouted and stuck one finger in my ear. "Sallie are you there?"

"Yeah?"

"It's Juicy," I said. "It's Juicy!"

"Yeah? What's up, Juicy?"

"Look. I know it's been a minute, but remember that favor we talked about?" I let out a big sigh. "I'm gonna need you to do it and do it real fast."

"I can't hear you, Juicy. Lemme roll up the window."

All I heard was the wind in my ear as he paused for a few seconds. And then he spoke again.

"A'ight. Now what favor?"

"You know," I reminded him, still yelling even though the noise in the background had died down. "The *favor*," I lowered my voice and glanced around and tried to whisper. "The favor I told you I might need you to do with that money Gino left with you!"

"Gino who?" Sallie said. He sounded like he wanted to make sure his words came through real loud and real damn clear.

I half-chuckled even though my situation was far from funny. "Look, I'm dead serious," I told him. "If you knew what kind of shit I've been going through you wouldn't even be playing."

"Who's playing?" He sounded dead serious too.

"Oh, so it's like that? All right then. I'll just call your aunt and uncle and tell 'em you're trying to fuck over me, Sallie."

"Call 'em," he said calmly. "Yeah, go 'head and do that. Since the Feds are on your ass, why don't you lead them straight to Renata and get her and Big Frank thrown in jail too."

"What?" I damn near screamed. "The Feds? What the fuck are you talking about?"

"You fucked up, Juicy. They know you stole all that drug money, and they know you blew up your own car and skipped town too."

"I didn't blow up no damn car!" I shrieked.

"Whatever. Tell it to the Feds. All I know is that you left The Organization in a bag, sweetie. I tried to tell Frank you weren't shit from the very beginning, but I'm not Italian so he wouldn't listen to me.

"And now look at what's happened. You brought trouble to their door and our entire family is about to go down because of you. Some kind of friend you turned out to be. Yeah, call Uncle Frankie and call Renata too. I'm sure she'll be happy to hear from you while they're throwing her ass in jail."

I felt like a train had just run over me. What in the hell was going on? My mouth went dry with fear. Gino had stressed out hard over the Feds tracking us down. Did I leave a trail for them to sniff me out? Was I gonna go back to jail?

My head was spinning. I couldn't believe what I was hearing. I refused to believe that shit!

"Yo, Sallie!" I barked. Mrs. Singletary was looking at me like I was crazy but I didn't care. "Sallie..." I took a deep breath and tried to calm myself down. "I don't know nothing about no Feds, but I'm telling you, mothafucka! I'm gonna need you to send me some of *my* goddamn money, outta *my* fuckin' *safe!*"

"*What* fuckin' money?" Slick Sallie's voice was colder and slicker than shit as he hung up in my face. "*What* fuckin' safe?"

$$$$$

At first I felt so ass-out that I just wanted to kill myself. Of course I clicked over to a dial tone and punched in Renata's number right away, but as soon as it started ringing I hung up again. I knew Sallie was gonna try to keep all my money, but what if he was right about the Feds? What if they had Renata's phone tapped and they were just waiting for me to call, waiting to draw a solid line between me and her so they could take her down too? I couldn't risk doing that to her. As fucked up as my situation was and as much as I needed some help, I just couldn't do it.

For the next two days straight all I did was cry and blow up Sallie's cell over and over again. He never even answered that shit. His phone just kept rolling straight to voicemail, and by the fourth day it was full and wouldn't even take no more messages.

My soul felt stripped and bare. No matter how I looked at things in my head, I was fucked. And not only was I fucked, I was also broke, hunted, and living in a homeless shelter way in Brooklyn with nowhere else to turn.

Mrs. Singletary had put me in a room with some other homeless chick, but I didn't talk to her and she didn't talk to me neither. Matter fact, she barely even looked at me, and I figured she probably thought I was laying there crying over some niggah who had beat my ass and kicked me out on the streets, but of course she was dead wrong.

The shelter was full of people coming and going, but I kept to myself and stayed mostly in my bed for those first few days. I felt so beaten down and depressed that I just didn't know what to do. I couldn't go back to California, and I couldn't go back to Harlem neither. I didn't have a phone, and I damn sure didn't have a plan.

It took me a minute, but I finally broke down and called Rita. I ran down all the shit that Flex had done to me and told her where I was staying, and she cursed me out for not calling her right away so she could come get me.

"You can stay with me, Juicy. Nooni's bedroom is empty, *chica,* and it's all yours. Every damn thing I have is yours if you need it."

"No, Rita, no," I begged her. Even with Nooni gone she still had her little sister Chub to worry about. "I'm not coming back to Harlem. I'm way too scared. Plus, I wouldn't feel right putting you in no bag."

She started crying.

"I'm just so fuckin' sorry, Juicy," she apologized through her sobs. "I'm the one who put you in this situation in the first place! All of this shit is my fault. I shoulda never let you come back here. If you wanna go back to California I'll come up with the money and buy you a plane ticket back, okay?"

Both of us knew that wasn't gonna work. Hell, I could have called Renata and asked her to get me a plane ticket back to the West coast, but what the hell was I gonna do when I got there? Where was I gonna hide? The Feds were after me and somebody had blown up my fuckin' car! My ass wasn't no safer out there than I was right here.

Grandmother popped into my mind. I felt her presence within me so deep that it made my bones ache. I could see every line on her wise old face. Every crease in her overworked hands. She was in my bones, but she was also in my ear too. I could hear her telling me to just be still. To trust God and to be still.

And what choice did I really have? I couldn't have moved if I wanted to. So I decided to give myself a couple of days until my ankle healed and I could walk without limping. I would just hide out in the shelter and chill for a minute and try to catch my breath. For once in my life I'd be obedient to my grandmother. I'd think and pray and try to see where I was being led, and wherever God's grace took me, then that's where I would go.

CHAPTER 11

Sal had covered about fifteen hundred miles and he was itching to get his ass to New York City. He pulled over for gas and food, and slept during the day at cheap motels so he could do most of his driving at night.

Tonight he was sitting in a booth at a truck stop diner as he feasted on a T-bone steak and a large order of French fries. He had pulled off the road to get some gas, and the smell of greasy burgers and fried onions had lured him inside the joint.

The food was good, he had to admit as he cut into his medium-rare steak and watched the juices run onto the plate, but that wasn't what was keeping him there. The diner was full of truckers and travelers, and four pretty blonde waitresses scuttled around serving every man in the house with bright eyes and big, phony smiles.

Sal noted the beauty of the waitresses, who looked so much alike that they had to be sisters, but not one of the four had caught his eye.

Nah, Sallie was staring at somebody who looked totally different, and the more he sat and watched her, the hungrier he got.

She was eating by herself at the counter, and her ass looked like it was molesting her stool. She was slim up top with long, straight hair, but her hips looked nice and wide, and he could tell she had a plump booty packed into her tight jeans. Her frame put him in the mind of Juicy, who was one moolie bitch he'd fucked without ever taking his dick outta his pants.

Sallie watched the girl at the counter as she lowered her full lips onto the straw that stuck out of her glass of lemonade. He caught a glimpse of her pink tongue as she inserted the straw deep into her mouth, and instantly his pants rocked up with a strong desire for her.

She was just what he was looking for. Her small hand gripped the frosted glass, and her earrings dangled seductively from her earlobes. She had smooth, mocha skin, and when she spoke to the cashier at the counter Sallie melted as he saw a deep dimple flash in her left cheek.

The girl must have felt him staring at her because every now and then she glanced in his direction with a shy look in her eyes, and then looked away.

She's flirting with me, Sallie thought. She was reading him and he was reading her too. The next time she snuck a peek at him Sallie nodded at her and winked. Her face seemed innocent and beautiful when she broke out in a bashful smile, and Sallie shot her his sexiest grin in return.

She was no local girl, Sallie could tell, and she wasn't the kind of cheap hooker he usually snatched up off the track either. His curiosity was quenched when she slid down from her stool and jangled a large set of keys in her hand. Waving goodbye to the cashier, she took one last look at him and then her hips swayed like a melody as she walked out of the diner and headed toward one of the large trucks that was parked right outside.

Sallie couldn't believe it. A chick like her was pushing a rig. He dug into his pocket and peeled off a fifty-dollar bill, and tossed it onto the table as he rushed outside behind her.

The trucker's name was Meesha and her and Sal were in the back of her cab smoking a little reefer and having a real good time. Sal told her he worked as an aide to a big-time Los Angeles politician, and that he was driving to New York for a vacation. Meesha broke out a bottle of gin and told him she was from Oklahoma and that she got off on a creating a little adventure during her long, lonely road trips.

The moment she slammed the truck's doors Sallie was all over her black ass. He knew her type very well. She was one of those black chicks who just loved to ride white cock. Well, Sallie had plenty of cock for her, but it didn't matter how white she tried to talk he saw straight through her. She was still a nigger.

It had been a minute since Sallie had gotten a taste of some good black tail, and he started out by asking Meesha if she wanted to play a little game.

"You're gonna love it," he promised as he watched her strip out of her jeans and shirt and then wriggle out of her underwear. Her body was fuckin' stunning. Her stomach was sweet and flat, and her hips looked like an artist had sketched them to perfection.

Sallie urged her to turn around, and he was damn-near slobbering by the time he saw her naked ass. It gave him a jolt. It was high and firm, perfectly round, and her thighs were tight and slender.

"Bend over and grab your ankles," he instructed her as he swept his hand over her thick black booty. Meesha giggled and did what she was told, and Sallie used two tie-down cords that were on the floor to secure her wrists to her ankles.

When he had her tied up tightly he stood up behind her and took off his pants. His white penis stood out from his body at an angle, and Sallie rubbed it all over her ass before reaching under her and cupping and squeezing her firm brown nipples.

"You're gonna love this," he whispered as he bent over her and planted kisses down the curve of her naked back. She shivered beneath him as his lips trailed along her sweet chocolate spine and he approached the crack of her ass with sheer heat coming out of his mouth.

Gripping her fine hips, Sallie slid his tongue between her ass-cheeks and stuck it deeply inside her tight hole. She moaned and squirmed as he withdrew from her back door so he could continue licking lower. Sighing, Sallie sniffed her gorgeous pussy and plunged his face in, rubbing her clit with his nose. He backed out and parted her lips with his thumbs, and peered into the pinkness that was surrounded by the kind of chocolate he wanted to eat every single day.

Sallie got down on his knees so he could have better access, and then he went to work eating that dripping pussy like it was the last meal he would ever have. He gulped and slurped and licked and moaned into her yummy as Meesha screamed and bucked her hips at him, cumming over and over as Sallie fucked her deliciously with his tongue.

The air was thick with the smell of hot sex in the cab and Sallie's dick throbbed with his need to burst. He fumbled for his pants and dug in his pocket and got a condom, then slipped it over his erection and rolled it down until his dick was all wrapped up.

By now Meesha was begging for it. Sallie was just about to give it to her, but he needed to taste that pussy just one more time. He massaged her clit with his fingers as he stiffened his tongue and probed her juicy insides. She came in his mouth again and flooded his tongue with her thick, hot cream. With one last lick at her asshole, Sallie stood up and rammed his prick inside her pink tunnel. He gripped her hip with one hand and spanked her ass with the other.

Meesha moaned and urged him on as he fucked and spanked and fucked and spanked. At some point the sound of his slapping hand got faster and harder as he pumped even deeper inside of her.

Excited beyond belief, Sallie went into a slapping frenzy. Meesha's moans were now turning into yelps and she began twisting and turning, trying to get away from him. She tried to fall over on her side, but Sallie hooked his left arm around her waist like it was a sling, holding her right where he wanted her as he dicked her all the way down.

Sallie slapped her ass with all the strength he could muster. Her pussy had dried up, but he didn't care. He reached way back and swung his hand down sharply, the splintering sound mingling with the girl's frantic yelps and screams.

It took him five more thrusts before his balls emptied out, and at the height of his orgasm Sallie pulled out of Meesha's pussy and snatched off his condom. He screamed like a bitch as he shot his load all over her dark ass, and he watched in satisfaction as his sticky semen slid between her thick cheeks and disappeared down her crack.

Meesha was really crying now, but Sallie barely heard her. He had come so hard that it took him a few moments to get himself together, and when he looked down at Meesha's ass he almost laughed out loud. Her left cheek was smooth and caramel brown, but her right cheek was swollen with horrendous welts, and countless red abrasions, some beginning to bleed, marred her beautiful flesh.

"You crazy mothafucka!" she screamed in pain as he shoved her over and then stepped across her so he could get his drawers. "Untie me!" she demanded. "Are you mental or something? What the fuck is *wrong* with your stupid white ass?"

Sallie ignored her and pulled on his clothes. He stuffed his dick back in his pants as the dumb black bitch called him every low-down dirty motherfucker she had in her vast vocabulary.

But Sallie was done. His tongue was starting to itch and he could feel her rotten juices churning around in his stomach. He reached into his shirt pocket and got two sticks of cinnamon gum and stuck them in his mouth. He was just about dressed when he glanced down at her and stared at the smooth skin of her left flank.

Taking a deep breath, Sallie pulled his belt out of his pants loops. Meesha screamed as he reached back over his shoulder and let his leather fly. The belt cut into her flesh with a hiss, and instantly a purplish bruise appeared on her skin. Sallie swung again and she screamed, and he swung again and Meesha screamed.

Sallie didn't stop swinging until he was sure her left ass-cheek looked almost as good as her right one looked.

And Meesha didn't stop screaming for a minute either. At least not until the crazy white boy that she had picked up on a whim had stolen her cell phone and the keys to her truck, and then locked her in the back of the cab with her beautiful ass cheeks bleeding and her wrists still tied to her ankles.

CHAPTER 12

The day was way too beautiful to be having a funeral. Especially for a child. While the Harlem sun shone above a perfectly cloudless sky, inside the Church of the Redeemer there were lovely pink and blue flowers on display everywhere.

There were bunches of them up on the pulpit and at the front of each pew, and a batch in the shape of a cross had been placed over the bottom half of the open casket that held the body of the pregnant young girl whose short life was being celebrated and whose tragic death was being mourned.

The mood inside the church was sad and grim. The organ player banged soulfully on his keys, and the church was packed with so many grieving mourners that they were spilling out of the door.

Almost the entire community of Harlem had turned out to show their respect for poor little Princess Howell and her unborn baby. Neighbors and friends had passed around a basket to collect money to purchase her a burial plot, and the small business owners in the community, especially those who were members of the Talented Ten, had dipped into their pockets to buy her a beautiful casket and pay for all of her funeral expenses too.

Trey Jackson had already announced a community scholarship fund he was establishing and dedicating in Princess' name, and right now him and the other nine members of the Talented Ten Crew sat in the front row of the church next to the dead thirteen-year-old's grandfather, Mr. Howell, and her best friend, Taleah.

Three of Princess' girlfriends from her poetry troupe called Street Talk N.Y.C had just finished reciting a beautiful poem that talked about the senselessness of her death and their vision of a world without street violence and drugs. Trey had organized the group under the wings of The Crossover Community Center where he'd once mentored Princess, and he was proud of the three young ladies who had spoken so passionately for their dead friend today.

The funeral director held out his hand toward Trey and Mr. Howell, indicating that it was time for them to stand and approach the coffin for the final viewing of Princess' body. Trey stood up and lifted the old man to his feet, and then matched his steps as the old man shuffled toward the casket.

Behind them, the Talented Ten Crew and over fifty youngstas that Trey mentored at the Crossover Community Center stood and followed them up to the front of the church. Each youngster held either a pink or baby blue flower in their hand as a gesture of their grief and love for Princess.

These throw-aside kids of Harlem had been Princess' friends and companions during the time she'd spent at the Crossover Community Center, and just like Princess they had been exposed to drugs, gangs, street violence, and dysfunctional families, and every last one of them knew it could have been them laying up in that cold box instead of her.

As the mourners filed slowly past the casket, everyone in the church seemed to moan and rock together like they were of one body. Their grief swelled up to the rafters and fell like a sad mist over everything it touched. The sight of Princess' stiff young body in her bright pink dress, with her stomach still swollen and carrying her dead baby inside, crushed the hearts of the entire neighborhood. The horror of the two deaths from an overdose of the drugs that were sold on the streets of their neighborhood sent rage through their collective souls.

A stylishly dressed older woman began belting out *Keep Your Eye on the Sparrow* in the most beautiful voice that Trey had ever heard. He returned to his seat and sat tall as Mr. Howell's thin shoulders heaved with cries and his body trembled in Trey's arms.

"My grandbaby was all I had," the old man moaned in a soft, pitiful voice as he clutched Trey's shoulder. "These kids is just killing they selves! Princess and that baby was all I had left in this *world*."

As much as it fucked Trey up to see a dead child laid up in her casket with her belly filled with the body of another dead child, he kept his emotions in check and an impenetrable mask of composure on his face. Over the past few years he had been to more funerals than he could count, and not one of the dead had been over the age of twenty-five. Between the outta control gun violence and the unchecked flow of drugs flowing through the streets of Harlem, youngstas like Princess were now an endangered species in their own neighborhoods.

Trey thought about his manz Mayhem and frowned inside. No matter how hard organizations like The Crossover and the Talented Ten fought for the souls of Harlem's children, the lure of fast money and pipe dreams never died, and the battle was uphill every single day. But regardless of what they were up against, Trey and his posse had vowed they would never stop fighting.

The last of the mourners had filed past the casket and returned to their seats, and the funeral director was about to lower the lid on Princess and her unborn baby forever, when the church doors banged open and a beautiful but deadly-looking chick walked in.

A hush fell over the large room as she headed straight down the center aisle, taking long, deliberate steps and draped in expensive gear and ghetto finery. She was tall and gorgeous. She wore a form-hugging silk sweater made of mint-green satin, a pair of silky black jeggings that hugged her stunning curves to a tee, a pair of black, stiletto-heeled leather boots that came all the way up to her knees, and a full set of glittering diamond jewelry.

Lil Lee's makeup was perfect and her hair was straight butter as she strode up to Princess' casket and glared down at the cold, stiff body before her.

Posing with her hands on her hips, the only female capo in the notorious Divine Nine click gazed around the church real slow to make sure she was commanding her proper respect, and then with a chilling glance at Trey she sniffed real deep and hock-spit loudly, right down in the dead child's face.

A deathly hush fell over the church like a smothering wool blanket, and then the air exploded with shouts of anger and clacking gats as people got swole and started brandishing burners like they had been transported to the Wild-Wild-West.

Lil Lee had been the first to pull her piece and she stood posted up by the open coffin looking deadly as hell as she gripped her tool and waved that shit around in the air.

But Lil Lee wasn't the only one carrying heat. The men of the Talented Ten were up on their feet and ready to blast too, and Trey instinctively pushed Taleah down to the floor and urged her to ball up under the pew.

It only took him a second to see what was up and assess the danger. About a dozen of Lil Lee's low-level underlings had blended in with the funeral mourners. They'd waited until she made her grand entrance, and then they'd taken her cue and jumped into position. They were all young'uns and they were all armed too, aiming their pistols recklessly around the church at kids, old people, and anybody else who was within bullet-range. Trey's blood almost boiled when he scanned the crowd and saw that Mayhem's younger brother Maleek was strapped up and standing amongst the Divine Nine crew.

"Uh-huh," the beautiful young drug queen barked as she sneered coldly at Trey and his crew. "We got us one of them Mexican standoffs." She nodded toward Princess' body. "And all because this lil dumb-ass fiend fucked around and got my best slanga murked!" She looked around the church. "Somebody out there gave J-Ugly a ride off a rooftop because this lil trick laying here wanted to get high, and I'm telling all y'all mothafuckas right now that *somebody* is gonna pay."

She reached in her back pocket and came out with a fistful of drug vials. Sneering, she flung them down at Princess and they rolled all over the corpse.

"Get high in *hell,* bitch!"

Shooting another glance at Trey, Lil Lee turned around and switched her bomb-booty back down the aisle, parting the crowd with a wide sweep of her gun. Her young'uns pushed out of the aisles and followed behind her like trained puppies, walking backward and keeping their wary eyes on Trey and every other pistol-packing niggah in sight.

"That's the guy!" Taleah stood up from her hiding spot and elbowed Trey as the posse of drug slangas moved toward the church's door. "Trey, that's him!" she half-whispered. "That's the guy!"

"What guy?" he leaned over and asked her as he watched Maleek and the others back outta the door. "What guy, Taleah?"

"The guy who so—" The teenager bit her tongue as she locked eyes with the fine skinny dude with the cornrows who had conducted the drug transaction with Princess and a chill zipped through her bones.

She took a quick glance at her best friend laying up dead in her coffin. "Never mind," Taleah said softly. "I don't know *what* the hell I'm talking about. Never mind."

By the time the church's door slammed shut there were plenty of gangstas left standing in the house of the Lord who were ready and willing to rush outside and go head up with Lil Lee and her crew. But Trey quickly checked them. He held his hand in the air signaling to let the Divine Nine posse leave in peace. There was a time and a place for everything, and with countless pews filled with scared women and children this wasn't the time for gunfire and mayhem, and it damn sure wasn't the place.

$$$$$

The church was finally settling back down as the people of Harlem regrouped from the rude disruption and continued to pay their last respects to Princess. The preacher had stood up from his crouched position behind the podium, and the funeral director had emerged from behind Princess' coffin where he had ducked and hidden when all the guns came out.

Trey and everybody else had taken their seats again, and the preacher was rushing to wrap up Princess' eulogy before any more ghetto nonsense could jump off.

"Yo," Trey's man Skeet leaned over and tapped him on the shoulder. He nodded towards the center aisle of the church where once again the crowd of mourners was parting, but this time it was to let four uniformed police officers get through.

"What the fuck is up with this?" Skeet muttered. "First this child gets disrespected by some come-up crew, and now the blue boyz is rollin'."

Trey's expression never changed as the cops walked through the grieving crowd and came straight up to the front of the church. The preacher looked confused, and he stumbled over the words in his sermon as the officers posted up in the front row directly in front of Trey and old Mr. Howell.

All four cops were well known in the community, and Trey knew exactly why they were there. He nodded at his boy Skeet, then slid Mr. Howell outta his arms. Skeet threw his arm around the old man as Trey stood up. He towered over the cops as he grilled them with a cold, neutral expression in his eyes.

"Yo, y'all niggahs straight buggin', son," Rain hollered as one of the cops went to grab Trey's elbow and lead him down the aisle. "We at a funeral, fool!"

Trey shot the cop a 'wish-yo-ass-would' look that was so dark and menacing that the little dude backed off and put his hands back down at his sides.

Trey strode unhurriedly outta the church with his head held high and his eyes full of love for the people in his hood.

"What y'all messing with him for?" A wrinkled old man hollered from the back of the room. A loud chorus of voices joined him. "Where the hell was y'all ten minutes ago when a gang of drug dealers was up in here about to shoot us down?" the people shouted. "Huh? Huh? Where was all of this so-called police presence in the community then?" they screamed.

Trey's kids from The Crossover were back up on their feet and yelling too. They looked swole and hyped and ready to wild the fuck out this time, but there was a calm authority about Trey as he motioned for them to sit back down and chill. Giving his boys an example of how to handle themselves under this kind of pressure was a big part of teaching them how to survive in this world as young black men, and the self-assuredness of Trey's mad swagger was all they had to see in order to confirm that he had everything under control.

Trey took his time leaving the church and the cops trailing behind him had no choice but to stop and wait each time he paused to hug an old lady or dap out some of the older men of Harlem. He lingered in the crowd accepting the love he was being shown from the young and the old alike, and there were tears in the eyes of countless mothers who reached out to hug, kiss, and thank him for saving their children from the same fate that had befallen the young girl they had all gathered to mourn.

Finally, Trey paused at the door, and looked back at the crowd of people who had turned to watch him go. He could tell they were still mad about the disrespect Princess had suffered, and male and female, young and old, they looked agitated and ready to get something started. Like they were just itchin' to jump all over the po-po if Trey would just give them the nod.

His Talented Ten crew had also followed him toward the doors, and the little peashooters the cops were strapped up with were no match for the superior firepower Trey knew his dudes were packing.

But Trey also knew this day was about honoring Princess and not about reckless rage. He gave the enormous crowd a fearless look that said, "I got this," and then he stepped calmly outside the church doors and into the bright sunlight.

"Dig, Trey," one of the cops who had been his manz back in high school reached for some dap as they walked toward the squad car. "We just out here doing our jobs, ya know?"

Trey didn't even look at dude as he folded his long legs and muscular body into the cramped backseat of the car.

"Then maybe y'all muh'fuckas need to do a *better* job," Trey spit coldly before the officer closed the door. "So a niggah like me ain't gotta keep doing that shit for you."

CHAPTER 13

My roommate's name was Egypt and she was a real sharp chick from the Brownsville section of Brooklyn. We had finally started giving each other a little convo after almost a week of doing the New York-thang and staying out of each other's space.

Egypt had stayed in this shelter quite a few times so she knew the drill and how they liked things done. The staff had put us on the schedule together to clean the kitchen, and now that the dishes were done and we'd wiped all the counters down with bleach and water, we were sitting at the table together tearing up some cheese doodles, onion and garlic Wise, twisted pretzels, and Dipsy Doodles corn chips that we had mixed together in a brown paper bag.

"I don't know, Egypt," I said, running my mouth as I crunched on a pretzel. "I've had some fucked up things happen in my life, but I never thought I would end up in a homeless shelter. I don't even know how I got here."

I was glad we had finally stopped igging each other and started talking. Neither one of us could believe that life had stomped us down so far that we'd ended up in our present situations.

"Well my ass ended up in here because I was stupid as hell," Egypt told me bluntly, without putting a drop of sugar on it. She was tall and dark-skinned and very, very, pretty. She had a stacked body, beautiful dreadlocks, and a gorgeous white smile, but there was something real sad and haunted about the look in her eyes.

"See, I used to be a crack-head," Egypt admitted as she dug her hand inside the greasy paper bag and came out with a handful of the mix. "Nah, hold up," she corrected herself. "I used to be a crack *hoe*."

I stared at her. Egypt looked so fly and sounded so smart that it was hard for me to believe she had been out on the streets smoking crack and I told her that.

"Oh, a minute ago I would have said the same thing about me too," she laughed. "From the outside looking in, I had it going on. My father owned a barbershop called Fat Daddy's on Livonia Avenue, right across the street from Tilden Projects. We lived in ghetto luxury in our apartment upstairs over the shop, and I had everything a little black girl from Brooklyn could ever want. But *anybody* can get caught up in a bad spin, Juicy. All it takes is a couple of hard knocks and one or two stupid-ass decisions and you can end up flat on your ass, you know."

Oh, I knew. I damn sure knew.

"For me," Egypt kept going, "it started when my dude Lamont—they call him Hood in The Ville—got knocked. And then right after that my father ended up getting murdered by some of the same drug slangers and power players that he had helped raise up in the streets. Those cats fucked him up, Juicy," she said miserably. "They tortured him without an ounce of mercy. I came home from school one night

314

and found his dead body in the kind of condition that no daughter should ever have to witness."

Egypt shivered and hugged her arms.

"I was only seventeen, and all of a sudden I was left by myself in the world. All of that loss was just too much for me. I mean, yeah, I was raised in the belly of the hood, but my father had spoiled the shit outta me. He'd shielded me from most of the ugliness that lived in Brownsville. In the world, really."

She shrugged.

"But after those same guys that he had fed and protected and trusted, upped and betrayed him and murdered him like that...I just slipped. I couldn't handle it. Girl, you just don't know. I miss my daddy so damn *bad*, but in a way I'm glad he's dead and he didn't have to witness all the gutter shit his baby girl went through."

"I *do* know," I said, thinking about my family and how it woulda killed Grandmother and Jimmy to know I'd been shot and in jail and was now sitting up in some damn homeless shelter.

"And what made my situation even more grimy and scandalous, " Egypt admitted," was that I fell into my addiction because I got blinded by the wrong niggah. By some mental case named Dreko. He was my dude's best friend. His main manz. His partner-in-crime. When Lamont went to jail that fool had me *and* Lamont's mother sucking his dick and eating his ass too. That's how low-down and shitty that crack had both of us living."

Egypt shrugged like she was over it, but her brown eyes got flooded with the deep pain of her memories.

I pushed the greasy bag of grub back on the table and kept my mouth closed. Egypt had a hard-knock story, but I wasn't about to tell her that my life had been even grimier than that. I thought about how G had damn near beat me to death, then peed all in my face and let them nasty tricks run endless trains on me down in that filthy Dungeon. I thought about how my baby brother had gotten tortured behind me and my stupid-ass foolishness. About how he had been forced to murder a man he loved and blow his own brains out just because of me. It was crazy. All that death and drama going down just because I had gotten turned out on the dick of my sugar daddy's only son. I didn't dare think about how I'd lost Gino and our baby with one single bullet. I just couldn't bring myself to think about that.

"I guess we all go through some shit," I said softly. "If we had lived our lives the right way then we probably wouldn't be sitting here talking about it now."

Egypt nodded in agreement. "I'm here to tell you, honey, I went from sugar to shit so fast that it was unreal. One minute my life was perfect and I had big future plans, and the next minute I was left with nothing, girl. Absolutely nothing. But the worst part of it was that I lost Lamont. I lost his love and I definitely lost his respect."

Egypt reached for the paper bag and peeked inside. She took out a couple of cheese doodles, then lined them up on the table in front of her and brushed the crumbs off her fingers. "You know, the best thing that ever happened to me was when Lamont drove me up on the Brooklyn Bridge and told me to get outta his whip and jump my ass into the East River. I had gotten to the point where I was so damn *gutter*, Juicy. I'd do anything for a hit. Anything. I was just stank and desperate and no damn good for nothing except suckin' dick and suckin' pipe."

I had never messed with crack, so I just shook my head as I tried to wrap my brain around that one. "But damn," I said frowning. "That was some cold shit! Your man told you to jump off a bridge?"

Egypt nodded. "He sure did. And it was good advice too because on the real my ass was already dead. Walking dead. See, Mont understood my condition even better than I did. First, he pulled out his gat and told me to suck it. I was so damn defeated that I actually put that burner in my mouth and pulled the trigger."

She wiped a tear from the corner of her eye.

"The gun jammed, though, and I took it as a sign that God was giving me another chance to pull my shit together and do something right."

She stared at me real hard. "Nobody *wants* to end up where we are, Juicy, but it's a whole lot better than sleeping in abandoned buildings and crack houses. I move my ass around from shelter to shelter every ten days because it benefits me. The people who run this system hooked me up with a drug treatment program, and then they helped me get my GED and some counseling too."

She shrugged and popped one of her cheese doodles in her mouth. "I'm telling you, God made me get humble when I fell down on my ass. I was two seconds away from graduating at the top of my class in high school, and my plan was to go to college and medical school and become a doctor and all that. And I believe I can still do it too. It ain't over. I'm just chilling here until the situation is right and I can make the move that's gonna take me to the next level, you know what I mean?"

She stopped chewing and looked at me real hard.

"You're a cute girl, Juicy. You don't look like a junkie or a hoe. Hell, other than those crazy lumps and bruises that were all over your face when you came in here it don't look like the streets been riding you that hard at all. So why are you up in a shelter instead of out there letting some investment baller keep you laced?"

I shook my head. Fuck how I looked on the outside, Egypt just didn't know how raggedy I was on the inside. The last thing I needed was another psycho-ass big willie who wanted to own me.

"Girl, I used to be caught up with this big-time drug kingpin in Harlem," I told her. "He was rich as hell and old enough to be my damn daddy, and any little thing I did he beat my ass real good for it. He took good care of me and my brother when it came to money and jewels and all that, but that just wasn't enough for me. I wanted to be regular, you know? I was only seventeen at that time too, and I wanted to hang out in the streets and do all the crazy shit my friends was doing. So I started creeping on him. Getting me some outside dick. And when that niggah found out he turned into the devil and tried to kill me."

I didn't have the heart or the energy to tell her why my fucking-out had hurt G so bad, or about how me and Gino had ran away and tried to build a new life together. And failed.

"Damn!" Egypt said with her eyes real big. "So you up in here hiding out from that fool, or what?"

I shook my head. "Nah, he's dead. My brother killed him."

Egypt shook her head. "You lucky then. It's better that niggah be dead than you."

I nodded my head and reached for the last little cheese doodle that she had left on the table. I picked that shit up and bit into it and whispered real low, "You ain't lying. For real."

$$$$$

Sharing a room with Egypt made my situation something that I could almost bear. I didn't really know my way around Crooklyn, New York's biggest borough, all that good, but Egypt was Brooklyn-born and bred, and she understood this town's unique brand of New York City flow.

We hung out for a little bit. Nothing big, since I was broke and Egypt didn't have a whole lot of money. But my foot was feeling almost all the way better so we walked up on the avenue and got a slice of pizza once or twice, and when Egypt went to class then I just sat around and tried to figure out what life had in store for me next.

On my fifth day at the shelter a big old Goodwill truck came and dropped off a bunch of used clothes and other stuff, and after the workers got it all sorted out then the residents were free to take what they needed.

I was one of the chicks in the house who needed every damn thing. Where I had once stayed draped in the best fabric that money could buy, every stitch of gear I now owned had come out of a donation box, and I wasn't mad about it neither. For one thing I wasn't tryna be fly and attract no attention, and for another thing I would rather wear another woman's used shit than depend on a man to put clothes on my back.

On Saturday morning Egypt got up and said she wanted to go downtown and buy some natural products for her hair. I asked her if I could go with her just to hang out. We rode the train to Nevins Street and got off and went upstairs. We walked up on Fulton Street so Egypt could get the stuff she wanted from a street vendor, and then we walked down toward Albee Square, just running our mouths and window-shopping.

We were right outside of a hair salon when a commotion broke out. I frowned as a bunch of chicks with half-done hair busted out the door fighting their asses off.

"Kick her ass!" a bunch of girls were screaming as the whole damn shop seemed to empty out on the sidewalk. It was a sight. Females had wet hair, weaved hair, wrapped hair, and creamy-crack perm all up in their hair, but not one of them seemed to give a fuck about their hair as the mass ass-kicking went down. "Beat that bitch's ass!" They swung haymakers and kicked and fought. "Fuck her up! Beat her ass!"

"Crazy sistahs," Egypt smirked as we jumped off the curb and walked around a parked car trying to get out of their way. "Black women need to stop that shit." She frowned and crossed her arms as we watched chicks scrapping and scratching all over the pavement. "And that big-ass trannie over there really needs to stop," Egypt pointed with her chin and rolled her eyes.

I looked over to see who she was talking about. There were three chicks fighting off to the side and they were really going at it. One had bleached blond hair and she was laying flat on her back getting her mug drilled by the trannie, who was sitting on her chest and banging her head on the ground. A real skinny girl with half of her hair braided in extensions and the other half flying everywhere had yoked the cross-dressing dude up from behind. She tried her best to pull him off her friend who was getting her head cracked on the concrete, but mami had no wins because the big dude was too much for both of them.

I blinked real fast as he reached behind his back and slung the skinny female down on the ground right beside her friend. Still sitting on the blond-haired chick, he leaned over and started beating the hell outta the skinny girl too.

I was just about to turn away from the fight when I caught a look at dude's face and my heart banged in my throat. I damn-near slumped over the parked car we were leaning on as the truth slammed me hard in the gut.

"Uh-uh. That ain't no damn transvestite!" I shouted to Egypt. And it sure as hell wasn't neither. It was that treacherous bitch from the West coast who had ruined my life and brought death down on my baby *and* on the only man I had ever loved.

It was DarQuese.

$$$$$

I lit into that two-faced bitch with the fury of a Japanese tsunami. I mean I jumped on her ass and got to kicking and punching and slapping and scratching her with the backed-up rage and fury that boiled all down in my bone marrow.

The two chicks she was already fighting didn't know what the fuck was going on when I jumped in wildin' like a madwoman. I grabbed Quese's head and brought my knee up hard under her chin. I slammed into her face as many times as I could before she twisted away from me and fell over on her side. Jumping over the girl she was sitting on, I gave a flying kick to DarQuese's nose, and when the heel of my shoe connected with her face I heard a snap and blood spurted outta her nostril and gushed all over the place.

Fuck her blood, I raged as I kept right on going after her ass. Me and Gino had spilled much more blood than that.

For a Harlem chick who couldn't fight for shit I wasn't doing all that bad. Quese reached up and grabbed me around my waist, and I banged furiously at her face as she took me down to the ground. My fists were slick with her blood as I kept swinging and started kicking and squirming even harder as we scrapped.

Egypt ran over and jumped in swinging when she saw that I was down. She boxed the shit out of Quese's ass like a true-blue Brooklyn girl, and all three of us was panting and breathing hard as we got it on.

"Stop fuckin' hitting me!" DarQuese screamed on Egypt as she wrestled me flat and laid her huge self on top of me. "I ain't hurting her!" she yelled over and over again. "Juicy is my fuckin' *friend!* I would never fuckin' hurt her!"

"They done called the cops!" a girl with a head full of white perm hollered as the rest of the fighting girls got ready to break out. "They called the cops!" She had fought so hard that her plastic smock had twisted around her neck and was flapping behind her like a cape.

DarQuese and Egypt both froze, and even above my rage I could hear the sirens in the distance. "Y'all better dip," the chick warned as she straightened her smock and ran back inside the hair salon. "Them mothafuckas are coming!"

$$$$$

"I swear, Juicy!" DarQuese pleaded. "On my dead *mama!* Girl, I put my right hand up to *God!*" she cried. "You gotta believe me. I didn't have nothing to do with it."

We were sitting in the back of Bella Pizzeria on Hoyt Street, and DarQuese was crying and babbling as she held a napkin full of crushed ice to her nose. That shit was swollen and crooked from the driving force of my thrusting shoe, and every now and then she dotted a fresh drop of blood from the tip.

"You *had* to know!" I barked on her. "If Pit was down with that shit then you was down too!"

"But Pit *wasn't* down with it, Juicy!" she insisted. "I'm telling you he didn't do nothing to y'all! By the time I found you and Gino laying on the floor Pit had already left the church!"

"But how did he know where we were gonna *be*, Quese? He wasn't *invited* to the goddamn church! Just like he wasn't invited to my wedding dinner the night before that either, but I caught his ass smoking weed outside in the parking lot anyway! That niggah warned me out of his mouth that night that my honeymoon was gonna be a nightmare and Gino was gonna get sat down. Nah," I waved my hand and dismissed her bullshit. "Pit did it. I know damn well he did it. And the only reason that fool knew where to find me and Gino is because *you* told him, DarQuese."

Her eyes were red as she continued to shake her head in denial. "Look," she sniffled and set her bundle of ice on the table. "This is God's truth, Juicy. God's *truth!* Yeah, I let Pit give me a ride to your wedding dinner and that's why he was there. And yeah, he came by the church the next day and I opened the side door and let him in. But I had left your wedding present in the back of his Range Rover, Juicy! Me and Cynthia had chipped in together and bought a big bag of freaky sex toys for you to take on your honeymoon, and I called Pit and asked him to bring the bag to the church for me.

"And I swear to God, that's all he did. He came inside and gave me the bag, and then I watched him jump back in his whip. As soon as he pulled off I came right back downstairs to your dressing room. And the minute I opened the door and saw you and Gino laying on the floor in all that blood...I started screaming."

I shook my head. That shit was unbelievable. Her story had to be bogus. It left too many questions unanswered. "So you're trying to say you was upstairs with Pit when me and Gino got shot?"

"I'm not *tryna* say it, that's what I'm *saying*. And that's what I told the fuckin' cops, too. It wasn't me, and it wasn't Pit neither."

I smirked at her, my rage still going strong. "Okay, if it wasn't y'all then who the hell was it, DarQuese? Tell me that. Who the hell was it? Who shot me and Gino?"

My old friend with the burnt up face took a real deep breath and stared me straight in the eye. "I think it was Gino's boy," she said quietly. "That greasy asshole who was always hungry and always scheming. I think it was Slick Sallie."

$$$$$

There was a time when I would have brushed off anything Quese said about Slick Sallie as pure bullshit, but after the ruthless shit he had just pulled with my money I didn't put anything past him anymore.

"I tried to tell you them Italians was shiesty," DarQuese insisted, "and you ran me some mess about them just being good businessmen and all that. But I told you I peeped Sallie from the gate. That cracker stayed up on the track creeping chicks out. He didn't want nothing to do with the Latino hoes or the Asian prostitutes. He went strictly after the black sistahs, and every last one of them came back with a wild story about some sick, twisted drama he had put them through."

DarQuese smirked and shook her head. "I never trusted his ass. He was all the time begging to lick my pussy. The way he stayed strapped up and brandishing his tool is what made me start watching his ass. You shoulda been watching him too."

"Sallie was Gino's friend, not mine. I didn't have no reason to watch him."

"Well them mafia fuckers didn't have no reason to do me and Pit the way they did us neither, Juicy! They came after us hard. They tore up Pit's shop and destroyed my salon too. Yeah, I ended up losing every damn thing I had worked for, but Pit got it worse 'cause they tracked him down like a dog. And when they sniffed him out they tortured him. They smiley-faced him and cut off his hand for some reason, and then those animals hung him up to bleed to death in his own shower so his mother could find his body."

I shuddered and crossed my arms. "They cut off his hand because whoever shot me also stole my wedding ring while I was laying there bleeding on the floor. At least that's what Renata told me."

"Well it wasn't Pit because he never got anywhere near downstairs where y'all were at! I swear I wanted to come tell you all this while you was in the hospital, Juicy, but I was running for my life. I got outta town as fast as I could too. Pit was dead, and the Italians had caught two of his boys out there and served them too. It was just a matter of time before they came looking to X my ass out, so I came back home. I figured it was better to take my chances here in Brooklyn with my crazy ex-boyfriend than to sit around like a duck waiting for the mob to make me disappear. It was really a no-brainer."

I shook my head. "None of it makes sense," I said, but in the back of my mind I was thinking how out of everybody me and Gino knew, Slick Sallie had known where our money was stashed, so he had the biggest reason to want the two of us dead. Hell, he'd had over half a million dollars worth of reasons to get rid of our asses.

I didn't wanna believe what Quese was telling me. I swear to God, I didn't. I'd spent a lot of time hating her and Pit. When I found out that the Italians had fucked Pit up I was happy that the animal who had killed Gino and caused me so much grief was dead. But if Quese was telling the truth and Pit wasn't the one who had fired that gun, where did that leave me? Who the hell was I supposed to hate now? Sallie?

"Juicy, just think about it," DarQuese continued to plead her case. "Why would I wanna set you up anyway? For what? I got crazy love for you! Do you really think I could hurt you or your *baby*, Juicy? I was gonna be lil man's *godmother!*"

Egypt shot me a curious glance when DarQuese mentioned my baby and I started crying. She reached out and put her arm around me and whispered that it was okay. I hadn't gotten around to telling her about that part of my life yet and if we hadn't ran into DarQuese, I probably wouldn't have ever told her.

"Why, Juicy? Why?" DarQuese asked again, demanding that I respond. "Why would I do something like that to you?"

"I don't know fuckin' *why!*" I spit as a river of tears fell from my eyes. "All I know is somebody in that church *shot* me! They shot me *and* Gino. My man and my baby *died*, DarQuese! They died and now I don't have nobody. That's all I fuckin' know!"

CHAPTER 14

Less than an hour after being escorted inside Harlem's 28th Precinct, Trey Jackson walked back out the front door on his own accord.

"I know what kind of cat you are," said the burly lead detective who was investigating the death of J-Ugly, the young drug dealer who had been thrown off the roof of a well-known crack den. "You got a lotta passion for the kids on these streets, Trey, but remember son, restraint beats overkill seven days of every week. I'm not saying I want you to stop all that good lookin' out you be doing out on these streets, I just need you to ease up sometimes and let shit play out through the proper channels, okay?"

Trey stared at the older man whose salt-and-pepper hair he had neatly trimmed only a few days earlier. Not only was Detective Bobby Peterson one of Trey's regular customers, he was also the cop who had arrested Trey after he pumped cold lead into two drug dealers in a dark, deserted parking lot what seemed like a lifetime ago.

"A'ight, Mr. P," Trey said, dapping his friend and mentor out. The proper channels of conducting police business had very little to do with handing out street justice, and both of them knew that if the cops didn't handle shit on their side of the law, then Trey and his men of the Talented Ten would take care of business in their lane.

Trey stood on the precinct steps shooting the shit with the detective while he waited for his manz Rain to pick him up. He grinned when a shiny new ride pulled in at the curb and a New York City probation officer got out.

"What it do, Dutchy?" he said, as he gave up a rare smile to a member of law enforcement. Dutchy was his sister Chiney's long-time P.O. and their families had been tight back in the day. Trey nodded at his boy. "I ain't seen you in a minute. What's good in your world?"

Dutchy Gaines grinned and reached out for some dap. "I ain't doing as good as you, Trey, but I'm handling mine. You know I got your sister Chiney on my roster again. She told me you still doing big things at The Crossover, man. That's what's up."

"Yeah," Trey said, stepping off as his boy Rain pulled up behind Dutchy's whip. "We do what we can. I'ma need you to come lay some rap on the kids when we have career night, cool?"

Dutchy nodded. "Oh hell yeah. I'm definitely down for that. Whatever you and those kids need, I'm down for whatever."

Trey climbed into the car with Rain and gave his boy some dap.

"I woulda got here sooner but shit got bad out at the cemetery," Rain said. "Mr. Howell passed out, man. We had to call an ambulance to come get that old dude."

"Muh'fuckas," Trey muttered, shaking his head and referring to the cops who had picked him up. "I wanted to be out there for Mr. Howell. Instead them fools had me in the station wasting my time."

"We got him through it," Rain said with his jaw set in a serious line. "But we still got some shit to handle. That bitch Lil Lee is gonna be a problem. J-Ugly was her boy and that little drama she popped off today is only the beginning. Matter fact, all of those Divine Nine fools are starting to act a little bit ill. That niggah Flex been sticking his toe across a couple of lines just a' probing and violating. He's tryna expand his territory and get real swole."

Trey frowned at the mention of Flex's name. He thought about the cold look he'd seen in Maleek's eyes during Princess's funeral. Just the thought that Mayhem's young brother was out there scrambling yay and everything else for Flex and his grimy crew was a painful blow to Trey's gut.

"Yeah," Trey grunted as he got out of Rain's car in front of his crib. "That stunt Lil Lee pulled today was unpardonable. Somebody is gonna have to teach her ass a little lesson."

CHAPTER 15

"All the goddamn toilets are backed up again," Salida bitched at Ace as she came out of G's bathroom drying her freshly manicured hands on a paper towel. "I already told you the building inspector is about to come through here. I thought your simple-ass partner said he unclogged all the pipes?"

Ace looked up from the plate of barbeque rib tips he was devouring and shrugged. He'd thought a whole lotta shit about Pluto his damn self, and he was starting to believe most of what he thought he knew about his boy was wrong.

The street grapevine had been whispering and tickling Ace's ears. He'd heard all the low-cutting jokes from the hardcore Harlem hustlers who ran hole-in-the-wall clubs, pool halls, and number spots. Them cats had been making ha-ha's and poppin' live shit about Salida and the new direction that she had taken the G-Spot in. Ace didn't like his woman being the butt of nobody's fuckin' jokes, and he couldn't help thinking that his manz Pluto was behind some of that noise.

The tension between the two men had grown thick as shit, and it wasn't that he had let a piece of pussy fuck up their partnership like Pluto claimed he did. Nah, it was about being a stand-up niggah and doing whatever it took to get what you needed out on these mean streets.

Not only had Salida launched a whole new flava and attracted new customers to the Spot, her club drug operation was booming like a muh'fucka and that shit she cooked upstairs was now being packaged for deep distribution all over Harlem.

Pluto swore Salida was just greedy and selfish, and he claimed she wasn't doing a damn thing to put any extra dollars in his pockets.

"You let that chick take over everything, man," he had complained one night. "You wanted me to go along with her shit and we was all supposed to benefit from it. As far as I can tell ain't nobody collected a dime off of nothing she got going except her."

"But that's the thing," Ace had countered, rushing to Salida's defense. "Just because her shit is jumping off don't mean me and you can just sit back and play with our nuts, son. We had a mission and we fucked it up and that's why me and you is broke. Haters gone hate, but who you think paid the back rent up in here? How is the damn cops getting their cut every week, and how you think we got squared up with the back utility bills and the liquor license too? All that shit got taken care of outta the doe Salida brought in. Me and you still gots to get our own."

It was this kinda talk that pissed Pluto off. Salida was all the time yakking about how bad him and Ace had fucked up their opportunity to get their hands on some big cash. She was still mad as fuck that Juicy had slipped through their fingers, and he figured she was withholding her cash from them as some type of punishment or some shit.

Pluto had smirked and waved his boy off. "Both of y'all can kill all that whining about G's missing doe, yo. That shit is gone somewhere out in Cali and what's done is done. Don't nobody know where that bitch Juicy is at, and don't nobody know where the money is neither."

"But see, that's where your thinking is all fucked up," Ace insisted. "We can't forget about that shit, man. We gotta keep pushin'. We gotta be diligent. We gotta go back in, ak. And we gotta go back in hard."

"That shit is dead, man. It's dead."

That's the same thing Ace had tried to tell Salida, but she had snapped on him with a quickness, telling him, "Dead my ass. I know damn well y'all ain't gonna just give up on that kinda goddamn money! I ain't the only one still scheming and dreaming up in here, am I? 'Cause if I am, what the hell do I need with you two broke-ass clowns?"

"Look, P," Ace had pleaded with his partner. Yeah, he had sent Izzy and Zero out on a death-mission over that doe, but what the fuck. His cousin Rabbit wasn't even speakin' to him no more. He told him he didn't give a fuck how much money Juicy mighta been hiding out in Cali. He had lost two good killers when that car bomb went off and Ace could kiss his black ass. "Pluto, that money is still out there somewhere, man. It didn't disappear. It's up to us to use everything we got to find it and get it back."

Pluto took a deep breath and grilled his old friend. "I tell you what, niggah. I ain't feelin' the kinda slimy shit y'all niggahs been pullin' on Nooni, ya heard? She's Truth's bitch, and that shit just ain't right. If we go at that money one last time and we still come up empty, then we gotta let that girl go."

With his eyes wide and innocent, Ace had nodded in agreement. He'd dapped his boy out as they settled on a course of action, but deep inside he knew releasing Nooni was never gonna happen. Somehow the young girl had become Salida's personal pet, and her junkie ass wasn't going nowhere. At least not no time soon. Shit, probably not never.

CHAPTER 16

Cigarette smoke hung heavy in the air as the G-Spot strippers gripped the golden fuck-poles between their thighs and performed tantalizing feats of sexual strength and provocation.

Monique sat at the bar pretending to rest her feet as she watched Salida put the moves on Nooni. That old lady had Nooni in her clutches, Monique saw. She was manipulating the girl with an expertise that was simply fuckin' mind-boggling. Acting all motherly. Pretending to be so nice and concerned about her. Gaining Nooni's trust by stroking her with one hand, while deep-screwing her with the other one.

And Nooni was simple as fuck too. For a wanna-be grown-ass who had been born and bred right there in Harlem, it had been too easy for Salida to get in the girl's head. That child had almost zero street smarts, and Monique couldn't help giggling as she remembered how she'd made the young girl believe that she had killed a white trick in Atlantic City, and then convinced her that the cops were looking to bust her and throw her in jail right here in Harlem.

It was hilarious. Twice already Mo had suckered the hell outta Nooni when the local police came to the G-Spot to pick up their weekly protection money. Monique had looked all scared and panicked in the face when she lied and told Nooni the police were there looking for her, and that they had her pictures from their hotel surveillance cameras.

That chick had broke out running like a goddamn racehorse. She'd jetted into one of the fuck rooms so fast that it was comical, and Monique had bust out giggling before Nooni could get inside the room and close the door good.

And it had been pure damn street smarts and the ability to think on her feet that had allowed Monique come up with that little caper she'd pulled on Nooni when they were in the car that day. Salida had sent them to pick up some supplies for the cut room, and Truth had been waiting at a traffic light. Monique had almost panicked when she looked up and saw that fuckin' bitch Rita crossing the street right in front of the car!

Using her street wit she had screamed, "Cops!" and told Nooni to duck down in the seat. She'd tossed Truth's jacket over the girl quick-fast until Rita had finished crossing in front of them and was all the way on the other side of the street.

Nooni had been so convinced that the cops were on her ass that she'd stayed crouched down in the car all the way to the store and all the way back. Even when Monique had told her the coast was clear, the girl had refused to pop her head up and she'd kept her face covered up with Truth's jacket.

Monique took a long drag on her cigarette as she watched Salida work the girl over. All those crazy drugs was fuckin' the young girl up, and if Salida didn't get up off the money she had promised her, then Monique might have to make herself an anonymous call and tell Rita exactly who was playing pusher to her little sister.

CHAPTER 17

Two days after I ran into DarQuese in downtown Brooklyn I saw a flyer posted on the bulletin board in the shelter's kitchen. There was a black-and-white photo on it of a spoken-word group called Street Talk N.Y.C., and the flyer said they were coming to perform that night for the kids who were staying in the shelter.

"What's Street Talk N.Y.C. about?" I asked Egypt when I went back to our room. Her ten days were just about up and she had just packed her stuff so she could move to whatever shelter had the next open bed.

"You never heard of them? They're from Manhattan but they visit shelters in every borough. They come through this one a lot," she said as she looked in the mirror and put on some huge silver hoop earrings. Her locks were parted down the middle and she had two big spiral ponytails on each side. "They're real creative. Sorta like the groups in that Russell Simmons show called Brave New Voices. They travel all over New York doing spoken word, poetry, rap, hip-hop, and all that. They even perform at hospitals, schools, community centers, everywhere." She chuckled. "Girl, I've even seen them bust out spitting fiyah on the buses and the trains too."

"Oh yeah?" I had heard a little bit of spoken word when I was in high school, and I'd always wished I had the guts and the talent to get up on a stage and let all the shit that was bottled up inside of me just come pouring out in a poem like that.

"Yeah. Those Street Talk kids are young, and they're real smart too," Egypt said. "Sometimes they visit shelters on the weekends and hold little workshops and writing sessions and stuff too. It's fun. All the teenagers up in here really seem to get into it."

I was ready to get into it too, and at seven o'clock I followed the shelter crowd into the dayroom. I was surprised to see that it wasn't just the teenagers who were showing up. Plenty of people of all ages were already crowding into the room and everybody seemed excited. All the couches and chairs were taken, and most of the littler kids were sitting in a circle on the floor. There was no place for me to chill, not even up against a wall, so I sat on top of a metal trashcan and waited for the show to begin.

They had turned all the lights off except for two lamps right behind me near the pool table, and a chubby light-skinned girl with long twists hanging down her back stood in the middle of floor and opened it up.

She told us that Street Talk N.Y.C. was dedicated to positive social change, and how they gave life to the concerns in our communities through their spoken and written word. And then her voice dropped low as she informed us that their performance tonight was being dedicated to the memory of their friend and fellow poet, Princess Howell.

"Princess was one of our brightest angels. Her light shined on everybody who knew her. And even though she was only on this Earth for thirteen years, she left a piece of her spirit with us when she died and we're here to share that beautiful spirit with each of you tonight."

Lil mami with the beautiful twists in her hair stood up there giving off some real positive energy about her girl Princess, and my heart felt heavy just hearing about the death of a child that young.

Those youngstas set Princess' eulogy to poetry, and I couldn't believe how powerful their words were. I felt kinda sad and empty inside, like I had missed something important in life. I had never had the opportunity to join no kind of poetry clubs or stuff like that when I was in high school. Living with Grandmother it had been all about going straight to school and coming my hot ass straight back home.

And life had been even worse with G. That niggah had squashed any thoughts of creativity and freedom of expression that might have even thought about popping up in my head.

I sat there mesmerized like a little kid as I listened to those youngsters lay their Black consciousness down on the entire room. They brought the joy and they brought the pain too. They talked it exactly the way it went down in the streets, and the words they spit were on point and realer than real.

By the time they were finished my hands burned from clapping so hard and my cheeks were sore from grinning. My ass was hurting from sitting on top of that open garbage can too, so I stood up so I could stretch a little bit.

The performers had taken their bows and were introducing their mentors and organizers when I leaned on the pool table and tried to wiggle some circulation back into my legs. I was yanking up the waistband of my tight jeans when I got a shock that touched me way down in my bones.

A tall, muscled-up dude with gorgeous dreadlocks, milk-chocolate skin, and deep, penetrating eyes had stepped up to the podium and taken the mic. He was so tall that he had to lean down to speak into it and I got so hypnotized by his looks that I couldn't hear a word he was saying. All I could see was his pretty teeth, his chiseled lips and his smooth pink tongue as my eyes stared past his curly moustache and straight down his freakin' throat.

Whatever dude was saying got everybody to clapping real loud, and when he looked out into the crowd and flashed a perfect grin, he busted me grilling him like I was in a trance.

Messiah. His name whipped through my mind. *Trey Jackson.*

I shivered as our eyes met across the room. A clap of thundering heat crept up my collar, down my back, and licked straight between the split in my thighs.

Ignoring the applause, Trey pinned me in his strong, sexy gaze and wouldn't let me go.

Goddamn muthafucka, I thought, and then I panted out loud as my nipples got stiff and I broke out in a hot, funky sweat. *Ahhhh, shit!* I moaned inside as ol' boy stood there sucking me deeper and deeper into his eyes. Flex's little ass had been right, I realized as I tried to stop myself from falling down a mental hole of yearning. My woman-thang wasn't dead after all.

Because for the first time in more months than I wanted to remember...my pussy popped.

CHAPTER 18

It was way past midnight when Trey got home from Brooklyn. His kids had done it up and made him real proud tonight, and he had dropped every one of them off and made sure they got inside their apartments before heading to his own crib.

He punched in his security code and turned his key in the door, letting himself in quietly so he wouldn't wake up his sister. Walking past the kitchen and living room, he entered his bedroom and went straight to his bathroom and stripped down naked.

Grabbing a washcloth, Trey stepped into the stone-tiled shower stall and let the water run nice and cold as he stood under the spray. The frigid pellets numbed his skin, but they couldn't put out the lustful fire that seeing her had sent burning through his groin.

Juicy.

He held his head under the spray and opened his mouth. He felt the cool mist of water rush over his tongue, and as it spilled over his lips and dribbled off his chin he mouthed her name again.

Juicy.

She felt good on his tongue. She felt real sweet sliding off his lips. Trey shook his head and tried to push her outta his mind. She was just a girl, he told himself. He had plenty of them. He could've had plenty of them right there in his bed with him tonight if he wanted to.

Trey stepped back and grabbed a bar of soap and rubbed it over his skin, but when his hand dropped down to his groin the proof that she was deep in his head was sticking straight out in the air.

Gripping himself, Trey gave his snake a brief squeeze and then soaped it up. His hand was slippery as he stroked himself. He squeezed his dick even tighter each time his clenched fist slid up his shaft and neared the head.

The muscles in his ass flexed as he jacked off with his eyes wide open. He didn't even need to picture himself pounding inside of her. It was like she was already there. Her sex appeal and the essence of her womanhood was enough to send him falling over the edge.

There were plenty of women that Trey Jackson could have called to help take his mind off of Juicy, but he didn't want none of them. None of them stacked up to her. Yeah, hitting them for some quick, hot sex would be real easy, but that would only serve as a distraction for what was riding him, not as a cure.

Trey's dick was still swollen and throbbing in his hand as he stepped back under the cold shower spray. He rinsed the soap from his body, and stood there until the cool pellets reduced his body heat and softened his wood until it hung down by his thigh.

In his bedroom, Trey dried off and put on a pair of boxers. He grabbed the remote

331

and turned on the television that was mounted on the wall opposite his bed, and then he sank back on his pillows to watch the news.

The usual fools were on Fox News talking all kinds of unintelligible shit, and Trey flipped through the channels surfing for something that would take his mind off what he considered to be a problem at hand. When he was just a young boy he had asked his mother what kind of woman he should look for when he grew up.

His mother, in all her wisdom, had rubbed his head and replied quietly, "You'll know when you know, Antonio. It won't be hard to recognize her. The heart always knows what it wants."

Closing his eyes, Trey tossed and turned for a long time before finally drifting off. A burning question was on his mind as he drifted off into the darkness. Ignoring the needs of his body, his subconscious mind came right out and asked his heart what the hell it wanted. The answer came to Trey just as he was entering the world of deep sleep, but he heard what his heart said just as clear as day.

It answered, "Juicy."

$$\$\$\$\$\$$

Chiney was scrambling eggs and stirring a big pot of cheese grits when her brother walked into the kitchen. Glancing over her shoulder, she slid the top on the pot quickly, and stuck the plate full of turkey sausage and beef bacon in the microwave so Trey wouldn't see it.

She had left her lady, Venus, chilling naked in her room. She was planning on serving her breakfast in bed as a reward for the hot loving she had laid on her, and she didn't want Trey to see how much grub she had cooked up and realize she was hiding somebody up in the crib.

And that wasn't the only thing Chiney was hiding from her brother. She had been steadily getting high behind Trey's back, and even though most street slangas avoided selling to her if they could, she could always cop the good shit from her old friend Maleek.

"What's up?" she asked and gave Trey a big smile. She had a red bandana tied around her short hair and was wearing a pair of loose red sweats on with a white belly shirt.

"Sup, Cool," Trey said and opened the refrigerator. He took out a container of fresh-squeezed orange juice and held it up to his mouth and downed it.

"Damn, get a cup!" Chiney said like she was disgusted. "Don't be up in here drinking out the carton like that!"

Ignoring her, Trey chugged the rest of the juice down and then belched.

"Uggh," Chiney complained, screwing up her face. "You so damn nasty!"

Trey laughed as he tossed the empty carton in the trash. As gay as his sister was, she was still a girlie girl in a whole lot of ways.

"Yo, I saw your friend last night," he said slyly.

"Friend who?" Chiney asked. She took a plate out of the dishwasher and put two big spoonfuls of hot grits on it and then put some scrambled eggs on top. She was trying to hurry up and fix Trey's food real quick so he could get the hell outta the kitchen and let her sneak two plates in her room for her and Venus.

Trey shrugged. "That dumb chick you was locked up with in Rosie. What's her name again? Spicy?"

"Oh, you real stupid," Chiney said with a smirk. "Her name is Juicy. And you know goddamn well her name is Juicy."

Trey shrugged again and sat down at the table while Chiney stacked three turkey sausage patties and several strips of beef bacon on his plate.

"Yeah, a'ight," he fronted. "Juicy. I ran across her last night."

"Eat," Chiney said, passing him a fork. "Where'd you see her at?"

Trey reached for the salt-n-pepper shakers and waited until she passed them to him and then he answered, "Down in Brooklyn. I took the kids to perform at a homeless shelter. She was there."

"For real?"

Trey dug into his plate. "Uh-huh," he said, chewing.

"Ah, man. I shoulda went with you. What's she up to? She got a spoken word group going too? Were they performing or something?"

"Nah." Trey shook his head. "She was by herself."

Chiney frowned. "Juicy was by herself at a homeless shelter way in Brooklyn? Why?"

"I guess 'cause she lives there," Trey shrugged. "That's where she rests."

"Oh, shit!" Chiney exclaimed. "Is that where she went when she got off The Rock? I thought one of her girls was gonna hook her up with someplace to stay when she hit the bricks?"

"I don't know," Trey sounded annoyed as he picked up a half-burnt slice of bacon. "Hell you askin' me for? I don't know nothing about that damn girl. I guess somebody fucked up somewhere."

"But that shelter shit is crazy," Chiney countered as she remembered all of her late-night conversations and crying sessions with her jailhouse friend. "Juicy don't have no family, Trey. She ain't got no peeps. She told me Cooter used to look out for her at the G-Spot. She said he was the one who helped her get outta there and saved her life."

She stared at her brother as he kept right on eating without a care in the world.

"I wanna go and get her, Trey. I wanna get her outta Brooklyn and bring her up here so she can have someplace decent to stay."

Trey chuckled and shook his head. "Negative, baby girl. That shit ain't gone happen."

"Why not?" Chiney looked around and challenged him. "All these empty rooms and ain't nobody up in here but me and you. I mean damn, it's cool for you to help every snotty-nosed kid you walk past on the street but I can't look out for my friend?"

Trey gave her a hard look. "What? You feeling her like that or something?"

"I'm feeling her like a *friend*, Trey. Juicy is straight. But what does that gotta do with it?"

"Nothing." He scraped the last mouthful of grits off his plate and stood up.

"For real," his sister said. "We can't leave her down in Brooklyn by herself."

"Damn, girl! She wasn't by herself. There's a lot of people living in that shelter. And they prolly got a waiting list a mile long with people trying to get up in there everyday. She a'ight."

Chiney stood up and put her hand on her brother's rocked-up arm. "You know what I mean, Trey. I wanna go and get Juicy. I wanna bring her here."

"Hold up, didn't you tell me them G-Spot niggahs was looking for her?"

Chiney nodded. "Yeah, that's what she told me when we were locked up. But so fuckin' what, Trey? You got a posse! Them fools at the G-Spot ain't crazy. If they know Juicy is up here with you and your crew them niggahs will chill with all that bullshit.

"Besides," Chiney said slickly, completely exposing Trey's weakness and blowing up his spot. "I saw how you was checking for her on the visit that day so don't even front. You feeling Juicy ya damn self, Trey. And I already know how you get down. If you feeling a chick then you ain't gonna let a damn thing happen to her."

CHAPTER 19

"Stop, Nooni," Truth begged gently as she moaned her way through yet another orgasm. She was flying higher than an eagle, and instead of experiencing pleasure her flushed face was twisted and contorted in pain.

"That's enough, baby," he pleaded as he pinned her shoulders to the bed and moved away from her violently thrusting hips. "Cut it out. That's enough!"

They had been fucking for over an hour and after cumming over and over and over again, Nooni's body was wrung out and physically exhausted, yet she still couldn't stop herself from going for just one more.

"Please," she muttered through cracked, parched lips as she grabbed his ass and tried to pull him close again. "I need it. Just a little bit more...please."

"Nah, baby. You need to come down, that's what you need to do. They fuckin' you up, girl. They tryna kill you..." Truth's eyes were dark with worry as he stared down into the sweaty face of the girl he had grown to love.

Nooni's shit was all fucked up. Her face had broken out in sores, there was dried vomit in her hair, and her mouth smelled rotten as hell.

Guilt and regret flooded Truth's heart. Nooni didn't look a damn thing like the fly-ass around-the-way-girl that he had fought over in T.C.'s Place that crazy night, or the sexy *mamacita* who had cut outta school and rode with him to the G-Spot the next day.

Truth didn't know how shit had gotten bad so fast, but it did. The only thing he'd been tryna do was get his hands on some cash. Nooni was supposed to be a simple pawn, and that was the only reason he had gone along with Monique and Salida's grimy ransom plan from the gate. But these G-Spot muh'fuckas had gotten all extra with their endless greed and lust for doe and power. When the money scheme got deaded, instead of letting Nooni go like they said they would, she had become their junkie fuckin' prisoner, and Salida had turned her out on a steady diet of hard-core drugs that had fucked up her body and were about to fuck up her young mind too. That is, if Truth didn't get her outta there in time to save her.

He had thought shit was bad when they were staying with Pluto and Monique, but when Salida got run over in that alley, Ace had come and packed up Nooni's shit and moved it over to Salida's place. It was a wrap for Nooni after that. She had been on an everlasting meth high ever since.

Monique had walked in while Truth was complaining about that shit to his uncle Pluto, and her skank-ass had wilded right out.

"Let that bitch stay her ass over at Salida's house! She ain't coming back up in here, I can tell you *that!*"

"C'mon, Mo. You see how Salida's doing her! She's fucked up, man. All the fuckin' time too! That shit ain't cool."

"Oh shut the hell up, Truth!" she had blasted on him. "When you thought you was gonna get paid off her ransom money it was cool, wasn't it? Don't play ya self, clown. You was down from the jump. Ain't nobody tell you to start catching feelings for her ass. Nooni don't belong to you. Salida owns that ass now!"

If Pluto hadn't been standing there Truth woulda pushed his fist into Monique's mouth. He woulda broken her squeaky fuckin' jaw. But he was already in the shit-house with the G-Spot crew, and smashing Monique woulda made everything worse.

Ace had already slashed his status and demoted him from being Salida's driver to hustling out on the trap again. That dreadlock niggah Bilal had gotten his driving job, and he made sure Truth knew how much he loved sliding into his spot.

Wasn't nothing going the way it was supposed to, and Truth knew it was time for him to make a big move. But first he had to get Nooni out. Get her away from Monique *and* that crazy bitch Salida, and back home to her family where she belonged.

And once Nooni was safe and sound and they couldn't hurt her no more, then Truth was gonna dip out the backdoor and beat his damn feet too.

CHAPTER 20

The morning after the spoken word show I was feeling myself. Egypt had gone out, so I went downstairs to the counselor's office and got a notepad so I could start writing in my Juicy Journal again. I pushed all my pain and bad times out of my mind as I laid across my bed and dug into that old spot where my sexual fantasies had once flowed.

Dear Juicy Journal,

I know I shouldn't have done it, but I was horny and I wanted to fuck.

It seemed like forever since I'd felt the hardness of a man pounding between my legs, and the moment he walked into the room I knew I wanted to do him.

The poets had just finished their last set when the crowd broke out in applause. I couldn't believe my eyes when he stepped up to the mic and thanked everybody for coming out and showing their support.

Mmmm...I moaned under my breath as I clapped. Goddamn he was fine. Even finer than I remembered him being back when I lived on 136th Street and he was a beast-ass high school baller pounding that rock up and down the court. Well I had something he could pound, all right.

Our eyes met across the room, and it felt like an inferno sparked up between us. He penetrated me with his piercing gaze and my womanly juices started to flow. I gazed at him without blinking as my clit throbbed in my panties. I panted and twitched in my seat as my pussy popped deliciously in that sweet, familiar way.

The man was a beast. A dick slanga. I could tell he could put it down just by the way he looked at me. Like he was already all up in my pussy and denting up my walls.

I was dying to suck his dick. I pictured it matching his dark, muscular body. His lips were moving as he spoke into the mic, but I had gone deaf and dumb and I couldn't hear a damn thing. I wanted to walk over to him and tangle my fingers in the black velvet of his locks. I wanted to feel his curly moustache tickling my pussy lips.

The applause sounded again, and then suddenly it was gone. The whole world disappeared as he walked across the room and headed straight at me. He stood in front of me and I watched a knot rise up in the front of his pants.

"Take it out," I whispered as he inched his zipper down and then reached into his boxers. Carefully, he extracted his throbbing dick, and it looked so damn good I wanted to lick it. My shit was on, and I had called it right. That dick looked just like him. It was thick, dark, and long, a stunning rock-hard slab of muscle, and my breath caught in my throat when he dropped his hands, releasing that monster and showing it off.

It had been a minute since I'd seen one as pretty as his, but I swear it looked like dope and I was shaking like an addict. He stood there and let me feen for it as it stuck out from his body like a battle sword.

337

I jumped all over that baby. Grabbing it with both my hands, I opened my mouth wide and made a popping sound as I sucked the head straight past my lips. I paused and ground it tightly between my soft tongue and the roof of my mouth, and then I jutted my neck and plunged my head straight down toward his groin.

Moaning, he palmed my skull like it was a basketball and pushed his meat deeper into my mouth. My tongue twirled all over that chocolate pop as I opened that trap door in my throat and sucked him in.

"Yeahhh," he groaned out his encouragement. "Suck this big dick, baby. Suck it."

I went to work even harder and I really put that neck pussy on him as he mouth-fucked me like he was really up in my guts. I cupped his balls and let my cheeks collapse, blowing his head and making him grunt for more.

Moments later he shuddered and pulled away. I grinned up at him, knowing that I had almost copped that nut.

"Your turn," he said as he pulled me to my feet. It was all about me as he covered my lips and slipped his tongue deep inside my mouth. He unbuttoned my shirt and my firm twins jumped right out, rowdy and free. My nipples stiffened like pebbles as he unzipped my jeans and slid his hand inside my panties.

My pussy juices burned his fingers as he inserted them in my snatch. He stroked my swollen clit, slowly at first, and then faster as my hips started to thrust. Slowly, he used his other hand to inch my pants down around my hips, and they were barely past my knees when he lost it and gripped the cheeks of my ass. He bent down and bit into my pussy like it was a big juicy apple.

I shuddered as soon as his tongue touched me. "Uh-huh, give it to me," he demanded as he parted my pussy lips with his fingers and plunged his tongue deeply inside my wet forest. I yelped as he lapped up my juices and then used his soft tongue to spread them all over my clit.

He ate my pussy like he was a starving man, and when I felt him gripping my ass, spreading me open wide, I arched my back and clenched my teeth. His tongue felt just like a little dick as he inserted it deep inside me, and when his finger pressed up against my back door and then slipped up in there too, it was my turn to palm his head as I screamed and spurted sweet cum in his mouth, coating his tongue and lips with the big load of honey that I had just spilled....

I dropped my pen and sat up. Sweat had dripped from my face and fallen onto the paper. My pussy was wet. It was hot and it was ready. I wanted to open my legs and get the dog shit fucked outta me but the problem was, it was all just a fantasy. The same type of crazy stories I used to write back when I was a sexually frustrated teenager who was dying to get fucked.

The words I'd written had started out small and neat, but by the end of my little story they'd gotten big and loopy. I closed the notebook and slid it under my pillow. I thought back to the days when I used to masturbate on the pull-out sofa in Grandmother's living room, and then to all those nights that I had fingered myself to a silent orgasm while laying in the bed right next to G.

I had always craved dick. It was just in my nature to want to fuck. And right now I wanted to reach down in my panties and rub my pussy until it exploded, but I didn't. Because it wasn't a finger or a fantasy that I wanted. It was a man. And hell, since there wasn't nobody around to judge me but me, I just went on ahead and admitted it.

I wanted Trey.

$$$$$

When Chiney showed up at the homeless shelter begging me to come back to Harlem I thought she had lost her damn mind. I was stretched across my bed reading a real sexy book called, "Knockin' Boots" when one of the counselors banged on the door to tell me I had a visitor.

"*Me?*" I said stupidly, "Somebody is here to see *me?*"

I glanced at Egypt, terrified. The first thing that ran through my mind was that Flex had found me and had come to finish my ass off.

"It's a young lady," the counselor said. "Kinda tall, light-skinned. Pretty in the face."

"Come with me," I asked Egypt.

Chiney was waiting on the front porch when we got downstairs. A white sedan was parked at the curb. She broke out grinning as I stepped outside and we hugged each other tightly.

"Girl, what the hell are you doing here?" I said after I introduced her to Egypt. "You scared the shit outta me! When they said I had a visitor I thought somebody had found my ass!"

Chiney laughed. "I did find your ass! I came to get you, Juicy. To break you up outta here."

"But how did you know—"

"Trey," she said quickly. "My brother told me he saw you living up in here and it fucked my head up. So I came to get you."

I shook my head. "Are you serious? You came to get me to take me *where?*"

"Home with me! To Harlem. I stay at Trey's crib and we got plenty of room. Ain't no reason for you to be living like this when you can stay with us until you get on your feet."

I chuckled a little bit and backed up. "Uh-uh, Chiney. I'ma stay right here until they put my ass out in a couple of days, and then I'ma move on to the next shelter just like everybody else does. I'm not staying at your brother's crib, and I *damn* sure ain't about to show my face in Harlem. Niggahs is gunning for me up there, girl. I'd be stretched out cold in less than 24 hours."

"Juicy. C'mon now." Chiney sat down on the top step and pulled me down next to her. She frowned and shook her head. "Don't insult me like that. Do you really think I would come snatch you up outta Brooklyn and put you in a fucked up situation? You think I would put you in any danger, girl?"

I shrugged. I had told her a lot about my past while we were locked up on Rikers Island together, but I hadn't told her everything. "No, not on purpose, but it's not about you, Chiney. It's about my life and my situation. Hell no, I don't think you would let me walk into nothing crazy if you knew about it. But there's a lotta stuff going on with me that you *don't* know about."

"Ya think?" she said.

I nodded.

And then Chiney proceeded to spit out all the gritty, embarrassing shit I thought I had kept secret. She knew practically everything about what had gone down in

Harlem. From my days with G, to how I ran off with his son, to how Ace and Pluto had put a bounty on my head, and of course how I was now living in a shelter way down in Brooklyn.

"Ain't no secrets on the streets of Harlem, Juicy. You should know that by now. But trust me," Chiney said. "I already talked to my brother, and if you come stay with us you ain't gotta worry about nobody fuckin' with you, Juicy. Trey's got a crew, and they got you covered."

"They?" I smirked. "Who the hell is *they?*"

"My brother and every other hardbody in Harlem who's down with his Talented Ten crew."

I shook my head, not feeling it at all.

"I really appreciate you looking out for me Chiney, but I don't know if I can live with your brother."

"Why not?" Egypt butt in. She had been so quiet I had almost forgotten she was still standing in the doorway. "Why you can't live with people who are willing to look out for you, Juicy? That's kinda stupid," she said in her typical blunt way. "I mean, you came up in here to live with perfect strangers, and trust me, if that dude who pushed you on the train tracks had busted up in here tryna get after your ass, wasn't nobody here gonna help you. I don't see why you wouldn't go somewhere where somebody you trust is willing to look out for you. Don't be like me. A shelter hopper. When you're single with no kids it's not easy to get a bed in this system, girl. You better jump on this opportunity and not let it get away."

I thought about the heat I had felt in Trey's eyes just last night and a spark zinged through me. "I know, but I just don't want to..."

"C'mon, Juicy," Chiney said and stood up. I got up too, and her eyes begged me to trust her. "We got all the room you could want, and Trey stays gone all the time. Get your shit and come home with me, girl. You won't even know his ass is there."

$$$$$

Being back on my side of Harlem affected me in a way that I couldn't have predicted. The last time I'd seen these streets I'd been running for my life. Even in my dreams. But now, all the old sights and sounds, the corner stores and pizza shops, all of it came down on me and made my heart hurt inside my chest.

As scared as I was of what might happen to me here, this was home. It had been Grandmother's home, Cara's home, and Jimmy's home, and no matter who was after a piece of my ass, Harlem was my home too. And even though I had suffered here and lost so, so much, I had missed it.

"A'ight," Chiney said as she pulled up outside of a wide, one-story building with a lot of small windows on it. "This is it."

Chiney had told me we were gonna make a quick stop to pick Trey up before we went to the crib. She said he ran a community center for the children of Harlem, and that he had convinced a bunch of other organizations to donate computers, workstations, tables, chairs, and even after school snacks and meals.

There was a sign near the top with a big basketball holding up a bridge, and the emblem read, The Crossover.

"This is Trey's place. It's where he sponsors basketball and boxing, and a lot of other programs for kids."

I got out the car and stood on the sidewalk. For the longest time I just stood there staring at the wide building as neighborhood children ran in and out of the front door. From the outside it looked like a real cool place. Some of the kids were high-school age, and others were a lot younger.

"This is what's up," I said to Chiney. "I wish we would have had something like this when me and Jimmy was growing up."

"Me too," Chiney nodded. "All we had was a playground with some broken up swings and see-saws to keep us occupied. But kids around here got choices now, ya know? Irish Baines' old joint No Limitz is only a few blocks away. His boy Menace is running it now. And Candy Montana is still mentoring girls over at Power Productions with her man, Knowledge. Between places like those and what Trey has going in the community, these kids don't have no excuse to be scrambling and slanging out on the streets unless they want to."

The front door swung open again as we were talking. This time, instead of a bunch of lanky boys in basketball jerseys pouring out, a tall, well-dressed brother with amazing dreadlocks and a curly goatee stepped out. His legs were all-day long in his expensive slacks, and his shoes were made of quality leather without going overboard with it like Flex did with his countless pairs of imported alligators.

He crossed his arms over his broad chest as he stared at me and Chiney. The look in his eyes was unreadable, but it was focused and intense.

"Sup!" Chiney said, sauntering over to her brother.

The contrast between the two of them was crazy. They looked alike, but they weren't alike. Both of them had smooth skin, but Chiney's was light and Trey's looked like yummy milk chocolate. They both had the same nice features too, but that's where it ended. Chiney was all street and Trey looked like he was all about his bizz. Chiney was small up top and round on the bottom and had on loose jeans and red and white plaid men's shirt, where Trey was beastly, all dude. He had a muscled-up chest, broad shoulders, and banging arms.

I watched as Trey reached out and hugged his little sister and then kissed her on her forehead. She threw her arm casually around his waist. I felt some kinda way inside as they approached me, and I realized it was jealousy. Trey and Chiney were a heart and a soul. I could tell just by the way they looked at each other. I wished my brother was still alive so we could show each other that kind of affection and he could look out for me. Even though I had been the oldest, Jimmy had always, always protected me. Hell, he had given up his life for me.

Trey never took his eyes off mine as he walked up on me and stared without speaking.

"Stop playing," Chiney laughed. "Say hi to Juicy," she said, nudging him with her hip.

"What's up, Juicy," he said quietly. His eyes were so dark and so damn sexy. "It's good to see you again."

He nodded toward the building. "Welcome to The Crossover. Come on in. I gotta finish up a couple of things before we head to the house."

A cool blast of air hit me as soon as he opened the front door. I had expected to see a smelly, dusty gym, but instead it was bright and white and sparkling clean inside. A huge mural hung from a gold-trimmed board, and I could tell one of the dudes in the picture was Trey when he was younger. He was with another young dude who looked real familiar to me.

"That's Mayhem," Chiney said, standing next to me as I studied the picture. "Trey's best friend. Messiah and Mayhem. You remember him?"

I nodded. I did. He had been real tall like Trey, and both of them had been real popular. I kept staring at the picture. Trey looked so young and innocent with his body covered in sweat as him and Mayhem hugged each other while walking off the court.

"Yo, y'all come on," Trey interrupted us as he held the foyer door open and motioned for me to walk through. He led us up about four or five steps and directly into a large, open room that had most of it sectioned off as a basketball court. There were a bunch of kids running and dribbling and shooting the ball at the six rims they were sharing. Leaving me with Trey, Chiney ran out on the court and stole the ball away from one of the boys, and then she hiked up her pants and took him straight to the hoop.

"You a coach?" I asked Trey.

He nodded. "Yeah. We've got about ten teams we sponsor through our Crossover league," he explained. "We catch these kids when they're about seven or eight years old, and then we train them all the way through high school. It ain't just about basketball, though. We teach them how to survive and prosper too."

Off to the right was a raised boxing ring, and the floor area around it was cluttered with weight benches, speed bags, and a bunch of different sized kettle balls and other gym equipment.

"Over there is where we make men out of our boys," Trey said, following my gaze. "We put 'em in the ring and give 'em a safe place to get all that anger and frustration out, nah'mean?"

I nodded as he stopped in front of row of vending machines along the wall. Instead of being packed with the usual junk food these machines were full of bottled water, and apple, orange and grape juice.

"What's ya poison?" Trey asked, clinking some change around in his front pocket.

"I'll take an apple juice. Thanks."

He put those eyes on me again, and then nodded. "Good choice."

"Oh, I got a little change," I said quickly, digging in my back pocket.

He waved me off. "I'm good. They only cost a quarter. We keep it cheap so our kids can afford to buy it."

I stood there feeling kinda useless as he fed the vending machine. On the one hand, I felt like I had just dumped myself on some dude I didn't even really know, but on the other hand I couldn't get him out of my head.

Trey handed me an apple juice, and then he got a grape juice for Chiney and led me into his small office.

He nodded toward the couch and then went around and sat behind his desk. His office was painted in the Crossover colors of royal blue and white, had large glass windows that allowed you to look out on both the courts and the entire gym area. I sat on a soft white leather sofa and waited while Trey shuffled through a stack of paper that was on his desk. His phone rang and when he answered it I stood up and started checking out the hundreds of photos and plaques and awards framed neatly all over his walls.

I checked out some of the framed articles that were about an organization Trey had founded called The Talented Ten. The newspaper said it was an alliance of businessmen who worked together to keep the drug dealers from taking over the community and extorting money from legitimate businesses. According to the article they provided security in the neighborhood, mentored kids, and generally worked to take Harlem back from the hustlers and playas that had run the town into the ground.

There was another article about them on Trey's wall, and this one said the Talented Ten was made up of a group of local entrepreneurs who owned barbershops, grocery stores, urban clothing outlets, communications franchises, fish markets, fast food restaurants, computer repair shops, dry cleaners, and check cashing places. They seemed to have their hand in a lot of pies, and although they ran on the right side of the street, they had a lot of clout and a lot of power.

"You ready?" he asked me when he finished his call. I held up one hand as I finished reading all the way to the end of the article. I could hear Trey behind me as he locked a few file cabinets and pulled down the shades and a few moments later he said again, "You ready?"

"Yeah," I pulled my eyes off the wall and kinda smiled a little bit without looking at him. I never knew he was so large in Harlem, but after reading all that I was even more impressed.

We walked out of his office together and it was like I didn't even know how to be around a man like him. He was hardbody and street, I could tell that. But he wasn't rough or gutter like most of the dudes I had been exposed to were.

Just like Gino had been, I could tell Trey seemed smart and educated. He was also fine and his game was silky smooth, and he smelled so damn good...every time I looked into his eyes I felt like I was gonna drown in my own juices.

Stop playing yourself, stupid, I fussed at myself. I'd seen plenty of cats like Trey before. Their fine asses had money, they had a little positioning in the community, and they were usually dirty as hell. And talk about women? They had chicks out the ass. A big, powerful man like Trey just had to be a pussy magnet. He probably had women hiding in his bushes, under his bed, and all up in his clothes closet too.

We were walking through the center when I noticed the crazy shadows that were being cast all over the floor.

"What's that?" I asked looking up. A skinny dude was at the top of a long ladder. The ceiling was made of thousands of panes of glass, and almost every one of them had something written on it in shiny gold lettering. The noon sun was beaming brightly down inside the gym, and it caught the outline of the letters and cast them as shadows on the floor.

"That's our roof of regrets," Trey said. He touched my shoulder and we both stopped and stood in place. "Every pane of glass we write on up there represents the loss of a Harlem kid to street violence. Guns, knives, drugs, beatings, it don't matter. If they die on our watch we have their name, age, and date of death inscribed on a panel of glass. Eli is up there giving Princess her pane. She was only thirteen when she overdosed and died."

He shrugged and stuck his hands down in his pockets. "As you can see we're running outta room up there. Once the ceiling is filled up we'll have to start writing names on the windows."

"Wow," I said softly. My eyes scanned the endless written-in squares. "If those kids up there were still alive there wouldn't even be enough room in this gym to hold them all."

"Exactly," Trey said. He put his hand on my arm again, but this time he kept it there as we started walking toward the door again. "That's why it's important to give a visual representation so people can actually see how many kids we're losing. Just hearing a number doesn't do their deaths no justice. You actually gotta see it to believe it, and then some kinda way you gotta work to change it."

I nodded.

"Look, Juicy," Trey said as we continued to walk. "Chiney put me down on your situation. I know what's up, and I know all the people who've been fuckin' with you. The good thing is, they know me too." He gave me a serious look. "I ain't saying you don't have to be careful, but I don't want you stressing about nothing either, a'ight? I got my whole team standing guard for you. We roll real thick, and we hold it down. Don't worry about that lil niggah Flex, and don't worry about the G-Spot crew neither. I'm about to put the word out on the street, and that means you'll be safe as long as you're here with us, a'ight?"

I was more than grateful, and I couldn't help but compare Trey to Flex as I waited while he went and got Chiney off the basketball court. Both Trey and Flex had killed somebody and done some time, but they were nothing alike.

Flex was just a dumb kid running a drug empire and trying to take over the world like a mad scientist, and Trey was a grown-ass man who had done some bad shit in his past, but had survived it and made something out of his life. As I walked out of The Crossover and stepped into the bright sunlight under the Talented Ten's protection I was thankful that I wasn't gonna have to deal with Flex and his madness no more. But as I would soon learn, just because I was done fucking with Flex, that didn't mean his crazy ass was done fucking with me.

CHAPTER 21

The early fall sun was beaming down on Harlem as Flex rode down the street in his brand new Hummer. He'd bought it for cash the day after his other one got towed out of a parking spot in the BK. Instead of sporting the whip in candy-apple red again, this one was money green with 18-inch shoes, and it was even fresher than the last one had been.

Music was blaring from the speakers as he surveyed his drug territory. He nodded in satisfaction as he checked on his trap boys as they manned the corners and hustled that yay.

An occasional police sedan cruised down the street, but after a brief glance to see exactly who was conducting business they kept on cruising. They weren't pressed about the drug trade on the streets of Harlem. Since they couldn't possibly beat it, most of them simply turned a blind eye and profited from it.

"Ay!" Flex hollered from the passenger window as his boy Shorty stood posted up on the corner supervising his five-man crew. Shorty was one of Flex's favorite aks, and he had been thinking about promoting him to Divine Nine capo status to fill the spot that Cee-Low had left empty.

Shorty flashed him a sign, then sauntered over to one of his sons to replenish his supply of tan goods.

Flex liked the way that gangsta Shorty worked. That niggah was all bizz all the time. He kept his little soldiers standing at attention and his take never came up short.

"Yo," Flex turned to his boy Dre who was driving. "I think we should promote that niggah Shorty and bring him up, yo."

"What?" Dre said. He eased up to a red light and turned the music down. "Run that by me again?"

"Shorty," Flex said. "He's a real dude. I think we should promote his ass. Give him Cee-Low's crew. Nah'mean?"

Dre thought about it for a second, then nodded his head. "Yeah. That niggah's chill. He's certified and legit."

"A'ight," Flex replied, his spirits lifted. He turned his head and spit out the window. "We'll put him to the gut test and see where his heart is."

But moments later, as they rode past a popular community youth center called The Crossover, Flex peeped something that immediately fucked his head up and dogged his mood.

"Yo!" he said, sitting straight up in his seat. "Pull over, niggah! I *know* that ain't who the fuck it look like it is! I know that silly bitch didn't bring her ass back to Harlem!"

Dre pulled up next to a fire hydrant and put the whip in park. He took one glance out of his boss's window and clammed right the fuck up.

"I'on't know, man," he said like he had amnesia. "I'on't know who the fuck that broad is."

"Niggah, you ain't blind! You know that's Juicy!" Flex said, shock and amazement making his voice squeak. "And that's that niggah Trey Jackson flossing wit' her too!"

Dre bucked and threw his hands up in the air. "Goddamn, muh'fucka!" he blasted on Flex. "The last time somebody recognized ya girl you shot his fuckin' ass! I don't know *who* the fuck that chick is!"

Flex clenched his jaw and breathed hot rage through his nose.

"It's *her*, man," he said as he eyed the fine bitch with the gangsta booty. She was standing there with another chick Flex recognized as his man Cooter's little sister, Chiney.

Flex fumed as he watched Juicy climb in the front seat of Trey's whip and Chiney get in the back. Him and Cooter had been mad tight. In fact, they had started out as partners in a bold quest to pull a takedown on the G-Spot crew for control of Harlem's drug trade. But a series of unforeseen and tragic events had unfolded that tossed a big rock in their game. They'd been forced to accelerate their agenda when G got popped, but the framework wasn't firmly enough in place yet and their timing was off. Flex had gotten gut shot, and Cooter ended up taking a street beat-down that cost him his life.

Flex eyed that niggah Trey with big disdain.

Trey was Cooter's younger brother, but there had never been any love between him and Flex. Where Cooter was of the streets and deeply vested in the game, Trey had gone to the joint and came out damn-near sanctified. He had opened up a bunch of barbershops and started mentoring young boys, and him and Flex inevitably bumped heads because they were constantly trying to draw talent from the same limited pool. Trey recruited the youngstas in the community to cut hair out of his shop, and Flex recruited those same youngstas to sell ooo-wee on his corners.

Flex eyeballed that niggah warily. Trey had a way of flossin' that made him wanna bust that niggah one. He was one of them big, handsome niggahs who used to ball back in the day, and all him and his Talented Ten posse wanted to do besides cut hair and sell bean pies was work to put a niggah like Flex out of business.

Trey got in the car with Juicy and Chiney. Flex stared at all three of them, grinding his teeth. He couldn't believe Juicy was rubbing up against that niggah and riding around Harlem in his cheap car.

He thought about the jump-off he had fucked just two nights ago as he fantasized about Juicy. He'd chosen her because she had a body type that was similar to Juicy's, but the bitch ended up being a beast in the face and a skank in the sheets. She was one of those ruff project bitches, and with all that thick and musty underarm hair she was sporting, the girl had thrown his fantasy totally off and it hadn't felt like he was fucking Juicy at all.

"That scandalous bitch!" Flex spit, breathing hard.

Dre shrugged and waved his boy off.

"You know Chiney's a dyke, man. She be out here fuckin' bitches without a dick."

"Not her," Flex growled, his eyes never leaving the scene. "Juicy."

He sucked his breath in sharply as he saw Trey throw his arm over the back of

Juicy's seat and pull out into traffic. *That grimy muh'fucka...*Flex thought, and then an idea popped into his head.

"Yo!" he punched Dre in the arm. "Ain't them niggahs down at the G-Spot still looking for Juicy? They got some money on her neck, don't they? A cash reward for that booty, right?"

Dre nodded. "Yeah. As far as I know they still want her."

Flex grinned like a little kid. "Good. Send that niggah Pluto a text message for me," he said and laughed real loud. "Tell him I got some juicy info I wanna drop on him."

Flex was still grinning when another idea popped into his head. This one was a grand opportunity for him to play one camp against the other and cancel both of his rivals out.

"Yo!" he said abruptly. "Forget what I said about bringing that niggah Shorty up."

"Huh?"

"Cancel all that shit I just said about Shorty! That fool is gone have to wait on that promotion."

"Cool. Whattup doe?" Dre asked. "You got somebody else in mind?"

Flex nodded. "Yeah." Trey wanted to fuck around with his property? Cool. He'd stick it to that big niggah by corrupting his son.

"Go find me that niggah, Maleek. Tell him he's next up in the Divine Nine queue. Put him out there to make his daylight hit, then bring him to the crib so I can give him the gut test and let him press the six-shooter to his head."

"A'ight," Dre nodded. He checked his side mirror then pulled back into traffic. "You got anybody special you want Maleek to smash?"

Flex thought for a few moments and then smiled. "Yeah," he chuckled at his own brilliance. "Tell him to hit one of them G-Spot niggahs. Let him pick one. I don't give a fuck which one he burns. Just as long as he gets it in."

Dre stared at his boss with an impressed, knowing look, and Flex put his head back and laughed like a mothafucka. He'd found himself an opportunity to aggravate two birds with one stone. He'd let the G-Spot niggahs take care of smashing that bitch Juicy, and let Maleek stick a knife in the hearts of the G-Spot crew. Either way, Trey Jackson was gonna learn some real fuckin' lessons and suffer some real fuckin' pain.

CHAPTER 22

Trey drove me and Chiney down a narrow block that was lined with brownstones. It was one of those Harlem streets where the homes had been remodeled and white people had started moving in. He got my small bag out of his trunk and the three of us walked up the stairs to the small stoop.

"Make yourself comfortable, Juicy," Trey said quietly as he unlocked the door and I followed him inside. He handed me my bag and walked through the doorway of a nice-sized kitchen. "Chiney can show you where your room is."

I could tell from the jump what kind of energy Trey was packing. It was a black man's crib and it was laid out. It was decorated in masculine colors of mocha brown, rust, black, and off-white. The air was cool and the scent of African candles met my nose.

There was abstract black art on the walls, the kind they sold on 125th Street, and a lot of African statues and masks and stuff like that displayed on shelves.

"C'mon," Chiney said, scooting past me. "All the bedrooms are back here.

We walked down a long, narrow hall and she told me there were four bedrooms and two bathrooms on the main floor.

"There's another bedroom with a bathroom downstairs that Trey uses as his office and," she pointed and looked up, "we've got two more rooms upstairs. Trey is an exercise freak, so one of the rooms up there is his work-out room, and I don't know what the hell is in the other one because he keeps that shit locked and ain't nobody allowed to go in there."

There were four bedrooms lined up in a row on the right side of the house, and Chiney explained that the first bedroom was Trey's and the last one was hers.

"This is his shit," she said and touched his closed door. "I wanted this room 'cause there's a real nice bathroom in there, but Trey wasn't having it. My brother is real protective, Juicy. His has gotta be the first room in the house. Just in case some shit pops off. A fiend would have to get past Trey's room before they could get to me in mine, you know?"

I nodded. I could see Trey being that kind of dude.

"This room is yours," Chiney said, stepping just one door down from Trey's room and twisting the door knob. "It's cool in here. You'll like it."

I peered into the room and took a deep breath. It was simple, but really nice. There was a queen-sized bed with a rose-colored chenille bedspread, and a mix of cream and rose-colored throw pillows were displayed at the head of the bed. The floor was made of a dark, shiny hardwood, and there were cream and rose drapes up at the windows. I stepped inside and got a whiff of the candle-scent that was circulating through the house, and immediately I loved the flow of energy that surrounded me.

"There's a television and a DVD player over there," Chiney said and pointed across the room. A flat screen TV sat on a beautiful table display, and somebody had put a vase of fresh flowers right next to it. "And the bathroom is right down the hall next to my room."

I took a deep breath and looked at her, then sighed. "Chiney, I just don't know about all this…"

"All what? It's just a room, Juicy, damn! Relax girl, and just accept the love, okay? This is how friends do each other, right?"

"I know," I sighed. "I just don't feel good about staying here and living off your brother, you know what I mean? I don't have anything to give up for rent and food and all that…"

Chiney gave me a crazy look. "Damn, Juicy. Is it that fuckin' hard to admit you need help? You turning down a bed when your ass was just in jail a minute ago, and you slept in a homeless shelter last night. You need to check ya ego and let go of some of that pride, my sistah. I want you to stay here. And Trey wants you here too. So chill, baby. If you feel like you need to contribute something then ask Trey if you can help him out at the center. They got mad young girls dropping by The Crossover every day. Those chicks are surviving on nothing but their tits and their wits. Maybe you can holler at some of them and make a difference in their lives."

$$\$\$\$\$\$$

Flex mighta had a lesson planned for Trey, but there were lessons to be learned everywhere. And later on that night while Trey was sleeping he experienced a lesson that his waking mind had been trying real damn hard to deny him.

He was in a strange place but for some reason the girl he was making love to had a real familiar feel. He was riding her from behind, and the further he thrust into her, the deeper something stirred in his heart.

They moved like they were one, their rhythm dynamic perfection as she rotated her hips and he pounded his groin against her ass. Her hair was soft and thick as she pushed it over her head and exposed the back of her neck. He nibbled behind her ear and sucked that tender spot right at the base of her shoulder, sending sparks of electricity surging back and forth between their damp bodies.

Trey reached around and cupped her breasts and her nipples stiffened and throbbed against his palms. She moaned and he sniffed her hair, then licked her neck and pumped inside her even deeper.

The heat between them was getting intense. Trey withdrew his dick until only the head remained lodged between her pussy lips, and then he dove back in as far as he could go, the last few inches of him still outside of her. She screamed and inched up slightly on her knees, opening herself wider to him, her body adjusting to accommodate him as she panted and urged him to bury his whole rod inside her.

Trey deep-dicked her and made her happy. Her insides gripped him like a perfect glove as she shuddered and came, and if he could have he woulda kept his throbbing wood buried inside her wetness forever.

But then she rolled her ass like she was tossing a hula hoop, and Trey almost lost it. Sucking the back of her neck, he bore down on her three times real hard, and her walls swallowed him. She clenched her insides around his thickness and milked his dick until he felt his nut rising.

Trey was just about to bust when his eyes flew open. Gasping, he reached for his dick and found it rocked up like a piece of iron. He inhaled deeply and the sweet smell of pussy teased his nose. Trey rolled over and groaned. This type of shit hadn't happened to him in a real long time. Not since his days in the joint. He was embarrassed by his dream but he hated to let that shit go too.

He sighed with disappointment. He couldn't believe it. She had been in his arms. Right there in his bed. He'd never gotten a look at her face, but he sure as hell had recognized that body.

She was beautiful. A stunna. A straight-up, bona fide brickhouse.

She was Juicy.

$$$$$

I had been staying at Trey's house for less than a week and already that cold sexy niggah was driving me wild. I had taken Chiney's advice and asked him if I could hang out at The Crossover and help out with some of the kids, and he had surprised me and said he actually thought that was a good idea.

"The word is out deep on the streets, Juicy," he assured me. "Those fools at the G-Spot know not to fuck with you, but you know how it can be out here sometimes. All it takes is one wild cowboy to act up and cause major problems. My crib is pretty safe, but I don't really want you staying there by yourself if you don't have to."

As much as I hated to admit it, I loved hearing those words come out of Trey's mouth. He was so big and strong and he gave off an aura filled with so much power, swagger, and confidence that being around him made me feel safe and protected like I had never felt before.

So I started leaving the house with him in the mornings. With Chiney sleeping in her room knocked out cold, me and Trey would ride out to his barbershops so he could open them up and get his staff ready for the day, and then we usually ended up at The Crossover by ten o'clock or so.

I told Trey I was willing to type or file papers, or do whatever he needed me to do to help out around The Crossover, and he put my ass right to work.

But as cool and nice as Trey was when we were around each other, I got the feeling that he was trying to keep a whole lot of distance between us on purpose. I knew he had a lot of women because they were always blowing up his phone, but I hadn't actually seen him with anybody yet.

It was real late on a Friday night when Mister Trey kicked up a hot spark in me that damn near blew me out of the water. The Talented Ten crew had hosted a talent show for some of the younger kids at The Crossover, and a lot of people had turned out to support it. Local businesses had donated prizes to be raffled off, and some of the parents had volunteered to make some chicken wing and French fry plates and sell them out of The Crossover's kitchen. It was a pretty big event, and most of the money that was collected was going straight to the scholarship fund that Trey had established in memory of the teenager, Princess', who had overdosed on drugs and killed herself and her unborn baby.

My job for the night was to keep track of the raffle money and all the cash that came in at the door, and to make sure the kitchen register was straight and they had enough change on hand to keep the food sales going. I counted stacks of money and stayed outta sight in the small room behind Trey's office all night long, scared that I might see somebody I knew, and scared that somebody I knew might see me too.

Besides Trey and Chiney, the only person who knew I was even in the building was Rita. I had called her from Trey's office and her and her man Dutchy swung by to see me. I was too damned glad to see my girl, and so happy to meet Dutchy too. Rita had told me he was a good guy, and I could tell by talking to him that everything she'd said about him was true.

I was happy for Rita. I really was. As kids, both of us had survived some fucked up situations. My junkie mother had offered up my life in an attempt to save hers, and Rita had been forced to take her child-raping father's life in order to save her own. But at least things had gotten better for her over the years.

It was kinda late when me and Trey finally got back to his brownstone. He punched in the security code and unlocked the door and let me walk inside first, but before I could get to my room he called my name and said, "Juicy. Um, check it out. Thanks for helping me out with the money and all that tonight. That was real cool."

I wanted to say something back, but instead I just nodded and went inside my room and closed the door. Thirty minutes later I had taken my shower and climbed in the big, fluffy bed, and I was knocked out before my head hit the pillow.

But I didn't stay out for long.

A strange noise woke me up. It was coming from Trey's room right next door, and it only took me a second to realize what was up.

"Oh yeah, baby. Dig it out. Fuck this pussy. Ummm...yeah. Just like that, Trey. Oh, baby....this your pussy, Trey."

I opened my eyes in the darkness. Trey's headboard was tearing up the damn wall, and by the way some chick was screaming and moaning, Trey must have been tearing up her stuff too.

I started to go down to Chiney's room and see if she was up, but my girl had been sneaking chicks in the crib almost every night and getting her wild thang on too. And what was worse, as hard as Trey and his manz were working to keep kids off drugs, Chiney was still out there getting high, and I didn't like being around her when she was zooted and flying.

There was nothing I could do except lay there in the blackness and listen to Trey and his girl get their freak on. I tried not to, but I couldn't stop myself from imagining what Trey looked like naked, and how good girlfriend must have been feeling as he blew her back out.

Whoever the chick was, she talked mad shit as she was getting hers. She screeched and moaned and gave Trey big props as the bed squeaked and banged up against my wall.

Biting my lip, I flipped over on my stomach and flung the pillow over my head. I could still hear them loud and clear, and to my horror my clit was starting to throb and I felt myself getting slick down there.

I rose up on my knees and scooted my butt back the way a baby likes to sit. I stuck my fingers in my ears, and rocked back and forth a little bit and tried to sing a song to block them out, but my body had a mind of its own and pretty soon I realized I was rocking my bed to the same fuck-rhythm that Trey was rocking his to.

Giving in, I pressed my titties into the bed, and then brought my hands up to find my nipples. They were stiff and aching, and it felt strange to touch them in this way after so many months of feeling dead inside. I pinched them through the fabric of my t-shirt and I moaned as a thin trail of slobber pooled in my mouth.

I flipped back over on my back and shuddered as the girl in Trey's bed hollered, *"Ayyy. Ayyy! AYYY Yeah! Throw that big dick, Trey baby! Throw it!"*

My shit was a wrap after hearing all that. I kicked off my pajama pants and slid my hand down in my panties. I mashed my clit and plunged my finger deep into my own wetness. I moaned real loud as I arched my back in the darkness and fucked myself with pleasure. I pictured myself in the girl's place with Trey moving on top of me and driving his pelvis into my hips. Gripping my left breast, I swirled my finger around my clit each time I dipped it deep on the down-stroke, and my hips fucked up to meet my hands like Trey was on top of me banging me out for real.

It didn't take me long to come, and when I did, I clamped my thighs on my hand and continued playing in my own pussy as I squeezed and crushed my clit until the sweet feelings began to fade.

But once it was over I felt like shit. I used to be a professional masturbator back in the day, and I had explored every nook and cranny of my own body so I knew what I needed and I knew what I liked. It was kinda creepy, though, to be listening while somebody else fucked and to get off so deliciously on that shit. I knew I probably wasn't the type of woman that could attract a man like Trey, and I felt like I had disrespected him a little bit by listening in on his intimate night with his lady, and especially by fantasizing about him doing to me all the things that I could hear him doing with her.

But something about what Trey was doing next door had changed. The bed had stopped hitting the wall and the chick had stopped moaning. Instead she was yelling now. Bitching. It sounded like they were arguing, but I couldn't tell what it was about. All I could hear was her hollering, "No! What's my name? What's *my* name, Trey? Call me by *my* fuckin' name!"

I got up out the bed and crept over to the door. I had to pee and I wanted to go clean myself up a little bit, so I eased outta my room and ran down the hall to Chiney's bathroom.

I wasn't in there very long, and I was halfway back to my room when the door to Trey's room was flung open.

A cute sistah in high heels and a pair of tight jeans barged out into the hallway with Trey right behind her. He was naked except for the towel that was wrapped around his waist.

"Debbie," he pleaded. He reached for her shoulders and she jerked away. "It ain't even like that," he told her. "C'mon, baby. I'm sorry. I fucked up. It was a mistake. I don't know what I was thinking. It was a mistake."

She turned around to face him and I could see that she was beautiful.

"Nah, Trey. It wasn't no mistake! You said what you meant, that's all. Just admit that shit!"

"Deb," he said, but then girlfriend looked past him and saw me coming down the hall toward them drying my hands on a paper-towel.

"Excuse me," I said softly as I got near my door. I yawned and ducked my head a little bit as I reached for the knob. I already felt like a slut for getting me a nut while they were fucking, and I sure didn't want Trey to know I had been wide-awake and listening to him bang her all that time.

But his friend caught me in her glare and barked on me.

"Who's *you?*" she demanded.

I paused with my hand on the doorknob and looked up slowly. "I'm Chiney's friend Juicy," I said, and suddenly I was real conscious of the fact that all I had on was a thin t-shirt and a pair of boy-shorts drawers.

"*Ohhhh,*" girlfriend drawled and glanced up at Trey, who sighed and shook his head like, *damn!*

"Okay, *now* I get it," she said nodding her head and narrowing her eyes like a light bulb had just gone off in her brain.

"So *you're* Juicy, huh?" She smirked and looked me up and down. "Well, since you're the bitch whose name this niggah be moaning out when he's fucking, I guess you're the bitch he really wants to be with then."

CHAPTER 23

It was now or never, and Nooni knew she had to act fast. Once again Truth had shaken her awake from a drugged-induced stupor, and she had staggered into the bathroom sick, but stone-cold sober and plagued with feelings of deep shame and disgust.

Last night had been crazy. Monique and Bilal had pushed her into the XXX cinema room, then put her in a sandwich and used her poor body every which way they could. They'd fucked her up against a wall, and Bilal had penetrated her anally while Monique had gotten down on her knees and stuck her face in Nooni's pussy. Bilal had lost his nut after just a few minutes, but Monique and Nooni had switched positions several times, licking each other out until they both screamed with orgasms. Nooni had hated every moment of it even as she was doing it, but between the drugs and her emotional frailty she'd been unable to fight or resist.

Just minutes earlier Truth had found her sprawled out naked on the XXX cinema room floor, and when he woke her up the sensation of Bilal's joint was still throbbing up her ass, and the scent of Monique's pussy was riding all up her nose.

Truth had hugged her and told her everything was gonna be okay. He told her he was about to get her the fuck outta the G-Spot, and after making sure she understood his instructions he dipped outta sight just as Monique walked in the room and said Salida wanted to see her in G's office.

The office was empty when Nooni walked in, so she sat down across from G's old desk and waited. It wasn't even lunchtime yet and she could hear Salida and Ace next door in the stripper's dressing room trying to sweet-talk the building inspector outta giving them a violation, as they explained that a plumber had come out and fixed all their sewage problems.

Nooni sat there chewing on the collar of her wrinkled blouse and praying for good luck as she watched the ticking clock. Truth was waiting for her outside in the car and she knew she was almost out of time. As soon as she heard the flushing of multiple toilets in the stripper's dressing room she made her daring move.

Jumping up from the chair, Nooni peeked out of G's office and saw Ace and Salida leading the tall white man over to the bathroom near the bar. She waited until they disappeared from view and the coast was clear, and then like lightening she darted down the short hall and pushed through the back door.

Daylight hit her as she sped across the pavement like a monster was dead on her ass.

But instead of being pursued by a beast, her man Truth was waiting in the car with the passenger-side door open, just like he'd said he would be.

Nooni dove head-first into the whip, yanking the door shut behind her and shaking like a leaf as Truth came up off the gas and peeled out of the narrow alley.

"Stay down!" he warned her, his eyes glued to the rear-view mirror as he stomped on the gas and she cowered on the passenger-side floor.

The coast was real clear as Truth turned onto the one-way street coming out of the alley, and then hit the brakes hard as the traffic light at the corner turned red. The squeal of the tires cut through the air, and several heads turned in his direction.

"Just stay down," he repeated, trying to keep his voice calm for Nooni. "We out, baby. I got you out. Now you just gotta stay outta sight as we ride past the front of the Spot, okay?"

Hugging the floorboard, Nooni trembled in fear.

"Can't you just run the damn light?" she asked. Her terrified eyes searched Truth's face, scared like hell that somebody might run outta the G-Spot and drag her back inside.

"Nah," Truth said. "It's too much traffic out here." He was scared and counting the seconds until the light changed too. It finally did, but Truth knew the most dangerous part was about to pop off. If anybody had noticed Nooni missing or seen her sneak out the back door, then more than likely they would be looking for her by now.

Truth eased up off the brake and flowed slowly through the intersection with the rest of the vehicular traffic. Approaching the front of the G-Spot, he glanced toward the entrance and was relieved to see the door closed and the outside area deserted.

He took a real deep breath, and was just about to let it out when the first round hit him in the neck.

Pop!

The passenger-side window shattered, sending thousands of pieces of tempered glass raining down on Nooni's head. She rose up and glanced outside and saw her ex-boyfriend Maleek aiming his gat dead at her. A terrified scream burst from her lips and she ducked back down again.

Pop!

The second bullet sank into Truth's right shoulder.

Pop!

The third slug whizzed in from the shattered window. It penetrated Truth's right temple, exited his eye socket, and blew out the driver's window as it continued on its path.

The chaos of tires screeching, horns honking, and the terrified screams of pedestrians filled the air. People ran like hell on the streets. Some squatted behind parked cars, while drivers ducked down and put the petal to the metal, doing their best to get out of the line of fire.

From the floor of the car, Nooni could only scream. Truth's dead hands had fallen away from the steering wheel, and the driverless car had turned left into oncoming traffic, barely missing a passing garbage truck.

The car continued, out of control, until it jumped the curb and the front bumper collided with a Johnny pump, bringing it to a halt not more than three steps from the front entrance of the G-Spot.

The safety inspector was the first one out the door. He was followed closely by Greco, Ace, Pluto, and Monique. They stared into the glass-shattered windows, eyeing Truth's lifeless body and listening to Nooni scream for help.

"Oh, no," Pluto moaned, rushing over to his nephew and snatching the car door open. Truth's body fell over and Pluto caught him in his arms. *"Ah, shit man!"* Pluto cried out, his face contorted in grief and horror. "What the *fuck?*" he hollered at the sight of his sister's son. "Ah, *nah,* man!"

Salida was one of the last people to push her way out the G-Spot door, but she was the first one who saw shit for what it was.

"The girl!" she pinched Ace's fat arm and hissed under her breath as Nooni screamed her head off from the front seat. "Get her outta that damn car and bring her back inside!"

Ace rushed over to the passenger-side of the car and flung the door open. In one movement he scooped Nooni's ass up off the floor and cradled her in his massive arms. He positioned her head so that it was in the crook of his left arm, and then he squeezed her in a bear-hug that almost took her breath away.

"Say one word, bitch," he warned her in a deep growl. "One word, and I'll break ya fuckin' neck."

Nooni went limp with fear. Her desperate screams turned into soft hiccups as Ace carried her toward the G-Spot.

"I don't think you should be moving that child." An old bag lady standing next to a shopping cart filled with junk chastised Ace as he walked past. "How you know she ain't broke her back?"

"Damn Miss Bag Lady!" Ace barked, as he carried Nooni over the threshold of the G-Spot with Salida quickly following them. "What? You's a fuckin' bag doctor too? Ain't nothing broken on this broad. I got her ass."

CHAPTER 24

When Ace told that old bag lady that he had Nooni's ass, he really meant that shit. She was a prisoner for real now. With Truth dead—cold slumped for no apparent reason—Ace and Salida were about to play her ass closer than close.

"Where the hell did you think you were going?" Salida grilled her as Ace smacked the hysterical young girl upside her head. They were sitting in Salida's small office upstairs in the cut room, and Nooni was hysterical and feening for a hit. Bits of blood and gore from Truth's blasted dome stuck to her face and arms.

"Please, Mizz Salida...I *need* it..." Nooni cried, ducking Ace's next blow as she begged and shivered and reached her trembling arms out toward Salida.

"You need your fuckin' ass kicked!" Ace bellowed. "You just got a good niggah killed, you dumb bitch!"

Nooni's head swirled in a vacuum of fear and grief. She couldn't stop hearing the sound those bullets had made as they sank into Truth's flesh. Or the gurgling noise he made deep in his throat, and especially the sight of his mangled eyeball after the bullet tore through his brain and continued wreaking destruction on its exit path.

"Please...she begged. Her mouth was dusty and her bowels were going loose. "Mizz Salida, help me. Gimme just a little bit. I'll do whatever you want me to do. I swear I will!"

"What *I* wanted you to do," Salida said sternly, "was meet me in the goddamn office like you were told to do! We could have avoided all of this," she took Nooni's hand gently and lowered her voice. "None of this would have happened if you had just listened to me and trusted me!"

"I *do* trust you!" Nooni shrieked. Her raw need was gnawing at her. That monkey on her back was demanding to be fed. She dry-heaved from her empty stomach and her entire body convulsed in agony. "I swear I trust you, Mizz Salida. You're the only person I'll *ever* trust!"

"It sure doesn't seem like it," Salida disputed. "You don't run away from the people you trust, child."

"He *made* me run!" Nooni blurted out. The young girl wanted what Salida had so bad that she lied like a mutha on her dead man. "Truth made me go outside and get in the car! He said if I didn't...." she searched for something to say that would get her what she needed, "if I didn't run then something bad was gonna happen to me!"

"Don't you know all the bad stuff is happening out *there?*" Salida pointed toward the window as she went inside her desk drawer and came out with a small vial and a set of works. Ace and Nooni watched in silence as she cooked the crystals in a spoon and sucked the liquid up in a syringe.

"The cops are already looking for you because of that man you killed," Salida reminded Nooni as she stood up and grabbed her trembling hand. She slapped up a vein in the crease of the young girl's arm. "What do you think the police are going to do if they find out you were in the car with Truth when those bullets started flying? They're gonna want to know who was shooting and why. They're going to want to talk to you, Nooni. They're going to take you in."

Nooni's eyes were wide as she stared at the syringe in Salida's hand. She knew she was being elevated to the next level, and while the thought of getting on the needle scared the hell outta her, everything else about her life scared her even more.

She trembled as she held her arm out and allowed Salida to shoot a syringe full of liquid meth into her veins. Salida made soft, soothing noises as she pressed the plunger and flooded Nooni's system with heat.

"There you go," she cooed sweetly as Nooni sighed and relaxed. The young girl leaned forward and rested her cheek against Salida's stomach like she was her mother. Above her, Salida wrinkled up her nose. The smell of fear, sweat, bloody gore, and unwashed ass came off Nooni in a thick wave, and as much as she wanted to push the girl away, Salida patted her back and stroked her hair instead.

She glared at Ace and craziness was all in her eyes. "Run downstairs and get Monique for me," she demanded. "This here baby needs a bath. Tell Monique and Honey Dew to come get Nooni cleaned up so she can be fresh and ready for tonight."

$$$$$

Pluto was on fire. His nephew was dead, and somebody was gonna have to pay.

"I'ma kill her. I swear to God I'ma smoke that hoe! That little bitch got my fuckin' nephew slumped, man!"

Ace pushed back at him hard. "Yo, your nephew was aiding and abetting, P! That lil niggah was supposed to be working for us, but instead he was out there helping Nooni's ass get gone. How you gon' justify that shit, homey?"

There was no justification for Truth's betrayal and Pluto knew it. It fucked him up that his sister's baby boy had taken one to the noggin while helping their prized piece of property sneak out the back door, and the only thing he could figure was that the pussy musta got to him.

The boy's nose musta been wide open on that young piece of ass he'd been snuggling up with every night. And as much as it hurt his heart to lose him, Pluto knew Truth had violated the most important law of a street niggah's nature: never let pussy rule you.

But still. The boy had fucked up but that didn't have nothing to do with him getting smoked. Whoever had popped him had disappeared down the crowded streets and gotten away, but the streets had a way of offering up what was due, and that was a fact.

Sooner or later, Pluto knew he'd find out whose finger had been on the trigger of the gat that killed his nephew. And when he did, chaos was gonna come to Harlem and the gutters would run red with that niggah's blood.

"I feel you though, my dude," Ace said sympathetically. "All this shit is Nooni's fault."

"Nah, it's *your* fault!" Pluto shot back. "Who the fuck was supposed to be watchin' her? That old bitch Salida got you so pussy-stumped you let the little mouse squeak right outta the goddamn trap!"

Ace eyed his boy evilly. His woman wasn't gonna be too many more of Pluto's bitches.

"Oh, so we back on that ol' bullshit, huh? Every fuckin' thing is Salida's fault, right? Well suck my dick, niggah! Truth's head getting split didn't have shit to do with Salida!"

Pluto was just about to blast on him when his cell phone vibrated. He yanked it off his belt and saw he had a text message, and he couldn't believe who the fuck it was from.

"Yo," he said as he scrolled to open it. "Fuck that niggah Flex doin' texting me, man?"

Ace waited impatiently while Pluto took forever to read the message. "What it say, P? What that lil niggah got to say?"

Pluto frowned.

"Flex said he's turning in the G-Spot's most wanted. He said Juicy's back in Harlem and she's riding with Cooter's brother Trey. Flex don't want our cash reward for the info, though."

Ace frowned. Niggahs like Flex didn't give up nothing for free. "Well what that fool want then?"

Pluto looked up from his phone and said quietly. "He wants some info. Since he's giving us Juicy, he wants us to give up the name of G's main drug connect."

$$$$$

"If her little ass can run, she can dance," Monique declared to Salida as she led a freshly washed and shampooed Nooni over to a glistening gold pole.

"Get your ass up here," Monique demanded as she pulled Nooni onto the stage. "Hey," she called out loudly, "lemme get some music!"

A hot, funky beat blared through the speakers and Monique shoved Nooni roughly into the pole.

"You ain't no damn baby no more, so pay attention," Mo ordered. "Do exactly what I do."

Monique took a deep breath in, and exhaled it slowly through her nose.

"Close your eyes," she said, flexing her waist as she bobbed slightly at the knees. "You feel that?" she asked. "Can you feel that beat?"

Nooni closed her eyes and let the music wash over her. She relaxed and let her body do what the drugs and the music was telling it to do.

"Yeah," Monique said with approval. "Yeah, start right there."

She watched as Nooni's upper body started to coil and uncoil.

"Put some hips in it!" Monique ordered.

Nooni placed her palms on her thighs and started gyrating her sweet hips, kicking them out from side to side and pausing to put a little dip in the middle.

"Now flex your back. Curl it and pop it. Like a hot snake."

For the next thirty minutes Monique taught Nooni how to make a man scream just by taking off her clothes. Nooni was a natural too. With her curvy young body,

359

Puerto Rican hips, and bangin' sistah-girl's ass, she had it going on in several different directions at once.

Monique shared quite a few of her ill na-na moves with the young girl, and she was surprised at how quickly Nooni picked up on the concept as well as the moves themselves.

"The trick is," Monique said, as she watched Nooni turn around and jiggle her blooming onion, "you gotta be feeling it ya damn self. You gotta be straight turning yourself on out there if you wanna get all them deep-pocket niggahs hot. I mean, your pussy gotta be straight dripping honey, baby. It's gotta be hot and stankin', cause once them freaks get one good whiff of it I guarantee you they *will* wanna taste it."

Monique went on to teach Nooni how to pull herself up on a pole and spin around without looking stupid or breaking her neck, and she showed her some in-the-air splits and gyrations that never failed to have her customers hollering for more. Nooni was a little slower to learn the pole moves, but Monique was patient, and eventually the girl got to a point where she was looking pretty good.

Later that night, after Salida filled up her veins again, Nooni made her breakout appearance on the G-Spot's stage. Under Monique's watchful eye she got up there and pretended she was a slithering snake, swirling her hips like a hula dancer and stirring up a storm in them old men's drawers.

She went through three whole numbers, and she remembered almost all the moves Monique had taught her, and when she forgot one she just shook her ass like she was cumming and that seemed to do the trick. The customers loved it as her young flesh wiggled deliciously under the hot lights, and cash money sailed through the air all around her.

Monique was up next, and Nooni knew she was supposed to get off the stage fast so she could clear out for the main event. Even though she'd done a damn good job, there wasn't no whole lot of clapping or fanfare when she finished because Monique was the show-stopper and Nooni's little amateur routine was designed just to entice the crowd and warm shit up.

So as soon as her music stopped Nooni reached down and plucked up her bra, her shawl, and the ten and twenty dollar bills that were laying on the floor just like she'd seen all the other strippers do. And when she climbed down the stage steps she strode off into the crowd shaking her hips with mad sex-appeal and confidence, like all the other strippers did too.

But instead of jetting straight to the dressing room like the other strippers usually did, Nooni walked her ass right through the crowd and straight outta the front door.

Barefoot, and dressed in nothing but a thong and carrying her bra and a handful of cash, the young girl tied the shawl around her naked breasts, then fled tearfully toward the busy corner and flagged down the first bootleg taxicab that drove past.

CHAPTER 25

Your useless ass has *got* to be retarded!" Salida exploded. Monique had just come off the stage after her stripper set clutching the twenties and fifties that had rained down and littered the floor. Salida had pulled her into G's office and told her that Nooni was missing. The girl was nowhere to be found in the club, and nobody had seen her for the last thirty minutes.

Salida was on fire. "First you let Juicy get past you at the airport with all that goddamn money, and now Nooni's ass done gave you the slip too?" She shot Monique a look of pure disgust. "I want you to explain how the hell you let that dumb little girl get out the goddamn door?"

They were alone in G's office and Monique was fed the fuck up. A ball of hot anger rose up in her and she based so hard and loud that she caught both herself and the older woman by surprise.

"Me?" she screeched, sweating mad as she backed Salida down. "Me? I was up on the stage shaking my ass! How the fuck did *you* let Nooni get out the door?" Sliding her hand down in her purse and gripping her switchblade, Monique got up in Salida's face and grilled her like she was just another slimy bitch out in the street.

"Bitch I'm *tired* of your fuckin' ass!" she spit, coming outta her purse with her blade and pointing it dead at Salida's nose. Rage had made Monique cross the line, and she was so hot she took it all the way. Dropping all that phony sweetness and fake-ass respect she had once shown G's bitch, she twisted up her lips and blew some real shit all over the older woman.

"You know what? You ain't shit, Salida! Every damn thing that goes wrong around here is somebody else's fault! But *you* the one who came up in here throwing salt in everybody's game and messing shit up! We shoulda left your fuckin' ass in that nut house where G stashed you at because you are one trifling, crazy-ass *bitch!*"

Fire flashed in Salida's eyes, but then just as quickly it simmered and died out again. She knew she was at a disadvantage with Mo's knife stuck in her face, and instead of jumping bad or trying to find a weapon of her own, Salida took a deep breath and blew it out slowly.

"Okay," she said and stepped off calmly as daggers continued to fly outta Mo's storming eyes. "I'll be that crazy bitch. But I tell you what, Monique." Salida turned her back on the stripper and went to stand in front of G's long mahogany-framed mirror. She smoothed a strand of her hair and adjusted her suit collar and gave it a little pop.

"There's a big difference between crazy and stupid, baby. You see, crazy is a bitch like me who took a bright idea and made it a half-a-million dollar reality. Stupid is a hussy like you whose only reality lives in her gutted-out pussy."

It was all Monique could do to stop herself from running across the room and plunging her knife into Salida's treacherous back. She wanted to stab that old bitch a million times, the same way she believed Salida had back-stabbed her.

But Mo didn't. Because as mad as she was, she was still street-smart enough to sense the truth of Salida's words. Salida had gotten outta the crazy house and commenced to making big moves, while Monique had been slaving away in the G-Spot for years, and the only moves she had made had been with her hips.

The realization that Salida was right and that she had wasted so much time conniving and tryna get ahead but had still ended up without a goddamn thing was a deep blow to Monique's gut. All the fight went outta her and she dropped her knife back into her purse and turned away.

"You better stay the fuck off my back, Mizz Salida," she said as she yanked open the office door. "I did everything you told me to do, and you still fuckin' with me. Just stay the fuck off my back!"

Monique stomped out the door and slammed it as hard as she could. She was so mad that she didn't even hear the loud crack the wooden door made as it collided with its frame. She didn't hear the loud cackle of laughter that erupted from Salida's crazy lips neither.

CHAPTER 26

Rita was watching little Chub and her friends pin the tail on a donkey when, for the second time in less than a year, she opened her door to a half-naked, beaten down girl who had ran up outta the G-Spot.

"Nooni!" she screamed and pulled the shivering teenager through the door. The girl was hysterical. Her eyes were bloodshot from crying, and she was shaking like a leaf.

"Lock the door!" Nooni shrieked as she jerked out of her sister's arms. She pushed the door closed quickly, and then flipped the three heavy deadbolts until the tumbler slammed in the lock.

Dropping her bra on the floor, Nooni ran over to the windows and pulled down the blinds and closed all the curtains. Her eyes darted toward the kitchen, and she skirted inside and pulled two butcher knives from the rack sitting on the counter before shrugging the shawl off her shoulders and glancing around uncontrollably.

"I'll kill those mothafuckas!" she gripped the butcher knives and threatened, wild-eyed and wearing only a thong. "I'll kill all of them!"

"It's okay, Nooni," Rita whispered, not wanting to alarm the three little girls who were playing in the back room. She grabbed Nooni's wrists and gently urged her to put the knives down and then took her into her arms. "It's okay," she said, sinking down to the floor and holding the girl like she was a baby. "You're safe now, chica. Nobody's going to hurt you. You don't need any knives. You're safe."

Nooni huddled in her big sister's arms, weeping like the child she was. She had been so fast and grown and hot in the ass that she had never considered how cold the world could be beyond the safety of her family's front door.

"I'm sorry." Nooni clung to Rita and whispered through her tears. She was ashamed of all the foul, dirty shit she had participated in. From faking her own kidnapping to helping lure her sister and Juicy into a money trap. "I'm sorry for everything, Rita," she moaned, meaning it from the bottom of her tender heart. "I swear I'm sorry."

Rita consoled the girl the best she could. She was so happy to see her little sister alive that she didn't even try to hold back her own tears. She just let them flow unchecked.

"It's okay," she whispered, rocking her little sister back and forth. "It's over. You're home now, and you're safe."

$$$$$

While Nooni was safe at home with her family, somebody else's child was about to take a ride with a stranger.

Pooch Johnson hated kids. It was just after two p.m. when he drove his big yellow school bus out of the yard where the large fleet was parked. His suburban New York route was one of the most sought-after in the Mount Vernon school district, but dressing up in a blue uniform and driving a bunch of hyped-up preschool brats irked the shit out of him every day.

Pooch pushed his tiny speaker plugs deep in his ear canal so he could listen to some tracks on his way to pick up the kids. Listening to music while driving was against the bus driver safety rules, but fuck all that. If he didn't have his sounds he wouldn't make it two blocks without tossing some of them whining-ass kids out the window.

He scrolled through the songs on his iPod and turned the music up as loud as it would go as he pushed the school bus down the road and headed toward the preschool he was assigned to.

He had just made a right turn and was taking his usual short-cut through an abandoned industrial park when a man staggered out of the woods and ran directly in front of his bus.

Pooch slammed on the brakes and the tires squealed loudly as they fought to grip the pavement.

"Oh, shit!" Pooch put the bus in park and ripped his ear-plugs out and flung his iPod to the floor. He stood up and peered outta the window and over the nose of the bus. Dude musta been laying under the front end, even though Pooch coulda sworn he'd braked in time to miss hitting him.

"What the *fuck?*" he hollered as he released the hydraulic lever and opened the door. He went down the steps in one big leap and ran around the front of his bus with his heart beating like a hammer in his chest.

"Why the hell you run out in front of me, you fuckin' fool?" he screamed on the downed man. He glanced around at the empty, deserted road. "And where the fuck did you come from?"

Pooch crouched down beside the still man and trembled. "Ah, shit!" Hitting a pedestrian would automatically get a niggah fired. What was wrong with this fool? Wasn't even shit out here! No houses, no cars, no *nothing!*

"Yo, you okay?" he asked, touching the man's shoulder. Dude looked like he was in his late twenties, and he was dressed in sweat pants and a dark hoody.

"Yo, muh'fucka!" Pooch shook him a little bit more and frowned. "Wake ya stupid ass up! That's what you get for running out in front of me! I couldn'ta hit you that bad anyway. I barely fuckin' touched you!"

Pooch reached out to shake the man one more time, and that's when dude got him.

"Be easy, muh'fucka," the downed man said, yoking Pooch around his neck and pressing the cold barrel of a Glock under his chin at the same time. The so-called "hit" pedestrian flipped Pooch over on the ground, then stood up and put his foot on the school bus driver's heaving chest as he held him at gunpoint.

Pooch lay flat on his back with his hands down by his sides. "W-w-what's up, man?" he asked as he stared up in fear and surprise. "I don't carry no money, niggah. So what the fuck you want?"

Dude's demand was real calm and real simple. "I want your ride, man. Give up the keys."

Even with a gat in his face Pooch couldn't help but chuckle. "Fool, I *know* you ain't jacking me for no fuckin' yellow school bus!"

Ol' boy nodded and looked Pooch up and down from head to toe. "Yeah I am. And for ya kicks and ya cool blue monkey suit too. Give 'em up, my niggah. Give 'em up."

$$\$\$\$\$\$$$

Out of all of Flex's capos in the Divine Nine, Lil Lee was the most beautiful and the most dangerous too. Niggahs got caught sleepin' on her all the time because from the outside she didn't look a damn thing like who she actually was.

Unlike the foolhardy dudes in her click, Lil Lee had escaped the urban trappings and moved outta the hood. Yeah, she ran her set there and did her business there, but she didn't live there, and there was definitely a good reason for that.

Lil Lee drove her nondescript black hatchback down the tree-lined streets of her suburban neighborhood. The houses were small, but the grass outside was green and the hedges and flowerbeds were neatly trimmed. She had come a long way from the projects of Harlem, and she had no problem making the commute back into the jungle early each morning because her sweet reward was always waiting for her when she returned in the afternoon.

But today was different. She noticed it as soon as she turned onto her quiet little street. Her daughter's school bus was there, parked right outside her house, and since her block was the driver's final stop she always made sure to leave the city in time to beat her little girl home by at least fifteen minutes.

The school bus was blocking her driveway, so Lil Lee pulled up behind it and jumped out as fast as she could. Her designer heels clacked on the sidewalk as the muscles in her toned legs flexed with each long, hurried stride.

She was almost up on her porch when she realized what time it was. The bus driver was sitting on her top step grinning with his little blue hat cocked to the side. Her four-year-old daughter, Yahyah, sat beside him holding a half-eaten McDonald's chicken nugget and sipping from the blue-ice slushy that the bus driver carefully held to her lips. At their feet the remnants of Yahyah's meal were laid out neatly on a napkin. An opened pack of ketchup, a few French fries, and half a chocolate chip cookie.

"That was good, Mister Keep Kids Safe!" Yahyah squealed, then tooted her blue lips up as the bus driver patted them carefully with his napkin.

"Come here, Yah," Lil Lee said quietly. She walked up two steps as she fought to keep the rage and fear out of her voice. She held her hand out to her daughter. "Come over here to Mommy."

The bus driver smiled at the little girl and nodded, then pat her back as she stood up and went to her mother. Lil Lee bent down and kissed the top of her head, and the little girl wrapped her arms around her mother's knees.

"What the hell are you doing here, Trey? How the fuck did you get my daughter?"

Trey grinned and spun his bus driver hat around to the back. "Who, Yahyah? Oh, I got your little girl the same way you been out there getting other people's little girls. I took her."

Lil Lee's lips twitched and her hand itched with the urge to grip her piece.

"This ain't part of the game," she growled between her teeth. "You made a big mistake going after my fuckin' kid."

"Ain't no rules in this goddamn game," Trey said coldly and stood up. He looked at Lil Lee's daughter and then back at her with disgust. "You somebody's mama and you out there spitting on dead kids and pushing poison in babies. What? You thought I forgot about that shit?"

He stepped down toward them and gave the little girl a small pat on the head before grilling her mother again. "You think just because you moved her outta Harlem your kid is gonna be safe while you line somebody else's kid up in your grimy fuckin' crosshairs?" He shook his head. "It don't work like that, baby. Anybody can get picked up and picked off in this game. *Anybody*."

Lil Lee pressed her daughter closer to her body and her eyes flashed with unbridled rage. "I ain't gonna forget this shit, Trey," she promised him. "I swear to God I ain't never gonna forget it."

Trey gave her a brief nod. "Good. I hope you don't. But remember, I brought your daughter home to you in one piece. I fed her and protected her, and I kept her happy until you got here. But if one person's kid ain't safe on our streets, then ain't *no* fuckin' body's kid safe. Not even yours. And that's some shit you *better* not forget."

CHAPTER 27

Once again, Ace and Pluto were going at it.

"This time we're doing every fuckin' thing *my* way," Pluto declared as him and Ace passed a fat blunt back and forth between them and chugged back three straight shots of gin.

They had studied Flex's text message and hit him back and exchanged a few comments, and once again they could see their way towards the possibility of bulking up their street business and putting some real ends in their pockets.

"Yo," Pluto said, "I think Flex is on the up and up about hooking up with G's distributer and us taking him down the middle, but before me and you jump off in any damn thing we gotta get some shit ironed out, ya dig?"

He stared at Ace, challenging his gangsta.

"You whipped niggah," Pluto said. "Your ass is whipped. You too fuckin' blind to see that Salida's doe is *Salida's* fuckin' doe. I don't give a fuck how much bank she's pulling in or how many light bills she's been paying. She ain't tearing me off and puffing up my pockets, so you can kill all that bullshit noise."

Ace nodded. This was about business, and it wasn't the time to dispute the truth.

"So if we get down like you wanna get down, then I say we do just like we been doing. We just do it with a different twist."

"Different how?"

"If Flex is right and Trey and the Talented Ten got Juicy under their wings, then it would be stupid for us to just pop off buck-wild and rush in on them tryna get at her. Shit would get real bloody in Harlem, and real quick too."

Ace nodded again. His manz had that shit correct. Right now there were three main factions runnin' shit. The G-Spot Crew, Flex and his Divine Nine, and Trey and his Talented Ten.

All three of them were hardbody and none of them would bend, and if shit ever got rowdy between them there would be some straight-up pandemonium, turmoil, and chaos, and there would damn sure be some bloody fuckin' combat.

"So, let's play this shit smart," Pluto suggested. "Let's keep right on squeezing Juicy. We might not be able to get G's money outta her, but we can use her to get the name of G's connect. And once we got that, we can get down with Flex."

Ace shook his head. "I been witcha all the way, baby. But I gotta jump off the train right here. Juicy is the *last* person who would know that kinda info. G would never breathe a single word to a bitch like Juicy about his business."

"I know all that!" Pluto barked angrily. "Niggah stay with me! Keep ya head in the game while I draw this line. Trust me, it links from Nooni to Juicy to Trey…and then to what all of us really want."

"And it starts with *Nooni?*" Ace smirked and shook his head. "Yo, son, we lost our pawn just now, remember? That bitch dipped out the door! We ain't got shit left to bargain with. How we gonna put the squeeze on Juicy with Nooni gone? That bitch is free as a breeze."

Pluto shrugged. "So what? Manhattan is an island, slime. She ain't gone but so far, my dude. All we gotta do is go get her ass. I got some sons in my pocket who can go in hard on that bitch and bring her ass back."

Ace still wasn't with it. "But you tryna draw a line between Nooni and Juicy and Trey and—"

"And ultimately to the *one person* who knew every fuckin' thing in the world about G. To include who his connect was."

Ace frowned and looked confused. "Who you talkin' about man, *Salida?*"

It was Pluto's turn to smirk. "Please," he said shaking his head in disgust at his boy's stone-blind inability to see. "Niggah, *please.*"

CHAPTER 28

After scrubbing herself from head to toe in the longest shower she'd ever taken in her life, Nooni had dried her hair and put on some clean underwear and a pair of Tweety Bird pajamas.

Paranoid like hell and coming down off her high, she'd peeked out all the windows and checked the locks on the door about twenty times before Rita made her go lay down in her bedroom.

"I wanna talk to Nooni," little Chub had whined as Rita stopped her from entering the bedroom where Nooni was trying to rest.

"Sorry, Chub. Nooni is tired, and plus you already saw her. Go back to your room and play with your friends, okay? They're gonna be leaving early in the morning so y'all better play and have some fun while you can."

"Well, can we have a snack then?" Chub asked hopefully.

Rita sighed. Not only was the little girl eating her outta house and home, she was gaining weight so fast it was scary. Dutchy had told her he'd caught Chub sneaking out the bed and creeping in the kitchen to raid the cabinets at night, and Rita believed him. She'd gotten rid of almost all the snack food she had in the house, but Chub was an indiscriminate eater. It didn't matter if it was cookies or kernels of corn straight out of the can, the little girl would eat any damn thing and it seemed like she had a bottomless stomach.

"How about an apple?" Rita offered her gently. Chub's doctor had suggested that she give the girl healthy snacks as opposed to denying her everything all the time. Rita kept fresh fruit in the house but Chub would grub non-stop on that too.

In the kitchen, Rita rinsed off three apples and sliced them, then put the shiny red chunks on a large plate and handed it to the little girl.

"Okay," she reminded Chub. "This is your last snack for the night, okay? Once I put you guys to bed you gotta stay there, do you understand me?"

Chub nodded.

"That means no getting up and sneaking in the fridge, or rambling through the cabinets while everyone else is asleep, *comprende?*" Rita held out her fist for a bump.

Chub grinned. She liked it when Rita spoke Spanish to her. She didn't know very many Spanish words, but she wanted to learn more.

"Comprende!"

They bumped fists and Chub took the plate of fruit into her bedroom to share with her friends, while Rita went back in her own room to check on Nooni.

To her relief the girl was fast asleep and clutching her pillow. Every few seconds Nooni's body would hitch and jerk, like she was reliving a terrifying nightmare in her dreams. Rita felt horrible for what she knew her sister had been through. She had wanted to call the cops and send them over to the G-Spot to shut that fuckin' joint down, but Nooni had begged her not to call anyone.

She'd babbled some nonsense about how the cops were after her for killing a man in Atlantic City, but Nooni seemed kinda spaced-out and paranoid and nothing she was saying was making a bit of sense.

Rita wanted to know about everything that had happened while Nooni was gone, but she knew it wasn't time to press the girl yet. She remembered how Juicy had described her time as a prisoner in the G-Spot. She had no idea how Nooni had managed to survive for as long as she did, but she was grateful that her sister had made it out of that hellhole alive and in her right mind.

Taking her cell phone from her night table, she tiptoed out of the room to call Dutchy. They were supposed to get together for some hot sex tonight, and since Chub had Lucie and Charlize over, Dutchy had agreed to wait until the kids were asleep before coming over to slip in bed beside her and get up in that gushy.

But Nooni was laying on his side of the bed right now, and she sleeping fitfully too. There was no way Rita was gonna put her sister in her own room by herself, and there was no way she wanted any man, even her good one, in her sister's space until she'd had a chance to recover a little bit.

Dutchy was supposed to drive her to a job interview in the morning, but he was gonna have to chill at his own crib for the night. He was a real good dude and Rita knew he would understand.

She quietly closed the door to her bedroom and went next door to Nooni's room. The bed was made and the room was neat, but it somehow felt cold and empty, like Nooni's essence was still missing from the house. Rita clicked on her cell phone and hit a number that was on speed-dial.

As she waited for Dutchy to answer her heart flooded with relief. Nooni was home. Her baby sister was back, and she couldn't wait to give Dutchy the good news. He answered the phone on the second ring, and for the next thirty minutes Rita told him everything that had happened since Nooni had stumbled through the front door.

And just as she thought, Dutchy understood completely.

"Take care of your sister, baby. You and me got plenty of time to do our thing, okay? Plenty of time. And don't worry. I'll be there first thing in the morning to pick you up for your interview. I love you, Rita, and I'm glad your sister came back home, baby."

Rita hung up the phone with a small smile playing on her lips and headed to the bathroom to take a shower. Something told her that life was about to get real good for her. She had her sisters with her, a shot at a damned good job, and the love of a good-ass man. She was looking forward to sleeping next to Nooni tonight, but a big part of her was looking forward to seeing Dutchy in the morning too.

$$$$$

It was slightly after three a.m. and the rumbling of her empty stomach woke Chub up from a deep sleep. She lay under the covers between her friends Lucie and Charlize, recalling every word her big sister had said about sneaking out the bed and stealing food in the middle of the night.

Moonlight streamed in from her window and she heard the faucet dripping in the bathroom sink. Chub tossed and turned, sandwiched between her sleeping friends, and trying hard to ignore the terrible gnawing in her growling belly.

Squeezing her eyes closed, she forbid herself to get out of bed, and tried to will herself back to sleep. She didn't want to disobey her sister, and the poor girl fought her hunger pangs for a good half hour, but as usual, she gave in to her overwhelming yearning to eat.

Moving slowly, she inched her way out of the bed, being careful not to make any noise. She was good at this, Chub was. Sneaking and creeping through the dark house while everyone else snored in their beds.

Mouse-quiet, she slipped out of her room and made her way down the hall. She paused outside of Rita's bedroom, where both of her sisters soundly slept. Chub continued on her journey, undeterred by the lack of light to illuminate her way. She knew every bump of the wall by heart. Every sharp edge of furniture, every squeaky floorboard, was imbedded in her memory.

In the kitchen she paused to debate whether or not she should risk opening the fridge. The last time she'd tried it Rita's boyfriend Dutchy had woken up and caught her, and she didn't want to see that disappointed look on her sister's face again.

Chub decided to go for the treats that were in the cabinet. Since Lucie and Charlize were staying over, Rita had relented and bought a box of white powdered donuts and a Louisiana Crunch cake. She'd also bought a box of red, white, and blue bomb pops, but Chub had already decided the fridge and the freezer were off limits.

Crouching down to the floor, she opened the bottom cabinet and reached into the darkness. Her hand had just closed over the soft bag of powered donuts when she heard heavy footsteps and knew someone was coming.

Panicked, Chub jumped to her feet and rushed from the kitchen. The footsteps were directly outside the front door, and she stopped in her tracks. Dutchy! Spinning on her heels, she waddled back into the kitchen as fast as she could. She glanced at the table, and considered yanking the chairs back and scooting underneath it, but there was no time as the front door opened violently and light spilled in from the hall.

Biting her lip, Chub snatched opened the broom closet and jumped inside. Using one finger, she pulled the door closed and then pressed herself as far back into the corner as she could.

She listened closely, breathing hard. Dutchy had brought company over. She could hear several men moving through the apartment, and they were moving very fast.

The first shot sounded like a car backfiring. But then one of her sisters screamed, and Charlize woke up and started crying.

The next two shots came back to back, one right after the other.

There were more screams after that. Terrified, frantic screams. It sounded like they were beating her sister Nooni and dragging her down the hall. Chub squeezed her knees together so she wouldn't pee, and then she pressed her fist deep into her mouth to stop herself from crying out loud.

Moments passed. There was no more screaming or crying now, but Chub could hear men cursing, and it sounded like her sister Nooni was begging and praying real loud. She wanted to go out there and see what was going on, she wanted to go help Rita and Nooni, but she was frozen in place with fear pounding through her veins with every beat of her young heart.

Suddenly there were more footsteps, and they were a lot closer to her now. Chub wheezed deeply as somebody walked into the kitchen and paused only steps away from where she was hiding.

"Ay! Let's get the fuck outta here!" she heard a man yell in the distance.

Whoever was in the kitchen answered him back.

"Hold up, niggah. I got the munchies."

Chub's wheezing grew deeper and louder. She lost control of her bladder as the sound of the man opening and closing cabinets reached her terrified ears. He was right on the other side of the door, and she trembled when she heard him say, "Ooohh, white donuts. These are the shit."

The bag of donuts made a crinkling sound as the strange man picked them up and stomped out of the kitchen holding them in his hand.

It seemed like forever that Chub waited in that hot, dusty closet, but she was far too terrified to move, even after the house grew eerily quiet in the early morning dawn.

Chub fell asleep, and she had no idea how many hours had passed before she awakened to hear footsteps, and then voices again.

"Rita!" a lady called out. It sounded like their next-door neighbor. "Marguerita! Why you go leaving your front door open for?" the Cuban lady yelled. "You want people should come in and rob you?"

The footsteps faded and disappeared down the hall toward the bedrooms. And then suddenly there was a loud scream.

"Oh my God! We need the police!"

Chub opened her eyes. The voice sounded just like their next-door neighbor, but she couldn't be sure. She closed her eyes again and drifted back into a fear-induced sleep.

Time passed, and sometime later the frightened eight-year-old was awakened again.

"I found another one!"

Chub squinted. A man with a blue uniform was peering into the broom closet and shining a flashlight in her eyes.

"She's alive. We've got one who's alive!"

Chub yawned and clutched her stomach. She was so hungry.

"Are you okay, little girl?" the officer asked. "Come on out, dear. You're safe now. Nobody's gonna hurt you."

Chub took the hand that was being offered. She stepped out of the broom closet and into the kitchen. It was morning time. The sun was shining. She glanced down at the floor and saw the dirty footprints and streaks of blood that had been left by the man who stole her powdered donuts.

As the policeman led her from the room Chub saw scratch-marks on the wall, like a cat had been dragged out of the apartment. The police officer called out to someone in the back of the house.

"That's a total of four, McNair. The first ambulance already left with the three victims who were shot, and I've got one survivor right here with me. The second ambulance just pulled up outside."

Chub stood there silently. The policeman had just said there were a total of four people, but there had been five people sleeping in her apartment last night.

And when Dutchy Gaines arrived on the scene minutes later to find crime tape stretched across his girlfriend's apartment door, he broke down crying at the carnage that greeted him.

"You okay, Chub?" he bent down and clutched the stone-faced little girl to his chest as they led her down the steps and outside to the ambulance. "Are you okay, baby girl?"

Anguish filled his heart as Chub stared straight ahead without a hint of emotion or recognition in her eyes.

Dutchy grimaced as they put Chub in the ambulance. What kind of fiends would pull a kick-door on a house full of women and shoot innocent little kids in the head?

"At least that kid survived," Rita's building manager called out as Dutchy hurried back to his car so he could follow the ambulance to the hospital. "They said Rita and two other little kids got shot in their sleep, but Chub was hiding in the closet so they missed her."

Dutchy heard what the man said, but it took him a minute to realize that something was out of order about the whole damn scene. He was halfway to the hospital when he remembered the long conversation he'd had with Rita about why he couldn't come by her crib last night.

They said Rita and two other little kids got shot in their sleep, but Chub was hiding in the closet so they missed her.

Rita has been babysitting for two little girls last night. Dutchy's heart pounded in his chest when he did the math and realized that yeah, Rita's baby sister Chub was damn lucky to still be alive, but once again, her other sister, Nooni, was gone.

CHAPTER 29

The brown-skinned beauty laying spread-eagle on the bed had Chiney straight-up pussy whipped. Dressed in a skimpy black thong and a sheer, front-snapping black bra that had come undone, her wrists were tied to the bedposts by silk scarves in soft shades of orange and yellow pastel. Her feet were tied as well, with similar scarves in pale pink and mint green.

Both women were flying high on some real good Red Devil, and the beautiful girl looked anything but stressed as she lay vulnerable and exposed, her taut stomach quivering with anticipation.

Chiney stared at the twin mounds of 38-D cup flesh that was being presented to her, and her mouth watered at the sight of the chocolate-chip sized suckable nipples.

"You think you so cute, don't you?" Chiney teased, crouched on her knees between the girl's lean, shapely legs. She reached down and grasped the heel of the girl's right foot and brought her manicured toes to her mouth.

"I think you cute too," Chiney whispered, parting her lips and inserting a perfectly polished big toe into her mouth. She sucked the girl's digit greedily, swirling her hot tongue around its elegant base. Pulling back, Chiney went to work on the other toes, attacking them with greedy kisses, and darting her tongue in and out of the sweet crevices between each toe.

She lifted the slim foot to her shoulder, and licked the girl's ankles, and kissed up her tight calves.

Chiney was strung out. And not just on all the crack, ice, and pills that she had been steadily ingesting since her release from Rikers Island. She was high on the sweet smell of pussy that seeped from the slit between Venus Kendrick's thighs. Of all the girls that Chiney had partied with over the years, out of all the seemingly straight chicks who were either bi-curious or straight up lesbians in disguise, none had ever rocked her the way Venus did.

And it wasn't just a sex thang, either, Chiney knew. It was a love thing. They had been together for the last three years, and even though Chiney fucked around and hit some outside pussy every now and then, no woman had ever gotten close to stealing her heart the way Venus had.

But being Venus's stud came with certain problems, Chiney had to admit. As a drug addict who was always trying to kick the shit and get her life straight, she struggled like crazy with her sobriety. But Venus never seemed to worry about hers. The only thing the girl wouldn't touch was crack, but she would fuck up some roofies, X, zanies, and ice seven days a week.

It was no secret that Trey couldn't stand the sight of the girl, and he damn sure didn't want her coming around the crib. He blamed Venus for causing most of Chiney's relapses, and he was all the time barking about how dumb chicks like her kept dope dealers in business.

But as much as Chiney loved her brother there wasn't a damn thing he could say to keep her away from Venus. It was more than her dimpled smile, her bowlegs, and that sexy sway in her back when she strutted her bold ass that had Chiney turned out on her chick.

She dipped her head lower and left a trail of kisses from the inside of the girl's knee and across the tender meat of her thigh. Inhaling deeply, Chiney pressed her nose to Venus's curly triangle and took a deep breath.

Chiney shuddered at the erotic scent, and her groin throbbed with need as she felt her clit swell between her legs and harden just like a dick. Using her forefinger and her thumb, she parted the glossy, cocoa-colored lips of her lover, and prepared to dive in.

"Hold up," Venus piped up, wriggling her hips seductively on the bed. "Femmes before studs," she declared with a giggle. "Before you eat, you have to feed me first."

Chiney grinned. She knew what time it was.

"A'ight," she said, and slapped Venus playfully on her hip, enjoying the way the flesh on her flank jiggled. Crawling across the bed on her knees, she reached up onto her dresser and grabbed a small vial that was filled with the stuff that made good sex even better.

Chiney opened the vial and shook two tablets into her palm, then crawled back over to Venus and placed one on the girl's pouty lip. Venus opened wide, dry swallowing the pill greedily, and Chiney crouched down and slid the second pill deep inside the mouth of the girl's wet pussy.

Moments later, she went to work. Her tongue was like a snake as she probed into that warm, dark cavity searching for her treat. The excitement of it all had both ladies moaning and dripping, and in her enthusiasm Chiney reached up to cup one of Venus's firm melons, and the empty vial fell from her hand.

Tiny sparks of pleasure were radiating through every nerve in Venus's body. She arched her back, urging Chiney's tongue deeper, as her hips rocked and shook with need.

Chiney met the challenge, penetrating that hole until the root of her tongue was sore, then whipping it back and forth in a fuck-frenzy against the girl's clit.

Venus bucked, and Chiney rocked.

Neither girl noticed when the small vial tumbled from the bed and fell to the floor. It rolled twice, and then landed on its side, the words DIVINE NINE facing straight up and standing boldly for all the world to see.

But moments later, what Chiney *did* notice was the sound of the breaking news report that blared through the television speakers. She had turned the volume up real loud so her brother wouldn't hear her and Venus fucking, and now the broadcast was all she heard.

"This is Channel Two News coming to you live from Harlem, New York. There was a home invasion and mass shooting in a Harlem apartment building during the night, and this morning several people are reported dead..."

Those few words were more than enough to spark Chiney's curiosity, but when she peeked up from her moist feast and glanced at the television screen, the sight of her parole officer Dutchy Gaines as he rushed through the hospital doors with tears streaming down his face was more than enough to make Chiney come up outta that good pussy she was licking and pay some real close attention.

CHAPTER 30

I was writing another erotic story in my Juicy Journal when Chiney busted up in my room with a look on her face that I had never seen before. Trey came through the door right behind her, and his normally dark eyes looked deep and sad, and real, real intense.

"What's wrong?" I looked at Chiney and frowned. When she didn't answer me I glanced at Trey. "What? Did something happen down at the center?"

He shook his head.

Chiney whimpered, "Nah, Juicy. It's, um…I can't…!" she pressed her face into her brother's chest. "I can't!"

"Juicy," Trey said, fixing me in his strong gaze as he grabbed both of Chiney's wrists in one hand and gently moved her out of the way. He stepped toward me with something so burdensome on his heart that I could see him struggling to get the words out of his mouth.

"What?" I demanded. I was doing like Chiney now. Whimpering. "What happened? Just fuckin' *tell* me! I wanna know!"

"I just got off the phone with my boy Dutchy," Trey said, pulling me deep into his arms. We had never been this close before. He hugged me, and I felt my titties pressed up against his rock-hard chest. His scent went all up in my nose and I started trembling in fear from head to toe.

"What's wrong?" I moaned. "What the hell is *wrong?*"

"It's your girl," Trey said quietly. He leaned down and softly kissed my ear. "It's Rita. Somebody pulled a kick-door on her crib and they shot Rita in her sleep." I felt him clutch me tighter as my head swooned and my legs went out from under me.

"They shot her little sisters too."

TO BE CONTINUED…

Order

TRICKERY: THE 6TH DEADLY SIN
at
www.Amazon.com or www.BN.com

PART SIX
OF NOIRE'S BLOCKBUSTER
URBAN EROTIC SERIAL TALE!

Harlem is caught in a vicious three-way scheme!
Will Juicy get tangled in the deadly web of violence?

Life is getting real tricky for Juicy Mo-Stanfield as she hides in plain sight right in the heart of Harlem. With the powerful Trey Jackson watching her back, Juicy-Mo just can't go wrong. Or can she?

When the major players in the game get greedy, scheming becomes second nature and former friends become distant, bitter foes. Are the hard knocks of the past over for Juicy? Or will the vicious hand of street life strike one more violent blow to her gut?

WARNING!

This here ain't no romance
It's an urban erotic tale
Thugs are straight up wildin'
And they're scheming for ya mail!
Tongues are slithering just like snakes
So you better watch your back
Grimy double-crossin' has
Become a hood-life fact!
Rival clicks are perpetrating scams to get it in,
TRICKERY is a mutha in this deadly ghetto sin!

Find out more in...
G-SPOT 2: THE SEVEN DEADLY SINS
Trickery: The 6th Deadly Sin

The Urban Erotic Serial Saga Continues!

NOIRE

G-Spot 2:
The Seven Deadly Sins
An Urban Erotic Serial Tale Told in 7 Parts

TRICKERY: THE 6TH DEADLY SIN

by
Noire

www.AskNoire.com
www.GSpot2.com
www.TheGSpotSaga.com

CHAPTER 1

I stood there trembling in Trey's arms as I tried to make sense of the craziness that was coming out of his mouth.

"It's your girl. It's Rita. Somebody pulled a kick-door on her crib and they shot Rita in her sleep."

"Nooo!" I shook my head and buried my face in Trey's chest as his arms tightened around my back. *"That can't be true!"* I screamed as my knees sagged a little bit and then straight-up collapsed and buckled.

"Ritaaa..." I threw my head back and wailed. Trey gripped me in his rock-hard arms and held me up on my feet as I screamed for my girl. A knot of grief swelled up inside of me and I cried from way down in my gut as a bolt of hot pain ripped through my heart. "Rita... *nooo!*"

"I'm sorry, Juicy," Trey kept saying as he held me close. "I'm sorry, baby. I'm sorry." My tears soaked the front of his shirt. His big hands rubbed all over my back and shoulders as he tried to comfort me with gentle, soothing words.

"Please, God," I begged as a fresh river flowed from my eyes. "Not Rita," I pleaded. "*Please* not Rita! Trey!" I hollered. "*Trey!* Please tell me that shit ain't true!"

But it *was* true. I could feel it in the way he held me. Like I was a baby bird who needed protecting. Like he was trying to suck some of my pain deep inside his heart so there wouldn't be quite so much for me to bear.

I looked up at him and in a quick rush of breath I asked him a question, even though I knew the answer might fuck me all the way up.

"Is Rita dead? D-d-did she die?"

He shook his head quickly and held me even tighter, "No. She's alive, Juicy. She's in a bad way, but your girl is still alive."

"W-w-where is she?" I moaned. My knees sagged again. My whole body felt weak.

"Harlem Hospital," Trey said quietly. His lips were warm on my ear as he clutched me close to his body and rocked me like a baby. "C'mon. Put your shoes on, Juicy." He sat me down on the bed and helped me into my sandals, and then he led me gently toward the door. "Come on, baby. Let me take you over there."

$$$$$

"But how could this happen?" I kept asking as we zipped down the crowded city streets in Trey's whip. I was riding up front with him, and Chiney was sitting in the back. "Rita don't have no money! Why would somebody break in her house to rob her and then just start shooting all crazy like that?"

"It was a kick-door," Trey muttered as he dipped in and out of traffic, "but it wasn't no robbery, Juicy. Them cats didn't go there looking to pull no simple lick. They went there to clean the whole house out, baby. That was their intention from the gate. To lay everybody down. That's why they shot the whole place up."

My mind was whirling in a tunnel of grief, and without even realizing it I slipped my hands under my shirt and pressed my fingers to the twisted scar that stood out on my lower belly. Poor Rita, I cried inside. Guns scared the hell out of me because I knew what it was like to get blasted. Clutching my stomach, I moaned as I thought about how gun violence had fucked up my entire life. Cara, Aunt Rea, Jimmy, Gino, me... and my unborn son. Every last one of us had taken a heat round from the tip of somebody's burner. And now so had my best friend in the whole world, Rita.

I opened my mouth and cried even harder. I couldn't believe this shit was happening! I just couldn't believe it! Chiney leaned over my seat and passed me a tissue, but there was no stopping the tears from falling from my eyes.

By the time we walked into the hospital I was totally shook. My old memories had sucked me deep into a heartbreaking pit of fear. Chiney waited in the car as me and Trey walked inside and headed down a long hallway. I was wobbling so bad on my feet that Trey looked down at me with a frown, and then he took my hand in his and steadied me. He pressed his thumb into my palm and massaged it in gentle circles, and then he wrapped his whole hand around mine and held me firmly as we got on an elevator and headed upstairs to the intensive care unit.

I was trying hard to keep myself together but just the smell of the hospital was giving me crazy flashbacks. My whole body broke out in a cold sweat as I followed Trey off the elevator. Every step I took toward the nurse's station made my heart pound harder and harder in my chest. I remembered being back in Cali and being wheeled down a hall toward Gino's room. There had been mad doctors and nurses running around looking crazy-panicked. I remembered how heavy my stomach had felt with my unborn baby still nestled inside me. Both of us had gotten ripped up by the bullet that had passed through Gino and straight into me. I started crying again. My feet felt so damn heavy, and my mouth was so damn dry.

"You gonna be okay?" Trey asked as he looked down at me. He stopped and waited while I gulped air and tried to get my shit together. His intense brown eyes were full of concern. He reached out and smoothed my hair back, and then he rested his strong hand lightly on the back of my neck.

After a minute I nodded and bit down on my lower lip. "Yeah." I took a deep breath and forced my feet to move the last few steps. "I'm straight."

The NYPD had posted a young cop outside of Rita's door, just like the Cali cops had posted one on me and Gino after we got shot. A big black gun was sticking out of the holster on his hip, and I couldn't help shuddering at the sight of it. Strapped cop or no strapped cop, I knew Rita was ass-out if somebody really wanted to get at her. Hell, this was New York. Almost every thug-ass cop in Harlem was notorious for being paid on the take and deep in some kingpin's pocket. I'd seen mad proof of their greediness and griminess back when I was still rolling around town as G's little on-the-stool bitch.

Dutchy was talking to somebody at the nurse's station when we walked up, and when he saw me and Trey he reached out to hug me and gave Trey some heavy dap.

"Yo, this shit is fucked up, Juicy," Dutchy told me with tears in his eyes. "It's all fucked up! It's bad enough that Rita got served like that up in there, but the two little kids she was watching got murked last night too, you know. Yeah," he said, nodding when he saw the look of shock and horror come across my face. "They got blasted. Rita was babysitting when the shit popped off, and Chub's two little friends didn't make it."

Dutchy had a few words with the police officer who was guarding the door and told him it was okay for both me and Trey to go inside and see Rita. Trey stepped into Rita's room ahead of me, and as bad as I wanted to comfort my girl and let her know I was there and praying for her, I was straight-up terrified of what I was going to see on the other side of that door.

Instead of walking in, I let go of Trey's hand and hung back a little bit, dragging my feet again. All kinds of shit was running through my head. What if Rita had tubes coming outta her everywhere? What if she was all swollen and messed up like Gino had been?

I wasn't ready to see all that. I just couldn't handle it. I had been through way too much in my young life, and my heart just couldn't take it. My instincts were screaming at me, telling me to turn my ass right back around and run down that hall. I felt new tears rushing to my eyes, and there was no way I could stop them.

"Yo, you up for this baby?" Dutchy asked. He had come up behind me and he put his arm around my shoulder and pulled me close to him. "Listen, they fucked her up pretty bad, Juicy," he said gravely. "I ain't gonna lie to you. They beat Rita until they thought she was dead. Hell, her heart stopped in the ambulance and the paramedics thought she was dead for a minute too. But my baby is mad strong, ya dig? They shocked her and brought her back and she's still alive now, Juicy. She's in a bad way, but at least she's still alive."

I swallowed hard and braced myself for what I was about to see. I knew Rita needed me right now. And no matter how scared I was there was no way I could justify closing my eyes and running away and not being there for my friend.

I nodded and sighed. "I'm good," I whispered to Dutchy. And when Trey held out his big hand again, inviting me to draw strength from him and follow him inside Rita's room, that's exactly what I did.

$$$$$

I did my best not to freak out when I saw what them mothafuckas had done to my girl, but trust me it was damn near impossible.

"Oh my *God*!" I moaned as my heart banged in my chest and my knees buckled. I almost hit the ground. Catching myself, I covered my mouth with one hand and then leaned heavily on the raised metal railing of the hospital bed as pain wracked through my body. My eyes were full of water as I gazed down at Rita, and then looked over at Dutchy.

"Oh my God!" I repeated. "What in the hell did they *do* to her?"

Rita was totally fucked up. Straight brutalized. Her whole face looked like it had been kicked in by five niggahs wearing spiked metal boots. Her gorgeous brown skin was black and torn. Her eyeballs were the size of two hardboiled eggs, and her upper lids had been taped closed with white hospital tape. There was a fat tube coming out of her mouth, and a skinnier one coming out of her right nostril. Her nose didn't even look like a nose. It was twisted and pointing way to the side, and it was almost as swollen as her eyes. The rest of her was either wrapped in gauze or in some kind of plaster cast. I wanted to touch her and let her know I was there, but there was no place safe to lay my hand. Even her damn elbows were all wrapped up.

Trey came over and stood beside me. I was shaking so bad I almost fell into his arms. He held me tight and kept me up on my feet as I cried. I felt Rita's pain. God knows I felt it in my heart and in my *bones*, and all I could do was hide my face in his chest as Dutchy broke the situation down for me.

"I'm sorry you gotta see her like this. I told you they fucked her up, Juicy. She's holding on, but it ain't looking all that good. Her doctor said she's got a slight chance of pulling through but her brain is so swollen that she could come outta this with a lotta mental damage too, nah'mean? Right now they're watching her real close, and if the swelling gets any worse they're gonna go 'head and take her in the operating room and open up her skull and give her brain some room to move. Otherwise, she could die for real."

I couldn't stop crying. I tried real hard, but I swear I couldn't stop.

"W-w-where did she get shot at?" I asked as my eyes scanned her battered body. The way she was all wrapped up she could have had a bullet hole almost anywhere.

Dutchy sighed with sorrow. "They shot her in her head, Juicy. Execution-style. They put a bullet right above her ear. Like I said, the doctors told me it's a miracle that she's still alive, and even if she makes it they don't know what her mind is gonna be like, nah'm saying?"

Dutchy's words cut deep into my heart, and Trey had to hold me up on my feet as I shuddered and remembered how the bullet that killed Gino had passed right through his body and into mine. I hated guns, and if I never heard about another senseless shooting for the rest of my life it would be too damn soon.

I wiped at my eyes as I managed to whisper, "D-d-did they catch anybody yet? Do the cops know who did this shit?"

Dutchy shook his head, and a cold, steely look came down on his face.

"Nah, them fools is still stumbling around in the dark, but trust, baby. Whoever it was, them niggahs is gone get found out. Found out and dealt with. You can believe that."

I nodded and then he dropped another bombshell on me.

"And yo, check this out," Dutchy said. His voice had gotten real quiet. "Nooni showed up at the crib last night."

"*Nooni*?" My eyes bucked open wide as unexpected joy jumped into my heart. "Y'all found her? She came back home?"

Dutchy nodded and frowned. "Yeah. She came back alright. And all this fuckin' time it was them G-Spot niggahs who was holding her! Rita said the girl looked like they had been getting her high and abusing the shit outta her. I didn't get the whole story, but some kinda way Nooni broke up outta that joint last night and made it back home."

"Oh my God," was all I could say. Just hearing those words made me feel so bad for Nooni. Those horrible nights of being chained to a pole and raped down in The Dungeon flashed through my mind and all of a sudden my body got real cold. I knew exactly what kind of hell Nooni had been through in the G-Spot. The way Granite McKay had whipped my ass and stomped a mud hole in my face and pissed down on me in that nasty little rat hole... all them dirty-dicked niggahs who had fucked the shit out of me, chewing on my titties and violating every hole in my body coming and going... *shittt*, my black ass had expected to *die* down there.

"Yo," Dutchy went on talking. He was hyped with rage and I could see the pain written all over his face. "I was supposed to be chillin' up in the crib with Rita and Chub last night you know, but Rita told me not to come over. She didn't want no man in the house since it was Nooni's first night back, nah'm sayin? She said the girl was so shook she didn't think she could handle having me or any other dude up in there, so I stayed home and went to sleep."

He gazed down at Rita's battered body and shook his head.

"She wanted me to swing by early this morning so she could fix me some breakfast, but as soon as I pulled up shit was mad chaotic. I saw all this crime scene tape across the door of the fuckin' building. There were cops everywhere. I'm in law enforcement and I couldn't even get up the stairs, man. The chick who lives next door told me they'd just taken Rita and some kids out in an ambulance, and the cops were bringing Chub out as I walked up."

I pulled away from Trey and frowned.

"Little Chub? Oh, shit! Is she okay?"

"Yeah," Dutchy nodded. "She looked okay. At least on the outside. The building manager said they found her hiding in a kitchen closet. Child Services took her into custody. They're grillin' her right now. Tryna find out who she saw and what she knows."

My heart broke wide open for Chub. That baby had already been through so much trauma in her young life.

"So what happened to Nooni?" I asked with dread creeping all up in my chest. "Where is she now? Did Child Services take her into protective custody too?"

Dutchy frowned. A funny look flashed deep in his eyes as he pushed his hands down in his pockets and shook his head slowly.

"See, that's what's so fuckin' crazy, Juicy," he said. "When the paramedics took Rita and them little girls outta the house there wasn't nobody left inside, and that tells just me one fucked up thing."

My breath caught in my throat. "What's that?"

"It tells me exactly why them niggahs rolled up like stompzillas in the first goddamn place."

Dutchy grilled me hard, and his eyes were dark and grim.

"Nooni is the one them fools was gunning for, because Nooni is the one who's missing!"

CHAPTER 2

The Dungeon in the basement of the G-Spot was just as nasty as it was the night Cooter Jackson had unlocked Juicy's handcuffs and set her free. Unfortunately for Nooni, with the recent busted pipes and clogged sewage issues at the G-Spot, the conditions down there were even wetter and filthier than ever before.

"Get ya ass on down them goddamn stairs!" Ace bitched as he twisted Nooni's wrist painfully and jerked her arm high up the center of her back. Balling up his fist, he punched her in the back of the head and then booted her hard in the tailbone with his big fat knee. Laughing, he flung the crying girl forward with almost all his strength, forcing her to sail through the air and land flat on her face on the wet concrete down below.

Nooni screamed inside as she hit the ground and her face splashed in a nasty shit-tinged puddle. She tried to cry out in terror as she lay there, but her lips were so busted up and her jaw was so painful and swollen that her cries came out sounding like baby whispers. She stood up slowly, then tripped over her own feet as Ace shoved her roughly from behind. Her arms flailed and wind-milled as she frantically reached for something to catch her and break her fall.

Collapsing in a wet puddle again, Nooni peered through her terrified, fist-dotted eyes. Already they were ringed in black from the bruised blood that had accumulated under her battered skin, and pretty soon they'd be too puffed-up for her to see out of them at all.

But right now she could see enough. More than enough.

And what she saw sent icy fear rushing through her veins. She was in a shit hole. It was hot and dark down there. Wet as hell too. The pajamas her sister had dressed her in were completely soaked through by the dank water, and so were her panties. She peered into the darkness and pushed herself into a sitting position and trembled as she looked around.

They called this place The Dungeon and that's exactly what it was. In fact, it was more than that. It was damn near a torture chamber. It was soundproof and dark, and the smell of putrid, stagnant water sent hot bile rushing to her throat. She looked down as her eyes adjusted to the darkness. There was at least an inch of murky water sloshing on the floor and she was sitting her ass right in it. A ripped and badly stained mattress had been pushed up against a wall, but there was no other furniture in sight. Through a doorway off to the left she could see a tiny bathroom, and judging from the foul smell of sewage that clogged the air all around her it was just as nasty as the rest of the room.

Ace stood behind her with his big belly jiggling as he laughed his ass off. Marching closer to her, he snatched her ponytail in his fist and wound her curls around his wrist. He dragged the screaming young girl through the huge puddle of slimy water, and then he jerked her up off the floor by her hair, tearing out her roots as he flung her with one massive heave and sent her sailing onto the soggy mattress.

"Ouch! W-w-why you do that Ace?" Nooni screamed as she plopped down on the bed and clutched her burning scalp with both hands. Ace came over and knelt beside her. His fat knees made deep dents in the waterlogged mattress.

"W-w-what you doing?" Nooni stammered as he grabbed her wrist and yanked her arm high over her head. She felt cold metal against her skin, and then heard a click and realized that his crazy ass had handcuffed her to a pipe that ran along the wall.

"*Nooo!*" She screeched into the silence. Her whole body broke out in goose bumps. "Don't lock me up! *Please* don't fuckin' lock me up!"

Gripped in terror, Nooni yanked and jerked at the icy metal that encircled her wrist and held her captive in place. Her eyes were wild in the darkness. She couldn't believe what was happening. All she knew is that she was feenin' real hard, and since she needed to be loose to get her some drugs, she didn't wanna be chained to nothing in this stankin' ass basement, not a *goddamn* thing!

But no matter how hard she struggled Nooni's fate was a clear as day. And deep in her heart she knew this was the punishment she got for trying to be so damn grown. Trying to be so damn fast, and so hot in the ass. Whimpering, she got on her knees and flailed her handcuffed arm back and forth. The hard metal bit painfully into her bony wrist as she tried her best to either slide her hand through the small circle or pull her whole damn arm outta socket. But the hole was too small. It was way too narrow to get her fist through. The tender skin at the base of her thumb tore and split, and she felt the warmth of her own blood as it trickled down her arm.

I'm having a fucking nightmare, Nooni told herself. She looked around in a panic as her eyes adjusted to the dim room and her heart sank down to her toes. This just had to be a nightmare! The kind that just kept playing over and over again on rewind and wouldn't let you go. Twice she had escaped from the G-Spot. And twice those fuckin' maniacs had caught her and dragged her right back through these haunted doors.

It was *crazy*. Everything about her life was crazy. She cursed the day she'd shook her ass with Truth up in T.C.'s Place and allowed him to introduce her to this madness she was living. And even though Truth had really loved her and he had died trying to set her free, she hated that she had ever loved him enough to step foot through the doors of the G-Spot Social Club.

Nooni thought about her sisters and the hardbody crew of street niggahs who had bust up in the house blasting tools, and she cried even harder. Who the hell were those dudes and why did they want to bring her back to the G-Spot so damn bad? It was all so confusing. One minute she was trembling in her sister's bed as her body cried out for drugs, and the next thing she knew there had been a crew of thugs standing over her waving gats, barking in her face, and kicking her mothafuckin' ass.

They had dragged her outta the bed, and Nooni had balled herself up in a tiny knot as mad fists got to swinging and crazy boots got to stomping her everywhere. Every damn body in the house took a beat down, but her sister Rita had gotten it the worst, and Nooni cringed as she remembered Rita's loud and pitiful wails.

And then there had been the horrible sounds of gunshots. She didn't even know how many, because her mind had gone totally blank after the first few. But what the hell had happened to Rita and Chub? To Charlize and Lucie? A moan of stark terror pushed its way up from Nooni's throat. Trapped down in this funky-ass dungeon, was her whole family dead and she the only one still alive?

"Please!" the terrified young girl whimpered, begging Ace from her knees. She knew he was Salida's man but right about now she just didn't give a fuck. "I need me a lil something," Nooni begged him. "I'll do whatever you want me to do. I'll suck your dick, or you can fuck me in the ass, just don't chain me up down here. Please... unlock this thing. I swear I'll do anything!"

Ace backed off the mattress and stood over her as he shook his head and frowned. He had absolutely no desire to fuck Nooni, and he damn sure didn't want her suckin' his dick. Nooni was a fiend and she'd fallen way off. She had sores all over her chin, and her teeth were black and rotten, like they would crumble into pieces if she bit down on anything too hard.

"You goddamn right you gonna do anything," Ace told her. "You gonna do anything and *every* goddamn thing I tell your ass to do. Believe that."

The door opened upstairs and they heard the sound of footsteps. Ace and Nooni both looked toward the stairs at the same time.

"Is somebody down there crying?" called a sweet, feminine voice.

It was Salida.

Nooni's face lit up and Ace's did too.

They waited in silence as a pair of slender ankles perched in elegant red high-heeled shoes appeared on the steps. She stepped down and they saw her slender calves and knees, and after one more step the flaming red skirt that sensuously hugged her hips and thighs came into view.

"Abraham!" Salida exclaimed, standing on the last step with her hand perched on her hip. She peered into the room with a phony expression of shock and disbelief on her gorgeously made-up face. "Uh-uh! What in the world is going on down here? You're not down here hurting this baby girl, are you?"

"Nah," Ace said and shrugged. "I ain't doing shit to her."

"Yes he is!" Nooni screamed. The sight of the older woman was the sweetest thing her eyes had ever seen. "Please, Mizz Salida," Nooni begged. Salida was just like a mother to her. She was a boss bitch who carried much clout in the G-Spot, and who controlled the happenings with just the look in her eyes. "He handcuffed me!" Nooni shrieked, pointing at her arm that was linked to the pipes. "He locked me up! Please make him let me go. Please, Mizz Salida. Help! *Help me!*"

Salida tiptoed carefully through the foul-smelling water trying not to mess up her expensive designer shoes. She made her way over to the trembling young girl and gazed down at her with caring, maternal eyes. She frowned and *tsked* with disgust and disapproval, and then she turned to Ace with fire blazing in her eyes.

"Who the hell done beat this poor child?" she demanded sharply.

Ace shrugged. "Ain't nobody beat her. I think the bitch fell down the stairs or something."

"Let her loose, mothafucka," Salida ordered him in a voice filled with rage. "You let this baby loose right goddammit *now,* you hear? I'm taking her home with me."

Ace hesitated for a couple of seconds, and then he shook his head. They had already rehearsed this part but Salida was playing her role like such a damn champ that for a moment he'd thought she was actually serious about wanting him to let

Nooni go.

"Nah, I can't do that, Mizz Salida," he said, shaking his head. "Monique told us to find Nooni and bring her back here. She wants us to keep Nooni strictly on lock until we find out where all that money is."

"*But I don't know where no money is!*" Nooni screeched at the top of her lungs. Great gulping sobs shook her traumatized body, and she arched her back and cried from her soul. "Y'all know I don't know where it is! I don't know nothing about no fuckin' *moneyyyy...*"

Ignoring the filth on the damp mattress, Salida sat down and perched daintily beside Nooni and gathered the distressed teen in her arms. Making soft, comforting noises, she stroked Nooni's long hair as big fat tears fell from the girl's swollen eyes.

"I'm sorry," Salida smirked as she delighted in the trickery she was using on the young girl. "I'm so, so sorry, Nooni. But you heard what Ace said. Monique doesn't want us to let you go. She'd cause a lot of trouble for us if we did that. But look, I'll try to talk to her, okay? You know, maybe I can convince her to let you come back upstairs, okay? I'll try that but I can't guarantee you anything. You know how evil Monique's ass can be."

A fresh wave of tears fell from Nooni's eyes as her body went stiff on the sodden mattress. A low moan erupted from her mouth that filled the entire room.

The smirk fell off Salida's face and she was shocked for real when the girl suddenly rolled away from her and began banging her head on the wall. Over and over again, Nooni bashed her head against the concrete cinderblocks, and Salida was forced to snatch her and throw her body on top of the child to stop her from splitting her forehead and cracking her own skull.

"Stop, baby," Salida murmured gently. "Don't do that. Don't you hurt yourself like that, sugar. Come on now. Let Mizz Salida help you. I know what you need."

Reaching inside her jacket pocket, Salida took out one of her new drug vials that had been stamped with her signature logo. Opening it quickly, she shook some powder into the palm of her outstretched hand.

"Here," she said, pressing her fingers right above Nooni's swollen, blood-crusted lips. "Hit this," Salida urged. "It'll make you feel so much better."

Hearing this, Nooni lifted her head as hope and desire surged through her body. Using her free hand, she pressed her left nostril closed and took a deep, grateful hit. Euphoria and bliss exploded in her brain as the potent drugs flooded her system. Nooni shivered in glee. Her pussy got wet. And then she took a second and a third hit as well until there was only a thin trace of powder left in Salida's palm, which the young girl licked greedily with her wet tongue.

"I'm gonna help you," Salida assured the shaken girl as the drugs seized control of Nooni's central nervous system and the girl fell back on the mattress in relief. "I swear I'll find a way to help you. But in the meantime you gotta stay strong, you hear?" Salida hugged Nooni goodbye, and then rose from the nasty mattress. "Stay strong, baby. Stay strong."

Salida signaled to Ace to follow her upstairs. Once they were behind the closed doors of G's office she shrugged out of her jacket, kicked off her shoes, and then unzipped her wet skirt and let it fall to the floor. With Ace watching closely, she peeled off her damp panties and tossed them into the trashcan.

Standing there with her yellow ass looking luscious in a red garter belt and thigh-high stockings, she opened G's armoire and flicked through the rows of skirts and dresses that were neatly hung on crush-velvet hangers. She selected a fifteen hundred dollar sleeveless, mango-colored Dior dress, then took it off the hanger and draped it over the back of a chair. Turning to face Ace, whose pop-eyes had been glued to her firm, perfectly shaped ass the whole time, Salida slid her hands down her tight waist and let them rest on her gorgeous round hips.

"What the hell you staring at frog-face?" she demanded. Salida knew she looked damn good and she knew Ace couldn't resist her no matter how much she demeaned him.

"You wanna stare at something? Come over here," she ordered as she sashayed her cute fanny over to G's desk. Without hesitating she swept her arm over the surface and sent everything on the desk flying to the floor.

With a look of pure disdain in her pretty eyes, Salida climbed her lithe body on top of the desk and struck a pose on her hands and knees. Her tooted-up starfish puckered and her juicy slit glistened with creamy need. "Bring them googly eyes over here and stare up my ass," she told him as she glared over her shoulder. She sneered at the horny look of adoration on Ace's face as he walked up on her and tried to cover the bulge in his crotch behind his cupped hands.

"Sssss..." Salida hissed and sucked air between her clenched teeth as Ace got up on her and parted her swollen pussy lips with his thumbs and tantalized her clit with his tongue. "Yeah, you muskrat-lookin' imp, you! Lick my stuff out. Lick it nice and soft, just like that."

Ace didn't care what kinda names Salida called him. She coulda called his dear mama a string of dirty-ass hoes for all he cared. The only thing he was concerned about was sucking out that na-na and making his baby feel good. He stiffened his meaty tongue and curled it inward like a flute. Teasing her asshole with his finger, he inserted his warm tongue deeply inside her pussy, marveling at the way her inner muscles locked down on him and squeezed deliciously as he mouth-pumped in and out of her.

Salida's fleshy ass jiggled and turned him on even more. Ace palmed both her cheeks and squeezed and kneaded the thickness of her booty as he continued his oral fuck-fest. Withdrawing his tongue from her dripping cave, he extended it and gave her a big long lick from her public mound all the way back to her asshole. Salida jerked and moaned at the sudden sensation of his warm tongue bath, and Ace repeated his long, slow pussy-to-ass licks as her back arched in pleasure and her body trembled exquisitely.

"Oh-oh-*oh*!" Salida cried out in ecstasy. Reaching around her hip, Ace briefly massaged her clitoris, then inserted his middle finger deep into her honey pot and pumped it. Moments later he felt her inner walls begin to spasm, and he withdrew his dripping finger and reached for her firm breast. Biting gently on the fleshy piece of meat right next to Salida's asshole, Ace cupped her titty and rubbed her wetness all over her erect nipple, causing sticky sparks of pure electricity to shoot through her body.

Sliding his mouth over just a bit, Ace licked her hole, pinching her nipples as he gently tossed her salad, and the moment he felt her body stiffen with intense pleasure, he pressed his palm down on her lower back and thrust his entire tongue up her ass.

Salida screamed in delight as an orgasm tore through her body and caused her to buck back at him with short, hard thrusts. Ace's tongue was a real muthafucka, but she needed something stiff and thick to put out the fire that was burning inside her pussy. She jerked her ass to the side as he tried to stick his finger up in her twat again.

"*Dick!*" she screeched madly. "Come on, you dog-faced mothafucka! Fuck me with your *dick!*"

Ace fumbled with his pants and extracted his monster dick. The head was so swollen it looked like it was about to bust, and a long string of pre-cum dripped from the tip.

Gripping it with his left hand, he guided his chocolate iron toward Salida's waiting pussy, and just as the head touched her hole, he hauled off and slapped her ass-cheek hard enough to make her scream.

"Agghh!" Salida threw her head back and yelped in surprise. Ace had never put his hands on her with nothing but a tender touch. Thrusting his meat deeply inside her, he slapped that ass again, and Salida felt lightheaded from the explosion ignited in her burning flesh and steam-rolled through her dripping pussy.

"Slap me again, mothafucka!" she demanded as Ace held her by the hip and monster-fucked her so deep she got disorientated. She was having multiple orgasms. One would barely subside before another one popped off inside of her again.

Behind her, Ace was almost in tears. Salida was a prime bitch, and this was the best piece of ass he had ever had in his life. He grunted as he pounded his meat between her sucking pussy lips, loving the way her asshole looked as it clenched and puckered with each stroke. Leaning forward, he slobbered on the smooth skin of her back, then licked it up as he cupped her grapefruit-sized titties and rubbed her nipples between his fingers.

He felt her body stiffen and suddenly her pussy clamped down on him and held him in a vice grip. Ace whimpered as his dick seemed to get harder and swell up to twice its normal size, and when Salida screamed and collapsed face-down on the desk of her dead ex-husband, Ace gripped her ass, gave her two more hard, fast pumps, then busted a whole grove of walnuts up inside of her and collapsed down on top of her.

Ace knew he had laid some demon pipe on Salida and fucked her so good she had shot a gallon of cream outta her pussy. But if he thought all that good dick-action had earned him a moment of tenderness from his boss-boo, his ass was sadly mistaken.

"Get your heavy tail up offa me," Salida barked just moments later. Both of their bodies were covered in sweat and Ace was still trying to catch his breath. He let go of her and straightened up on his feet as his softening dick slid outta her pussy with a loud slurping sound.

His dick was still at half-mast as he stood there with the scent of her twat on his lips and her tangy juices coating his skin.

Salida eased herself down from the desk, and then walked naked over to the armoire. It was back-to-bizzness time and she looked down at the wet skirt suit that she had recently pulled off and discarded, then kicked it in Ace's direction and snapped, "Get rid of this stankin' shit. Toss them damn soggy-ass shoes I had on somewhere too. And when you're finished," she ordered, smoothing her hair and checking her fine self out in the mirror, "send somebody back downstairs to get Nooni high, and then I want you to go down there and kick the shit outta her ass again."

CHAPTER 3

I stayed up at that hospital praying over Rita practically 24/7.

The cops claimed they had searched the G-Spot and Nooni was nowhere to be found, and Chub was being held somewhere by child protective services. The homicide detectives were acting all clueless and they told me and Dutchy there were no leads pointing toward the identity of the gunmen who had pulled this bloody caper.

"Fuck the cops," Dutchy kept saying over and over. "This is *me* right here! Lemme find out who did this shit, man. Just lemme find out. The streets are gonna start talking in a minute and somebody is gonna get X'd the fuck out," he swore one night as he stared down at Rita's battered face with tears in his eyes. "That's word to my mother. The muh'fuckin' streets are definitely gonna talk."

I was scared as hell behind all this. I didn't know whether Rita getting shot was just a random act of violence, or whether it had something to do with all the people who were out there gunning for me. I got even scareder one day when I was sitting in the waiting room and Chiney called to tell me a big bouquet of sympathy flowers had been delivered to the crib. She said the card was made out to me, and it wished Rita a speedy recovery.

"Who is it from?" I had asked her, suspicion jumping all up in my throat.

Chiney didn't answer for a second, and then she said, "You ain't gonna believe it, but this shit is signed, "Love, Flex.""

My heart pounded. That little buck-toothed fool had a lot of nerve sending me some damn flowers to Trey's house. Yeah, him and Rita was cool and she was the one who had arranged for me to stay with him when I first got outta jail, but he didn't really give a damn about her getting shot. Flex didn't care about nobody but himself. Rita had thought she was protecting me from the G-Spot crew by sending me to hide with him, but she just didn't know how twisted that niggah was. But I sure as hell did, and I wasn't about to give him the kind of attention I knew he was trying to get.

"Is your brother home?" I asked Chiney. "Is Trey there?"

"Nah. He's at the Crossover Center."

"Good," I said. "Take the whole bouquet outside and throw it in the curbside trash. Get rid of that shit, Chiney. Just dump it."

I had gone back to Rita's bedside clenching my jaw and making worry lines pop up all over my face. Even though the nurses only let me sit in Rita's room for about thirty minutes at a time, I tried to be there for her the way my Italian friend Renata had been there for me when I got shot. Rita was still in a coma, but I still talked to her like she could hear me, mostly telling her not to worry and that everything was gonna be okay.

And Dutchy was a dedicated soldier for her too. He took a week off from work right after it happened, and when he went back he still came up to the hospital every day on his lunch hour, and then he came right back to see her again as soon as he got off work at night.

Trey hung out at the hospital with me sometimes too, and I appreciated all the concern he was showing for me and for Rita, especially with all the other stuff he was juggling on his plate. Trey was a real active businessman and he stayed on the run all the time working on projects that benefited the community of Harlem. His Crossover Center was scheduled to host its first annual D.I.V.A. Day soon, so Trey was busy running back and forth taking care of all those last minute arrangements that would assure its success. Still, he swung by the hospital every day so I could give him an update on Rita's condition, and he always found time to sit and keep me company for a little while.

Our relationship had definitely gotten closer since all this had happened, although I kept telling myself not to read anything into it. Before Rita got shot it seemed like Trey was forever either avoiding me or fronting me off, and he wouldn't even say two damn words to me in a row unless he had to. But it seemed like he had a lot more conversation for me now. He had more patience, and definitely more compassion in his eyes for me too.

I hadn't forgot about the way he had held me real close in his arms and softly kissed my neck when he broke the bad news to me, but I didn't dwell on that shit neither. People did all kinds of shit and acted outta themselves when a tragedy jumped on them. I knew Trey had just been trying to soften the blow for me, and that little kiss hadn't really meant nothing to him. He had plenty of women in his life, and I didn't wanna read too much into his actions and twist our friendship into something it would probably never be.

But I was real grateful for his concern right now, and I was happy when Chiney came up to the hospital later that day too. She had brought me a couple of cute outfits that her girl Venus had boosted, and even though I was liked what she brought, I was worried too because every time I saw Chiney with Venus they were both high as hell. Trey had already told her she better not bring Venus back up in his crib no more, but that didn't stop Chiney from hooking up with the girl on the streets. I stared at her real close and there was no way for her to hide the fact that she was flying high.

"You better slow down on that shit you smoking. I know you not sneaking no chicks in the house and getting lifted are you?" I asked with a warning in my voice. "You know how your brother is."

Chiney grinned. "Nah, I'm straight. I don't be smoking no shit in the crib, man."

I gave her a be-for-real look. I knew Chiney was lying, but what could I say? I didn't like what was going down with her, but I didn't know what to do about it neither. I wasn't about to bust on her to Trey though. Chiney was my girl and she always looked out for me. I just hoped one day I could find a way to look out for her too.

"Yo, you hungry? Did you eat anything today? You want me to go get you a hero or some Chinese food or something?" she asked.

All I could do was smile at her. Chiney was such a giver. She was always trying to do something for somebody else. I thought about that time when we were locked up on Rikers Island and that stud freak named Psycho had come at me in the shower.

That grisly bitch had laughed in my face, and then pinned me down to the shower floor and tried to get all up in my coochie.

Chiney had come to my rescue outta nowhere and saved me from that humping-ass hood bitch. I was grateful to have a chick like Chiney down on my team, but I shook my head no on the food request. The truth was, I really didn't have much of an appetite because my nerves were all fucked up. It was bad enough that Rita was all laid up the way she was, but Chub and Nooni stayed on my mind too.

The day after Rita got shot I had called around to find out where lil Chub was and how she was doing. I pretended like I was Rita's sister from Puerto Rico and I spoke to a white lady who told me that Chub was still in state custody and receiving around the clock protection. She said she couldn't give me any additional information, but hell, she didn't have to. After witnessing a straight-up bloodbath, the murder of her two little friends, and being taken away from her sister and stashed with strangers, it wasn't hard to figure out what kind of hell poor little Chub was going through.

And going through hell went for Nooni too. Trey and Dutchy both had put some feelers out on the streets trying to find her, but nobody had seen the girl, and when the cops went to the G-Spot looking for her they didn't find her there neither. In a nutshell, the shady po-po in Harlem still had Nooni listed as a runaway teenager, and when I tried to tell them that Nooni had gone back home to Rita's apartment and then disappeared all over again when the bullets started flying, they told me I didn't have no proof that she was ever there, and then they acted like they didn't give a good goddamn.

The one bright spot that I could see in all this was that even though Rita still had a bullet lodged in her head and she was in a coma, her doctors said she was holding her own. I wasn't surprised because I knew my girl was a warrior and I knew how bad she wanted to live. Even though she was unconscious I could see the fight she had in her, and how hard she was struggling to stay here in this world. I had Rita's back to the max, and I pulled for her every day as I talked to God and whispered a bunch of scriptures and prayers that Grandmother used to say back in the day.

A day or so later while the doctors and nurses were examining Rita, I went down to the waiting room to watch television and in walked long-legged Mister Trey.

I couldn't take my eyes off him as he moved toward me in a smooth, unhurried pace. This dude had some shit about him that was just uh-uh-fuckin'-*uh*. He was so damn tall and so fuckin' *beastly* with his flow that he made every other dude in the room look tired and weak. I can't lie, I started sweating and my coochie lips spread wide open like a blooming flower.

All kinds of heads turned as Trey approached. Females, young and old, couldn't help but be impressed because his shit was truly well put together. He was tall, and the way he dressed was real casual but sharp and stylish, and his locks looked like hand-spun black velvet. His cologne was expensive but mild, and my heart banged in my chest as he sat down next to me and we just started kicking it.

The waiting room was overflowing with poor Black and Hispanic people, and every last one of them were there because somebody in their family had either gotten shot up or stabbed up, or run over by a car, or maybe they had a heart attack or some other sickness that had brought them to death's door. People were yakking away in English and in Spanish, but somehow the only voices I could hear were mine and

Trey's.

At first we talked a little bit about Rita, and then about Chub, and then we just started vibing about shit that went on in everyday life. It seemed like all the good stuff I had ever thought about him was right on point, and I wasn't surprised that his convo got deep and passionate when he talked about drugs, guns, gangs, and all the other madness in the streets that had led us to the point that we were at today.

And yeah, papi was fine as hell, but even more important I liked the way this dude's mind worked. I could tell Trey was a thinker and a strategist. I had figured that out right off the bat just by the way he had organized his profitable Talented Ten click in Harlem.

He wasn't the type of dude who just ran off randomly at the mouth neither. Everything that flowed from his lips seemed like he had considered it real careful first. Chiney had told me that he used to be a high-post lawyer and he had worked in the stock market too, which was where he had made all the money that he now invested back into the community.

After a while we gave up our seats to two old black women who had come in, and we walked down the hall to get something from the vending machines. I got a cup of hot chocolate and Trey got a cold bottle of water.

"You know, Harlem is my shit, Juicy," he said as we took our time walking back to the waiting room. I love this hospital 'cause I was born here, but I hate this place too because it symbolizes sickness and death, nah'm sayin?"

I looked at him and nodded. Harlem Hospital was a big part of the community. Me and Grandmother had sat up in this place with my brother Jimmy on many, many days. That boy had stayed getting hurt. If he wasn't busting his head open or damn-near cutting off one of his fingers, then he was being mentally evaluated because of that crazy bug that lived in his head and kept him acting off the wall. I used to beg Jimmy to stop talking idiotic shit and act right because I was scared the doctors would cart his ass off to the psych ward at Bellevue where our father was locked up at.

"You had a lot of sick family come through here or something?" I asked Trey as we walked back inside the crowded waiting room. The intensive care unit was on jam, and people were steady coming and going.

"Yeah," he nodded as he held the door open and let me go in first. "Family and friends too. Actually," he said offhandedly, "I got knocked from here. Matter fact, they slapped the cuffs on me right here in this room."

I sucked that scalding hot chocolate in my mouth so fast it burnt my tongue.

"You got arrested up *in here*?" I gave him a crazy look as we leaned against a back wall. "Oh, you's a gangsta in disguise, huh, Mr. Messiah? What did you get busted in the hospital for? What in the world did you do?"

"I killed a man, Juicy," Trey said quietly, and I could tell by the look in his eyes that he wasn't bragging about that shit neither. "Matter fact," he added, "I killed two."

$$$$$

All I could do was sit there and listen as Trey put me up on what had happened the night his manz Mayhem died. I had heard so many rumors about it that it was impossible to know what was really real, but now I was getting the bullet straight out of the shooter's mouth.

I sat there mesmerized by Trey's story. In a crazy way it was sorta like mine. Tragic. Both of us had been through a lot in life, and both of us were out here in the world practically by ourselves. Trey's mother was dead just like mine was, and his sister Charlene and brother Cooter had lost their lives fuckin' around with G, just like my brother Jimmy had. Trey felt like he shoulda done more to save his boy Mayhem, and Lord knows if I coulda just left G alone, then my girl Dicey woulda never got her tongue cut out her mouth and my brother Jimmy woulda never blown his own brains out of his own head.

"By the time I went looking for Mayhem that night," Trey continued, "my dude had already made his decision, and them two niggahs had made them one too. They were gonna do him."

"So what happened then?" I whispered. "What did you do?"

Trey pushed off the wall and stood up straight and frowned. He looked down at me and stared dead into my eyes and said quietly, "I killed them mothafuckas, Juicy. I blasted them niggahs with they own gats. I emptied the clips and made sure they was both dead."

A cold look entered his eyes and I felt so sad inside. Shyly, I reached over and touched the back of his hand. Spreading my fingers, I slid them down between his, and then I curled my hand into a tight fist.

"Chiney told me how close you be playing Maleek," I said softly as we squeezed each other's hands. "Is that why you try to look out for him so hard? Because he's Mayhem's little brother?"

Trey nodded a little bit and shrugged, but he didn't look at me when he spoke. "Yeah. Prolly. But Mayhem was way more than Leek's brother. He was that boy's daddy too. When their moms passed all they had was each other. And when Mayhem got killed, Maleek went bonkers. I mean that cat got straight-up reckless with his shit. Even the hardest nigs on the streets got enough sense to have a fear of dying, but not Maleek. When Mayhem got shot it was like that young boy caught a fear of living or something."

Trey shook his head. "I started wondering if he had some kinda death wish, nah'mean? Word, I started thinking the boy might jump off a roof or run out in front of a truck or some ill shit like that. So I stayed real close to him and kept him in pocket. I tried to look out for him the same way Mayhem woulda looked out for me and minez."

Trey's hand had swallowed my fist and he was holding onto me real tight as he spoke. There were eight million stories in the naked city of New York, and Trey had trusted me enough to tell me his. But I was a New Yorker with a story to tell too. So standing against a hard wall in that crowded hospital waiting room next to a dude that I was feeling all down in my bones, I opened up my heart just a little bit, and even though I told Trey about some of the dirt that life had thrown down on me, I damn sure didn't tell him everything.

CHAPTER 4

Flex mighta been moaning like he was in heaven as he got his top done by a chick who favored Juicy, but even though his nut was rising, his mind was way on the other side of town.

He gazed down at the chick who was slobbering on his balls and frowned. She looked good in the face and she had a nice ass on her, but she damn sure wasn't no substitute for the girl he really wanted. The girl he planned to wife and own someday.

Flex moaned as the hoe he'd picked up off the track gripped his fat dick in both her hands. She had looked real surprised when he pulled his bone out and she saw how big it was. Like she had expected him to have a kid-sized lil pee-pee or something. His shit was man-sized, just like his gangsta. Matter fact, this bitch could barely throat his shit. Every time she dove down and tried to swallow his meat, the sheer length of it stopped her and she fell back, acknowledging his superior structure.

Flex let his head loll back as the young girl gave up trying to deep throat him and went into her hoe bag for a couple of new tricks. She pulled up her shirt and clapped his dick between her swollen bubble-breasts, then squeezed them babies together and swirled her tongue around the head while titty-jacking his shit to a perfect rhythm. He closed his eyes and imagined it was Juicy squeezing his wood, Juicy's tongue licking all over his dick, and Juicy's hands gently gripping his swollen nuts.

In due time, Flex told himself as he snatched the girl by the head and pumped deeply up into her mouth. He'd get Juicy in his bed in due time. Sex and power went hand and hand for Flex, and just thinking about how he was gonna reign large as fuck one day turned him on.

Yeah, he admitted, his shit mighta got twisted a lil bit to the left when he got mad and pushed Juicy down on them train tracks, but hell, she could forgive him and his basic plans could still stay set. He was *still* gonna be running Harlem one day, he thought as he thrust his meat halfway down the hoe's throat. He was *still* gonna take over the G-Spot. And no matter what nobody said, he was *still* gonna get Juicy.

Juicy. *Juicy.* Juicy... he moaned her name and an avalanche of cum raced up outta Flex's nuts and spewed outta the tip of his dick. He shuddered as his muscle jerked and his seed scalded the back of the girl's throat. *Juicy. Juicy. Juicy.*

Flex kept his eyes closed as he pulled his wet dick outta the skank's mouth and stuffed it back inside his drawers. He waved the bitch off, dismissing her from his presence as he tried to hold on to the remnants of his pleasure and his thoughts of Juicy. Flex well understood that wifing Juicy would be the greatest sign of his evolution as a G. Because in the street world it was all about progress and gain. Gain and progress. If you wasn't growing then that meant your black ass was dying, and even though he lived in a funeral parlor underneath the cold and the dead, Flex wasn't planning on dying anytime soon.

Instead, he was plotting on multiple avenues of expanding his business sector, and there was one shifty bitch who was throwing up roadblocks on one of his key paths.

Salida McKay.

That chick had a mind for business, and it burned Flex up to know that for months now she had been out-thinking him three steps to one. He had figured the old bird was harmless when she first came to him looking to cop some low-priced ingredients to cook up her own club drugs, but outta nowhere her shit had blew the fuck up into a booming money-pit.

Her Strawberry Snake meth was severely undercutting the Divine Nine crack sales, and people were flocking to Harlem in droves for that shit. At the rate Salida was selling there were gonna be more meth heads than crack heads left on the streets pretty soon, and Flex wanted him a piece of that icy action.

Actually, it was only right that he should get a piece of it. He had helped Salida tap into a virtually underexposed market, and since he was the one who provided her with the raw materials she needed, damn straight he should be getting him a lil cut on each vial of shit she sold.

But just like Juicy, Salida was a hardheaded bitch who didn't wanna cooperate. When Flex sent a couple of his boys to tell her about his new shakedown rules where she was either gonna have to dig real damn deep in her pockets to keep purchasing his shit, or slide him a cut off the top of her profit, that bitch sent him back a note with only two words written on it.

Fuck you.

Oh, I'll fuck you, you old-ass bitch, Flex fumed. He didn't know what the world was coming to when some elderly come-up bitch thought she could cross him and get away with that shit.

Flex had read the note and then stared at the kid she had sent to deliver it with cold contempt in his eyes. "So this how them G-Spot niggahs wanna do me, huh, Bilal?" he barked on him. "I gave them pussy niggahs the scoop on Juicy, and this is how they let this trifling bitch Salida do me? A'ight," he had nodded his head and balled up the piece of paper and hurled it across the room. "You go tell that bitch Salida we gone see who's got the biggest dick in this town."

Flex had immediately called a meeting with three of his most trusted members of the Divine Nine. The four of them had sat in his basement battle-den plotting and scheming on that bitch Salida, as Flex tried to figure out how he could fuck her shit up and teach her a lesson at the same time.

He gave less than a fuck about the broad being old enough to be his mama, or about her being G's ex-tramp neither. She was just another trifling money-hungry bitch in his book, and somebody shoulda taught that dried-up slice of pussy how to stay in a pussy's place a long time ago. All he had to do was figure out what was in Salida's shit that kept feens flocking to it, and he'd be ready to make his move.

Luckily, every last member of Flex's inner circle was a thinker and a schemer, and by the time their meeting was over Flex and his small crew had figured out how to drive Salida McKay outta business and launch a highly profitable new branch of their own business at the same time. *Shiiit,* Flex laughed to himself. Salida wasn't the only one who could feed club drugs to the rich white kids who were all of a sudden so fuckin' in love with Harlem. Yeah. Flex was about to get his hands on that jawn's secret formula, cook up his own batch of chemicals, and bone in on all Salida's action and her fuckin' customers too.

And if them G-Spot niggahs had a problem with that shit, then let them chump ass niggahs just try to jump. Flex hoped the fuck they would! He was already planning to twist Ace and Pluto's shit up by stiffing them on the joint-connect deal he had told them to work out with Moonie. He didn't have the slightest fuckin' intentions on sharing a common supply line with Ace or Pluto, and if either one of them bear-lookin' fags got fancy he would send his lil hooligan Maleek out to bust a cap in their asses.

Regardless of what them niggahs did, Flex was still aimed and charging toward his original agenda. All of his dreams were gonna come true in due time, but in the meantime, Flex knew he had to keep his cool and let his plans unfold naturally. *All things in time*, he calmed himself as he wiped off a dirty Smith and Wesson that had about ten bodies on it. Once he got his hands on that clean stash of burners that he'd ordered from that Italian boy, he'd be ready to storm the G-Spot and press a tool to that bitch Salida's forehead and squeeze the trigger as many times as he wanted to. But until then he just had to wait.

Flex's grandmother had come to New York City outta the deep South, and the churchified old lady had always told him that the best way to kill a snake was to cut off the head. Flex grinned. Salida McKay's head was about to get chop-chopped.

CHAPTER 5

A'ight, this shit here looks a whole lot better, Mizz Salida."

Freeze Dodson held out a bright pink sample of the crystallized mixture of meth that him and his crew had just spent the last few days mixing, cutting, and cooking upstairs in the G-Spot's cut room. He was Salida's number one street pharmacist and he was damn good at churning out batches of crystal and powder for her left and right, but just a couple of weeks earlier he had almost got himself fired for pissing Salida off.

It wasn't his fault though, Freeze thought. Salida was bent in about twenty different directions, and she had gone off on him when she dumped some special chemicals into his mix and he complained that it made the batch come out too strong.

"This shit ain't even smokable," Freeze had told her. "We put this out on the streets and it's gone fuck around and give them fools a heart attack. I think we need to cut it again."

Salida had narrowed her eyes and shaken her head. "Hell no. We ain't cutting shit! Put it out there just like that. We'll get these fools hooked on it first, and then when they're jonesing so hard till they start banging down our doors, that's when we'll cut the mixture back."

Freeze didn't have no choice but to cook the overload of toxic chemicals in the mix like she had ordered him to. But Salida had been right 'cause that shit had worked. The corners they manned had turned into Meth-Head Central, and they couldn't produce the shit fast enough to meet their growing demand. The nice-sized batch of strawberry-scented crystals they were about to package today would bring in a quick hundred grand on the streets, which Salida would promptly pocket and make disappear.

Freeze knew their young clientele could go through that much ice in just a day or so. Bizz was booming, and they were drawing in droves of white boys and Asian kids from colleges all over Manhattan and the Bronx.

"Let me see," Salida sauntered over to the table where he was working. She tipped around cautiously on her toes, careful to avoid any of the chemicals and paraphernalia used to produce their lethal product.

"You burn any yet?"

Freeze nodded. He had burned a small amount, but he hadn't smoked none of that shit. He mighta been a dope dealer but he wasn't no fool. He had been around hardcore drugs all his life, but the most he did was fuck with a little weed and occasionally hit a couple of lines of blow. Besides, he was way too fuckin' handsome to get high on his own supply. That shit woulda had him walking around digging holes in his face tryna get at the imaginary bugs crawling around under his skin. Nah, he was cool on all that. Give him some good Cush any day of the week, but smoking meth was for the dummies of the world.

"Want a tester?" Freeze asked Salida, partitioning off a small portion and scooping it into a small vial that was stamped with her custom-designed neon-pink serpent logo.

"Yeah," she said. "Give me two. One crystal and one powder."

"You need a dun dun?" he asked as he passed her the drugs.

"No. I already have one," Salida said as she thought about Nooni who was still chained up in the Dungeon and jonesing like a feen. She took the first vial Freeze gave her and stuck it inside her jacket pocket, and she placed the second one inside the top drawer in the cut-room's office. She glanced at Freeze and narrowed her eyes. This new shit better be as good as he said it was. Some of the early batches they had cooked up had just been pretty good in terms of quality, but Salida had wanted more than good. At the time wasn't nobody complaining or coming back for a refund, but they weren't turning flips over her product neither.

That didn't sit well with Salida at all. She was a boss bitch and she wanted her customers to be straight up feenin' for her shit. Itchin' and scratchin' for it. She had wanted they asses to turn flips, do headstands, and break out with some cartwheels too.

So that's when she did some research and got creative and came up with a bright idea for a new formula. Yeah, it was risky, but so the hell *what*! Life was risky. She stared at the pink lump of powder sitting on the table before her. The sweet aroma of a strawberry milkshake rose to greet her nose and she grinned. It had been a kick-ass idea to start dying her powder and her crystals pink. She called her product Strawberry Snake, and between the sweet smell, the hot, tantalizing color, and the sexy dice-tossing snake logo on the package, it made her shit memorable and caused it to stand out on the market. Not to mention the special ingredient she had added to make the high it gave her customers simply unforgettable!

She laughed out loud. Her reorganization of the G-Spot was nearly complete, and she couldn't wait to get this new batch out on the streets and to distribute it to her customers on Rave nights. Those mindless youngsters were going to suck her strawberry product up with a crazy straw! Tapping the vial she had placed in her jacket pocket, Salida unlocked the cut-room door and tipped her hips down the stairs.

$$$$

The minute Salida was gone Freeze Dodson jumped his ass into action. "Crazy bitch!" he growled under his breath as he glanced at the closed door and then jetted over to the stack of boxes that lined one wall. Salida wasn't nothing but a troublemaker. A crazy-ass shit-starter! That toxic shit she was selling was gonna *kill* some goddamn body!

Freeze slid two boxes off the top, then dug into his front pocket and pulled out the carefully printed list of ingredients that he had written down. He folded the list and slipped it through the crack of one of the boxes, and then glanced at his watch and frowned as he shook his head.

C'mon, niggah! Freeze muttered under his breath. His brother Naj was supposed to show up ten minutes ago, and even though he hated it that the boy was all the time runnin' late, he was grateful that Naj hadn't shown up while him and Salida was conducting their lil bizz.

As Freeze carried both of the specially-constructed boxes over to the window, he thought about his elderly grandmother who was back at the crib sitting in her wheelchair with a tool pressed to her dome. The boxes were light. Real light. He set them down gently to make sure the objects inside were in no danger of breaking. Freeze put one box on top of the other, then secured them together by wrapping a nylon cord around them as tightly as he could, and then he left one end real long.

He was a loyal soldier and he wasn't tryna cross Salida, but he wasn't tryna get his own fuckin' grandmama popped neither. He remembered the look of stark terror in the old lady's eyes when he walked into her crib that morning and found her trembling in her wheelchair as two of Flex's capos force-fed her breakfast.

The smell of a shitty diaper was in the air, and the home health nurse who took care of the old lady six days a week was stretched out on the floor with her ankles bound and her wrists tied behind her back. A thick white gag had been stuffed in her mouth, and bloody knots had swelled up all over her forehead.

But them Divine Nine fuckers had done a whole lot more than just crack the young nurse in the dome with their pistols. They'd shot the poor girl through both her eyes, and half her brains had sprayed out the back of her head and splattered all over his Gramma's swollen ankles and feet.

"Dig, I want two things," Flex's right-hand man Dre had told Freeze as he stroked Gramma's face with his warm metal tool. Standing beside him, that crazy bitch they called Lil Lee was forcing spoonfuls of cold, lumpy oatmeal into the old lady's mouth. "I want the formula for that shit y'all been cookin' at the G-Spot, and about five hunnerd of them lil snake vials y'all be dishin' that shit off in."

There wasn't a moment's hesitation in Freeze when he agreed to their demands. His grandmother had raised him and Naj up from babies. Their own moms had taken them to McDonald's for fries one day, then left them waiting for their order as she skipped town with a Panamanian drug lord and never came back.

Gramma was all they had in the world, and relief washed over Freeze as his cell phone vibrated and he read a text message from his brother.

Naj was downstairs, and he was ready for his delivery.

Raising the window up as high as it would go, Freeze looked down into the back alley below, and then pushed the boxes of vials outta the window and used the nylon cord to lower them down into the waiting arms of his baby brother.

CHAPTER 6

It had just stopped raining and the streets were still wet when Lil Lee stepped out of her little black hatchback on Lenox Avenue and tipped her round ass around the corner. Dressed in a thigh-baring lilac skirt, black tights, and a black off-the-shoulder tank, her hips swayed and her breasts bounced as she strutted down the block dodging rain puddles in her six-inch heels. She was rocking her accessories to the max too. She had an expensive silk stole draped over her shoulders, and twin 9mm Glocks were strapped to the outside of both of her upper thighs.

Earlier in the day she had attended an emergency meeting that Flex had called with her, Dre, and Chickie, and now she was hyped as fuck and ready to get some shit popping. Lil Lee was a loyal soldier, so when Flex told her what kind of caper he wanted to pull to run Salida McKay outta bizzness, she had been one hunnerd percent down with his program.

But a few minutes later, when she turned around and told that niggah Flex that she wanted to pull a slick move on Trey and Chiney Jackson, he had bucked on her and told her to stand the fuck down.

"Why I gotta fall back?" Lil Lee had barked with icy anger flying from her eyes. "That mothafuckin' Trey snatched my fuckin' daughter, Flex! He touched my *blood*. That niggah gots to pay for that!"

She had been stunned at the look that crossed her boss's face when he waved her off and told her to forget about that what Trey had done.

"Fuck all that bullshit," Flex had said with an unconcerned shrug. "You too focused on that niggah. Your numbers been sliding ever since that shit happened, and that's what the fuck you need to be worrying about. Besides, it's your fault you let somebody get that close up on your daughter. You need to keep a better eye on that little girl. Word."

And even now, Flex's reproachful words were burning in her ears as Lil Lee's sharp eyes scanned her drug sector and she judged the level of heat on the streets. The rain had driven a lot of people indoors, but there was still a lot of die-hard meth addicts and pipe heads who didn't mind getting wet just as long as they could get high.

Lil Lee's face hardened as a dude-looking chick in baggy jeans and an oversized Polo shirt came around the corner and approached one of her best soldiers looking to conduct some business. The chick was light-skinned and had one of them telltale buzz cuts that a lot of stud females wore. Lil Lee's mind whirred as she observed the deal go down. She watched closely as the girl copped her shit, and then dapped Maleek out like a man and bopped her ass back around the corner.

On the outside Lil Lee appeared to be handling her business like the cool professional that she was, but fumes were rising off her as she stared a hole in the girl's back. When the dyke had disappeared, Lil Lee got with her trap boys one by one and discreetly went about picking up their excess cash and replenishing the street supply.

"Wassup?" Maleek greeted her as they walked up the steps of the drug spot and made their switch. Lil Lee frowned as she collected a thick knot of money from her very best corner boys. She was about to lose Maleek from her team, and she hated that Flex had chosen to promote him from a slanga to becoming a full member of the Divine Nine, because Maleek was one cutthroat niggah who truly belonged out on the streets.

"Nah, wassup with you? You getting ready to do big things, huh?" Lil Lee said as she grinned at the tall, lanky young boy.

"Yep," Maleek said coolly. "Today is my last day hustling the block."

Lil Lee was gonna miss her best street soldier when he took over Cee Low's old drug sector, and she knew he would be damn good at controlling his crew.

"Yo," check this out," she told him smoothly as her brain kicked into deep-scheme mode. The details of her meeting with Flex churned in her mind and she felt a wave of defiance rise up in her. What better way for her to get some payback and profit-up her pockets at the same time?

"That was Chiney Jackson you was transacting with a minute ago, wasn't it? She be hitting you up on the regular? I thought her brother put a stop to all her buys?"

Maleek shrugged and shook his head without a lick of concern over Chiney, Trey, or nobody else. "Yo, I don't get involved in no family drama, man. If she buying then I'm selling. Word."

Lil Lee nodded and a spark of excitement flashed in her eyes as she saw an opportunity to give Flex her ass to kiss and to do unto Trey Jackson exactly as that mothafucka had done unto her.

"Damn right. Stacking cream is how you stay in bizz in this game. Check it out, my manz Fitted is gonna take over your spot when you leave tonight. And when he comes on, I want Chiney to cop all her packages from him and only him, you got that? I'ma tell Fitted, but I wish I woulda caught you before Chiney left so you coulda told her that."

Maleek shrugged again. "It ain't no thang. I'll be conducting bizz with her again before the night is over. Chiney's eating for two, nah'm sayin? Her bitch is a real feen. That jawn'll be back as soon as her last hit runs out. I'll tell her."

With her eyes still on the corner, Lil Lee was thinking hard. This block used to be one of her top money-making territories, but business had been bad ever since J-Ugly had taken that ride off the rooftop of their main drug spot. Just remembering that shit made her frown up her pretty face and narrow her eyes into deadly slits. She didn't appreciate what her drop in sales revenue had done to her ranking in the Divine Nine, and she damn sure didn't appreciate what that niggah Trey Jackson had done when he snatched her little girl off a school bus and took her hostage neither.

But what she didn't appreciate the most was what her fuckin' boss had told her to do about it. *Stand down.* She smirked as she struck a sexy pose in her six-inch heels. Stand down, hell. Leandra Lee didn't stand down for no niggah! Matter fact, she was about to raise the fuck up. And raise up hard.

"Cool," Lil Lee told Maleek as she walked away with a grin. "Tell Chiney. Make sure you do that." Trickery was about to be a real mothafucka! Lil Lee didn't give a shit what Flex had said. She was making plans to go after Trey's blood the same way that mothafucka had went after hers!

CHAPTER 7

It was dull and rainy the morning Slick Sallie finally arrived in New York City, and he was damn glad that the city of Los Angeles was finally a thing of his past. He had driven across the entire country and had been on the road for so many days that he'd lost count. At some point, while driving through the state of Colorado, he had put in a call to one of his old Asian friends from Brooklyn. Lin was the son of an intelligence engineer, and they'd run a couple of Internet schemes together in the past. His great-grand father had bought up patches of real estate in Chinatown in the early 1900's, and Lin had joined the family business as a slumlord building manager.

Sallie was looking for someplace to stay that was out of sight and deep in the cut, and Lin knew just the place. One of his old immigrant relatives from China had just died in her sleep, and her one-room walk-up apartment above a Chinese butcher store was vacant. The place wasn't air-conditioned, but it had decent heat in the winter and best of all, it was already fully furnished. Lin was careful to inform Sallie that he had a waiting list of Chinese families fresh off the boat who were willing to pay top dollar to cram ten people inside the one-room flat, but because of their friendship and the big money that Sallie had promised to pay him, Lin was willing to hold the apartment for him.

The two friends had agreed to meet at a restaurant near the walk-up, and when Sallie arrived Lin was already there. They ate a small meal and then Lin suggested they head over to Sallie's new apartment.

The stench of bloody pork and gamey chicken coming from the butcher shop downstairs and the meat storage unit upstairs was almost suffocating, but Sallie sucked it up without complaint as he followed Lin up the chipped, rickety stairs. Once inside the apartment he took a long look around. There was a pullout sofa in the front room that doubled for a bed, a tiny kitchen, and a bathroom that was roughly the size of a closet. It was way too small to hold a bathtub, and the rusted-out sink was in the same stall as the jerry-rigged shower.

There was one other thing that Sallie noticed. There was a fake statue of Buddha pushed up against the wall. Sallie crossed the room and touched the statue. It was about six feet high and had been carved from antique Cambodian wood. He knocked three times on its fat, round belly. It was hollow, and nice and broad across the navel.

"I'll take it," Sallie said, holding his hand out for the keys.

Lin frowned as he toked on his blunt. "Take what? The Buddha?"

"No, asshole," Sallie said, snatching the stick of weed from his boy as he eyed the statue critically. He puffed and passed, then stared. If he positioned his stolen bricks of cash just right he could probably stuff most of the cash right up inside this guy's protruding beer belly. "I'll take this funky little shit hole. I wanna rent it for the next three months."

$$$$$

"I'm telling y'all idiots that boy Maleek is the one who pulled the trigger on Truth!" Salida swore up and down as she argued with Ace and Pluto. She knew damn well that after turning down Flex's business proposition and sending him a note that said, Fuck you! she needed to come up with a plan to take that young niggah all the way down.

She raised her voice and glared at Ace, trying to punk him. "You heard me! Maleek was the shooter and Flex put him up to it! Don't tell me y'all niggahs is too scared to go over there and pay that fool back!"

"Nah," Ace said, shaking his head as he challenged his boss-woman and displayed a rare moment of opposition to her will. "I'on't think it's like that, Salida. Me and Pluto got us a bizzness agreement going on with Flex. An arrangement. I'm telling you we gotta know for sure before we start talking outta our necks like that."

Salida broke. She needed to get these fools on her side and quick. Flex was just a younger, greedier version of Granite McKay, and she fully expected him to retaliate against her in some kind of vicious way. She didn't mind going to war with Flex's twisted ass, but she knew she couldn't go up against him all by herself.

She sneered at Ace in disgust. "And *I'm* telling *your* dumb ass that it was him! Besides, we got a witness! Bilal saw his ass!" she insisted.

Gripping Bilal's arm, she turned away from Ace and pushed the dreadlocked young'un up in Pluto's face instead. "Tell Pluto what happened, Bilal! Tell him! You saw Maleek shoot Truth with your own two eyes, didn't you?"

Bilal stood there shaking as he swallowed the rock in his throat. The young'un was so shook he could only nod. Salida had tortured the shit outta three of her cut-room boys before one of them squealed on him and told her that Bilal was the one who had run her ass over in the back alley that dark night. Not only had Salida gotten a crew of her corner boys to roll up on Bilal's younger brother and smash him until he was halfway dead, she had threatened to drop a dime to Ace and Pluto and tell them that *Bilal* was the shooter who had actually slumped Truth.

"Yeah, it was him," Bilal confirmed when he finally managed to get his tongue unwrapped from around his nuts. Salida was a big-ass liar! Not only didn't he shoot his boy Truth, he hadn't seen Maleek pull no trigger on that niggah neither!

"Not only did I see him do it, but Maleek even *told* me he did it," Bilal said, lying through his teeth. "That niggah told me he put the tool on Truth over a bitch. He said he popped him because Truth stole his girl. *Nooni.* I guess that Puerto Rican chick was suckin' Maleek's dick first and that niggah got mad when Truth boned in on that and snatched Nooni up. It was all about payback. Revenge."

Bilal felt like shit inside as he mixed a little bit of truth with his lie. That piece of ass Monique had paid him with had been real good, but it wasn't worth all this. She'd let him run his dick up in her chocolate dookey in exchange for bouncing Salida off his bumper, but nobody had told him he was gonna get his brother's face stomped in and have to play like he was an eyewitness to a goddamn murder.

"For real, I saw him, dude," Bilal told Pluto, and then he added something slick, just in case that crazy bitch Salida tried to renege on her promise and cross him up.

"And word on the streets is that Maleek was the one behind the wheel of the whip that crashed into Mizz Salida too. Matter fact, Maleek bragged to all his boyz about pulling a hit-and-run the night she got hit."

Frowning at his bold game, Salida cut her eyes at Bilal, and then glared at Ace and Pluto. "See? Told y'all! Bilal saw Maleek blast Truth right in the neck!"

Pluto stared at Bilal and then bellowed, "Niggah if you seent that shit go down then why the fuck you didn't *tell* nobody?"

"'Cause he was *scared*!" Salida barked, stepping in front of the boy and using her body to shield him from Pluto's deadly glare. "He didn't tell nobody because he was too scared that Flex and the Divine Nine was gonna put a target on his forehead just like they put one on Truth! Besides, if Bilal had told y'all then who was gonna look out for him? Who was gonna protect him? Everybody already knows y'all asses are way too soft to go up against Flex anyway! The only one Bilal felt safe telling was *me*. And that's why I'm telling you. And it ain't because I give a fuck about you, Pluto, because you already know I don't, but I loved me some Truth and I just figured you would wanna get some justice for your murdered nephew!"

The look on Pluto's face was one of deadly rage. That grimy niggah Flex! Truth had been his manz. His fam. His nephew. His blood. Them niggahs had capped him in the head and blown out his goddamn eyeball, and that shit was unpardonable.

Pluto pondered on that little distribution deal Flex wanted to get down on where they would go in hard together for G's old connect, and then split the supply channels right down the middle. Hell naw! That shit was off! Flex could kiss his ass! He wasn't doin' no bizz with his enemy! If Bilal was telling it right and the Divine Nine was behind Maleek's cowardly slump of Truth, then that lil sawed-off, rat-faced runt muh'fucka Flex was gonna get handled. Matter fact, Pluto thought as his heart burned hot in his chest, Flex was gonna get tricked *and* fuckin' handled. He was willing to put his last money on that shit.

Pluto knocked over his chair as he jumped up and stormed out of the room. If he hadn't been so blinded by rage and deafened by the need for revenge, he woulda been able to peep the scandalous Salida as she grinned real wide and snickered in satisfaction.

CHAPTER 8

It was just after two o'clock in the afternoon when the front door of Second Chances barbershop swung open wide.

"Yo! Trey!"

A down-ass white dude named Skeet busted up wildly inside the shop like somebody was chasing after him with a pit bull. Skeet was the owner of an urban clothing store called Empire Attire and a dedicated member of the Talented Ten, and right now his blond hair was wild, his pale cheeks were flushed red, and a look of pure rage was clouding his face.

Trey looked up quickly, surprised by the disturbance. He had an old-timer from the neighborhood in his chair shining his baldhead, and six of the other nine chairs had customers in them too.

"Yo, them fools hit my delivery truck, man!" Skeet barked. "And my safe too! I had Hill posted up at the back door waiting for a shipment to come in, and they got past his ass! Fizz had just emptied the safe and was about to go make a bank drop when they bum-rushed him too."

Skeet was red and swole with fury. His urban clothing store brought in big loot in the hood, and he sold his trendy gear at cut-rate prices so he could keep it affordable to his customers. His father and his grandfather had both been businessmen in Harlem, and Skeet had grown up on these mean streets and had been married to his sistah-girl honey from high school for five years. Just like the other members of their coalition who owned grocery stores, fish markets, dry cleaners, rib shacks, deli shops, check cashing places, and even AT&T franchises, Skeet had joined the Talented Ten to help keep his small business, and the neighborhood, thriving.

"You mean Fizz just gave your cash up just like that? That cat didn't even try to stand his ground?"

Skeet shrugged. "Them bandits was brandishing from the gate, my brother. Fizz said he had a Glock stuck halfway up his nose before he could even reach for his piece."

Trey set his clippers down and glanced out the window. He peeped two members of his street security team roving outside. They were posted up and standing watch just like they was supposed to be.

He shook his head. "Yo, Skeet man, how your soldiers let that kinda thing happen? What's bad for your business is bad for everybody's business. Why didn't nobody sound the alarm so we could rally up and take them cats down?"

Skeet frowned. "Hill said it happened too fast. Them boyz was layin' in the cut. They musta been hiding in the back of the truck when it pulled up. Zack was supposed to be on guard too, but that fool had just went to take a piss when they rolled up."

Trey smirked. "I told you before about that slow cat Zack, didn't I? When you put a weak dude on security ain't nobody gone be safe. How much they get? Is Fizz good?"

"Fizz is stable, man. He's madder than a muh'fucka, but stable. He said they got everythang out the register. Every fuckin' dollar. But we ain't sweating the doe, man. We just ready to get up in somebody's ass, you feel me?"

"Yeah, I feel you," Trey said. "But that's why we put all these systems in place, ya dig? To make sure shit like this don't happen. Them fools musta been real desperate to come around here violating like that. These local cats know they can't match up with us."

"It's all them new drugs," the old-head sitting in Trey's chair butt in. "These young boys is losing their damn minds over them new drugs."

A cute chick in her early twenties scooped her toddler out of the barber's chair right next to Trey's. His clothes were all brand name, and his little shape-up was slick and tight.

"Hell, the crack craze was bad enough," she said, shaking her head. "But now them fools is out there chasing that crystal meth too. That's even worse."

"You ain't lying," Skeet agreed quickly as he followed Trey to the back of the shop. "Check this out," he said once they were behind the closed doors of Trey's office. He reached into his front pocket and pulled out a small vial and held it in his pale, outstretched palm. "Fizz said he recognized them dudes, and one of them dropped this shit on his way out."

Trey peered into his manz hand. The small vial held icy-looking crystals and had the words Divine Nine stamped on the outside.

A hot ball of rage jumped in his chest and his dark, piercing eyes narrowed and became even darker.

"That little muh'fucka," he said. "That's Flex and his crew."

"Flex? That young boy who used to run around with your brother Cooter? I thought he got popped?"

Trey nodded. "He did. But them fools messed around and got him in the gut when they shoulda crashed his dome. I had a talk with that youngsta right after my brother got killed, man. Him and Cooter was scheming on bagging the drug trade all over Harlem. I told him if he ever brought his little ass anywhere near here he would regret it. That niggah's testing us, man. Inching his fucking toe over the line."

"Yeah, you right. He sent them boys," Skeet agreed as he studied the vial. "This is definitely his work. Fizz said it was Rome, Boog, and that lil cat Maleek you be sonnin'. He was ridin' with 'em too."

Trey froze and grilled the white boy. "You sure about that? You sure Fizz said it was Maleek? Little Leek?"

"Yep," Skeet nodded. "That's who I'm talking about. That cat might be young, but he's real twisted. So what we gonna do about this shit?" he asked. "Call the cops?"

Trey chuckled and shook his head like Skeet was crazy. He touched his front pocket and felt the cold slice of metal that was resting against his thigh.

"Nah, we don't call no cops when a faded niggah like Flex pulls a lick on us, homey. We assemble us a war council, dude. And then we get ours in."

"Cool," Skeet said with a nod of satisfaction. "Them lil cats is prolly up on the Ave right now styling my shit! Rome and Boog are gonna get served, but whattup witcha boy, Maleek? We gonna get in his ass too?"

An unreadable look washed over Trey's face.

"Nah," he said. "Don't fuck with Leek. Don't even think about touching him. Maleek is mine. I'll handle that lil cat."

CHAPTER 9

Money-making Monique was busy fake-moaning her ass off, when in reality she was steady scheming and her pussy was numb and couldn't feel a goddamn thing.

"Yeah, Daddy!" she screamed as she bounced up and down on Pluto's lap. "Gimme that good dick, baby. *Ooooh*, yeah, fuck this shit up!"

She was facing away from him and impaled on his wood, and behind her Pluto was gripping her small waist and raising and lowering her on his pole. Babbling sexual gibberish, Mo arched her spine and thrust her bold chocolate cake way out so he could really get up in it. Smirking as she worked her ass-cheeks, she rolled her eyes up toward the ceiling and gripped Pluto's fat thighs to brace herself upright.

Trying her best to get him to blow his load, Monique started shuddering and stuttering like she was turned on to the max and just about to cum. She made her pussy muscles get soft and loose, and then she contracted her pelvis and grinded down real hard, making her coochie walls suck him in deep and tight as shit. Performing like a mothafucka, Mo moaned and yelped like Pluto's slimy dick was a stiff, delicious bomb-pop, but every bit of it was just part of her professional hoe-act because Monique knew she couldn't get off on this niggah's wood if she tried.

While he was back there grunting and humping and waxing her ass, she was busy thinking about the slick one that she had just pulled on him. Mo had deliberately come home from the G-Spot early, and then waited in the living room until she heard Pluto's key turning in the lock. Jumping up quickly, Monique had run into their bedroom and pressed her cell phone to her ear, and pretended to be having an intense conversation while she looked for something in her nightstand drawer.

"I just don't know," she sighed into the phone, making sure her back was turned as Pluto approached their bedroom. "I mean, if I tell Pluto that Ace and Salida set his nephew up to get shot, then how the hell is my man gonna feel? I mean, on the one hand he'll probably wanna *kill* both of their grimy asses, but on the other hand Ace is his partner! His *manz*! Them two go way back together to the early days with G, and the *last* thing I wanna do is drop a dime and come between two best homeys, you know what I mean?"

Monique paused with her hand on his hip like she was listening to somebody on the other end. Never mind that she had turned her phone completely off so that shit didn't mess around and ring and blow her game up. She could feel Pluto's eyes crawling on her back as he stood listening to her fake convo, and she could even hear his fat ass wheezing behind her like a pissed off asthmatic old man.

"I know," she finally said, sounding torn and tortured. "Yeah, you prolly right girl. Matter fact, you *are* right. I know. I gotta tell him. I can't let them bastards play my man for no fool! Pluto *deserves* to know what kinda slime he's fuckin' with. Girl, can you believe they got him thinking Maleek killed Truth over a stank piece of ass? Now you know that's a lie! On the real, Ace and Salida actually *hired* that young boy to

412

shoot Truth!" Monique said passionately. "They *paid* him! They wanted Truth dead 'cause his lil ass got open on Nooni and started fuckin' up their plans. They knew he was trying to sneak her outta the G-Spot so she could go home to her sister. That's why Truth had to die. Not because of no bullshit beef between him and Maleek. That poor boy died to keep him from fuckin' up Ace and Salida's dirty plans for Nooni!"

Monique jumped and whirled around as Pluto stormed into the room behind her with his eyeballs lit on fire.

"Oh, shit! I gotta go," she whispered fearfully, then pretended to turn off her phone and look shocked and terrified.

"Who in the fuck was you just talking to?" Pluto demanded and snatched the cell phone from her hands. His fat cheeks jiggled and his pig-nose flared. "Who in the fuck was you just tellin' all my fuckin' business to?"

"N-n-nobody!" Monique stammered, acting her ass off as Pluto turned her phone on and started scrolling through her call history. "I was just talking to my sister Marva, that's all. Just my sister, Pluto. Nobody else."

Monique watched as his fat fingers found her call folder. She had definitely dialed her sister's number, but she hadn't spoken to that bitch. Marva owed her a hundred dollars and when she caught up with that trick Monique was gonna put her foot up that ass. But Pluto liked Marva, so it wasn't a total crime for Mo to be talking to her. Sometimes Monique thought he liked her sister Marva a little bit too damned much.

She stiffened as Pluto flung the phone down on the floor and took a menacing step toward her. He was gonna kick her ass. Straight fuck her up. Monique had figured this would be one of the consequences of her plan, but if it meant exposing that bitch Salida and getting Pluto to go after Ace's throat, then this was one ass-kicking she was down to take.

"You grimy-mouth bitch!" Pluto said, and pounced on her. Monique let her knees sag and she dropped to the floor as he slung her by her hair and back-fisted her upside her head. "You better not never get on the phone and blab nothing about my fuckin' nephew to no fuckin' body! You hear me?"

Monique took the blows that rained down on her head and back in stride. She balled up in a knot and protected her face, and she winced as Pluto threw a flurry of haymakers at her exposed arms and legs.

Yeah, yeah, yeah, niggah! she thought as his fury exploded and he took his rage and frustration out on her. Keeping her chin tucked, she rolled left and right as he swung his feet and fist wildly and beat the shit outta her until he was winded and his anger was finally spent.

Monique waited patiently until he had stopped swinging, and then she pleaded with him from her knees. "You ain't gotta beat me like this, Daddy!" she beseeched him with fake tears falling from her eyes. She clutched at his ankles, and then his knees, and then she rose up a little bit and clutched at Pluto's belt buckle.

"Mo-Mo is sorry," she meowed like a sweet kitten as she massaged his joint through his pants. She looked up at him through soft, adoring eyes as she threw her femininity down on him and appealed to his masculine nature. "You know your baby didn't mean no harm," she cooed as she expertly undid his belt and his zipper and went to work on his love muscle like it was the prettiest one she had ever seen.

Above her, Pluto was still breathing hard from exertion, but Monique had no trouble detecting the moment he went from winded to wanting. Manipulating his hardening dick in her expert hands, she had his joint standing up nice and tall in no time, and even though the foul stench coming off his ass smelled like he hadn't touched a drop of water in about ten days, Monique jumped on his greasy dick and gobbled it up like that grimy thang was made of pure gold.

"Yeah," she whispered as she planted tiny kisses up and down his thick shaft. She reached down into his pants and cupped his nuts, cringing at the disgusting sensation of his stubbly ball hairs raking across her palm.

Wiggling his hips, Pluto shook his baggy pants off until they sailed down to the floor and fell around his feet like a deflated balloon. He hooked his thumbs in the waistband of his drawers, and backing off slightly so Monique would lose her suction grip on his dick, he peeled his tighty-whities down over his plump thighs and pushed them below his knees.

Monique tried to moan, but that shit came out like a gag and a groan. The crusty disaster staring up at her from the crotch of Pluto's drawers almost made her go blind, but unless she wanted this niggah to really bust her ass, she knew better than to let him catch wind of her disgust.

Monique stayed on her knees sucking his dick for a long-ass time. It was like that niggah was deliberately holding on to his nut. Every time she got him in a grip and a motion that she just knew would make him blow his load, Pluto would push her off and make her change her rhythm and position so she would have to get his arousal built up all over again.

When he finally got tired and had to sit his fat ass down in a chair, Mo was happy as hell and she promptly obeyed him when he told her to back her big ass up and ride him motorcycle-style. She climbed on and rode that funky niggah like a jockey, and when he finally thrust his thumb up her asshole and shot his wad off in her pussy, she sighed with relief and squeezed her thighs on him real tight, milking every ounce of liquid from his balls.

As soon as he caught his breath, Pluto pushed Monique off of him and she sank down to her knees on the floor. She didn't even look up when he stomped angrily into the bathroom and slammed the door, instead she just sat there and listened to the sound of his putrid farts and his fat turds of shit plopping into the toilet bowl.

Climbing slowly to her feet, Monique picked up her cell phone from the floor and then looked in the mirror to inspect the damage that he had put on her body. Her arms were welting up with fat purple bruises, and her legs felt like she had run a marathon, but her smile was bright and her face was untouched.

Mission accomplished! she thought, giggling inside with evil satisfaction. She knew Pluto had overheard more than enough of her phony conversation to make him go after Ace and Salida and chop both of them fools straight through the neck. And all Monique wanted in exchange for her clever trickery and the ass-whipping she had just taken, was a front row seat when it all went down so she could flash a big grin at her enemies when their severed heads rolled on the ground.

CHAPTER 10

New York hadn't changed much since he'd left and that made Sallie really happy. All the little rat holes, and grimy digs he used to do business in were still right there where he'd left them, and they were even dirtier and grimier than he remembered.

He'd spent his first two nights in the city just making sure his surroundings were secure. He was a white boy in Chinatown, and the re-emergence of gangs in the Chinese underworld was a problem he didn't want to deal with.

Plus, Sallie knew that Juicy was hiding somewhere in this town and the last thing he wanted to do was run into her and any of her moolie friends. He'd have to kill that bitch over the money he'd stolen from Gino's safe, and while he didn't have a problem taking her out, it would be messy, and a mess was the last thing Sallie needed right now.

So, he had to be careful and he had some work to do too. It took him a while to carve a hole in the base of the Buddha statue, but it was all cream after that. He stashed Juicy's loot as far up in the guts of the statute as he could, and then he slid two handguns up in there too.

Sallie spent his third night on the East Coast in a state of deep thought. He mulled over his pending arms deal with the young kingpin from Harlem and carefully laid out his plan. When everything was organized and crystal clear in his head, he called the fast-talking dude to confirm that he did indeed have the necessary funds to conduct such a large transaction.

"Don't fuck with me," Sallie warned the slimy young kingpin. "I'm fronting a load for you and everything better be in order. 'Cause if it ain't I'm taking you down."

"Muh'fucka!" the kid had barked. "Suck my dick, white boy! A niggah like me is sittin' on plenty of cash! You just get me them fuckin' tools and make sure ere' one of them shits is squeaky clean, a'ight?"

Sallie hung up and made another call. This time he hit the arms trader who had promised to supply him with the shitload of clean guns. Unlike the greedy young moolie who was planning to spray the shit outta Harlem, this cat was a true professional. He was semi-retired and only popped his head up to do special jobs on special occasions, and just as Sallie expected, the trader confirmed that his arsenal was well-stocked and he was ready to do some heavy business. Satisfied that all his ducks were finally lined up and his dots were all connected, Sallie slept like a baby in his shitty little Chinatown flat.

On his fourth night in town Sallie stepped out to find some action. Chinatown was ablaze with activity and bright lights. He walked toward the busy avenue where he'd parked his car, passing by storefronts, restaurants, and Asian whores who were looking to turn a quick couple of dollars.

Sallie walked by and never even looked their way. There was no need to. These flat-assed, bony-butt chicks weren't his flavor. Instead, he headed north on the East

River Drive and drove until it became the Harlem River Drive. He exited at 116th Street, then cruised the neighborhood leisurely. Sallie had to admit that Los Angeles hadn't been all that bad, but there was no place in the world like New York. It had a pulse all its own, a smell of its own, and a vibe that was unlike any other city he knew. Wondering if he'd run into Juicy somewhere on the streets of Harlem, he drove past pizza shops, beauty salons, travel agencies, and more bodegas and storefront churches than he could shake his nuts at.

Sallie might have appeared to be wandering aimlessly, but he knew exactly what he was looking for, and he knew this town would surely deliver. He'd spent part of the afternoon watching and rewatching Beyonce's Single Ladies video on his laptop, and no offense—but fuck that broad Beyoncé! It was the chocolate-skinned girl with the thick, muscular ass that Sallie couldn't get out of his mind. She was exactly the type of chick he wanted to bang tonight, and this town had plenty of hoes who had the same kind of luscious body as hers.

Sallie headed for one of the popular spots where prostitutes worked the track and flaunted their business openly on the street. There were lots of chicks on the stroll tonight, and as soon as they spotted a clean-shaven white boy like him their eyes lit up like they could just taste their jackpot.

The block was on buzz as Sallie pulled his ride over and slid up to the curb. Black girls with big tits and monster asses were posted up in mini-skirts, short-shorts, tight pants, and high heels. Sallie's well-trained eye sifted through the assortment of women like he was looking at the menu at a greasy fast food restaurant. There were about fifteen of them flagging down cars and working the curb, and every last one of them made a bee-line over to his whip like they were competing in a relay race.

With a crowd of hoes surrounding him, it only took Sallie a minute to spot the kind of chick he had a taste for, and when he got out of his car and stood up so he could see her better, his drawers immediately rocked up and he had to stop himself from drooling.

Ignoring the vulgar propositions from the other prostitutes, Sallie motioned to the young girl with the smooth brown skin and bright eyes, and she smiled and shook her hips and she pushed her way through the crowd and walked toward him. As usual, all the hoes he hadn't chosen got loud and salty and started talking mad shit.

"Damn! You can only handle one of us, white boy?" a cute light-skinned chick reached out and grabbed Sallie's arm as he turned back to his car with his prize for the night. "One is fun, but two is terrific, baby. Karisma ain't been out here a good damn minute. She don't know shit about pleasing no real man like you! But I'm a professional, baby. Take me with y'all and I'll lay some head on you that will blow your fuckin' mind!"

Sallie grinned as he brushed past her and held the car door open so the young hoe she'd called Karisma could get in. "Next time," he told the older hoe as all the other working girls started screaming for him to come back and get them when he was finished so they could show him what he was missing out on.

Sallie slammed his car door and turned and looked at the black girl he had chosen. She had big, juicy titties and a small waist, and he could tell how wide her hips were by the way her thighs spread out all over the car's seat. She was real young, but at closer glance he didn't see the innocence he had expected to see in her face. Instead, there was something fun and mischievous in her eyes, and she looked like she was ready to hang out and have a good time.

"How much?" he asked her as they grinned at each other.

She shrugged. "Depends on what you like."

Sallie nodded. "What I like, huh?"

"Yep," she said, "what you like."

"I tell you what," Sallie grinned even wider and slid his arm around her slender shoulder. "How about we do something that *you* like?"

The girl's grin disappeared and she gave him a quick, suspicious look like, *what the fuck you talking about, trick*? She held up her wrist and tapped her watch.

"Oh, I know," Sallie said smoothly. "Time is money. But I'll pay you good for your time, baby. Real good. Check this out. Do you like Chinese food?"

She nodded. "Hell yeah. Who don't?"

"Cool," Sallie said as he turned his key in the ignition and pulled out into Harlem's night-life traffic. "Let's go get us some then."

$$$$$

Less than an hour later Sallie's stomach was full of Chinese food and his dick was full of action. He had driven the young hoe down to Chinatown and brought her an egg roll, and then taken her to a meat and poultry storage unit that was upstairs in the building he was staying in.

Sallie had busted the padlock on the door to the storage unit pretty easily, and then he led her into a large office across from the industrial freezer where the duck, chicken, pork, and beef that was sold in restaurants all throughout Chinatown was stored.

"Eeew," the hood chick had the nerve to wrinkle up her nose and complain as soon as they walked through the door. "What's that nasty-ass smell? It stinks like a mothafucka up in here!"

There were three windows on the far wall and Sallie walked over and opened all three as wide as they would go. They sat on a small couch in the office and smoked some weed and tossed back the bottle of E & J that Sallie had picked up from the liquor store next door to the Chinese restaurant. The girl was young, but she had a real long throat, and after she sucked up the Erk and Jerk they were both loose enough to get down to business.

"Let me undress you," Slick Sallie said softly as he touched the girl's hair. He let his fingers slide down her toned neck and trail over her arm. Her body was young and perfect. Her skin looked like solid milk chocolate. Sallie gathered the bottom of her shirt in his hands, then raised it up over her deeply indented navel, her bulging breasts, and finally over her head.

She sat on the raggedy couch naked from the waist up, looking like a nubile African princess sitting on a throne. Sallie stood up and took her hand, pulling her to her feet. She reached for the top button on her pants, but he brushed her hands aside gently.

"Let me do it," he whispered. His face was flushed red from the liquor that was burning in his belly, and the smell of her black pussy that was tantalizing his nose.

He dropped to his knees in front of her and opened her tight pants and slid her zipper down. Sticking his fingers in her waistband, he inched her pants down over her wide hips, looking past her yellow thong, and surprised to see her plump pussy had been shaved naked.

Sallie pulled the crotch of her thong aside with two fingers and gasped. Her clit was dark and glistening, nestled snuggly between the juicy outer lips of her beautiful cunt. He could hardly wait to get her pants off. He just couldn't help himself. He dove in with his tongue and took him a big wet gulp of that gorgeous pussy right then and there.

Above him, the girl stiffened up.

"You gonna eat me out?" she asked, like having a white trick slurp her pussy was the most insane damn thing she had ever heard of.

"Yeah." Slick Sallie nodded. "I'm gonna lick your kitty dry."

And that's exactly what he did.

Sallie yanked her pants all the way down and waited patiently as she stepped out of them. Her bright yellow thong he ripped right the fuck off, the flimsy material giving away like toilet tissue in his hands.

"Hey!" the hoe protested as she stood there in nothing but her high-heeled shoes. "What you do that shit for?"

"Ssshh..." Sallie pressed one finger to his lips. "I'll buy you another one," he promised. He reached into his front pocket and pulled out a fifty-dollar bill and pushed it into her palm. "I'll buy you ten of those cheap shits."

Karisma clenched the money in her fist and thrust her hips out at him. She spread her legs a little bit more so his probing tongue could lap up the clear sticky juices that were beginning to flow down her toned inner-thighs.

Sal was in hog fuckin' heaven as he opened his fly and took out his erect dick. He couldn't get enough of the girl's scent, or of the way her liquid sugar just seemed to melt into a sweet mist on his tongue. Still on his knees, he gently cupped her big ass in his palms and weighed her cheeks like they were two ripe honeydew melons. Her flesh back there was a solid hunk of meat, and he gripped and massaged her with a frenzy, pressing his tongue as deep up in her snatch as he could get it as he pulled her ass toward him and guided her gyrating hips.

Karisma was a spicy little freak, Sallie observed with delight. She cupped her own titties and played with her dark, raisin-sized nipples as he slithered his tongue in and out of her clenching pussy. But pussy wasn't all Sallie wanted. After a while he shifted his position, and with his dick still hanging out of his fly-hole, he bent her over the small table and parted her ass-cheeks wide. A pink slice of her inner walls smiled at him, and Sallie stuck his tongue deeply inside her sex cave and gathered about an ounce of her cream. He held it in his mouth for a second, and then used his tongue to smear it around her asshole in a tight figure-eight motion.

The girl moaned out loud as Sallie attacked the hell outta that chocolate! Going back and forth rapidly with his expert tongue, he stabbed her fiercely in the pussy, and then he swirled his tongue around the rim of her ass, reaching between her thighs and playing with her clit the whole time.

And the young hoe was loving that shit! She tossed that ass back at him with wild strokes and opened her legs wider so he could put his whole face up in her. She had nutted twice already, and now she was bent over at the waist with her elbows on the desk, making all kinds of sexy fuck noises and telling him how good her pussy felt. Sallie was willing to bet that no other man had ever licked that chocolate up the way he was licking it, and he sucked her swollen clit until he felt her body convulse and begin to shudder. At the moment of her release he covered her pussy hole and sealed it with his lips so he could catch every drop of sweet juice that flowed from her tunnel, and as she shivered and filled his mouth with her delicious creamy nut, he stroked himself off and shot a huge wad of hot cum into the palm of his own hand.

Slick Sallie wasn't done yet though. Ignoring his itching tongue, he stood up and rubbed his slime all over the girl's full breasts and erect nipples, and at the same time he reached into his back pocket with his free hand and pulled out his cuffs. Thrusting his tongue into her ear canal to distract her, he slapped one cuff onto her right wrist, and then grabbed her left wrist with his sticky hand and tried to bring her hands together so he could get the other cuff on her too.

But Karisma was hood-quick. The moment she felt that cold metal bracelet click around her wrist she started swinging and fighting and making a break for the door. Caught off guard, Sallie lunged for her. He bodied her from behind and wrestled her naked ass to the floor.

"What the fuck is you doing!" The young girl blurted in astonishment. Her big brown eyes were wild and fearful as she kicked up at Sallie with both feet and caught him on the chin with the heel of her shoe. Instead of answering, Sallie reached down and capped her in the face like she was a full-grown man. Karisma mighta been young, but the bitch had some beast in her. She took that blow and rolled with it, then jumped to her feet with her naked titties heaving and threw two real nice power jabs that took Sallie by surprise. The first one caught Sallie in the nose, and the second one thumped his chest so hard it sent an involuntary cough flying from his mouth.

Then the bitch put up her dukes like she was ready for some more.

Sallie was in a panic. None of his tricks had ever fought back like this before! He rushed at the girl and bear hugged her around her waist, squeezing the shit outta her. Karisma started screaming and swung her fists, punching him all over his head in short, furious blows. And then the bitch got clever. Her hood instincts kicked in and she leaned forward and sank her bright white teeth deep into Sallie's forehead, puncturing his skin and biting into his dome like it was a sweet red apple.

It was Sallie's turn to scream now, and trust and believe, he shrieked like a muthafucka! Grabbing a fistful of her hair, he wrenched his head out of her mouth as her vicious teeth tore through his flesh. Dark rivulets of blood trickled into his eyes and slid down the tip of his nose. The girl screamed again. And this time the bitch screamed the type of shit that made people stop and pay attention.

"Fire! Fire!" the young hoe screamed as she tried to break free of his grasp. "Call the fuckin' cops! The building is on fire!"

"*Shit*!!!" Sallie cursed and lunged for her naked, slippery body again. He spun her around and yoked her up by the neck, then smushed his other hand over her mouth, cutting off her cries.

The girl reached back and fumbled wildly around Sallie's head, and then suddenly an excruciating burst of pain exploded in his ear canal. He screeched like a bitch as the hoe grabbed his ear again and stabbed her nail tip even deeper into his crevice, pushing her that porcelain into his flesh like she was trying to puncture his ear drum.

Sallie cringed in pain and let up on her just for a second, and that was all the time the prostitute needed. She swung her cuffed fist at Sallie's bloody face and the empty end swung free, slamming into his cheekbone as it raked across his nose.

He yelped and grabbed at his face, stunned like a muthafucka. But then young the chick stunned Sallie even more as she sprinted across the room like a track star, and with one panicked, terrified look back at him, she threw one leg over the window ledge, then crawled her naked ass the rest of the way out and simply fuckin'... jumped.

Sallie heard a sickening thunk as her body hit the concrete ground, and he coulda sworn he heard her bones snap on impact. The rank taste of her pussy rose on his tongue, and his stomach heaved as he ran over to the window and peered down at the ground in the alley below. The young girl was laying on her side, still as death, and under the glow of the street lights he could faintly make out the edges of a small puddle of blood that was forming around her head.

"You dumb bitch!" Sallie shrieked into the night. "What the fuck did you do that for?"

It took him less than two minutes to stuff his dick inside his pants and throw his sweatshirt back on, and then run down the stairs and around the corner to the alley. The girl was still laying right where she'd landed, and Sallie rushed over to her and grabbed her shoulder and shook her real hard.

"Are you okay?" he demanded. "What the fuck you jump like that for, stupid ass!"

The girl moaned and her eyelids fluttered open. Recognition and fear flooded her face at the same time, and in a wild, terrified frenzy she swung her cuffed fist at Sallie again. Hard.

"Owww!" he yelled and jumped back as the metal bracelet sent fire flaming through his nose. The girl turned over onto her stomach and all four of her limbs moved like crab legs as she tried to climb to her feet. Favoring her left leg, she made it upright and took off screaming and limping down the alley, hollering Fire! at the top of her lungs and glancing back over her shoulder like Sallie was some kind of serial killer or something.

Moments later, people started peering anxiously from the windows of Sallie's building as well as from the building next door. Their garbled Asian words sounded frantic and concerned, and Sallie cursed when he heard somebody say call 911 in very clear English.

Pressing his fingers to the bloody bite-mark on his forehead, Sallie darted into the shadows against the building, and then he threw his hoodie over his head and hauled ass around the corner and jetted toward the safety of his parked car.

CHAPTER 11

D.I.V.A. Day at the Crossover Community Center was coming to a close, and even after the drama that had jumped off the day had been a big success. I was highly impressed with Trey for investing so much of his energy in his Developing Initiative and Values for Achievement program, and for bringing hope and joy to the young girls of Harlem.

Trey Jackson was the type of dude who attracted light, and there were corporate ballers and big willies out the ass up in the house all day long. It was obvious to everybody that he had mad status and pull in the community, and people not only loved him, they respected him too.

And his Talented Ten business owners were just as dedicated as he was. It didn't matter if they were Asian, Hispanic, Black, or white, the small business owners of Harlem had jumped in together with their money and their products to contribute to Trey's vision. Food and juice had been donated and delivered from local delis, coupons were being handed out for free groceries from corner stores, there were fifty-percent-off vouchers being passed around from two local dry cleaners, and a couple of nail salon owners had set up booths and were giving young girls free manicures.

There had been mega young chicks rolling in off the streets to learn about HIV/AIDS testing, and to get free condoms and stuff. There were representatives on hand from cosmetology schools showing young girls how to do their hair and makeup, while career counselors from local colleges gave demonstrations on how to fill out applications for college admission and free financial aid.

Even though the day was supposed to be all about empowering young girls and giving them a clear road to follow for their future success, plenty of young boys from Harlem had turned out in droves to take advantage of all the free information and services too.

And me? I was working my ass off! My girl Egypt road the train uptown from Brooklyn, and I kept her busy cutting material and threading needles as I led a bunch of short sessions I called, "From Fabric to Finery in 15 Minutes or Less".

I had chicks strung out, oohing and aahing as I picked a girl out of the crowd at random, then posted up at my sewing machine and measuring her body dimensions with just my eyeballs, I whipped her up a sexy, banging JuicyOriginal summer dress in less than fifteen minutes. After a few sessions everybody in the joint wanted them a free JuicyOriginal! Those crazy teenagers started lining up real thick at my station and fighting over who was gonna look the best in their gear.

There were entertainers from the music industry in the house too, and one of my old friends showed up and stole the show. My girl Candy Montana used to be the lead singer in a hot female trio called Scandalous! And I got amped when her and her man Knowledge Graham walked in looking like Jay-Z and Bey.

I had known Candy from my old neighborhood, and she had been through the same type of craziness with her man Hurricane Jackson that I had been through with G. Or maybe even worse. Candy was one of those real gorgeous chicks who had such a beautiful voice and a different look about her that no matter where she went she made people stop, stare, and take notice. Me and her were about the same body size, and back in the day whenever I got a chance to sew something hot and slutty that I knew G wouldn't let me wear, I would send it to Candy and she would style my gear and publicize my JuicyOriginal line.

Today, Candy got up on the stage they had set up in the middle of the basketball court and gave a real good speech that motivated all the young chicks and had them jumping up and down and screaming her name. She started her session out with a little prayer that was dedicated to her baby sister Caramel, and her two best friends from Scandalous! Dominica and Vonzelle.

The prayer was sad and tragic because all three of the people she had dedicated it to had died when a fire broke out at the House of Homicide and everybody in the joint got trapped behind the chained doors. Folks had stampeded like crazy as they tried to get outta the building anyway they could, and the few who didn't go down from the smoke and the flames ended up getting crushed to death under other people's feet.

It had been a real miserable time in Harlem when that happened, and for a while the word on the streets was that Candy had lost her mind from all that grief, but time heals everything, and eventually she had come back to being herself, and back to doing the things she loved; singing, dancing, and helping young girls make something out of their lives.

Because Candy's life had definitely been real fucked up. Everybody knew that Hurricane Jackson had dogged her out and forced her to do a lot of unspeakable shit, and when word got out about the nasty XXX sex tape he had made her star in with his dog, a lot of people said her singing career was dead. But instead of being embarrassed and running and hiding from all that humiliation, Candy had embraced her life journey and owned it. Today, just like she did at every live appearance she made, Candy got up on that stage and made them shine a light dead on her. She pointed at the ugly scar on her face and then proceed to tell all the young girls in the audience exactly how she got that shit.

"Look at me!" she barked into the mic and demanded as she pulled her long red hair back from her face and made sure everybody could see what she needed them to see. "I said, look at *me!*" she yelled and pointed into the crowd. "Y'all see my face? Y'all see my scar? It's ugly as hell, ain't it?"

"Noooo!" people in the crowd screamed. "No!"

"Yeah it is!" Candy shouted back. "It's ugly and it's *permanent!* It's *always* gonna be there. I'ma take this scar with me all the way to my *grave!* And you know why?"

She peered out at all the young girls with a look of quiet seriousness on her beautiful face.

"Because I was *just like y'all* a minute ago! I was *hardheaded!* I was caught up in the hype and chasing the lights! I was silly and naïve! *Greedy!* Impatient! Attracted to the madness! Tricked out on the money, the fame, and the *game!*"

The whole gym was in an uproar as people clapped and whistled at the pure truth

Candy was spitting down on them.

"My little sister *lost her life* because of this industry bullshit! My best friends Dom and Vonnie *died* because we got blinded by this impossible dream! So I'ma need y'all to be way smarter than we was!" Candy hollered into the mic as the young girls of Harlem screamed and clapped.

"I'ma need y'all to keep your eyes *open*. To see straight through the fake glitter and the gold in this industry! I'ma need y'all to have *vision*, and *direction*, and to recognize this shit for what it really is—a *trap* baby! It's a booby-trap! An ambush! A young girl's graveyard! Chasing ballas will *kill* you! Do you hear me? Chasing dollars and drugs will *kill* you! But check it out, little sisters. What happened to me and my girls don't have to happen to you! Y'all can be better than we was. Y'all can *do* better than we did! Y'all got a scar-face sister like me standing up here today to make sure you don't step on none of those landmines and booby-traps that blew our lives away! I'm standing here today to give you a little bit of *knowledge* so you can turn it into a whole lot of *POWER!*"

The crowd went off. Every hand in the joint was clapping. The young girls were screaming and the dudes in the house were all whistling. Candy's man Knowledge Graham was standing in the background just a' watching her. He was a fine-ass investment baller who everybody said was rich as hell. They were a power-couple who had clawed their way up outta the trenches in a real rags-to-riches story. I could tell how much he loved her just by the way he looked at her, and when all the clapping had just about died down, he was still putting his hands together and giving it up for his girl.

Candy got back on the mic and called five teenage girls up on the stage and challenged them to freestyle a rap or a song by finishing the sentence, "My life has meaning because..." The first teenage girl got up there and took the mic and started getting hers in. She had a sweet face and a strong voice, and the lyrics falling out of her mouth were full of gutter street pain mixed with hope and determination.

"Look at Taleah!" Trey said from over my shoulder. I glanced up at him and saw that he was smiling real big and had a look of pride on his face like the young girl was his daughter or something.

"She's good," I nodded and agreed. "Real good. Who is she?"

Trey beamed up at the stage. "Taleah's an 'around the way' lil sis that I look out for when I can. She used to hang out with my goddaughter Princess before she overdosed on some bad shit and died. Taleah started hanging around the Crossover a lot after that."

Lil Mama was up on there on that mic cutting up hard and stealing the show. The girls who got up there behind her were pretty good too, but none of them could match her delivery or her flow. When the contest was over Candy gave all five girls one of her business cards and invited them to join the Girl Power! mentoring program she held over at Knowledge is Power Productions.

The Crossover was on a happy buzz by the time Candy got off the stage, but you know how niggahs are, and just a few minutes later some kind of scuffle broke out near the door.

I peered through the small group of people who were crowding around. I saw two girls and I recognized one of them. They looked just alike, except one was taller and older than the other one. They younger chick was crying and the older one looked mad as hell.

"I thought I told you to stay your stupid ass away from here!" the older one screamed on the teenager as she grabbed her by the back of her shirt and yanked her toward the door. "Get the fuck outta here!" she spit, pushing the young girl around as the kid looked up at her like she was mad as hell. I didn't know what was going on, but I could see Big Sister wasn't no joke. Every time I'd ever seen this chick she was flyer than fly, and I couldn't understand why she would wanna be down with a dude like Flex. She was a lace-front junkie with curls falling down her back. She had on a real tight jean jumpsuit that fit her ass like a second skin, and her two-thousand-dollar Manolo Blahniks were just like a pair I'd seen Beyoncé sporting at a basketball game.

"Wassup, Lil Lee?" Trey bust through the crowd out of nowhere. He towered tall over the two girls and everybody else in range as he quickly took control of the scene. "You came out to get your D.I.V.A on today?" he said like they shared a joke.

Joke, hell. That chick Lil Lee hit him with a look so hot and venomous that her cat-eyes narrowed all the way down to slits. "Don't fuckin' play with me, Trey. I came to get my sister up outta this shit hole. Didn't nobody give her permission to come up in here, but hold up. When it comes to you having your way with little girls you don't need no fuckin' body's permission right?"

The sounds of, "Ooooooh," rose in the crowd like she had burned Trey a big one.

Trey never dropped his smile.

"C'mon, mami," he said easily. "Can't you come down off ya gangsta horse for just one day? Today is for the kids. All of them. Let your sister stay. I took good care of your daughter, didn't I?" He gave her a real slick smirk. "I'll take care of your sister too."

And then he added, "Or anybody else you make me take care of."

Lil Lee looked like she was ready to start throwing blows. Instead, she nodded, then snatched her sister up again and headed out the door. "A'ight, Trey. A'ight, you muthafucka, you. Remember, you gots to bring ass to get ass! You better watch your fuckin' back, son. You heard? Me and you got a whole lotta unfinished bizzness. You better watch your fuckin' back."

Trey laughed. "I will, baby, but you better watch more than that, Lil Lee. You better watch more than that."

CHAPTER 12

It was getting late when fourteen-year-old Taleah left the Crossover Community Center and walked back to her apartment building. An alarm was ringing loudly as she entered the lobby, signaling that once again that the elevator was stuck between floors, probably from some hoodlum kicking the shit outta the exterior door.

Sighing, the young girl headed towards the building's stairwell. She held her breath against the familiar onslaught of pissy air as she pushed against the door and began dashing up the stairs, taking them two at a time. Taleah made it all the way up to the third floor before she was forced to take some air into her burning lungs, and after inhaling one deep breath she sped up to the fifth floor. Exhaling with relief, she pushed through the exit door, turned the corner, and to her horror and surprise, she ran dead smack into a monster from her nightmares.

"Sup, Taleah," the tall, skinny dude with the cornrows said as he stared at her from a pair of cold, merciless eyes. Taleah was mute with fear as he pushed up on her and forced her back through the door and into the pissy stairwell.

She had been terrified of running into him ever since the night her best friend Princess had been found dead and she was forced to tell Trey where Princess had copped her drugs.

Unbeknownst to Taleah, she had been spotted spittin' fiyah on the stage at the Crossover Community Center earlier in the day. No, not by an A&R agent or by a big-time executive of a music label, but by a chick who was so diabolical and cold-blooded that she had busted up in a church and spit down into the casket of a pregnant thirteen-year old girl, and then viciously flung a handful of crack vials into the face of the corpse.

"I want you to get that lil bitch Taleah," Lil Lee had placed a call and barked an order to the undisputed most brutal member of the Divine Nine. "I want you to fuck that stank ho up!"

Lil Lee pictured the way Trey had sat with his arm wrapped protectively around young Taleah at Princess's funeral that day, and how he had pushed her safely to the floor when the gats came busting out. That niggah was gonna learn that nobody he cared about was safe from the grip of Lil Lee. Nobody.

Locked in the glare of a murderer's eyes, Taleah trembled. She had feared this day was coming. She had dreamed of it. She knew Trey had made the wrong drug dealer pay for Princess's death, and now her best friend's real killer had come to snuff her life out too. Tears fell down her cheeks. Her entire body was stiff with terror as the nightmare from her dreams fumbled in the pocket of his hoodie and came out with two small vials.

"You know the rules, baby. Around here snitch-bitches get all kinds of stitches," the young man said quietly as he backed her up against a cold wall. "But that ain't always true." He put his head back and laughed, and the cruel, eerie sound bounced off the concrete walls and echoed throughout the empty stairwell.

"Sometimes snitches don't get stitches," he told her as he pulled out a clear glass stem and started packing it with crystals. "Sometimes them muh'fuckas just get... high. "

$$$$$

It was real late when we got back to Trey's apartment, and the house was so quiet that I could tell right away that Chiney wasn't there. I didn't have to wonder where she was because I already knew she was somewhere out on the streets chasing her girl Venus and chasing a high too. I understood how much it hurt Trey to see Chiney getting strung out on that street shit, but my mama had been a stone-cold junkie and I didn't think barring Venus from his crib was gonna stop his sister from getting her fix.

"You hungry?" Trey asked me as we walked into the living room. I plopped down on the couch. "Yeah," I said. "A little bit."

I sat there while he went into the kitchen. I leaned my head back when I heard the water running, and the refrigerator door opening and closing. He was rattling pots and pans, and pulling drawers opening and rumbling through silverware. I wanted to get up and go help him fix whatever he was fixing, but I was just too exhausted to move.

I must have dozed off, because when I opened my eyes again Trey was setting a Cherry-wood serving tray on the coffee table. Two small candles were glowing from the tray, and he'd even folded two napkins in a cute little design. He'd fixed us a plate of Ritz crackers with grape jelly spread on top of them, and he'd sliced up some strawberries and apples and put them on a separate plate.

"Yum," I said, sitting up with a smile. "That looks real good."

Trey grinned, "It's just a little something for you to sleep on so your stomach ain't making a whole lotta noise tonight. You know the walls are thin as hell, and I ain't tryna hear your stomach growling all night long." He sat down next to me and reached for my hand.

I hesitated for a moment.

I swear I tried not to, but I automatically thought about Gino and how he used to hold my hand and say grace over our food. It used to make me feel so good when my man did that. Like we were bonded in the world together and he was asking God to bless us both.

Trey was still reaching for me, and slowly I gave him my hand. He looked at me with real patient eyes, then lowered his head slightly and began to pray.

"Father in Heaven, the Master of our world and the Owner of the Day of Judgment. Bless this food and those that are about to receive it. Allow it to nourish and sustain our bodies and souls. Amen."

I didn't realize how hungry I was. I tore into them jelly crackers like they were little hunks of fried shrimp. Trey ate a few crackers too, and he played with a couple of strawberries, but he pushed most of the food toward me and told me to knock myself out.

While I was busy eating Trey slid down to the end of the couch near my feet, and leaned back into the plush sofa. I crossed my legs at the ankles and nibbled on the sweetest strawberries I'd tasted in a long time.

I looked over at him and I was surprised to see how intensely he was staring into my eyes. I got kinda embarrassed and coughed nervously, and then out of nowhere I started rambling off with the mouth.

"I know I already said this a whole bunch of times before, but thanks for letting me stay here with y'all. I mean, I appreciate being here, I just don't wanna cause no trouble between you and your girl."

I wanted to kick myself. Now why the hell did I say that?

But Trey played it real cool. "My girl? What girl?"

"Oh you know what girl," I said, thinking about the fuck noises I had heard coming from his room the night he was over there pounding her pussy and blowing her fucking back out. I felt my cheeks flush as I remembered how I had fantasized that it was *me* he was over there deep-drilling, and I remembered how I had gotten my pussy nice and sticky as I masturbated to the sounds of them fucking and beat my own stuff up deliciously.

And then I remembered how ashamed I had been after I had nutted all over my fingers and then heard the two of them arguing. That chick had been steady hollering, "No! What's *my* name, Trey? Call me by *my* fuckin' name!"

Man, that chick had been raging on fire when she busted on me out in the hallway and asked me who I was. And after I told her, I would never forget how I felt when she stared at me and said, "Oh, so *you're* Juicy, huh? Well since you're the bitch whose name this niggah keeps moaning out while he's fucking, I guess you're the bitch he really wants to be with then!"

All of this flashed through my mind as I stared into Trey's dark, intense eyes, and I could tell that he was remembering that shit too.

"Yo, I don't know what you talking about, Juicy. I don't even know no other girls," he joked and bust out laughing. Then he reached over and tickled my feet with his big hand, making me giggle too.

"Yeah, uh-huh. Remember, the walls are thin Trey, and you sure as hell knew that chick that night. Inside and out."

"Oh, you real funny," he said, grinning. "But don't worry about Debbie. Ain't nothing going on between me and her no more."

I gave him the "niggah please" look.

"What? You don't believe me?"

I shrugged. He was rubbing my feet in both his hands now, and I squirmed a little trying to ignore the sudden wave of heat that was being stoked up in me. "I'm not saying you're lying... but I could tell that girl was really into you."

His eyes bore into mine as his sexy lips moved.

"So you can tell all that," he said, pressing his thumb into the arch of my foot and teasing me with small strokes, "but you still can't tell when a man is really into *you*?"

A ball of fire flashed through me. I squirmed and squeezed my thighs tightly together. I didn't wanna feel what Trey was making me feel. I loved it and I was damn near feening for it, but I didn't want it.

"Trey—" I said, "I'm just really tired."

He rubbed my feet once more lightly, and then he nodded and let them go.

"I know you are," he said quietly. "You've been through a whole lot, Juicy. And I ain't talking about just today either." He stood up, and I couldn't stop my nasty eyes from zooming straight to the bulge that had formed in the front of his pants. "Come on," he said, reaching for my hand. He pulled me easily to my feet and looked down at me. We were only inches apart and just his manly scent had every nerve in my body screaming.

"You ready for bed?"

I swallowed hard. His six-foot-six inch muscled-up body damn sure had me ready for something.

I don't know what came over me, or what the hell I was thinking, but I just stepped into him. I stepped straight up on him, crushing my titties to his chest as my arms went around him, and then his arms went around me too.

I felt like a starving woman who had accidently stumbled into a food fest.

Trey was all man as I pressed myself into his rocked up chest and felt the hardness of his thighs pressing against mine. I don't know who went for it first, but I think we met halfway. His lips were on mine, and I opened my mouth to him. Our kisses were hot and greedy. You couldn't tell who wanted it more. Who was loving it more. I melted in the middle as his tongue probed my mouth. He teased me with it, giving and taking at the same time, fucking me orally just the way I needed it.

"Juicy," he whispered, pulling away even as I was pushing forward and going in for more. "You ain't ready for this, baby."

I knew he was tryna think about me but I was on fire. The only way he was gonna get me off him was if he poured a bucket of cold water over my head.

I stood on my tiptoes and reached for him again. My arms wound around his neck as my nipples tingled against his chest. My hips started moving on their own, grinding on the boulder that stood out boldly from his groin.

Trey cupped my ass with both hands and squeezed. He pulled me to him, letting me work my hips the way I wanted to. I almost came as I moved back and forth against his dick, scraping my clit on his hardness through our clothes.

I found his lips and nipped the bottom one gently between my teeth. I sucked it the way a baby sucked a nee-nee, with my eyes rolling back in my head as I inhaled the scent of sweet strawberries on his breath.

Somehow we ended up on the couch.

For somebody whose woman thang was supposed to be dead, my poor panties were soaking wet. It was shameless the way I threw one leg over the back of the sofa and invited him in. Trey lowered himself on top of me, his tongue never leaving my mouth.

He grinded into me, his hardness trying to penetrate me through my jeans. I threw my pussy up at him. We were humping like two kids trying to sneak a nut on the back staircase in school. Trey took off his shirt, then pulled my blouse up. My breasts jumped free from my bra like two wild beasts. My nipples pointed at the ceiling, and I practically screamed as he cupped them and brought his soft lips down to cover them.

I was in Heaven as he licked and nibbled and sucked all over me. I was alive! I was *alive*! It had been so long since I'd allowed myself to feel any type of sexual stimulation from a man that I was like a virgin, experiencing pleasure for the very first time.

I reached down between us and felt for his dick. Dude was a piper! I almost screamed when I felt the long, thick imprint standing out prominently from his body. Trey held himself up with his arms, hovering over me as I undid his belt and yanked at his zipper. When his pants were open he lowered himself down on me again and we kissed and moaned into each other's mouths.

We were panting and sweating. Fucking through our clothes, and I wanted to be closer to him. I reached between us again and started fumbling with my top button. Trey moved my hand aside and opened my pants and pulled them down just below my hips. I arched my back and shuddered as I felt his big dick stroking between my pussy lips, with just our underwear as a thin, moist barrier between us. I knew he was gonna split my pussy wide open when he finally got up in me, and just imagining how good he was gonna pound my guts and mash me out had me about to cream. I couldn't even wait to get my panties down. An intense storm of bliss had started barreling through my groin and pushing its way out of my dripping tunnel, and I was just about to tip over the edge of steaming hot pleasure when Trey's cell phone started bleeping in a very strange pattern.

He pushed himself up on his forearms and listened.

"That's a 911 call," he muttered under his breath. He leaned over to get it from the table and I clung to him, damn near dragging him back down on top of me. I threw my pussy up at him again, my body desperate to cum, and even with the phone bleeping in his hand, his hips started grinding and working me over once more.

The bottom halves of our bodies were glued together and moving to a serious fuck-beat as Trey pushed the talk button and pressed the phone to his ear.

First his hips stopped moving. And then I watched his whole face change. By the time his short conversation was over that bucket of ice water I said would be the only thing that could separate us came splashing down on both of our heads.

Trey pushed himself off of me and stood up. His chest was still heaving and his dick was about to explode through his drawers like a mothafucka, but there was nothing but frozen rage in his eyes.

"What happened?" I whispered. The first thing that came to my mind was that something bad had gone down with Chiney, but then I realized I was way off when Trey finally answered me.

"That was my boy, Rain," Trey said quietly. "Somebody found little Taleah on the staircase in her building and took her to the emergency room."

"What?" I shrieked and sat straight up. My eyes darted back and forth as I searched his face for the answers to the questions that rolled off my lips. "What happened to her? Is she okay?"

He shook his head. "She's in intensive care. She took a beat-down and got all her front teeth knocked out. Somebody musta given her some dope too, because she OD'd in the ambulance on the way to the hospital."

"*Nooo*," I moaned as I sat up and clutched Trey around the waist trying to comfort him. I pressed my face to his belly and squeezed him tight. Just a few hours ago that beautiful little girl had been up on a stage rapping about her self-worth and having the time of her life. And now she was in the hospital fighting for her life!

"And that ain't all," Trey said coldly as he pulled away from me and started zipping up his pants. "Rain said Taleah can't talk and tell nobody who did that shit to her, but she did write a name down on a piece of paper."

"She did?" I asked, as I stuffed my titties back inside my bra and started fixing my clothes too. "Well if she knows who the dude was then the cops can go get him and lock his ass up! Well what did she write? Who did that shit to her?"

To my surprise I saw a single tear forming in the corner of Trey's eye. And then he opened his mouth and said the last word I had expected to come out of his mouth.

He said, "Maleek."

CHAPTER 13

There were several jiggle joints that Slick Sallie coulda found his pleasure in that night, but the part of him that was Irish had always been drawn to danger. He chose a nightclub that had once been known as the grandest in all of New York City. The cover charge had been a grand a head, and the owner of the club had attracted such high-profile, crucial, and iconic celebrity clientele that his spot used to be busting at the seams as he turned away droves of customers at the door each night.

Sallie knew he coulda picked up another piece of trim right off the track if he'd wanted to, but the prominent bite mark standing out on his forehead was a stark reminder of how dangerous and unpredictable street girls in Harlem could be.

Besides, Sallie was done picking up hoes like Karisma. Tonight he was going to a place where he knew he could find the kind of woman he craved and they could do their thing without a whole lot of drama. And he was also going to the one place in the world that he knew Juicy Stanfield was guaranteed *not* to be.

Slick Sallie was going to the G-Spot.

$$$$$

"Make that money-money! Make that money-money! Make that muthafuckin' money-money, honey!"

The heat was spiked up sky-high at the G-Spot Social Club and Monique was stripping mad.

Kiss my ass, perverts! Lick my twat, assholes!

Mo-Mo had an attitude as she performed for the crowd of drunk, horny men. Yeah, these fools were tossing mad green doe on the stage and making it rain all over her head, but these bastards still wasn't *appreciating* her shit the way they shoulda been!

She frowned out into the crowd as them hard-dicked mothafuckas got off on the scent of her pussy as it blew through the air. It was an all-out freak-fest up in that joint as she turned her back on them and made her thick booty cheeks jiggle wickedly, clenching and flexing one well-defined hump at a time.

Those niggahs loved it!

"Mo-Mo! Mo-Mo! Mo-Mo!"

They screamed out her name as she worked her hips and performed her nasty dance under the filtered spotlight, bucking and gyrating like a glistening silver pole was about to come sliding outta her twat.

"That's birthday cake!" A hustler with a row of gold fronts screeched as he stared mesmerized at her stunning bottom half. Monique knew she looked crucial as hell up on that stage. She completely understood why every niggah in the joint wanted to fuck her lights out.

But what she couldn't understand was why three magnificent titties and an extra-

431

large hunk of tail is *all* they saw when they looked at her? Yeah, every last one of them were ballin' and would toss down good money to spend a few hours knocking her back out. But didn't these niggahs know she had a heart too? A soul? Didn't these fools understand that she was a woman who wanted her a paid-out-the ass, halfway-decent man?

Twisting up her lips, Monique squeezed her firm knockers in her hands and raked her nails back and forth across her inch-long nipples. Ducking her chin to her chest, she did the same old tired shit that never failed to get the club jumping. She extended her tongue and gave the tiny third nipple in the center of her chest a nice long lick.

Niggahs wilded out! Everybody loved a freak!

But a freak wasn't all Monique wanted to be. She'd had her sights set on becoming a real classy business woman, an icon of fashion and style, the kind of bad-ass bitch who dressed in silk and expensive jewels and ran corporate shit from top to bottom.

All this gutter action has to go, Mo thought as she dipped her chips and gyrated her hips down to the floor. *She wasn't never gonna get more than a stiff dick doing this type of freaky shit.* She stretched out seductively on the stage and lifted her shapely, and perfectly proportioned legs high in the air.

The noise in the room amplified, and Monique frowned up her face, disgusted by the unseen wads of cum she knew niggahs was about to start shooting off in their drawers. She arched her back up real high until only her shoulders and her thick mound of ass were touching the ground. She clenched her stomach muscles and rotated her hips in tight, suggestive circles as she pretended to be fucking an imaginary lover.

Closing her eyes, she shivered as multiple C-notes fluttered down and stuck to her moist skin. The lover of Monique's fantasy pressed his pelvis down on top of hers, and she threw her pussy at him like she was a wild animal going for broke during mating season.

The crowd was now at the height of excitement, and Monique spun around quickly and gapped her stunning legs open wide. Licking her index finger, she gazed out at the men with a blank expression on her face, and then she thrust her finger deeply inside her twat and began masturbating her wet pussy in deep wet strokes.

Normally, she would be getting to the part she loved best right about now, but not tonight. Yeah, all three of her nipples got hard and her pussy began to simmer and leak, but in reality Monique wasn't feeling a damn thing except disappointment and disgust. She wanted *out* of the strip club scene. *Out* of the G-Spot. She wanted the high-post glamorous life that had been promised to her right before G went and died and fucked up all her dreams.

Using both of her hands, she spread her lower lips wide and gave every man in the house a bird's eye view of her pink inner walls, silently inviting each of them to examine her uterus.

Dudes stared and drooled, anxious to see what she had for them next, and Monique knew if she wanted that doe to keep raining down on the stage, then she better not disappoint them. She had tons of routines to choose from, and she lay back on the stage floor with her heels up near her butt like she was about to deliver a baby. Slowly, she let her curvy thighs fall open wide as she rubbed her clit and prepared to fuck the hell outta her middle three fingers.

Going through the motions of her deep na-na act, Mo slid one finger up inside herself first, and then gradually she thrust all three in all together. Dudes screeched and stood up on tables as she gripped one of her massive breasts and then reached down and licked her lil titty again. This was usually enough to get her nut to rising, but the sparks that normally ignited in her sensitive little mini-breast failed to catch fire and Monique had to fake her way through the rest of her set.

And that's exactly what she did, too. The way her hips heaved and shuddered, and all the moans that spilled from her mouth and the puddles of sweet cum that leaked on the floor, not a single dude in the crowd could tell she wasn't up there having the orgasm of her life for real.

But by the time it was over, instead of feeling powerful and triumphant the way she usually did, Monique felt surprisingly humiliated and thoroughly unappreciated.

Y'all dumb-ass niggahs don't know nothin' about a mothafuckin' woman! she cried inside as she ended the show by rubbing her glistening pussy juices around in the crack of her ass. *Nothin' goddammit! Y'all don't know nothin!*

The room exploded in applause as a bunch of satisfied customers wiped sweat from their brows and adjusted their dicks in their pants.

Selfish bastards! Mo-Mo mouthed at the crowd as she snatched the money she'd earned off the stage and ran off that bad boy steaming mad. She didn't wanna be just another hot piece of pussy-for-show no more. She wanted a man who was gonna elevate her status and treat her like a queen.

"Girl, you fuckin' killed that shit!" her girl Honey Dew grabbed her arm and beamed as Monique stormed angrily through the crowd of bodies. "You about to have a long-ass night cuz these fools done bought up almost all your chips!"

Shit! Monique grimaced, wondering how many stank dicks she was gonna have to suck as she stomped her way back to the dressing room. It was definitely time to look for a new gig. Time to find herself a whole 'nother line of work. She hardened her heart and prepared herself for a long night of misery as she flat-backed for her doe.

Monique glanced toward the back door of the G-Spot and she was real tempted to just walk straight outta that shit. She could clearly see the dead-end sign that loomed large at the end of her road. There wasn't the slightest chance in hell that she was gonna find the kinda life she wanted up in a joint like this, and even if she got fired she was about to tell every last one of them niggahs who had stood in line and bought her chips, that they could kiss her fuckin' ass!

$$$$$

Sallie couldn't stop himself from drooling.

Never had he seen this much ass and attitude in one hot and gorgeous body. He stared at her with his mouth open and a look of utter amazement in his eyes. It was all he could do to stop himself from running up on the stage and begging her to sit on his face. No wonder there were so many big black dudes pulling security around the stage. This girl had something that could be worth billions if somebody found a way to bottle it up and sell it on the stock exchange. Sallie couldn't help himself. He leaned over toward a guy at the table next to him and asked, "Who was that chick? What's her name?"

"They call her Money-Making-Monique," was the man's response, and Sallie could tell by the thick tone of impressed admiration in the guy's voice that he had enjoyed the visual stimulation just as much as Sallie did.

The room had been hazy with smoke, but the spotlight had shone down on Money-Making-Monique like she was the only chick in the universe. She'd worn a sexy little pout on her face as she pressed her chin to her chest and extended her tongue. Sallie had shivered in his seat as she licked the stiff little nipple that sat prominently in the middle of her chest.

"This broad has a freakin' birth defect!" he had whispered out loud in amazement. Well, if you had to be born with something extra, Sallie reasoned, better it be an extra nipple than an extra nose, chin, or eyeball.

Sallie had watched as Monique split her legs in the air like a pair of scissors, then went down to the floor and lifted her legs over her head, then spread them as wide as the ocean. She'd gyrated her hips wildly as her hump of butt bounced and jiggled like it was about to break a hole in the stage floor. All kinds of hoots and hollers had cut the air when she sat up and fingered herself, then parted her lips, took her engorged clit between two fingers, and milked it until a stream of liquid sugar formed a puddle on the floor.

Now that her act was over Sallie found himself covering his crotch and breathing heavily through his mouth. He had never been so turned on in his entire life. There was only one thing left to do, and he knew he had to make his move real quick.

Bolting from his seat, he almost knocked the table over as he rushed across the room to the cashier's window that was near the bar.

"How do I get the girl I want?" he asked the old man who sat behind the glass handling the money.

"We're back to selling chips again. They cost two bills and they're good for fifteen minutes a pop."

Sallie asked, "How many chips can I buy?"

The old man chuckled. "How much ass can you handle?"

Sallie thought for a moment.

"How much time does that girl Money-Making Monique have left tonight?'

The man punched a few keys into the laptop in front of him and said, "Monique is almost booked, partner. It's not even midnight yet and she's down to her last four chips."

"Only four chips left?" Sallie whined.

"Yep, only four."

"Cool," Sallie said, reaching for his wallet. "I'll take 'em."

$$\$\$\$\$\$$

Look at that soft-ass muh'fucka! Pluto sulked angrily as he lurked in the shadows of the G-Spot. He sat back in a corner, sipping gin and evil-eyeing Ace and Salida as they stood near the bar cutting up like two silly young lovers.

No matter how much alcohol he slugged back Pluto couldn't stop hearing

Monique's words in his ears as she talked to her sister on the telephone. The words that had revealed to him exactly who was responsible for cold-smoking his fuckin' nephew Truth.

It had been painful to hear that shit though. Truth was a good soldier and he didn't deserve to go out the way he did. And to top it off, all this fuckin' time it had been Ace and Salida who had really set his fam up. Set him up and took him out!

Pluto watched the two of them and fumed. His boy Ace was all up on that old hag tryna smooch his lips on her neck while she laughed and pulled away like his breath stank.

"Niggah so soft he done got fluffy," Pluto muttered and tossed back another drink. He was getting liquored up and tipsy. But one thing he was not getting was weak and sloppy. Quite the opposite. He felt betrayed, disrespected, and burning fuckin' mad. Matter fact, he was so mad he had to force himself not to pull out his tool and pop both of them muh'fuckas right there where they stood.

It was a good thing G wasn't around to see how bad his boy Ace had slipped, Pluto thought, lighting a blunt as he forced his anger to ease back. If the boss had been around that cold-crushin' niggah woulda slit Ace's punk-ass throat for letting this shrewd, diabolical bitch kill his street cred and stuff his gangsta deep in a trick bag.

Pluto tapped his foot furiously as he sat back in the cut puffing his blunt and grilling the pair. His bottom lip was turned down in disgust and his mind was clicking and whirling as he thought about what kinda tools he was gonna use to smoke his ace-boon niggah and get some revenge for his nephew. And once that fat-necked niggah was deaded, then Pluto would grab him some of Salida's loot, and blow this fuckin town. Blow it and never look back.

Pluto didn't have a drop of hesitation in him behind smoking Ace. Yeah, they used to be partners, and they had fought their way up on the streets side-by-side, running shit together. That right there dictated that he take the niggah out fast and not let him suffer. But their history together wasn't enough to make him spare Ace's life, Pluto thought with a storm brewing in his eyes. What that fool had done was unpardonable. In fact, he didn't deserve no fuckin' mercy. At the whim of some used-up bitch, Ace had pulled some sucka shit that no real rider woulda ever pulled on his manz.

Pluto fumed from his corner as he watched a strange white cat leave the cashier's cage and walk toward the fuck rooms. White boy had a niggah bop on him. That ice Salida was selling had brought all kinds of new clientele into the G-Spot, just like she'd said it would, and the joint was almost back up to its old standards and will probably exceed them shits too.

Pluto grimaced. He had been born and raised in the heart of Harlem. This city ran through his veins just like his blood. He'd never thought the day would come when he would despise this club, these streets, and all who walked them. But that day was here now, and he was about to dip on all of them. He was gonna dip out on the G-Spot, on that worn-out trick Monique, and he was especially out on that bitch-niggah Ace. But before he left, he was gonna handle that fool. Handle him well.

Pluto forced himself to chill as he glanced at his watch and waited for his phone to ring. It wouldn't be long before he got the call he was waiting for. And whenever his phone did finally ring, he knew exactly who was gonna be on the other end of the line too.

Just wait, he thought coldly as he got up and walked through the crowded club and toward the Dungeon where Nooni lay chained to a pipe. She was stank and grimy, and looked a real mess. Ace and Salida had hidden that poor girl away like she was a retarded relative, and he couldn't believe fine little Nooni had turned into a rotten-toothed little hag. Pluto didn't like what them bastards had done to the young chick one fuckin' bit, and outta love for Truth, he was planning on letting the poor girl go one day soon. But not yet. Nooni still had some work to do. She had to help him find Moonie before that niggah Ace got to him, and then he'd worry about letting her go later.

Because right about now Pluto was about to go Lone Ranger and pull some trickery on these fools. He was gonna get his hands on some of that profit Salida was always hollerin' about, and then teach his boy Ace a fuckin' lesson that he musta never learned in school: pussy might have a whole lotta power, but a fat dick like his came packed with some major fuckin' muscle.

CHAPTER 14

Me and Trey rushed over to Harlem hospital and took the elevator upstairs to the intensive care unit. I felt funny coming up here knowing that I wasn't coming to see Rita, and even though my heart was bamming hard with dread for poor little Taleah, my coochie muscles were still humming with horniness for big bad Trey too.

That call from Rain had come just in time. Both me and Trey had been grinding so hard and hot on his couch that we could have easily taken shit to the next level, regardless of what kind of drama might have come out of it. I felt horrible that yet another Harlem child was in the hospital because of violence and drugs, but that didn't stop me from reliving the memory of Trey's hard dick pushing against me or his wet lips and strong hands roaming all over my half-naked body.

I couldn't lie. I knew what I wanted now, and I wanted me some of him. I wanted him the way I used to want Gino, and admitting that shit excited me and scared the hell outta me at the same time. It shamed me like crazy too, because I felt like was betraying the memory of Gino and of our unborn baby too.

Rain was waiting for us when we got off the elevator. I kinda moved to the side and let him and Trey talk, but I could still hear what they were saying. I watch Trey's shoulders get real stiff as Rain told him that Child Protective Services had taken emergency custody of Taleah and that her doctors were trying to find out what kind of crazy drugs she had been forced to take.

We walked down to the nurse's station and one of the young nurses I knew from being on the floor with Rita all the time told me that no one was being allowed to see Taleah for the rest of the night. She said she was sorry she couldn't give me any more information, but when I asked her if we could peek in on Rita for a quick minute she said okay.

When we walked into Rita's room my girl was still bruised up and swollen, but she was looking a little better than she had before. I held her hand and smoothed her hair back, and her eyelids tried to flutter a little bit. Once or twice I even thought she tried to squeeze my fingers.

"Everything is okay," I told her, wondering if she could hear me. "You're doing real good, Rita. I'm here for you, girl. Just rest, that's all you gotta do. Everything is gonna be just fine."

Trey put his arm around me and I leaned on his rocked up shoulder and took a deep breath. He looked down at me, and his hand slid along the length of my arm and he gently cupped my hip.

I was grateful that Rita was at least stable, and I wanted to say something about Taleah that might give Trey a little comfort too, but before I could get my words together the nurse from the front desk walked in the room holding out an envelope for me. My name was scribbled on it in scrawny chicken-scratch letters, and whoever wrote it had spelled it "Jucy" like they forgot to put the letter i between the u and the c.

"Sorry, I meant to give this to you," the nurse said.

I frowned as I took it. "What is it?"

She shrugged. "A letter, I guess. One of the night orderlies brought it upstairs and left it at the nurse's station for you."

"Thanks," I told her, and then I glanced at Trey as she left the room.

"I can't think of nobody who would be sending me no letter up in here," I said suspiciously, all the while thinking of those flowers that Flex had sent to Trey's crib.

"Go ahead and open it," Trey said calmly.

It didn't look like nothing but a plain white envelope. The kind that people send letters in every day. I tore into it and pulled out a single sheet of paper. The writing on it was scratched out and raggedy. It said: *Call Nooni rite fuckin' now 917-555-1213.*

I stared at Trey as I passed him the note. "Uh-uh. It's a set-up. I know damn well Nooni didn't write this. Somebody else musta wrote this shit."

We got up outta Rita's room so we could talk. We both agreed that I should call the number, but Trey told me to wait until we were back in his whip before dialing it. He had one of them Bluetooth systems in his ride, and that way the call would be blasted through all the car's speakers and he could listen in and hear what was being said.

Sitting beside him in the front seat of his whip, I pushed the numbers from the note into his cell phone and the call was answered on the third ring. Immediately the sound of music and a partying crowd blared from the speakers and exploded in our ears.

A dude with a deep voice barked over all that noise and said, "Speak, muh'fucka!"

"Um... somebody left me a note that said to call this number," I stammered.

"Yo, who this?"

I strained, listening close.

"This is Juicy. Who is this?"

He answered by laughing.

"Juicy, Juicy, Juicy," he shouted into the phone. "It's been a real long time, baby. You doing a'ight?"

Immediately I knew exactly who the fuck I was talking to. I had a quick flashback and I clutched my throat as the taste of his fat, nasty dick washed over my tongue and almost made me throw up in my mouth.

"Where's Nooni?" I snapped.

That foul niggah laughed again. "She's the same place yo azz was at the last time I saw you. Remember? That night I was gonna bang you? Hold on a minute. I'm going down there right now."

He was talking about the G-Spot. The Dungeon. I shuddered inside as I heard his big feet stomping down the stairs. I remembered how bad that niggah had done me when I was trapped down there in that shit hole and I just couldn't resist taking a jab at him.

"You talking about the night I almost bit your lil nasty dick off?"

"See now, Juicy. That shit wasn't right boo. I'ma get you back for that one. Or maybe I'll just take it out on Nooni."

The noise of the music was gone, but right on cue I heard a loud, smacking sound of flesh hitting flesh, and then a young chick screamed and whimpered, begging for mercy, and right away I knew it was Nooni for real.

"Pluto!" I hollered. "Why the fuck you hitting on her like that? Y'all need to let that girl go, Pluto. Let her the fuck *go!*"

"Oh, I'ma let her go," he said easily. "'Cause this lil feen is sick. Sick enough to die. But first I'ma need you to do me a lil favor."

I didn't say anything.

"You there, Juicy? You hear me, girl? You there?"

"I hear your ass."

"Good," he said. "'Cause you gone hafta do me a lil solid if you want this little bitch back home safe and sound, nah'mean?"

"A solid like what?"

"Well, I ain't gonna ask you to suck my dick no more, but you *are* gonna get down on a little swappy-swap exchange with me. Ya feel me? You gonna get me the name of G's old drug connect, Juicy. That's what the fuck *you* gonna do. And in return, I'm gonna give you Nooni"

I sucked my teeth real loud at his bogus offer. Pluto knew goddamn well G had never told me shit. I was the last person the great Granite McKay wanted up in his business, and I reminded Pluto about that.

"You know G didn't tell me nothing. He never told me a damn thing, so I don't know *who* the hell he got his drugs from."

"Oh, I know *you* don't know who G's connect was," Pluto said happily. "But Moonie damn sure does."

"*Moonie?*" I said in amazement. I hadn't thought about him or heard his name in a long time. "What Moonie got to do with me? You think I been hanging out with some Moonie?"

"No, dumb ass," Pluto said. He sounded real exasperated, like I was retarded or something. "I know *you* don't know where Moonie is, but you know that real swole niggah you been fuckin' with? The one who's listening in over the goddamn speakerphone right now? That niggah sure as hell knows."

$$$$$

Bitter bastard! Ace thought as he watched his manz roll his fat frame out of a chair and amble toward the back of the club. He had been chillin at the bar with Salida, acting all nonchalant like ere'thang was ere'thang, when in reality he had been checking his boy Pluto as he sat in the shadows shooting venom from his eyes.

Shit, if anybody shoulda been on broil it was him. Pluto had convinced him to go along with some whack-ass plan for them to use Nooni to squeeze some info outta Juicy, and then he had hired some off-brand juveniles to do it. Of course shit had gotten all fucked up. Them young'uns didn't have no experience in kidnapping nobody. Instead of dipping in to get Nooni and then sliding back out like they was supposed to, them wild cowboys had rolled up in there and sprayed the whole joint with lead. They'd popped Nooni's sister and slumped two little kids, and for what? To have their crime splashed across every television screen in Harlem during the six o'clock news? And even after all that pandemonium Juicy was still safely under the protection of the Talented Ten, and now Ace and Pluto were no closer to finding out who the fuck G had been in bizz with than they were before all this shit started.

The whole scenario had pissed Ace off because Nooni's sister Rita was down with a family full of NYPD cops. Word on the street was that her man Dutchy Gaines and his crew were on the prowl for Rita's shooter, and this shit had the potential to bring unnecessary heat down on all their heads. Bottom line, it had been a stupid ass plan, and Ace couldn't help barking on his boy over it neither.

"Yo," he had spit when he found out how bad shit had gone, "why you send them lil knuckleheads in there to fuck everythang up, man? You said snatching Nooni was gonna send Juicy running straight to us and make her give up the connect. Well, we got Nooni feenin' like a muthafucka down in The Dungeon, but where that bitch Juicy at with the info? I'on't see her helpful ass nowhere around here."

Pluto had stared at him through glazed, deadly eyes. Ace could see a vein jumpin' on the side of his man's temple like that niggah was about to pop a fuckin' vessel.

"We can't get close to Juicy right now," Pluto lied. "That Talented Ten got her on deep lock. But tell me something, ak," Pluto hit him, coming outta nowhere with a blast from their grimy past. His eyes had bored into Ace's and his words were flecked with ice. "Wuss good witcha cousin Rabbit out in Cali, man? That west coast niggah a'ight? What about his dudes? You know, the two fools you hired to put in that work on Gino. What they call them niggahs? Izz and Zero? Yeah. How them two hot-headed muh'fuckas been doin'?"

Ace had swallowed hard as guilt crept up his cheeks. How the fuck did Pluto find out about the side deal he had made with his cousin? That was the first time that Ace had ever betrayed Pluto or gone behind his man's back. He'd cut an under the table agreement with Rabbit to send Izz and Zero to confiscate Juicy's whip, and them idiots had fucked around and gotten blasted into small, bloody chunks when the car blew up from an ignition bomb. To this day his cousin Rabbit still wasn't speakin' to him behind that shit, but how the fuck was Ace supposed to know that Juicy's whip was rigged?

That there conversation had confirmed the status of their relationship in both Ace and Pluto's minds. There was no more loyalty between them, and only the illusion of an alliance. Their cards had been dealt and now they each had to play out their hands. Neither one of them had meant for their bond to get all fucked up the way it did, but sometimes shit just happened, and every gangsta in the hood had learned to roll with them kind of punches.

Ace shook his head as he patted Salida on the ass and stared at the spot where Pluto had just been sitting. There was a time when he woulda laid down his life for that niggah. A time when he had trusted Pluto like he trusted the right hand that was attached to his right arm.

"All good shit gotta come to an end," Ace muttered without a moment's sadness. Some niggahs just didn't have enough vision. They couldn't handle the raging river that flowed in the gutter of progress, so they had to keep their feet dry and get left standing safely on the curb.

"Small-minded, bitter *bitch*!" Ace mumbled under his breath. If there was one thing he had learned from G, it was how to think on his feet. That niggah G had stayed three steps ahead of the competition, and the only reason he had been able to reign over the largest patch of drug territory in New York City was because he'd had the foresight and the heart to go out there and get that shit.

Ace didn't even wanna imagine where the Spot would be right now if Salida hadn't come along with all of her grand ideas. Fuck what anybody said about that lady, she had a calculating brain that could think laps around even the coldest ghetto kingpin.

Not only had Salida brought back a lot of the G-Spot's old clientele, she had opened up a whole new drug market for them. A meth market that neither him nor Pluto woulda been able to tap into on their own.

Ace glanced around the club. G woulda been real proud to see his shit all glossed up and shiny again. Salida had done a lot of hard work and remodeling around the joint to prepare for her Grand Re-Opening party that was coming up soon. She had brought in a brand new cleaning crew and had shopped for new sheets for the fuck rooms so that her new Asian and white clients would feel nice and comfortable paying for some trim.

"Hell yeah I let them white muh'fuckas up in here," Ace laughed out loud as he thought about how mad Pluto got every time he saw a cracker roll up in the club. "Them white niggahs came knockin' at the door with cash money!"

The kind of money that made the world go around.

The kind of money that Ace had was willing to pay to get rid of the problem that was standing in the way of the G-Spot's progress. He visualized the cut-throat scene of trickery that was gonna pop off when shit came to a head between him and his former slime.

Outta him and his manz, when the dirty deal was all said and done, only one of them was gonna be left standing. Standing and breathing. And Ace was gonna make damn sure of that.

$$$$$

Hours later Slick Sallie had drank so much of Monique's honey that his cup was damn near full. Not only had they engaged in the kind of hot, nasty sex that blew his freakiest fantasies out the water, they had also lay around in the fuck room talking and laughing in between their sheet-drenching bouts of animal-like bed play.

Monique, Sallie discovered, was very smart and she had a sharp wit about her too. Of all the hookers he had picked up off the streets and tied to bedposts over the years, Sallie couldn't ever remember having a real conversation with a Black chick. Up until now, he'd never thought he had much in common with them, but after just a few hours with Monique he was beginning to realize that he'd been dead wrong because him and Mo-Mo really vibed together. They grooved. They *clicked*. She was digging his drift, and he was damn sure digging hers too.

Monique told him she had lived in Harlem all her life, but that she'd always dreamed of escaping the city and going somewhere far.

"What would you do when you got there?" Sallie asked her.

He was stretched out on his back with a sore dick, and Monique was laying on her stomach, resting her head on his shoulder as she played with the soft blond hairs on his chest.

"I don't know," she said with a sigh. "I'd probably open up a real classy club somewhere in Baltimore and be a sexy hostess every night. You know, the kind of club the G-Spot used to be, but better."

Sallie nodded. He had never been inside the G-Spot before, but he'd heard all about its iconic rise and the legend of G McKay.

"So why don't you just do all of that right here?" he asked.

Monique's eyes narrowed. The answer was, because slimy-ass Salida had practically fucked her out of her First Lady status, leaving Monique to play second fiddle way back on the sidelines. Matter fact, that bitch had played every last one of them like boo-boo fools, but she'd gotten up in Ace's head the worst. Monique thought it was real slick the way him and Pluto went at it these days. They had actually let a bitch throw salt in their partnership and run it into a ditch.

"There's only room for one First Lady up in here," Monique finally answered truthfully. She had never been one to shy away from competition, but it was hard to go head-up with a twisted chick like Salida who had lost most of her marbles.

"Besides," she told Sallie as her fingers twirled in his hair, "I wanna start my own place. The kind of joint where millionaires roll up in limos and you gotta have velvet ropes and security guards outside to keep the paparazzi back."

Monique closed her eyes and grinned as she imagined herself strutting through a high-class club styling labels out the ass. If she could, she'd step out on some fine niggah's arm every night wearing a dress that cost at least five g's and a pair of matching designer shoes that cost even more.

"I just wanna run my own show, you know? I wanna have total say-so over everything from the way the place is decorated to what kind of liquor is stocked. I would do all the hiring and firing too, "she said, indulging herself in her fantasy. "You saw what kind of talent I got on the stage, right? Well, if I had my own place I'd choreograph all the strip routines. Wouldn't be no stiff-ass chicks up on my stage doing the same old two bends and a wiggle all night long! I would teach them some of my signature moves, and if they did them the right way, hundred dollar bills would come raining down on their heads. So, basically," she said simply, "I would build me a social club from the ground up and run it exactly the way I wanted to."

"Wow," Sallie said. This girl had talent and dreams, and he was definitely impressed. He ran his hand across the smooth, ebony skin on her back. It felt like fine satin.

"I agree. You are very talented, Monique. So what's stopping you from doing all those things you wanna do?"

She lifted her head and gave him a smirk.

"Money! What's stopping everybody in the world from doing all the shit they wanna do? It's always money!"

"Not for everybody," Sallie contradicted her. He thought about all the crisp bills he had amassed back in Chinatown stuffed up Buddha's ass. "Money isn't stopping me from doing anything. I pretty much do whatever I want."

Monique stared at him for a long moment.

Was my dumb-ass just now dreaming about stepping out every night on some fine niggah's arm? Scratch that, she corrected herself. A fine white boy would do just fine.

Sallie touched her hair as her lips curled into a bright smile.

"Are you serious? You can do whatever you wanna do and not have to worry about no money?" she asked.

Sallie's mouth watered as he eyed her breathtaking body again. "Yeah," he said. "Pretty much."

Monique giggled. "Cool!" She slid down until her head was resting on his stomach. Sallie's aching dick shot up in the air at the sight of her delicious Hershey's flesh pressed up against his.

"Well then you came to the right room tonight, baby boy," she said sexily. "Didn't nobody tell me I was partying with a VIP!"

Monique bent her head and inserted his dick inside her hot wet mouth. She slid her lips down his shaft so deeply that it felt like the mushroom crown kicked in a back door that was hidden in her throat.

Sallie could only take so much of the sweet hurting she was putting on him before he became desperate to get what he needed. Monique was sucking the white boy off like a mothafucka and she was surprised when he extracted his dick from her mouth and flipped her over onto her back.

Sallie lowered his face to her groin and delved into her pussy with wild abandon, licking and sucking and sniffing like it was the last piece of chocolate punanee in the world. And even though they'd been going at it hard and strong for hours, hands down, Monique's pussy was the best he had ever tasted in his life.

An hour or so later Sallie made his way out of the G-Spot. His chips had run out long ago, but Monique had insisted the overtime was on the house. He stepped out into the crisp morning air and turned his eyes eastward toward the new sun. Thoughts of beautiful Monique were heavy on his mind, and her sweet taste still lingered deliciously on his lips.

Sallie was amazed as he walked toward his car. This was the very first time that he had eaten a piece of chocolate that didn't make his mouth itch. He ran his tongue over his teeth and swallowed the last bits of her sugary residue, and instead of making him nauseous it made his tummy feel nice and warm inside.

Sitting behind the wheel of his car, Sallie thought about the two complex business transactions he was about to conduct. Thanks to Gino and Juicy he had plenty of cash, but hey, a man with his appetites could always use more. Besides, Monique had shared her dreams with him, and with the right kind of bank he might just be able to make some of them come true. She'd said she wanted to open up her own nightclub down in Baltimore, and Sallie could definitely go for a change in scenery.

He pondered on the upcoming matter he had going on with the young drug dealer from Harlem, and the large cache of clean arms that he was gonna sell the dude. Sallie was due to collect a whole lot of cash at the completion of that deal, but now he wondered if there was any way he could pull a little switcheroo trickery on the young cat who lived in a funeral home, and perhaps scam him out of a few bucks.

He figured if he dipped in on the shipment he got from his supplier, and then discreetly shifted a few pieces around, he might be able to hide a number of dirty gats at the bottom of the crate and resell the clean ones and make himself a nice little extra profit.

Sallie mused on this as he opened his glove box and pulled out a large pack of cinnamon gum. An early-morning wino was bobbing and weaving against a light pole on the corner, and Sallie rolled down his window and tossed the pack of gum in the bum's direction.

Let the poor fellow have it, Sallie chuckled with thoughts of sexy Monique on his mind, because after the kind of sweetness he'd had on his tongue tonight, he sure as hell wouldn't be needing it anymore.

CHAPTER 15

While Flex was in the early stages of being double-crossed by Slick Sallie, he had just about perfected his method of beating Salida at her own game.

"This shit better be right," he told Freeze Dodson as he sifted through their latest batch of crystal ice. Flex had bum-rushed Freeze's precious Gramma again and turned Salida's number-one street pharmacist into an undercover double-agent.

Flipping Freeze had been a matter of operational necessity. For the longest time Flex and his crew had tried to cook their own meth using the crazy list of ingredients they had stolen from Salida, but every batch of shit they turned out had ended up a useless, gooey mess. Finally Flex had decided he needed to go straight to the source, and his boyz had rolled on Freeze's fam and put him in charge of mixing their brew and stirring their pots.

"Make sure you put just enough rat poison in that shit to get them feens real sick," Flex directed him, leaning over his shoulder. "Don't put enough in there to kill 'em, but make sure once they smoke this shit they ain't gonna be in a hurry to come back and smoke no fuckin' more."

Flex thought his plan was some real genius shit, and he figured while he had Freeze under his thumb he could use his weak ass to help him kill a few other birds that were lurking in the bush too.

"Yo, Freeze," Flex said casually as he thought about how he was gonna get his guns and ammunition where he needed them to be when the time was right. "I bet you know the G-Spot like the back of your hand, don't you niggah?"

Freeze shrugged, and Flex could see this fool's brain working overtime as he tried to figure out what kinda hammer was gonna fall on his head next.

"Yeah, I guess. I know it pretty good."

"Fuck pretty good, ak. I bet you know every corner of that bitch. Every closet and every little cubbyhole too. You could prolly hide all kinds of shit up in there if you needed to. Tell me something. They got a back door on that place, don't they?"

Freeze nodded.

Flex grinned. "Something tells me that if somebody needed to sneak something in that back door and hide it, you'd be just the muthafucka to pull some shit like that off."

"What you talkin' about man?" Freeze looked scared and confused at the same time. "What you tryna say?"

Flex shrugged. "Nothing, man. I ain't tryna say a goddamn thing. At least not yet."

$$$$

I was pissed off and I wanted Trey to know it. As soon as I hung up from that call to Pluto I had begged Trey to tell me where Moonie was so I could get those fools to let Nooni out of the G-Spot.

"I can't do that," Trey had told me shaking his head. "That niggah Moonie is done. It's over for him. He gave all this up and he's living another kind of life. If Moonie wanted to be ass-deep in the G-Spot's bullshit he woulda never left Harlem."

"Let Moonie tell me that!" I had insisted. "All I'm asking you to do is hook me up with him. Give me his phone number. Tell me where he lives. Let me ask him to help me, and if he don't wanna do it then let him be the one to tell me no!"

Trey gave me a look that had ice in it. We were back at the crib and sitting in his bedroom, and if I wasn't so mad I would have appreciated being in his intimate zone. Trey was a real man. Everything in his area told you he was the king of his castle, a dude in control of his space, and even though I was concerned about Nooni, I wasn't immune to the way being close to this man made me feel.

"Be for real, Juicy. You think this lil shit we got going on here is important enough for Moonie to risk his life over? My manz got all kinds of cops and crews gunnin' for his throat out here on these streets. You think he's gonna roll up and cooperate with Pluto just because he's holding some girl down at the Spot?"

"You trying to say Nooni ain't that important? What? I'm just supposed to let her rot down in there in that damn Dungeon?"

"I'm saying we got time to handle Nooni! We know where she is, and we know who's got her. Pluto ain't stupid, baby. He ain't gonna let nothing happen to that girl. If he fucks with her then he loses all his leverage, and even his dumb ass is smarter than that. Nooni is gonna be chill for a minute, Juicy. I'ma help you, and I'ma help her too. But right now I gotta handle Maleek."

I stared into his strong brown eyes and saw the truth of his promise looking back at me. A picture of Taleah's battered little face flooded my mind and my whole body went soft. I knew how bad Trey felt for that poor child, and how hurt he was that Maleek was the one who had fucked her up and put her in that hospital bed in the first place.

"Okay," I said quietly with my shoulders slumped. "Okay."

$$$$$

Trey Jackson was putting in some mean work.

For the past ten minutes he had been on a staircase in Manhattanville Projects slapping Maleek around. Fury bubbled in him as he dragged the tall, slim youth up the pissy stairs leading from the sixth floor to the seventh, tagging his ass with killer blows with every step.

Trey had been stalking the boy for hours. Maleek had peeped him coming out of the lobby of a project building in his drug sector and tried to fly up the stairs and get away, but Trey had been on that ass like a track star. He'd caught Maleek by the back of his jacket on the third floor landing, and had beaten and dragged him up further and further from there.

"Fuck is *wrong* with you?" Trey exploded as he gave the tall, skinny kid a man-sized beat-down. "You out here tryna kill *little girls* now, niggah? Huh? Is that the kinda grime you into man?"

"Yo, get the fuck offa me!" Maleek yelled as he flailed his arms and kicked out at

Trey. "You don't know me, niggah! You don't *know* me!"

Trey doubled down on the ass-kicking. He was way bigger and stronger than Maleek, and he was way madder too. He was in a fist-flying frenzy, blinded by his rage, but there was some guilt flowing through his fists as he beat up on Maleek as well. The boy cowered on the dirty concrete. His lip was busted and one of his eyelids was swollen damn near closed. Blood dripped from his nose, but nothing but anger and stark defiance shone in his dark eyes.

"Yo why you always on my fuckin' *dick*, Trey? Who the fuck is you? I'm tellin' you man, you need to stay outta my fuckin' bizzness, ya heard? You don't know me, niggah! You don't fuckin' *know* me!"

Trey froze as he stared down into the cold, empty eyes that squinted up at him in rage. The truth was in those eyes, clear as day. He had failed this cat. Lost him. Maleek's soul had been eaten by the streets, and his brother Mayhem was prolly rolling over in his fuckin' grave.

"You better check ya'self," Trey warned the boy as he tried to slow his own breathing. "That little girl was fourteen, yo. And she was innocent. You keep fuckin' around like you doing and you gone be headed upstate for good. Believe that."

"I didn't fuckin' do nothing!" Maleek barked from the ground. From where Trey stood the boy resembled a cornered animal. He looked like one, he sounded like one, and he smelled like one too.

Trey just nodded. He got it now. He got it. Maleek, Flex, and that whole fuckin' squad was throwed off. All them lil cats was bent.

"A'ight. Run that 'didn't do nothin' shit on the fuckin' judge when the blue boys roll up on you and bust yo ass. If you was any kind of man you would go ahead and turn yourself in 'cause I'm done fuckin' with you, Leek. I'm done."

A disrespectful noise burst from Maleek's lips as Trey turned and headed back down the steps. He had only made it down three steps when Maleek reached deep into the waistband of his jeans and pulled out a glistening silver Beretta. Wrenching his bruised body into a sitting position, he gripped the tool with both hands and pressed his right index finger to the trigger action and aimed.

"Pow," the boy whispered as he sighted an imaginary bulls-eye target on the center of Trey's back and pretended to fire his gat. "Pow!"

CHAPTER 16

A dusty white van with painted-over windows rolled down 125th Street at a moderate pace. From the outside it appeared no different than any other vehicle moving through Harlem's Saturday morning traffic, but inside there were two bloody and naked men with their wrists shackled together in handcuffs.

"Y'all niggahs is making a big mistake," the larger of the two young dudes spit through his busted lips. His name was Boog, and him and his partner Rome had been on their way to the count room at Three Brother's Funeral Home to make their customary money drop, when suddenly some old smelly bum had rushed up to them and started grabbing all on their clothes and hollering some crazy shit about the world coming to an end.

Boog and Rome had dropped the grub they were munchin' on and started kicking the shit outta the bum-ass dude, when outta nowhere a van pulled up at the curb and mad niggahs rushed out and snatched both of their asses inside. The next thing Boog knew their drop bags full of drug money got ripped outta their crotches, and then both of them got straight-up stripped outta their trendy new clothes. Them fools even yanked them outta their drawers!

Boog trembled in rage and embarrassment as them crazy niggahs joked him about his flabby, ashy body. This is what the fuck he got for listening to that bent niggah Maleek. He'd known better than to violate a business that was protected by the Talented Ten, but Maleek had insisted he had shit covered. Covered hell! Where was that niggah now that the retribution was about to go down?

"Y'all cats is making a big mistake taking them drop bags!" Boog hollered again. "We down with that dude Flex! You fuck with that niggah's money and ya dead! Ya heard? Ya dead!"

"Shut ya fat ass up!" Fizz Williams barked. He was breathing hard from the ass-kicking he had just laid on the two naked men. Him and his boyz had watched them come outta a local Chinese restaurant gnawing on jumbo shrimp and greasy fried chicken wings, and proudly sporting the gear that they had stolen from Empire Attire's delivery truck.

"Pull over right here," Fizz reluctantly instructed the van's driver. Him and Hill had wanted to snuff these two fools out and dump their dead bodies in the East River, but boss man Trey had vetoed that idea.

"Nah, don't plant 'em," Trey had forbidden him. "We just gonna send our manz Flex a lil message, that's all."

The van came to a stop on a packed-out portion of 125th Street. Vendors, shoppers, and every day Harlemites were crowding the streets in droves. Fizz grabbed Rome's wrist and unlocked his cuffs. He slid the door open and planted his big foot so deep in the boy's chest that he flew out the door and landed hard on the concrete, his naked back slapping painfully against the ground as his shriveled-up dick and balls jiggled freely.

A lady screamed, and a bunch of young dudes selling mix tapes started laughing real loud. Rome rolled over onto his stomach, then jumped to his feet and hauled ass down the block with the sound of loud laughter rising in the air behind him.

"Yo, you kickin' us outta this bitch naked?" Boog shouted in disbelief as his wrists were freed too. He grabbed desperately for the jeans he had been stripped out of, as Fizz brought his knee up hard under his chin and sent a semi-circular arc of blood spraying from his mouth.

"These is my boss's muthafuckin' clothes!" Fizz screeched, wanting for all the world to plant a hot one in that niggah's chest. Instead of kicking Boog out the door, he lifted his saggy body under the arms and hurled his fat ass out into the street, frowning in satisfaction as brakes squealed and tires screeched as drivers tried to avoid running that fool over.

Boog had attracted mad attention, and all eyes were on him as he lay naked in the street. He balled up into a knot and shrank inside himself as a bootleg taxi sped past and clipped his shoulder. He jumped to his feet and tried to cover his dick and balls as he darted toward the curb with everybody laughing and pointing at his loose, ashy ass.

With blood running from his mouth and dripping down his chin, Boog ran up to the first young cat he saw and collared him with one hand.

"Gimme ya fuckin' pants!" he demanded hysterically as the crowd of people stared at his flabby bare ass. "Give 'em up goddamn it, or I'll shoot ya ass!"

Dude looked him up and down and stiff-armed the shit outta him.

"Shoot me with what, homey? Ya flabby, stretch-marky dick?" He raised his knee and put his foot in Boog's stomach, pushing him off. "Get ya jiggly ass the fuck outta here!"

With the sound of laughter tormenting his ears, Boog stumbled backwards with embarrassment leaking from every pore on his exposed body. Once again he was the ugly fat kid, and his worst nightmare had suddenly come true. He glanced around and saw a wino leaning against a light pole and sipping from a bottle of cheap drank. Dude had on a faded trench coat that was so grimy and caked with dirt that it looked stiff. He rushed over and slapped the bottle from the old man's hands, then jerked the coat down his back and tried to tear it off his body.

Desperately, Boog tried to stick his arm through the coat sleeve, but he quickly realized that he was way too fat. With tears of rage forming in his eyes, he gave up and wrapped the coat around his waist as best he could, and then he took off running down the block.

$$$$

Daydreaming about her growing romance with Slick Sallie and deep in economic scheme mode, Money-Making Monique was walking toward the avenue when a naked dude ran past her and damn near knocked her down.

"Damn, niggah!" she stumbled and hollered at the sight of his fat ass jiggling down the street while he tried to cover the front of his body with a trench coat. "Watch where the hell you going, dude!"

Shaking her bomb booty in a five-hundred dollar designer skirt, Monique kept on tipping down the street as she tried to figure out exactly what to do about her little issue. Life was really looking up for her now that she had a paid white boy eating outta her ass, and if Sallie's shit was as legit as she thought it was, then she damn sure wouldn't be slumming around Harlem much longer.

But before she left the Big Apple there was some unfinished business that Monique needed to attend to, and no matter how sweet the road ahead was looking for her and her new boo, there was no way in hell she was gonna leave Harlem without paying that snake-eyed bitch Salida back for all the conniving, double-crossing, and humiliating shit she had done to her.

Just thinking about Salida made Monique's face get hot as she waited at a corner for the light to change so she could cross the street. She had tussled, fussed, and scuffled with a whole lotta bitches in her day, but she had never hated a chick as much as she hated Salida.

All that fake love the bitch had shown her. The lies about them being partners for life. The empty promises to hook her up with some big-time cash. Monique didn't even wanna think about the way Salida had pulled a gat on her and mushed her forehead in. Or about how she had been forced to stand up at the stove after Bilal ran over the old bitch, and cook Salida's meals morning, noon, and night.

Speaking of cooking, a small idea began forming in Monique's brain as she crossed the busy intersection, and by the time she was on the other side of the street a sly smile was playing on her lips. Yeah, Salida liked it when people waited on her and cooked for her, and slaved over her like she was some type of queen. It didn't matter how much you did for the bitch, or how nice you were to her, her greedy ass sucked up your kindness and then demanded more.

Monique was giggling under her breath now. She could barely hold her laughter in. She was gonna wait on Salida's ass, alright. She would give that throwed-off bitch something that would make her feel real special. Something that had been made especially for her.

"Yeah!" Monique pumped her fist and shouted out loud, ignoring the curious looks she got from people on the sidewalk. She had something for that crusty old heffah. Something that was gonna blow her rotten-ass mind!

CHAPTER 17

It was a real sweet plan if Flex had to say so himself. Tapping Maleek as his ninth man was a slick, bold move, and it had definitely gotten the attention he had intended it to get. Right about now, that community-organizing niggah Trey was all over Flex's dick hoping he could pull Maleek outta the game.

Trey had sent him a message earlier saying they needed to have a face-to-face, and Flex was on his way to meet with him right now. They were gonna hold court at a Chinese restaurant down near South Street Seaport, and although Flex had used the spot for business transactions many times before, he still made sure to get there much earlier than he had to. His chief of security had checked the place out thoroughly, then posted his team in strategic spots that covered their boss from every angle.

Trey was part of a known click. The Talented Ten were businessmen first, but they were gutter all the same. They held down their side of the street and were known to pounce when they needed to.

Flex had expected Trey to post up in the joint at least ten deep. Instead, the muscled-up ex-baller slid in alone, which made Flex respect him way more than he wanted to. He watched as Trey took his time following Dre to the table he was sitting at in the far back corner of the room. In a way, Trey was almost family. Next to crazy Jimmy Stanfield, Trey's brother Cooter had been the best dawg Flex had ever had.

But Trey was nothing like his brother. Cooter was older and grimier, and he had been deeply entrenched in the street life. That niggah was so loyal to the game that he had stayed on G's team even after G had his sister Charlene bumped off in an alley and discarded in a Dumpster.

Trey was built real different. He had set his sights on playing professional ball, and when he ran into that lil trouble over his manz Mayhem and got sent upstate to do him a lil bid, he had come back to Harlem on some kinda "Ungowa" Black Power trip.

Flex was all about blacks being in power, and the only real beef he had with Cooter's brother was the fact that they always seemed to be going after the same thing at the same time. They both wanted the cream of the crop. The best and brightest and most beautiful that Harlem had to offer, and whether it came down to having Juicy, or controlling the dun duns on the street, only one of them could come out a winner and take home the prize.

These were the thoughts on Flex's mind as Trey sat down in the chair across from him. Killer vs. Killer, they stared into each other's eyes. Trey made the first move. His big hands hit the table with a thud as he got right down to it.

"I thought I told you Maleek was off the table, yo?"

"I thought I told you not to be in my bizzness, ay?" Flex shot right back.

Trey leaned forward and grilled him for a few cold seconds.

"Leek is just a kid, man." He chuckled and then shook his head and went in hard. "Yo, your ass is just a kid too, son!"

Flex felt his face turn to stone. Trey was Cooter's blood, but that wouldn't stop him from peeling this muh'fucka's wig back. The cool steel of his burner pressed into his side and made his skin tingle. Flex took a deep break and tried to get himself under control. This niggah had one more time to try to son him. It was dead disrespectful.

"Maleek is a soldier," Flex said finally. "Soldiers go to war."

"Soldiers take orders too," Trey barked. "So order him to sit the fuck down."

Flex shrugged. He knew how bad Trey wanted the kid off the streets. "Now why would I do some shit like that, man? Maleek is one of my most fearless, most reliable troops."

"Yo, I heard about what happened to that kid Truth," Trey said quietly, coming outta the blue. "He got popped on a busy street in broad daylight. Right outside the G-Spot. Maleek wouldn't have nothing to do with that, would he?"

Flex shrugged again, lookin' like he could give less than a fuck about what Trey was saying. "Maleek is a soldier," he repeated. "Sometimes soldiers go to war."

"Cut him loose, Flex," Trey said point-blank. "Maleek is talented. He could make it outta here. Cut him loose."

"Oh you right about that," Flex agreed as he mentally assessed how strong his bargaining power was. Maleek was highly valuable. Give him an order and he would jump right on it. Leap all over that shit. Without the slightest regard or concern for his personal safety or anybody else's. "Maleek's got a whole lot of talent, that's word."

The men stared at each other like they were playing a game of chess. They were like two wild dogs with their dicks hard and their tails sticking straight up in the air. Neither was willing to give up an inch of their square.

"I tell you what," Flex relented with a grin. "How about we come up with a little compromise?"

Trey tilted his chair back on two legs.

Flex leaned forward and put his elbows on the table. He spread the fingers on both his hands, then pressed the tips together. He rested his chin on his middle fingers like he was deep in thought.

"How about I give you Maleek," he offered slowly. "And you give me something I want in return."

Trey chuckled mirthlessly. "Yo what the fuck is up with that you'll "give" me Maleek shit?"

"That's what I said, niggah. I'll give him to you. I'll toss his ass off. He won't be down with my crew no more, and he won't handle no more of my product. I'll cut him off. That niggah won't even be allowed to walk on my side of the street ever again."

Trey frowned, but the fact that he was still listening told Flex he was interested. Straddling his seat, Trey leaned forward until the front legs of his chair were once again on the floor. "And what would I have to give you in return?"

"A name," Flex said simply. "Just a name."

Trey looked suspicious. "All you want is a name? Niggah, who's name you looking for?"

"The name of a connect. G McKay's main connect."

Trey stiffened deep inside. This was the second time he'd heard this request made. Keeping his cool, he remained perfectly calm and unfazed on the outside as he said, "Man, you must got me confused with my brother Cooter. G was Cooter's pizo. Not mine. How the fuck I'm supposed to know who them slimes did their business with?"

"I ain't sayin' you know who the man is personally," Flex conceded. "But I bet your ass knows how to find out."

Trey made a cold, disrespectful sound in the back of his throat.

"Muh'fucka if you know what the fuck I know then why can't you find out ya damn self?"

"Because your fuckin' brother wouldn't tell me, that's why!" Flex shot back. He sat up straight, fuming as beads of sweat dotted his forehead. He had known this fuckin' question was coming and he should have been better prepared to answer it. It wasn't like he hadn't tried to find out who G's main manz was on his own. He had. But the only niggah left in Harlem who knew the answer to that question had refused to give it up. No matter how hard Flex's boys had kicked Cooter's face in on that crowded street that day, that stuttering fuck had refused to give up the name.

A small smile spread over Trey's handsome face. He had kept his head and Flex had clearly lost his. Round one was under his belt.

"So," Trey said, pushing past the cloud of anger that now surrounded the baby-faced killer sitting across from him.

"Let's get this straight. You think I'm the man sitting next to the man, who's sitting next to the man?"

Flex nodded once. "That's right."

Trey stared at him.

"So who you *really* looking for, Flex?" he asked, knowing he already knew the answer.

"Moonie," Flex barked out the exact name Trey had expected to hear. "I'm looking for Moonie, ak. Hook me up with that niggah real quick and Maleek is all yours."

Before Trey could respond, Flex's dun dun Dre came over and spit something in his ear. Like the stupid kid he really was, Flex looked puzzled for a second, and then that niggah bust out laughing.

"They put 'em out there *naked*?" he asked his boy, unable to contain his glee and surprise. "*Butt-ass* naked?"

Dre nodded and went back to Flex's ear. But now the laughter on Flex's lips dried up and his eyes were filled with a look of cold rage. "Fuck you mean they got my drop bags, niggah?" he growled in a deep, deadly voice.

Dre backed off like he felt an ass whoopin' coming on, and Flex jumped to his feet like he was ready to wild out. He glared at Trey as he knocked his chair over and it fell to the floor with a loud clang.

"It's time to dip my niggah. So now you know what I want, and I know what the fuck you need. I'ma hafta holla at you later though 'cause I got some bizz to take care of."

I bet you do, niggah, Trey muttered under his breath as he leaned back in his chair and watched Flex and his flunkie jet toward the door. A robbery for a robbery, he thought with cold amusement. Fuck with a niggah's pockets and it would get his feet moving every time. *Damn right you gotta get going, niggah. I bet the fuck you do.*

CHAPTER 18

I was polishing my toenails in a real nice shade of baby blue when Trey walked up and stood in the doorway to my room. He wasn't even dressed up but he still looked good as shit. Like he could have been one of those fine-ass male models in a photo spread. He didn't say anything for a few seconds, he just stared at me with an easy expression in his eyes.

"How you doin'?" he finally asked quietly.

I shrugged. "I'm good. You?"

He nodded and pushed his hands down into his pockets. "Chillin'."

I nodded back. I hated that the air was all thick and awkward between us. Ever since I'd talked to Pluto and asked Trey to help me Nooni out of the G-Spot, it seemed like our love thang had cooled off.

"You hungry?"

I shook my head. "Nah. Chiney brought me a slice of pizza earlier. But thanks."

He lifted his chin, then nodded real slow.

"Yo, check it out, Juicy. I wanna apologize to you, okay?"

I shrugged. "It's cool. I understand how it is between you and Maleek."

Trey shook his head. "Nah, I'm not talking about that. I'm handlin' Maleek. I'm talking about how I behaved when we came home after the D.I.V.A. Day at the center. I pushed up on you in a way that made you uncomfortable, and I shouldn't have done that. I apologize. I shoulda had more control."

I stared into his deep brown eyes, and shook my head quickly.

"Uh-uh, Trey. That wasn't your fault. It was late and we both got carried away, that's all. It's okay. I'm good with it. For real."

"Nah, it's not okay, Juicy. Not for a woman like you. You already been through enough and I ain't tryna put you through nothing else. Trust me, it won't happen like that again."

I didn't know what to say to that. Of course I had wanted him to fuck my brains out that night and I couldn't hardly even look at his ass without my pussy getting wet.

But I had also confided in Trey a little bit about me and Gino. About how we'd both gotten shot on our wedding day, and how hard it was for me when I ended up losing him. Of course I had left out some parts of the story, especially the ones that had anything to do with G's crazy ass, but this was Harlem. It was Trey's town. He probably already knew a whole lot more about me than I had told him.

Since I couldn't just come right out and tell this man how bad I wanted to fuck him, I just nodded and accepted his apology. I couldn't hardly get no sleep for laying in the bed and fantasizing about Trey right there on the other side of the wall. I wanted to ride his dick, suck him off, and spread my legs so he could eat the shit out of my pussy, and here he was feeling bad about pushing up on me.

Men, I thought as I dipped the brush back into the small jar of polish and started putting another coat on my toenails. Dudes could be a real trip sometimes.

$$$$$

Trey had made a bogus deal with Flex to exchange Moonie for Maleek, but when it all played out neither one of the Harlem killers was gonna hold true to his word.

"You still wanna go see Moonie?' Trey asked Juicy the next morning as he chugged back some orange juice and plotted his next move. The smack-down that he had put on Maleek just stayed fuckin' with him. And not because he felt bad for manhandling the boy, but because he was afraid he hadn't fucked him up good enough.

Juicy nodded. "Yeah, I still wanna go. Cause if we don't give Moonie up then I don't see no other way of getting Nooni outta the G-Spot. Do you?"

Trey shrugged. He cared about Nooni and no matter what Juicy thought, he really was down for getting her back, but right now it was Maleek's fate that weighed heavily on his mind. Trey knew these streets. He knew their paths and their pathology. Even if Flex stood tall on his word and tossed Maleek off, it would only be a matter of time before the boy worked his way back into the click and was back out on the corners starting trouble and wrecking shit again.

Trey had been crushed by what Maleek did to Taleah, and he'd come real close to cutting him off for good. But then he remembered the promise he had made to Mayhem. And the one he had made to himself. As bad as he wanted to make Maleek suffer for his sins, he had decided to give the boy one more chance. One *last* chance.

And that's why he needed to find Moonie. Not so his manz could give up G's connect and flood the streets of Harlem with more illegal drugs. But so him and Moonie could come up with some intellectual trickery that would shut Flex, and maybe even the G-Spot too, down for good. Because if Trey had even the slightest chance of saving Maleek's life, that's what it was gonna take, and that's what he was gonna have to do.

"A'ight, cool," he finally answered. "I'll take you to talk to Moonie, but we gotta roll out fast. I'm about to take a shower. Go 'head and get your stuff ready so we can get outta here as soon as possible."

CHAPTER 19

The air was stale and musty in the little Spanish store on the corner. Lil Lee was standing in a long line to buy a bag of Wise Onion & Garlic potato chips and some squirrel nuts for her daughter, when her big opportunity walked in the door.

Her heart started pounding as she stared at the light-skinned chick with the short, curly hair. She knew exactly why this bitch was on this side of town and what she had come around here to cop.

Chiney grabbed her crotch and hiked up her imaginary dick and Lil Lee scoffed inside. Fuckin' poser! This bitch's gear and her swagger mighta made her look like a man, but Lil Lee knew she bled from between her legs once a month just like every other female.

She turned her head and watched as Chiney Jackson walked toward the back of the store and started talking to a chick who had a cute little toddler with big eyes and long hair riding on her hip. The chick was posted up in front of Chiney and grinning like it was a dude tryna hit up on her or something. Even though she was now up at the counter, Lil Lee stepped out of line and darted down an aisle where the household cleaners and bug spray and stuff was kept.

Her eyes quickly scanned the shelves as she looked for something that almost every resident in Harlem had in their cabinets. Chiney was still throwing her rap down on the girl when Lil Lee paid for her purchases and jetted back to her car. She climbed in her backseat and opened up her package, and then she took out five of the vials that Freeze had stolen from the G-Spot and handed off to the Divine Nine crew.

Lil Lee knew Flex had already had his street pharmacist spike their bogus Strawberry Snake with a little extra bang for the buck, but for the type of satisfaction she was seeking, that little bit wasn't gonna be enough.

She sat in the backseat of her whip grinning like crazy as she mixed up some special shit just for Chiney Jackson. She had to force herself not to add too much to the mixture because she wasn't tryna take Chiney out fast. Nah, she wanted that bitch to suffer first.

It had blown Lil Lee's mind when she had read down the list of ingredients that Freeze had given up in exchange for his Gramma's life. Lil Lee knew for sure that Salida was a mad-ass beast when she saw the words rat poison written on the piece of paper.

"Rat poison?" she had asked Freeze in surprise.

"Yep," he'd said. "It's like a boosting agent. It dilates the blood vessels and gives a killer high." He shrugged. "The toxic ingredient in that shit comes out as a byproduct of cooking meth anyway. Salida just adds a little bit back to the mix so it can give them fiends a bigger rush. That's why they keep coming back to get more."

That shit had seemed real risky to Lil Lee, but she'd shrugged it off thinking, what the hell. Fiends didn't give a fuck what they smoked. As long as it made they hearts pound and their heads swirl, they were on cloud nine. Besides, this was Harlem, and some rats could take a lot more shit than other rats could.

Lil Lee giggled as she shook up the vials and made sure everything was mixed in good. "That dyke bitch wanna act like a fuckin' man," she muttered under her breath, "let's see if she can handle her poison like one then."

$$$$$

Ten minutes later Lil Lee was up in her boy Fitted's grill. "Here," she told him as she passed him the vials full of potent pink shit. "This here product is only for Chiney, you hear me? If that feen comes to buy one, then you give her two. If she comes to buy two, you give that dyke bitch all four. I want her to get double what she asks for, and you make sure you tell her she can always get more. You got that?"

Fitted nodded.

"Good," Lil Lee said, as she walked away looking sexy-scrumptious and completely evil at the same time. "Make that shit happen."

$$$$$

Chiney Jackson was feeling herself as she walked out of the corner store. She had just run into her old boo-thang Lincy inside and they had a real long conversation. Mami had been looking fat in the ass and sweet in the lips, and they had agreed to hook up for a little booty call. Chiney was in mad love with her girl Venus, but she couldn't help remembering how that nasty chick Lincy used to eat her pussy out until her walls were bone dry. She figured she could bang Lincy on the sneak tip for a few minutes before going home to her real boo.

Chiney walked around the corner and headed up the street where she planned to score her some shit. Today was Venus' birthday, and since Trey and Juicy were going outta town Chiney had a nice lil romantic surprise planned for her girl.

The streets of Harlem were alive with flavor. Little girls were jumping rope on the sidewalk outside of their stoops, and a bunch of grown-ass teenaged mothers pushed their babies up and down the block in expensive strollers.

Chiney looked around for her new hook-up, Fitted.

"Yo, whattup?" Chiney said, lifting her chin as she approached him to make a quick transaction. "I'm feelin' icy today my dude."

They walked a few steps together, and when Chiney slid him enough cash for two vials, Fitted slid her twice that amount in meth.

Grinning, she headed back down the street and toward the Spanish store where her old sex-boo was coming out carrying her two-year-old daughter and a bag of Pampers.

"So whattup?" Chiney asked in a low, deep voice. "You still gonna treat me right or what?" She stood wide-legged and eyed Lincy's thick, sexy frame as her swollen clit throbbed double-time in her boxers.

Lincy grinned and shifted her two-year-old daughter on her hip. "Not if your bitch Venus is gonna get all stupid like she did the last time we hooked up. I'm telling you Chiney. Next time that chick roll on me I'ma hurt her ass."

Chiney grinned. She loved it when bitches fought over her.

"Don't worry about Venus," she said, knowing how much her girl hated the sight of Lincy. "Me and her got an understanding. So you gonna treat me right or what?"

Lincy grinned. "That depends. You gonna treat *me* right?"

"Always," Chiney said, thinking about the four nice vials of meth she had just copped for the price of two. "Why you askin' stupid questions, girl? You know your Daddy *always* treats you right."

CHAPTER 20

The early morning meeting of the Divine Nine was just about to come to a close.

Without mentioning Boog or Rome or the robbery that had recently gone down, Flex had reviewed the sales performance of every territory, and praised those who deserved it and gave a verbal ass-whipping to those teams that had been slacking on their grind and coming up short. It was all about productivity and expansion, and he reminded his niggahs of that. If their operation wasn't constantly growing then that meant their shit was slowly dying, and Flex told them he would smack his burner on every niggah in the room before he let that happen.

"Yo, man, speaking of burners," Stamp, the fourth man, spoke up from the back of the room. Flex shot him a look. Stamp was one of the main niggahs whose crew was lookin' weak. For the last couple of weeks their take had either dropped, or they'd turned in the same amount at each count.

But like every other dude sitting before him, Flex trusted Stamp explicitly or he woulda never made him a member of the Divine Nine. He knew his soldier wasn't stealing, but if that niggah didn't start showing some progress soon he might have a problem.

"Whattup?" Flex asked, giving Stamp permission to speak.

"Nah, I'm just saying... you know, my man here," Stamp turned around and nodded at Maleek, who as the ninth man and the most recent member of the team, was sitting at the back of the room, furthest away from Flex. "Leek is a hardbody niggah and all that, but um, to my knowledge, this cat ain't never played our game, man."

A hush fell over the room, but a murmur of agreement soon rose in the air.

Flex moved to shut it down.

"Nah, nah, nah," he held his hand up high. "Maleek was a special appointment. He popped his intro niggah in broad daylight, just like the rest of y'all niggahs so he's good, my dude. He's proven himself."

"Willing to kill, willing to die," Stamp reminded him of their secret motto. "Yeah, Leek popped his intro man, but that niggah didn't *play*."

Flex pushed back. He had a feeling Stamp was tryna work some trickery into the mix. "Yo, hold the fuck up. The main reason Leek got on—besides the fact that as a young'un he's got more heart than most grown men I know," Flex looked hard at a couple of cats so there was no doubt in their minds that he was referring to them, "is because that niggah Cee-Low lost his head. Now, I'm the number one man up in here. I make the decisions and I make the appointments. Anybody got a problem with that," Flex barked, grilling his posse as he looked around the room, "open ya goddamn trap. Speak the fuck up and let a niggah like me know."

Most of his dudes clammed up tight. They knew all about Flex's quick temper and his even quicker draw. The sight of Cee-Low's dead body sliding down the wall was still fresh in their minds.

460

But Stamp wasn't finished yet.

"I respect you, Flex," he said calmly. "And I ain't got no problem with your authority or your decisions, man. I just don't think it's right that we all get to walk around out here on these streets gettin' our proper respect and Maleek don't get him none. It's a respect thing. That's all I'm sayin'."

Flex opened his mouth to say something, but Maleek beat him to it.

"Yo, Stamp is right, man," he said, rising to his feet. Weaving through the other click members, Maleek walked to the front of the room. "Yeah, I popped my intro niggah," he agreed with Flex, "but I'm just a kid so you know I like me some games. Hell yeah. I want my respect *and* I wanna play."

Flex nodded. Maleek had become even more valuable to him since the meeting he'd had with Trey. In fact, he had that niggah Trey by the balls. Now that Trey had agreed to put him on with Moonie, Maleek's worth was suddenly a million times steeper than the gold standard, and Flex wasn't about to let nothing fuck that up.

But rules were rules. And besides, Flex controlled the game. He wasn't soft, and neither was Maleek. He watched as the youngsta walked over and sat down at the table like it wasn't no thing. Maleek had absolutely no fear in him as Flex took out his six-shooter and loaded it with a hollow-point round. The room was mad quiet as Flex spun the cylinder on the revolver.

Taking a seat across from Maleek, he extended him the burner.

Maleek took the tool without so much as a tremor in his hand.

"These are the rules," Flex grilled Maleek in the eyes and said the same words to him that he had previously said to the other seven members of the Divine Nine.

"You press the barrel to your right temple, and when I give you the word you pull the trigger. I'll tell you when, so don't get ahead of me. But the game ain't over until I say it is, ya heard? If you bitch up and your gut can't take it, you're out."

Maleek nodded his understanding with steady nerves and a demeanor that was cooler than a whole bucket of ice. He pressed the barrel against his temple and waited for the word.

"Pull," Flex said simply.

Maleek squeezed the trigger.

Click.

The sound of the hammer falling on an empty chamber was the only sound in the room.

"Pull," Flex said again, twirling his onyx ring.

Click.

Maleek didn't even blink. His eyes were locked tight on Flex's.

Flex took a deep breath. He usually made 'em go to four, but this would be the last squeeze for Maleek. Fuck what these other niggahs said. Flex wasn't about to jeopardize the goose that was gonna lay his golden egg.

"Pull," Flex said for the third time.

Maleek squeezed the trigger.

Pop!

Maleek's upper body slumped and his forehead cracked hard against the tabletop just moments after a plume of hot brains and gore shot outta the left side of his head.

"Ahh, *shit*!" Stamp screamed as blood and bits of flesh splattered all over him, gooing up his face as it blinded him and dripped from his lips.

Flex almost blacked out.

Jumping to his feet, he snatched the six-shooter from Maleek's dead fingers and aimed it down into Stamp's bloody face. Ignoring the warning cries of his other seven soldiers, Flex pulled the trigger, squeezing it over and over as it clicked harmlessly on the empty cylinders.

"Chill out, man," Dre said, grabbing Flex and prying the revolver from his fingers. Flex fought hard against Dre as he swung the gun at Stamp, and almost every other man in the room had to rush over and help Dre hold the hysterical Flex down.

It was now clearly obvious to them all that the Divine Nine was once again back down to eight, but what they didn't realize is that the expansion of Flex's empire, in fact the key to fulfilling all of his dreams, had been severely compromised.

Because with Maleek dead, Trey had no reason to give up Moonie's whereabouts. And if there was no Moonie, there was no connect. And no connect meant no progress. And if there was one thing Flex insisted on above all else, it was progress.

$$$$$

Dre watched as two staff members from the funeral home upstairs lifted Maleek's body onto a stretcher zipped him into a waiting body bag. Flex had instructed him to run upstairs and have one of the morticians send a crew downstairs to clean up the mess and to put young Maleek in the meat cooler.

Dre had watched his boss lose it before, but Flex had been well-justified this time because the stakes were sky fuckin' high.

"So how you wanna handle this shit?" Dre had asked cautiously. Flex had ordered everybody else outta the meeting and just Dre and Doc, his number two and three men, his war council, remained.

Flex sat there fuming, the fingers on his left hand moving in a blur as he twirled his onyx ring.

"We gonna do just like we planned to do," Flex spit. "Don't nothing change. The minute Trey hooks up with Moonie we should get a call. When Moonie calls, we set up a meeting. Ain't nothing gonna change."

"And what about Maleek?" Dre ventured.

Flex grilled him coldly. "What about that niggah? He's dead! We bury him! Didn't that fat-ass, short eyes preacher Reverend Flashlight up the street just clock the fuck out? I think they having his funeral today, right? Go tell Mr. Santiago to throw Maleek in the coffin with that preacher. Maybe Leek can shine a light and show that fraud-ass Bible-thumper how to get his child-molesting ass to Heaven."

CHAPTER 21

I didn't know how to feel as I climbed in the car next to Trey and we got ready to head out on our trip to see Moonie. Trey wouldn't tell me exactly where we were going, he just said we were probably gonna be gone for one night, at the tops two, so there was no need for me to bring a whole lot of stuff.

I threw two pairs of jeans and two shirts in a small backpack along with a bunch of underwear and my toothbrush and all that, and then I stuffed a sweater, my comb and brush, and a few other items into a stylish Marc Jacobs shoulder bag that Chiney's girlfriend Venus had boosted for me.

My body was still tingling from a hot, erotic encounter that me and Trey had shared earlier in his shower, and that shit had been so sexy and felt so good I couldn't stop replaying it in my mind over and over again.

Chiney looked happy as hell to see us leaving, and of course Trey noticed that. He had a million last-minute rules to dish on her, and I could tell by the look on her face that she wasn't hearing none of them. Especially his rule about bringing Venus up in the crib. I had a feeling Chiney was gonna have herself a five-chick orgy while we were gone, and I just hoped she didn't let none of her little friends go in my room and do the nasty in my damn bed.

Trey said he needed to stop at the Crossover Center and take care of a few things before we hit the highway, and as he drove us over there I was nervous, sad, and amped all at the same time. Even though I tried hard not to think about it, I couldn't help remembering the first time I had gone on a trip with a dude I was feeling. It was back when my brother Jimmy had disappeared while making a drug run for G, and me and Gino had been sent down South to look for him.

Back then I had been real young and dumb as hell. I had been scared for my brother, but rebellious against G and turned out on Gino at the same time. The end result of that trip had been a disaster and it had changed the course of my life forever. And now, as I sat in the car waiting for Trey to take care of his business inside the Center, I didn't know how this trip was gonna play out either.

Because on the one hand my goal was a hundred percent for getting Nooni up outta the G-Spot, but I wasn't blind to this game the way I used to be, and I knew exactly why Pluto wanted to get hooked up with Moonie. Yeah, of course I wanted Moonie to do whatever it took to help me get Nooni back, but I damn sure didn't want him helping Pluto build up his grimy drug empire either. My feelings were kinda twisted on all that because I didn't wanna be responsible for helping those fools put no more drugs on the streets of Harlem.

Put your trust in God, I could hear Grandmother whispering in my ear. *He will never leave you or lead you astray.*

So, as I sat in the car outside of the Crossover Center waiting for Trey, I prayed real hard and asked God to make this situation play out in a way that all the innocent souls like Nooni were set free, and all the guilty ones were made to pay in full for their sins.

And then, just to take my mind off the deadly dilemma that I knew lay ahead of us, I reached deep inside my Marc Jacobs bag and pulled out my Juicy Journal and a pen and started to write.

Dear Juicy Journal,

This morning I did some crazy shit that I just couldn't resist!

I was supposed to be packing my bags for our trip outta town, but instead I was listening to the shower running next door in Trey's bathroom, and trying my damnest to ignore the bursts of heat that kept sparking up between my thighs.

For some reason I was extra-hot in the ass and my imagination was working overtime. I kept picturing how Trey must have looked naked in the shower as jets of water sprayed down on his dark chocolate body. I imagined every last one of those delicious muscles that bulged on his shoulders, arms, and chest. Letting my eyes fall "down there" I stared at the white trail of suds that cut a line through his six-pack and slid down into the curly black forest of his pubic hair.

I was all over that thang now and I couldn't stop my eyes from dipping down even lower. And when they did, I moaned out loud and straight-up embarrassed myself as I licked my lips like I was ready to start sucking!

On the real, I felt like a dick-hound. A sex fiend. A nasty little nympho. My poor grandmother didn't raise no loosey-goosey chick in the streets! She had raised me to have some morals in my life, so I tried to tamp down on all my freaky fantasies because I knew most chicks just didn't crave sex the way I did.

I knew the way to play the game was to hook up with a dude in a serious relationship and then make him spend a couple of months dropping doe and earning the right to get up in my pussy.

But then again I had also been through enough shit in this world to know that time didn't wait on nobody. I could hear my girl Dicey hollering at me from her grave. "Life is too short, Juicy! You know damn well tomorrow ain't promised to you. You want that dick? Then go get that shit!"

I couldn't believe it when I found myself standing up and walking over to my bedroom door. I was wearing a cute pink undershirt and a pair of silky black boy shorts, and I couldn't tell if the air conditioner had suddenly gone on the blink, or if the heat simmering on the surface of my skin was coming out of my own body.

But what I did know, is that it was a whole 'nother Juicy who put her hand on that doorknob and twisted that shit. It sure as hell wasn't me. That other Juicy walked out of that room just as bold and horny as she could be, and then she went next door and stepped up in Trey's crib without even knocking.

That new-and-improved chick Juicy was bodacious as hell, lemme tell you. She followed the sound of running water and then she opened the door to Trey's private bathroom and stepped inside. The air was moist and swirling with hot steam, but it was no match for the fire that was burning between her legs.

There was a large Jacuzzi bathtub in the middle of the floor, and a double-wide shower stall made out of clear glass panes was up against the far wall. The swirling steam had fogged up the glass a little bit, but that chick Juicy could see inside the shower good enough to peep what was going down.

Trey was standing in there naked with his extra-long dick gripped in his hand.

It was rock-hard and coated with sudsy bubbles, and he was stroking that shit up like a mutha.

Juicy watched quietly for a second as her eyes zoomed in on his monster like it was a heat-seeking missile. Trey's body glistened under the spray of water as he fisted his wood and pounded it to his own beat.

Suddenly their eyes met. Trey didn't move, but he didn't miss a stroke neither. He kept up his steady rhythm as he stared at her and went right on beating his throbbing meat.

There wasn't a drop of hesitation in that bold bitch Juicy as she pulled her shirt over her head and stepped out of her panties. Her pussy was already damp and hungry, and her nipples were so hard they tingled and ached.

By the time she realized she was on the move she had already crossed the room. Her eyes were locked on him as she pulled the glass door open and stepped inside the wet stall. Immediately, a warm mist blanketed her bare body and tiny pellets of water hit her skin. Juicy stood in front of him honest and naked, showing him what she wanted and checking out what he had to offer her too.

Trey's eyes straight-up molested her.

They roamed over her firm titties and paused to admire the peaks of her nipples with mad appreciation and crazy lust. His gaze traveled down her toned stomach and paused at the 'V' accenting her waistline before heading further south toward the urgent explosion of her hips.

Directly above her neat mound of pubic hair, his eyes took in the dark, twisted wound on her belly. It was a treacherous scar, left by a killer's bullet, and for him it was a cold reminder of just how delicate she really was.

And that's when everything changed.

"Juicy," he breathed quietly. "Gone back to your room, baby," he said gently. "You shouldn't be in here with me. Ga'head, baby. Gone back."

"Trey," she whispered as she shook her head, no.

He tried to explain. "You ain't ready for none of this girl. Yeah, I know you want it. And you might even need it. But you damn sure ain't ready for it."

"How do you know what I'm ready for? I'm grown, Trey. And I'm ready too."

He shook his head again. "The next time I put my hands on you I'm gonna do it the right way. There ain't gonna be no regrets involved, Juicy. It's gonna be right. But it ain't gonna be today."

Even though his dick was still swollen, the look in Trey's eyes told her that he meant exactly what he said. He wanted to fuck her, but he wasn't going to.

"I'll tell you what," that horny chick Juicy said, scheming on a way to get her sticky off. "You don't even have to touch me... and I won't touch you neither. Just..." she reached for the shower gel and spread a big glob in her hands. "Just touch yourself," she whispered. "And I'll touch myself too, okay?"

That wild-ass Juicy dipped her hands into the falling spray of water, and then she crossed her arms over her shoulders and gently massaged the scented suds into her skin.

With her eyes locked on Trey's, Juicy's hands crept downward and her palms slid under her titties. Balancing their fullness in her hands, she lathered them up with soapsuds and fingered her stiff nipples as Trey stood there and watched. A low moan escaped her lips as a pleasure chord hummed from her breasts all the way to her clit, and Juicy sighed as she released her nipples and allowed her fingers to trail down and across her belly.

By now Trey's eyes had taken on a whole different look, and the fingers gripping his penis were tightly clenched. His breathing was getting deeper too, and Juicy could see his manhood responding to her visual stimulation.

Squeezing more gel into her hands, Juicy worked up the foam between her fingers and then delved through the tangled curls of her pussy hairs and gave her punanee a sexy shampoo. She dipped low between her legs and tantalized the fine tufts on her lower lips, and then without warning she brought both hands back up and spread her pussy open wide as her stiff little man leaped right out of his boat.

Trey stared between her legs as her clitoris stood swollen and exposed. Her tender knob of pussy meat looked sweet as hell and his mouth started watering.

He started jacking his dick again, slowly at first, but then when Juicy suddenly mashed down on her clit and slid her middle finger deep inside her pussy, his fist moved faster and slid up the length of his pole with hard, demanding strokes.

Turned on to the max, they fucked each other with their eyes and masturbated to a common beat. And when the groove finally got too hot to handle, Trey put his head back and moaned, and Juicy rotated her hips as the sugary walls of her pussy collapsed and squeezed down on her plunging fingers.

Their self-induced orgasms were powerful and explosive, and by the time Trey's dick jerked in his hand and his nut spurted through the air and landed on Juicy's naked belly, her own orgasm was tearing through her too, and she gripped her pussy in her palm as her juices seeped through her fingers and dripped to the shower floor.

By the time their breathing slowed down the water was turning cold. Trey wrapped an extra-thick towel around her, and Juicy looked up and sent him a sexy message with her eyes.

You was wrong, Mister Jackson. Dead wrong. I'm ready for everything you got, baby. Ready and waiting.

If anything, Juicy wanted Trey even more now. She wasn't sure exactly how he had done it, but some kinda way this dude had just gotten down with the part of her that had needed it the most.

Her mind.

And he did it without laying a hand on her body.

CHAPTER 22

Happy birthday to ya! Happy birthday to ya! Happy *biiiirthday*!"

It was early afternoon and Monique smiled brightly as she sang and danced and carried Salida's beautiful made-from-scratch birthday cake over to the bar where her boss sat sipping champagne. The cake was tiny and real cute, just enough for one person really, and she had decorated the shit outta it with creamy hot-pink frosting and thinly sliced strawberries on top.

"Is this for me?" Salida said, her greedy eyes lighting up brighter than the single candle that blazed from the center of the small cake. "Mo-Mo!" she exclaimed. "You baked this pretty cake just for me?"

Monique beamed and nodded at her boss-lady. "I sure did. I know your birthday ain't until tomorrow, but I wanted to give you something right now. Hell, you do so much for everybody else around here Mizz Salida that you deserve to have something sweet of your own."

Bitchy-ass Bizzie had the nerve to stand behind the bar and twist his chicken neck. "Oh, so don't nobody else get no cake?"

Monique shook her head quickly. "Not none of that one there, they don't. I made another one for y'all though. See?" she angled her head over her shoulder as young Bilal walked outta the kitchen carrying an identical, but much larger cake in his hands.

"So y'all back off and let Mizz Salida eat her little birthday cake in peace," Monique chastised the hungry men. "That big one right over there is for the rest of y'all greedy asses."

CHAPTER 23

Y ou didn't have to do this but thank you, Mrs. Washington," Trey said as he reached out his open car window and accepted the freshly baked sweet potato pie that one of the older residents of Harlem was offering him.

Mrs. Washington had caught Trey just as he was about to pull out of his parking spot at the Crossover Community Center and get on the road heading south. She was the grandmother of Gerard Brown, one of Trey's most improved protégés. Two years earlier Gerard had been out there on the avenue bangin' and wildin', and he had messed around and gotten caught in the middle of a street-corner crossfire.

The bullet that struck Gerard had severed his spine and paralyzed him from the chest down and left him a sixteen-year-old paraplegic. For months after his shooting the boy had been desperate to check out on life. Not a day had gone by that he hadn't begged his grandmother to give him an overdose of his pain medication and put him out of his misery.

Lolly Washington had taken the boy to see several psychiatrists, and every one of them had assured her that her grandson's mental anguish was a natural reaction to his life-changing physical condition. They told her that over time he would come to accept the confines of his body and learn to live within his new limitations.

But after failing to see any progress for many months, Mrs. Washington was unable to bear her grandbaby's death-pleas any longer. Her older grandson had played basketball with Mayhem and Messiah back when they were in high school. He was in the Army serving in Afghanistan right now, but during a phone call home he suggested she take Gerard over to the Crossover Community Center to get hooked up with his old friend, Trey.

Mrs. Washington knew Trey and his family from the neighborhood, and she had always felt bad about that trouble he'd gotten into. She took Gerard down there to meet him, praying that Trey would accept Gerard into his program and find some kind of way to reach the boy.

Things had turned out far better than she had expected.

Not only had Trey agreed to admit Gerard to his program, he had taken the boy under his wing without an ounce of pity, and he'd treated Gerard the same way he woulda treated him if the boy was healthy and up running around on his feet.

Trey had arranged for a Handi-Van to bring Gerard to the center four days a week, and even though the state paid for him to have a full time nurse, Trey kept the boy close to him, often wheeling him around with him wherever he went. Gerard felt real special when he got to sit in on staff meetings with Trey and watch basketball games and boxing matches right by his mentor's side. Slowly, Trey trained the boy to use all the things that the stray bullet hadn't been able to destroy: his eyes, his ears, his brain, and his heart.

"Y'all enjoy the pie," Mrs. Washington called over her shoulder as Trey waved goodbye. He passed the pie to Juicy, then started backing out of his parking spot. The sun was high in the sky and sending warm rays of heat down on the streets of Harlem. He turned the whip's air conditioner on blast, and cool streams of air rushed out and washed over him. But just as Trey started to roll up his window Lolly Washington called out to him again.

"Trey!" she hurried back over to the car with a worried look on her face. "I'm getting old, dammit. I knew I was forgetting to tell you something!"

Trey pushed a button and slid his window down again and let the cool air drifted back outta his ride. "What's going on?" he asked her.

"I know y'all heard about Reverend Flashlight, right?"

Trey nodded. The slimy Harlem preacher had gotten busted naked in the bed fucking two fourteen-year-old cousins from his congregation. When the girls' uncle bust up in the room waving a burner, the Reverend had passed out on the spot and dropped dead of a heart attack.

"Yeah, I heard about all that craziness. It's a shame."

"Well, they had the Reverend's funeral today at Three Brothers Funeral Home. His dead tail wasn't allowed across the threshold of his own church no more on account of what he did with them poor little girls, but the reason I'm telling you this is because the Reverend's wife asked me to bake some pies for his repass after the funeral."

Trey sat there waiting for her to get the point.

Mrs. Washington's voice fell a tone lower.

"I dropped six pies off at the house and gave them to one of his sisters, and she told me that something really crazy happened when they were carrying Reverend Flashlight's body out of that funeral parlor."

Trey shook his head. "Something crazy like what?"

"Well, she said them pallbearers threw the Reverend right out in the floor!"

"Threw him out on the floor?"

"That's right," she nodded vigorously. "He fell clean out. Right in the floor."

"I don't get it," Trey said and glanced at Juicy hoping she could make some sense outta what the old lady was saying. "Did somebody drop him outta the casket, or did he fall out?"

"He *fell* out!" Mrs. Washington said. "Came busting clean out the bottom! They sure don't build them things the way they used to. But the crazy thing was, Reverend Flashlight didn't fall outta that pine box by himself."

"Huh?" Trey said frowning. He was ready to get on the road and the old lady was fuckin' with his head.

"What I'm trying to tell you is that Reverend Flashlight fell outta his box, but he wasn't the only one layin' up in there!"

Trey frowned. "Who was in there with him?"

"It was that *boy*," Mrs. Washington said, lowering her voice as tears sprang to her eyes. "Maleek. Your friend Messiah's brother. Maleek was running the streets with Gerard the night he got shot, you know, and I guess the Lord figured it was his turn to get shot too."

Trey froze as a look of disbelief spread across his face. "What are you talking about Mrs. Washington?"

"I already told you I'm talking about that *boy*! Gerard's friend, *Maleek*! They said that poor baby's head was blown wide open when him and Reverend Flashlight hit the ground all tumbled up together. It's just a shame before God how them greedy funeral folks be doing our people because both Maleek and the preacher was just as stiff and dead as dirt!"

CHAPTER 24

Chiney was in Trey's bathroom getting her dick sucked. Her brother had left to take Juicy somewhere down south, and Chiney and Venus had the whole crib to themselves.

Chiney knew how her brother felt about her girlfriend, but she just didn't give a fuck. She loved her some Venus and she was gonna be with her regardless. So the minute Trey and Juicy walked out the door Chiney had hit Venus on her cell and told her to rush over so she could give her a little birthday surprise. By the time her girl showed up Chiney had her brother's bathroom lit up with scented candles, and had a tub full of hot bubbly water with rose petals floating on top, just waiting for her boo-thang.

"Yeah, baby," Chiney panted, straddling Venus's body with her right foot propped up on the edge of the tub. Using both hands, she spread her outer vaginal lips apart and thrust her hips forward. Her clitoris pointed straight out from her body. Its fleshy knob was erect and throbbing just like the head of a dick.

Venus took the succulent piece of meat between her lips and toyed with it. Sitting in the warm, bubbly water, she wiggled it back and forth and slithered her tongue around its swollen base.

Chiney palmed her woman's head and pumped her hips back and forth. She was a straight up man, mouth-fucking the hell outta her bitch, at least that's what she imagined in her own mind.

"Ah, shit! I'm about to cum again," Chiney moaned as she felt a nut pressing against her asshole and trying to bust through her coochie. She had already licked Venus to three orgasms and had two herself. This is where Chiney had a big advantage over a real man. She could have back-to-back nuts and still be ready to wear Venus out again five minutes later.

"Here it comes!" she squealed, curling her toes and clenching her ass-cheeks tight as Venus's head rapidly bobbed on her mini-dick.

"Ughh!" Chiney screamed as her muscles stiffened and she came hard and heavy. "Ugghhh!" Her titties jiggled as her body trembled and convulsed like a dog shaking off water.

Her knees were weak and shaky, and she was forced to lean against the wall in order to keep from sliding down into the tub.

"Whew!" she said after a few moments. She looked down at Venus, who was reclining in the warm water with a slight smile on her face.

"That was real good, baby," Chiney praised her, even though Venus's head game was nowhere near as good as her jump off Lincy's neck action. Chiney stared down at her woman with mad admiration. She loved the way her girl's light-brown coconut-shaped breasts looked as they floated in the soapy water. She hoped Venus was soaking the soreness outta her pussy because she was gonna want her another taste of it real soon. "Are you hungry?" Chiney asked.

Venus shook her head. "Nah, but I'm thirsty and I'm starting to come down though."

Chiney bent down and pulled the stopper from the drain. The sucking sound of water rushing into the plumbing filled the air.

"What you doing?" Venus murmured.

"Letting the cold water out," Chiney said. "Just relax. I'm gonna fill it up again and make it warmer."

Venus lay back as the water swirled down the drain near her feet. The candles flickered and glowed around the room, and the rose petals that Chiney had sprinkled in the tub stuck gently to her beautiful brown skin.

Chiney waited until almost all the water was gone, and then she stopped the tub up and began filling it up again. She poured two capfuls of strawberry-scented bubble bath under the rushing tap, and then stepped out of the bathtub and onto the micro-fiber floor mat.

"I'll be back," she said. "I'm gonna go fix us a couple of drinks." She grabbed a clean towel from the shelf and wrapped it around her body. "You good?"

Lounging sexily with the soapy water filling up the tub, Venus nodded yes.

"Wait!" she said as Chiney's hand hit the doorknob. "Let me get another hit before you go," she said.

Chiney reached for the vial they'd been smoking out of, but it was empty. She picked up the pants she'd been wearing and dug into her front pocket and pulled out the last of the dope that she had copped from Fitted that morning.

Chiney studied the small vial. It was stamped with a peculiar logo that said, "Strawberry Snake." A pink snake was on the front, and it was shaped like the letter "S". The snake's tail was curled at the end, and two dice were gripped in the tip like they were about to be rolled. Both dice were showing just one dot, which Chiney knew stood for "snake eyes." This wasn't the same Divine Nine stuff she usually copped, but hell, half of it had been free so who was she to complain?

She set up the hit for Venus, placing the pipe on a dry washcloth and putting about a quarter of the glistening crystals in the stem. She handed the whole thing off to her girl, then gave her a lighter and told her to spark up whenever she was ready.

"Save me some," Chiney said over her shoulder, knowing damn well Venus would prolly try to smoke the whole damn thing up in one blast.

Venus laughed. "Yeah, a'ight."

"You good?" Chiney asked one more time before she walked out the door.

"Yeah, baby," Venus said sweetly as she prepared to get her head sparked up. "I'm always good when I'm with you."

$$$$$

Chiney moved around the kitchen still wrapped in her towel. Humming under her breath, she turned on the small flat-panel television that sat on the counter. A crooked Republican politician was on a talk show talking a bunch of yang, and Chiney shook her head as she listed to his twisted bullshit pitch.

She got two crystal wine glasses off the portable bar and set them near the sink.

Then she took a fat lemon out of the refrigerator and rolled and kneaded it until it was soft. She washed it off and sliced the tip off one end and squeezed a little bit of juice into each wine glass.

Back at the bar, she chose a bottle of Puerto Rican rum and poured it until each glass was halfway full. She opened a can of Coca-Cola and poured again until the glasses were almost up to the rim. Then she added a few cubes of ice and sliced the lemon and stuck the pieces onto the edge of the glass.

She arranged the glasses on a sterling silver serving tray that one of Trey's bitches had given him for his birthday, then rummaged through the fridge and found a hunk of cheddar cheese. She put it on a plate with a couple of grapes and then broke off a corner of the cheese and popped it in her mouth.

Giggling under her breath, Chiney let her towel fall and stood in the kitchen butt naked. Picking up the chocolate colored vibrating dildo she had retrieved from her closet after leaving the bathroom, she positioned it around her pelvis and strapped it on tight with the leather belts and buckles coming to a close on her right hip. Flexing her ass-cheeks in and out, she pretended she was stroking Venus down, getting deep up in that pussy. Nodding in satisfaction at the ten erect inches that stuck out at an angle from her body, Chiney felt more like a man than ever before. She had just picked up the sterling tray to take it to the sexy chick who was waiting for her in the bathroom, when she heard a voice on the television say:

"Breaking news coming to you live from Channel 7, Eyewitness News. Our top story this half hour...a two-year-old child has died after ingesting crystal meth left on a table by her mother. Eyewitness news reporter Martin Solter joins us live from Harlem, New York. Good afternoon, Martin.

"Good morning, Gloria. Yes, a twenty-year-old Harlem mother has just been taken into custody in connection with the suspected drug overdose death of her two-year-old daughter. Earlier today the emergency call center received a 911 call about a woman convulsing and a baby not breathing in an apartment on Eighth Avenue. Officers responded and found the mother overdosing on methamphetamines, and the child in full cardiac arrest. At this hour it's being reported that the mother's condition has been stabilized, however, the child was transported to Harlem Hospital where she was pronounced dead. An autopsy will be conducted, but according to authorities the mother admitted the baby may have ingested some crystal methamphetamine that was mistakenly left near her Sippy cup.

As you know, Gloria, the rise in meth usage in Harlem has become a concerning trend, and this is not the first case of an accidental overdose that has been reported after the use of the fashionable pink crystals that seem to be popping up all over the city. And sadly, this particular drug may have attracted the baby because it looks and smells like Strawberry Quik. However, I must add that the two-year-old was also reported to have several burns on her body and at least one broken bone, and child abuse charges may also be filed. We're live at Harlem Hospital, Martin Solter, Channel 7, Eyewitness News...Back to you, Gloria."

"Venus!" Chiney screamed as a picture of a meth vial with a Strawberry Snake logo flashed across the television screen. The sterling silver tray she was holding hit the floor and the wine glasses shattered in a thousand tiny pieces.

"Don't smoke that shit!" Chiney screeched, jetting toward the bathroom with her stiff

dildo waving from side to side in front of her. "Don't smoke no more, Vee! *Don't smoke it*!"

Chiney reached the bathroom and flung open the door. The running water had overflowed from the tub and thousands of frothy bubbles were spilling out on the floor. Venus was lounging with her eyes closed and her head propped against the wall. Chiney was already halfway to the tub when she noticed the meth pipe and the empty glass vial floating in the bath water.

"Venus?" Chiney blurted, panic in her voice.

Her feet splashed in warm water as she ran the rest of the way over and placed two fingers on Venus's face. The girl's head lolled to the side, and then her chin dropped to her chest like her neck was just a limp spaghetti noodle.

"Venus!!" Chiney screamed. "Venus, Venus, *Venus*!" Chiney cried as she jumped into the warm tub of overflowing water and cradled her lover in her arms. "Oh baby...baby...my *baby*..." Chiney wailed at the top of her lungs. Grief and desperation made Chiney's cries grow even louder, but still Venus could not answer. Venus could not hear her. Because Venus was no more.

CHAPTER 25

Leaving Mrs. Washington standing in the street, Trey peeled outta his parking spot and left remnants of burnt rubber on the pavement. He ignored Juicy's questions as he reached behind him and grabbed a bag from the backseat. He had just retrieved it from his safe at the Crossover Center, and there were three loaded gats inside. Two Glocks and a lightweight Ruger five-shooter revolver. Trey had a concealed handgun permit to carry them and his burners were all clean, but if he so much as smelled that little niggah Flex, that fool was gonna be a dead man.

Trey drove down the streets of Harlem passing by tons of corner boys working the drug sectors of Harlem. Some scrambled meth and yay for the G-Spot, others were small factions holding it down for low-level dealers, but the vast majority were young cats just like Maleek had been, out there on the street peddling product for Flex.

For the first time ever Harlem looked like a wasteland to Trey. It was a great big cemetery filled with walking skeletons. When you got right down to it, it was all about the drugs and guns in this town, and every young Black kid walking the streets could expect to die from one or even both of those things.

Ten minutes later Trey pulled into a parking spot down the block from the Three Brothers Funeral Home. He nosed up close behind a FedEx truck and killed his engine, leaving the keys in the ignition. His face was harder than stone as he reached into his gun bag and retrieved the three firearms. He set them on his lap and briefly examined them, then pushed the two semi-automatic pistols down into the waistband of his pants and slid the revolver beneath his seat. And then, for the first time since Mrs. Washington had dropped her bomb on his head, Trey turned and looked at Juicy.

"Stay right here," he barked on her. "Lock the doors and don't get out, you hear me?"

Her eyes were wide and solemn as she nodded, and Trey felt his gut clench. He had never taken *anybody* with him to put in work, especially a female he was digging on so hard, but Trey was way past thinking straight and reasoning right now. He was operating in a blind rage, and the only thing he could see stretched out in front of him was a childhood promise unfulfilled, a racketeering funeral home, and the cold certainty of death.

$$$$

Shit was getting critical in Flex's world.

With Maleek dead and Ace and Pluto's bitch-asses acting flaky with the connect, it was looking like he was gonna have to blast the info he needed outta them fools. Salida's Grand Re-Opening of the G-Spot was about to be up on them in a minute, and Flex had put in an emergency call to the white boy who was brokering his arms

475

deal, and they had arranged to meet at a pizza shop in Harlem to finalize the details.

This muthafucka better be ready to deliver my tools, Flex fumed inside. It had taken a whole lotta hard scheming, but he had finally constructed a deadly plan that would not only allow him to gain control of the G-Spot, he would also gain a major share of Harlem's drug trade and finally take his rivals and enemies all the way down to the mat.

"Push this bitch," Flex told his dun dun Dabu as he climbed into the passenger seat of the white Rolls Royce that sat idling in the funeral home's parking lot.

Following orders, Dabu backed away from the building and then drove toward the parking lot's entrance. Both men looked left and saw the FedEx truck that was parked at the curb, and then Dabu whipped the wheel to the right and pulled out into traffic.

Neither man noticed when the FedEx truck pulled out behind them and made an illegal U-turn as the driver rushed to make his next delivery. And they damn sure didn't notice the mid-sized car as that had been parked behind it, or the tall, beastly-lookin' dude who had jumped outta the driver's seat and was now striding purposely through the parking lot and over toward the funeral home's doors.

CHAPTER 26

Salida was sick as a dog, Monique realized gleefully as she watched her boss-lady vomit up blood in the sink by the bar. *Yeah! Hurl, bitch! Hurl! I hope you puke up a whole fuckin' lung!*

Bizzie rushed his swishy-ass over and patted Salida on the shoulder, and then he pressed the back of his hand to her forehead, tryna act like he was some fuckin' kinda night nurse.

"Ace!" Bizzie's bitch-ass screeched at the top of his lungs. He looked like a dollar-store RuPaul but not half as cute. "Ace! Salida is *sick*! I think you better come see about her!"

Monique giggled like a mothafucka as Salida slumped over the sink making nasty sour-stomach-all-up-in-ya-throat noises.

That's what her ass gets for eating all that cake! Monique rejoiced as she remembered how good it had felt to take a nice long piss in the gooey pink cake batter that she'd sprinkled with a vial of Strawberry Snake.

Salida's body heaved and trembled as her system fought off the same venom that she had been pushing into the bodies of kids all over New York City for months on end.

"I wonder was it the rat poison or the pee-pee?" Monique muttered under her breath as Salida hit her knees and pressed her cheek to the floor as she moaned and slobbered in pain.

Oh, Monique thought. *This bitch was sick all right and she wasn't fakin' neither!* Anytime a prissy chick like Salida got her uppity ass on the floor in a three-thousand dollar dress then you just knew it was time to call a damn doctor!

And that's exactly what Ace did as he rushed over and found Salida with her ass tooted up and her face on the ground. By now her body was jerking and shuddering, her nose was dripping blood, and the gut-twisting sounds coming outta her mouth were straight-up pitiful.

It won't be much longer, Monique thought as she peered around Ace's fat shoulder and watched Salida wiggle like a dying cockroach. Her face was drenched in sweat and her skin looked gray and soggy.

"Oh, shit!!!" Ace shrieked as he dropped to his knees and cradled Salida's twitching body in his arms. "Call a fuckin' ambulance!" he bellowed. "She's fuckin' *dying* over here! Some fuckin' body dial nine-one-one!"

$$$$$

I couldn't even find the words that would comfort Trey at a time like this, and something told me it would be useless to even try. The look on his face when Mrs. Washington explained to him how Maleek's frozen body had fallen out of that casket and hit the ground was simply fuckin' heart-breaking. I had wanted to reach out and hold him and let the womanly part of my arms bring him some type of relief, but Trey wouldn't even look at me, and he damn sure wouldn't answer me when I tried to talk to him.

Matter fact, he had tried to make me get out of his car right there at the Crossover Center, but I had decided on the spot that I wasn't going no damn where. I knew a lot about grief and rage, and I knew both could make you do some crazy-ass things. So when Trey pulled out into traffic and took off speeding down the streets, I braced myself and made a commitment to stand by his side through whatever was gonna happen next. I didn't have a clue about where he was going, or what the hell he was planning to do when he got there, but whatever went down I was gonna be his ride-or-die, and my head and my heart were both good with that.

Trey was scary-silent as we drove down the crowded streets. His foot was heavy on the gas and light on the brakes, and I could feel the rage from his soul humming in the vibrations of his whip.

I knew Harlem well, and it didn't take me too long to figure out what direction we were heading in, but no matter what I said or how much I tried to caution Trey not to rush off into anything, there wasn't a damn thing I could do as we pulled up behind a FedEx truck just a few feet down from the Three Brothers Funeral Home.

Just thinking about how bad Flex had scared me in that basement apartment underneath all those dead bodies had me shaking in my seat, but I didn't have time to get too shook because as soon as Trey cut off the engine he turned to me and told me not to get outta the ride.

"Stay here, Juicy," he said. His voice sounded cold and scary. Every bit of emotion in it was gone. "Lock the doors and don't get out the car. You hear me?"

I nodded and held my breath as he jumped out the ride and slammed the door, and it was that cold closing sound, like a lid slamming on a casket, that brought out the absolute worst fear in me.

You know Flex is gonna kill him down there, a little voice screamed inside my head as I watched Trey walk into the gated parking lot and head toward the side door where they brought the dead bodies in. *Go 'head. Get you one last look at him Juicy 'cause just like Gino, you ain't never gonna see that man again.*

I sat there with my whole body stiff with fear as I watched Trey slip through the doors that I knew led down those steep basement steps. I started counting the seconds that he was gone, and at some point I decided that if he didn't come back out by the time I counted up to five hundred then I was gonna have to find a way to call his boy Rain, or maybe even call the cops to bust up in there and see what was going on.

In the midst of all the madness five hundred seconds seemed pretty reasonable to me, and I would have counted all the way up that high if I would've gotten the chance. But when I saw a small black hatchback pull into the funeral home's parking lot, and a fly gangsta-sister wearing a short-short mini-skirt got out with a small pistol strapped to each of her thighs, I sat up real straight and watched her like a hawk.

And when she rested her palms lightly on her guns and switched her ghetto booty over to the funeral home doors, then I knew damn well I had to do something and I had to do it real quick.

So I did.

$$$$$

Ordinarily there would be no way in hell that Trey would let a cat sneak up and get the drop on him, but deep in the belly of the home of the dead, these were no ordinary times and this was no ordinary gangsta.

"Sup, Trey. You looking for something?" a familiar voice cooed from behind him as Trey was examining the mega locks on the outer doors of the basement fortress where the leader of the Divine Nine rested.

Trey's hand was halfway to his waistband when the deadly click of a chambered round echoed in the small hallway.

"Uh-uh, big boy," the chick posted up behind him warned. "Don't reach, baby. Just gone and put 'em up in the air. You reach and I'ma have to pop you. It's as simple as that."

Raising his hands halfway in the air, Trey turned around slowly and faced Lil Lee. She was dressed in a sexy green mini-skirt, with white tights and a pair of green high-heels, and her pierced belly-button winked at him from under her short shirt as a string of tiny diamonds dangled from her caramel-colored navel.

"You like what you see?" she sneered and glanced down appreciatively at her stacked hips. "Want me to lift my skirt so you can bust up in a lil bit of this before we get it in?"

When Trey didn't answer she gave a short, cruel laugh.

"Know what I should do? I oughtta make you eat my pussy before I blast your head off, Trey, you know that? I should make you lick out my ass crack and suck my fuckin' twat, boy-o. That's what I oughtta do."

Lil Lee's hand was rock steady as she raised one of her baby Brownings and aimed it at the center of Trey's chest.

"But you don't deserve to taste my stuff, Trey. I mean, you fine and you look like a piper who can really sling that dick, but you could never get none of this. Not even a lick. And you know why? Because you violated my blood! You snatched my daughter up and gave my baby nightmares, niggah! You fucked with my little girl's head. Real bad. And I gots to *kill* your ass for that!"

It wasn't the first time that Trey Jackson had stared down the barrel of a loaded gun, and the unflappable look of defiance in his eyes made that shit real clear.

"What?" Lil Lee got swole and frowned at his lack of fear. "You think your ass is bullet-proof or some shit? You think you solid enough to go head up with my gat? Then try me, muthafucka! C'mon. Try me!"

Lil Lee was ready to splatter his brains all over the wall, but suddenly the look of defiance in Trey's eyes disappeared and the fear she had been waiting for washed over his face like a raging flash flood.

"Oh—I didn't know y'all was—" The girl came down the last step and stopped suddenly. She was digging inside her shoulder bag for something and looked up in surprise when she saw Trey and Lil Lee.

"I told your ass to wait in the car!" Trey barked and took a bold, involuntary step forward.

"Back ya ass up!" Lil Lee said, gun-checking him hard. She glanced to her left and recognized the chick who had put the kind of fear in Trey's eyes that she had been trying to produce with her burner.

"Damn!" she barked when she saw Juicy standing there looking stupid and clutching her Marc Jacobs bag. Lil Lee shook her head in disgust. "Juicy what the hell is you doing here? What? You came back to get with Flex or you fuckin' this niggah now?"

Lil Lee waved her gat. "Get your stank ass up against that door," she ordered and motioned for Juicy to go stand beside Trey. "Get the fuck over there and get real close so I can blow a hole in both of y'all muthafuckas with one goddamn bullet!"

But as Juicy tried to scramble past her and rush over to go stand by Trey, Lil Lee reached out and yoked her up with one swift, manicured hand. Keeping the business end of her burner trained on Trey, Lil Lee slid her forearm around Juicy's neck and squeezed hard, smashing Juicy's face into the pit of her underarm, right beside her breast.

"So this your new bitch, huh?" Lil Lee taunted Trey. Her eyes were filled with cold specks as she stared at him in contempt. "You been sloppin' up ol' Flex's slimy seconds?" She laughed and choked Juicy tighter as the terrified girl gagged and stumbled forward on her feet. "Just for that, I'ma do her first and make your ass watch her bleed."

The barrel of Lil Lee's gun swung around and caught Juicy right in its crosshairs.

Trey stiffened. He was calculating the odds and they weren't in his favor. If he so much as acted like he was reaching for his tool Lil Lee was gonna sink a hot one right in Juicy's gut. Could he yank his shit out and get his shot off before Lil Lee got hers off too?

"Nah, it ain't gonna work," Lil Lee said, reading his mind and yoking Juicy even harder as she jammed the gun barrel deep into her stomach. "I'll blow her fuckin' back out before your finger can hit the trigger."

"No!" Juicy's terrified plea was muffled as she screamed into Lil Lee's breast. "Please," she moaned, and her gut-twisting cries sent Trey's heart surging into his throat. "Don't shoot me," Juicy begged as Lil Lee tightened her neck grip and Juicy swayed and lost her footing and stumbled against her helplessly. "Please. I don't wanna get shot again!"

Lil Lee laughed as Juicy struggled against her, and the sound was so cruel and diabolical that there was no doubting her deadly intentions.

She's gonna kill her, Trey thought as fear crawled through his gut and he reached for his burner in stark desperation. *This crazy bitch is about to pop her—*

Pop!

Pop!

Two hollow gunshots rang out in rapid succession, and all three of their eyes met in a deadly, confused triangle.

The cracking sound was still bouncing off the basement walls as both of the women stared at Trey for a long, endless second. And then Juicy slowly turned her head and gazed up at Lil Lee, and Lil Lee turned slightly and gazed down at Juicy, and that's when Trey looked down and saw the blood.

TO BE CONTINUED...

Order

REVENGE: THE 7TH DEADLY SIN

at

www.Amazon.com or www.BN.com

**PART SEVEN
OF NOIRE'S BLOCKBUSTER
URBAN EROTIC SERIAL TALE!**

It's about to go down in Harlem!

A speeding bullet always strikes the closest target in its path, and there are plenty of bodies in the line of fire!

With double-crossing plans set in motion by gutter henchmen, who's gonna walk away with the crown in this gritty urban battle?

Will Flex and his grimy Divine Nine posse pull off the stick-up of the century? Will Salida's conniving scheme shut the G-Spot's enemies all the way down? Will Monique get the devious payback she's been dying for? Will Trey and the Talented Ten Coalition keep the youth of Harlem from falling prey to the streets? And will Juicy-Mo Stanfield escape her horrific past, or is there more gut-wrenching violence and tragedy in store for the poor little girl from 136th Street?

WARNING!

This here ain't no romance
It's an urban erotic tale,
Slimy double-crossers
Settin' rivals up to fail!
If PRIDE is the mother,
Then BETRAYAL is her son.
GREED is steady feenin' hard
And ENVY packs a gun!
LUST will have you drippin'
TRICKERY will make you cringe,
But out of all the Deadly Sins
The sweetest is **REVENGE!**

**Find out more in...
G-SPOT 2: THE SEVEN DEADLY SINS
Revenge: The 7th Deadly Sin**

The Urban Erotic Serial Saga Concludes!

NOIRE

G-Spot 2:
The Seven Deadly Sins
An Urban Erotic Serial Tale Told in 7 Parts

REVENGE: THE 7TH DEADLY SIN

by

Noire

www.AskNoire.com
www.GSpot2.com
www.TheGSpotSaga.com

CHAPTER 1

The cracking sound of a spent bullet exploded in the bowels of the funeral home just as Trey gripped the butt of his burner and took a deadly aim.

Pop!

A bright flash of orange light exploded outta the side of Juicy's designer handbag and the warm air rippled as the acrid scent of gunpowder filled the basement hallway.

Trey stood stunned for a split second as his dark eyes whipped back and forth at the crazy scene that was playing out. The two gorgeous young stunnas who'd just been tussling around in a catfight were now frozen in place and still intertwined with each other. One of Juicy's hands was thrust way down in her pocketbook. The rest of her body was clutched up in a battle-embrace with the notorious Lil Lee.

The crack of the gunshot had come outta nowhere and all three of them got shook. Both girls stared up at Trey in straight-up astonishment, but it was Lil Lee, Flex's vicious female capo, who broke the silence first.

"Yo, dude..." the gangsta diva hissed as she loosened her grip on Juicy, whose neck was still wrenched in the crook of her arm. "Sh-sh-she fuckin' *shot* me."

Lil Lee's gun hand fell slackly to her side and she stared up at Trey with shock and disbelief shining in her pretty, killer eyes. "Yo, my niggah. This fuckin' bitch *shot* me!"

Trey's eyes darted away from Lil Lee's gat for the briefest of seconds. He saw the gaping black exit hole that the bullet had left in Juicy's bag, but he just couldn't wrap his head around that shit.

Pure silence fell down on them. A thin stream of bright red blood dripped from the wound in Lil Lee's side. It ran down her slim, sexy thigh and stained her white tights crimson as it seeped over her open-toe designer shoe and puddled down to the cement floor.

Lil Lee gasped. The warm red liquid flowing down her leg freaked her ass right the fuck out, and in a pure panic the hardcore diva started catching death vapors. Fear flooded her eyes as she stared down at her life's fluids in mad disbelief. In a quick flash of rage, the ghetto gangsteress raised the muzzle of her burner and whipped it around toward Juicy aiming for a clean headshot.

A second explosion shattered the still air.

Lil Lee coughed and sputtered as a round of lead tore through her neck and sent a spiral of blood spraying from her torn-out throat in all directions. The impact of the bullet spun her fine, stylishly-dressed body around in a tight arc. She stumbled against Juicy as her unfired burner slipped from her hand and clanged harmlessly to the floor. Gurgling for air and clawing at her throat, Lil Lee's eyes were wide with fear as bright blood spurted from her neck like plume of water shooting out of a busted pipe.

A moment later her knees sagged and her shapely legs folded, and Trey's next shot, the bullet of mercy, caught her flush in the forehead and put her out of her misery before she could hit the ground.

With the hollow echo of the gunshots still bouncing off the walls, a jumble of heart-wrenching cries spilled from Juicy's mouth.

"Oh my *God*!" she screeched as she jerked her hand outta her pocketbook and the gun she had taken outta Trey's whip hit the ground with a loud thud.

Lil Lee's dead body had fallen hard to the ground too. Fallen hard and landed right on Juicy's foot. The thug-gangsteress stared up blankly from the cement floor with her ruptured dome flapping wide open. Her punctured noggin' was leaking bits of slimy gore and looked like a busted-up Chinese apple. The odor of gunpowder mingling with body matter was thick in the air, and Juicy's hair was frothy red from the sticky blood that had washed over her and was clinging to her skin.

Biting down hard on her lip, Juicy squeezed her eyes closed and let her world go completely black. Suddenly she was a dirt-ball, pissy little seven-year-old girl back on 136th Street again. Somehow she had landed right back in that funky hoe-bed where her dead mother and Aunt Ree lay on the cum-stained sheets—wide-eyed, ass-naked, and shot full of bullet holes. Somehow she was right back in the bed where her younger brother Jimmy had blown a trick's brains out and splattered the warm goo all over her innocent little face.

"I didn't wanna shoot her!" Juicy shrieked as she opened her eyes and yanked her foot out from under Lil Lee's corpse. "Oh *Lord*," she moaned. "I swear to God I didn't wanna shoot no fuckin' body!"

Trey was on her. He stepped over Lil Lee's dead body and wrapped Juicy in his arms and pulled her close. He smoothed her soft hair back and kissed her forehead as she trembled in shock and fear. He let her cry into his muscled chest for a few moments, but their time was short and Trey knew he had some work to put in.

"Don't cry, Juicy," he begged her as she moaned and whimpered. "Please don't cry, baby. Everything's gonna be a'ight. I can promise you that. But I need you to stop crying baby, 'cause I got something I need you to do for me real quick, okay?"

He took her trembling shoulders and turned her around gently until she was facing the gray cinderblock wall. "I need you to face this way for a few minutes, Juicy, okay? Can you do that for me, sweetheart?" His deep voice was like sweet velvet. Smooth and soothing. "Don't turn around, and don't look down no more, neither. Just stay right here until I get back, okay baby? Can you do that for me?"

"But I didn't wanna shoot anybody!" Juicy moaned as she pressed her forehead to the rough cinderblock wall, then bent over at the knees and clutched her stomach. "I swear to God, I didn't..."

"I know, baby," Trey said quietly as he got ready to put shit back in order. "I know."

$$$$

Less than fifteen minutes later Trey's work was done.

He had carried Lil Lee's limp body down the hall to a large room where all the empty caskets were stored, then lifted the lid on a big brown coffin and tossed her dead ass right on in there. On the way back he found a small supply closet and grabbed a mop and a jug of industrial strength disinfectant. He tore off almost half a roll of paper towels and wet them under a trickling faucet. Then he took the cleaning supplies back to the hallway where Juicy stood waiting with her face turned toward the wall, just like he had asked her to.

She looked over her shoulder when she heard his footsteps, and Trey's stomach clenched at the pained expression of fear he saw in her eyes.

"Here, let me get you cleaned up a lil bit," he told her as he used the wet paper towels to wipe some of Lil Lee's blood from Juicy's pretty skin. That shit was every damn where. On her face, caked up in her eyebrows, and in her hair too, but Trey wasn't about to tell her that. Instead, he asked Juicy to close her eyes and then he cleaned her up the best he could, knowing that no matter how much he wiped at her with his balled up paper towels it still wasn't gonna be enough to wipe what she had done outta her mind.

When he finished cleaning Juicy up, Trey went to work on the floor. He mopped up Lil Lee's blood and scrubbed a few streaks of gore off of Flex's steel door, but there wasn't a damn thing he could do about the blood splatter that had sprayed onto the cinderblocks, or the chinks in the cement walls from the speeding bullets that had torn straight through Lil Lee's body.

Trey worked quickly and methodically, and his body was covered in a light coat of sweat by the time he was finished. Juicy had done like he'd told her and stood facing the wall the whole time, but she was still shook as hell when he finally touched her shoulder and urged her to turn back around.

"W-w-where is she?" she asked, looking down at the wet floor where Lil Lee's body had been. "What did you do with her, Trey?"

"She's a'ight," he said gently. "Don't worry this is a funeral home, baby. Lil Lee is straight."

"I just can't believe I *shot* somebody!" Juicy whispered. "I just can't fuckin' *believe* it!"

Trey nodded. He couldn't believe it either, and it hurt his heart to know Juicy had taken his gat and pulled the trigger just for him. Whatever kinda feelings he had felt for this girl before, he felt them even stronger now. He owed Juicy his life, and he would never, ever forget that shit.

"Don't worry, Juicy. Trust me, you ain't never gotta worry about *nothing*," Trey swore to her as he took her hand then gripped his gat in his fist, cocked and ready to spit pure fire. "Besides," he added quietly as he led Juicy toward the funeral home's steps and straight up outta the bowels of the home of the dead. "You ain't kill that crazy chick, baby," Trey reminded her as his voice dropped down into the freezing zone. "*I* did."

CHAPTER 2

Harlem Hospital was on jam as Ace paced the floor in the emergency room. He had rode in the back of the ambulance with Salida and had sat there looking helpless as the paramedics did all kinds of shit to try to bring her back.

His boss-baby had looked half-dead as they rolled her outta the ambulance and ran with her on the gurney before pushing through a set of swinging double doors that led to the ER. The last part of his woman he'd seen was her slender, elegant hand as it hung off the side of the stretcher, and then the doors had closed and Salida was gone.

Ace had never felt so fuckin' helpless in his life. Or so alone, neither. Bizzie and a couple of Salida's dun duns had busted up in the emergency room wildin' out a few minutes later, but security had quickly put them niggahs out the door and Ace was too worried about his baby to try to raise up and make any noise for his boys.

So, as the doctors and nurses worked feverishly over Salida in a back room, Ace paced the floor wracking his brain and trying to figure out what the fuck coulda happened to her.

One minute it seemed like she was licking cake frosting off her fingers and talking her usual manner of snappy shit, and the next thing he knew she was foaming at the mouth like she had rabies and flopping and twisting all over the goddamn floor!

A surge of relief rushed through his body when the doors finally opened and a doctor walked into the waiting room asking for the family of Salida McKay. He pulled Ace to the side and explained that Salida had ingested a dangerous dose of some very potent drugs, and told Ace that it was a damn good thing they'd gotten her to the hospital when they did.

"This could have been a fatal incident you know," the young Asian doctor said shaking his finger sternly. He looked like he shoulda been passing out fortune cookies at somebody's greasy Chinese take-out restaurant, but instead he was posted up in front of Ace chastising him like he was some kinda fuckin' lil kid.

"How long has Mrs. McKay been abusing methamphetamines?" he demanded.

Ace shook his head dumbly.

"Nah, Doc. Salida don't fuck with no meth. That's word. She ain't nobody's fuckin' feen."

The doctor shrugged. "She's either a user or she's a producer. We found toxic levels of the primary chemicals used in methamphetamine production in her blood system. Her saturated lab results tell us she's been exposed to these potent chemicals for quite some time. So which one is it? Does Mrs. McKay use the drugs, or does she produce them?"

Ace swam like a fish and didn't miss a stroke.

"Man! I been tryna get her to stop fuckin' with that shit for the longest, Doc! Salida's hardheaded as hell though, and smoking that meth got her by the ass. I tell you what," Ace said, bullshitting like a mutha. "The minute you let her up outta here I'ma see about getting her into a drug treatment program, you dig? I'ma tryta help her kick that ice habit. I swear I am."

The doctor nodded. "I suggest you do that. Crystal meth is not the kind of drug a woman her age wants to play around with. Especially now. For the past few days we've seen countless addicts who've overdosed on that stuff. We've even had a couple of fatalities too. Like I said, Mrs. McKay is no spring chicken. At her age she should be very concerned about the effects that street drugs can have on her blood pressure and her heart functions, because here lately our local meth addicts have been dropping on the streets like flies."

$$$$$

Trey stole a quick glance at Juicy's sleeping face as he pushed his whip down the turnpike at a steady speed. This girl was beautiful beyond words and in her sleep she looked sweeter than a slice of pie, but deep down where it counted his baby was a combat soldier. A straight-up rider. It fucked him up the way she had rolled down them basement steps packing mad heart and cold heat. Shit, if it wasn't for Juicy popping Lil Lee thru her purse then Trey mighta got his melon tossed down there.

He had pulled off the road when they hit North Jersey and got a room at a small, but nice hotel so Juicy could take a quick shower and wash the rest of Lil Lee's blood and brain goo outta her hair. Juicy had still looked real shook when he guided her outta the shower and gently dried her skin off with a soft towel. She had cried when she leaned on him and let him help her get dressed, but she had also insisted that they keep heading south so she could get in touch with Moonie.

So when they got back in his ride Trey had reclined Juicy's seat back as far as it would go, then kissed her gently and told her to close her eyes and try to get some rest while he drove.

Trey's eyes mighta been on the road as he cruised down the highway, but his head was definitely back in Harlem. Back in the basement of that funeral home where that lil rat-faced niggah lived. Trey was gonna kill Fletcher Boykin. That's the reason he had rolled down in that basement in the first place. To take that niggah out. And he was still gonna do it too. He was gonna kill Flex for making Maleek pop himself in the dome, and for forcing his baby Juicy to have to shoot Lil Lee.

Time passed fast as he schemed and planned, and a little more than three hours after he'd tossed Lil Lee's body into an empty coffin, Trey and Juicy were rolling through the toll plaza at the southern end of the Jersey Turnpike.

With thoughts of murking fools consuming his mind, Trey paid the toll and jumped on I-95 going ten miles over the speed limit. He was pushing his whip hard down to Virginia, and it wasn't because of no bullshit deal he'd made with Flex back in New York City, neither. Nah, it was "demolish a muthafucka" time in his world, and Trey couldn't want to get up with his manz Moonie so they could collaborate on a plot to take Flex, Pluto, Ace, and anybody else who fucked with his woman or stood in the way of progress in his beloved town of Harlem, all the way down.

CHAPTER 3

Back in Harlem Monique was grooving on the G-Spot's time, but the only clock she was watching was the one that told her it was almost time for her sugar-daddy-eat-pussy-like-he-had-a-Hoover-in-his-mouth, white-knight-with-the-swole-pockets to snatch her up so they could head south to warm weather and tropical beaches.

She was laid up in a fuck room with Slick Sallie. They were scheming and planning to dip outta Harlem on the sneak tip, and Monique couldn't wait to get gone! Matter fact, her suitcases were already packed and stashed under the bed she slept in with Pluto, and it took everything in her not to slap the shit outta his fat ass while he was laying up there snoring and farting and scream, "Deuces, niggah! I'm out!"

But Mo knew better than to blow her own cover, and when the right time came to tell Pluto to kiss her black ass she was gonna do that shit over the *phone*, from about five states away! Until then, she concentrated on sticking her pussy in Slick Sallie's face every chance she got. She had never given one man so much good ass in her entire life, and with the kind of bank this dude was holding he deserved every lick of it.

"You makin' me so fuckin' *hot!*" she exclaimed as she rode Sallie's dick like he was a little white pony with a satchel full of dollars around his neck. She arched her back and thrust her pelvis forward. Leaning back on her arms, she contracted her thigh muscles and bounced up and down with a smile of pure glee widening her lips.

Stretched out beneath her, Sal gripped her fleshy black ass and rotated his pelvis in a wide circle. He was trying to knock a hole in her slippery inner walls as he probed the softness of her every crevice.

"You said it stays hot down there in Florida all the time, right?" Monique suddenly asked him, sitting upright again as she flicked her little titty and fantasized about being laid out on a warm sandy beach dressed in a thong and nipple pasties and looking real yummy. She closed her eyes and a grade-B movie showing nothing but a life of luxury and riches began playing on the inside of her lids. She was bent over this white boy. She had even put a picture of them on her facebook page and changed her relationship status from single to married!

"Yeah. It stays hot as hell," Slick Sallie panted as he worked his hips deeper and faster. "Just like this sweet black pussy!"

"And they ain't got no nasty-ass snow down there, right?" Monique asked, slowing her hip motion.

She thought about the grimy, dirt-caked snow mounds of a New York City winter, and how it was white and pretty when it was new, but ended up looking like lemon slush after stray dogs finished pissing all in it.

She turned her top lip up in disgust, then pushed the image of nasty snow outta her mind by popping her hips and forcing herself to visualize a brand new life where she rocked the latest bangin' fashions and styled custom-made jewelry out the ass, just like Salida did every day up in the G-Spot.

"Oooh," Monique moaned, quickening her pace. Her na-na was getting nice and gummy as she imagined the humungous mansion she was gonna be ruling over; the fancy whips, the endless weed, and all the maids and servants and shit.

"Baby can you buy me a Por-sha?" she begged in a little girl's voice, twerking her ass real hard as she sucked Sallie's dick deeper into her tunnel. She thought about how Pacho used to chauffeur that bitch Juicy around all over Harlem like she was a queen or something. She wanted somebody to do her like that too! "For real, baby. You think I can get me a Por-sha and a driver too?"

"You mean a Porsche?"

"Yeah." She humped the shit outta him. "That's what I said."

All Sallie could do was nod and slobber. Monique was throwing her sex thang down on him like a certified professional, and as long as she kept this up she could get any fuckin' thing she wanted because this was the best black pussy he'd ever had in his life.

"Yeah," he panted as he encircled her tiny waist with his pale hands. He loved the way their chocolate and vanilla swirled. "Hell, yeah. A Porsche, a Maserati... whatever the fuck you want..." he slurred as he lifted her off of his midsection and raised her up until she was floating above him with her thick cum dripping down into his face.

He looked up into her glistening snatch and shivered. He couldn't believe he had such an insatiable appetite for this prime chocolate candy with the gooey pink in the middle. He licked his lips as his mouth began to water. Then he stuck out his tongue and stiffened it before urging Monique lower and guiding his thick piece of mouth-meat straight up in her slit.

"Get it," Monique commanded above him as she felt his warm tongue probing around inside her tunnel. "Get it and get it good!"

She let Sallie slurp up all the oral he could handle, and by the time she was on her third nut he finally exploded too, humping hard on the bed and shooting his seed onto the red satin sheets.

Afterward, they smoked a blunt together as Monique continued entertaining notions of flyness and splendor in her head.

"It's gonna be great for us down there," Sal hyped her up as he exhaled a thick plume of smoke. It had been easy to let his guard down and catch Monique's vapors because her big dreams and excited energy was real contagious. He'd become a lot more open to shit since coming back to New York. Back in L.A. he would have never even thought about taking a chick along for the ride. Especially not a Black one. But what the hell. It was a new day and a new time. Time to do new shit.

"We can be whoever the hell we wanna be when we get to Miami," he told her. "We can start our whole lives over, ya know? Fuck the past! We can even change our names, if we wanna. We can live any damn where we feel like living too. It's gonna be fun. I can't wait."

Monique nodded in agreement but then asked, "You really serious about taking me down there though, right Sallie? You ain't bullshittin', is you? I mean, you really do wanna be with me, don't you?"

Money-Makin'-Monique couldn't even imagine no white boy coming up in the Spot tryna run game on her, but you just never knew these days. One thing she was sure of was that if she skipped town with a square sucker like Sallie she could never bring her ass back home to Pluto. *Never*. That mad gorilla would kill her. Choke her ass clean dead. Nah, when Monique left Harlem she had to be outtie for good. There would be no turning back.

She slapped the shit outta Sallie's arm. "I *said* do you really wanna be with me, dammit!"

"Of course I wanna be with you!" Sal laughed and he meant it too. He squeezed her bulging titty and grinned. He had always wanted to floss on the beach in Miami, and he dug the shit outta Monique. Yeah, she was Black, but everything about her was sweet as hell. Besides, there were lots of dark Cubans and other ethnic girls all over Miami. Monique would look real good on his arm.

"So," she said pouting, "we still gonna get us some matching tattoos, right? Not one of them ugly ass sleeves, though, yuck! Nah, we gonna get each other's names, right? You gettin' minez and I'm gettin' yours, right?"

"Right." Sallie nodded.

"Right? That's all you got to say? Hold up. You ain't gonna get me way down there and diss me and treat me like no jump-off, is you?"

"Of course not," Slick Sallie said soothingly. "I wanna be with you, Monique. I wanna be with you in a way I ain't never wanted any other girl. And that's the truth."

Monique nodded, finally satisfied, and then settled back in his pale arms.

"You got us a place picked out for our bizzness yet?" she asked.

Sal shook his head. "Nah. I figured we could do that together when we got there, ya know. Since you're gonna be the First Lady of Money Makers, I think you should help decide where we set it up."

Monique nodded, this here white boy had her ass feeling straight up important, valued, and excited all at the same time.

"I know just how we should hook our shit up, too," she grinned and told him. "I been studying how the Spot is run from the front door to the back, and I can handle it all. The hoes, the bar, security, the cut-room—but we ain't cookin' up no goddamn meth!" she said shaking her head. "That shit stanks like a muthafucka! I don't want none of that nasty shit in our place, you hear me?"

Sallie laughed. "Cool. No meth," he said. With all the paper he was gonna stack from the weapons he was about to sell, combined with the jackpot he already had stashed away in his shitty little rented joint in Chinatown, him and Monique could afford to go into business without getting involved in no kinda club drugs at all.

"Yeah, boss lady," he said, thinking about his upcoming meeting at the pizza shop as he fingered Monique's chocolate chip nipple that looked like a sun-sweetened raisin sitting on top of a fluffy mocha cloud. "Whatever you wanna have in our goddamn club, is exactly what's gonna be in there."

CHAPTER 4

Paulie's Pizzeria smelled like garlic stix and stale pepperoni when Flex and Dabu barged through the door with murderous looks in their eyes. Pausing in the entryway, Flex narrowed his gaze and scanned the joint, tryna spot his arms dealer in the thick crowd. Seconds later he locked eyes with a hard-looking white cat with blond hair who was sitting in a booth toward the back, and dude gave Flex a short nod to let him know he was his man.

"Yo, *bitch*," Flex barked the moment his ass touched the seat across from the thugged-out white boy. "I'ma need yo pale ass to be about this bizzness, slime."

The blue-eyed cat shrugged and said coldly, "Then let's be about it, muh'fucka."

Flex sniffed, and placed his folded hands on the table. He grilled Slick Sallie hard and deep, like he was about to go up in his ass raw.

"You know what the fuck I want."

Sallie nodded with no emotion. "And I got what the fuck you need."

Flex felt the weight of his gat pressed up against his side as he stared across the table. Dude was right. He needed those clean tools, but this muthafucka bet'not dance with him. He had left instructions for Lil Lee to meet him back at the funeral home so they could get up in the count room and bag up the bank to handle this transaction, and if one fuckin' thing went wrong he was gonna flap this honkie's forehead back and open his dome up wide enough for the whole world to read his thoughts.

"A'ight, so dig. I'ma need my dead bitches all laid out together in one wooden coffin," Flex said, speaking in code. "And every last one of them ugly broads betta have a hard dick stuck up her ass, you feel me?"

Slick Sallie nodded again. It was an unusual request to have a shipment of firepower delivered fully locked and loaded with ammunition, but for the kind of bank Flex was paying him it could certainly be done.

"The funeral is gonna be open casket," Flex told him. "So I need all my shit to be in top viewing condition. You know the date, you know the muh'fuckin' time. Make sure my dead bitches are there."

"I got you, homey," Sallie said casually as he slid outta the booth and stood up. Indiscriminate killers like Flex instilled fear in the souls of the hardest street cats, but this fool didn't make Sallie's heart pump not one beat faster.

"Bitches gotta be fed, you know," Sallie spit over his shoulder as he walked away from the table. "Even dead ones. Make sure you bring me that cheese in real small slices, homey. You know *that* date, and you know *that* time."

$$$$

I was chilling in the passenger seat next to Trey with my eyes closed but I damn sure wasn't sleeping. I couldn't believe that I had actually pulled the trigger and shot Lil Lee, and my hands and feet were still shaking like hell.

I had calmed down a little once we got in the car and headed out of town, but then I freaked out all over again when we stopped at a motel so I could clean myself up. The sight of all that bloody water running off my body and outta my hair, and swirling around my feet in the bottom of the tub was a stone-cold reminder of what I had done.

"But you didn't kill her, Juicy," Trey had told me over and over again as he took me outta the shower and kissed the tears from my eyes. He wrapped my body in a towel and used another one to help me dry my hair, and I felt like a baby as he helped me step into my panties and get my clothes back on. Even though I was scared, I knew he was right. Lil Lee had gotten exactly what was coming to her ass. That crazy bitch had earned that fuckin' bullet, and it had had her name on it. Hell, it was all about survival of the fittest on the streets of New York, and if I hadn't gotten her ass first she damn sure woulda gotten either me or Trey.

So no matter how pressed out I was behind shooting her, I stuffed those feelings way in the back of my brain and I didn't let them stop me from being aware of the other stuff that I was feeling in my head and in my heart.

Because riding beside Trey had me feeling some kinda way. Sad. Guilty. It put me in the mind of the ride that me and Gino had taken to Atlantic City. Except, the trip me and Gino took had been a treacherous set-up arranged by G so he could bust me and his only son getting our fuck on. A set-up that had led to me being gang-raped, my brother Jimmy blowing his own brains out, and me and Gino hauling ass out of New York to save our lives.

Yeah, I was still shook about pulling the trigger on Lil Lee in that funeral home, but I wasn't in pure panic mode like I had been when Gino was driving through all that snow trying to help me find my brother. Instead, this time I was older, stronger, and I was damn sure smarter. And it wasn't just about me either. I sat there with my eyes closed just praying like hell that Trey would find Moonie so he could give up the name of G's main dope connect and help us get poor Nooni outta that Dungeon alive and in one damn piece.

I shivered as I thought about what that girl must have been going through down in that Dungeon. As much as I couldn't stand Monique's skank ass, I had been real grateful for them purple pills she had slipped me when Ace dragged my young ass down them Dungeon stairs. If it wasn't for them drugs lifting me up and taking me out of my battered and brutalized body, I woulda lost my damn mind as I laid there getting my coochie raped raw.

I sure hoped Nooni had found something to take her mind outta her body too while she was trapped down there. Because if she didn't, her body might be straight by the time we got to her, but her tender young mind was damn sure gonna be throwed off.

CHAPTER 5

Deep down in the basement of the Three Brothers Funeral Home, Flex was back from his meeting with Slick Sallie, and he was also smelling him a real stank rat.

Earlier in the day he had sent Lil Lee a text telling her to meet him in the count room so they could pack up the cash they were gonna exchange for his upcoming shipment of brand new gats. Her ride was parked right outside so he knew she had swung by like she was instructed, but for some reason his head hench-chick wasn't nowhere in sight and something churning in Flex's gut felt suspicious as hell.

"Yo, what the fuck is this?" he barked, then peered closely as he ran his finger over a nick in the bullet-proof steel frame of his door. He knew damn well that shit hadn't been tore up like that when he left earlier in the day, and suddenly his eyes narrowed into slits and his street instincts kicked in hard.

"Ay, boss," Dabu said as he ran his fingers over a rough area of gouged concrete in the cinderblock wall. "Something skimmed the fuck outta this shit right here, man. Skimmed it and took a nice chunk outta it too."

Immediately both men jumped into action and their gats appeared in their gripped fists. "Go that a' way," Flex nodded over his shoulder. He sent Dabu down the hallway to his right, and he headed down the narrow corridor to his left. They conducted a quick recon of the basement area, and when they met back up outside the door to Flex's joint both men were shaking their heads in confusion.

"Nothin, son?" Flex asked. "You ain't see shit on that end either?"

Dabu shrugged. "Not a damn thing, boss. It don't look like nobody been back there, and I can't see nothing outta order."

"You looked everywhere, niggah? Even in the storage room and in that lil broom closet?"

"Yeah," Dabu lied. He had gotten as far as the room where they kept all those empty fuckin' caskets and then he caved. Just the sight of them dead-bed jawns had given him the creeps and he'd bounced in the other direction after that.

Flex frowned and looked around, his eyes scanning the basement like a radar. "Then why the fuck is shit feelin' so funky down here then?"

Dabu shrugged. "I'on't know. Doc or Dre or one of them other niggahs prolly swung by while we was gone," he speculated, "but ain't no fuckin' body down here now but me and you, man. Word. I looked."

Flex shook his head and frowned again. *Some* fuckin' body had been down here violating his muh'fuckin space, and this he knew for sure because his gut intuition was raising a hood alarm.

"Yeah, a'ight, niggah," he said suspiciously, and then he hit Dabu with a question that his manz sure as hell didn't have the answer to.

"Yo, my niggah. Where the fuck is Lil Lee?"

$$$$$

My eyes were open real wide as Trey turned into a driveway that was long and narrow, and led up to a big house that looked like a log cabin. There were a whole bunch of big green trees and pretty flowers everywhere, and there was even a pond with a boat dock off to one side.

Two little girls were outside playing on a colorful swing set, and if they weren't chocolate black I would've sworn all out we were rolling up on some rich white people's property where we sure as hell didn't belong.

I stared at the little girls as Trey coasted the whip to a stop. I'd seen them before, but it seemed like that had been two lifetimes ago. Two lifetimes ago since my grown tail had snuck off to hang out all over the city with Rita while G took Jimmy with him to California to go to Gino's college graduation.

I thought about how me and Rita had spent five days slumming around New York City, just being wild and free like regular teenagers, and other than the little bit of time that God had given me with Gino, those five days was probably the best days of my life.

I remembered that shit like it was yesterday, too. Rita had dragged me all over the place like I was a tourist. And I had damn sure felt like one. She couldn't believe I had never done the usual shit that every New Yorker does, like going to the Statue of Liberty, the Radio City Music Hall, or even the Bronx Zoo.

And it was while me and Rita was chillin' at the Bronx Zoo that I saw something that shocked the hell outta me. I saw G's right-hand man, Moonie. He was coming out of the stank-ass monkey house. He was holding hands with his woman, and one of these cute little girls right here on the swings had been riding high on his shoulders.

The grimy underworld that G had thrust me into had been full of gangsters, murderers, strippers, and thieves. It had really messed my head up to see somebody from the G-Spot living an ordinary sherm life. As far as I had known, Moonie was just a quiet, deadly killer. G's top capo, the underboss who oversaw every little detail at the G-Spot and kept the flow in deep check.

But, as I realized that day at the zoo, Moonie was way more than a killer. He was a schemer. A coldblooded, calculated conspirator. He might have perpetrated and passed as a regular dude during the day, but papi turned into somebody totally different when the ballers and the freaks came out at night. I knew this for a fact because when the shit hit the fan and G's shiesty empire began to crumble, damn near every soldier in town had either gotten popped or knocked.

But not Moonie. He had jetted up out of Harlem and gotten away clean, and according to what Cooter had told Chiney, Moonie had rolled out with a gwap in cold, clean cash, and he had even more cheddar stashed away where couldn't nobody ever find it.

So while I knew Moonie was a treacherous criminal, I also knew he was cool as hell too. I hadn't forgotten about the good-looking-out he had done for me by sliding me that fat envelope stuffed with cash when I was chained up in that Dungeon. Cooter had given it to me right before I ran my naked ass up outta the G-Spot, and I had been damned grateful to him and to Moonie too.

And now, as me and Trey climbed out the whip and walked up to the house I couldn't take my eyes off the small-framed man who stood on the porch peeling an orange. The bottom half of his face broke open in a wide grin as he watched us, but the telltale signs of a cold-blooded killer was still lurking in his eyes.

"Juicy," he said, reaching out to hug me with one hand as I stepped up on his spotless porch. "Damn it's good to see you, baby girl. You been a'ight?"

I nodded as he held me close, and I couldn't help thinking about how righteous Moonie had always treated me. There had been plenty of times that he had busted my hot, hard-headed ass getting loose and pushing my luck with G, but for some reason Moonie had never snitched on me. He had never once dropped a dime or gotten me in trouble, and I loved him for that.

"I'm good," I said when he let me loose. "I been pretty good. How about you?"

"Oh, I'm chillin'," he laughed as him and Trey dapped each other out real quick. "I'm chillin' just like always baby."

Without a drop of hesitation Moonie looked into my eyes and went ahead and laid all the cards right out on the table.

"A'ight, check it out. I know what happened to you and Gino, mami. And you got my sympathies for that shit too. Gino was a real good dude. As solid as they come. It's fucked up that we lost him but I'm glad you pulled through shawty. You was lucky as hell, you know. Real lucky."

A wave of pain hit me as the old memories flooded over me. Moonie had that shit right. Gino had been a good man. A damned good one. And I had been real, real lucky.

"So," Moonie put his arm around me again. "My rowdy Trey told me them fools Pluto and Ace are tryna make a comeback, huh? Them bitch-niggahs been leaning on you? Tryna use you to catch up with me?"

I nodded. "They shot my best friend and snatched her sister right outta her bed. She's only seventeen. Just like I was when G brought me up in the G-Spot. I think they got her down in that basement, Moonie. Down in that filthy-ass Dungeon."

I swallowed real hard after I said that shit. If no damn body else knew how much I had suffered when I was chained up like a dog in that hot, stinking-ass little torture hole, Moonie knew. He was the one who had comforted me and washed me up with my own bloody t-shirt after Jimmy blew his brains out all over me.

"Pluto said I was gonna have to give up a big name before he would let Nooni go. So that's why I asked Trey to bring me to you."

Moonie laughed. "So I'm just supposed to tell you who G's major connect was, huh?" he shook his head. "It don't work like that in the bizzness world, baby girl."

I nodded. I thought about that crazy night when Rita had cracked the code to the safe that G had hidden behind a picture on his bedroom wall. I was sweating and happy as hell when she opened that shit because I just knew there was gonna be some mad cash, stocks, bonds, gold bars, and Swiss bank accounts up in that baby.

But other than a few old pictures, about five large in twenties, and a key that had the words RENO SUPREME engraved on it, there wasn't shit else in there except a thin black binder. The binder had a list of the names and contact information for all of G's front men and his connects, but I had already checked them out and they were all low-level dealers. One or two of them were still operating in Harlem on a real small-time platform, but most of them had gotten knocked in the police sweep after G died, and the rest were either in jail or outta business. None of them were large enough to have been his main man.

"Look, I'm not tryna put you in no trick bag, Moonie, and I know you retired and you don't deal in no street bizzness no more. But a young girl's life is depending on me. I need some info that I can take back to Pluto, or Nooni is gonna be dead."

Moonie tossed his orange peels over the porch rail and into some thick bushes. "So Big P is using you to get up on G's connect," he said, then he laughed. "That's some funny shit because his partner Ace hollered at me on the side tryna get with G's connect too, yo!"

I stared at Moonie. What the fuck was I supposed to say?

"On top of that, my manz Trey here is telling me that lil niggah Fletcher from 136th Street is tryna find out who G's connect is too. Goddamn! *Everybody* wanna get in the bed with G's fuckin' connect!" Moonie stared back at me with his dark, killer eyes. "Yo, this is a big boy's game we playin', Juicy. Do you *really* wanna know who the connect is? Are you *sure* you wanna know, baby girl?"

I thought about my friend Rita who was still laying up in Harlem Hospital all shot up, and about poor little Nooni trapped downstairs in that filthy-ass Dungeon suffering like a muthafucka, and I nodded.

"Yeah. I wanna know. I *need* to know."

"A'ight," he said, turning toward the front door. "A'ight."

Moonie walked into his house and motioned for me and Trey to follow him. We stepped into a large living room that was full of expensive-looking furniture and stuff.

"Juicy-Mo," Moonie said, nodding toward a big dude who was sitting on his sofa guzzling from a tall can of beer. "Lemme introduce you to Granite McKay's major power player. The *consigliere* who once controlled the biggest drug distribution network in not just the city but the whole fuckin' *state* of New York."

All I could do was stand there with my mouth wide open as I eyeballed the dude who was chillin' on the couch and puffing a cigar. Wasn't no introductions necessary between me and this cat because I already knew him. I knew him pretty damn well.

He was my old friend Renata's husband.

It was Frank.

CHAPTER 6

Salida was burning up on fire and causing everybody all kinds of heartburn.

She had signed herself outta the hospital, but not before every fuckin' body in Harlem found out that she had passed out in the G-Spot and got taken away in an ambulance. That lil idiot-ass broad Nae Nae had even called her sister Lourdes way downtown in Brooklyn and told her it looked like Salida was about to die right there on the floor!

Poor Ace had been worried as fuck that he might lose the only woman in the world that he had ever loved, but now he was baby-stepping around Salida as she went from foaming at the mouth and throwing up all over the floor, to snapping with the tongue and bossing him around. She had gotten mad as hell when she found out he'd told the doctor she was a meth head, and she couldn't stop blastin' on him about it.

"What in the fuck was your dumb ass thinking?" she said as she stood in the mirror in G's office bathroom curling her hair. She was posted up with one hand on her hip, and she had on a hot pink bra that was so sheer her thick nipples were poking through. A sexy garter belt in the same hot pink color rode her curvy hips, and it was clamped to the silkiest pair of thigh-high stockings that Ace had ever seen.

"You told them idiots I was some kind of mess head!" she bitched. "Them fools was tryna talk me into checking into some goddamn residential rehab program all because of your stupid ass!"

"Yo, I ain't have no other choice!" Ace tried to explain. "The doctor said he found that shit in your system, Salida! He said your ass was either a producer or a user. You prolly got it in your blood from all them fires you been settin' upstairs in that cut room. You can't be breathing in all them damn fumes, baby. That shit'll kill you!"

"When's the last damn time I set a fire?" Salida demanded at him in the mirror. Yeah, she used to set one at least every other week, but ever since Freeze took over the mixing they hadn't had a single damn blaze. "Huh? When's the last goddamn time? Besides, jail'll kill me faster than some damn meth will! Your stupid ass shouldn'ta told that doctor *shit*!"

"Yo!" Ace spit, "it was either Rikers or rehab! I was just tryna stop them from lockin' your ass up!"

"Who the fuck is you yelling at?" Salida whirled around and froze him in her icy glare. "Don't you *never*," she panted, pointing the hot curling iron up in his face, "raise your voice at me again, you buck-toothed, knock-kneed, jiggly-belly gorilla! You got that shit? You *got* it?"

Ace stared cross-eyed at the hot curling iron that Salida was brandishing at the tip of his nose as he tried to understand the anger that had his boss-baby all twisted up. Nobody never woulda believed he had lost his gangsta and allowed a chick to put her foot on his throat the way Salida was doing him. He had knocked plenty of birds on their asses just for looking at him wrong, let alone basing on him and disrespecting

498

him the way Salida did whenever she got ready to snap.

But there was something about this woman that brought out the little boy in him. He entered the pussy-lickin' zone whenever he was near her, and she could make him do any damn thing she wanted him to do by just saying the word.

Salida was just sexy as hell.

Especially when she got mad. And especially when her stunning body was looking and smelling like this.

Ace eyeballed her. Her bra was so sheer that her nipples stood out like targets. Her titties looked like puffed-up buttery biscuits as she breathed hard and her chest rose up and fell down.

His eyes traveled down to her trim stomach and tight waist, and then paused at the explosion of her hips before sliding down her perfect thighs and beautiful legs.

"What you lookin' at me like that for?" she demanded in a husky voice.

He swallowed hard and shook his head. He wanted to fuck her. What the hell could he say?

Ace stood there looking hopeful as Salida's eyes changed. She was still mad, but she liked to fuck when she was mad.

"Put me up on the sink," she demanded.

Oh hell yeah, Ace thought as the front of his pants bricked up and his dick started uncoiling like a snake. He licked his lips as she unplugged the curling iron and set it on top of the toilet tank, and then he cupped her hips and lifted her up on the edge of the sink.

She parted her thighs and let him get a whiff of her sweet pussy.

Ace moaned and dipped his head to get at those thick nipples that were now poking out like pencil erasers. He parted his lips and took one into his hot mouth, twirling his tongue around the peak and sucking it right through her bra.

Salida moaned and his fingers slipped between her warm thighs and found her steamy pussy. He rubbed her swollen clit and rammed his thick middle finger deep inside her wet snatch. He sucked her and fucked her as Salida threw her head back and opened her legs even wider. Her firm ass gyrated around on the sink as she gripped his wrist and humped on his finger.

Ace was just about to switch sides and get at her other titty when she demanded the dick instead. He unzipped his pants and extracted his meat outta his drawers, and almost fainted at the sight of her gapped-open pussy as Salida lifted her knees and drew them shits back to her shoulders and braced her heels on the edge of the sink.

With his dick aching in his hand, Ace dove face-first into that dripping pussy.

He ate that sweet pink meat like it was the last meal he was gonna get in his whole life. He sucked her clit and then licked her pretty pussy up and down, catching each spurt of warm cum as it seeped outta her snatch.

Jacking his dick with one hand, Ace fingered Salida's asshole and then gently inserted his fingertip inside. She whimpered and he felt the muscles of her tunnel squeezing and contracting, drawing him in even deeper.

He brought his mouth up to her nipple, then finger-fucked her asshole and jacked his dick at the same time. A few moments later Salida pushed his head away and guided it back down to her pussy. He licked and pumped and fingered and sucked, and when she clenched his ears and pressed his face down hard into her pussy, he took charge like a real man and snatched her ass down off the sink.

Ace flung her up against the wall and gripped her hips, jerking her ass backwards toward his groin. He pushed his monster dick up in her with one deep stroke, then he leaned his elbows on her back, forcing her to bend over real deep as he doggy-fucked her so hard her head banged up against the wall.

Salida was whimpering and moaning as he beasted the shit outta her hot pussy. Ace reached down and ran his hands up and down the silkiness of her stockings, then took her melon-sized titties in his palms and rubbed and squeezed them until Salida started to scream.

Bucking back at him, her pussy blossomed like a flower and his dick slid in two inches deeper. The wet heat percolating in her tunnel was too much for both of them to take, and as Salida arched her back and came in a rush of spurting hot pussy juice, Ace thrust his thumb up her ass and slammed his dick into her pussy hole with five strokes that were so deep and hard it felt like the gallon of cum he blasted up in her snatch was gonna come shooting straight outta her mouth.

Yeah! He thought with mad satisfaction as Salida mewed like a cat and nutted again. It didn't matter how much shit his baby liked to talk. He could always shut her up with just a few good strokes of his rock-hard dick.

$$$$$

"Juicy!"

The man on the sofa stood up grinning and I couldn't help but walk into the arms that were held out to welcome me.

"*Frank?*" I stammered as my mind reeled like a mutha. Confusion had me looking dumb in the face. "You down with *Moonie?*" I shook my head a few times. "Hold up. I don't get it."

"Oh, Frank's the man," Moonie said. "He's down with a lotta important people, Juicy."

Frank gave my shoulders a squeeze.

"Moonie and me, we go way back," he explained. "In fact, he was the only person Granite ever trusted when we made our deals. Who would have thought that one day me and Moonie would be making a few deals of our own?"

I couldn't believe this shit and I knew my feelings were showing on my face. "So all that time me and Gino was out there lying our asses off in L.A. you already knew the truth? You knew who we were? You knew Gino was really G's son?"

Frank nodded.

"Yeah, I knew. Moonie was worried about you. He asked me to take you under my wings, so I hired Gino to work for me so I could keep my eyes on you."

I glanced at Moonie real quick and then back at Frank.

"So, hold up. That means you and Renata was just frontin' like y'all was our friends then, huh? Y'all was just babysitting us for Moonie and playin' some kinda role?"

"No," Frank held his hand up and checked me. "Not at all. My wife's the real deal, Juicy. She loves you. We had a daughter a long time ago, but we lost her. Renata got attached to you. She was worried out of her mind when you just walked away and disappeared."

I took a deep breath and then nodded. I believed him. Renata was my friend on the real, and she was definitely legit. Out of all of them greedy leeches who was at the church when I got shot, Renata was the only person who was still by my side when I woke up in that hospital bed with my baby boy dying in my stomach. It was Renata who had held me in her arms and cried with me when I grieved outta my head, and she was the one who had suffered with me after Gino died too. There's no way she coulda been faking the funk on none of that.

I turned back to Moonie and I almost started crying.

This dude was amazing. Moonie had been looking out for me for a real long time, and I truly appreciated him. I remembered how he used to step in between me and G whenever that fool went too far and lost his head. He was real good at getting G sidetracked with some bullshit issue just to get him off of me. Shit, Moonie wasn't no fool. He had known good and damn well that I was out there trying to run the streets and have my fun just like any other teenager. But he had never snitched on me, not even when my hot-booty drama ended up getting him in trouble with G.

Yeah, Moonie was a rider for real. He was the one who had told me that G had set me and Gino up for the kill. It was Moonie who had washed my naked body after my baby brother shot G and blasted his own brains out all over me. Hell yeah, *Moonie* was the one who had stepped up for me when Ace and Pluto and the rest of them niggahs wanted to shoot me down like a dog after G got slumped. I owed this man so fuckin' much. True, he was a gutta henchman and he was a certified killer, but he had also been my guardian angel.

I walked over and put my arms around him, squeezing my eyes closed tight as I tried not to cry. I hugged him real hard, the way I would have hugged my father or my brother Jimmy, if I could have.

"I wanna thank you for everything you ever did for me, Moonie. Everything. Cooter gave me the money you left for me that night," I said softly, and he knew exactly what I was talking about. "I was young and dumb, and I didn't really understand the way you was looking out for me at the time, but I do now."

"You was just young that's all, Juicy," Moonie said as he held me in his gangsta arms. "Not dumb, just young. I got two daughters myself, baby girl. I wasn't gonna let G toss you off in a Dumpster the way he did all them other chicks. You ain't deserve that type of shit, baby. You ain't deserve it."

I turned back to Frank.

"I'm sorry I left California without saying anything to you and Renata. Believe it or not, I was only supposed to be gone for one night."

I thought about how I had gotten knocked at the airport and thrown in that grimy cell on Rikers Island and shuddered. "So much crazy shit happened to me that I couldn't even catch my breath," I admitted. "I was trying to help one of my friends and I ended up dead broke and I couldn't get back home."

"We were worried about you, Juicy," Frank chastised me a little bit. "You should have called me. Or at least called Renata."

"Like I said, everything got all fucked up," I told him. "I had thought I was rolling with a pretty decent plan, but then I got arrested and your slick-ass nephew Sallie fucked me over!" I said heatedly.

"Salvatore?" Frank spit the name off his tongue as his face went dark. "That low-life little bastard!"

I smirked. "Low life ain't the word. For some reason Gino trusted Sallie to hold on to our safe full of money. It was all the money we had, and we brought it with us all the way from New York."

I turned to Moonie. "Me and Gino took G's money, Moonie. We found it stacked in my grandmother's grave."

Frank and Trey both looked at me like, "What the fuck?" But Moonie was chill because he already knew and wasn't surprised to hear nothing I was saying.

"Yeah, Gino really trusted your nephew, Frank. And I trusted his grimy ass too. Matter fact, Sallie was the only one who knew I was leaving Los Angeles that night. He even offered to give me a ride to the airport but I told him I would drive my own car and park it in a lot." I shrugged. "I guess since I never made it back my little green ride probably got towed a long time ago."

"Nah," Frank said. "It got blown up." He waved his hand dismissively and puffed on his cigar. "Salvatore had my cousin Earl rig your car with an ignition bomb, Juicy. If you had come back and tried to drive it off that lot you would have ended up looking like a bloody can of Chunky Soup."

"What!" I said, totally rocked off my spot. "You mean Sallie was gonna try to kill me?"

"He wasn't just going to *try*, Juicy," Frank said coldly. "He was going to get it *done*. My nephew is a snake. He ran away from California not long after you left. And that's why I'm here," Frank added.

I shook my head. "I don't get it."

"Mick's dead," Frank said, and again my brain got rocked.

"*Mick*? What the hell happened to him?"

Frank shrugged, but I busted the look of pain and rage that crossed his face.

"The short version of the long story is that his cousin Salvatore killed him."

I blinked real quick a few times and shook my head again.

"So you came here to get Sallie for killing Mick?"

"No," Frank said coldly, shaking his head. "I came here to get *Moonie*."

A look of pure ice frosted up his blue eyes.

"Moonie is gonna get Sal."

CHAPTER 7

She was scheduled to be at work in less than an hour, but Money-Makin'-Monique was stretched out on her living room sofa smoking a blunt and playing in her pussy hairs as she watched the local news. All kinds of crazy shit happened in New York City on a daily, and most of the stupid shit people did in the ghetto cracked her the hell up.

She was breathing hard and pinching the nipple on her third little titty when the camera panned to a white woman sitting at the news desk.

"This just in. According a recent report, crystal methamphetamine is wreaking havoc on communities all over the United States and more than 12 million people have already tried it at least once. What began as a problem that was largely confined to rural communities has crept into major urban centers like ours right here in New York City, and local police tell us that dangerous meth labs are being discovered everywhere.

Known by trendy names like, "crank", "speed", "chalk", or "ice", crystal meth has grown in popularity because it's relatively easy to produce and it's far less costly than other street drugs like cocaine or heroin. The drug can be taken orally as a liquid, snorted, smoked, and even injected. While meth is very popular in so-called rave club scenes, many young people in our inner cities have begun using it as an alternative to crack cocaine. But today, here in Harlem, it was a potent mixture in a small vial such as this—"

Monique's eye's bucked open wide as the camera cut to a blown-up image of a small vial filled with pink crystals. It was stamped with the words "Strawberry Snake" and it had a hot-pink logo of a snake shooting dice with his tail on the side.

"It was something almost identical to this 16-ounce packet of fruit-flavored "candy" that recently caused the death of a very small child in Harlem. According to the National Institute on Drug Abuse, this explosion of crystal meth is infiltrating our cities at a rate unrivaled by any drug in recent times."

"That crazy *bitch!*" Monique shrieked as she tossed her blunt in an ashtray and jumped up from the couch. That damn Salida was putting out some *bad* shit! Wasn't no telling what kinda chemicals she was fuckin' with upstairs in that cut-room! All that drain-cleaner and battery acid and ammonia and shit. Who the fuck knew what the right combination of all that stuff was supposed to be? Salida's bent ass sure as hell didn't!

"See, this right here is why they shoulda never let that bitch get outta pocket," Monique fumed as she opened her closet and yanked out a bright orange skirt Prada and a matching low-cut blouse. As soon as the cops found out where that Strawberry Snake was slithering at they was gonna come down on the G-Spot like giant flies on ten piles of horse shit. Good thing it was a black baby that had died and not one of them rich white college kids who couldn't keep their fascinated asses up outta the Spot buying dope! The whole damn joint woulda been raided by now.

G had worked hard to keep his drug operation above the board. Everybody knew he had the best product in town because he was real careful with that shit. He had copped from some of the best suppliers in the country, and he didn't put none of that crazy cut on his goods tryna stretch it out and squeeze a buck.

Hell yeah, there had been a certain high quality that was attributed to Granite McKay's dope. Even the lowest junkie on the streets knew that if the shit came outta the G-Spot then it had to be good.

But not no more.

Salida was about to bring the G-Spot all the way down this time. Monique could feel it. And since them stupid niggahs Ace and Pluto had refused listen to what she tried to tell them, Monique hoped both of their funky asses went down with it! That's exactly what they should get for taking up for that wrinkled old bitch instead of her!

"Hell yeah!" Mo muttered under her breath as she styled her extra-long weave in the bathroom mirror and ran her tongue over her pearly white teeth. "I hope the cops knock the shit outta Salida for selling that nasty-ass meth and throw her ass straight out on the Rock! Yeah, fuck the G-Spot! Let that bitch fall! Let that bitch fall *hard*! And let all 'a them mothafuckas who thought they was better than me go down with it!"

$$$$$

I've heard people talking about six degrees of separation, but the crazy shit that we had going on in Moonie's living room was taking the cake. I'd always known Moonie was sharp as hell. G had been the brutal, big-name force behind the G-Spot, but Moonie had definitely been one of the craftiest brains up in that joint.

Cats who didn't know about him used to underestimate him all the time because Moonie looked soft and low key. He'd be standing behind the bar drying glasses looking harmless as hell. But if you watched close enough you could tell that Moonie's little rat eyes was seeing everything that moved. All that bar-wiping stuff he did was just a front because in reality he was running security, the cashier's cage, the staff in the cut-room, the strippers, and the hoes in the fuck rooms too.

The four of us sat in his living room and talked for a real long time. Scheming, collaborating, connecting dots, and calculating our revenge. As I listened to Moonie and tried to follow the logic of his thinking, I could see exactly how he had been able to work all the money-making magic he did for G and still have him a woman and kids on the side too. The brother was lethal as shit and he had a brilliant mind.

One of the major things that came up in our convo was the fact that Slick Sallie had hooked up with Moonie looking to buy some brand new guns. A whole fuckin' lot of guns.

"Yo, me and him did a little bidnezz a long time ago," Moonie explained. "I tore him off some damn-good pieces at a damn-good price, and now he's looking to make the same kinda deal again. 'Cept this time dude wants to buy up an entire *arsenal*. Twenty handguns, twenty-five semi-automatics, ten shotguns, about a dozen fully automatic AR-15s, and enough ammunition to keep all that shit spittin' fire for hours."

"Yo," Trey said. "What the hell is that fool tryna hit? A vault?"

"Nah," Moonie said. "He's gonna flip 'em. He said he's got a buyer lined up for a sweet transaction in Harlem. And knowing Sallie, he'll prolly sell them gats for three times the amount he pays for 'em."

Frank was steady frowning. "I don't know. Twenty-five assault rifles? That sounds like some entry work to me. You know, the kind of guns you need for busting through some armored doors. The kind that lets you throw down a whole bunch of bullets in a hurry."

Frank nodded. "Yeah, whoever he's selling to must be going out on a pretty big job if they need that type of capability. If I had to bet I'd say it had something to do with Don Rosarita and his Family. But of course they wouldn't be moving around in Harlem. It's out of their territory. Besides, if Sallie's involved in the deal then that means the Family definitely isn't involved."

Something got triggered in me and I remembered something I had overheard when I first got out of jail.

"I think I know who Sallie might be planning to sell those guns to."

They all swung their heads around and looked at me like they had forgot my lil tail was in the room or something.

"Who dat?" Moonie asked.

I glanced at Trey real quick and said, "Fletcher Boykin. From 136th Street. You know. He goes by Flex."

Moonie chuckled. "Yeah, that scrawny bucktooth niggah used to scramble for G in Taft project a few years ago. Is that lil come-up swellin' up that big?"

I nodded. "Uh-huh. I used to stay with him for a quick minute down in the basement of the Three Brothers Funeral Home. I heard him talking on the phone one night when he thought I was sleeping. He said something about buying up a bunch of tools. He called them 'dead bitches' and he kept saying over and over that they had to be clean."

Trey sat up straighter in his chair. "Ay, if that fool is lookin' for G's connect and he's tryna bust down some doors at the same time, then you know what he's scheming on."

"What's that?" Frank asked.

"The G-Spot. He's gonna take that joint down."

"Yo, are you serious? Lil Fletcher done got that big?" Moonie asked, skeptically.

Trey shrugged. "He's been wildin', man. Wildin' hard. He's tryna be the next G McKay. But even bigger. He's been steppin' on Ace and Pluto's toes and they ain't happy with his ass neither."

"Steppin' how?"

Trey shook his head. "Ace and Pluto done got soft, man. They couldn't handle the overhead in the Spot no more and some of G's properties went up on the auction block. Flex laid down the cash and scooped them shits up at a discount, and then he cut Ace and Pluto completely outta the profits."

Trey frowned. "Them two fat cats ain't no match for his crafty young ass. Flex is already slanging more dope in his sector than any other distributor in Harlem. But that lil bastard still ain't satisfied. Whatever Granite McKay had, that niggah wants it and I mean he wants *all* of it. Including the G-Spot."

Moonie smirked. "If them sherm niggahs ain't strong enough to hold the Spot down, then he might just get it then."

"But the problem is," Trey said, "Flex is still brand new, man. That cat still got warm milk on his breath. He don't know it but he could never be G. He ain't got the rep G had, or the mental muscle to put behind that shit neither. Yeah, that fool is crazy and he'll pop a niggah in a hurry, but it takes more than a loaded gat to rule an empire like Harlem."

Trey leaned forward with his elbows on his knees.

"And that's why *I'm* here. The only reason Flex asked me to get at you is because I told him to toss off my boy Maleek and kick him outta his set."

Moonie frowned. "He got lil Maleek? Mayhem's baby brother?"

"Yeah," Trey nodded and I saw his jaw clench and something catch fire in his eyes.

"He put Leek on with his Divine Nine, man. Even though he knew that kid wasn't right in his head, he still put him on. Flex made Leek one of his capos. He took him off the corner grind and gave him his own squad. That boy was heading straight upstate. I could see it coming. He wasn't but one drug bust away from the state pen."

"So I called a meeting with Flex and told him to put Leek's ass up on a shelf. Flex agreed to call Leek in, but only if I hooked him up with you."

"Did he send Leek to the corner?" Moonie wanted to know. "Or is the kid still out there grindin'?"

I saw Trey's shoulders stiffen.

"He iced him, man. Flex made him play the double-R game and Maleek caught a bad spin. He's dead, man. He blew his brains out."

Moonie shrugged and nodded. Life was short in Harlem.

"So I guess your deal is off now, huh?" Moonie said.

"Yeah. But Flex tried to get rid of Leek's body, man. He double-stacked him in a coffin with a Harlem preacher so he could hide that shit. He still don't know that somebody hipped me to that shit."

We sat in silence for a few minutes and I could almost hear their minds clicking and calculating.

"So, lemme lay all this shit out real quick," Moonie finally said. "We got Ace and Pluto holding a lil girl in the Dungeon tryna use Juicy to get some bargaining chips. Slick Sallie is rollin' around New York with a shit-load of Juicy's money and tryna make a sweet deal with me so he can turn around and sell some gats to Flex, right? And Flex is tryna use Trey and Sallie to pull off a two-way heist: that lil come-up wanna take over the G-Spot and buy up the best raw cocaine in the city of New York."

Everybody nodded.

Moonie shrugged.

"Ay, then we ain't got no fuckin' problems then! All we need to do is give ere'body what they want and make all them niggahs happy." He grinned. "At least until we fuck 'em up."

"You said Salvatore wants every piece you give him to be squeaky clean, right?" Frank asked.

Moonie nodded.

"Damn. You got that much shit on hand that's clean?"

Moonie shook his head and grinned again.

"Nah. *Hell* fuckin' nah. But I got plenty of shit that's dirty."

CHAPTER 8

Dutchy Gaines stood by his woman's hospital bed and stared down at her sleeping face. Her bruises were fading and scabs had already formed over most of her cuts and scrapes, but her body had been so brutalized that the doctors had warned him it was gonna be months before she was back on her feet.

Waiting patiently was cool with Dutchy. He could handle Rita's healing period just as long as his baby could come off all that life support shit. His eyes followed the thick tubing that ran outta her mouth and disappeared into a large plastic bag that hung from the side of her bed. There were more tubes coming outta other places on Rita's body too, and every time he looked at her he thought about how sweet it was gonna be when he murked them slum fuckas who had done her this way.

And he wasn't just thinking about that shit neither. He was planning it. Dutchy had made his baby a promise on the day they wheeled her in here. He had vowed that he was gonna find the gritty bastards who were responsible for pulling that kick door and straight *slump* their asses for shooting his woman and killing them lil kids.

And he had a real good idea of where to start looking too.

Dutchy had mad family in New York City's law enforcement, and once he found out exactly who had put that bounty out on Rita's head it was just a matter of time before he smoked that ass. Because of his job position he was gonna hafta be real sly and strategic about his shit, but it was gonna get done regardless. And it was gonna get done soon.

It was with a heart filled with grief and a mind swirling with a murderous rage that Dutchy had received an unexpected phone call.

It was from one of his former probation felons. One of them *La Cosa Nostra* niggahs. A career-criminal whose entire family had come through the justice system and who, despite his vast unlawful business network, had earned Dutchy's trust and his respect.

Dutchy had listened closely as the grimy names of the men who had ordered the hit on Rita were spit into his ear. His old probationer had come up with a real sweet plan to catch a whole lotta fish in one big net, and he needed Dutchy's cooperation. In exchange, he would make sure Dutchy got his shit off on the right niggahs, at the right time, and in the right place.

Dutchy's heart had ached for immediate retribution as he fought the intense need to rush off wildly and plant a hot round of slugs in them niggah's domes right then and there.

But when his former client gave him the run down of the big-picture plan, who all was involved, and the grand scheme of what was about to come, Dutchy was more than happy to exercise a little patience so he could jump onboard and use this lil collaboration to get him some get-back.

To get him some *revenge*.

$$$$$

The meeting Slick Sallie had arranged with Flex was scheduled to take place in a record shop in Harlem later on that night. Sallie was amped about getting his hands on all that crisp green cash, and since he was feeling pretty good and had a couple of hours left to kill before he was scheduled to show up, he had dipped over to the G-Spot to check out his baby girl, Monique.

"So no more stacking room chips for you, right?" Sallie asked, sipping vodka as he gave Monique a stern look like he was her daddy for real.

She laughed. "Damn right," she agreed fast as shit. "This is it right here, baby. No more chips." Monique flashed him a sexy grin and reached over to hug his neck one more time. "No more *mothafuckin'* chips!"

She kissed Sallie passionately, licking his mouth out in a way that she had never kissed any trick before. Her tongue felt like a thousand snakes as it slithered around in his mouth stirring up heat. Monique could have kissed this white boy for *months*, that's how grateful she was to him. Because of Sallie she had flatbacked for the *last* time in the mothafuckin' G-Spot! Never again in life would she have to strip outta her thong and play in her own slippery pussy just to turn a funky ass dollar!

Because Sallie was retiring her ass. He was gonna get her the fuck outta Harlem and set her up in her own damn club, and Monique couldn't wait to get gone. Blowing exhaust dust on Harlem was gonna be the best move she had ever made in her life, and thanks to Sallie that day was almost here.

Sallie broke away from their embrace first, breathing hard. He gazed down at the package of warm chocolate pudding cuddled in his arms and his heart skipped a beat. The sexy powder-blue thingie she had on was silky and see-through, and he had never met a woman who stunned his eyeballs the way this gorgeous black girl did.

"Just a little bit longer until we get our asses outta here, right?" she asked, pooching up her lips.

He nodded. "Just a little bit. I promise." Sallie grinned. "And then we can say 'fuck you' New York! Florida here we come!"

Monique squealed. She could see herself down there right now. Slaying those Flo-Flo bitches! Them Miami haters was gonna be straight jealous of her strut! She didn't care how hot their bodies was, or how much fun them beach-bitches was used to having in the sun. They didn't have *shit* on her. Money-Makin'-Monique was gonna take her New York spice down to the hot shores of the Magic City and show them what was *really*, real!

"Look, I gotta get to this meeting," Sallie said, kissing her deeply one last time as he headed out the door. "But the next time I see you I want your bags packed and ready to go, you got that?"

Grinning broadly, Monique nodded.

"Okay, daddy," she said, baby-talking him. "I'll walk you to the door, okay?"

"Ah-ah-ah—" Sal corrected her, shaking one finger. "Not *daddy*. Whatever you do, don't call me daddy. That's whore talk. Call me Papa, *capisce*?"

Monique giggled her ass off. "Cap-eesh, Big Poppa!"

They kissed again.

"I'ma walk you out," Monique said.

The pair stepped out of fuck room number 3 linked at the arms. They walked past half-naked strippers leading their customers to their designated fuck huts, and party-goers heading to the triple-X room or to the other side of the G-Spot to hit the gambling rooms.

Sallie and Monique were strolling past the main bar when a beautifully-shaped older woman with a tight waist and killer hips came into view. She was sashaying toward them and Sal's eyebrows furrowed as his brain worked to figure out why she looked so familiar.

As the woman approached she swung her hips left and right in her tight dress, catching countless appreciative eyes, to include Slick Sallie's. For a white boy he was an ass-watcher extraordinaire. Never had a Black woman walked past him without his eyes zooming in on her fanny and taking a mental snapshot. He couldn't see this woman's ass yet, but he could tell by the curved shape of her fleshy hips that she had a fat hammer banging in the back. And as his eyes traveled up from her waist and over her plump titties to her mature, but still gorgeous and sexy face, Sal was finally able to place where he had seen this woman before.

"Hey, what's up?" he nodded at her as Monique hung on his arm. "What a surprise running into you way out here on the East Coast."

The woman stopped in her tracks and gave him a fake smile.

"Hello," she said dryly, playing her role. "Nice to meet you and welcome to the G-Spot. I'm Salida. Your hostess. Is this your first time joining us?"

"Nah," Sal said, shaking his head. "I been here before. And I met you before too. Remember? Out on the West Coast, right?"

Salida's cold smile froze on her face.

"Who the hell are you talking to?" she hissed, dropping her pose as she blasted on Sallie in a low, stank voice. "Keep it movin' white boy! You got me confused with somebody else."

"No I don't," Sal insisted. He was feeling his liquor and he was more than a little bit tipsy off of Monique's loving, but his memory was tight as shit. "It was you. There's no way in hell I could ever forget a woman who looks like you."

Salida stepped up on Slick Sallie and let her gangsta hang straight out.

"Look'a here you honkie *mothafucka*!" she beasted at him with her twisted lips just two inches away from his face. "You can bring your retard-looking ass up in here and smoke you a little ice, hit you some caine, and stick your dick in all the stank black trim you can pay for! But don't you *bring* you your pale ass up in here questioning me! You got that, mothafucka? YOU GOT THAT???"

"Hey!" Monique screeched, jumping in front of her man. "Who is *you* to be fuckin' yelling at *him*?"

Ace stepped up and barked on Monique. "Silly *bitch*! Get ya ass back there in that fuck room and earn ya fuckin' paycheck!"

"Wait now, hold on," Sallie said calmly. He was slightly liquored up but he wasn't no fool. He raised his hands in the air a little bit to show that everything was cool and he didn't want no trouble. But by now Greco had gotten a sniff of the static and four of his biggest bouncers were rolling up to provide Salida with some serious security.

"I ain't trying to start nothing, Miss," Sallie told Salida in a real respectful tone. "All I'm saying is that I *saw* you," he insisted again. "I spoke to you, remember? You walked right past me. I looked in your pretty face and checked out your phat ass..."

Sallie ate the next word out of his mouth. Ace drilled him with a hard right to the grill and a solid round-house blow to the temple.

Sal went down hard and Monique started jumping up and down hysterically.

"You dirty bitch!" she screamed on Salida as Greco's security crew charged and started banging Sallie up on the floor.

"Fuck him up!" Salida yelled as the bouncers swung their booted feet at the white boy's head and guts, kicking snot and slobber outta him in a vicious frenzy. "Yeah! Kill his ass!" Salida urged them wildly. "Stomp his fuckin' brains out!"

Sallie rolled around in a helpless ball as the brothahs put a Harlem hurting on his ass that he would never forget. Monique was helpless too. She couldn't do nothing but screech and cry as she darted from one haymaker-swinging bouncer to the next, climbing on their muscular backs, grabbing at their iron-hard arms, and trying her best to pull them off her man.

She was sweaty and weak with relief when Greco finally called his boyz off the ass-beating and Sallie managed to roll over and scoot up on his knees. She rushed over as he pulled himself to his feet, but he shook her off and ran his bloody ass straight toward the door.

"Sallie!" Monique cried and chased behind him in her powder blue stiletto pumps. "Wait for me, Sallie! *Wait*!"

The security crew busted out laughing as the white boy jetted out the door holding his bloody nose.

Salida called out some deadly words of caution at Sallie's back as she nodded at young Bilal to follow his ass.

"You better not *bring* your narrow ass back up in here!" she warned him as she ran over and stuck her head out the door. All traces of the charming, graceful hostess of the G-Spot disappeared as she showed her true gutter colors. "If I ever so much as lay my *eyes* on you again you's a dead man!" she threatened Slick Sallie from the pit of her soul before heading back inside. "A fuckin' *dead* man!"

Monique ran down the dark street after Sallie screaming out his name the whole time, but he was already halfway down the block and hauling ass toward the corner.

"You coming back?" she yelled desperately at his retreating back. "You coming back to get me, right? Right? *Right*?"

Sallie never even heard her and Monique was utterly devastated as she stood there sweating and trembling as her meal-ticket disappeared into the crowd on the busy Harlem street.

"He ain't hear you," she muttered to herself. "He's coming back. He just ain't hear you."

She'd uttered the words to comfort herself, but there was no denying the heavy ball of doubt that pressed down on her chest as she whirled around and flung open the door to the G-Spot and stormed back inside. With her monster booty-cheeks bouncing and swaying, Monique rolled up on Salida with nothing but pure fury in her eyes.

"You crazy *bitch*!" Monique screamed as the G-Spot's hostess stood near the bar looking cool and calm again as she waited for Bizzie to serve her a drink. Snatching a full shot glass outta the hand of a fat old man, Monique slished the straight Bacardi Dark dead in Salida's face.

Salida gasped and sputtered as the hundred-proof alcohol stung her nose and burned the shit outta her eyes, but then she shrieked even louder when, quick as shit, Monique smashed her in the forehead with the glass, then drilled her with a round-house right to her temple, and caught her with a sneaky left hook straight to the chin.

"Help!" Salida staggered and screamed as she tried to dodge the blows and rub the burning liquor outta her eyes.

Sensing a wall of rushing movement coming up behind her, Monique went in for the quick kill. She drove her fists flush into the older woman's nose and then busted both of Salida's lips with two short jabs.

And then them niggahs swarmed on her.

Greco's crew grabbed her arms and legs and started yanking and jerking her around in all directions, like they was breaking chicken wings off a yardbird.

Stretched out like a human starfish, Monique screamed in pain and started arching her back. She kicked out with her feet until them niggahs finally let her go.

Ace quickly snatched her by the neck and yoked her up in a headlock. He pressed his muscular forearm into her throat and squeezed until her vision went hazy and her cries were strangled off.

"Yo what the fuck you doin'!" Pluto rushed over in a rage. He'd been taking a shit in the men's room and the first thing he saw when he came out was his ex-slime roughing up his bitch.

"Fool!" Pluto roared as he planted one big hand against Ace's shoulder. He clamped down on his manz fist and jerked that shit way back, and then twisted the shit outta his wrist until it popped, forcing Ace to yelp in pain and turn Monique loose.

"This *my* fuckin' property right here, homey! What the fuck is you doin' slime!"

"What *I'm* doing? Niggah you need to handle yo bitch!" Ace barked, clenching his twisted wrist and hoping like hell that shit wasn't broke.

Salida ran over half-blind and swung a weak lil punch at Pluto. He stiff-armed her mug and gave her a little push that sat her down hard on her ass.

"Nah, niggah!" he turned to Ace. "Yo ass need to handle *your* bitch!"

With Pluto on the scene taking up for her, Monique got bold and let her rage fly again. Clutching her bruised throat, she went in for one more go 'round on the throwed-off bitch who was tryna ruin her life. While Salida was still sitting on the ground Monique darted over and snatched her by her hair and drove her knee dead into the older woman's grill.

"Get this bitch offa me!" Salida screamed as she turned over onto her stomach and tried to crawl away. She was a schemer, not a fighter and she wasn't trying to get into no close-combat tussling match with Monique's stupid young ass!

Pluto stepped up in the mix and grabbed his bitch. He gripped Monique by her shoulders and shook the shit outta her until she calmed her ass down.

"Y'all broads done went crazy or something?" he demanded. "What the fuck is going on around here?"

"Ain't nobody crazy!" Salida yelled. "Your bitch got mad and started passing licks because I had to go off on her pussy-whipped white boyfriend!" she said, blowing Mo's shit up. "She got stupid and broke a goddamn glass on my head just because I put his disrespectful ass up outta here!"

Monique did a real quick assessment of the situation. It was so quick, that when she opened her mouth to lie she never missed a single beat.

"Uh-uh! She ran my best fuckin' customer off for no reason! That dude been buying out the bar and tricking up drinks and chips left and right, and this crazy bitch just ran him off!"

Pluto shot a look at his dude Ace, then he glared at both women and smirked like he knew the deal. Fuck Salida and fuck Monique too. He didn't give a shit if these two psycho jawns beat each other into the dirt. Because Pluto was Chicago-bound. He had a sweet little hustle and a dumb little snow bunny named Coco out there in the Windy City just'a waiting on him. He had met the big-titty white chick on Facebook and started giving her some Internet bone, and in a hot minute it wasn't gonna matter if these here bitches slit each other's throats or if the G-Spot crumbled all the way to the ground. He was gone!

"Both of y'all need to chill with the mouth and cut that shit out," he said, playing his role and not tipping his hand. "All that noise is bad for bizzness."

Eyeballing Ace again, Pluto turned around and barked over his shoulder at all the nosy strippers and hoes who had run half-naked off the stage and outta the back rooms so they could watch the catfight go down.

"The rest a' y'all tramps get back on ya fuckin' grind! If y'all ain't heard then ya better check ya wallets! Time is money, bitches! Time is *money*!"

CHAPTER 9

"We gots to do something about that mothafucka," Salida said coldly as Ace stood behind her and massaged the knots outta her shoulders. Monique had put a crook in his baby's neck with that round-house blow, and they'd retreated into the comfort of G's office so Salida could recover.

"Who?" Ace asked her. "That white boy? Or that trash niggah Pluto?"

"Both of them mothafuckas," Salida snapped as she put her head back and let Ace work the tension outta her neck.

"Cool. You got something planned?"

She sat up and shrugged his hands off, then peered up at him and smirked.

"Damn right I got a plan. I *always* got me a plan. *Don't I?*"

She damn sure did, Ace had to admit as Salida settled back in the chair and gave him permission to touch her once again. And as he rubbed her shoulders and listened to her latest grimy plot unfold, Ace's chest got filled up with mad respect and admiration for Salida. He had to be bangin' the mostly brilliantly diabolical chick in all of New York City, and tears almost rushed to his eyes as his head and heart got swollen with pride.

Hell yeah his baby was fuckin' *gifted*! The kind of gritty shit Salida was talkin' 'bout would not only throw the scent off their trail from all that contaminated Strawberry Snake that had mess heads passing out and foaming at the mouth, it would also make sure that his ex-ak Pluto got his ass planted like a tree too.

"But what we gonna do about that lil fool across town? Flex."

Salida smirked and waved her hand. "That wanna be Granite poser?" She snorted. "His young ass ain't nobody to worry about. I got a feeling he's gonna get caught in somebody's crossfire anyway. Fake-ass gangster! Hell, I can be a better G than that greedy little bastard ever could."

Ace nodded and grinned like a muh'fucka as Salida continued to lay it all out for him. It was as tricky a scheme as he had ever heard in his life, and he couldn't wait to get up on it. That lil white boy Monique was fuckin' didn't mean shit in Ace's book, but he was geeked as fuck about doin' his manz Pluto. That bitch-niggah was a part of his grimy past life under Granite McKay's rule, but with Salida steering the ship there was a new boss in Harlem now, and it was time to put those old loyalties to bed and get up on some revenge.

$$$$$

Pluto was sweating like a greasy black pig as he climbed the stairs up to the cut room. He had just stomped a big mud hole in Monique's ungrateful black ass, and even though he had probably broken that bitch's nose, he gave less than a damn because she deserved that shit. That bitch was feeling herself for real. Instead of

514

taking her ass back to work after scrappin' with Salida like he'd told her to, Mo had called herself throwing the rest of her chips in and taking the night off.

At first Pluto had just grilled her ass with an intense fire glowing in his beady little eyes. That white dick she was getting musta been goin' to Mo's head because lately her whole attitude had changed and she had gotten a real swole noggin'. Whereas she used to keep her ass in a cluck-cluck's place most of the time and play her fuckin' role, for the last few days she had been gettin' real slick wit' the mouth and she always had some off-the-wall smart shit to say like she didn't love her life no more.

"Uh-Uh. I ain't fuckin' with no more tricks!" she had twisted her lips and told him as she stood in front of him in the stripper's dressing room and wiggled out of her powder blue camisole. Her hands were perched on her lusciously stacked hips and her big juicy titties were just 'a bouncing all around. "Nah, I'm taking my ass *home*, Pluto! Y'all just stood up there and let that bitch Salida run my best customer out the door. That white dude *paid* for them chips and since he ain't here to use 'em I'm going home!"

Pluto's backhand dropped her to her knees so quick that he shocked his own damn self.

"Bitch!" he bellowed as she balled herself up in a knot and cringed on the floor. "Who the fuck is you tellin' what you gonna do? You betta unnerstand sumpthin' real quick, hoe! You do what the fuck I *tell* you to do!"

"I ain't doin' *shit*!" Monique jumped to her feet and lunged at Pluto, swinging her arms wildly in the air. "Niggah this the last fuckin' ass-kickin' I'ma take from you, okay?" she screamed as she threw random haymakers at Pluto's head and chest. "You ain't *never* gonna beat my ass no more! *Never*!"

Pluto's hand shot out and caught her neck in a crushing vice grip. He squeezed so hard her voice box hummed, then he pimp-slapped her to the left with all his might, then backhanded her to the right with a pile-driving upward sweep that took her knees right out from under her.

"Trifling skank!" he growled. He loosened his grip and Monique plopped to the floor with her arms and legs splayed out like she was just a bucket of skeleton bones. The force of his killer blow had rocked her head halfway off her neck and her face was boiling with white-hot pain. It felt like her nose had gotten swept way down into her ear canal, and like all the flesh had been ripped from her cheek.

"I'm sorry, Daddy!" Monique had shrieked hoarsely with her eyes bucked out in terror as Pluto roared like a beast and started kickin' shit around and tossin' the whole damn dressing room up. "Please! Please! *Please*!" she begged as he smashed mirrors and flung racks stacked with thongs and garter belts across the room, sending all the strippers breaking out for the door tryna get outta ass-kicking range. Monique could tell by the way his right eye was twitchin' that Pluto was about to fuck her up real bad again, but the last thing she wanted was to get another taste of the big black fist at the end of that niggah's hand!

"Mo-Mo *sorry*!" she shrieked, turning over on her stomach and folding her body up real tight. "I'm sorry! I'm sorry! *I'm sorry*!"

"You fuckin'-a-right you sorry!" Pluto spit as he swung his fat leg back and tried to kick her tailbone way up into her throat. He was fed up with Monique's guttersnipe ass and he couldn't have stopped himself from knucklebustin' her if he *wanted* to.

Pluto beat the shit outta her until his fists and his feet were tired and he couldn't hardly catch his breath no more. And still, he didn't get offa her until one of the other hoes ran and got Greco and his crew and they came and *pulled* him off.

But that shit was all good, Pluto thought now that he had calmed down and stopped hearing bells and seeing red. Mo's scandalous ass mighta thought she was slick and tricky, but he was way up on her grimy game. He knew all about that Italian dude she'd been fuckin' and suckin' in the back rooms! That punk wasn't just no ordinary customer, neither. Nah, that fool had gotten bent on Monique's scuffed up pussy, and he was tryna push up on Pluto's game and violate his property!

Not that he really gave a fuck, Pluto reminded himself as he pushed all thoughts of Monique from his mind and opened the cut room door.

He eyeballed the young hood pharmacist Freeze, who sat at a table full of chemicals that had been mixed in large glass vats. Pluto was surprised to see the young'un slumped forward with his head hanging down tryna stop a tear from rollin' outta his eye.

"Yo! What it do, what it do, what the fuck do it *do*?" Pluto spit, forgetting all about his mash up with Monique.

Freeze glanced up and then tried to duck his head and dry his eyes on his sleeve, but by then it was way too late. Pluto had peeped the boy's inner weakness, and like a snake stalking a mouse he was eager to exploit that shit.

It took him less than five minutes of fatherly talking to convince Freeze to trust him and tell him what had him so damned pressed out that he had to cry about it.

"Ay, you remember my nephew Truth, right?" Pluto asked him, tryna draw him out.

A look of grief crossed Pluto's face.

"Yo, my lil dude caught a bad one out here fuckin' with these niggahs, man. It hurt me to my heart when he got popped and I stopped fuckin' with a whole lotta these slimes after that. On the real, my dude, if there's anything I can ever do to help you, just holla, a'ight? You 'bout the same age my lil nephew was, yo. But Truth was hardheaded, man. Trust me. I couldn't look out for my lil fam, but Big P can look out for you. You just gotta trust me."

It took a few more minutes of bullshitting and tongue-twisting for Freeze to open up and run shit down to him fully, but when he did Pluto was shocked by what he heard and saw.

"Damn!" he said as Freeze held his cell phone out and showed him a picture that had been messaged to him of a badly charred body. "Yo, who da fuck is *dat*?"

"It's my little brother, yo," Freeze said with his voice cracking with grief. "Naj."

Pluto eyed the corpse with a look of deep disgust on his face. It was sprawled on top of a pile of trash inside of a Dumpster, and a pair of red Puma sneakers had practically melted on its feet.

"Man, that niggah ain't got no face or nothing! Ain't nothing left on him but some sneaks and some teeth. How you know that's Naj?"

Freeze tapped the picture and spread its borders with his fingers, enlarging it.

"Because ain't nobody seen him in two fuckin' days, and then they sent me this one too," he said, swiping the screen to go to the next photo. This one was taken from a distance, probably from a second or third floor project window. Two big words had been spray-painted in black on the front of the Dumpster, and Pluto squinted as he read them out loud. "Gramma's Next."

"Oh, I see what's up," Pluto said and let out a long, slow whistle. "Somebody's gunnin' for you, word? Gunnin' for you and ya fam." He frowned and tapped his finger twice on the phone. "They done did this here terrible shit to your brother and now they going after ya grandma next, is that right?"

Freeze nodded and Pluto shook his head.

"Muh'fuckas ain't got no respect these days," he said like he was straight-up disgusted with his criminal homies out on the streets. "Yo, you can't be fuckin' with nobody grandmama and expect a niggah not to raise up on you!"

Pluto shook his head again. "So tell me this," he said moving closer and putting his meaty arm around Freeze's shoulder like the dun dun was his son for real. "Whose cocaine you done pissed in? Who's fuckin' wit'chu, my lil slime?"

"It's them Divine Nine niggahs," Freeze reluctantly confessed. "Flex and his crew. Them fools been squeezin' on me, man. Squeezin' on me *hard*. They want Harlem, man. All of it. And they don't give a fuck who they gotta slump to get it neither."

Pluto mulled that shit over for a few quick seconds and suddenly a bright light flashed behind his beady little eyeballs. Why should he care about Flex and his crew taking control of Harlem? Yeah, he owed that lil niggah one over his nephew Truth, but why not let Flex and Salida go at each other's throats and X each other out? Hell, Pluto was about to hit Chicago and get up in that grimy Midwest game! He gave less than a fuck about who stuck a hard dick up Harlem's shitty ass once he was gone.

"I tell you what, son," he said to Freeze like he was about to be real generous with his advice. "You look out for me and I'll look out for you, bet? Flex is my lil rowdy. He used to slang rock for me back in the day. I'll holla at that niggah and tell him to get the fuck up offa ya dick, a'ight? All you gotta do is hit me wit' a lil solid. Cool?"

A wary look crossed Freeze's face. He had a funny feeling that he was about to be squeezed some more.

"C'mon, now. What kinda solid, yo? What I gotta do, man? What the fuck I gotta do?"

Pluto shrugged. "You ain't gotta do nothin' that's too hard for a niggah who loves his grandma! I just need you to show up where I tell you to and take care of somebody that I wanna get off *my* dick. Is you down with that, my niggah. Is you down?"

"A'ight," Freeze said, sitting up straighter in his chair. He'd do any fuckin' thing to get his Gramma's throat outta Flex's teeth. "A'ight, yeah. I'm down."

CHAPTER 10

We left Moonie's crib way after midnight and Trey checked us into a banging room in a sweet hotel. It was one of them real fancy joints with bellhops and a concierge and great big chandeliers, and it put me in the mind of the kind of place that G would have stayed in.

It was a slow night and there wasn't much of a crowd, so the young African dude working at the registration desk upgraded us to a suite and smiled when he told me it came with a full kitchen and one of those rainfall spa showers too.

We were only gonna be staying for one night and I wasn't planning on doing no cooking, but the suite was laid out from one end to the other. It had real marble floors and expensive leather furniture, and the king-sized bed looked nice and fluffy.

"Are you hungry?" Trey asked me as he carried our small bags inside the room and set them down next to the dresser.

I shook my head. Moonie's woman had fried us some dope chicken wings while we was at their crib and I was still full from that.

"You tired?"

"Nope," I said and shook my head again. Resting my bones wasn't hardly on my mind. Besides, there wasn't but one bed up in the room and all I could think about was whether or not both of us were gonna get in it.

"I'm gonna go take a shower," I told Trey and picked up my backpack and headed towards the bathroom. I felt his eyes on me as I walked away and I knew exactly how my ass looked in my jeans.

The bathroom smelled like lemons and everything in it sparkled and glistened. I stripped out of my clothes while I waited for the water to get hot, and then I took my ponytail down and twisted my hair up in a big ball at the top of my head.

I walked over to the long brass mirror on the wall and stared at my naked self. At my titties, my belly, my hips, and my thighs. All of a sudden I was feeling some kinda way and I looked deeply into my own eyes as I tried to figure me out.

I knew damn well what my problem was.

I was craving dick and feeling guilty about it.

The first time I had slept in a hotel with a dude other than G, was when me and Gino had checked into the Taj Mahal in Atlantic City one night. I had been a real stank chicken back in those days, hell-bent on putting out the fire in my hot young pussy and blind to the price that I was gonna have to pay for my scandalous ways.

But being up in here with Trey tonight was way different though. *I* was different. True, my pussy was still as hot as it had always been, but now there was something mature and real intimate about sleeping in a hotel room with a fine dude who turned me the fuck on.

Trey Jackson's game was deeper than the ocean, and there was so much I wanted to know about him. So much I wanted to share too. I wondered how he would take it if

518

I read him one of them nasty stories I liked to write in my Juicy Journal. Better yet, I wondered how he would act if I walked out there and made one up right on the spot, just for him.

Shit, after that mutual masturbation shower that we had taken together I already knew Trey was a piper, and I couldn't get the sight of his hard dick jumping around in his soapy hand out of my mind.

I wanted his ass.

I wanted him so, so bad. His thick chocolate meat had looked like a delicious hunk of tube steak to a starving woman, and I actually felt like a sex freak for feening over that shit the way I was doing.

Backing away from the heat that was lurking in my eyes, I stepped into the shower and stood under the hot spray of water until my skin started tingling. I reached up and peeled the wrapper off a bar of perfumed soap and started rubbing myself down.

My soapy hands felt like they had electricity flowing through them. My nipples started aching and I squeezed my thighs together. It had been a real long time since I'd had a nice hard dick up in me, and I wanted that again. I missed it. I needed it. My body was craving sex. I had been having toe-curling orgasms in my sleep damn near every night. Sometimes I woke up with my pillow jammed between my legs. Just a' humping the shit out of it.

Just knowing Trey with his big black dick was right there on the other side of the wall fucked my head up. I soaped up my pussy and pressed down on my throbbing clit. I knew damn well I wasn't gonna be satisfied with just a little finger rub, and as I massaged my nipples with one hand, I fantasized about Trey and gave my pussy a serious beat-down with the other one.

My face felt flushed and hot when I walked outta that bathroom. I was ashamed of pounding my own pussy so hard that I had to bite my lips as I squirted sweet cream in the palm of my hand and came.

Trey was kicked back in a chair with his feet up on a small round table. He was aiming the remote at the television as he surfed through a bunch of sports channels. I busted the intense look in his dark eyes as I walked past him wearing a pair of jogging shorts and a t-shirt, but he didn't say nothing and neither did I.

I found some bottled water in the fridge and a deck of cards on the counter next to one of them Keurig instant coffee machines. While Trey went in the bathroom to take his shower I fixed myself a cup of hot chocolate and sat on the couch and started playing me some solitaire.

I had just finished my second game when Trey came out the bathroom wearing some white basketball shorts and carrying a big towel. He had a thirty-six pack on that toned chocolate belly of his that made me want to lick it. His locks hung over his shoulders like black velvet licorice, and his rocked up chest was naked and bulging.

"What you playing?" he nodded toward the cards as he came over and sat down next to me.

I grinned a little bit. "Solly."

"Can I play?"

I started laughing. "Boy you know only one person can play this game! That's why it's called solitaire. 'Cause you play it by yourself."

"Yeah, that's right." He grilled me. "What else do you know how to play, Juicy?"

"Ummm..." I was embarrassed to tell him the only other card game I was really up on was pitty pat, because even though Grandmother used to play her some numbers every single day she didn't allow me and Jimmy to do no whole lot of card playing in her house.

"You know how to play poker?"

I shook my head. Hell no. I'd seen plenty of dudes gambling up in the G-Spot but G had never let me get close to them so I really didn't have a clue.

"Well scoot over," Trey said as he scooped up the deck and slid closer so he could get a piece of the table too. "'Cause tonight I'm 'bout to teach you something new."

$$$$$

I found out real quick that Trey was a big-ass cheater.

We started out playing us some poker all right, but damn if it didn't end up being *strip* poker!

It was getting hot as hell in that hotel room. We were sitting cross-legged in the middle of the bed and I was down to nothing but my bra and my thong. Trey had been buck-naked ever since he had started losing in the first hand, and he wasn't the least bit concerned about the fact that his long black dick was pressed up against his belly, nice and hard.

"You gonna show ya hand or you folding, baby?" he asked me with a grin.

All my cards were shitty so I knew I didn't have no wins, but I showed them anyway because I was horny like that!

Trey was holding two pairs when I threw down my old raggedy hand, and since I was the loser I knew exactly what I had to do.

I stood up on the bed and reached between my titties and unsnapped my bra. My twins bounced out freely and I heard Trey growl, "damn!" under his breath.

I took my time taking the bra off, slipping the straps down my shoulders sexily and then letting it flutter like a satin ribbon as I circled my breasts with it and tantalized his eyes.

I wasn't no stripper by no means, but I had seen that shit done enough times to pick up a few nasty moves. I hooked my fingers under the elastic waistband of my thong, and then slowly twerked my ass. Then I popped my spine a few times and made like I was about to pull my thong down and expose my pubic mound.

Trey's dark eyes were all over me. Molesting me. Appreciating me. Promising me that he was gonna *handle* me.

I removed my thumbs from my waistband and let the elastic snap. Then I turned around and stood there for a minute and let his eyeballs feast on my ass. I knew what kinda package I was holding back there, and I knew how much men loved to look at it. I got turned on like fuck as Trey made the, "uh-uh-uh," noise, like he just couldn't believe what his eyes was seeing.

I crouched down a little bit and made my booty bounce the way I had seen the best strippers do in the G-Spot. Then I stood up and vibrated my ass cheeks, letting my jelly quiver like crazy as I held the rest of my body perfectly still.

After that I hooked the elastic on my thong again and turned back around.

This time I really did pull that baby down and expose my pussy, and as it slid past my knees and around my ankles Trey reached out and helped me get it all the way off.

He sat in front of me with one hand around my calf and the other one cupping my hip as he pressed his face into my pubic mound. He didn't even go for the pussy, he just rubbed his face all over my trimmed forest and inhaled deeply like he was tryna suck me inside his soul.

And then his hand slid over the hump of my ass and he pulled me closer. He squeezed my calf and parted my legs. I leaned my hands on his strong, muscular shoulders as I felt him probing deep between my legs, and then I gasped as he opened his mouth and covered my clit with his warm, tender lips.

I fought not to cum right then and there. It had been so long since a man had touched me like this that I had absolutely no control. And when he licked my clit and then stuck his tongue between my hot lower lips and started eating my pussy out slowly and calmly, and better than it had ever been eaten in my life, I couldn't even fight no more as I clenched my ass cheeks and grabbed his head and nutted. It felt so beautiful.

Trey held me up as my knees buckled and sagged, but he didn't slow down not one lick, neither. His tongue was fuckin' amazing as he played with my clit and kept up a pressure and a rhythm that had me feeling faint.

He grabbed my ankle and lifted my leg over his shoulder, and then he palmed my ass in both hands and licked me out until there was nothing I could do except hold on to him as tight as I could and again, bust the most beautiful nut in the world.

I was breathing harder than hell as Trey gently lowered me onto the bed, and ran his hands all over my tingling body. I closed my eyes as he touched me everywhere. My face, my breasts, my stomach, my legs, and my feet.

I needed to catch my breath and calm down a little bit, but as soon as my ass was half-way recovered I jumped all over him. I crawled up on my knees and gently pushed him onto his back. Then I turned around and straddled his hips backwards, with my ass in the air and my wet pussy mashed down on his chest.

My man was a piper. I leaned forward and took his long black pussy-poker in both of my hands and just gripped that shit. It was thick and hard and had a strong vein running down the underside of it. I closed my eyes and nuzzled it against my lips, nose, and chin, just like he had nuzzled my stuff, and then I opened my mouth and let all my fantasies come true.

I deep-throated that shit.

I pounded my head down on it until I felt like I had a golf ball stuck in my throat.

I hummed all over the tip, giving up my neck-pussy like a pro as I tightened my lips around the base of his dick and slurped with my cheeks.

I moved my hips like I was on a horse. Riding his chest as I rubbed my wet pussy all over his warm skin. Trey held me by the waist and watched my ass move as I slurped his dick and jockeyed my hips.

I was a freak for getting my pussy licked, but I was also one of them chicks who loved giving head too. I stretched my legs out and we started sixty-nining like a mothafucka. Wasn't nothing to be heard up in that room except slurps, swallows, and moans.

I loved the way his meat-bone felt sliding on my tongue. I loved how my jaw ached when I opened that shit wide and let all that hardness in. Trey had a dick that was big, thick, and powerful, and I coulda sucked that baby seven days a week and *still* been wanting more.

But right now I could tell more was what *he* wanted.

I let go of his dick and turned myself around until I was facing him. I stretched out on top of him and he held me tight as his tongue snaked inside my mouth and we dry humped to the same beat.

Trey gripped my ass cheeks and massaged them in his strong hands. I tickled his ear with my wet tongue and then sucked up a hickey on his neck.

"Put it in," I whispered as I spread my legs open wide and came up slightly on my knees. My pussy was dripping. I wanted that dick. I couldn't wait to feel his thickness going up inside me. I wanted him to impale my na-na and bang it up real hard.

But Trey slowed down. He put his hands on my hips and started pushing me off.

And I damn near broke.

"C'mon, now!" I whispered in his ear, crawling back on top of him and humping my naked ass even faster. "Don't start that *'you ain't ready for this'* shit! I'm ready! I'm fuckin' ready! You feel how hot this pussy is? I'm *ready*!"

He slapped me on the ass and chuckled.

"Yeah," he said, reaching between us and sliding one finger deep up in my wet pussy. "You're ready, baby. You sure are. But I want you to feel *safe* when I get up in you, Juicy. So hold up a minute baby and lemme get wrapped up."

$$$$$

It was hard to describe what I was feeling as Trey lay on top of me kissing me and sparking up crazy heat in my body. Yeah, my coochie was on fire and I wanted that dick, but something else had me feeling real good too. Something about being in his arms that ain't have a damn thing to do with sex.

I moaned as Trey tried to ease the head of his big dick inside of me. I had already cum twice, and damn if I wasn't ready to cum again. I grunted and dug my nails into his strong back as he inched his wood in deeper, little by little.

Juicy, he whispered in my ear as he bit down on his lip and strained to hold his need back.

Trey, I whispered, as my legs fell open even wider and my pussy felt like a tree trunk was trying to barge up in it. I raised my pelvis to take more of him inside me, and then I yelped real loud as that monster dick damn-near split me.

"You okay, baby?" he whispered. Every muscle in his body was straining as he smoothed my hair back and licked all over my neck.

I shivered under his touch. I was like a fuckin' virgin. Wanting way more than I could handle at one time.

And Trey seemed to know this as he took it nice and slow, creeping up in it easy-like as my pussy flooded with hot cream and then stretched out little by little and let him in.

"That's right, baby," he whispered trying to control himself and slow me down a little bit at the same time. "I don't wanna hurt you. So don't rush, Juicy. *Uh.* You ain't gotta rush. This dick gonna be right here for you. *Damn.* Right here whenever you want it."

He lost his head a little bit after that and thrust two more hard inches up in me, and once Trey was in there, he was *in there.*

I gasped and moaned as he fucked me silly, stroking my pussy with long, deep grinds, as he gripped my ass-cheeks and drilled me nice and hard.

My pussy was filled to the brim and he still wasn't all the way in as he got to knocking my back out in that hotel bed. He fucked me so good till I couldn't hardly breathe. My titties was jiggling up and down as he gripped my hips and pounded me into the mattress. I was in heaven as we sweated and groaned and listened to our wet bodies slapping together, hot skin on hot skin, as we fucked to our own delicious beat.

"Pussy good—" Trey blurted as his hardness pressed down on my clit and got my nostrils to flaring. He licked all over my bouncing titties as he rammed his dick up in me and banged down my deepest walls. "*Ahhh* this pussy *good*!"

I creamed all over him as my coochie squirted and I came twice back to back.

And I *still* wanted more!

The kind of heat this dude had ignited in me was blowing my fuckin' mind, and his dick control was so damn superb that after damn near an hour his bone was still rock hard and putting in mad work.

"I want you to cum," I begged him after I had gotten me another nut and Trey seemed like he was ready to pull an all-nighter. "I want you to get yours too."

Trey hesitated. He extended his arms out and raised up off of me. The muscles on his broad chest rippled and his dark skin was covered in our slick sweat. With his piercing dark eyes, brown skin, and gorgeous white teeth, he looked fine as hell as he stared down at me.

"You want this shit?" he asked me, breathing hard. "You ready for this?"

I nodded, and Trey went to work.

He banged his hips into my pussy so hard my whole body shook.

I arched my back and screamed as he pulled his dick all the way outta me, then rubbed the head around on my clit before plunging back inside me. My pussy was bubbling as he cupped my ass and held real still, then pressed his dick inside of me as deep as it would go. He withdrew slightly, then went back in, pressing down on my mound so hard that I screamed and came again.

And this time my man came with me. His dick felt like it was drilling its way outta my back bone as he yanked me up to him by my hips and held me there tightly. He rocked me on his pole two times real quick, and then his dick exploded like a bomb in my pussy as he shot a hot load of endless cum outta his nuts that scalded my insides, even through his glove.

My body went limp as I collapsed exhausted into the sheets. I couldn't even open my eyes and Trey kept his dick lodged up in me as he planted small kisses all over my neck and cheeks. I wanted to tell him thank you for what he had given me, but all I could do was lay there and enjoy the kisses because bruh-man had just knocked my back out and I fell into a deep, happy sleep.

$$$$$

And it was all good until I started dreaming.

I was back in the city again. On a walking path in Central Park.

It was bitter cold outside and big, fluffy snowflakes were spinning through the air all around me. The clouds were thick and gray and the wind howled in my ears and tossed me on my feet with the force of a blizzard. Just up ahead on the path I strained to see into the whiteness as a deep layer of snow sucked at my feet.

And then I saw him.

Gino was there. Running away from me.

"*Wait up!*" I screamed as I reached out for him in the storm. I was worried about him because it was cold as hell outside and all Gino had on was the white tux he was wearing at our wedding. "It's too cold out here, baby!" I shouted out to him. "You need to put a hat on, Gino! What happened to your coat?"

I started running down the path toward him and Gino started running again too. I was scared and it worried me to see him out in the cold with hardly nothing on, but no matter how fast I ran he kept leaving me in the dust.

"Gino *wait* for me!" I begged him. "Let me catch you this time! *Please* let me catch you!"

"I'm not running anymore, Juicy," Gino said quietly, and suddenly he was standing right there in front of me.

"Gino," I moaned as he opened his strong arms and I fell into them crying. Instead of freezing in the storm, I melted like butter inside as a rush of pure love surged through my body like electric honey.

"Gino..." I pressed my face into the warmth of his neck and then my lips were all over him as we stood there kissing each other greedily and squeezing each other tight.

Gino was real. He was with me and he was *real*. I smelled him. I *tasted* him. I shivered and moaned under the heat of my man's touch.

"Oh God, I missed you so much baby," I cried as he held me in his arms and kissed away my tears. "I thought I lost you, Gino. I thought you were gone."

"I *am* gone," he whispered as a frigid wind suddenly blew over us. I felt him slipping away from me. The heat in his touch was disappearing and I was growing cold again. "I'm gone, Juicy. Gone."

"No!" I screamed and lunged at him. I fought my way back into Gino's arms, digging myself into his solid flesh as I tried to keep him and the warmth of his love close. "Don't leave me baby," I whined as I clung to him desperately. "Gino *please* don't leave me!"

"I didn't wanna leave you Juicy," he said sadly, and his eyes were full of sorrow. He pulled me close to him and kissed my forehead, my nose, my lips. "I swear I didn't wanna leave you, baby. You're my heart, Juicy. My love will *always* be with you girl."

Gino pressed his trembling lips to the tip of my nose one more time, and then he smoothed my hair back and gazed so deep down into my eyes that I felt our souls collide.

"I love you, Juicy. You were the best thing in my life, baby. But it's time to let me go. To *really* let me go."

"Gino *noooo*!" I screamed as I tried to wrap my arms and legs around him. Gino was *here* and I had to keep him with me. I *needed* to keep him with me!

But the heat was fading and Gino was starting to drift away. He stroked my cheek and kissed me one last time. On my lips. Sweet and long. And then he stood up straight and looked off into the distance where a single ray of sunshine had broken through the dark, cloudy sky.

"You've got a beautiful son," Gino told me. "He's amazing, baby. Just like you."

And then I opened my eyes.

CHAPTER 11

Y'all find her yet?" Flex barked as his number Five and Six men came through the door of his basement battle-den the next morning. He had been hopeful when he heard the beeping codes being punched into his door panels, and when the secret knock of the Divine Nine sounded on his last door of entry he had hoped like hell that it was Lil Lee standing out there.

But it wasn't. It was Mannie and Rome grubbing on some Lemon Heads and Jaw Breakers. Both of them fat fools stopped chewing when they saw the look on his face.

"Nah, boss. We ain't seen her," Mannie muttered.

Flex felt his temperature spike about a mile high.

"Yo, where the fuck is that damn girl at?" he spit. Lil Lee's car was still parked outside the funeral home and Flex had about five search parties out there sniffin' for her ass like bloodhounds, but couldn't nobody find the girl.

That shit straight puzzled Flex. Combat soldiers like Lil Lee didn't run off right before a major battle, and they damn sure didn't just disappear into a puff of smoke. Flex couldn't shake the uneasiness that had crept up on him. Something wasn't sitting right in his gut, and he didn't like it. He'd already put his foot on the necks of every niggah Lil Lee had ever fucked with, and none of her slangas had seen or heard from her either.

Flex shook his head. He couldn't spend no more time worrying about Lil Lee's ass right now 'cause there was bizzness to handle and shit to be done. He stood up and motioned for his crew to pick-up the suitcase full of cash that he was about to go deliver to his arms supplier. They were gonna pass the doe off at a record shop in the hood that doubled as a number joint in the back, and Flex wanted to get there before the white boy did.

"So what we gonna do now that Lil Lee ain't around?" Boog asked as the small crew walked through the Funeral Home's parking lot and past her abandoned whip.

Flex shrugged angrily. "Fuck you mean, 'what we gone do' niggah? We gone keep on doin' like we been doin'. We gonna handle our bizzness transaction so we can get these burners and get ready to set the muh'fuckin' G-Spot on fire!"

$$$$$

Virginia was way behind them when Trey glanced at his Rolex and pulled over at a busy rest stop in Maryland to get some gas. They'd stayed at Moonie's crib until late-night scheming up on a plan, and then he'd taken Juicy to one of the best hotels in town and had one of the best nights of his life.

Trey had been with enough honeys to know what kind of woman he wanted to wife, and loving on Juicy all night had not only felt right, it felt better than anything he

526

had ever done before. The girl was in his heart. She was in his blood and up under his skin. He wanted her in a way that was everlasting, and he woulda laid his life down for her without a question or a thought.

He had put his master dick game down on her until she couldn't take no more, and then they'd fallen asleep naked and wrapped in each other's arms, but when he opened his eyes that morning he wasn't surprised to see Juicy sitting propped up against the headboard and staring down at him.

She looked sad and confused, and Trey felt his heart reach for her. He saw what was in her eyes. He knew what that kind of guilt felt like. He knew what a harsh muthafucka it could be.

"You all right?" he had asked her as he reached over and placed his big hand on her smooth thigh. It had been a rough night for Juicy. Trey had woken up at dawn to find her tossing and turning in her sleep, but when he stroked her cheek and kissed her deeply on her lips, she seemed to calm down and whimper a little bit before falling back off.

"Yeah, I'm okay," she nodded. "I just feel so..." she shrugged and shot him a small smile. "I feel good, Trey. I really do."

She was real quiet later that morning as they took a shower together. He had soaped up her back and watched as the warm sudsy water ran over her round, delicious breasts. Juicy had stepped up close to him under the rainfall spray of water, and pressed her cheek up against his wet chest.

And as the water sprinkled down on them Trey held her quietly and let her work it out. He knew what was fuckin' with her, and he respected it. He also knew it was something she was gonna have to come to grips with on her own. But he was damn sure gonna be right there for her to lean on. He would be right there to catch her if she ever started to fall.

They had gotten dressed and jumped in the whip to dip back to New York, and Juicy had nodded off almost as soon as he pulled onto the highway and headed north.

And now, after waiting in a long line at the gas station Trey drove up to the pump and cut off the car. Juicy sat up and looked at him, and then both of them stepped outta the ride to stretch their legs.

Trey ran his eyes over her bangin' frame as he pumped gas. Even though shit was kinda crazy in their world right now he appreciated the love she had shared with him last night and he told her so with his eyes.

After the tank was full they walked inside the rest stop plaza holding hands, and Trey bought two vanilla ice cream cones from a vendor while Juicy went to use the bathroom. She looked a lot better when she came out. She even cracked a little grin when she saw her ice cream melting and dripping down the sides of the cone and spilling all over Trey's hands.

"Lemme get that," she said softly, reaching out to take it from him. But instead of taking it she pulled Trey's wrist toward her and gently licked the dripping sweet vanilla cream from his skin. Her tongue lingered in the soft spot between his thumb and forefinger before sweeping from side to side and sending sparks of heat shooting through both of their bodies. With her eyes burning sexily into his, Juicy extracted the cone from Trey's grasp and took three long, slow licks, giving him a hot reminder of the way she had licked his dick just hours earlier, before filling her mouth with the soft vanilla deliciousness that exploded with sweetness on her tongue.

"You got that lick technique on lock, huh," Trey muttered as his meat stiffened in his pants and strained toward her. He swept his thumb across her soft lower lip, wiping away a small trace of ice cream.

"Yeah," Juicy said, her voice getting thick. "You damn right I do."

Trey was bending down to kiss her on her nose when his cell phone sounded off. He kissed her anyway, even though the ringtone told him it was a call from a member of his Talented Ten crew. It was hard to pull himself away from Juicy, and Trey took a real deep breath before he answered.

"Ay, whattup?" he asked his main manz Rain.

"Yo, man, I hate to holla at you when you outta town and shit, but it's your sister."

Trey frowned as he felt his chest tighten up. "Chiney?"

"Yeah. Her and that chick she be swingin' with. Venus."

Trey's face got hard.

"What happened man? Chiney brought that chick up in my crib, didn't she?"

"Yeah," Rain admitted. "She brought her up in there to *die*. Venus is dead, man. She OD'd right in ya bathtub, dude. Her and Chiney was partying and getting high off some bad shit and it took her out."

"Yo! Where's my *sister*?" Trey spit, fearing the worst. Whatever Venus had been smoking he knew Chiney had been smoking that shit too. "Where's Chiney, man?"

"She's cool, dude. She's cool. But niggahs been ODing like crazy around here so the cops took her downtown for questioning and ended up holding her on a probation violation. I just now got word about it from ya boy Dutchy Gaines. He said he's gonna see about getting Chiney released as soon as he can, my dude, but it's gonna take him a minute. Swing by his office and holla at him as soon as you get back in the city, a'ight? Dutchy'll prolly have your sister out by then."

$$$$$

"What happened?" Juicy asked as Trey led her back to the car. He held her door open as she climbed in the passenger seat, and he knew she could feel the heat coming off of him from where she sat.

"Venus is dead," Trey said quietly as he cranked up his ride. "She overdosed. Probably on the same shit everybody else been choking on out there on the streets."

Trey's voice was composed but his jaw worked with fury. After the long hours he had spent collaborating with Moonie and Frankie he knew some real unholy alliances had been formed on the city's streets. All types of criminals were either double-crossing each other or climbing in bed and humping each other's legs over the profitable club drugs that had infiltrated Harlem.

They got back to New York quicker than shit.

Trey went straight to Dutchy Gaines' office and Chiney fell into his arms before he could get in the door good. Clinging to him in grief, his baby sister wet his shirt up with her tears as she cried over the loss of her boo-thang.

"Tell me what went down," Trey said gently as Dutchy pulled up some chairs for him and Juicy.

Chiney swallowed and said, "Okay, I know Venus wasn't supposed to be up in the house and shit, but I'm sorry Trey!" her face crumpled into a mask of pain as a fresh wave of tears started to flow. "It was her birthday and that was my *girl*, man. My baby! I loved that chick and I wanted to show her a good time. I was planning on having her outta there before y'all got back and everythang... but shit just got all fucked up! All I know is that I copped some ice from up the block and me and Venus got to hittin' that shit before we started messing around."

"Afterwards, I ran her a nice lil bath and shit, and then I went in the kitchen to fix us a lil drink. And when I came back the water was still running and Venus was out. Gone. I swear she looked just like she was sleeping. Except she wasn't."

"Tell me who you copped that shit from," Trey said quietly. "And don't lie to me, Chiney. Don't lie."

She sighed as she took a deep breath. Trey had promised to get in the ass of any slanga who transacted with her, and Chiney knew she was about to burn a bridge right now.

"I got it from my dude Fitted. He usually keeps some pretty good weight on him and he's reliable. But something about the shit he gave me and Venus to smoke up was different."

Trey sat there thinking and frowning. He was familiar with that cat Fitted. Dude was one of Flex's slangas in Lil Lee's sector, and he managed a pretty busy corner where cocaine thrived.

He shook his head because shit just wasn't adding up. "Yo, Flex ain't no chemist, baby. Lil Lee keeps Fitted and his boys out there transacting crack and duji all day. You telling me that niggah is hustlin' meth now too?"

Chiney shrugged. 'I'on't know, I guess so. Fitted sure nuff had some on him yesterday because that's who I got it from! All I know is that shit said "Strawberry Snake" on the vial. It came on the news and that's why I tried to warn Venus before she smoked it!"

Trey shook his head again and shot a questioning look at Dutchy.

"But that ain't Flex's hustle, baby. Strawberry Snake comes straight up outta the G-Spot, Chiney. Flex's product got Divine Nine stamped on it. You couldn't have picked that shit up from Fitted."

"Yes I *did*," Chiney insisted. "I copped four vials from him but he only charged me for two. I usually only hit him up for fish scales or rock, but yesterday I told him I was feelin' icy and that's what he handed me off."

Trey's mind started whirring like a computer. Just what in the fuck was Flex's Divine Nine crew doing selling polluted vials of G-Spot product? "Are you sure about that, Chiney? Are you *sure*?"

"Hell yeah. Like I said, a report about it had just flashed on the news when I hollered at Venus not to smoke that shit. You remember my old jump-off Lincy?"

Trey frowned and nodded. He could never understand what his sister had seen in that ape-looking chick.

"Well, Lincy is in the hospital on critical and her little daughter *died* from that shit," Chiney said, her voice thick with guilt. She wasn't about to tell her brother that Lincy had ate her asshole out and she'd left her a vial of ice as payment. "I'm telling you, that Strawberry Snake shit is poison. They said Lincy's lil baby got hold of it by mistake and it took her out instantly," Chiney snapped her fingers and sniffled back some big fat tears. "Just like it did Venus."

CHAPTER 12

"Y ou can think I'm bullshittin' if you wanna. I swear on my junkie-ass, duji-sniffin', one-toofed, wine-guzzlin', dopefiend *mama*," Flex spit as he stood in the back room of a local record shop and handed over the cash to buy his arsenal of burners. "If you fuck over my money I'ma fuckin' kill you, a'ight? I'ma cut out your fuckin' tongue and pour gasoline down your throat and set you on fire, niggah. You got my word on that."

Sallie shrugged indifferently as he closed the large bag full of cool green cash that Flex had brought to the table. His greedy eyes had lit up like a starry night sky at the sight of all that doe stacked up in neat little rows of banded moolah, ten piles deep.

"Ain't nothin' but fitties and hunnerds in there," Flex had told him as Sallie fingered a few random stacks and fanned the edges of the bills, and Sallie knew better than to insult the young gangsta by trying to count that shit.

"Cool," he said, closing the bag and playing it hardbody like he got his hands on this much dirty doe every day. "Now all you gotta do is wait for my call. I'll let you know what the combination to the lock is and where your bitches can be picked up. And then we'll be squared up."

"All them bitches is clean, right?" Flex grilled Sallie hard. He was expecting a bloodbath full of mass casualties at the G-Spot and he didn't want a single piece of ballistic evidence traceable back to his organization.

Sallie nodded. "Clean and stuffed with some nice big dicks. Big *black* dicks," he laughed. "You got my word on that and my word is *always* good."

"It better be, muh'fucka. It better be ya bond."

$$$$$

Even after taking a beat-down in the G-Spot, fear wasn't something that came naturally to Slick Sallie McCain, and there wasn't a drop of Kool Aid running through his veins as prepared to meet with his gun supplier and conduct the transaction of his young life.

He'd slept like a baby that night and early the next morning he got down on his knees in his Chinatown flat and dug his hands all the way up Buddha's ass. Sallie was all smiles as he reached up in those guts and pulled out the money he had stolen from Juicy and hidden in the hollow statue. After counting it out carefully, he packed the huge stash of greenbacks inside a duffle bag, and then separated the bank he had gotten from Flex and packed it in right on top of the pile. And then without a backwards glance, Sallie walked outta the tiny room and abandoned everything he'd brought to New York City as he headed downstairs to his car.

What a workout, he laughed and told himself as his muscles strained under the weight of the heavy duffle bag. He was making an unbelievable profit on this gun

531

deal, and he had already ganked Flex outta three times more than what he was about to lay out for the shipment. *Sheiiit*, Sallie thought, cracking a wide grin. If he kept making deals this fuckin' sweet he was gonna have to put all his cash in a shopping cart and pull that shit around behind him.

The meeting with his arms dealer was scheduled to take place in a warehouse in North Jersey, and once Sallie handed over the moolah he would be given the address to the location where the guns were stashed. The arrangements he had made with his gun trader were a little bit outta the ordinary, but Sal hadn't protested too much because logistically things worked out better for him in the long run this way.

Besides, his strategy *had* to be different now that his entire Family was *persona non grata* in the city of New York. Back in the day when his clan was still sitting pretty at the top of the heap, Sallie would have had enough resources at his fingertips to call the shots any way he wanted them. Ideally, he would have been the one who to decide on the location for the drop, and then both the guns and the money would have been handed off at the same time. But fuck all that, he figured. He woulda had to come up with a truck to transport the weapons and a trusted crew on hand ready to help load that shit up. Yeah, that kind of set up would have been the safest and it would have protected him from any type of slick double-cross, but right now it just wasn't practical. Sallie was riding solo. He didn't have a crew of ready henchmen that he could call on to watch his back. The days when he could turn to the so-called "Family" of New York mobsters and tap into their internal bank of criminal resources were over. Besides, Slick Sallie needed to keep his head down and fly real low under the radar. If word got out that he had crossed even one fuckin' *toe* into the New York metropolitan area, the cut-throat mobsters running the city would plant a bullet in his brain and toss his dead ass into the East River with a slab of concrete tied around his neck.

This was something Sallie knew for a fact, so when his arms dealer had told him to meet him in New Jersey with the cash, and then promised to give him the combination to a lock and the address to a brand new sub-division where a portable storage Pod was parked in the driveway of an unoccupied house, he had jumped on that shit.

Once the transaction had been completed and Sallie verified that the guns were where they were supposed to be, then he was gonna call that punk from the Three Brothers Funeral Home and tell him where to pick up his ugly dead bitches.

And after that, Slick Sallie was gonna hit the bridge back to New York City, and then call Monique and tell her to hop in a cab and meet him at the Chinese restaurant around the corner from the G-Spot. He was gonna swing by that restaurant and snatch his baby up outta that joint, and take her down to the beaches of Miami, where they would buy themselves a club and make that shit larger than any titty bar that New York City had ever seen.

With his head filled with dreams of blue waves, white sand, and endless black pussy, Sallie was hyped as hell as he drove out to Jersey. He turned up the music and rolled down all the windows, and pushed his whip just under the speed limit. He'd have to be fuckin' stupid to get himself stopped for speeding when he was carrying hundreds of thousands of dollars in cash on him, and if there was one thing Slick Sallie definitely wasn't, it was fuckin' stupid.

$$$$$

Traffic wasn't too bad and Sallie reached his destination in just over an hour. His slick eyes took in the scenery around him and he sneered. Whether it was New Jersey or New York, the northeast was one big congested shithole, Sallie thought as he sped down the streets of North Jersey and drove toward the address he had already memorized.

The area he was looking for was a deserted industrial center that had a lot of abandoned warehouses and dilapidated storage facilities. Sallie drove down the alleys between the empty, gutted-out buildings until he found the right one, and when he saw a beat-up Ford parked on an angle outside of a deeply recessed doorway, he knew he was at the right place.

With a tingle of excitement zipping through his balls, Slick Sallie pulled up just a short distance away from the Ford and hopped outta his ride. He retrieved his extra-heavy duffle bag from the car's trunk, and when he slammed it shut a loud and chilly echo rose into the air and sent a cold trickle of fear running down the back of his legs.

"Hell the fuck *nah*," he chastised himself sharply, wondering where the sudden sliver of dread had come from as he forced that shit to go flying outta his heart. "Slick Sallie McCain ain't scared of a goddamn thing," he reminded himself as he gripped the ever-present gat strapped to his waist. Nah, men like him weren't scared to live, and they damn sure weren't scared to die, and Sallie gave himself a harsh mental reminder of his mobster heritage as he pushed through the creaky warehouse door and stepped into the darkness inside.

CHAPTER 13

The meeting with his arms supplier was going down real lovely, and so far Sallie was impressed. The warehouse was obviously used by big willies to conduct a lot of illegal trade, because while it was beyond shitty-looking on the outside, the interior was totally laid out. Sallie and the guy he was meeting had done a little business together in the past, and Sallie felt big-time respected when the small Black man greeted him with a spread that coulda been set out for a Mafia goodfella.

With his ego swollen up to the max, Sallie sat across from the dealer as they drank from a bottle of fine Scotch and smoked imported cigars. When they were done and he was about to dig into his duffle bag and slide the moolie the cash for the guns, Sallie reminded him of the specific terms of sale they had agreed upon.

"You packaged it up like I told you to, right?" Sallie asked with one eyebrow raised up high. He thought about the big bank he had collected from Flex and the fact that he was about to lay out less than half of that for the shipment and pocket the rest as pure profit. "The clean stuff is at the top of the crate and all the cheap dirty pieces are on the bottom, right?"

The little man peeled the skin off of a red orange and nodded. "That's right, boss. I made sure it got in there just like that."

"And every single piece is loaded right?" Sallie spit gruffly, posing like a wiseguy and grilling the dude like he was a badass Godfather or something.

"Oh yeah," the cat said quickly, nodding his head as he tossed the peels into his empty glass. "Every one of them babies is packed to the rim with first class ammo. The best money can buy."

Sallie paid the dealer from the banded money that he had gotten from Flex, and then nodded in satisfaction as the dealer slid him a piece of paper that revealed the combination to a lock and the address to the location where the guns were waiting for him. After folding it up and slipping it into his pocket, he drained the last of the Scotch from his glass and eyeballed the half-filled bottle.

"Ga' head. Take it with you," the small man said, nodding at the top-shelf liquor. "Consider it a parting gift, my manz."

Sallie snuffed out his cigar, hoisted his half-full duffle bag onto his shoulder, grabbed the bottle, and dapped the moolie out.

"It's been good doing business with you," Sallie said, smirking as he headed for the door.

"But the pleasure is minez." the Black man chuckled his ass off. "Hell yeah, the pleasure is all minez."

$$$$$$

Whistling happily as he closed out his meeting and walked outside, Slick Sallie headed around toward the back of his whip to place the bottle of liquor in the trunk. He frowned when that shit popped open before he could even turn the key in the lock.

"I coulda sworn I slammed that shit," he muttered under his breath. Sallie looked around the deserted industrial area where nothing was moving except a few stray pieces of trash that blew in the breeze, and then that tingly feeling of fear exploded in his nuts again, making him feel like a paranoid little bitch.

"Man, chill the fuck out!" he bitched hard at himself as he slammed the trunk closed then got inside his whip and heaved the duffle bag in the back seat. Everything had gone down perfectly, and once he checked out the shipment and called Flex with the combination to the lock, he planned to swing over to Harlem and scoop up Monique, and then the two of them would get outta town.

Cruising toward the address he'd been given, Sallie thought about that last delicious night he'd spent with Monique. Not even the punches and the stomps from all them gorilla-ass black dudes could make him forget how good her chocolate cookie had tasted. He couldn't wait to handle this last bit of business and then go snatch her up. The plan was for him to give her a call when he was on his way, and then she'd bring her suitcases around the corner to the Chinese restaurant where he would pick her up.

Sallie was amped about getting out on the open road and heading down to the beach. One thing he had loved about California had been the smell of the ocean breeze, and he was looking forward to hitting the beaches of Miami with nothing but sunshine and sweet Monique to keep him occupied.

Traffic was steady as he zipped down the streets of a residential community. He wasn't all that familiar with New Jersey, but he figured he wouldn't have too far to go. A nagging thought crept up on him as he drove. The coast wasn't clear on this deal yet. On the real, he had left outta that warehouse totally empty-fuckin' handed. For all he knew the storage pod might be full of rocks. Or even worse, he might get to the address just to find there was no storage pod parked in the fuckin' driveway at all.

This was the shitty part of the situation and Sal forced himself to chill out and have faith. In every criminal alliance there was a certain level of risk involved. And for a dude with Slick Sallie's track record, risk was just one of them things.

He drove down the streets of Jersey taking stock of the neighborhood. Blacks and Hispanics and other minorities were now dominating the areas that whites had once occupied when they fled the ghettos of Brooklyn and Staten Island.

The directions the moolie had written down led him to a residential area that had recently been developed. Signs of ongoing construction were everywhere. Concrete pads, framed-out lots, and building materials were scattered throughout the subdivision. Some houses looked like people had just moved into them, and others were still sitting empty. Sallie drove down a block lined with brand new starter homes that were set back off the road. About half of the houses were occupied, and construction work was still being done on quite a few.

He cruised down the street at a normal speed trying hard to look ordinary.

It was already getting dark outside and he was surprised when he passed by a little girl jumping rope on the sidewalk, a middle-aged man who was mowing his lawn, a couple of Mexican landscapers planting flats of colorful flowers, and four masonry guys spackling bricks to the exterior walls of a ranch-style house.

Sallie spotted his destination when he was halfway down the block but he kept right on driving. He had already seen what he was looking for, and his heart jumped with excitement even though his facial expression never changed.

The street ended in a dead-end, and Sal swung his whip around in a wide circle and headed back out. Driving toward the house that had a large portable storage pod sitting at the bottom of a long driveway, Sallie swerved around the container and parked in front of the house.

He climbed out and glanced at the Mexican workers, and when the old man pushing the lawnmower next door nodded, Sallie nodded back.

Whistling, he walked over to the back of the pod real casual-like. Using the backlight from his cell phone, he punched the combination code into the panel and then he disengaged the lock as fast as he could. With one slick glance over his shoulder, Sallie pulled the door open just wide enough so he could slip inside, and then he quickly shut it behind him. Holding his phone out in front of him, Sallie used the glow of the backlight to see what was up.

There was a big-ass wooden crate in the Pod.

Unhooking his Leatherman knife from his belt, Sallie pried the top off the crate and busted out in a big-ass grin. That baby was full of guns. A shitload of them. There were assault rifles, submachine guns, semi-automatic pistols, and countless revolvers.

"Yeah, mothafucka!" he yelled, hyped the fuck up. In the back of Sallie's mind he had been shitting bricks that he might get ganked on this deal, but his little moolie friend had come through for him once again.

"Mo-Mo, baby!" he crooned, "I hope you got your shit packed because we are getting the fuck *outta* here!"

Mopping his sweaty face with the end of his shirt, Sallie dialed a number and gave up the address and the combination to the lock. All he had to do now was get back to Harlem and get his baby, and this shit was a wrap. *Finito*. Done.

Sallie was feeling like a big-time willie as he stepped outta the storage Pod and slammed the door. He made sure the lock clicked securely and pulled out his keys so he could jet back to New York, but as he headed over to his car he saw something that made his heart go cold.

A New York Police Department cruiser was rolling by with all the lights off.

NYPD?... what the *fuck*... Sallie mouthed as he watched it go by.

The cruiser didn't slow down or nothing and he didn't get a look at the cops inside, but instinct told Sallie that shit was critical and he needed to think fast.

He glanced around real quick.

The old man next door had abandoned his lawn mower and gone inside his house. The two gardeners were busy arguing in heavy accents over where the fuck they should plant the rose bush and where they should put the tulips. The little girl with the jump rope had disappeared, and the masonry workers were still on their knees smearing concrete under the darkening sky.

At the bottom of the dead-end street the cop car had turned around and was now circling back.

Quick as shit Sal stuck his car keys in his pocket and cut across the front lawn of the house next door. He primed the lawnmower twice and as soon as it caught and the engine sputtered to life, he ducked his head down and started cutting grass for all he was worth.

Nervous sweat started running down his back in waves as he pushed the lawnmower in long even lines across the stranger's front yard.

"Stay your old ass inside, muthafucka," Sallie prayed under his breath as his eyes flickered toward the house, hoping the man didn't hear his mower running and come outside to investigate. "Just stay the fuck inside!"

But just moments later the worst fuckin' thing that could possibly happen, *happened*.

The police cruiser pulled up in front of him, right under a streetlight, and two blue boy moolies stepped out with their hands on their holsters.

Sallie swallowed hard. His gut was screaming at him to dip, but the cops were standing right between him and his fuckin' ride!

Abandoning the lawn mower he took off running across the grass. His knees were pumping like a muthafucka and his feet were kicking so high that he was kicking his own self in the ass.

"Yo!" One of the cops yelled. "Don't fuckin run!"

Sal hit the concrete, zipped down the driveway, and darted out into the middle of the street.

He snuck a quick look over his shoulder and saw the cops running hard on his ass, and they were being followed real close by the old man who had been outside cutting his grass.

Ignoring their warnings to stop, Sal broke into a whole nother gear and opened up some distance on them. He tore that street up like he was one of them champion sprinters from Kenya racing toward the finish line.

Right up ahead of him were the two masonry workers.

Those mothafuckas jumped to their feet when they saw Sallie coming and started fanning out like they was gonna catch him in a net. One of them held a walkie-talkie up to his mouth, and his eyes were trained dead on Sallie.

Veering right, Sallie ran across the street determined to make it back toward his car.

But to his horror, the Mexican landscapers had abandoned their pansies and were coming at him crouched real low with their arms held out like they were playing some tough defense on a basketball court.

"Get the fuck outta my way!" Sal panted as he ran dead into the shorter guy and barreled over his ass.

That squat little Mexican wrapped his arms around Sallie's waist and put a wrestling move on him that had him stretched out on his back in two seconds flat.

The bigger guy ran over and pressed his muddy boot into Sallie's chest. The fake gardener planted his weight down, then leaned forward so hard that he damn near cracked Sallie's rib cage open.

Screaming, Sallie yanked on the big guy's foot and twisted his ankle hard to the left. Dude shrieked and went down flat on his back, as Sal kicked up at him and punted the toe of his foot deep into the shorter guy's nuts.

Gunshots exploded in the air as the two cops ran toward him shooting. It was nothing but pure fuckin' panic that sent Sallie springing to his feet. Running in a zigzag and dodging hot bullets, he made it over to his ride in about two seconds flat. Yanking the keys from his pocket Sallie snatched his door open and dove behind the wheel. Then he ducked his head down low and stomped on the gas, peeling up outta that cul de sac so hot and fast that he left ten layers of rubber plastered to the concrete.

CHAPTER 14

Yo," Flex said cautiously as he answered his cell phone and got the call he had been waiting for. His gun dealer had called him about an hour earlier and given him the address and the combination to the storage Pod where his shipment was located. Flex had passed that information straight to his crew, and right now he was listening as his number Eight man Chickie spit some shit in his ear that made him feel like a million bucks.

Chickie was out in North Jersey standing in the driveway of an empty house. The crate of loaded gats was exactly where the white boy Sallie had said it was gonna be, and after using the combination to the lock Chickie was happy to report that him, Boog, and Mannie were about to load the crate onto a flatbed pickup so they could make their way back to Harlem with it.

"Good shit," Flex said loudly as a smile of excitement spread over his face.

"Yo, y'all open that shit up real quick and make sure it ain't full of bricks!" Flex ordered.

"Yeah. It's legit, ak," Chickie said after a few minutes. "This baby is full of black bitches."

"Don't touch none of 'em!" Flex barked. "Remember, I told y'all niggahs not to put ya hands on none of my pieces until I give you the go!"

"Nah, ain't nobody touching shit. Word."

"Good," Flex said. "Now y'all niggahs need to hurry up and get to the G-Spot and get that crate stashed in a closet somewhere, ya heard? That punk-ass niggah Freeze is gonna be waiting at the back door to make sure ere'thang goes real smoove and easy, and if that fool act like he wanna buck or give them G-Spot niggahs a headz up signal or somethin'," Flex told Chickie coldly, "you *pop* his punk ass! But first you do his Gramma witcha big belt, homey. Pull off her dirty fuckin' granny drawers and spank her wrinkled ass! And you make that niggah watch you do it too, ya heard?"

Chickie responded with the right words and Flex nodded, satisfied that ere'thang was ere'thang and all his ducks was lining up in a row. And they just oughtta be lining up, too. Flex had a knack for planning intricate shit down to the smallest detail, and his diabolical mind had been working overtime as he thought about the entrance he was gonna make at the G-Spot later on that night.

He had picked out a Granite McKay-inspired suit he was gonna wear to the Grand Re-Opening party with a whole lotta care because he was plannin' on making a real clear statement to every niggah up in that joint. All kinds of ballers and hustlers were gonna be rollin' up in the cut, and while everybody else was showing up to attend a hot party, Flex was gonna bust up in that bitch to get a party started as he knocked the G-Spot crew straight off the throne and sent them tumbling into the gutter on their grimy asses.

$$$$$

The streets of Harlem were bustling with fast-moving nightlife. Pluto drove with the windows down and a smoldering blunt clutched between his lips. His eyes were ice-cold as he gazed at the familiar people and places on the crowded avenue. This was gonna be his last night fuckin' around in shitty-ass Harlem, and he couldn't wait to get gone. He was heading to the G-Spot to pick up Ace so he could take his slime downtown to dish off the thousands of vials of Strawberry Snake that Salida needed to get rid of before the DEA came down on her ass.

Silly bitch, Pluto thought and shook his head. At least ten mess head fiends had either dropped dead or ended up on critical after smoking Salida's homemade shit, and Pluto wasn't the least bit surprised. He'd tried to tell her dumb ass about mixing up all them chemicals and making them look all pink and pretty. That bitch wasn't no damn chemist, and she didn't know shit about lighter fluid and decongestants and whatever other shit she cooked up in them glass bowls and sold to them fiends who was out there chasing a high.

And she had brought the heat down on herself too. Ace said he had gotten a headz up from his manz in the police department who told him the local DEA office had Strawberry Snake aimed dead in their crosshairs. Salida's 7:30 ass had gone into a panic, and now she wanted him and Ace to take every single vial she had left and sell them shits to a Polish dude in the East Village who exported club drugs outta the state.

Salida was about to take a lil hit in her pockets 'cause a transaction this hot was gonna have to come with a real deep discount. She prolly figured taking the hit was better than letting the po-po roll up in the G-Spot and catch her holding more than half a million dollars worth of product. Pluto didn't care either way, 'cause once him and Ace dropped off all that meth and picked up the cash from the Polish dude, they were gonna zip across the bridge to Jersey so Moonie could hook them up with G's old connect.

Or at least that's what the fuck Ace thought.

But it wasn't happening.

Pluto was gonna help Ace sell off that meth all right, but not a dime of that cash was *ever* gonna touch Salida's hands. And yeah, he was gonna drive Ace out to Jersey for that hook-up they had scheduled with Moonie, but he damn sure wasn't gonna be driving that niggah *back*.

Because Ace wouldn't be coming back from Jersey at all. Unless it was in a pine fuckin' box.

With all the details of his grimy back-door plan running through his mind, Pluto parked his ride in the alley behind the G-Spot. Inside his trunk were two designer suitcases that he had stolen from Monique. That trifling bitch thought she had some moves on her but she wasn't half as slick as he was.

Earlier in the day Pluto had found the suitcases hidden underneath his bed stuffed with a whole bunch of Monique's cheap, frilly shit. He had waited until she got her slick ass in the shower and then he dumped all her shit out and re-stuffed the suitcases with his own travel gear. After that he'd snuck downstairs and locked both suitcases up in the trunk of his whip where they were gonna stay until he slumped Ace's punk ass and then dipped over to Newark Airport to hop on his flight to Chicago.

"Yo, whattup!" Pluto greeted his dude Ace with a shitload of fake love as he walked casually into the front area of the club. The event staff was in a frenzy as they scurried around getting shit decorated, polished, and shined up for Salida's Grand Re-Opening party that was gonna officially pop off at midnight. Pluto looked around. Shit was all glossed up. He had to admit that Salida had brought the G-Spot way back up, even though her crazy ass didn't bring it up *right*.

"What it do?" Ace nodded, standing up from his barstool to dap his manz out.

"It do ere'thang it's 'posed to do." Pluto said then nodded in the direction of the cut room. "So, Salida got that shit all packed up and ready to go? We gonna get rid of them vials and make that run, and still be back before the big crowd gets here tonight, right?"

"Yeah," Ace said, turning around to lead his boy deeper into the club. "All that shit is lined up my dude. After we drop that weight off and pick up Salida's cash, then we can head on out to Jersey real quick and see what that niggah Moonie is talking about, cool?"

"Definitely," Pluto agreed as he followed Ace up the steps to the cut room.

Ace twisted the doorknob and walked inside.

"Catch that so it don't lock," he reminded Pluto, holding the door open with his toe.

Pluto planted his large frame in the doorway and looked around at the gigantic chemistry set that Salida had constructed. The cut room looked like the laboratory of a mad fuckin' scientist. Bottles of liquids, churning vats, stank, monstrous chemicals, twisted rubber tubing, and cooking apparatus was everywhere.

Ace crossed the room and knocked on the door to the small office. Salida opened it and Ace stepped inside for a quick minute, then he came back out lugging two huge black plastic storage containers with their lids taped down tight.

Salida walked outta the office behind him and smirked at Pluto as he took one of the big containers from his manz.

"That's a whole lotta work y'all taking up outta here," she warned sharply, and Pluto could tell she was real nervous over her doe. "Ya'll idiots betta not fuck up my money, you hear me?"

Pluto just grinned as he held the door open for Ace with dollar signs glowing in his eyes. Hell yeah it was a lotta work to get rid of. That's why she was giving it to him and Ace to dish off in the first fuckin' place. With all them fiends dropping dead and putting the blame on Strawberry Snake, Salida's product was gonna be in low demand around town until shit cooled off a lil bit. But that was okay because there were plenty of mess heads who lived in other cities and they were gonna love that shit.

Salida gave him a real nasty look as they walked out the door. Pluto wanted to smash her fuckin' face in, but he forced himself to chill. Wasn't no need in gettin' riled up. That bitch was gonna get hers in due time. Besides, thanks to Salida there was a real nice gwap riding on this transaction. Cash that Pluto was definitely gonna enjoy filling his pockets with once his manz Ace was dead, Salida was neutralized, and everything else was said and done.

CHAPTER 15

W WGD?

What would G do? Flex had asked himself one last time before making the call.

"Yo, Boobie," he barked into his phone madder than a mutha. "I'on't know where the fuck yo sister at but I'ma need you to hurry up and get ya ass over here so we can put this work in tonight!"

It was time to go to war and Lil Lee's ass was still missing in action. And even though Flex had good eyes out on the streets scoping for her, hadn't nobody seen the girl. Not a soul. Not even her fam.

Flex wasn't about to sit around worrying about her ass though. With the Grand Re-Opening of the G-Spot kicking off at midnight and every soldier in his click out there on the streets working on crucial aspects of his plan, Flex couldn't afford to let nothing knock him off his game. Not even Lil Lee. Right now he needed all his warriors in the trenches and ready to pull some fuckin' triggers. And since Lil Lee wasn't around and Flex needed to have a beautiful cut-throat bitch on his arm when he made his grand entrance at the G-Spot tonight, he had decided to use her little sister Boobie in her place.

It was a good decision and Boobie was a damn good pick. She was way more than just Lil Lee's baby sister. She was also one of the Divine Nine's best street slangas, and she trapped from a corner that was notorious for bringing in top bank and taking down full-grown men. Yeah. Boobie was a true hooligan out there on them streets, and even though she didn't have the cleverness or the cunning mind that her older sister had, she was trustworthy and she was solid. Flex had tested her gangsta plenty of times in the past, and the girl had ice-water pumping up underneath all them big 'ol pretty titties she had on her.

"You gonna be my decoy tonight," Flex explained to Boobie over the phone. "So make sure you ready to skull drag a niggah at the first sign of static. You can bring ya burners with you but you gonna have to leave 'em down here in the basement," he warned her. "Them niggahs at the door is gonna be finger-fuckin' pussies and assholes too looking for gats tonight, and beside we got all our firepower completely covered. Just hur'rup and get ya ass over here, girl. We got us an empire to take down."

$$$$$

Slick Sallie was shaking like a bitch as he drove across the bridge from New Jersey to New York. His foot was trembling so bad on the gas pedal that he had to brace his elbow against his thigh to hold that shit steady.

Moolies from the NYPD rollin' out in Jersey! Them fools had damn-near bagged him!

He just couldn't believe it! That little rat-faced niggah had set him up real fuckin' good, and for the first time in a long time Sallie was forced to admit that he was scared as shit. He had paid Moonie some top fuckin' dollars on this transaction and he never woulda thought that muthafucka was gonna stab him in the back! What the hell made that lil fucker cross him up like that? Sallie didn't know, and at this point he really didn't give a shit. All he knew was that the heat was suddenly scorching hot on his ass, and the most important thing in the world was for him to get back to Harlem and pick up Monique and then get the fuck outta town.

$$$$$

Chiney was missing her girl Venus and taking her death hard.

The fact that her boo-thang's life had been snatched away over some bullshit drug territory beef was burning her up and she couldn't get the sight of Venus' dead body floating in Trey's bathtub outta her head.

"*Why?*" she kept asking herself over and over as she walked the streets of Harlem in a lonely daze. Trey was scared that her grief was gonna send her on a mission and she was gonna crawl up in some crack house and get blasted outta her mind, but he was wrong.

Chiney didn't even wanna get high no more. She wasn't jonesing for no hit, and the taste for drugs had completely left her mouth. All she wanted to do was understand why this shit had happened. It coulda been her who had smoked that bad shit instead of Venus. Both of them coulda been dead right now. If there was one thing a trap boy didn't wanna get known for it was for passing off bad shit. That was the quickest way to scare off your customer base and that's why Chiney couldn't understand why her boy Fitted had done some stupid shit like that.

So she asked him.

"What the fuck kinda shit did you give me, niggah?" she demanded as she pressed her knee into his throat and smashed his teeth in with her burner. She had waited in the stairwell of his mother's building and caught him taking a bag of trash to the incinerator, then she snuck up behind him and tried to crack his skull open. "That shit killed my lady, you stupid bitch!" she bashed him in the head again as he dropped the bag of garbage and sank down to his knees. "She's dead, niggah!" Chiney beat him in the face as he fell to the ground. "She's dead!"

"I'm sorry, Chiney," Fitted rolled over and mumbled through his bloody lips. He coughed and spit out a few shards of broken teeth before taking a deep breath through his nose and muttering again. "I didn't mean to kill nobody, Chiney. Vee was real cool with me. That's word."

"Then why you gimme me that bad shit?" she screamed, swinging her arm back to smash him in his grill again. "What the fuck did you put in it?"

"It wasn't me!" Fitted shouted. "I ain't fuck with none of that shit, girl! It was Lil Lee, man. She gave me some special shit to give to you! She mixed it up herself and told me to make sure you got double what you asked for."

"You *lyin'*!" Chiney smacked that niggah's nose over to the side of his face. "Lie again, muh'fucka! Go head! Lie again! I want you to," she aimed her gun toward his mother's apartment, "so I can walk right in that door and pump a cap up ya mama's narrow ass! Lil Lee ain't have nothing to do with it! That work you gave me had

Strawberry Snake on it! Y'all Divine Nine trap boyz don't even *sell* that type of shit!"

Fitted cringed as he thought about his dear mother sitting at her kitchen table about to get her back blown out. "We sell that shit now, goddamn it." He cupped his broken nose and got ready to tell Chiney all about Flex's grimy scheme to chase the meth fiends of Harlem away from Salida's bestselling product. "We sell it now."

$$$$$

I didn't know what kind of bug had gotten up Trey's ass but he was acting real funny. We were eating dinner in the kitchen when Chiney came in the house crying and said she needed to speak to him in private. Her and Trey had gone in her bedroom and stayed back there for a real long time with the door closed up tight.

I had sat out in the kitchen by myself eating some Chinese food, and when they finally did come outta the room Trey was real quiet and there was a dark look in his eyes that kinda put me on edge.

"You said you was gonna help me get Nooni out of the G-Spot, remember?" I said softly as he sat down in front of his cold Chinese food. I hated to bring it up while he was looking so intense, but every day Nooni spent trapped below ground in the G-Spot was a day she moved closer to her grave. "You told me to wait until you handled all that stuff with Maleek and then you was gonna help me."

"I *am* gonna help you, Juicy," he said. "In due time, baby."

"In due time? When is that gonna be, Trey?"

"Soon," he said. "I need to handle some crucial business real quick tonight, and as soon as I'm done with that I'm gonna help you get Nooni out."

"But that's what you said the last time!" I snapped. "First you had to handle Maleek and now you got some other 'business' that's more important than Nooni!"

I sucked my teeth and got up from the table and snatched my paper plate.

"That's okay, Trey," I said, talking shit as I flung my food in the garbage can. "Thanks, but no thanks! I don't need *nobody* to help me do what I gotta do!"

"C'mon, Juicy. Don't be like that, baby. I'ma help you as soon as I get back tonight, baby. I promise."

"Nah, that's all right. I'm good, *baby*," I said sarcastically as I switched my ass up outta the kitchen. "Thank you very much."

$$$$$

Traffic was thick and Sallie was cruising deep in the heart of Harlem when he peeped them. Two cop cars. One marked, one unmarked. Both of them were a couple of cars behind him, but they were definitely on his ass. Panic jumped into Sallie's throat and his mouth went bone dry. His eyes darted around as he searched for a possible escape route. He cut a hard right at the next corner and pulled over in front of a fire hydrant. Hauling the heavy-ass bag of loot from his back seat, Sallie knew better than to venture down the congested block filled with drug dealers and violent junkies. Instead, he abandoned his car and fled around the corner to the main avenue and quickly ducked into a crowded pizza shop.

Pushing through the door, he bowled over two young chicks who immediately started yapping at the mouth and cursing him out.

"Damn, muthafucka! Watch where the fuck you goin', yo!"

Ignoring them and their loud ghetto noises, Sallie got on line behind a fat black lady and hid behind her as he peered out of the plate glass window. He breathed a sigh of relief as he watched the two cop cars drive slowly past the shop. He followed them with his eyes as far as he could, and he was grateful as their tail lights faded into the distance.

With his eyes glued nervously to the window, Sallie hoisted the heavy bag to his other shoulder and snapped his cell phone off his waist clip. Pressing a number on speed dial, he took a deep breath when Monique answered on the second ring.

"Boy where the hell are you?" she sounded damn near as panicked as he felt.

"I'm on my way," he reassured her as he moved forward in the line and craned his neck, still searching out the window for cop cars. "I'm coming, baby. I had to make a quick stop at the pizza shop. You want me to bring you a slice?"

"A slice?" Monique damn near shrieked. "I been waiting on you all goddamn day and you wanna bring me a slice? I thought you left town without me, Sallie! Hell nah I don't want no goddamn slice! I wanna get *outta here!*"

"It's all good, baby, I would never leave without you. I promise—" Sallie paused, suddenly distracted as he narrowed his eyes and peered out the window again. A small crowd of sexily dressed corner hoes had started gathering outside and they were looking inside the pizza shop and pointing their fingers.

Right at him.

"Shit!" Sallie cursed as he recognized one of the girls standing out there. She was leaning on crutches and she was actually one of the chicks that he had almost knocked down as he rushed to get inside the pizza shop.

"So what time do you want me to catch a cab over to the Chinese restaurant?"

"Shit!" Sallie said again.

"Shit?" Monique barked into the phone. "*Shit*?"

"My bad, baby," Sallie said quickly as he eyed the crowd of chicks that was growing outside. "I was thinking about something else. Check it out," he said as he stepped up to the counter to place his order. "If you don't want no pizza, then how about I bring you a nice hot knish?"

"Hell nah," Monique said catching an even bigger attitude. "I don't want no nasty-ass knish! Bring me a beef patty instead."

CHAPTER 16

Ace and Pluto carried the large black containers downstairs and headed toward the back door of the G-Spot, but as soon as they got outside in the alley Pluto realized his mistake.

"Ay, we gonna hafta take your ride, man," he said, kicking himself up the ass. He had forgotten all about the two big-ass suitcases in the trunk of his sedan. Wasn't no way in fuck he was gonna get these huge containers full of meth in his ride too, and he couldn't take the suitcases out in front of Ace neither.

"C'mon, now niggah! I thought *you* was driving. What's the matter with your whip?" Ace asked looking puzzled.

"I'on't know. My shit keeps cuttin' off on me," Pluto lied. "Might be the ignition switch."

Damn! This was fucked up! If he didn't drive his own car to Jersey then that meant he was gonna have to leave his whip and his suitcases at the G-Spot when he dipped and catch a ride to the airport after the meeting with Moonie!

"Yeah," Pluto played his lie all the way through, "that shit was actin' like it didn't wanna start before I left to come over here. I don't trust it. We don't need to be takin' no chances on the road while we holdin' all this work."

Ace bucked. "Damn, muh'fucka! You shoulda told me this shit before!"

"I just fuckin' did!" Pluto blasted back. *Fuck them suitcases*, he fumed. After he robbed this here niggah he'd have plenty of bank to go shopping with! He could replace all that shit!

"C'mon, ak," he fronted as he headed toward Ace's ride gripping the bottom of his container. "This shit is heavy as hell! What Salida got in these things? Bricks?"

Ace frowned for a quick second then he shrugged and started hauling his container toward his flashy money-green Hummer too.

"A'ight, my niggah. But you know my whip gets a whole lotta attention. I figured we was gonna need to fly real fuckin' low considering how much work we holding, ya dig?"

"Yeah," Pluto nodded and shrugged again. "I feel you, ak. Just drive slow and don't be runnin' no red lights or nothin' and we gone be a'ight."

After loading the containers into the back of the Hummer, Pluto settled his large frame in on the passenger side of Ace's ride. His manz shit was sweet and flashy all right. It was butter-smooth and spotless inside and out.

Leaning back in his seat, Pluto put his hand over the spot on his waist where a hard bulge of metal shoulda been. He felt real naked without his trusted burner. He had given that shit to his lil young buck Freeze so he could blast Ace's skull open when he showed up in the East Village to put in that work.

Half a fuckin' mil. Pluto smiled inside. He was a clever muh'fucka if he had to say so himself! Because the minute they handed off that meth and got that moolah in their hands, he was gonna reach down in his trickbag and pull out some revenge on one of the greasiest muh'fuckas he knew!

$$$$$

Charmaigne's Polish-American restaurant was located off East 13th Street, just a couple of blocks away from Stuyvesant Park. Ace pushed his sparkling green whip down the FDR Drive at a moderate speed, being careful not to draw any unnecessary attention with his driving.

Charmaigne's was one of those greasy East Village joints that had a loyal following of Polish customers who loved the old-country food that reminded them of their homeland. The drug distributor that Salida did business with was the owner's oldest son, and him and his sister not only cooked the food and ran the restaurant, they also distributed cut-rate meth all over the country.

"Yo, that's a lotta shit Salida's gotta dish off at a bargain, my dude," Pluto said, making idle convo as Ace threaded the Hummer through the traffic. He angled his head toward the back of the whip. "How much cash you think it's gonna bring in?" he asked again, even though he had already been told.

"A gwap," Ace admitted. "At least five hunnerd g's. Even at the discounted rate."

Pluto whistled greedily. He could chill with his lil snow bunny Coco for a long fuckin' time offa that much doe.

"But it's all good," Ace said, "'cause that's Salida's bank. Hers and the connect's, if Moonie hooks us up the way we want that niggah to."

Pluto nodded agreeably but inside he was screaming, *Fuck Salida! Fuck that connect! And fuck you too, you pussy-whipped lil snake!*

Ace drove carefully as they approached the restaurant. They cruised past the front door at a slow clip and double-parked outside.

"Whattup?" Pluto said, staring out the window with his eyes darting back and forth. The restaurant's iron shutters were rolled up and he could see right through the clear plate-glass window and there wasn't a soul in sight.

"Yo, ain't nobody in there, man. That shit looks closed."

"Nah," Ace said quickly as he stepped on the gas and pulled around the corner and into the side alley. "They open, ak. Salida told dude we was gonna be here around this time. You just gotta go around to that door on the side back there and knock, that's all. Ga'head back there and knock."

Pluto got out and did it, but three minutes later Ace was still sitting in the ride with the dope while Pluto stood in the filthy alley banging his fast fist on the side door.

With visions of half a million big ones dancing in his head, Pluto watched the alley and pounded on that shit until his knuckles felt cracked. Then he turned around and mule-kicked that shit with one foot. The door rattled in its frame, but nobody came to open it.

Glancing toward the whip, Pluto strode outta the alley and walked around to the front of the restaurant. He yanked at the door, but it was locked too. Cupping his hands to the window he peered inside. It looked like people had been sitting around eating but then everybody had gotten up and left in a hurry. Plates of food and shit were still on the tables, and glasses and more plates was all over the long counter, but otherwise the joint was deserted.

"Yo, what kinda shit is this?" Pluto wondered out loud as his eyes scanned up and down the street. "These muh'fuckas ain't even clean up from last night yet!"

A knot of rage and disappointment sat heavy on his chest as the thought of missing out on five hunnerd g's clouded his mind. Checking his watch, Pluto yanked out his cell phone and punched in a number.

"Niggah where you at!"

"I'm on the highway, man! We got a flat!"

Pluto cursed. "We *who*, niggah? Who the fuck is *we*?"

"Me and Bilal. He was already headin' out that way so I caught a ride wit' him."

Stupid muh'fucka! Pluto fumed. "Yo, you was supposed to be here by now and you was supposed to come by ya muthafuckin' *self*! Hurry the fuck up and get here, fool! Hurry the fuck *up*!"

Hanging up, Pluto stormed back into the alley and snatched open the whip's door.

"Ay, niggah! You sure this the right place man?"

"Hell yeah!" Ace said as he craned his neck and peeped outta the window and down the alley. "This the fuckin' place, P. I been here with Salida before. Dude is gonna show. He should be pulling up in a minute."

"Well," Pluto said, climbing his bulk back into the whip, "ain't nobody in there right fuckin' now! Yo, hold up. You got dude's number, right? Call that fool!"

"I did already." Ace said, holding his cell phone up in the air and looking mad as fuck. "I called him three fuckin' times, man. He ain't picking up."

Pluto shook his head as he saw his big plan going up in smoke. "I don't know what kinda game these Polish fools is playing but we ridin' too dirty to be fuckin' around out here like this. We gotta get rid of this meth and pick up that money, son."

Ace looked furious in the face. His eyes were glued on the entrance that led into the alley. Cars were swishing by left and right up on the avenue, but not a single one turned in. Finally, after about fifteen minutes he glanced toward the empty restaurant and said, "I tell you what. Let's go take that ride to Jersey and get with Moonie and the connect real quick, and then on the way back we can swing through here again. And if that greasy Polish sausage ain't waiting here with the cash when we get back then we find out where he lives and roll up at his fuckin' crib and smoke him!"

Pluto had no choice but to sit his fat ass back in the Hummer and chill.

Calm ya ass the fuck down, he told himself as he took a few deep breaths. Even the best of plans sometimes got delayed, but this little pebble thrown in the game wasn't gonna stop no show.

Ere'thang was still gonna be ere'thang.

All he had to do was text his lil niggah Freeze and tell him to meet him at the restaurant a little later, that's all. Yeah, Pluto was prolly gonna miss his flight to Chi-Town but there'd be other flights. His plan was still his plan and Ace was still a dead man. Pluto was gonna roll with his homeboy over to the hotel to wheel and deal with G' cocaine connect, and then when they swung back through the East Village and got their hands on that all that meth money, he'd smoke him.

CHAPTER 17

Ace didn't look it on the outside, but on the inside he was sweatin' the fuck outta the change in their plans. Traffic was gonna be too heavy to fuck with the Holland Tunnel, so he zipped over the George Washington Bridge steering with one hand and texting like crazy with the other.

"Yo, drive with two hands, niggah!" Pluto bitched as Ace swerved all outta his lane. "You can text that bitch later, fool."

"You over there textin' too, niggah! Besides, Salida needs to know her Polish boy done fucked around and left us hangin'," Ace said as he used one thumb to click away on his cell phone. "I'm telling her to holla at that muh'fucka and tell him he better be there waitin' with that paper when we get back tonight."

Pluto frowned, then nodded. "Yeah tell her to make that muh'fucka bring us a little sumpthin' extra for wasting our fuckin' time too, yo."

"I'ma do that," Ace said, steady texting. "Word, slime. I'ma tell her that shit."

But in reality Ace wasn't telling Salida a damn thing. Because while Pluto had been out there in the alley bammin' on the restaurant's side door, Ace had called his dun dun Bilal and blasted him for being late for the scheduled execution.

"Ya fuckin' ass is *late*!" he had hissed into his cell phone as Pluto stood out there kicking on the door just like a lil kid. Salida had gone through a lotta fuckin' trouble and laid down a whole lotta doe to get these Polish fools to close up their restaurant and clear out the goddamn alley! Bilal had been paid good money to creep up on the side door and sink a slug in the back of Pluto's dome, but instead that fool was on the phone stuttering about him and Freeze being stuck on the highway with a flat fuckin' tire!

"Freeze? Who told you to bring that pussy-niggah along for the ride???"

Ace was mad as hell. And while he had been pretending to text Salida just now, he had really been texting Bilal directions to the hotel in Jersey so dude could meet him out there and finish off this job and get this murder *done*!

Traffic was light and it didn't take no time at all to get to Newark. Moonie had sent them a message to check into the Howdy Motel and it was only a few miles away from the exit.

"Dig," Pluto muttered. "We ain't been down with Moonie in a minute, yo. You still trust that niggah like that?"

Ace shook his head so fast his cheeks jiggled. "Hell fuckin' nah. I don't trust *no* fuckin' body, ak. *Nobody*."

The Howdy Motel was right next door to a busy Mickey D's and Ace spotted it right away. Stalling for time to give Bilal a chance to catch up after changing his flat, he drove past the motel on the first go by and circled around the block again. The second time he approached it he actually pulled into the parking lot and drove around the building twice before pulling back out on the street. Then he got right back on the highway and drove down two exits before turning around and heading back again.

It was only after their fourth sweep and much reconning of the area did Ace park his whip in the front of the building and get ready to go inside the cheap motel.

"Yo, we can't both go in and leave them containers out here," Ace said, angling his head toward the rear of the Hummer where the drugs were stashed.

"Hell nah, man," Pluto quickly agreed. "That's way too much cheese to let outta ya sight, partner."

Pluto waited in the whip with the drugs while Ace went inside and paid for a room. He was being real fuckin' funny when he signed his name as Mister Mass Murderer on the registration card, but the young desk clerk who was talking on her cell phone and flipping through a magazine didn't even bother to read that shit.

The motel was only three stories high and the entrance to all the rooms was from the outside balcony. Ace got the key and went upstairs and checked shit out. The room was old but clean, not that he gave a fuck. Going over to the window, he pulled the curtain back slightly and peeped down at his money-green Hummer. It was parked right under a streetlight and he could see his manz still waiting patiently in the front passenger seat.

Ace wiped a trail of sweat from his face, then pulled out his cell phone and punched in some digits. "Yo!" he barked when Bilal answered. "Where you at? Your stupid ass got ten fuckin' minutes to get here and put in this work so hurry the fuck up!"

With his murderous plan once again set in motion, Ace went back downstairs to help Pluto carry up the containers full of drugs. They wheezed up the iron steps, and when they got in the room Pluto plopped down in a chair and Ace collapsed on the cheap sofa as the breeze from the air conditioner blasted over them.

"Whattup now?" Pluto said after a few minutes.

"Dig, Moonie s'posed to call us and let us know which room to come to. We sit tight until we get that call."

Pluto glanced at his watch. He had a fuckin' flight to catch. After they went back to that restaurant and picked up all that money first, that is.

"Ay, that niggah need to hur' the fuck up and call. It's already late as hell."

"Yeah," Ace said, rising to his feet. He stuck his car keys down in his pocket and then stretched his arms over his head and yawned. His big belly jiggled like a muthafucka as it hung low over his waistband.

"Dig, watch the dope for a minute, slime. I'ma slide across the way and get me a Big Mac real quick. You want somethin'?"

Pluto frowned. "Damn! You gots'ta eat *right now*, niggah? We got bizz to handle, son! What if Moonie and them show up while you gone?"

Ace snorted. "Hell yeah, I gotta eat *right* now! Shit, I'm only going across the way! If them niggahs show up just tell 'em I'll be right back!"

Ace busted the look of suspicion that crossed his dawg's face and smirked, "But hey. If you gonna sit there and wet up ya panties then I'll stay here and *you* can run across the way and pick up some grub."

Shaking his head quickly, Pluto frowned again. "Nah, you go." He wasn't about to leave his ex-partner alone with half a mil worth of meth *and* the fuckin' car keys. It wasn't happenin'.

"Yeah," he said, settling back in the comfortable arm chair. "You ga'head. I'll wait. Matter fact, bring me back a Big Mac too, muh'fucka," he said coolly. "And throw in two apple pies."

$$$$$

Biting into a hot calzone, Sallie walked out of the pizza shop carrying his duffle bag full of money on his back and cradling Monique's hot Jamaican Beef Patty in his hand. He tried to pretend that his attention was focused strictly on his food, but there was no way to ignore the big crowd of junkie-looking hoes who were leaning against parked cars and light poles and talking big shit.

"Hey white boy! You remember me?"

Sallie kept his eyes on his calzone as he beat feet toward the corner with the mob of street yummies following close behind him.

"Yeah he remember you!" an older woman's voice rang out as all the other hoes hyped her on. "You one of them white niggahs who like to kick black ass, ain't you honkie boy! Well you done fucked with the wrong hoe this time, *beeaatchhhh*!"

The prostitutes laughed and talked shit behind him as they closed in on his stride.

Slick Sallie's steps were long and quick as he rounded the corner and headed toward his car. He was reaching for the passenger door handle when he felt an explosion rock the right side of his temple. The calzone and the beef patty went flying from his hands, and as he sank to his knees under the force of the blow, his stomach clenched with nausea and he realized his head had been flown by a baseball bat.

"What the fu—" was all he managed to mumble outta his mouth as the gang of painted-up hookers swarmed on his ass, kicking, punching, scratching, and beating the shit outta him any which way they could. Sallie screamed and tried to cover his head with his duffle bag as the crazy black bitches swung sticks, threw bricks, and even cracked open beer bottles on the curb and stabbed at his arms and legs with the sharp, jagged edges.

"Yeah! Karisma gonna be the *last* fuckin' ho you pull that shit on!" A bright-skinned woman with big titties and a fat face shouted. "Get him, Karisma! Get over here and fuck his ass up!"

Hot rage surged through Slick Sallie as the young bitch whose pussy he had feasted on raised one of her crutches in the air and started wailing on his back and legs in fury. He cried out loud as she swung her metal pole down on him like she was chopping firewood, and all Sallie could do was shriek and scurry beneath his duffle bag and try to ball himself up into the smallest knot possible as a crowd of junkies and winos gathered around to witness the slaughter.

"Monique!" he cried out his baby's name as a tall street-walker grabbed the other crutch and started cracking him up and down his spine. He cried even louder and tried to flip over onto his back as she started jabbing the tip of the crutch deep into the crack of his ass, tryna poke it up his dookie-shoot right through his pants!

It seemed like they beat on him forever and ever, and each time one of them tried to yank his duffle bag away so they could get at him better, Sallie would use what was left of his strength to wrench it back and hide under it again as he begged for mercy. But these hoes were merciless. They were hot and brutal as they beat him viciously non-stop, and Sallie didn't know how much longer he could hang on.

He was starting to give up and fade out when a sneaker slammed into the side of his face, and then the sharp pain of broken glass sinking into his upper thigh sent stars exploding behind his eyes. One of the hookers plopped her ass down on top of his duffle bag and started banging his face into the concrete so hard that his front tooth cut right through his lip, filling his mouth with warm, salty blood. Sallie was almost done. He was real close to blacking completely out when he heard a man's deep voice commanding the prostitutes to fall back.

It took a few more kicks and stomps before them crazy chicks obeyed him, but just a couple of moments later Sallie found himself being helped to his feet by a tall, massive-muscled gangsta who looked like he'd just got outta the joint where he'd been eating heavy weights for three meals every day.

"Damn! What the fuck you do to them bitches?" the dude asked in a Haitian accent as he lifted Sallie under the arms and tried to hold him up on his feet. Sallie swayed as he heaved his duffle bag onto his back, and all he felt was pain as blood ran down his face and into his eyes and he stumbled over to his car damn near blind.

"Don't be helping his ass, Gutta!" the prostitutes hollered when they saw Sallie was gonna get away. "This the trick who fucked Karisma up! Uh-uh Gutta! This cracker right here beats on hoes!"

Slick Sallie's hand shook badly as he fumbled to get his key in the lock while the crowd of wild women screamed and threatened to finish his ass off.

"No!" Sallie mumbled through his busted mouth and broken teeth as the thick-necked Haitian dude tried to hold his duffle bag for him while he unlocked the car door. "No! I got it!"

He groaned in pain as he opened the car door and pushed the heavy bag full of money into his passenger seat, and then he flung himself down behind the steering wheel. He had just managed to stick the key in the ignition and fire up the engine when the gang of crazy black bitches ran up on him tryna get a little goodbye love.

The hoes swarmed around his car, banging on his windows and trying to kick dents in the body of his ride. Sallie clenched the gear stick and shoved it in drive, then he turned the wheel into traffic and straight-up floored that baby, giving not a damn if he put a black bitch up on his bumper or flattened her dirty ass under his squealing tires.

The car lurched forward with sudden movement, and then to Sallie's horror the engine coughed twice, then flat-out died and shut completely off. His whip was drifting slowly out into the middle of the street when,

BOOM!

An incredibly powerful blast shattered his windows and a bright flash of light enveloped the entire car and shot thirty feet up in the air, taking chunks of burning metal with it.

Screams of fear and anguish rang out in the warm Harlem night, but Slick Sallie McCain never even heard them. The explosion that had rocked his car and blown his engine straight through the roof took Sallie's head with it and sent his bloody brains, along with the contents of his precious duffle bag, raining down all over the car, the street, and the sidewalks of New York.

The shock wave and shrapnel from the delayed ignition bomb that Slick Sallie's uncle Frank had rigged in his car left three hoes laying dead in the street, but the moment the smoke started clearing the other hookers sprang into action with the quickness of true city slickstas. They fought through the heavy smell of gunpowder and twisted-up metal, and scrambled around the wreckage snatching up the scattered hundred dollar bills, some ripped and burning, but many others fully intact, grabbing as many pieces of precious green paper as they could get their desperate little hands on.

And as the sirens of emergency vehicles began sounding in the distance, every dollar that had been left over from Granite McKay's massive stash of ill-gotten cash was snatched up by the junkies, winos, and whores of Harlem and returned to their rightful hands.

CHAPTER 18

It was almost time to head out to the G-Spot and Flex couldn't wait to stomp up in that muh'fucka pressed out in gangsta-white from head to toe. He had put on a pearl-white double-breasted suit he had special ordered from France, and slipped his feet into his white, thirty-thousand dollar Amedeo Testoni alligator shoes. He'd bought a bottle of top shelf cologne that cost more than a yard an ounce, and he had laid out a grip for a diamond-studded white top hat that had a smoove-ass dove feather laid against the side.

The rest of his crew had already headed over to the G-Spot, and Flex had his dun dun Dabu standing by to chauffeur him across town in a fresh-outta-the-showroom white Maserati with gangsta whitewalls and shiny chrome spinners.

The only thing about Flex Boykin that wasn't gonna be white when he hit the G-Spot was the black onyx ring that he wore on his finger. It was an exact match for the shade of black greed that he carried in his cold-blooded young heart.

Flex and his crew had put in some long hard hours tryna coordinate this take-over real lovely, and by the end of the night their hard work was gonna payoff a thousand fold. Ere' last one of his soldiers was thoroughly trained and ready to go to war when they got out there on the battlefield in the G-Spot Social Club, and like all good commanders-in-chief Flex was gonna lead the charge and cut his unsuspecting enemies off at the neck.

The only thing that was even slightly outta order right now was the fact that he'd had to make that last minute stand in for his number Nine capo, Lil Lee. But even that was cool. Flex was gonna have Boobie strut up in the club hanging off his arm looking like a stunning piece of dick-rockin' eye candy, but rolling like a brutal killer in a drug cartel.

He had paid a designer ten large to sew Lil Lee a foxy-ass evening gown made from a piece of fabric that matched his white suit to a tee. Her gorgeous calves woulda been set off by a pair of Italian stilettos with diamond buckles on the side, and her innocent-looking face and fuckable body woulda been the perfect camouflage for a vicious, go-for-the-guts hood assassin.

That key element of his plan woulda had to get completely tossed if it wasn't for Boobie being down to put on that dress and take her sister's place. She wasn't as pretty as Lil Lee in the face, but she had all-day titties and an ass on her that could make a niggah's head swirl. And not only was Boobie the type of ride-or-die soldier who could be trusted to follow orders, she was pretty damn good at slicin' throats and splittin' skulls too.

$$$$$

Ace jetted outta the motel room and let out a big sigh of relief. The smell of greasy hamburgers and salty fries drifting across the parking lot from McDonald's wafted up his nose and made his stomach growl.

"Aw, *damn!*" he said as he peeped a little old lady who was taking her time tryna climb down the motel's steps. She was a wide-assed old white woman and she was holding onto both rails and had a cane hooked over one of her wrists.

Ace frowned as he got up behind her. The old chick was going down just like a baby. One foot at a time.

Move bitch! MOVE!

Ace didn't have no time to waste. His lil dun dun Bilal was gonna be rolling through with his burner cocked in just a few minutes, and he had to make sure shit went down the right way this time!

He grilled the top of the old lady's gray head. One foot, step. *Pause. Pause. Pause. Pause.* One foot, step. *Pause. Pause. Pause. Pause.*

At the rate her ancient ass was moving Ace figured it was gonna take him at least an hour to get down to the ground floor, and that shit pissed him off. He got up even closer behind her and started breathing fire down her fuckin' neck. He wanted to push her flabby ass down the steps, or at least karate chop the bitch's wrinkled-up hand so she could let go of the rail and let him slide past. But then he thought about his own dead grandmama, and how it had been his fault that she had gotten her wig split when the cops came gunning for him right after G got murked.

"I'm sorry, young man," the old white lady stopped halfway down the steps and spoke to him sweetly over her shoulder. "I know I'm moving pretty slow today but that's because I was out dancing all last night!"

"That's okay, Grandma," Ace said, fake-laughing at her ol' corny-ass joke. "You ain't gotta rush. Take your time and just be careful you don't slip and fall, okay?"

Ace walked behind the old lady slow as hell. If he wasn't so fat he woulda jumped over the railing and beat her down to the bottom, but he was way too big for that kinda athletic shit. He prolly woulda hit that damn concrete and got up with two broken ankles.

It was a relief when they finally reached the bottom of the stairs, and by that time Ace was hungry for real. He left the old lady fiddling with her cane as he looked around for Bilal and checked his watch, then he jetted across the parking lot and through the doors of McDonald's.

The air was cool and crisp inside, and the smell of burgers and fries slid up his nose.

"Hurry up, muh'fuckas," he muttered under his breath as he waited in line to place his order.

"Yeah, lemme get a Big Mac, two cheeseburgers off the dollar menu, a large order of fries with extra salt, and a ice-tea."

Bring me back a Big Mac too, muh'fucka And throw in two apple pies.

Muthafuck Pluto and his apple pies! Ace thought with satisfaction. He wasn't getting that niggah *shit!* The next meal that fool ate was gonna be served in hell and come with a burning fork!

Five minutes later his food was packed into a large white bag and Ace pushed through the door and headed back toward the motel. He was almost halfway across the parking lot when he stopped to let a Mister Softee truck go by. The next step he took was a bad one 'cause outta nowhere he got bull-rammed hard from the left and his entire hip caved in.

"*Aaaah!*" he screamed as the impact tossed him into the air and white-hot pain shot straight through his hip and down into his ankle. The container full of sweet tea hit the ground and busted wide open, and his bag of food went flying from his hands as the fast food spilled out and scattered across the pavement.

"*Aaaah!*" Ace shrieked again, clutching his left hip. He was face down on the hood of a large sedan with the crack of his ass exposed to the moon. The same little old lady that he had followed down the stairs was peering at him through the windshield as she gripped the steering wheel with both hands and looked at him like, *what in the fuck is this big niggah doing on top of my car?*

Ace pushed himself up with his hands and tried his best to scoot off the hood, but the slightest movement sent another jolt of agony lancing through his shattered hip.

"Shit!" he gasped with pain, hurling himself sideways and using his good leg to support his weight. "You hit me, you blind old bitch!" he screamed on her. "You fuckin' *hit* me!"

But no sooner than the words came outta his mouth did Ace realize he had a much bigger problem than his spilled tea and broken-up hip.

His little accident had suddenly attracted big attention. People came runnin' outta everywhere to see what had happened, and when he glanced up at the balcony and toward the room where his ak Pluto was waiting, Ace spotted something that made his blood run cold.

Cops. Two of them muh'fuckas. Both of them was brothahs too. One was right outside his room door, and the other one was coming down the *stairs*.

"*Shit!*" Ace shrieked, pulling away from the hotel clerk who had run outside dressed in her little Howdy Motel shirt and was tryna help him stand up. Ace knew he had to get gone, and get gone quick.

"Lemme go, bitch!" he snapped as he pushed himself up and started hopping away on one foot. His hip was broke like fuck, he could tell. Somewhere underneath all his layers of jiggly fat there was some bone scraping against bone. He knew this for certain because every time his foot hit the ground a bolt of hot agony surged through his whole fuckin' body. "I said lemme go, goddammit bitch!" he screeched again as the motel clerk grabbed his arm told him she was calling an ambulance.

"Well *forget you* then!" her lil ghetto ass snapped. "I was just tryna help yo fat ass! You ain't gotta get shitty, *damn!*"

Sweating bullets and gritting his teeth, Ace hopped faster than shit as he tried to get as far away from the motel as he could. The cop up on the balcony started yelling something down to his partner, but Ace igged both of their asses and kept on hobbling. He was moving slow, but he was moving steady. He had made it past two more parked cars when he looked up and saw something that made his eyes light up and a wave of relief wash over him.

"Yo! Yo! *Yo!*" he jumped up and down on his good foot and waved his arms as a familiar sight greeted his desperate eyes.

It was his boy Bilal. Pushing Salida's white whip and coming to the rescue!

Ace hurled himself away from the parked car and hopped out into the middle of the lot. He peeked over his shoulder and saw one of the cops heading his way real fast. He waved frantically at his boy and the car slowed down as he started hopping toward the passenger door. But before he could get there an icicle of fear pierced his heart as the passenger window slid down and he saw that fool Freeze aiming a sinister-lookin' gat dead in his face.

"Niggah what the fuck is you doin'?" Ace squeaked as he ducked instinctively and fell to the ground. He looked up just in time to see the police officer rushing up on them real fast, but that bitch-ass niggah Freeze musta peeped the cop too because he hollered for Bilal to punch the gas pedal and them niggahs burned rubber getting outta that parking lot.

There wasn't shit Ace could do but lay there like a scared fat baby, helplessly on his back as the cop charged at him. His shit was so fucked up that Ace almost wanted to laugh as he held his hands up in surrender.

"Officer!" Ace hollered, tryna play a role as the other Black cop ran up and stood over him with his heat drawn too. "Thank God y'all are here! Can you get me a ambulance, my dude? I just got hit by a blind fuckin' old lady driving a raggedy ass hoopty, word! Can you be'lee that shit? I just got *hit*!"

Ace's eyes got real wide when he realized he was staring down the barrels of two big black burners. He glanced up at the nametags and logos on the shiny silver badges that both cops wore. Both of them said,

GAINES. NYPD.

Them niggahs looked just alike and right away Ace knew what time it was.

The cops lunged at him and started punchin' and kickin' the shit outta him left and right. Ace couldn't hold back his screams as his hip seemed to burst into a million flames, and that shit hurt so deep and so bad that he actually peed on himself a little bit.

"Yo!" Ace screeched as he slithered around on the ground dodging their brutal kicks and blows. "Hold up! This ain't New York! This is *Jersey*!" he whined as he tried to ball up in a tiny fat knot. "Y'all niggahs ain't from Jersey!"

"Nah, muh'fucka," Dutchy Gaines snarled as he aimed his gat down at the fat piece of scum who had put that treacherous hit out on Rita and her little sisters. Dutchy's tool spit and jerked, sending fire exploding from the tip as he launched a heat round straight into Ace's forehead and X'd him straight out. "We some Harlem niggahs, my dude. We from *Harlem*."

$$$$$

Pluto had gotten the warning call while he was peeking out the window and waiting for Ace to get back with the food. He had heard some fumbling around at the door and figured Ace had his hands full of grub and couldn't get to his key, but when he pulled the curtain back a lil bit and peeked outside, he saw a blue boy walking away from his door and heading toward the stairs.

Pluto had almost shit. His eyes slid over to the two suitcases full of drugs and he broke out in a cold sweat. His cell phone vibrated and scared the shit outta him, and he snatched it off his clip in about two seconds flat.

"Get the fuck outta there, Big P!"

It was Freeze.

"Yo! Ace and Salida walked you into a trap, my dude! They hired Bilal to pop you! Get the fuck up outta there!"

"Shit!" Pluto barked as his life and his freedom flashed before his eyes. "Flip his ass!" he hollered into the phone. "Flip him! Tell Bilal to slide over to my team and I'll pay him double!"

He stuffed the phone in his pocket and jetted across the room to the two large containers. His black ass was gonna get planted *under* the fuckin' jail if them po-po caught him holdin' half a million big ones worth of meth!

He almost cried when he ripped the tape off the lid on the first container. Staring at him from the inside of that joint was nothing but a bunch of junk. A crusty toaster, a bunch of chipped red bricks, some beat-up old shoes, and some nasty cummed-up sheets that had come outta the fuck rooms at the G-Spot.

"Them *bastards*!" he shrieked as he grabbed the other container and damn near ripped the lid off with his bare hands. The same type of shit was stuffed inside this one too. A broken up blender, some old copies of *Black Booty* magazine, more heavy bricks, a dookie'd up toilet bowl brush, and a big musty pillow, all wrapped in a nasty G-Spot sheet.

Pluto knew what time it was, and for a real heavy niggah he moved like a ballerina. Jumping over the containers he ran for the door and almost tore that shit off the hinges. He peeked over the railing just in time to catch Ace screaming and causing a big commotion as he hopped across the parking lot on one foot. The next thing he saw was two Black cops, and they were heading fast in Ace's direction.

And that was all he fuckin' needed to see.

Pluto squatted down low and duck-walked down the pathway as he tried to find somewhere safe to hide. Getting downstairs without being peeped was outta the question, so he ran into a vending area and crammed all three hundred and seventy five pounds of his jiggling black ass into a small crack between a Coke machine and the wall.

And minutes later, after he heard the gunshots ringing out in the parking lot below, Pluto got another call from Freeze.

"What?" he wheezed when he was finally able to pry his phone outta his pocket.

"Come on downstairs," Freeze told him. "Them cops just slumped Ace and took the fuck off! That niggah's wig got twisted, man! That fool is done!"

CHAPTER 19

Back in his bedroom Trey cleaned both of his Glocks and oiled the chambers, and then he changed into a pair of baggy jeans and a long-sleeved shirt. He pulled his thick dreadlocks back and put on a comfortable pair of Timbs as he strapped up and got ready to hit the streets.

The story that Chiney had beaten outta that trap boy Fitted was disturbing on several levels. Not only was Flex and the Divine Nine tryna amass the biggest chunk of Harlem's drug trade ever, they were feeding unsuspecting junkies lethal doses of rat poison as they tried to squeeze the G-Spot crew outta their stronghold on crystal ice.

And if that wasn't bad enough he had gotten a call from Mrs. Washington, the busy old lady who kept her nose in everything in the neighborhood. She was crying her eyes out when she told Trey that Mayhem's mother had just passed away. The poor woman had been eaten alive by cancer and she had died without even knowing that her baby boy, Maleek, was already dead.

Trey walked past Juicy as he headed for the front door. She was coming out of the bathroom and he wanted to reach out and hold her in his arms but she still looked mad. Instead, he put all of his love in his eyes and hoped she could feel it as he gave her a deep, lingering look.

Juicy rolled her eyes and looked away as she brushed past him, and Trey watched her back as she stormed inside her room and slammed the door.

"Juicy," he called out to her. "Juicy."

She didn't answer, but Trey knew she had heard him.

"I love you, Juicy," he muttered as he headed toward the door, knowing that this time she really didn't hear him. "I love you, girl."

Taking a deep breath, he forced himself to push his woman outta his mind so he could focus all of his attention on the work at hand. Mayhem's whole family was dead now, but Trey's family was still here. And he was planning on keeping them here too. Fuck depending on Moonie and Frank to work the plan they had come up with in Virginia. Because the only way Trey could assure the safety of Juicy and Chiney, the two people he loved most in this world, was to walk up on Fletcher Boykin and blast a hole in his heart.

And that's exactly what he was gonna do.

$$$$$

Boobie turned into the parking lot in the back of Three Brothers Funeral Home and killed the engine on her flashy red Ford 250. Hurrying, she glanced at her watch and hopped down outta the truck smelling good and lookin' like a big-titty cover model for *Ass Almighty* magazine.

Flex's newest capo in the Divine Nine posse was ready to prove herself as an invaluable member of the set, and even though she was worried about her sister, she wasn't mad about the opportunity to play a role in a take-down mission that was gonna change the flow of power in Harlem forever.

Boobie was so focused on getting inside that funeral home and proving to Flex that he had gotten him a number-one draft pick when he chose her to replace Lil Lee, that she never even noticed when a tall, ferocious-looking killer stepped out from behind a shiny black hearse and followed her through the door.

$$\$\$\$\$\$$

There was something about Boobie that reminded Trey of his dead sister Charlene, but that didn't stop him from rolling up behind her and smashing his pistol across the back of her skull.

"Reach for it," he said as she yelped and her hand shot down to the small of her back where her burner was tucked. He'd caught her going through the service entrance of the Three Brother's Funeral Home where all the dead bodies rolled through.

"Ga'head," Trey said calmly, pressing the barrel of his gat deep into the soft skin of her neck. "Go for your shit, baby. I'll wait."

Boobie sneered at him over her shoulder. The look on her pretty face was as vicious and deadly as Trey had seen on any man's, and he knew if this chick had beaten him to the drop she woulda twisted his cap back real nice for him.

"Check this shit out while you squirming," Trey said, pushing his cell phone under her nose. He clicked on a video and watched Boobie's eyes get wide as what she saw made her blood run cold.

It was her three-year-old son. He was wearing the Batman pajamas she had put on him when she put him to bed at her mama's crib earlier that night. Man-Man looked real sleepy as he rested his head on the shoulder of the strange black dude who was carrying him down the steps of his grandmother's front porch.

"What that tell you? Huh? *Huh*?" Trey said, snatching his phone back.

A single tear of rage rolled down Boobie's cheek.

"You got my son, dude?" she sobbed bitterly. "My fuckin' *son*?"

"What? Your sister ain't tell you about me?" Trey said sounding surprised. "Baby ain't no fuckin' body off limits these days," he laughed and pushed her toward the basement steps, careful to keep his gun barrel kissed up real tight against her slender neck. "*No* fuckin' body."

He paused at the top of the steps.

"Lemme get that tool you holdin' real quick."

"What you want, Trey?" Boobie asked as she gave up her burner and stumbled down the steps totally under his control. The sight of her son had taken her initial fury and replaced it with hopeful cooperation. "What you want me to do?"

"I want you to decide which one of them cats you love the most," Trey stated bluntly. "Flex or ya lil shorty. Get me through that basement door, ya heard? Use the right codes and say all the proper words, baby girl. 'Cause if you fuck around and miss one step you gone have to buy lil Man-Man one of them itty-bitty caskets they keep in that storage room downstairs."

He shook his head and gave her a bitter look.

"I tried to *tell* y'all muh'fuckas," Trey said and pushed her forward again. "If one kid ain't safe ain't *no* kid safe."

CHAPTER 20

The G-Spot was jumpin' by the time Pluto got back to Harlem, and the Grand Re-Opening party was going on in full force. Freeze and Bilal had scooped him up down the street from the Howdy Motel and given him a ride to the Spot, where he snuck in the back door and then slipped inside a bathroom so he could lay low and try to figure out his next move.

Them two NYPD cops had definitely been on a manhunt out in Jersey. They had executed his manz Ace in cold fuckin' blood, and Pluto knew they woulda routed his brains out too if Freeze hadn't sent up a warning signal in time.

He wracked his brain tryna figure out exactly who besides Ace and Salida had put a hit out on him, and it wasn't long before the truth of it materialized. Yeah, Ace and Salida had set him up, just like Freeze said. They'd sold him a bullshit story about selling off all their meth just to get him alone in that alley where Bilal was supposed to stretch him out cold. The only problem was Bilal had caught a flat and Ace wasn't gully enough to pull the trigger his damn self. Ace didn't have no choice but to go ahead and ride out to Jersey after that, but while ya bullshittin, that fool had still been plannin' on smoking him. Ace woulda had Pluto's ass shot dead right there in that motel room if Freeze hadn't flipped Bilal, and them cops hadn't shown up looking to kill both of them.

Them fuckin' cops! Pluto shook his head at that one. There was no way in hell no New York City blue boys shoulda been rollin' that deep in New Jersey and poppin' niggahs off. The fact that they were that far outta their jurisdiction meant they had some high level crooks in both police departments who had given them a nod of approval and had turned their heads and looked the other way. There was only one reason Pluto could think of that some rogue New York City cops would want both him and Ace dead, and the name *Dutchy Gaines* flashed brightly in his mind.

Yeah, it had to be that fool Dutchy. It just had to be. That niggah had prolly slumped Ace in retaliation for that kick door his dun duns had pulled on Rita's crib when they was tryna get Nooni back. Shit had gone down all fucked up that night, and a couple of lil kids had ended up dead.

But how the fuck did Dutchy know him and Ace was gonna be waiting for Moonie at some raggedy off-the-road motel? Who the fuck had told him *that*? There wasn't a doubt in Pluto's mind that his melon was on the chopping block to be the next one split. And that meant he still had to dip. Even without the cash he had planned to steal from the sale of Salida's meth, he had to get the fuck outta New York City.

But before Pluto left he was gonna hafta play the last card he had up his sleeve.

There was more than one way to skin a fuckin' snake, and even if Pluto didn't have the kinda bank he needed, what he *did* have was knowledge. It was the Grand Re-Opening night and the G-Spot was packed out with ballers from one wall to the other one. The crowd was just as big as it used to be back when G was runnin' shit, and as of tonight the cover charge was once again a cool, crisp grand.

Pluto visualized all the bodies that were jamming in the house and did a quick mental calculation. *Sheeiiit*, the door alone was prolly gonna bring in over two hundred grand before the night was halfway through, and that wasn't counting all the sales they were gonna rack up from the liquor, the pussy, and the blow too.

My ass is gettin' paid, Pluto swore. He knew the G-Spot operations inside and out, and he knew what he had to do. The cash cage was gonna have to be emptied at least three times before the night was over, and that money was gonna be taken straight into G's office and stashed in his safe to be counted up after the club closed.

Pluto was gonna hafta hit that safe.

He was gonna have to get in that office and open that safe, and then stick Salida's ass up for every penny the G-Spot raked in. Of course he was gonna have to time his move just right and hit the safe in between the second money drop and the third one, but that wasn't a problem. He was gonna be patient and lay in the cut until the time was just right, and then he was gonna empty that fuckin' safe and get the hell outta town.

$$$$$

As soon as Trey left the house I dialed Pluto's cell phone and got him on the line.

"Yeah." His voice sounded funny and I heard a muffled echo. Like he was in a closet or a small bathroom or something.

"Pluto, it's Juicy. I got in touch with Moonie and I did just what you told me to do," I lied.

There was a big long pause on the line. Like he could see right through my bullshit story.

"Yeah? So?"

I stared down at the phone.

"So I got you the hook-up like I said I would! Moonie's gonna call you and set up a meeting with G's connect. Now all I need you to do is what you said you was gonna do."

There was another pause on the line like his fat ass was thinking hard.

"You fulla shit, Juicy. Get up outta my ear with that bullshit girl."

"Hold up!" I started protesting like I was telling the God's honest truth. "I had to go through a lotta shit to find Moonie and convince him to hook you up! You said if I did all that y'all would let Nooni go!"

"You really want that lil bitch?"

"Yeah! I want her!"

I heard him chuckle. It didn't sound funny. It sounded diabolical.

"Well you betta come and get her ass then. I'm about to blow this joint Juicy-Mo, and if you ain't here before I dip then you might as well not come 'cause that lil run-through chick is prolly gonna be dead."

$$$$$

Pluto hung up the phone, then snuck outta the bathroom and made his way into the front of the club. He checked hard for Salida but she was nowhere to be seen. He kept his eyes on rotate and tried to blend in with the crowd as he walked through the room and over to the crowded bar where he slid pushed through the gate and took a key out of a small drawer that was hidden beneath the main cash register. He knew Juicy was lying through her damn teeth about hooking him up with Moonie, but he also knew why Dutchy Gaines was on the hunt for his ass, and he figured letting Nooni go might just buy him a lil time, and maybe even a lil mercy.

"Ummm... *what the fuck is you...*" Bizzie said from behind him, and Pluto turned around and busted the suspicious look in the bartender's mascara'd up eyes.

"Fuck you lookin' at?" Pluto lifted his chin and grilled his swishy ass. He could tell by the look on dude's face that Ace and Salida had already flipped this fool and he was workin' for the other team.

"Yo, gimme a goddamn beer and get the fuck outta my face," Pluto said, getting swole as Bizzie shook like a bitch and jumped right to it. Pluto snatched the icy bottle the bartender held out to him and then pried the metal cap off with his back teeth and spit that shit dead in Bizzie's face.

"Bitch ass!" Pluto muttered as he stomped outta the bar area and pushed his way back through the crowd and walked past G's office. Swigging from his brew, he used the key he'd just taken from the bar to unlock the door leading down to The Dungeon. A foul blast of funky hot air hit him as he yanked the heavy door open, and even though he almost gagged and choked on his brew, Pluto took a deep breath as he stepped into the darkness and headed down the stairs anyway.

CHAPTER 21

C'mon, you fat-faced fuck!" Salida bitched as she stood looking in the mirror in G's private bathroom and blowing up Ace's phone. She had been calling his ass for the longest but he wasn't picking up and she couldn't understand why. By now Pluto shoulda been a dead-ass dog, and Ace's meeting with Moonie and the connect shoulda been over. Even if traffic was heavy coming over the bridge, he still should have made it back to the G-Spot by now.

Especially since it was their biggest night of the year. Sometimes being a control freak was a real good thing because if Salida had'a been depending on Ace to help her launch the Grand Re-Opening she would have been shit out of luck. She had single-handedly organized the entire affair from the bottom to the top, and judging by the packed out crowd that was out there getting their party on she had done a damn good job too.

Salida tried Ace's number one more time and then she clicked off her phone. She didn't know where the hell he was, but there was champagne to be poured, pussy to be sold, and a whole lotta cash money to be made.

She smiled inside. She had just supervised another large transfer of money from the cashier's cage to the safe in her office. One more large haul of cash like that and she was gonna have to start sticking money all up in her bra and in her shoes because the safe was gonna be completely full.

She thought about Ace again. If his ass didn't show up soon somebody was gonna have to go looking for him. But in the meantime she needed to get back out there to her high-rolling customers and get her floss on and bask in the limelight of her success.

Salida was proud of herself. Proud of the power she had earned and the money she had stacked. All them celebrities, politicians, hustlers, and Fortune 500 mothafuckas out there partying had come back to the G-Spot because of *her*. *She* was the one who had built this baby up after them fools let it fall apart. *She* was the one who had put her foot down on some necks and got shit under control. *She* was the one who'd been smart enough to figure out how to make a dollar outta fifteen fuckin' cents!

Yeah, she'd come a long damn way since Granite had locked her ass up in that sanatorium all those years ago. She coulda fuckin' died up in there! She coulda lived the rest of her life as a drugged-up babbling fool and missed out on the joy of taking over a crumbling empire and lifting it up higher than it had ever been before.

She checked her shit out in the mirror.

Her slick, glittering cocktail dress was a Valentino special she'd splurged on for six grand, and her diamond earrings and matching necklace had cost her over ten bills apiece. Salida smoothed her feathery hair down and smiled brightly at her reflection.

She was one fine bitch if she had to say so herself.

And she was a smart bitch too.

$$$$$

Pluto was feeling some kinda way as he stood in two inches of stagnant toilet water and stared down into the pleading eyes of the once-beautiful teenager that his nephew Truth used to bang.

"Please Pluto," Nooni begged him from a set of cracked lips and greenish, rotted-out teeth. "I need a lil something real bad. Just one hit!" she moaned and strained against her handcuffed wrist. "Just gimme one lil hit Pluto! I'll suck your dick real good and you can even fuck me too! Just *please...*" she whined, twisting and turning on the damp, filthy mattress. "*PLEASE!* Gimme something. Gimme *anything!* Help me out just this one time, Pluto. Help me."

Pluto was stunned speechless. This young chick didn't look nothing like the Nooni that used to sleep on his couch and suck his nephew's dick every night. Her shit was *hit.* Crusty sores had popped out all over her grimy face, her hair was limp and dirty, and he could smell her rank pussy even over the foul stench of sewage comin' outta the bathroom.

Pluto knew meth could do you bad, but he couldn't even move as Nooni lunged at him and started going at his pants with one hand. She yanked his zipper down and stuck her grimy fingers in his drawers so fast that he didn't have time to react to the disgust he felt inside.

But beneath the disgust was something else, too, Pluto realized as Nooni's small hand started jacking his dick and massaging his sticky balls. He couldn't help squeezing his eyes closed as his joint started stiffening and growing under her frantic touch. And by the time he opened them again his dick was already deep inside her foul mouth, halfway down her sucking throat.

"Ahhhh, shit!" he shivered, both with pleasure and revulsion. Nooni pulled back and grinned up at him, and even in the near-darkness the sight of her stumped-out teeth was enough to make him sick. He closed his eyes again and imagined how good Nooni's thick ass had looked one night as he watched her get on her knees and give Truth a monster dick-licking.

"Yeah," he muttered replaying the x-rated movie in his mind as her warm tongue swirled around the cap of his fat meat. "That's the way you did it, baby. Yeah, you did it just like that."

Pluto took a swig from his beer bottle and then looked down as Nooni got up on her knees and started jutting her neck like a pigeon.

"You gone gimme something?" Nooni pleaded from below as she planted tiny wet pecks up and down the shaft of his throbbing dick. "You gone give me something too, right?"

"Here you go," he muttered thickly, tipping the beer bottle downward until the golden liquid splashed out over his dick. Nooni lapped that shit up greedily and then peered up at him hoping for some more.

And Pluto didn't disappoint her neither. Gripping the bottle of beer tightly in his fist, he rammed his fleshy dick deep down in her throat and gave her all he had.

$$$$$

Yoking Boobie up by the neck, Trey followed the young sister soldier down the basement stairs. His chin dug hard into the top of her head, and his burner dug deep into the soft meat of her throat. They moved stealthily through the gloomy service hall of the funeral home. The cinderblock walls and exposed wires and raw piping was a sharp contrast to the comfortable furnishings of the chapel upstairs.

Boobie led Trey through two security doors. The first one was made outta steel and it required a pass-code to get through to the next one, which was made outta concrete. Pausing at the second door, Boobie put in a different pass code and then punched in a bunch of numbers on a panel too.

Trey stayed up real close on her. Like he was spooning that phat hunk of ass in a bed.

"You better let me get up on that last door by myself," she said, stopping in her tracks as the second door closed. "Flex got a two-way mirror on that joint. He's gonna see you if you walk up on it with me. And if he peeps you, he pops you."

Trey nodded and backed off a little bit. He'd been testing her gangsta and he knew she spoke the truth. If she had let him walk up on that door with her he woulda put a hot one in her throat without a moment's hesitation. And then he woulda blasted the lock on that bitch and planted a bullet in Flex's head too.

"A'ight, but when he opens up that door I want you to wait a second before you walk in," Trey told her. "Let me get up on you just in case ya boy got any stupid ideas. I'm telling you," he warned her, "you try some funny shit in there and not only will ya lil shorty catch a bad one, I'll blow ya throat out for you, dig?"

Boobie nodded, and Trey pushed her toward the last door. The one that had a big shiny mirror across the top half. This time, instead of keying in a code Boobie rapped a secret pattern of knocks on the door and then stood up tall so she could be clearly seen.

Trey heard movement inside the room, and then four or five locks were turned and the door swung open.

Boobie paused for a few seconds, just like she had been told to, giving Trey enough time to make his move.

In a flash, Trey was on the inside of Flex's lair. He had both of his gats pressed hard to Flex's forehead before the young muthafucka could think a single thought.

"Don't do it," he warned. Trey kept his guns checked on Flex as his manz Dabu went for his action. "I'll cap his ass! Matter fact, toss your shit over here and go stand in that corner," Trey ordered Flex's dun dun. "You move, you die, my niggah. I can promise you that. If you move you *die*."

With Dabu gun-naked in the corner, Trey turned his attention back to Flex.

"Wassup, tyke!" Trey greeted him with a cold, calculating grin. "Didn't I tell you the next time I had to chastise your lil ass I was gonna spank you?"

Flex stood stock-still. His eyeballs moved like deadly snakes as they slithered over to rest first on Boobie, and then on Trey, before going back to rest on Boobie again.

"Ay, Nine," Flex said calmly, iggin' Trey and his guns as he addressed Boobie coldly. "You brought this ill-actin' muh'fucka to my door?"

"They got my son!" Boobie moaned with fear and rage in her eyes. Trey mighta been the niggah brandishing the tools, but Flex was the psycho-nutcase that Boobie feared the most.

Flex bucked. "Fuck yo son—"

Trey smashed his burner hard against Flex's nose and gun-checked the shit outta him as blood trickled down his lip.

"Shut the fuck up and get in there!" Trey barked as he pushed Flex deeper into the crib and kicked the door closed behind them.

"A'ight, what the fuck you want, man?" Flex said calmly as a drop of blood slid from his nose and landed on the jacket of his pearl-white suit. "Fuck you brought your sherm ass down here to do, niggah? Get murked so I can run up in ya crib and take ya bitch Juicy?"

"Nah, I came to punish you, Flex," Trey said calmly. "I came to *discipline* your stupid ass. You worse than a lil bad-ass fuckin' kid, ya know? Just hard-headed and wild as fuck. You want everybody else to play by the sandbox rules while you wreck shit and minimize ya risks."

Flex smirked. "Niggah what the fuck is you yappin' about? That shit right there don't even make no sense!"

"That's cause you too young-minded to understand it, niggah! You's a sucker, Flex. A cupcake. A punk-ass lil pup. Like I said, every fuckin' body else is supposed to play fair except you. You the only kid on the playground who can have your marbles and eat them shits too."

"Yo," Flex growled like he gave less than a fuck about Trey and his two loaded burners. "I ain't gone tell you no more, slime. I ain't no kid."

He cupped his nuts and shook his big dick at Trey and sneered.

"Go ask ya girl Juicy about me! Ask that chicken-hoe about that hurtin' I put on her tight lil pussy, ak! She'll tell you. I'm a cutter, niggah! I'm a grown fuckin' man!"

Trey ignored that noise. He could feel the rage and frustration rumbling around all up in Flex's chest. He had pushed that niggah's red-hot button and he was about to push that shit some more too.

"Ay, I heard what happened to Leek, man. That shit was cold, yo."

Flex shrugged, calming down.

"Maleek played a grown man's game. That niggah knew the risks."

"Yeah," Trey nodded. "But you knew them shits too. That's prolly why you ain't never played, huh?"

"What?" Flex frowned and his eyes narrowed into deadly slits.

"You heard me, *young'un!*" Trey chuckled. "You call that game your gut-test, right? Then how come everybody in your whole fuckin' click done played except *you*, niggah! Yo, Maleek got his gangsta tested. Hell, even Lil Lee's fine-ass played! BUT YO SCARED ASS AIN'T NEVER PLAYED, *FLETCHER!*"

Trey let his voice drop and then repeated softly.

"You never played, man."

"Bitch, *please!*" Flex exploded, his grill a mask of rage as he walked right into the trap Trey had laid for him. "Ain't a muth'fucka in *Harlem* who got a stronger gut than minez! I ain't scared of *shit,* you big gorilla-ass bitch! Not of *nothin'* and no fuckin' *body!* You better check the street reports, homey! You better *ask* about me!"

"I did ask about you, baby boy," Trey said quietly. "And everybody I talked to told me your punk-ass *never played.*"

"Fuck who you talked to!" Flex exploded. "I ain't no punk! I'm a man! I'm a *man!*"

"Prove that shit," Trey said. "Put your burner where your mouth is, home boy! Matter fact," Trey shrugged then looked around. "I'll play witcha ass. How about that? You wanna gut-test me like you gut-tested Maleek, niggah? Get your tool, homey."

Trey waved Flex on with his pistol. "Ga'head. Grab that lil pussy-ass revolver y'all lil niggahs like to play with. Then me and you can play us a grown man's game."

"Bet!" Flex said, crossing the room in three long steps. He reached between the pillows on the sofa and came out with his trusted Magnum six-shooter. Waving Trey over to the table, he slammed the gun down on the surface and then smirked and grilled him hard.

"Let's play, muh'fucka. You wanna go first or you want me to go? Take your pick."

"This your house." Trey stuck his gats down in his waistband next to the one he had taken from Boobie. "You go first."

Trey wasn't worried about Flex tryna pop him on the sneak tip. The young boy's street cred and his manhood had been called into question, and the only thing burning through Flex's juvenile mind right now was the need to prove Trey wrong.

Flex flicked open the revolver's cylinder and started shaking out all the rounds. "One for me," he said, holding up two brass-colored bullets. He pushed them back into the empty chambers. "And one for you."

Trey frowned. "Yo, hold the fuck up. We ain't about to play none of them tired-ass lil kid games y'all niggahs be playin', is we? C'mon, now. Man-up, baby boy! Let's take this shit to the next level and see if you can grow some hair on ya fuckin' chest!"

Flex snickered. "I'm cool, fool. What you got?"

"Let's play your bitch-ass gut-game," Trey suggested, "but with a lil twist on it, a'ight? Let's call this shit 'reverse roulette'. Yeah. Instead of taking out all the rounds except two, let's flip that shit and do the exact opposite. Take two rounds out and then leave all the rest of them babies *in there.*"

Flex thought for a second, then grinned. "Hell yeah, that's even better, my nig. That's even better!"

He loaded two more alternating chambers with full metal jackets and left the last two chambers empty. Then he pushed the assembly closed and spun the cylinder with one hand before setting the burner on the table.

"Nah, you first, niggah," Trey reminded him.

A disrespectful smirk appeared on Flex's face.

"Chump-ass *bitch,*" he grinned as he sat down in the chair and leaned his right elbow on the table. He picked up the six-shooter and pressed it to his temple for a quick second, and then suddenly he reversed the motion and let the first bullet fly.

POP!

Boobie slumped to the floor with her eyes wide open and a small red circle darkening her forehead. The back of her dome had busted open and sprayed the contents of her skull on the wall where she'd just been standing.

"Sorry 'bout that," Flex said as he put the gun back down on the table and leaned back easily. "Bizzness before pleasure, my niggah. You know how it is. That was bizzness. Watching you blow ya fuckin' brains out is gonna be pure pleasure."

Trey barely glanced at Boobie's body as Flex picked up the pistol and aimed it at his own head again. Trey was standing on Flex's left and he was almost on an even path with his body. If there was a bullet in the next chamber it would definitely blow Flex's head off, but it would take Trey's chest out as well.

"Hold up. My bad," Trey said quickly. He took one step backward and out of range of Flex's potential round, and without missing a beat that niggah Flex pulled the trigger.

Click.

The hammer fell harmlessly on the empty chamber and then the room was silent. Nothing happened.

"Hah!" Flex laughed crazily, jumping up outta his chair. "Yeah, muh'fucka! *Yeah!* Your turn now," he said, passing Trey the gat. "Your turn you big fuckin' *bitch!*"

Trey nodded and switched places with Flex.

He spun the cylinder then pressed the barrel of the gun to his own head and looked hard at the young boy who had so much to prove.

"Killing muh'fuckas don't make you no man, you know, Flex," Trey said quietly. "It just makes you a killer."

Flex cracked the fuck up. His gut had already been tested. He had done his dance with death and survived that shit. "C'mon, now," he waved Trey on. "Get at it, niggah! You ain't tryna bitch up on me now is you son?"

Trey adjusted his grip on the revolver and braced himself for what was about to come. The odds were in favor of there being a live round in the next chamber of the gat, and this was understood by everybody in the room. Trey also knew what kind of risk he was taking by playing Flex's game, but he too had a point to prove.

"Nah, I ain't bitchin' up," Trey said gazing up to his left as he grilled Flex dead in his eyes. "Nah, niggah. I ain't bitchin' up at all."

Flex's eyes glinted with pure evil as he spit the next words.

"You know I ain't forget about the way you stole Juicy from me, right?"

Trey nodded. He felt his chest get tight. "Yeah, niggah. I know."

"You know that bitch is gonna be minez, and I'ma run my dick up in her thick ass just as soon as you bust ya noggin' open, yo."

Trey nodded again.

And then he took a deep breath, and started to squeeze.

And at the last possible second he leaned back in his chair and put a slight shift on his aim and let the hammer fall.

POP!

Trey damn near went deaf as the hot slug sped past his face.

Dabu hollered from the corner as a spray of blood splattered down on the table.

Flex clutched his blasted chest and stared down at Trey as he staggered on his feet. The smoking pistol was still gripped in Trey's dark hand, and the realization that he had been sucker-shot twisted Flex's face into a mask of pain and rage.

"Oops," Trey said as the red stain on Flex's sharp white suit widened and the young'un sank down to his knees and took his last few grimy breaths in this world.

"My bad. I guess I need to head back to the sandbox too 'cause I don't know how to play by the fuckin' rules neither."

With Flex gasping on the floor and choking on his own blood, Trey turned the gat on Dabu and aimed.

"There's two more where that one came from, bruh."

"C'mon, Trey! Don't pop me, ak!" Dabu screamed like a scared bitch. "You told me to get over here and don't move! Well I ain't *moved,* niggah! I ain't fuckin' *moved!*"

Trey stepped over Flex's dead body and stood above the terrified street thug as he cowered in the corner. For long, hushed moments he stared him down coldly. In Dabu's eyes Trey saw everything that was wrong with Harlem. The greed, the drugs, the criminal-minded street niggahs, and the low-down gutta way of living.

"Yo where that niggah keep his ends at?" Trey demanded quietly.

"Back there!" Dabu pointed. "He got mad safes, man. Right back there in the count room!"

Trey thought about the hundreds of thousands of dollars worth of product that Flex moved on the streets on a daily basis, and mentally calculated the kind of yardage the young druglord musta been sitting on. Cash money. *Untraceable* cash money that could go a long way toward helping the Crossover kids gets scholarships and job training that would prepare them to be the future leaders and business owners of Harlem.

"You know the combination on them locks?" he asked Dabu as he raised the muzzle of his burner until it was flush with the young dude's forehead.

Dabu nodded like a muh'fucka, his head bobbing up and down like his neck was a yo-yo string.

"Cool," Trey said, lowering his gat about an inch. "Get yo ass in there and open them shits."

CHAPTER 22

Seconds after he shot his nut off, Pluto stuffed his limp joint back inside his pants.

He had gotten him a real good blow out, but now his dick itched like Nooni had liquid crabs in her muh'fuckin' mouth.

"'Kay, I gave you something," Nooni reminded him as she knelt on the wet, putrid mattress. "Now it's your turn to gimme something, P."

The foul stench coming offa her made his stomach roll and slosh, and Pluto took a step backwards as he offered her the beer bottle that he still clutched in his hand.

Nooni cursed and smacked that shit to the floor. "What the hell am I supposed to do with that! I need me a hit, Pluto! A lil shit to smoke! Something that's gonna take care of my head!"

"I'ma give ya nasty ass a hit all right," Pluto said as he glanced around. The party was kickin' live upstairs and the Dungeon was soundproof like a muh'fucka. He checked his waistband for the trusted gat he had taken back from Freeze, and then pulled it out and aimed that shit toward Nooni.

"What the hell are you doing?" the young girl screeched in terror. "That ain't fair, Pluto! I sucked your dick for you! That shit ain't fair!"

"Shut the hell up, bitch," he snapped as he yoked her around the neck and pulled her toward him until her wrist strained against her handcuff. "Your ass stinks like horse shit," Pluto muttered under his breath.

And then he pulled the trigger.

$$$$$

There were four dead bodies in the basement of the Three Brothers Funeral Home when Trey walked up the stairs carrying two large seaman's bags stuffed with money. The Saturday night crowd in Harlem was getting ready for some good times and good music as people scurried up and down the sidewalks and headed toward their favorite party joints.

Trey was a big strong dude, yet he struggled with the weight of the money bags that he gripped in his hands. He made it over to his car and set the bags down to unlocked his trunk. He threw his gats in there first, then he lifted the bags one at a time and pushed them deep into the back of the trunk compartment as his cell phone buzzed with a text message.

Pausing, Trey looked down at his phone and saw the message was from Juicy.

I'm on my way to the G-Spot to get Nooni. And I don't need your help!

Shit! Trey slammed the trunk closed on hundreds of thousands of dollars in cash and hurried around to the driver's side of his whip. He tried to call Juicy's phone but she didn't answer. Pausing again, he sent a quick text message to his manz Rain and told him to assemble the crew and meet him at the G-Spot. He tried to call Juicy's number again too, but her phone just rang and rang.

A heavy sense of dread settled in Trey's stomach as he clicked the remote and unlocked his car door. He was just about to yank on the door handle when a sweet young voice called out behind him.

"Trey! Hey Trey, Look over here!"

Trey stepped away from his whip and saw a familiar face smiling at him. It had been a minute since the last time he'd seen her, and she was waving at him and flashing him a toothless grin.

"Taleah!" he waved back and called out to her. "I gotta make a run real quick but I'ma swing by and check you out later—"

Bang!

The cracking sound of gunfire reached Trey's ears just a split second before the bullet pierced his chest. It spun him around and bounced him up against his car as he crumpled to his knees and lay bleeding in the street.

"Just tell me, Taleah," the young girl said, imitating Trey's voice as she walked up and stood over him with a smoking gat gripped in her hand. *"Tell me who it was Taleah and I swear I ain't gonna let nothin' happen to you!"*

Tears fell from her eyes as her rage bubbled over and spilled outta her tender soul.

"You lied, Trey!" the fourteen-year-old screamed from her toothless mouth as warm blood seeped from Trey's chest and got soaked up by his shirt. "You fuckin' *lied!*" the young girl cried.

And then she shot him again.

CHAPTER 23

Monique had been sitting around all day long with a sinking knot in the pit of her stomach. It was the Grand Re-Opening night at the G-Spot, and even though she was supposed to be shaking her ass up on stage she had known from the jump that she wasn't gonna be reporting to no damn job.

Instead, she had sat around and made herself sick with worry, and all she could think about was how all her dreams seemed to get killed before they could ever come true. She had been blowing up Sallie's phone left and right ever since he had called and asked her if she wanted a slice of pizza.

That had been hours ago and he still hadn't shown up. Monique didn't know where her man could be, but she couldn't help remembering how Salida's goonies had kicked his ass and chased him up outta the G-Spot. The last Mo had seen of her boo-thang was the back of his head as he ran down the street tryna get to his car.

She had dialed Sallie's cell phone number over and over and eventually she put that shit on speed dial and pressed one button so many times that her finger got sore.

She didn't wanna think the worst about her man, but as the minutes turned into hours and she didn't hear shit from him, her mind started fuckin' with her and the silent emptiness got all up in her head.

Monique thought about the two suitcases stashed under her bed that she had packed on the sly with all the shit she was gonna take with her when she dipped outta town. The bags were big and expensive and she had copped them from a pregnant booster on 125th Street. If Sallie didn't show up she was gonna have to chase that lil thief down and get her damn money back.

She sat in the darkness just waiting and worrying. The apartment was silent except for the clock on the dresser that was steady ticking. Ticking and workin' her last fuckin' nerve.

Monique jumped up and slapped that shit right off the dresser. It went flying against the wall and crashed to the floor where the glass front shattered into a thousand pieces. She cleared the rest of the dresser off next, sweeping every fuckin' thing to the floor with one crazy swipe of her arm.

"My fuckin' life ain't *shit!*" she raged as she threw a lamp across the room and tore pictures off the walls and tossed them like Frisbees. She yanked the curtains down after that and the dirty venetian blinds got ripped down too.

Crazed, Monique flung open her top drawer and dumped all her shit out on the floor. Wasn't nothin' left in there except a few old bras, some worn-out thongs, a tube of Monistat, and some mix-matched socks, but she flung that shit to the floor anyway.

She had just yanked opened the second drawer, the one that was Pluto's, and was about to turn that baby over and empty it out too when she realized that shit was *already* empty.

Monique froze for a quick second. Bending over, she yanked open three more of Pluto's drawers and got the shit shocked outta her when she saw those bitches were all empty too.

Monique jetted outta the room and dashed into the bathroom. She snatched open the medicine cabinet and saw a squeezed-out tube of toothpaste and a rusty disposable razor.

Everything else was gone.

She peered under the sink looking for Pluto's electric shaver and the two bars of designer soap she had brought him for his birthday. All that shit was gone.

Running back to her room Monique flung the closet door open real wide. All the decoy shit that she wasn't planning on taking with her but had left hanging up so Pluto wouldn't get suspicious was still there. But Pluto's shit was gone. His side of the closet ain't have nothing but spider webs and few pregnant cockroaches scurrying around in it.

Back at the bed Mo dropped to her knees. She lifted the comforter up and reached into the darkness feeling for her suitcases. *Them shits were gone!* In their place was a big pile of fluffy shit. Her hands sank into the mound and when she grabbed at it and pulled it out she realized it was the clothes that she had packed in her suitcases, all her fly dresses and her sexiest thongs!

Monique sat back on her heels, straight up stunned.

Her mind worked hard to put two-and-two together, and as soon as she added that shit up she opened her mouth and screamed at the top of her lungs.

"Plutooooooo!"

That fat slimy bastard had *left* her! He had dumped all her shit outta the suitcases so he could pack his shit up in them instead! Her heart felt like an elephant had kicked her in the chest. She wanted to cry but all she could see was red. She was way more mad than sad. Way more mad.

All kinds of murderous thoughts were speeding through her mind as the program on television was suddenly interrupted and the local news announcer cut in.

"Breaking news coming to you live from Channel 7, Eyewitness News. Our top story this half hour… a DEA raid has taken place in Chinatown and an arrest warrant has been issued for a man suspected of manufacturing the most toxic mixture of methamphetamines sold on the streets of New York City in years. As reported by us previously, three young children have died and at least fifteen people have overdosed on the particularly lethal mixture of crystal ice commonly known as Strawberry Snake.

Eyewitness news reporter Martin Solter joins us live from Chinatown. Good evening, Martin, can you give us an update on any developments?

"Yes, good evening, Gloria. I'm reporting from Chinatown tonight where drug enforcement agencies have released the name of the man they believe is responsible for the wave of toxic methamphetamine overdoses that have been sweeping across the city. Law enforcement officials have converged on a one-room flat above a butcher shop in Chinatown in an attempt to find this man and stem the rising tide of terror.

Take a look at this police sketch, New York, and see if you recognize this man. His name is Salvatore McCain, and his landlord Lin Wu tells us that he recently rented McCain the walk-up apartment when he showed up on his doorstep desperate for a place to stay.

According to our sources, the local DEA received a tip from a concerned business owner in Harlem who was appalled at the recent wave of deaths in the area. This business owner informed authorities that Salvatore McCain AKA "Slick Sallie" had been caught attempting to distribute the crystal ice called Strawberry Snake at her nightclub just a day or so ago, but he was chased off by her security staff and hasn't been seen there since.

I just got word that the police have come up empty-handed on their raid thus far, but thanks to the diligence of one savvy club owner, the hunt for Salvatore McCain continues...

Salida!

Monique's heart stopped beating as she stared at the television and a life-like sketch of her man's face appeared on the screen.

That grimy bitch! She got them fools thinkin' Sallie's the one pushin' all that bad dope!

"I'ma *kill* that old bitch," Monique swore under her breath as she stripped off her jewelry and put on her sneakers and tied them up in tight knots. She snatched up a big plastic container of Vaseline that she had knocked to the floor. Snapping the lid off she slathered goo-gobs of greasy gel all over her face. "I ain't *even* fuckin' playing! I'ma run up in the G-Spot and *kill* that bitch!"

$$\$\$\$\$\$$

Laying out a grand to walk across the threshold of the G-Spot Social Club was no big thing to the high-rollin' set of the Divine Nine. They'd pulled up in a plush white Rolls Royce, and after waiting on the red carpet line for an hour behind the long velvet ropes, Dre, Doc, Stamp, Boog, Chickie, Mannie, and Rome submitted to a thorough pat-down from the goonies on security, and then forked over the cash for their cover charge and walked into the Spot like they were ordinary customers.

The plan was for them to split up and position themselves in strategic spots once they got inside, and Boog, Doc, and Rome headed for the gambling rooms, while Chickie made his way to the triple X movie room. Mannie waited on line at the cashier's cage to buy up a bunch of pussy chips, and Dre and Stamp strolled over to the packed out bar to get a few drinks.

It had taken a whole lotta shrewd planning and detailed preparation but all of the necessary elements were firmly in place and the G-Spot's ownership was about to get flipped like a pancake. Nobody in the click was comfortable rollin' up in hostile territory buck-ass naked and defenseless, but thanks to Freeze they had a crate packed with fully-loaded weapons just waiting for them in the G-Spot's boiler room.

"Yo, it's about time to get this fuckin' bloodbath started," Stamp said impatiently as him and Dre bought double shots of straight Bacardi and headed toward the tables near the stage.

"No it ain't time, muh'fucka," Dre warned him in a low voice. "You heard what Flex said. Don't nothin' jump off until he gets up in here and gives us the signal, fool."

Stamp shrugged and tossed his shot glass back and drained that shit. "Then that niggah need to hur'rup and get his ass up in here then."

$$$$$

I caught a taxi over to the G-Spot, and I won't even lie. I sat in the backseat of that gypsy cab dressed in a hoodie and jeans and cried like a baby all the way there. The closer we got, the worse I felt. I started having crazy flashbacks. I saw G standing over me holding his big dick and pissing all in my face and hair. I felt every last one of them killer blows he had swung on me, and those hard-ass alligator shoes that had dented my forehead and burrowed into the pit of my stomach too.

And all those nasty-dick niggahs he had let come downstairs to fuck me... routing my pussy and plunging out my ass...

I was sweating real bad under my hoodie and my mouth started getting dry. I had a little switchblade stuck down in my sock that I had snuck outta Chiney's room, and I pictured myself stabbing the shit outta every dude who had ever violated me.

And violate me was exactly what they had done. Them niggahs had held my feet up in the air as they dug me out from all directions and left me screaming in shame and agony down in that Dungeon. They had climbed on top of me one right after another. Some of them took their sweet time and just wallowed in it, others just wanted to hit it and quit it, but every last one of them bastards had degraded and brutalized me... treated me worse than a dog... body and soul.

And now... I was about to walk right back into that lion's den.

All by myself without a damn soul to protect me.

My fear started choking me and I put my hand on the door handle ready to jump outta that cab while it was still moving. I was terrified all down in my bones, and wailing sirens of caution started flashing in my head. Danger was waiting for me in the G-Spot, and this I knew.

Death mighta been waiting there for me too.

I could hear Grandmother chanting all in my ear.

Yea, thou I walk through the valley of the shadow of death, I will fear no evil...

That was a goddamn lie.

I feared that evil, honey. Matter fact, I was *terrified* of the evil that lived in the G-Spot. I had to bite my lip to keep myself from screaming at the cab driver and telling him to turn the fuck around! To go back! I didn't give a damn where he took me, just as long as he didn't take me back inside that house of horrors they called the G-Spot Social Club.

But I didn't yell at the cabbie. I didn't scream for him to turn around. Because deep inside my heart I knew the deal. Going back to the G-Spot was something that I absolutely had to do. Something I *needed* to do.

Not just for Nooni and for Rita, but for that scared little pissy-tail girl from 136th Street that they called Juicy-Mo too. Because if I didn't stand up and face that evil then I was gonna have to run from the devil for the rest of my life. I would *never* be able to escape the wrath of Granite McKay in my dreams. I would *never* be able to lay Gino to rest in the memories of my heart. And I would *never* be able to be Trey Jackson's woman from the bottom of my soul.

So I forced myself to hold still in the backseat of that taxicab and let that driver take me deeper and deeper into the belly of Harlem. Because as terrified as I was, on the real tip I knew he was taking me to my destiny.

$$$$$

I'm not sure what I thought was gonna happen when I punched in the security code that my friend Dicey used to use and stepped through the side door of the G-Spot, but whatever it was it didn't happen. Didn't no harps from heaven start playing, I didn't have no sudden revelations about the deeper meaning of my life, the sky didn't light up with a million bolts of lightening, and G's black ass didn't rise up from the dead and choke the shit outta me neither.

Instead, I stepped into the middle of a real big party going on. There were flashing lights and balloons and banners everywhere announcing the Grand Re-Opening of the G-Spot. The music was pumping and high rolling gangstas were balling harder than hell. There was a long line at the cashier's cage where dudes lined up to buy pussy in their favorite flavor, and the bar was packed out and top-shelf liquor was being tossed back like it was city gin.

There was a show going on up on the stage and it had everybody's attention. That old skank Honey Dew was front and center leading the charge. She had on a white cowboy hat, a spiked white leather thong, and her plump honey-colored titties were bubbling up out of a tight white leather bustier. Hundred dollar bills rained down on the stage like confetti, and Honey Dew cocked her legs open in her thigh-high, open-toed, white leather boots and showed every hustler in the house what the inside of her pussy looked like.

I followed behind a waitress who was tipping across the floor wearing a push-up bra and a pair of fuck-me pumps with red feathers sprouting from the heels. A skinny chick with ass for days was giving a lap dance in one of the semi-private booths, and the dude she was straddling screamed out loud like he had just nutted in his pants.

All around me I saw countless girls volunteering to get used and abused. Losing their minds and giving up their souls as they chased the next dollar, the next high, the next dream.

I put my head down and moved with the crowd as I headed toward the back of the club. Towards G's former office. Towards the pit of hell.

$$$$$

I remember the first time I saw somebody getting dragged down into the Dungeon. He was a young dude, probably just a little bit older than me. Ace and Pluto had kicked him up and busted his grill real good for him, and by the time I peeped him he was rolling around on the floor begging for his life.

I would never forget the look in his eyes when he saw me. He looked at me like I was a life preserver and he was a drowning man. His eyes was pleading for help from the bottom of his soul, and I could smell the fear as it rolled off of his brutalized body.

Later, I found out that dude was one of them 'Licious Lovers. Smoove-A-Licious. The NBA rapper they called Thug-A-Licious was his cousin, and to my surprise G had worked dude over and held him in the Dungeon for some ransom money... the same kinda low-down shit that Ace and Pluto had tried to with poor Nooni.

I approached the stairs to the Dungeon with my gut all twisted up. I remembered jetting up out of that darkness like it was yesterday, terrified as hell that somebody was gonna find out that Cooter had unlocked my cuffs, and then come throw my ass right back to the wolves. Never in my wildest dreams could I have seen myself walking willingly back down those stairs. But here I was. Turning the knob, pushing through the door that Pluto had unlocked for me, and stepping down into the muggy darkness.

My ankles felt like jelly as I went down those steps. My balance was off, and I teetered on my feet like I didn't trust them to hold up my weight. I held my breath against the rancid smell that cloaked me, and when I got down to the bottom step I cried out so fast that I messed around and sucked down a whole mouthful of that foul-ass air.

The room was almost pitch black but the little bit I could make out sent a sharp pain stabbing through my gut. I stepped further inside and yanked on the light switch and a dim bulb half-glowed.

I thought my ass had been brutalized in the G-Spot, but what I saw down in that Dungeon was enough to make my heart stop.

"Nooni..." I whispered and clutched my hands to my mouth.

I knew it was her but my mind just didn't wanna believe it. The girl who was stretched out on the same pissy mattress that I had come to know so well looked more animal than human.

She had on a pair of stained, filthy pajama bottoms and a torn orange bra.

Her hair was a tangle of matted-up curls, and her eyes darted wildly, every which way as she sucked from an empty beer bottle she gripped in her hand.

Her face looked like it was covered in either sores or cigarette burns, and the rest of her body was bruised up with pus-crusted sores everywhere.

"Nooni!" I rushed over to her, my feet slogging in the nasty stagnant water that seemed to be everywhere. As bad as the Dungeon had been when G had thrown me down here it was worse, much, much worse now. I couldn't say exactly what Nooni had been through since she'd been down here, but she looked on the outside the way I had felt on the inside. There was a handcuff around her wrist that had once been chained to a pole, but now the handcuff looked like it had been busted up. It wasn't even attached to nothing no more, but she still had her hand up there like she couldn't move it. And then I saw the bullet cartridge that was laying on the mattress and I knew what was up.

"Nooni." I pulled her toward me and cupped her dirty face in my hands, and the creepy glare in her eyes told me that something had slipped from this child's brain. She looked spaced out. Mad crazy. Unzipped.

"Nooni," I repeated. "It's Juicy. It's Juicy. Do you remember me? I came to get you out of here and take you home. I'm gonna take you to see your sister, Rita."

"I know who you are," she said, and her voice sounded dead. Soul-less.

I looked around for something to throw over her, but there was nothing else in there except the moldy-smelling mattress. I wasn't about to go look in that filthy little bathroom, so Nooni was gonna have to go out just like she was.

She let me hold her grimy hand and I led her up the stairs real slow. It had been a long time since she had been up on her feet so she moved like a baby, sometimes stumbling and sinking down to her knees. But I kept holding on to her, trying my best not to cry the whole way up.

"Just a few more steps," I whispered over and over again. "You doing real good, Nooni. Just a little bit more and I'm gonna get you outta here."

They say a journey of a thousand miles begins with one small step. Well, I didn't know it but me and Nooni's journey wasn't quite over yet. The door to the Dungeon loomed right in front of us, and but little did I know there was about to be some real crazy shit waiting for us on the other side.

CHAPTER 24

There wasn't a single parking spot within five blocks of the G-Spot so Monique double-parked her whip near the corner and approached the gentlemen's club on foot. She had a razor blade tucked in her mouth and she walked fast and mad with her arms swinging wildly back and forth. There was a long-ass line held back with velvet ropes at the front door, so Mo ran around to the side door that the strippers used and punched in the code to the lock.

She stepped up in the joint and started blinking her eyes real fast so they could hurry up and adjust to the dim, smoky interior. As soon as she could see good she pushed through the thick crowd, and like a heat-seeking missile she started searching for her target. She didn't see Salida yet but she saw plenty of tits and tail prancing around the club. Over by the bar Bizzie's sweet ass was bossing his crew of bartenders around, and a bunch of low-level strippers were up on the stage wiping pussy juice all over the brass fuck poles.

Ducking her head, Monique was pushing her way toward the back hallway that led to G's office when she spotted exactly who she had been looking for.

"Hey, you skanky bitch!" she screamed over the loud-ass music and started knockin' bitches outta her path. "Move, trick!" She pushed one skinny broad and elbowed the shit outta another one. "Let me through! Get the fuck outta my way!"

$$$$$

Me and Nooni came up outta that Dungeon, turned the corner, and stepped right into a cat-fight.

"You dirty bitch!"

A real beautiful woman was standing near the cut room's stairs. Her hair was pure butter, and she had on a sweet designer dress that looked like it had cost at least five grand. She was dripping mad jewels everywhere, and even from where I stood I could tell the long spirals of ice that glinted from both of her ears was the real thing.

"You ain't shit, bitch!" she screamed on a chick who was standing with her back to us. "You just a stank piece of shit in the gutter that don't *no* man want!"

"Fuck you!" the chick screamed back. "You crazy old wrinkled-ass, crusty-coochie wench! You just jealous cause don't no man wanna lick all them gray hairs on your ol' antique pussy! "

I took one look at the bubbalicious ass on the girl who was standing with her back to me and instantly I knew who she was. It was that crazy-jealous bitch with the killer body who had tried her best to make my life a living hell.

It was G's top-dollar stripper. The notorious three-titty-bitch they called Money-Makin'-Monique.

Monique took a step toward the steps like she was gonna make a slick move and the other lady backed up. She was pretty as hell and something about her looked real familiar, but with all that bitching and hollering going on I couldn't think hard enough to place her.

"Hmph! Well at least I still *got* me a *pussy!*" she ragged on Monique. "That worn-out thing hanging between your legs ain't nothing but a used-up cum bag! That's why that ugly white boy don't want no more of it. He done saw how stink and nasty it was!"

"I got ya fuckin' nas—" Monique went to holler, but the flying kick I planted straight up her jelly ass killed all that stupid noise coming outta her mouth!

"Bitch!" I lifted my knee and sank my foot in her ass again! *Hard!*

She stumbled forward as her lower back caved in and tried to stop herself from hitting the ground.

And then something just came the fuck over me. Something in my mind just snapped, and I wanted to be all over that gritty bitch like a dog on a bone. All the scandalous, grimy shit she had done to me over the years just washed over me like a hot boiling wave and sent my temperature percolating right through the roof.

Money-Makin'-Monique had been fuckin' with me ever since the day G brought me through the front door. This jealous hoe had lied on me, shit on me, teased the hell outta my baby brother, and pulled all kinds of grimy capers to get me in trouble so G could bust my ass on the regular.

And what she had done to poor Nooni was just unforgivable. There was no way in the world this bitch deserved to walk around breathing air, and I didn't even think twice about it before I jumped on her ass again.

I charged up behind her and followed up on my kick with a killer blow that caught her on the side of her face and got a nice piece of her eye too. She spun around yelping, and I grabbed a handful of her horse-hair and drove her face down toward the ground as I brought my knee up and connected hard with her nose.

My ass was outta control as I beat the brakes offa her trick-ass!

I was off the damn charts as I punched and kicked and slung that skanky three-titty bitch left and right, mopping up the floor with her trifling behind.

And after all the cash-shit this bitch had talked over the years, she couldn't even fight!

I yanked at about two-yards of her extra-long curly weave and roped that shit around her neck like a lasso. I got her in a headlock and started choking her with that shit. With her neck in the crook of my arm, I used my weight to pull her hair tighter and tighter around her scrawny chicken neck.

She stomped her feet and bucked up and down, then started scratching and punching and trying to bite into my titty but I didn't feel none of it.

I wanted to kill Monique. After everything she had done to me I wanted this bitch *dead*.

I probably woulda choked her until her empty-ass head popped off her body if I hadn't gotten distracted by some real crazy laughter. It was that rollin' on the floor type of shit. Loud as hell and kinda scary. Cackles of pure delight that were just a' flying outta that lady's mouth as she pointed at Monique hemmed up in the crook of my arm and cracked the hell up.

Breathing hard, I eased up off Monique for a quick second, and then slung her gasping ass down to the ground. Then I glanced over at the lady who was still laughing her ass off and got the shock of my goddamn life.

"Umm, excuse me," I cut into all that cackling and interrupted her.

My mouth popped open as I stared real close at her ass and said, "Umm, who are you?"

She stopped laughing and stared right back at me. "Umm, who the hell are *you*?"

"I'm Juicy," I said, and it was right at that moment that I knew.

I fuckin' *knew*.

I knew exactly who the fuck she was! I could see it all in her face. I had snuck in G's office and studied the picture that was turned facedown on his desk mad times while he was gone.

I looked into her eyes. I remembered the first time I'd seen eyes like those hovering over me, looking down at me from my man's handsome face.

And all that butter hair... it was just like mine. This is where Gino had gotten all those wavy curls from.

No, Salida McKay didn't have to tell me who she was because I already knew.

But what she *did* have to tell me was why the fuck she was wearing the engagement ring that Gino had put on my finger when he asked me to marry him.

And where the fuck she had gotten it from!

$$$$$

"That's my ring," I said with my eyes glued to the sick hunk of ice that dangled from the glittering diamond chain Salida wore around her neck. I could hear Gino's voice in my ear.

It was my mother's engagement ring. It's one of a kind. G got it made somewhere in Asia.

"*Your* ring?" she stared at me from a pair of real evil eyes as her hand shot up to the jewelry that hung between her breasts. "No the fuck it ain't! This here is mine. *Mine*."

"No," I shook my head and started moving in her direction. "It's *mine*. It got stolen off my finger. On my wedding day. How the hell did *you* get it?"

"*Oooooh!*" Monique squealed from the floor and then got up real quick. I saw the noogies I had put on her head as she pointed at Salida and started jumping up and down on both feet.

"*Ahhh-haaa!*" she hollered like a light bulb had suddenly gone off in her brain and she had just put two-and-two together.

"You dirty, stankin', grimy, low-down-trifling, no-good dog-ass *bitch*!" she screamed. "You said you was going to *Queens* when you left my crib that day! And you did too! Your crazy ass went straight to the goddamn *airport*!"

Monique turned her whipped-ass around and stared dead in my eyes.

"Juicy," she said quietly. "This bitch right here shot y'all. Salida shot you and Gino. I know you don't fuckin' like me, but if you ain't never believed shit I said to you before I swear on my dead momma that you can believe this here shit *right now*. Salida was at your wedding. That's how she got your damn ring. That bitch was there! She flew from Queens right to California and she shot y'all."

I looked up at Gino's mother with crazy hope in my eyes. Praying that she would deny that shit. Praying that there was some other explanation she could lay on me.

For the longest time I had wondered about her. Where she was at, what she was like, what kinda grimy shit G had done to her, whether or not she had been young and dumb like me, and if G had tried to throw shade on her inner glow the same way that he had done mine.

I used to think of me and Salida as sisters in a crazy kind of way. Both of us had been caught in G's grip and totally under his control. We wasn't no different than his shiny new whips and all his fine shoes and clothes. Just glittery props to hang on his arm and boost up his ego. We were eye candy that made him look large in pubic. But in private we were trapped gutter rats who had no way out of our cages unless G's evil ass felt like letting us out.

"S-s-Salida?" I said softly. Her name came out of my mouth with a question mark on it because there was no way in fuck I wanted to think what I was thinking as I asked her again.

"How did you get my ring?"

"How the fuck you *think* I got it?" she mocked me like a kid, teasing me in a crazy, singsong voice. "I took it off your goddamn *fanger!*"

Pain and horror came crashing down on me as the naked truth rolled outta her mouth and glinted in her insane eyes.

"B-b-but Gino was your *son...*," I whimpered, pleading with her to somehow make this thing right. "Your only son! He was your *baby*. He *loved* you! He thought you was dead... everybody thought you was dead."

She started that crazy-ass laughing again and I swallowed real hard as a ball of rage rose up out of my stomach.

"Gimme my ring," I said pushing past Monique as I headed straight for her ass. "Gimme back my *mothafuckin' ring!*"

"You ain't getting *shit*," Salida spit, and turned around to run up the cut room stairs. But I was on her ass. Like a long-legged hurdler I leaped all over that bitch.

I wasn't a fighter by nature but I caught Gino's mama by the back of her dope-ass dress and swung her crazy ass around and capped the shit outta her. I started throwing the same kinda heavy-weight killer blows at her that G used to throw at me, and them shits was really doing the job too.

I was fucking her ass up. Pounding my fists into her grill as hard as I could.

But then I heard glass shattering behind me and Monique screamed and wailed real loud like she was dying or something.

I glanced down the stairs. *Nooni.*

I had forgotten all about her. The poor girl had cracked open her empty beer bottle on the floor and jumped on Monique's back, and now she was stabbing the shit outta her. Monique was screaming and trying to fight the girl off as blood gushed from her wounds.

Nooni had a death look on her face as she brought her hand up high and plunged the thick glass into Mo's neck and shoulder over and over again, like she was trying to take her straight out. I wanted to scream at Nooni and tell her to stop! I wanted to tell her that she was too young for this and that bitch Monique just wasn't worth it. I wanted to tell her that there was nothing more precious than a human life.

But for some reason when I opened my mouth only three words came out.

"Kill that bitch!"

And then that's all the fuck I said because that murdering heffa Salida had almost made it to the top of the stairs as she tried to get away from me, and I wasn't about to let that happen!

I caught her and jumped on her ass again, and we fought like grown men on them steps. My rage and fury was so deep that for only the second time in my life, scared-ass lil Juicy-Mo Stanfield was straight-out kicking a mud hole in somebody's ass and I didn't have a drop of mercy in me neither!

I punched her over and over in the face, busted open her lip, banged her head on the banister, and damn near kicked my whole foot through her chest as I tried my best to kill that bitch and get my ring back.

As crazy as she was, Salida wasn't no match for me. She kept swinging her arms and twisting and turning trying to keep me from getting close to her neck, but I just kept right on knocking the shit out of her, dotting her eyes, and smashing her nose as I tried to snatch her diamond chain and pull off my ring.

I almost blacked out when Salida caught me with a right jab that damn near broke my nose. My knees sagged and I cried out in pain as sparks went off behind my eyes and a stream of blood ran down my lips and into my mouth.

And that's when I bent over and reached into my sock and pulled out my knife.

I went at her crazy ass again, determined to get my ring! Determined to get me some goddamn *revenge*!

But Salida got stupid. "Oh, you tryna cut me?" She started swinging on me real hard. "Bitch you tryna *cut* me?" She laughed. "Just face it, Juicy! Bitch you just wanna *be* me!"

And suddenly I understood what people meant when they say they just "snapped."

I straight-up *snapped* on that bitch, and before I knew it I was stabbing the hell out of her, jigging that lil switchblade at her everywhere I could get her!

"This is for Nooni!" I hollered as my blade sliced across her face as we tussled like two wrestlers. "She was a child, you evil old bitch! She was just a child!"

"Child *hell*," Salida panted and grabbed my wrist as she scrambled to grab hold of my knife. "You shoulda seen the way them young legs climbed that pole..."

"This is for Gino!" I screamed as I slapped her hand down and tried to stick her dead in her heart.

That bitch rolled to the left and I cut her deep in her shoulder instead.

"And this is for my fuckin' *son*!"

I aimed at her chest again but she twisted and scooted and I got her in her side.

I didn't give a fuck where I got her. Just as long as I got her!

I was tryna kill that bitch as I thrust the thin blade at her wildly. She brought her hands up and tried her damnest to dip and dodge, but I got in there and was able to stick her in her chest anyway.

"Owwwwwwww!" she howled and grabbed at my wrist as hot blood spurted from her wound and she rolled from side to side. *"Get the fuck offa me!"*

Oh, I was gonna get offa this bitch all right! Just as soon as her black ass was *dead*!

I jerked outta her grasp and raised my arm up high again, but this time when I plunged the knife down in her shoulder the handle was slick with her blood and my whole hand slipped.

I sliced through my entire palm as my flesh slid down the length of the sharp blade. White-hot pain exploded as my cut-up meat split wide open. I cried out and reflexes made me open my bloody hand and drop the knife. It fell to the steps with a clang and Salida scrambled to kick it all the way down.

I didn't need no fuckin' knife as I lunged for my ring again.

She cursed, and struggled to squeeze it tight in her fist so I couldn't get to it.

"Get the hell offa me!" she screamed.

I just went bonkers and started stripping that bloody bitch. And not only did I bend them fuckin' fingers back until they cracked like twigs and I got my ring, ignoring the burning pain in my palm, I ripped the shit outta her fancy lil party dress, I knocked to her to her knees and made one of her fuckin' shoes go flying off, I grabbed that little squiggly bracelet on her wrist and yanked that shit until it popped, and then I punched her upside her head so goddamn hard those icy-ass earrings she had on ended up on the steps too.

And then I looked down at the ring I was holding in my bloody hand and all the fight went outta me.

I was rocked with grief as I remembered laying under Gino's bloody body as his very last gift to me was stolen right off my finger. So much blood had been shed for this one piece of jewelry! There was so much pain behind it! I leaned against the railing and opened my mouth to cry, and that's when Salida slammed her foot into my chest and jumped all over me.

With a stupid-loud scream she went straight for my face and tried to poke her long fingernails right through my eyeballs.

I slapped at her clawing hands and tried to twist out of range, and the ring went flying out of my hand and sailing over the banister.

It fell in slow motion, flipping over and over in the air as it hurled down toward the ground below.

"*Noooo!*" I screamed and lunged out desperately to catch it, and then the next thing I knew Salida had grabbed me and flipped me and I was sailing over the banister too.

$$$$$

Juicy's body sounded like a sack of flour when it hit the ground.

She landed right near the spot where Monique was fighting off Nooni, and Mo used the split second distraction to gain the upper hand.

"Crazy bitch!" she screamed, dripping blood as she grabbed two handfuls of Nooni's wild hair and slammed the girl's head on the floor. She cracked the back of Nooni's dome at least five times before she realized the girl was out cold and wasn't fighting back no more.

But by that time Monique had realized something else too.

That bitch Salida was getting away. She was dragging herself up the last few steps and heading toward the cut room.

"Uh-uh," Monique muttered as she abandoned Nooni and took off up the stairs to get a piece of Salida. "Oh no you ain't. Your ass ain't going *nowhere*, bitch! You ain't going *nowhere!*"

Mo ran up the stairs three at a time, forgetting all about her wounds. She caught

Salida just as she pushed through the door of the cut room and Monique busted up inside right behind her.

"You's a *dog*," Monique taunted Salida as she punched the old bitch in her bloody face and picked up the ass-kicking where Juicy had left off. "You slumped your own fuckin' son, Salida! You's a muthafuckin' dog!"

The two women tussled all over the cut room, tripping over hoses and triple beam scales and boxes and crates filled up with meth-making materials. Monique fought Salida like they were two hoes in the street. She threw a series of punches that busted the skin over Salida's eye open like a cherry, drawing dark red blood as the older woman shrieked for help.

"Oh you want some, help?" Monique laughed as she nailed Salida with a deep gut shot that buckled her knees and sent her lurching forward gasping for breath. "I got ya fuckin' *help*."

Salida made a run for it and Monique laughed and followed her as she staggered toward a mixing table. Slumped against the table and using the last of her strength, Salida waited until Monique was right up on her and then she grabbed a large glass vat and hurled a gallon of clear liquid dead in Mo's face.

AGGRRRRRRRRRRRAAAAAAAHHHHHHHHHHHH!

Monique screamed and gasped in agony as she rubbed at the acidic fluid that had splashed into her eyes and was burning through her skin.

AGGRRRRRRRRRRRAAAAAAAHHHHHHHHHHHH!
AGGRRRRRRRRRRRAAAAAAAHHHHHHHHHHHH!

She was on fire! In hellacious agony! She had never felt pain like this in her whole fuckin' life and she was running blind as she tripped and staggered toward the door with her eyes poaching and boiling in their sockets and horrible shrieks of torture flying from her mouth.

"Help!!!!!!!!!" Monique screamed, begging for aid now that the tables were turned and she was the one in big trouble. "I'm burning! *I'm burning! Help!!!!!!!!*"

Whatever the fuck Salida had hurled outta that vat felt like it was disintegrating her face down to the bone. She could hardly catch a breath as she felt around wildly for the doorknob, and she was way too pain-crazed to remember she needed a key to get out. And when she couldn't get the door open Monique knew she only had one option left.

She raced desperately toward the window with all rational thoughts replaced by the torture of unbearable pain. And when she crashed blindly through the glass and went sailing out into the night sky, the concrete that rose up to break her fall was kind enough to put her right out of her misery.

CHAPTER 25

The crowd had swelled up thicker than shit and Flex still hadn't made his grand entrance at the G-Spot yet. He wasn't answering his texts or calls neither, and now Dre was starting to get worried and that crazy young soldier Stamp was starting to get itchy.

"Yo," Stamp elbowed Dre and set his drink down on the table as they watched a pair of strippers masturbate on the stage. They had ordered up a bottle of Krug and slid into a small booth across from the bar. "Ay man, that dude Fizz from the Talented Ten just walked in with his set," he said, nodding toward a click that was rolling through the G-Spot. "Fuck is them square niggahs doing up in here?"

Dre shrugged. "Chill ya ass out, Stamp. It's a fuckin' party, remember? Maybe they swung by to show the crew some love."

"Uh-Uh," Stamp said as he hawkeyed the enemy group of small business owners and their loyal crew. He watched as three dudes got up in Greco's grill and started spittin' some yang he didn't need to hear in order to know what it tasted like. "Ain't no love being spread around over there. I can guarantee you that."

In the blink of an eye, Greco's security click came swarming from all corners. More dudes from the Talented Ten swarmed outta nowhere too, and before you knew it a straight-up club fight had broken out and all kinds of ballers and hustlers started getting caught in the cross punches.

"What the fuck!" Stamp ducked halfway under the table as a bottle shattered against the wall right over his head and sent glass shards raining down on him. Up on the stage the half-naked strippers pulled their fingers outta their pussies and came up off them golden poles screaming and running with their arms crossed over their fat, jiggling titties. The real slick bitches was screaming too, but they were bending over scooping up fifty and hundred dollar bills as they ran.

It was pure chaos up in there. Shot-glasses was getting zinged at niggah's foreheads left and right. Some lil sweet-looking bitch came out from behind the bar and climbed up on the counter and started jumping up and down and stomping his feet.

Dudes from rival sets all over Harlem had come rushing up outta the gambling rooms and the XXX theater and the fuck rooms too. They was jumpin' into the melee, swinging pool sticks, knockin' knuckles, and flinging chairs.

Dre was furious as he sat in his seat and watched all of their carefully orchestrated plans evaporate. These fools didn't know how to act! The Divine Nine was posted up and ready to pull off the take-down of the year, and these dumb-ass niggahs was tossin' furniture and wildin' out!

The music stopped playing and the fruit loop standing on top of the bar started looking around frantically and screaming at the top of his girlie lungs.

"Ace! Ace! Where the fuck you at! Ace!!!!"

Dre stood up on the table so he could see shit better too, and he had just peeped his partner Rome getting slammed over the head with the fat end of a pool cue when the first shot rang out and shut everybody the fuck up.

"Damn!" Stamp screamed and dove back under the table again as bitches shrieked and ran and niggahs started lunging for cover. Stamp was crouching down on his knees when more shots sounded off and something fell hard to the floor right in front of him. When he lifted up the long table cloth and peeked out toward the bar, all he saw was running feet and staring eyes.

Dre's eyes.

They were bucked wide open as his manz gurgled on a fountain of blood that was bubbling outta his shot-out throat.

"Dre!" Stamp hollered and snatched his dude by the shoulder and dragged him halfway under the table. Wet, whishing sounds was coming outta Dre's throat as Stamp reached up and yanked off the tablecloth and pressed it to his boyz neck.

"Hold up, niggah," he begged as Dre's chest started rising and falling real fast and blood soaked through the tablecloth and got all over his hands. "Don't you fuckin' die on me, Dre! Just hold the fuck up!"

Dre's eyes focused real sharp for a quick second, and then they glazed over as his heart stopped beating and he stared flatly at nothing at all.

"Dre!" Stamp screamed, and pounded on his friend's chest. But Dre was dead and gone, and when the whizzing sound of multiple speeding bullets started getting closer and closer, then Stamp knew it was time for him to get gone too. Covering his manz face with the bloody tablecloth, Stamp jetted out from under the table and broke out toward the back of the G-Spot.

He was heading for the boiler room so he could get to that crate of gats.

$$$$$

Pluto had both of his grimy hands deep inside of G's cookie jar when he thought he heard shots poppin' off in the front of the club. Frowning, he stopped filling up his garbage bags just long enough to hear another round of blasts before he started tossin' stacks of money outta the safe even faster.

A gun battle at the G-Spot was fuckin' unheard of, and Pluto didn't know who the hell was out front doing the shooting, or what the fuck Greco and his armed crew was doing about it, but he damn sure wasn't going out there to find out.

His hands moved in a blur as he cleared the shelves of the huge sum of cash that had been taken in so far. He felt some kinda way crouched down in G's office committing larceny on his old boss's safe, but he shrugged that shit off and kept on stacking paper. G was long gone and now Ace was gone too. It was look-out-for-self time, and that's exactly what Pluto was doing as he knotted both full garbage bags at the neck and slung them shits over his shoulders.

He was gonna slip out the back door and beat feet to his whip, then jump behind the wheel and get the fuck up outta New York as fast as he could. And he damn sure wasn't going back to Jersey neither. Not even to the airport. Nah, Ace had already made that mistake and he wasn't about to repeat it. Pluto planned on heading over to Connecticut instead. He was gonna zip through the Bronx real quick and get on the parkway and head for Hartford where he would ditch his whip and then lay low until the smoke cleared and he could get to Chicago and hook up with Coco.

"Yeah, that's what I'ma do," he muttered under his breath as he peeped outta the office and looked down the hall. He jumped back inside as some niggah ran around the corner like his ass was on fire and he had on gasoline drawers. Pluto peeped his head out as the dude ducked into the boiler room and slammed the door, and then he crept down the hall toward the back exit hoping like hell that whoever the fuck had run up in that boiler room stayed his ass in there until he got safely outside.

If that fool busts outta that door I'ma mash him, Pluto thought, eyeballing the boiler room door as he crept up on it. *Stay ya ass on in there niggah 'cause if you come out I'ma mash—*

BOOM!

A massive explosion went off in the boiler room and a raging ball of metal and fire blew through the wall. The entire building shook from the percussion blast, and nasty sewage spewed outta the pipes of every bathroom and saturated the walls.

Stamp was liquified instantly. He never knew that he had ignited the trip wire that Frank and Moonie had rigged inside the ill-fated crate of guns.

Pluto never knew what hit him either.

Projectile shards of iron and metal ball bearings ripped up his flesh and sent his body parts scattering in a spray of chunky pulp.

And the flames from the raging fire melted the plastic bags and sent the G-Spot's magnificent bounty of Grand Re-Opening cash up in a cloud of thick black smoke.

CHAPTER 26

Y eah, you ugly black wench!" Salida leaned out the window in the cut room and screamed at the chick who was sprawled out in the alley below. "That's what you get! I got your fuckin' *help*!" she taunted Monique and laughed like hell. "I got ya fuckin'—"

BOOM!

The G-Spot shook on its foundation as the boiler room on the other side of the building exploded and went up in blistering flames.

Every window in the building blew out in a shattering spray of heated glass, and thick metal shrapnel blew through the walls and obliterated everything in its path.

Salida was rocked off her feet and barely escaped being blown outta the blasted window. Burning smoke rose from the floor as huge jars of mixed chemicals exploded and the liquids stored in metal buckets and plastic containers splashed throughout the room. The loud music coming from the club had been strangled off and was now replaced by shouts of terror and screams of pain.

Salida coughed and staggered across the dark room, choking on smoke and slipping and sliding in the caustic chemicals that had seeped out on the floor. With only one shoe to protect her feet from the acidic liquid, she reached for her armband as she hopped toward the door.

She almost panicked when her hand came up empty. Her wristband was gone. And so was the key to the cut room. Holding her breath and hopping back toward her office, Salida made it inside and felt around underneath the rubble of the shattered desk until she found her gun.

She could hear the sizzling sound of burning noxious chemicals as she hopped over to the door again, and squinting to see the lock in the darkness she took aim and fired.

The hammer struck a bullet cartridge and ignited with the fumes in the air, creating a deadly spark that quickly turned into a blazing fireball. It rolled over Salida as it swept through the room and spread across the ceiling where the toxic fumes had collected in the air.

Engulfed in blistering flames, Salida opened her mouth to scream but she sucked in a wave of fire instead. She stumbled wildly toward the door and twisted the knob and fell out onto the landing. Trying to breathe and scream at the same time, she staggered toward the steps and tripped over her own feet. She reached out to catch herself but the railing was no longer there. She stepped right off the balcony and into the black nothingness of air, and as she fell into the darkness Salida McKay finally found her voice and screamed all the way down.

$$$$$

I was having one of my crazy dreams again.

But this time it wasn't Gino who was running away from me.

It was Trey.

I was back in Central Park and it was bitter cold outside.

Trey was sitting on a bench and I was standing across the street on the corner, waiting for the light to change. Huge snowflakes were falling all around us and my feet were sinking deep into multiple layers of thick ice and slush.

"Hurry up, Juicy," Trey hollered, grinning with his fine self.

His hairline and sideburns was edged up tight and his goatee had been nicely trimmed. He had on a black leather coat and some fresh Timbs and a pair of jeans. His smile was ultra white in his dark, handsome face and his jet-black locks were dotted with tiny flakes of white snow. A diamond earring glinted from his earlobe. He got up from the bench and walked toward me. Still grinning, he picked up a handful of snow and packed it between his hands.

He started laughing when I acted all scared, and then he tossed the snowball gently in my direction and turned around and started running into the park.

"You missed!" I shouted as I ran across the street and chased after him. "You ain't get nowhere near me boy!" I screamed.

Trey kept running. Sprinting. I started crying as he got further and further ahead, pulling me deeper into the park. The snow started sucking at my feet like I weighed a thousand pounds. Trey was dusting me and no matter how fast I ran I kept losing ground and getting more and more behind.

"Wait up!" I screamed as he turned into a shadowy blur against the winter whiteness of the snow. "Hey Trey! Wait up for me!"

"You gotta run faster, Juicy! *Faster!*"

I hauled ass through all that ice and snow.

My legs pumped like crazy as my chest burned from a blast of air that was so cold it damn near froze my lungs.

And then suddenly the world went completely dark.

Like somebody had pulled a thick wool blanket over the sky.

Ahead of me, where Trey should have been, was just an endless black road of nothingness.

And then I heard his voice. And I felt him and I saw him too.

Juicy, he said softly. *Ahhh... Juicy. I love you, baby. I love you.*

"Trey!" I screamed and ran toward him in the darkness. "Trey! Wait! Don't leave me!"

He slowed down so I could catch up to him.

He smiled and reached for me.

I grabbed at his hand and held on tight. He pulled me into his arms and kissed me, and I felt safe. I didn't know what was happening, but wherever this dude was going I was going too. And he was taking me with him. Leading me down that cold, dark path where there was only darkness ahead.

I felt so happy as I held his hand and walked beside him. I wanted to be with him so, so fuckin' bad. There was mad strength in Trey's touch. Mad love. And as long as me and him stayed together then I knew both of us were gonna be all right.

But I was still cold.

So damn cold. Cold Cold Cold Cold COLD.

I was so cold until I actually felt hot.

Hot Hot Hot Hot Hot Hot HOT HOT HOT!!!!

I woke up in a haze that felt just like a dream. But I knew I couldn't be dreaming. I just *couldn't* be. Because something was all pressed up against me and it had my arm hot as hell.

Burning hot.

I opened my eyes. And I was on *fire*.

$$\$\$\$\$\$$$

I sat up screaming in pain with the sleeve of my hoodie engulfed in flames.

Somehow Salida was on the floor laying up against me and she was on fire too, but almost half of her body was burning as she cried out and thrashed in agony.

I scooted away from her and started beating out my flames with my bare hands. It was dark in the G-Spot, and as I snatched my sweatshirt over my head and screamed for help I realized that the club was filled with heavy smoke and there were a whole lot of other people screaming for help in the darkness too.

It looked like whole walls had been knocked down by some sort of blast and the ceiling had caved in and collapsed in a bunch of spots. I peered across the room and saw a small, ragged hole that had been blasted in the outside wall. If I held my head the right way I could make out a faint glow from the streetlight in the alley outside. My mind was numb with shock as my eyes adjusted to the darkness. The G-Spot looked like one of those bombed-out buildings that you saw in war zones on the news. There was broken glass and twisted metal everywhere.

The room was starting to fill up with smoke, and if I wanted to live I was gonna have to get the fuck up out of there. I flung the smoldering hoodie away from me and tried to stand up. I couldn't. My lower back throbbed and the heel of my right foot felt like it was cracked in a million pieces. I was in way too much pain to support my own weight, and every time I moved, a sharp burst of agony jolted up and down my spine.

I strained to see through the smoky darkness as I called out Nooni's name. There was sounds of pure chaos coming from the other side of the club, and I could only wonder how many people were dead or hurt from what I just knew had to be some kind of terrorist attack.

I didn't know what the hell had happened to Nooni and Monique, but I could still hear Salida moaning and wriggling around in pain as her clothes burned off and her flames died out. I stuck my nose down in my t-shirt as I tried to breathe through the thick fumes that were closing in fast, and I was grateful as hell when I heard the sound of fire engines in the distance getting louder and louder.

"Nooni!" I lifted my head and screamed as I gasped and tried to catch my next breath. "Nooni where are you!" There was a faint sound of crunching glass coming from my right, and I half-crawled and half-scooted over to the twisted form that was laying where the bottom of the cut room stairs used to be.

"Nooni!" I screamed and reached out to shake her. Her face was all sliced up and her hair was slick with blood. She moaned a little bit but she couldn't talk, and all I could do was pray for both of us.

"Dear God," I pleaded in a panic. "Lord please save us. Get us out of here! Please get us the hell outta here! Help us!!!!"

Grandmother used to tell me that God looked out for babies and fools.

Well since Nooni was a baby then I musta been a damn fool because I recognized the voice of my savior right off the bat, and this wasn't the first time the Lord had sent this chick to look out for me neither.

"Juicy! Juicy! Where you at? *Juicy*!"

"I'm over here!" I screamed as Chiney's voice grew closer and shadowy silhouettes appeared by the ragged hole in the wall. "I'm by the stairs! With Nooni! Hurry up, Chiney! We're right over here!"

I was crying grateful tears as Chiney and Rain made their way to us through the darkness.

"Be careful, Juicy," Rain said as he helped me get up on my feet. I winced as he grabbed my sliced-up hand and I snatched it back. "Okay, you hold on to me, then," he said. "Hold on to me."

Chiney went to help Nooni, and I held on to Rain as he led me through all the twisted, burning rubble on the floor. We picked our way slowly and I panted with extreme pain as I followed him toward the opening in the wall and the faint glow from the street light that was shining outside.

Rain reached back and tried to hold me up, but I brushed him off. I was grateful to him but this time I was walking outta the G-Spot on my *own*. My whole body was busted up and wracked with pain, but I was determined to get the hell outta that house of horrors standing up on my own two feet.

A rush of emotions almost buckled my knees as we walked past Gino's mother. She looked half-dead laying there stretched out on the debris-covered floor. Her clothes had been burned almost completely off her body, and almost every strand of that butter hair had been singed off her head too.

As much shit as I had been through, and as weak and broken up as I was... I still had a heart. And as I limped past my dead son's grandmother I gazed down into her once-beautiful face... and then I raised my busted-up foot as high as I could get it and I *stomped* that bitch!!!

TWO MONTHS LATER...

"Breaking news coming to you live from Channel 7, Eyewitness News. Eyewitness news reporter Martin Solter joins us live from Harlem, where he is standing outside of the ruins that were once the grand social club known as the G-Spot. Good evening, Martin, can you tell us anything about the conclusion of the investigation of the rubble that used to be the premier gentlemen's club in the tri-state area?

"Yes, Gloria. I'm reporting live from Harlem today where authorities have finally concluded their investigation of the tragic bombing at the G-Spot Social Club. As you know, just two short

months ago rescue personnel were called to the scene when some sort of volatile explosive gutted the notorious gentlemen's club. To date, over a hundred party-goers were either killed or injured as a result of that bombing, and at least two unidentified victims remain hospitalized as social service personnel attempt to contact their next of kins . . .

"Who in the world turned this on?" a young psychiatric nurse walked into a patient's room at Bellevue Hospital and picked up the remote control from the night table. Shaking her head at the nightmarish footage of hundreds of people screaming and running out of a bombed-out Harlem nightclub, she aimed the remote toward the television and clicked it off.

She glanced down at the woman who was laying outstretched in the bed.

"That's the last thing you need to be watching," she said, shaking her head as she pulled the crisp sheet up from the foot of the bed and smoothed it around her patient's chest. "You need to be thanking God you made it out of there alive and survived all those surgeries too."

The nurse picked up the clipboard from the end of the bed and started flipping through the notes from the previous shift. They read the same as they always read.

Patient refuses to communicate and expresses no emotions.

The nurse shook her head. It was a damn shame what had happened to all those people up in that nasty club. It was even worse for people like this pitiful woman here who managed to escape that night, but was left psychologically damaged.

The young nurse set the clipboard down and did a visual examination of the patient. She had been rescued from the gutted club with third-degree burns over forty percent of her body. Large strips of her skin had been seared down to the flesh, and her poor scalp had been scorched completely bald. The woman had received several skin grafting operations, and it had been touch and go for a while, but just when it looked like she was on the mend the poor patient had suffered a mental break down and they'd been forced to transfer her to Bellevue.

They'd brought her up on the psychiatric ward in full body restraints, suffering from hallucinations, delusions, and homicidal tendencies. But that was weeks ago, and she seemed to be doing a lot better now that her anti-psychotic medication was beginning to take effect. In fact she'd been so calm that her doctors had moved her to the step-down ward, one of the least restrictive wards in the entire psych building.

The young nurse eyed the hideous scars on the woman's face and tried to be optimistic. Things might get better for her. A few more surgeries to correct some of her facial disfigurements, and maybe a whole lot of intensive therapy and who knew? This woman might end up as good as new.

Or as good as she could get considering her circumstances. Not one person had come to visit this patient since she'd been brought in, and even though the woman was perfectly capable of communicating she had refused to speak or even tell the doctors or the social workers anything about her. Not even her name.

Trauma, the nurse thought sadly, then scribbled something on her clipboard before walking out of the room to check on another patient. There was a stomach virus going around and it seemed like the whole staff had caught it. Every ward in the hospital was severely short on personnel tonight so her already heavy load had been doubled.

Moments after the nurse left the room, her patient flung the sheet back down to the bottom of the bed again.

Sunny Hills had been bad enough, but Bellevue was a goddamn dump!

It had been a long time since she'd been up on her feet, and struggling against the lingering pain and stiffness of her burned, but healing skin, she inched over to the edge of the bed and then crawled out. Three times she attempted to stand on her feet, and three times she failed and slumped back down to the mattress.

But on the fourth attempt she made it. Wobbling and holding onto the footboard for support, she staggered over to the doorway and peeked out.

She had places to go and people to kill.

And as soon as she saw her busy young nurse enter a room at the other end of the ward, the patient slipped out the door and hobbled down the hall toward the staircase and disappeared.

$$$$$

Every time a new clown was hired they gave him to Willie to train.

"Brang your slow ass on," the old man told the youngsta who had just reported for his first day of work at the busy city hospital. This one wasn't gonna last long, Willie knew. He could tell just by looking at him that the boy didn't have a lick of goddamn sense.

They went room by room mopping floors, cleaning shitters, and emptying trash cans. The damn boy was slow and lazy and he was stupid too. He couldn't figure out how to take one garbage bag outta the can and put the next one in, and they wanted *Willie* to be messing around with him all day? Wasn't gonna happen!

They came upon a room at the end of a hall where a young black lady was laying in the bed under a thin sheet. One of her legs was up in the air suspended in traction, both of her eyes were all bandaged up, and there was a thick tube clenched between her dry, crusted lips.

"Get in there and clean that shit bowl," Willie directed the dumb boy toward the bathroom. He looked just like one of those drug dealers who hung out on Lenox Avenue. He wouldn't be surprised if the fool wasn't high right now.

"Clean it for what?" the idiot said, staring at the woman under the sheet. "Wit' all them burns and broken bones she ain't been shittin' nowhere but right there in that bed."

Willie wanted to backhand this fool something terrible. But instead he ordered the boy to mop the floor and empty the trash, and then he walked into the bathroom and started scrubbing the sink, the shower, and the toilet himself.

"What the hell you doin'?" Willie almost fainted when he came back outta the bathroom with his wet rag in his hand. That lil twisted fool had done pulled back the poor girl's sheet and was peeking all up under her hospital gown!

"Yo! This chick got three titties!" the dumb-ass boy hollered, and Willie couldn't even help himself as he slapped that fool upside his head with the nasty toilet bowl rag.

"Get your black ass outta here!" Willie hissed, pushing the young boy outta the room. "Ain't nobody losing they damn job over you! *Three titties!* That's what's wrong

596

wit' all y'all young kids today! Been messin' around with all them drugs and ruining ya damn minds! Three titties!" Willie swung his dirty rag at the new hire again. "Boy get yo' dumb ass outta here before both of us get fired!"

Moments after the two men left the room, the broken-up blind chick laying in the bed took a deep breath and wiggled her big toe. And moments after that, she moved her whole damn foot. She had just had her third surgery and she might not be able to see yet, but she could damn sure think. And as long as she could still think she could still scheme.

Revenge was a mothafucka!

She wiggled her toes again. And then the crusty lips that were clenched around the tube did something they hadn't done in two whole months.

They smiled.

ONE YEAR LATER

It had been a long cold winter in New York, but today the birds were singing in the trees as I sat outside on the front stoop chillin'. I sipped on a cup of warm tea and watched a trail of ants crawl around my feet as they did their damnest to pick up a dead beetle. I wasn't mad at them for being willing to work hard for what they wanted. On the real tip, that's what life was all about.

Life. After all the craziness I had been through I was definitely trying to live mine to the fullest. It was hard to believe a whole year had passed since the G-Spot had crumbled to the ground, and so much had changed in my world that I couldn't even wrap my head around it. My body had healed and thank God my mind had too. It seemed like all that awful shit had happened to another girl. To some other chick named Juicy-Mo.

But when I looked back over my life I could see so much loss. So much damned grief. So many bad breaks and hard knocks. Shit, I had suffered through nightmares and daymares too. Devastating trials and mind-blowing tribulations.

I glanced down at my feet. It was damn sure an ant-eat-beetle world out there and I watched as a bunch of tiny brown bodies marched around like soldiers, dividing up the load to make sure everybody ate and everybody got fat.

Like me. Yeah, my behind had gotten kinda fat too.

The front door swung open behind me and I looked over my shoulder.

"Juicy! Now you know you need to get your big booty up offa that cold concrete! Just watch. You gonna tryta push that baby out and a hemorrhoid is gonna fall out ya ass!"

I shook my head and laughed.

"Chiney, please! Girl where you be getting all that crazy shit from? You need to stay off all them pregnancy websites reading them old wives tales. You sound just like somebody's superstitious old grandmother. *Mine!*"

We started cracking up and Chiney reached out and pulled me up to my feet.

"*Sheeeit,* grandmas be knowing what the fuck they talkin' about, Juicy. Remember, your baby ain't gonna have no grandma, but she *is* gonna have a real smart auntie. That's why I be reading up on all that stuff. So one of us can know what the hell we doing."

I gave Chiney a big hug. She was right. The baby I was carrying wasn't gonna have no grandparents but she was damn sure gonna have a whole lotta other people in her life who loved her.

Like Candy and Knowledge Graham. After the G-Spot blew up they had rushed over to the hospital to see me. They had stayed by my side for days and I had gotten real close to both of them.

Me and Candy was really feeling each other. Hell, we both used to be the type of hot-in-the-ass, dumb-as-fuck guttersnipes that predatory hustlers in Harlem zoomed in on every single day. Hurricane Jackson had dragged Candy through the sewer in the House of Homicide, and G had damn-near buried my ass alive in the G-Spot. Both of us were survivors of a whole lotta brutal abuse, and we had the battle scars to prove that shit. But on the real, if we had just had *somebody* around to pull our coats and hip us to the game, *and* if we had been smart enough to listen, then maybe our young asses wouldn't have gotten shit on like that in the first place, you feel me?

So me and Candy had just kinda clicked up together. I liked what she was doing with her girls at Knowledge is Power and I definitely respected her grind. Candy had lost her whole family too, so both of us were learning how to build a new family outta the trusted friends that we had in our lives.

Candy and Knowledge had been right at my bedside with Chiney after the G-Spot got bombed. The cops had come to tell us that Trey had been shot down outside of a funeral home just like a dog in the street.

My whole world had straight-up flipped when I heard those words. But my poor heart had been so damaged, so fuckin' beat down and broken up, that it almost wasn't even a surprise. Part of me had expected something bad to happen again. It was almost like I had just been *waiting* for it to go down. Like losing the people I loved was my fate. My *destiny*. Like there was no way in the world that a chick like me deserved to get a second crack at happiness.

Candy had cried right along with me and Chiney. The three of us had clung to each other and cried so long and hard that it felt like we were soaking the whole damn world with our tears.

News about the explosion at the G-Spot was all over every channel in New York. It made the front page of the Daily News and the Post too. Almost forty people had died up in there and way more people than that had been hurt. The fire department said a bomb had gone off inside of a box of loaded guns, and that somebody had planted it in there on purpose.

Almost everybody in Harlem knew about my life at the G-Spot, and my friends had come outta the woodwork and kept my hospital room on jam. My girl Brittany and her old-ass sugar-daddy Cecil had showed up to check on me, and so did Pacho, the Samoan dude who used to drive me all around town when G was alive.

My girl Egypt had rushed over from Brooklyn, and DarQuese did too. A nurse had just brought me back upstairs to my room and I was happy as hell to see them sitting there waiting for me. Quese had opened up her own shop in Crown Heights and she was relieved that I was okay that she didn't even act funny over that ass-kicking me and Egypt had put on her.

"I got something to tell you," I had taken her hand as she stood her gigantic self next to my hospital bed smiling down at me. Yeah, half of her face was still all burnt up and the other half was still beautiful, but I knew in my heart that DarQuese Middleton was a hundred percent a true blue friend.

"I'm so damn sorry, Quese," I told her as tears welled up in my eyes. "I was so damn wrong. I know who shot me and Gino now, and it damn sure wasn't Pit. He mighta been at the church that day, but he didn't kill Gino. Pit was your man and I know y'all had a good thing going. I'm sorry he caught a bad one behind that debt because it truly wasn't his to pay."

Egypt told me that she had hooked up with her dude Hood again and they were taking things real slow. Trying to find their way back to what they used to have. Hood was still doing his music thing and touring and all that, but at least they were talking again. And sometimes they were hooking up to get that gushy on too.

"We're picking our issues up thread by thread," she said simply, even though her pretty eyes were sparkling. Egypt was the kind of chick who looked just like her name. Strong, beautiful, natural, and powerful. "Lamont just signed a new recording contract and I'm tryna get in medical school. Ain't no telling what's gonna happen. We just gotta wait and see what's up."

And now, as I stood up on the front porch and stretched my arms over my head I was real glad that these was the kind of aunties my daughter was gonna have in her life to look up to. Chicks like Rita, Candy, Egypt, Chiney, and DarQuese who were smart and powerful and who had made a whole lotta dumb-ass mistakes in their lives, just like I did.

And who had *paid* for those dumb-ass mistakes too.

Just like I did.

Between the six of us there was a helluva lot about the streets that we could teach my little girl. The question was, when the time came would she be willing to learn?

"You ready?"

I was grinning my ass off as I turned around.

He reached out and pulled me close to him and his strong hands slid up the back of my thighs, scooped over my fluffy ass, and then slipped between our bodies to palm my big belly.

I nodded at my fine-ass husband and stood up on my tippy-toes to get at his warm kiss.

Trey had gotten shot by one of the teenagers that he used to mentor over at the Crossover Center. The poor little girl had been traumatized outta her mind by the horrors she had suffered through, and she had blamed Trey for telling her to trust him and then not being there to protect her.

"She's right, Juicy," he had told me when I went to see him in his hospital bed the day after the G-Spot burned down. They had him in a room right downstairs from mine, and this time instead of some crazy ass doctor tryna stop me from getting to my man when he needed me, my nursing staff had been instructed to put me in a wheelchair and take me downstairs to see Trey any damn time I wanted to.

"This was all my fault," Trey had told me as he laid in that bed with a bullet hole in his chest and another one in his shoulder. The blast to his chest had barely missed his heart, and the doctors said he was damn lucky to be alive.

"I don't blame Taleah for none of this," he said, "because I gave that little girl my word that nothing was gonna happen to her, Juicy. I *made* her tell me who sold

Princess those damn drugs, and even when she told me I still got it wrong."

"What are you talking about, Trey?" I had asked him. "What are you trying to say?"

"I'm saying I thought it was J-Ugly who was out there transacting with Princess that night. But it wasn't. It was Maleek's violating-ass. Just like it was Maleek who got hold of Taleah on that staircase and took her whole damn childhood away."

The cops had locked Taleah up even though Trey had made a call to the district attorney and begged him not to prosecute her. We didn't know what was gonna happen when she finally got a trial date, but Trey had hired his friend from law school to represent her, and he was keeping her commissary up and paying all her legal expenses too. Me and him took that nasty bus ride over the Francis Buono bridge to Rikers Island to visit Taleah every week, and she was studying for her GED and getting counseling too, and she was beginning to believe the promise we made her that me and Trey were both gonna work hard to get her released, and that we were gonna be there for her for as long as she needed us.

And Taleah wasn't the only one who me and Trey had vowed to be there for neither.

My girl Rita was out of the hospital and doing a whole lot better. She had gone through a lot of complicated surgeries and then spent six months in a rehab facility learning how to function again, but Rita was a Harlem soldier, and aside from a few headaches every now and then she was slowly getting back on her game. No, she wasn't no math-mama like she used to be, but she was taking care of Chub again and she was working part-time too, and her and her dude Dutchy was planning on getting married in a couple of months.

And Nooni? Just thinking about that poor girl made me sadder than sad. Unfortunately, we lost Nooni. Lost her to the streets. But she had shown up when me and Trey got married in a small church around our way, and I was hoping like hell she would pull herself together and show up at her sister's wedding too.

"That damned Nubia!" Rita had cried when I went to see her one day. "They really fucked my sister up you know, Juicy. Her mind is gone! She runs away from every rehab program I put her in. She's gonna end up dead or in jail, just watch. She's out there turning tricks up on the avenue, waving down cars at all times of night," Rita had shaken her head and sniffled in my arms. "She's steady chasing them drugs they got her hooked on in the G-Spot. Chasing, chasing, *chasing*! She just can't stop chasing those damn drugs!"

That dirty bitch, I had said to myself as I held Rita in my arms and thought about Gino's dog-ass mother, Salida. Nooni had told us that Salida was the one who had gotten her strung out on meth in the first damn place, and none of us had been surprised. Shit, if that trifling bitch could kill her own child she could damn sure kill somebody else's.

But I felt for Rita and I felt for Nooni too. I had put my life on the line to get that girl outta the G-Spot, and a lot of other people had tried to help her get clean and get her shit together too. But even still. I knew it was hard for her and I didn't regret a damn thing I had done. For Nooni or for myself.

Spring was feeling almost like summer as me and Trey walked down the streets of Harlem holding hands. I dug the hell outta my husband. I loved going to bed with a dude like him every night and waking up safe in his arms every morning. It felt good to have his baby growing inside of me, and being pregnant was really a wonderful thing. Chiney swore all out that my nose and my titties had gotten big as hell, and maybe she was right. My stomach was poked out a whole lot too, but Trey said I was carrying mostly in my ass.

I glanced up at him as we walked. My man was gonna be a damn good daddy. His little girl was gonna grow up the exact opposite of me. She was gonna be loved and protected and she was most definitely gonna be hipped to the game and prepared for the joy *and* the pain in this world too. I wasn't gonna stifle her the way Grandmother had stifled me. I wasn't gonna shut her down and keep my foot on her neck so hard that she fell for the first slimy niggah who patted her on the ass and told her she was fine.

Me and Trey had talked about all that. We had confessed a lot about our pasts to each other and we fully agreed on how we was gonna raise our baby girl. And hopefully our baby boy one day too. I didn't want my daughter growing up as the only child. I wanted her to have the same thing that me and Jimmy used to have when we was growing up. Somebody to be close to. Somebody to share secrets with.

Somebody who loved her enough to die for her.

Somebody who could be her heart so she could be his soul.

And Trey was totally down with having more kids too. He had been right by my side throughout my entire pregnancy. Cooking me all kinds of healthy food, taking me on long walks, making sure I took my vitamins and drank plenty of water. Just spoiling the hell outta me.

I felt so damn lucky. Trey wanted this baby. He wanted her bad, and he had been one hundred percent involved in choosing her name.

Shops up and down 125th Street were beginning to open for the day, and newspaper stands were being stocked. Street vendors were unloading their trucks and setting up their tables and stands. An old man pushing a cart filled up with everything he owned stopped to dap Trey out and congratulate us on our baby. I smiled as Trey kicked it with the homeless dude like he was one of his old stockbroker friends or something. My man was smart and paid and slanging big dick, but he was still humble and giving and connected to the community that we were helping to rebuild.

Yep, that's right. I said *we*. I took a deep breath as we stopped across the street from Trey's barbershop. I had opened up a store-front boutique called, *JuicyOriginals* and I specialized in sewing all the hot summer dresses and funky urban attire that big-booty Harlem chicks like me loved to wear. I had also gotten back to work on my *Birthday Cake* clothing line, and my girl Candy Montana rocked the hell outta my sexy signature pieces every time she went out on stage.

I stood in front of my shop waiting patiently as Trey went through the same routine that he went through five days outta every week. Wasn't nobody *never* gonna get the drop on me no more. Trey had set me up with gats, mace, tasers, switchblades... all that. And he had taught me how to use 'em too. The next time trouble came my way I was gonna be ready.

Trey unlocked my door gratings and pulled them up real high. Then he punched in the alarm code and unlocked the door. He made me stay outside while he went in the boutique and searched every inch of it from top to bottom, just to make sure nobody had snuck in there and was waiting in a corner to get at me or our precious unborn baby girl.

When he was finally done with all that, he flipped my CLOSED sign over to OPEN, and then held the door open wide so I could walk in. I grinned as he told me he loved me and kissed me goodbye. I stood in the window as he nodded at his man Rider who was opening up the check-cashing place down the block, and then walked across the street looking like a tall, fine-ass beast.

Trey stopped outside his barbershop and turned around knowing full well that I was still right there in that window watching him. He waved and blew me a kiss, and I waved and blew him one right back. Inside my stomach our baby kicked, and my heart got heavy with grief and light with joy at the same time.

Once upon a time I had carried another baby in my belly.

A little boy who I had loved so much. And that little boy had had a father who I had loved with my entire body, heart, and soul too.

But like people kept telling me, *life is for the living* and I'm definitely a witness to that. I'm here right now to tell you that even after all the pain and the heartache life *does* go on.

I looked outta the window again. Trey was still standing there. Watching over me with his love. I glanced up at the big sign above the awning on his shop. It said, SECOND CHANCES.

I waved at my man and grinned.

I had *loved* Gino. I would *always* love Gino.

I glanced up at the sign again and for a second I coulda sworn that bad boy blinked like a traffic light.

SECOND CHANCES.

Yeah, that's exactly what God had given me.

A second chance at life. A second chance at laughter. A second chance at love.

A second chance. With Antonio "Trey" Jackson III.

AND AT THE END...

Warning before destruction, Grandmother used to tell me and Jimmy all the time.

"Push, Juicy! Push!"

It seemed like everybody and their damn uncle was crowded up in my labor room looking up my coochie. Trey, Chiney, Candy, Rita, Quese. My baby girl had a whole posse waiting to welcome her into the world. They were all grinning and cheering their asses off, but I was twisting and turning in that labor bed and having second thoughts.

This shit was hard! Labor pains wasn't no damn joke! I had told my doctor I wanted a natural childbirth, but when that very first labor pain kicked me in the back I had changed my mind in a hurry.

"Gimme some drugs!" I hollered as another wave of pain rolled over me. "I can't take it no damn more!"

"She's almost here, baby," Trey held my hand and started doing all those crazy breathing exercises we had learned in our prenatal class. I had made him promise not to let the doctors give me anything, no matter how much I begged. I wanted to experience every minute of this. To really feel it. I wanted to keep my mind clear so I could appreciate every detail of this miracle that I was about to perform.

But I was in so much crazy pain that my mind didn't have no choice but to go to another place. And when I got there I heard my grandmother's voice in my ear. I heard her clear as day, and I even saw her too.

Grandmother! I screamed out in my mind.

She was standing between me and Trey. She was holding one of my hands and she was holding one of his hands too. Grandmother was just'a preaching and praying, just like she used to do back in the day. But instead of saying all kinds of crazy stuff that used to scare the shit outta me like, "The wages of sin is death, Juicy! Walk by faith and not by sight. My God is a *jealous* God! You can't serve two masters, honey! You gots to pick one. The devil or the LORD!"

Nah, Grandmother had tears in her eyes now. Happy tears.

Like maybe she was proud of me or something.

I heard her whispering, "Love is patient and love is kind, Juicy-Mo! It does not envy, it does not boast, it is not proud. It is not rude, it is not self-seeking, it is not easily angered. It keeps no record of wrongs, you hear me girl? Love does not delight in evil but it rejoices with the truth, baby! It always protects, it always trusts, it always hopes, and it *always* perseveres. Love never fails. Believe me, my child. No matter what befalls you in life, these three things shall *always* remain: faith, hope, and love. But the greatest of these, is love. And trust me, daughter, love doesn't die. It doesn't die, Juicy! It does *not* die!"

Love.

That's what this story is really all about anyway, isn't it?

Love.

I felt something big and warm tryna push its way outta me.

Love.

Rita screamed and Trey hollered and grabbed my hand as they stared between my legs.

Love.

Antonia Gina Jimmia Jackson

Love.

I felt my grandmother's cool kiss on my forehead.

Love.

Passing down all the secrets a Harlem chick like me would ever need to know.

Love.

And then somewhere in the deepest part of my heart,

Love.

I heard my daughter's cries.

The End

NOIRE

G-Spot 2:
The Seven Deadly Sins
An Urban Erotic Serial Tale Told in 7 Parts

REVENGE: THE 7TH DEADLY SIN

ALTERNATE ENDING

An Original Noire Twist

by
Noire

www.AskNoire.com
www.GSpot2.com
www.TheGSpotSaga.com

WARNING: Read at your own Risk!
The scenes you are about to read are graphic in nature.
If you don't have the stomach for the horrors of the street life, then
DO NOT READ ANY FURTHER!!!

ONE YEAR LATER

It had been a long cold winter in New York, but today the birds were singing in the trees as I sat outside on the front stoop watching the happenings at the three-story brownstone right across the street. Things had been real crazy over there for the past few days, but now the crime-scene tape was being taken down and thrown away, and it looked like the top-floor apartment was being totally emptied out.

Four maintenance workers wearing yellow rubber gloves kept running up and down the brownstone's steps bringing out big plastic bags and tossing them inside one of them portable little Dumpsters that they put at small construction sites.

Last Sunday morning, the hunched-over old man who had lived there had shot his wife to death. And once she was gone, he had pressed the gun to his own head and taken himself out too.

I had been straight-up shocked when the ambulance and all the cop cars had pulled up over there. I knew the old man's wife had been real sick and suffering with Parkinson's. He had been taking care of her by himself for a whole lotta years, but I never would have predicted this. All their kids were grown and gone, and the two of them had been all by themselves in that small apartment for a real long time. The old man had left a note saying he killed his wife because he couldn't stand to see her suffering like that no more, and that he was killing himself because he couldn't stand to live without her.

I wasn't mad at the old man because I knew how it felt to love somebody so much that you just didn't think you could live without them. On the real tip, loving hard like that is what life is all about.

Life. After all the craziness I had been through I was definitely trying to live mine to the fullest. It was hard to believe a whole year had passed since the G-Spot had crumbled to the ground, and so much had changed in my world that I couldn't even wrap my head around it. My body had healed and thank God my mind had too. It seemed like all that awful shit had happened to another girl. To some other chick named Juicy-Mo.

But when I looked back over my life I could see so much loss. So much damned grief. So many bad breaks and hard knocks. Shit, I had suffered through nightmares and daymares too. Devastating trials and mind-blowing tribulations.

I glanced up at the window where the old man and his wife used to live. I was gonna miss seeing the soft light shining from that window. Every night I used to sit in my window and look up there, and every night that old man used to look down at me and smile and wave. And now, there was one more person gone from my life. Fate had given me one more loss to live with.

The front door swung open behind me and I jumped and looked over my shoulder.

605

"Juicy! Now you know you need to get your big booty up offa that cold concrete! Just watch. You gonna tryta push that baby out and a hemorrhoid is gonna fall out ya ass!"

I shook my head and laughed.

"Chiney, please! Girl where you be getting all that crazy shit from? You need to stay off all them pregnancy websites reading them old wives tales. You sound just like somebody's superstitious old grandmother. *Mine!*"

We started cracking up and Chiney reached out and pulled me up to my feet.

"*Sheeeit*, grandmas be knowing what the fuck they talkin' about, Juicy. Remember, your baby ain't gonna have no grandma, but she *is* gonna have a real smart auntie. That's why I be reading up on all that stuff. So one of us can know what the hell we doing."

I gave Chiney a big hug. She was right. The baby I was carrying wasn't gonna have no grandparents but she was damn sure gonna have a whole lotta other people in her life who loved her.

Like Candy and Knowledge Graham. After the G-Spot blew up they had rushed over to the hospital to see me. They had stayed by my side for days and I had gotten real close to both of them.

Me and Candy was really feeling each other. Hell, we both used to be the type of hot-in-the-ass, dumb-as-fuck guttersnipes that predatory hustlers in Harlem zoomed in on every single day. Hurricane Jackson had dragged Candy through the sewer in the House of Homicide, and G had damn-near buried my ass alive in the G-Spot. Both of us were survivors of a whole lotta brutal abuse, and we had the battle scars to prove that shit. But on the real, if we had just had *somebody* around to pull our coats and hip us to the game, *and* if we had been smart enough to listen, then maybe our young asses wouldn't have gotten shit on like that in the first place, you feel me?

So me and Candy had just kinda clicked up together. I liked what she was doing with her girls at Knowledge is Power and I definitely respected her grind. Candy had lost her whole family too, so both of us were learning how to build a new family outta the trusted friends that we had in our lives.

Candy and Knowledge had been right at my bedside with Chiney after the G-Spot got bombed. The cops had come to tell us that Trey had been shot down outside of a funeral home just like a dog in the street.

My whole world had straight-up flipped when I heard those words. But my poor heart had been so damaged, so fuckin' beat down and broken up, that it almost wasn't even a surprise. Part of me had expected something bad to happen again. It was almost like I had just been *waiting* for it to go down. Like losing the people I loved was my fate. My *destiny*. Like there was no way in the world that a chick like me deserved to get a second crack at happiness.

Candy had cried right along with me and Chiney. The three of us had clung to each other and cried so long and hard that it felt like we were soaking the whole damn world with our tears.

News about the explosion at the G-Spot was all over every channel in New York. It made the front page of the Daily News and the Post too. Almost forty people had died up in there and way more people than that had been hurt. The fire department said a bomb had gone off inside of a box of loaded guns, and that somebody had planted it in there on purpose.

Almost everybody in Harlem knew about my life at the G-Spot, and my friends had come outta the woodwork and kept my hospital room on jam. My girl Brittany and her old-ass sugar-daddy Cecil had showed up to check on me, and so did Pacho, the Samoan dude who used to drive me all around town when G was alive.

My girl Egypt had rushed over from Brooklyn, and DarQuese did too. A nurse had just brought me back upstairs to my room and I was happy as hell to see them sitting there waiting for me. Quese had opened up her own shop in Crown Heights and she was relieved that I was okay that she didn't even act funny over that ass-kicking me and Egypt had put on her.

"I got something to tell you," I had taken her hand as she stood her gigantic self next to my hospital bed smiling down at me. Yeah, half of her face was still all burnt up and the other half was still beautiful, but I knew in my heart that DarQuese Middleton was a hundred percent a true blue friend.

"I'm so damn sorry, Quese," I told her as tears welled up in my eyes. "I was so damn wrong. I know who shot me and Gino now, and it damn sure wasn't Pit. He mighta been at the church that day, but he didn't kill Gino. Pit was your man and I know y'all had a good thing going. I'm sorry he caught a bad one behind that debt because it truly wasn't his to pay."

Egypt told me that she had hooked up with her dude Hood again and they were taking things real slow. Trying to find their way back to what they used to have. Hood was still doing his music thing and touring and all that, but at least they were talking again. And sometimes they were hooking up to get that gushy on too.

"We're picking our issues up thread by thread," she said simply, even though her pretty eyes were sparkling. Egypt was the kind of chick who looked just like her name. Strong, beautiful, natural, and powerful. "Lamont just signed a new recording contract and I'm tryna get in medical school. Ain't no telling what's gonna happen. We just gotta wait and see what's up."

And now, as I stood up on the front porch and watched the maintenance men carry the last bit of stuff outta the brownstone across the street, I was real glad that these was the kind of aunties my daughter was gonna have in her life to look up to. Chicks like Rita, Candy, Egypt, Chiney, and DarQuese who were smart and powerful and who had made a whole lotta dumb-ass mistakes in their lives, just like I did.

And who had *paid* for those dumb-ass mistakes too.

Just like I did.

Between the six of us there was a helluva lot about the streets that we could teach my little girl. The question was, when the time came would she be willing to learn?

"You ready?"

I was grinning my ass off as I turned around again.

He reached out and pulled me close to him and his strong hands slid up the back of my thighs, scooped over my fluffy ass, and then slipped between our bodies to palm my big belly.

I nodded at my fine-ass husband and stood up on my tippy-toes to get at his warm kiss.

Trey had gotten shot by one of the teenagers that he used to mentor over at the Crossover Center. The poor little girl had been traumatized outta her mind by the horrors she had suffered through, and she had blamed Trey for telling her to trust him and then not being there to protect her.

"She's right, Juicy," he had told me when I went to see him in his hospital bed the day after the G-Spot burned down. They had him in a room right downstairs from mine, and this time instead of some crazy ass doctor tryna stop me from getting to my man when he needed me, my nursing staff had been instructed to put me in a wheelchair and take me downstairs to see Trey any damn time I wanted to.

"This was all my fault," Trey had told me as he laid in that bed with a bullet hole in his chest and another one in his shoulder. The blast to his chest had barely missed his heart, and the doctors said he was damn lucky to be alive.

"I don't blame Taleah for none of this," he said, "because I gave that little girl my word that nothing was gonna happen to her, Juicy. I *made* her tell me who sold Princess those damn drugs, and even when she told me I still got it wrong."

"What are you talking about, Trey?" I had asked him. "What are you trying to say?"

"I'm saying I thought it was J-Ugly who was out there transacting with Princess that night. But it wasn't. It was *Maleek's* violating-ass. Just like it was Maleek who got hold of Taleah on that staircase and took her whole damn childhood away."

The cops had locked Taleah up even though Trey had made a call to the district attorney and begged him not to prosecute her. We didn't know what was gonna happen when she finally got a trial date, but Trey had hired his friend from law school to represent her, and he was keeping her commissary up and paying all her legal expenses too. Me and him took that nasty bus ride over the Francis Buono bridge to Rikers Island to visit Taleah every week, and she was studying for her GED and getting counseling too, and she was beginning to believe the promise we made her that me and Trey were both gonna work hard to get her released, and that we were gonna be there for her for as long as she needed us.

And Taleah wasn't the only one who me and Trey had vowed to be there for neither.

My girl Rita was out of the hospital and doing a whole lot better. She had gone through a lot of complicated surgeries and then spent six months in a rehab facility learning how to function again, but Rita was a Harlem soldier, and aside from a few headaches every now and then she was slowly getting back on her game. No, she wasn't no math-mama like she used to be, but she was taking care of Chub again and she was working part-time too, and her and her dude Dutchy was planning on getting married in a couple of months.

And Nooni? Just thinking about that poor girl made me sadder than sad. Unfortunately, we lost Nooni. Lost her to the streets. But she had shown up when me and Trey got married in a small church around our way, and I was hoping like hell she would pull herself together and show up at her sister's wedding too.

"That damned Nubia!" Rita had cried when I went to see her one day. "They really fucked my sister up you know, Juicy. Her mind is gone! She runs away from every rehab program I put her in. She's gonna end up dead or in jail, just watch. She's out there turning tricks up on the avenue, waving down cars at all times of night," Rita had shaken her head and sniffled in my arms. "She's steady chasing them drugs they got her hooked on in the G-Spot. Chasing, chasing, *chasing!* She just can't stop chasing those damn drugs!"

That dirty bitch, I had said to myself as I held Rita in my arms and thought about Gino's dog-ass mother, Salida. Nooni had told us that Salida was the one who had gotten her strung out on meth in the first damn place, and none of us had been surprised. Shit, if that trifling bitch could kill her own child she could damn sure kill somebody else's.

But I felt for Rita and I felt for Nooni too. I had put my life on the line to get that girl outta the G-Spot, and a lot of other people had tried to help her get clean and get her shit together too. But even still. I knew it was hard for her and I didn't regret a damn thing I had done. For Nooni or for myself.

Spring was feeling almost like summer as me and Trey walked down the streets of Harlem holding hands. I dug the hell outta my husband. I loved going to bed with a dude like him every night and waking up safe in his arms every morning. It felt good to have his baby growing inside of me, and being pregnant was really a wonderful thing. Chiney swore all out that my nose and my titties had gotten big as hell, and maybe she was right. My stomach was poked out a whole lot too, but Trey said I was carrying mostly in my ass.

I glanced up at him as we walked. My man was gonna be a damn good daddy. His little girl was gonna grow up the exact opposite of me. She was gonna be loved and protected and she was most definitely gonna be hipped to the game and prepared for the joy *and* the pain in this world too. I wasn't gonna stifle her the way Grandmother had stifled me. I wasn't gonna shut her down and keep my foot on her neck so hard that she fell for the first slimy niggah who patted her on the ass and told her she was fine.

Me and Trey had talked about all that. We had confessed a lot about our pasts to each other and we fully agreed on how we was gonna raise our baby girl. And hopefully our baby boy one day too. I didn't want my daughter growing up as the only child. I wanted her to have the same thing that me and Jimmy used to have when we was growing up. Somebody to be close to. Somebody to share secrets with.

Somebody who loved her enough to die for her.

Somebody who could be her heart so she could be his soul.

And Trey was totally down with having more kids too. He had been right by my side throughout my entire pregnancy. Cooking me all kinds of healthy food, taking me on long walks, making sure I took my vitamins and drank plenty of water. Just spoiling the hell outta me.

I felt so damn lucky. Trey wanted this baby. He wanted her bad, and he had been one hundred percent involved in choosing her name.

Shops up and down 125th Street were beginning to open for the day, and newspaper stands were being stocked. Street vendors were unloading their trucks and setting up their tables and stands. An old man pushing a cart filled up with everything he owned stopped to dap Trey out and congratulate us on our baby. I smiled as Trey kicked it with the homeless dude like he was one of his old stockbroker friends or something. My man was smart and paid and slanging big dick, but he was still humble and giving and connected to the community that we were helping to rebuild.

Yep, that's right. I said *we.* I took a deep breath as we stopped across the street from Trey's barbershop. I had opened up a store-front boutique called, *JuicyOriginals* and I specialized in sewing all the hot summer dresses and funky urban attire that big-booty Harlem chicks like me loved to wear. I had also gotten back to work on my *Birthday Cake* clothing line, and my girl Candy Montana rocked the hell outta my sexy signature pieces every time she went out on stage.

I stood in front of my shop waiting patiently as Trey went through the same routine that he went through five days outta every week. He had installed security cameras and red-button alarm panels all over the joint. He had put one in my office near my desk, one behind the counter under the cash register, one on the wall next to my sewing machine, and there was even one in my bathroom, right above the toilet tissue holder. Trey was my personal security guard. He had called in a hi-tech crew to hook up a remote receiver and a screen in his barbershop so he could flip channels and see me in every room in my boutique.

He looked real serious as he unlocked my door gratings and pulled them up real high. Then he punched in the alarm code and unlocked the door. He made me stay outside while he went in the boutique and searched every inch of it from top to bottom, just to make sure nobody had snuck in there and was waiting in a corner to get at me or our precious unborn baby girl.

When he was finally done with all that, he flipped my CLOSED sign over to OPEN, and then held the door open wide so I could walk in. I grinned as he told me he loved me and kissed me goodbye. I stood in the window as Trey nodded at his man Rider who was about to open up the check-cashing place down the block, and then walked across the street looking like a tall, fine-ass beast.

Trey stopped outside his barbershop and turned around knowing full well that I was still right there in that window watching him. He waved and blew me a kiss, and I waved and blew him one right back. I waited until he went inside and then I got out my appointment book and looked over my schedule for the day.

It was pretty light compared to the load I used to have when I first opened up my doors. Shoot, chicks used to be lined up waiting for me to take their measurements and sketch them a hot personal design. I used to have 'em squeezing their bootys in on my couches and standing all up against the walls, but I had to stop all that because I got sick and started having a lot of headaches and blurred vision and stuff like that.

My blood pressure had shot up too, so my doctor had put me on bed rest for a good minute, but once I started taking my medicine and feeling better he gave me the green light to come back to the boutique full time, just as long as I promised to cut back on my work load and take a nap every day.

So I had to shut a lot of my business prospects down and just start taking appointments. I only booked about six or seven a day, and this way I could take my time and really get a feel for a chick's style and personality so I could figure out what kind of designs would look good on her and bring out her body's best features.

By eleven o'clock I had met with three urban fashionistas and sketched them out some extra-sexy designs, and I had about an hour left before Trey came across the street to pick me up for lunch. Me and him ate lunch together almost every day. Sometimes we walked back home and ate leftovers or something from the crib, and sometimes we went up the block to the deli and got us a hero or something like that.

But today we was gonna do something different. I was almost nine months pregnant and my juicy booty was craving a slice of pizza with garlic and crushed red peppers sprinkled on that bad boy, so today I was gonna ask Trey to give me a walk to my favorite pizza shop up the street.

I flipped my OPEN sign to CLOSED and then I locked the front door and went in my office and cut on some music. I punched in the security code on the alarm panel next to my desk, and then I texted Trey and told him I was about to catch me a couple of z's until it was time to go get something to eat.

I pulled out my fuzzy pink blanket and my favorite satin pillow and tossed them on the plush little lounging sofa that was pushed up right beside my desk. I couldn't wait to crash out and get my late-morning snore on, and that's exactly what I was about to do, but first I was gonna jet into the bathroom real quick and pee because sweet little baby girl was pressing down real hard on my bladder!

$$$$$

I don't know what it was that woke me up, but suddenly my ass was wide-awake and cold as hell. I had been sleeping like a baby, with slobber coming out of my mouth and all that.

But the moment I opened my eyes my mouth dried up like a bowl of dirt. My heart banged twice *real hard*, and then it seemed like it stopped beating altogether.

How in the hell did she get in here?

My eyes slid over to the alarm panel. The "armed" light was still blinking red and all the other lights were off.

How the FUCK did she get in here?

The words pounded like a fist in my mind. I had no idea, but the bitch was standing right over me. Bald-headed and scary as hell. Her face looked crunchy. Like a piece of meat that had been scorched on a hot barbeque grill. Her cracked-open skin was burnt and crispy, but the healing flesh showing underneath it looked pinkish. Like a bad piece of fried chicken that was burnt on the outside and raw in the middle.

My hand shot up to my neck and I felt around for the treasured piece of jewelry that I always wore on my chain. It had been found when they sifted through the last bit of rubble in the G-Spot, and my ass had been so grateful to them firefighters that I had cried for days.

"You got my ring again," I blurted, shocked outta my mind as I stared at what was dangling from the diamond necklace around her burnt neck. "How in the hell did you get my ring again?"

"I already told you! I took it off your goddamn *fanger!*" that crazy bitch snarled as she pounced on me and went straight for my throat.

"Get offa me!" I gasped as she clamped her hands around my neck and cut off my breath, choking the lights outta me. I grabbed at her wrists. Them shits felt like man-hands, rock-hard and strong as hell.

I tried to dig my chin down toward my chest and break her hold, but that crazy bitch climbed on top of me and went for broke. She dug her feet into the lounge sofa like she was doing a push up, and then she leaned all of her weight down on her forearms and forced me to sink deeper into the cushions.

Noooooo!

I reached for the red panic button that was mounted on the wall by my desk, right above my head.

Trey!

He had installed five of them buttons all around my boutique, and I slapped up at this one over and over again in a mad panic, missing it by less than an inch each time.

Helppppppp!

Her hands felt like iron vice grips around my neck.

I needed air! My *baby* needed air! My mouth was stretched wide open as we struggled. I sucked in as hard as I could but I couldn't get my next breath. I couldn't get it! Lightening flashed behind my eyes and I saw tiny explosions underneath my lids. I swung my knees up between us and started kicking the mule shit outta her, bicycling both my legs like a mutha.

Her crazy ass didn't feel shit. Her lips was twisted up in a pit-bull snarl, and she had the purest look of hatred in her eyes that I had ever seen in my life.

I wheezed and bucked as tears ran down my cheeks.

A big bubble of pressure was swelling up in my head as I reached desperately for her clenching fingers and tried to pry them shits backwards and loosen her grip.

But she had me. She had my ass *good*.

I was gurgling now. I started tossing my head left and right, fighting for just one drop of air as she squeezed and squeezed until my ears started ringing and my vision started going dark.

Trey!

I screamed for him in my mind as I felt my baby ball herself up in a knot in my stomach. I slapped up at the panic button again and missed. My eyeballs felt swollen, like they were about to bust open and pop right out of my head. A sudden heaviness pressed down on my bladder. Like my baby girl was tryna crawl outta my coochie and escape this madness, and I started fighting even harder then.

I was swinging hopeless blows. Wild, crazy punches that didn't do a damn thing. Salida was slobbering all down on me. Grunting with mad exertion as her hot spit landed in my face.

I reached up blindly tryna get to her eyes, and when I raked my nails across her skin it felt like I was digging into crunchy cookie dough.

I thrashed at her blindly and arched my back. My fingers caught her nose and skimmed down her top lip. I felt the inside of her wet mouth and dug my nails into her gums and yanked. That bitch opened wide and bit the shit outta me.

I tried to scream and go for her eyeballs again, but Salida leaned back outta my reach and my hands flapped harmlessly around her face.

I was getting real weak and it felt like my head was about to explode. I raked my fingernails up and down her arms, scratching the shit outta her burnt skin as I twisted my hips and tried to buck her off.

The last thing I saw before the lights went out and my world went completely dark was the lens on the security camera that Trey had installed in my office. It was up in the corner, right above the doorway, and just before I lost my vision I noticed something about the camera's lens.

It was shattered.

$$$$$

The next thing I knew I was laying on the cold floor of my bathroom.

That bitch was sitting on me.

My arms were stretched above my head and tied around the bottom of the toilet bowl. My wrists had been duct-taped together real tight and my ankles were taped together too. I started struggling like hell, but she was sitting her ass on my thighs and I couldn't really move.

But I could scream. Damn right I could scream, and when I saw what Salida was holding in her hands I screamed louder than I had ever screamed in my entire life.

That bitch had a scalpel. The blade looked sharp as hell, and it glinted just like the crazy gleam in her eyes.

"What the fuck are you doing?" I screeched as she slid backwards until her butt was straddling my knees.

"Please!" I begged from the bottom of my soul as she pulled up my shirt and yanked at the front of my pants.

"*Salida nooooooo!*" I wailed as her psycho-ass picked up a bottle of rubbing alcohol and sloshed that shit all over the bottom part of my stomach.

I was in a pure panic.

I sucked in the sharp vapors of alcohol as the cold liquid soaked the front of my pants and pooled around my hips and ass. I bucked around on the floor in a wild frenzy, and Salida held on and rode me like a pony.

"Why the hell are you doing this?" I screamed hysterically. "Why are you trying to kill my baby?" I yelled.

"Why? Why? *Why?*"

"Because," she said quietly as she pressed down hard on my bulging belly and went at me with her knife. "Because a trick like you don't deserve no fuckin' baby, bitch!"

And then she sliced me.

Quick and deep.

I didn't even feel the pain at first. Just the sensation of my whole stomach opening up and the hot spurt of blood that sprayed up into Salida's face and landed all over me and the bathroom sink and walls.

And then the pain came. And a whole damn lot of it too.

I almost blacked out.

I could hear her muttering something crazy as she cut into me even deeper, damn near to my backbone, and all I could think was that this bitch was about to kill another one of my babies!

Please God. Please. Don't let her hurt my baby. I don't care nothing about me. Just don't let her hurt my baby!

I started going crazy outta my mind when I felt her hands digging around inside of me. She was up to her elbows in my gutted stomach and there was blood shooting everywhere. I felt her pulling and tugging around real hard inside of me and I arched my back and screamed as loud as I could.

"Don't take her!" I begged that crazy bitch as she lifted my unborn child right out of my torn-open womb. My body felt like a shell. Empty and worthless. My spirit was in so much fuckin' pain that I just wanted to die right then and there.

"Please don't take her away from *meeeeeee!*"

"This lil bitch is *mine*," Salida panted as she tried to keep my squirming baby girl from slipping right outta her hands. She gripped her under the arms and held her up high in the air so I could see her.

I sucked in my breath and my eyes bucked open wide as my newborn daughter wiggled around silently in the hands of a killer. She was covered in my blood, and as I stared into her face I knew why she wasn't crying.

Because she was dead.

I closed my eyes and I screamed the screams of a mother who had once again been denied her child.

"*Nooooooooooooooooooo!*"

"Look at her!" Salida growled as my broken-hearted cries bubbled up outta my soul. "Bitch open your goddamn eyes and look at her!"

"*Nooooooooooooooooooo!*"

"Open your eyes, Juicy!"

I took a deep breath so I could let out another scream.

"Open your eyes, Juicy! Open your eyes so you can see our baby girl!"

Trey.

And then I heard it. The faint cries of a newborn.

And then nobody had to tell me to open my eyes no more after that.

They flew open and there she was.

Up in the air. Screaming mad, and gripped in my doctor's gifted hands.

I cried out and reached for her, and somebody gently grabbed my wrist and pulled my hand back down to my side.

"Not just yet, Mrs. Jackson," I heard a woman's voice say. "The doctors aren't quite finished with her yet."

My heart pounded and my lips trembled as I watched my daughter being carried away as she disappeared from my view.

But then suddenly she was right there next to me.

Safe.

In her daddy's big, strong arms.

Safe.

Antonia Gina Jimmia Jackson.

My baby.

Our baby.

Our child.

Thank you God!

My daughter was here and she was *alive!*

$$$$$

It was a quiet, tree-lined street with expensive brownstones on both sides. The smell of fresh paint was in the air as the building superintendent led his new tenant up the narrow stairs to the small third-floor apartment.

"This is probably a lot of steps for you," he said over his shoulder as they approached the vacant apartment. "But don't you worry. There are a lot of good men on this block and they'll be more than happy to carry your furniture upstairs for you."

"I don't have no furniture," the woman said in a low, hoarse voice that sent a chill down the Super's spine. It was bad enough that this lady looked like she had run through a raging fire, but her sizzling eyes and raspy voice gave him the sho-nuff fuckin' creeps!

He shrugged it off and unlocked the door. He knew he was real damn lucky to find somebody who was willing to rent the place just a few days after it had been released from its crime-scene status, and since the woman behind him had paid cash money for the place sight unseen, he didn't give a hoot if the only thing she had to her name was the one big bag she had swinging from her shoulder.

He let the woman in and waited as she stood in the middle of the living room floor, just looking around. A few seconds later he followed her as she walked over to the front window and pulled the curtains back and stared down at the street outside.

The Super watched as his neighbor across the street came outta his crib and loaded up his car with a baby seat, a bunch of stuffed animals, and a big bouquet of flowers. His sister came outta the house right after him. She was carrying a big bundle of balloons as she got in the car on the passenger side and slammed the door.

"You like it?" the Super asked anxiously, all the while thinking *her ass just oughtta fuckin' like it because if she didn't, she wasn't getting her damn deposit back!* "You think this is gonna be okay for you, ma'am?"

The woman let the curtain fall back in place as she stood up straight and nodded.

"It's gonna be perfect," she said coldly. "It's gonna be just *perfect*."

AND AT THE END...

Warning before destruction, Grandmother used to tell me and Jimmy all the time. But when I looked into my daughter's beautiful face it was hard to believe there was evil in the world.

But there was. And I knew good and damn well there was.

"We're home!" Chiney hollered as Trey pulled up outside of our crib. I had stayed in the hospital for a whole week after giving birth, and as sore as I was, I could tell it was gonna take me awhile to bounce back from the emergency C-Section that I'd had.

Thanks to Trey and all his crazy security cameras he had seen me when I passed out in the bathroom in my boutique. My man had dropped his clippers and ran up outta his barber shop dialing 9-1-1 as he rushed across the street to get to me.

And thank God he did. My butt had had a seizure and fallen into a coma from a condition the doctors called eclampsia. My blood pressure had shot up so high that they'd had to give me some quick-acting drugs and perform an emergency Caesarean-section to try to save me and my baby's life.

"Let me get her!" Chiney yelled. She jumped outta the front seat before Trey had even parked good so she could be the first one to get to the baby. Chiney was gonna be a damn good auntie. I could already tell. She unbuckled baby girl from her car seat and snuggled her in her arms.

"Hey, somebody moved into that apartment across the street while you was in the hospital, Juicy," Chiney said as we walked up the front steps.

Trey was behind us busy getting stuff outta the car.

"Already?" I asked as I glanced up at the window that my old friend used to wave at me from every night.

"Yeah," Chiney said. "Already."

I peered up at the window. For a split-second I coulda sworn I saw somebody up there looking at me, but then the curtain fell closed and my heart banged all in my throat.

"Who's that up there?" I put my hand on my sleeping daughter and asked Chiney quickly. "Who moved into that apartment?"

She shrugged as Trey ran up the stairs carrying my suitcase and all kinds of other stuff that I had brought back from the hospital.

"I'on't know," she shrugged as Trey punched in the alarm code and unlocked the door. "I heard it's an old lady but I ain't seen her yet."

I stood on the stoop staring up at that window.

For some reason my heart had crawled all the way down into the pit of my stomach, and I felt my eyes narrow as I kept them aimed on that window.

Warning before destruction!

I ain't see her yet.

"C'mon, baby," Trey said, grinning as he took my arm and led me inside our crib. "The doctor wants you to rest, remember? Let's get you inside so you can get a little nap before the baby wakes up, cool?"

I nodded and let my husband pull me inside the house, but you can best believe a big piece of my mind was focused on that apartment across the street.

$$$$$

We got settled into our space, and me and Trey had just put our beautiful daughter down for the night when my man pulled me into his arms and kissed me on my lips.

"You been real quiet, Juicy. I don't want you worried about nothing, okay? You're safe, baby." He nodded toward the crib. "*She's* safe. All that other stuff was just a dream, okay?" He held me close. "It wasn't real, baby. It wasn't real. I just want you to relax and get some sleep tonight, okay?"

I looked up into his eyes and saw his love and his concern. I nodded, then pressed my face into his chest and took a real deep breath.

That fuckin' bitch Salida had come to me in my dreams every single night while I was in that hospital. I had been a nervous fuckin' wreck, and I couldn't hardly close my eyes without waking up crying and screaming just like a little baby.

But it wasn't gonna go down like that tonight. Or no other night either.

Trey had armed his crib like a military fort a long time ago. I had been real impressed by all his high-tech security systems when I first came to live with him and Chiney.

And while I was in the hospital he had hired a crew to come out and install even more features. Cameras out the ass and alarms everywhere.

But I knew something Trey must didn't know.

It didn't matter how far you ran or where you tried to hide or how many panic buttons or screech alarms you got installed. If somebody wanted a piece of your ass they was damn sure gonna try to get it.

And that's why, late that night after Trey and Chiney was both snoring and my little mini-me baby girl was sleeping peacefully in her crib, I got up outta the bed and opened up my closet and got my shit.

I gripped my Nine in my hand and walked into the living room and sat down in my rocking chair by the bay window. I peered up at the top-floor apartment across the street where a dim light was shining behind the curtains in the front window. A lot of people had died in the G-Spot, and the funeral homes in Harlem had been busting at the seams, just full of cold dead bodies.

But as far as I could tell there had never been a funeral for either Salida or Monique.

To date, over a hundred party-goers were either killed or injured as a result of the bombing at the G-Spot Social Club, and at least two unidentified victims remain hospitalized as social service personnel attempt to contact their next of kin...

That news report had stood out in my mind, and even after all this time I had never forgotten that shit.

... at least two unidentified victims remain hospitalized as social service personnel attempt to contact their next of kin...

Come on wit' it, I thought as I sat under the glow of the street light and rocked back and forth with my gat on my lap.

Them bitches was still alive. Both of them. I could feel it all down in my bones, and no matter what nobody said I knew this shit wasn't over yet.

And it wasn't gonna be over until I saw the bodies of Salida and Monique. Stretched out cold in somebody's fuckin' morgue.

I picked up my Nine.

Yea, though I walk through the valley of the shadow of death, I will fear no evil...

I had another loaded gat in my purse, and there was one in my kitchen and one in my bathroom too.

I was ready for them bitches.

Wasn't *nobody* gonna hurt my baby girl.

Bring ya ass, Salida, I thought coldly.

Yeah, bring ya ass and make sure you come correct.

'Cause when you get here Juicy-Mo is gonna be ready!

THE END
For now...

AVAILABLE NOW!

Excerpt From

B4 The G-Spot: The Legend of GRANITE MCKAY

AN URBAN EROTIC TALE

by

NOIRE

A Note from Noire

Dear Readers,

Well, who knew that ten years after penning G-Spot and creating the Urban Erotic genre we would be going back to that sexy Harlem Gentleman's Club to handle some unfinished bizz!

So many of you were captivated by the tale of Juicy Monique Stanfield and the saga of her tortured young life with the notorious kingpin Granite "G" McKay. I received endless emails and messages from you wanting to know more about G and wanting to hear his side of the story and to find out how he was able to do some of the coldblooded ish he did, and why he became the most brutal and fearsome capo that Harlem had ever seen.

My biggest compliment on G-Spot and on all the stories I write is when you tell me that my books read like movies, and that you can actually visualize everything that is going on in my plots as though you were standing on the sidelines watching the story play out on a big screen. Thank you. That is my goal each and every time the Urban Erotic train pulls outta the station.

I say it over and over again: I'm proud to have the most intelligent readers in the world. You guys expect quality writing and original stories, and you're the type of careful readers who can follow the most intricate plot lines created.

Almost ten years ago, I started the literary technique of interweaving different characters from my Urban Erotic Tales throughout my books, and I get a kick when somebody says, "Hey! Wasn't so-and-so from Thug-A-Licious in the G-Spot?" That's a Noire original twist for ya! No gimmicks, just some real good shit.

I really lub the fact that you guys are sharp and can spot these types of plot connections and twists, which is why I will continue to be original and ground-breaking in everything I bring you.

And what I'll be bringing you soon is some straight-up literary fiyah from my magic pen! I have an upcoming collaboration called A NEW YORK STATE OF MINEZ! with artist and actor Reem RAW that is going to be so dope! I know my loyal readers and fans will support our first novel together and show Reem some big-time lub! I've included a gripping excerpt from A NEW YORK STATE OF MINE! "The Chronicles of Crooklyn" at the very end of this book. Hit Reem up on FB at Reem ShortyGotHerHandsOnMe Raw and on Twitter @ReemRaw609 after you read it and let him know what you think!

If you check out my new website you'll see my versatile writing style on display in my SOME LIKE IT HARD, SOME LIKE IT HOT!!! section. (Let's see which author swagger jacks that ish first!)

I also highlighted a new addition to my new "Flirty Dirty" line of novels that are filled with sex, scams, drama, and hilarious hood double-crosses. RED HOT LIAR, the next installment in my Sexy Little Liar series: the Misadventures of Mink LaRue, is now in stores!

Thanks 4 riding this Urban Erotic train every time it pulls into your station. Once again, it's on!

Bringing you a movie in a book,

Noire

Sign up for my email contact list at **bit.ly/noiresignup**
Like my Facebook page at **bit.ly/noirefanpage**
Follow me on Twitter at **twitter.com/AskNoire**

WARNING!

This here ain't no romance it's an urban erotic tale
These gutter plots I drop will have you biting off your nails!
A menace has arrived, a terror Harlem's never seen
He started from the bottom and turned a dollar into a dream!
Before the ballin and the stuntin and the sexin and the flexin,
Brutal vision and ambition is how this gangsta manifested!
So let's stand up and salute the ruthless boss who paved the way
Let's go back B4 the G-Spot to: The Legend of GRANITE McKAY!

In the beginning...

Have you ever played Russian roulette with the Devil? Did you post up at the front end of his burner and stare that fuckin bullet down? Did you roll the dice with your life, ready to pay the cost no matter how high it might be? And when that trigger popped, did you catch that bullet between your teeth and snap that shit in half?

Check me out. I didn't come to Harlem riding shotgun. I came *packin* one. And I wasn't gonna stop spraying until I had every block in the city on lock. Failure wasn't an option. Weaknesses, I had none. It was the gun or the grave for this nigga right here. I had my guts and my fists, and I was either gonna *do*...or I was gonna *die*.

Yeah, I know what they told you about me. But their truth ain't the *whole* fuckin truth! I risked my life for my hustle in the belly of the *Badass*. I lunged at Big Sonny's throat with nothing but my teeth and my bare hands. I'm a made nigga! I made *myself*! From the dirt up. I'm a gangsta chiseled outta concrete. My name is Granite McKay, and now that you've heard it from everybody else, it's time for me to tell my *own* muthafuckin story!

CHAPTER 1

Alabama

I was raised in a whorehouse and I got my first taste of pussy when I was just six years old. They called her Juicy Lucy and she sat on my face and rode the shit outta me down in a musty old potato cellar.

My wino Aunt Rosie was watching me and her eight raggedy kids. We were outside chasing chickens around her shitted-up yard when my cousins Skooch and Boobie snatched me across the road and tossed me down into the neighbor's potato cellar.

"C'mere, Gerald!" Skooch was fourteen, and he laughed as he swung his big hand and knocked me down the rickety wooden steps. "Juicy Lucy wanna meet you."

"But why we goin' down-dere for in the dark?" I whined, tripping over my bare feet as I fell into the damp, moldy-smelling clay. I was pretty big for six, but I still wasn't no match for them two cats.

"Shut the fuck up, boy!" Skooch clamped his rough hand down on the back of my neck. "Quit whining like a goddamn baby! We goin' down there 'cause Juicy Lucy said so!"

Boobie struck a match across the bottom of his shoe. The flame of a large candle flickered in the darkness and threw scary shadows up against the dirt walls.

"Who dat?" I fought even harder as I blinked into the shadows and peeped a plump, big-titty girl stretched out naked on an old wooden pallet and fingering her nipples. "W-w-why y'all call her Juicy Lucy?"

Skooch laughed even louder as he twisted my ear and pushed me toward her cocked-open legs.

"You'll see," he said as he gripped my neck and shoved my face down into her big hairy pussy. "Just stick out ya tongue and give her a few licks and you'll find out."

$$$$$

It was a bitter cold Wednesday afternoon and the winter sun shone brightly over the sensational town of Harlem.

The dark-eyed young man stood deep in the cut, observing the street happenings from the shelter of a narrow doorway. He was a smasher; tall, muscular, and barely twenty years old, but already his heart was hardened and a predatory look of hunger and brutality lurked in his eyes.

In front of him 125th Street was all the way live. Shoppers bustled back and forth, ducking in and out of stores as they spent their last bit of change buying delicious trimmings for tomorrow's Thanksgiving meal.

The young man huddled in his thin jacket and watched closely as shiny whips zipped past, their big-rimmed tires kicking up soft tufts of grimy Manhattan snow.

Harlem was Big Sonny's town; Scheme City, USA, but even the most ruthless criminals adhered to the borough-wide holiday ceasefire held on the last Wednesday and Thursday of November.

Pussy, liquor, heroin, and cocaine were still sold 24/7 at a premium, but in the spirit of Thanksgiving all robberies, kidnappings, and blackout murders were called off for those two agreed-upon days of truce.

The young man in the doorway sniffed and wiped his nose with the back of his tattered sleeve. Winters were a whole lot colder in New York than they had been back in Alabama, but he didn't mind. He had been born in Harlem but a series of unfortunate circumstances had led to him being raised in the south. He'd come back to the Big Apple seeking power and retribution, and his first order of business was to land a prime spot on Big Sonny's drug squad.

The wind bit sharply at his legs as a tired young mother with five snotty-nosed children walked by, unaware of the pending danger. She was pushing a rickety shopping cart that was empty except for a small frozen turkey and two bunches of limp collard greens. The turkey wasn't much bigger than a young chicken, and between the five of them kids they'd probably get about two good bites each.

The young cat took a long look at the stark hopelessness in the young mother's face and made himself a promise, *one of these days every Thanksgiving turkey in Harlem is gonna be on me.*

The scruffy little family moved on as he scanned the street with his piercing eyes. Up ahead on his right was a club called the *Badass,* a player's joint where booze, drugs, and pussy reigned supreme.

A barbeque rib shack was attached to the side of the joint, and right next door to that was the jam-packed Associated Supermarket where last-minute holiday shoppers were lugging out brown paper bags filled with sweet potatoes, salt pork, chitterlings, and black-eyed peas.

Keeping his eyes trained on the hunt, the young cat ignored his growling stomach as he waited for his meal ticket to show up, eyeing the door to the supermarket like a rat on a piece of cheese.

His hand slid up to his waistband and he tapped the frigid piece of metal pressed against his side. The mark he was lining up had been inside the store for over an hour but he couldn't stay up in there all day. He had to bring his ass out at some point and when he did...

No sooner had the thought crossed his mind did the doors to the Associated swing open and a tall, well-dressed gentleman wearing a dark wool coat saunter outside pushing a cart overflowing with groceries. A lit cigarette dangled from the corner of his mouth and he moved with the finesse and confidence of a tried and true street gangster.

Beside him waddled a squat old lady with gray hair, her crooked smile broad under her flat nose. The gangster clenched his cig between his lips and grinned as the old lady happily eyeballed the endless bags of food that her favorite son had purchased for the next day's feast.

The young man standing in the doorway smirked as he sized up his victim: imported leather shoes, mohair wool coat, Barney's top hat, Cartier watch, a one-hundred watt smile and the million-dollar swagger to go along with it. He'd been scoping dude out for weeks and it was easy to see that the second-in-command capo was living on Big Street and his tailored pockets were stuffed with fat knots.

Without blinking the young dude reached onto his waist and unchecked his heat. He stepped outta the cut and calmly approached the mother-and-son pair. He didn't even feel the slushy snow under his feet as it seeped through the flapping holes in his cheap shoes and soaked his thin socks. He'd been trying to get a meeting with Big Sonny for over a month now but them cats had ghosted him, like he wasn't even there. Them niggas was about to see him real clear now.

He sauntered down the bustling street maneuvering through the crowd and swinging his arms with the heat right out in the open, gripped tightly in his fist. There was a single-minded determination in his stride. He wasn't rushing and he wasn't hiding from nobody neither.

"Oh, *shit*!" a street thug muttered and scrambled to duck behind a parked car as the young man strode past. "That nigga's about to *stick* somebody...."

The young man walked up on the well-dressed gangster, who he knew to be Big Sonny's right-hand man, and posted up in a shooter's stance.

"Yo, muthafucka," he growled as he raised his toolie to eye-level. "Lemme get one of them Newports, man."

His gun glinted in the sunlight and the flash of fear and surprise in the startled man's eyes was all he needed to see.

"You can keep ya lighter," he said, cocking the hammer. "Cause I got the heat right here."

"Nigga!" the man protested, "You know the rules! It's Thanksgiv—"

Pop!

There wasn't an ounce of holiday cheer in the youngsta as he squeezed the trigger and planted a hot one right between his target's eyes. The sound of scattering feet, abandoned turkeys, terrified screams, and the sight of the old lady fainting and collapsing on the ground next to her son didn't press him out not one fuckin bit.

He moved like he had all day as he reached down and rambled through the pockets and snatched what he wanted off the wide-eyed corpse. A gold money clip, thick with a folded stack of crisp Benjamins, was stuffed in the man's front pocket, but he didn't give a fuck about the cash so he left it there.

Ignoring the chaos unfolding behind him on the street as shoppers ducked and ran and screamed, the young man stared into the unseeing eyes of the dead gangster stretched out on the ground and then spit square down in his face.

"Y'all bitch-ass muthafuckas gonna see me now," he promised coldly as he turned and walked away.

The young cat was unhurried as he moved west for several blocks. He didn't look left and he didn't look right, and he didn't look over his shoulder neither. He knew what was coming and there was no turning back now. For better or for worse, he'd set the wheels of wrath in motion and his destiny was at hand.

With an unwavering stride he cut through a trash-strewn alley and entered the back door of a dilapidated tenement building. He paused at the stairs real quick and glanced down at the cold slice of metal he still gripped in his fist.

Fuck what it *was*, he thought, moving on with a purpose. He knew what it was gonna *be*. Today he was just a raggedy ex-convict from Alabama with shitty clothes and holes in his shoes. But tomorrow he was gonna rise up outta this bitch like pure cream, breaking backs and crushing throats until he was standing at the top of the heap.

Yeah, *all* them niggas out there were gonna see him now. They had been playing him like he was invisible, but come hell or high water he was gonna get that meeting with Big Sonny Dawson. He hadn't clawed his way up outta the dirty south so he could hustle for pennies with an empty stomach and shabby drawers. And he wasn't about to scramble on these mean city streets forever like some low-level slanga, number runner, or stick-up kid neither.

On the contrary. His greatness awaited him and this town was his for the taking.

He had his wits, his merciless ambition, and his sights aimed on high, and no matter who he had to slump or how many grimy niggas he had to roll, Granite McKay was gonna become more than just a menace on the coldblooded streets of Harlem.

He was gonna become a *legend*.

Download B4 The G-Spot and read the rest of the G-Spot Saga now!
Available on Kindle, Nook, SmashWords, and More!

Turn the page to read an excerpt from A New York State of MINEZ! by Reem RAW and Noire

COMING SOON!

Excerpt From

A NEW YORK STATE OF MINEZ!

By

Reem RAW

&

NOIRE

THE CHRONICLES OF CROOKLYN

A Nightmare in Crooklyn

"How can you mendddd a broken heartttt..." Lil Slick listened to his daddy sing off key as he slow-danced with his number-one baby momma, Kea.

"Damn boy," Kea said laughing as her man grinded against her mound and palmed her fluffy ass. She was young and pretty and enjoying every moment of his attention. "You know you can't sang for shit baby but I luvs ya anyway."

Lil Slick's parents, Kea and Big Slick, had grown up together in the same projects. Their families had been real cool with each other, and as far back as either one of them could remember they had always had a love thang going on.

Big Slick was a ladies man though, very charming and good-looking. He had always wanted to have a big family, so Kea got pregnant quickly when she was in her mid-teens and gave him three babies, damn near back-to-back. Even though Kea knew she was Big Slick's favorite woman, she knew she would never be his only woman. Kea had made peace with that knowledge because she had something none of Slick's other bitches could give him: His firstborn son.

Kea had named her baby boy Samir Jr. to create an unseverable bond between him and his daddy, and it worked. Big Slick loved the ground their little boy walked on, but when one of his on-the-side tricks pushed out a baby boy of her own, she tried to get clever by naming her son Samir II.

Kea had hit the fuckin' roof. It was one thing to watch some off-brand bitch pushing her man's seed around in a baby stroller, but it was something else to hear everybody calling the baby by her *son's* name!

So Kea came up with a sly plan. Fuck a Samir. Niggas in the know called Slick by his street name anyway. She killed all that "Lil Samir" shit and started calling her son Lil Slick, and she made sure everybody else did too.

But name or no name, Big Slick could have a whole damn tribe of sons named after him but none of their mamas would ever have his heart the way Kea did. She had started from the bottom with him. She was Slick's rider, his right-hand, through thick-and-thin bitch, 25/8. She lived for his slick ass, and she was willing to die for him too.

Like a true soldier, Kea had helped Slick rise to the top of the cocaine market in Brownsville, working right by his side as he schemed and strategized, yet she still found time to be a freak in the sheets and a damn good mother to their three kids.

Through all the ruthless shit Big Slick had to endure running the projects, holding shit down and evading the law, what he held most dear, even above the easy money, was his kids.

Regardless of how any of his baby mommas felt about him, not a damn one of them could ever say he was a bad father or didn't do right by his shorties. Big Slick knew his seeds were his only weakness so he kept his business in the street and never brought it back to the house with him.

But on this night, as Big Slick's oldest son watched him play with his mother sweetly and serenade her with songs, he had brought his two outside-the-house kids with him to Kea's crib to enjoy a big Sunday dinner.

In addition to having all of Big Slick's kids in the apartment, Kea was also babysitting the pretty little girl who lived next door with her drunk uncle.

As young as she was, the little girl called herself having a crush on Lil Slick, and every time Kea looked up she was asking if she could come across the hall to play. Kea felt sorry for the poor child. She was often left home by herself while her alky uncle ran the streets and got his drink on, so she invited her to eat dinner with them almost every night.

And tonight, all eight of them sat around the table like one big happy family. They were stuffing their faces on barbequed chicken, baked macaroni and cheese, and collard greens. After they ate and washed the dishes Kea took the kids into the living room where her and Big Slick put on some more music. They sang, danced, and enjoyed their family time with the children, like good parents often do.

After an hour or so of singing and playing with the kids a hard, desperate knock came at the door.

Kea didn't hang out in the streets or have any unannounced company in her house, so the bamming on her door caught her off-guard and had her a little concerned.

"I'll get that baby," Big Slick told her, noticing the look on her face. Lil Slick had noticed the look too, and as young as he was, he didn't like it.

"It's prolly my brother," Big Slick said, moving toward the door. "I told him I was gonna be chillin' over here with the kids and he said he might swing by so he could rap with me about something."

Big Slick answered the door and let his brother in. Hassan, or Crazy Haz as they called him, was Slick's little brother, even though he was just as tall as Slick, a little bit heavier, and a whole lot meaner.

Growing up, Haz had wanted to be just like his big brother but he wasn't as smooth with his shit and he couldn't get the ladies to like him the way they liked Slick either.

Compared to the bull muscles Slick was packing, Haz was un-athletic and on the pudgy side. They was both street niggas to the bone, but Big Slick was smarter and well respected on the streets, while Crazy Haz was feared and thought of as a grimy gangsta.

Haz was the leader of a crew of stick-up kids who ran around Brownsville, Bed-stuy and Canarsie jamming anybody who looked like they had some money or some product. As a kingpin, Big Slick was far from a punk himself and he could definitely handle his own. But even the come-up hungry wolves were too leery to test him because they knew how gutter his crazy brother Haz got down.

"Yo w'sup bro, what's going on wit'chu," Big Slick said as he grinned and gave his little bro a hug and showed him some love.

"Ain't shit, Slick. I'm chillin," Haz responded, sniffing and shifting his eyes back and forth.

Right off the cuff Big Slick smelled the aroma of Kush mixed with burnt cocaine on his brother's clothes. Haz's eyes were bloodshot red and slightly glazed over.

"Yo, you smokin' them dirties again huh nigga? Got you lookin' all crazy in the face and shit. You odee-dumb for fucking with that shit!" Big Slick said, openly pissed that his brother had showed up around his kids high as a fucking light bill to try to talk some business.

"Fuck you mean?" Haz bucked, swaying on his feet and looking more fucked up the more he talked. "Yeah, I'm high. So what? I do what the fuck I wanna do nigga! You ain't my pops muffucka!"

Big Slick got swole. "Naw nigga I ain't ya raggedy-ass daddy! I'm Big *Bro* that's who the fuck I am, not one of them lil dumb-ass flunkies you be getting dusted with, so watch ya tone! Now let's roll to the kitchen so we can talk, a'ight?"

As they headed towards the kitchen, Kea turned up the music and continued to entertain the kids so their dad and uncle could talk in private.

"Yo Slick, I need five ounces of that girl from you, just to show this nigga over in Marcus Garvey I got the product before I stick his ass. I'll give it right back to you, word," Haz pleaded, almost whispering it to Big Slick in a low desperate voice.

Big Slick shook his head. "Hell naw. I ain't fuckin' with you like that Haz. Not for nothing. Last time I gave you some work you was supposed to bring it right back too, nigga. Bad thing is, you didn't even take it and flip it, you just fucked the package up."

"Man, shit happens!" Haz exploded. "I hold you down in these streets, nigga! I keep the wolves offa yo ass boy! Now when I need a little help right quick you mister high-and-fucking-mighty?" screamed Haz, who was trembling with hot rage. The weed mixed with the cocaine fueled his deep-seated jealousy of his brother and allowed him to totally dismiss the fact that he really *had* fucked up the last package that Big Slick had given him.

"Yeah, nigga you must be high," Big Slick spit as he scowled at his baby brother. "Who the fuck you think schooled you on this game in the first place? I hold *myself* down out here, little nigga! You ain't grinding for yours! You just out there robbing and stealing from niggas who tryna make a lil change to feed they families! I'm a hustla baby, and my gun bang just like yours do! I don't need you for shit and you ain't getting *shit* from me. *Period*!"

The verbal lashing from his big brother was too much for Haz to take. Inside his warped, cocaine-filled mind Big Slick owed it to him, and everybody under the sun who breathed air and owed him *anything* had to pay the fuck up. Brother or no brother.

"Well *fuck you* then, nigga, ante-up!" Haz shrieked as he reached on his waist and pulled out a .38 long nose and cocked the hammer back.

"We mighta came outta the same pussy but I want that *work* nigga, or I'ma dead you up in this bitch!"

Above the sounds of the music Kea heard the commotion and began to focus her attention on the conversation going down in the kitchen.

"I'ma tell you what's gonna happen right now," said Big Slick in a calm, but firm voice. "You gonna put that gun down, apologize to me, and then get the fuck outta my crib right fuckin' now before I make you swallow that shit! And you ain't getting so much as a nickel bag from me you ungrateful fuck!"

BANG!!! BANG!!!

Two shots rang out and Big Slick flew backwards against the stove and crashed down hard.

In the living room, Kea screamed and dived on top of all six kids, covering them with her body.

Haz stood over Big Slick in the kitchen, wild-eyed and frightened at the sight of what he'd just done. He was in a state of shock and confusion. The drugs had his head spinning and he paced back and forth as he watched the only brother he had gasp desperately for air with two bloody holes darkening his chest.

"I told you to gimme the damn work nigga!" Haz cried out in regret. "Look what the fuck you made me do, man! FUCK! Why you had to try to play me like that? I told you... I told you... I *told* your fuckin' ass..." Haz mumbled as he watched his brother's life fade away.

"YOU *MOTHAFUCKKAAA*!!" came a roar from the doorway. "I'LLL KILL YOUUU," Kea screamed as she charged into the kitchen and jumped on Hassan's back, scratching, clawing, and biting at every part of him that she could get hold of.

Haz swung around violently trying to get Kea off of his back for a few seconds until he flipped her over and she landed hard on the floor.

"You stupid *bitch*! I ain't never liked your narrow ass anyway!" he spit as he raised his leg into the air and brought his size fourteen boot down square in the middle of Kea's face.

SPLAT!

Kea's nose broke instantly, exploding in a spray of snot and blood as she reflexively reached for her face and tried to take cover.

Haz began viciously kicking and punching her around the small kitchen. He bounced her petite frame off the cabinets, the table, and the refrigerator too.

Lil Slick jumped up from the living room floor where his mother had left him and peeked into the kitchen at the carnage that was taking place.

"You fucking slut!" his uncle was screaming as he kicked his mother around like a football, "This shit is all your fault! You turned my brother against me you fuckin tramp! I'ma dead ya dumb ass just like I did him, hoe!"

Haz gripped Kea by the hair and swung her in an arc. Her head cracked against the porcelain sink like a bat slamming a baseball into homerun land. Immediately she went limp and slumped to the floor, blacked completely out.

Kea stayed cloaked in merciful blackness for long, long minutes, and when she awoke she could barely move.

The pain radiating throughout her body was almost unbearable, but somehow she managed to crawl over to a chair and pull herself up to her knees, and then to her feet.

She glanced around in a daze. Blood was smeared all over the kitchen like thick red paint. She looked down and saw Big Slick sprawled out on the floor nearby, bullet holes dotting his body and his glassy eyes opened wide.

Kea's battered face crumpled in grief as she reached toward her man, but a scream from the living room snatched her attention and caused her adrenaline to kick into over-drive.

She crawled out of the kitchen on her hands and knees and turned the corner, then froze in her tracks, gasping in breathtaking shock.

Five of the six kids lay sprawled out across the living room, blood splattered everywhere with multiple stab wounds all over their tiny bodies. Samira, Samille, Samir II, and Samika, were all laying on the floor, deathly still.

To Kea's horror, Hassan was kneeling over a struggling Lil Slick, muscling the boy down and jabbing at him with the sharp tip of a dripping butcher knife.

She threw her head back and shrieked in pain and heartache as she watched Haz plunge the blade deep into her baby's chest. Her nose gushed blood as tears of rage and grief streamed from her eyes.

"Noooo..."

Haz looked up and eyed Kea wobbling on her knees with her bruised hands outstretched toward her bloody children.

"Noooo..." she moaned again as Lil Slick's small body shuddered and fell limp. "My babies...*noooo...* "

"Shut up, bitch," Haz muttered. "You know the fuckin drill," he said as he looked down coldly at the body of his firstborn nephew.

"I'm laying every fuckin body down, baby. Lotty-Dotty and *every* fuckin body's gotta go!"

Hassan raised the knife in the air to stab her son again, and bloodied and broken Kea growled deep in her throat. She glared at him from murderous eyes, and her entire body burned with the vicious rage of a mama bear.

With nothing but her teeth and nails as a weapon, she came up off her knees and made a swift, desperate lunge toward him.

Crazy Haz grinned as he watched his brother's bitch advance like a beast. She was almost upon him, arms extended like hammers, fingers reaching like claws, before he drew his heat and cocked the hammer, and shot her once, square between the eyes.

— From the **Chronicles of Crooklyn** in **A New York State of MINEZ!**